D0649172

CROSSFIRE

CROSSFIRE

JEANETTE WINDLE

KREGEL
PUBLICATIONS

Grand Rapids, MI 49501

CrossFire

© 2000 by Jeanette Windle

Published by Kregel Publications, a division of Kregel, Inc., P.O. Box 2607, Grand Rapids, MI 49501.

All rights reserved. No part of this book may be reproduced, stored in a retrieval system, or transmitted in any form or by any means—electronic, mechanical, photocopy, recording, or otherwise—without written permission of the publisher, except for brief quotations in printed reviews.

While careful research has gone into every aspect of this book to ensure an accurate portrayal of the Bolivian drug war, this novel is a work of fiction. Names, characters, places, and incidents are either the product of the author's imagination or are used fictitiously. Any resemblance to actual persons, living or dead, is entirely coincidental.

Unless otherwise indicated, Scripture quotations are from the *Holy Bible: New International Version*®. © 1973, 1978, 1984 by International Bible Society. Used by permission of Zondervan Publishing House. All rights reserved.

For more information about Kregel Publications, visit our web site: www.kregel.com.

ISBN 0-8254-4116-1

Printed in the United States of America

1 2 3 4 5 / 04 03 02 01 00

To the agents of the DEA in Bolivia,
both those of you who I am privileged to count
as friends and acquaintances and those
I know only for the work you do.
With heartfelt appreciation for the service
you render to my country and yours
in a job that can be dangerous and dirty
and not always pleasant—thank you!

The daughter of missionary parents, Jeanette Windle grew up in Columbia and Venezuela and has spent the last fifteen years in Bolivia. *CrossFire* and its characters are entirely fictional. But the situations, settings, attitudes, and opinions in its pages, as well as the details of narcotrafficking and the anti-narcotics effort, are as accurate as careful research and personal acquaintance can make them. The drug war in Bolivia is an ongoing drama of real people in a context of greed and addiction, unimaginable wealth and economic hardship, conflicting political ideologies, right and wrong motives—and of occasional simple heroism as well. *CrossFire* is the story of that drama.

3 0053 00507 5349

PROLOGUE

The dead fish gave them away.

Something always did, no matter how clever the *narcos* thought they were. The small anti-narcotics unit had seen other signs along the perimeter of the lake. A tangle of dead water snakes washed up on the shore. Birds fallen from the sky without a mark on them. An iguana lying dead next to the half-eaten fish that had been its last meal.

But nothing like this.

Hundreds, maybe even thousands of dead fish lay piled up on the shallow bank, sightless eyes and gaping mouths protesting the indignity of their end, the white fungus of decomposition already blurring their outlines. The soldiers—as tough as they professed to be—retched at the overpowering smell. Their guide was already backing away, his black eyes round with terror. "Then it is true! There is a curse on the lake. Evil spirits are killing the fish."

"Don't be a fool, old man!" one of the soldiers growled. But the *teniente* in charge of the unit snapped, *"Basta!* Enough!"

He patted the old Guarani farmer on the shoulder. "Not evil spirits, *compadre*. Evil men. Go home now. You have done well in telling us. After today, your lake will no longer be poisoned. In time, the fish will return."

Covering his nose with his hand, the young lieutenant knelt down next to a *pejerrey* that was threshing its final gasps at the lake's edge and dipped a small flask into the water. The sample would be sent to headquarters, but he needed no analysis to know what it contained. Somewhere nearby, a cocaine lab was flushing its deadly soup of toxic wastes into the water table that fed the lake. He turned to scan the jungle behind him.

Wilt marked the trail as neatly as any map, and the small band of soldiers followed the obvious signs until the sound of voices told them they were getting close. They covered the last hundred meters on their bellies, but their precautions were hardly necessary. The *narcos* hadn't bothered to post sentries along the perimeter. Lying motionless under the broad leaves of the jungle vegetation, the *teniente* drew in a sharp breath of satisfaction.

The lab was easily the biggest he'd ever seen. A large open structure of wood planks and canvas sheltered the mixing tubs and makeshift metal frames of the drying hammocks. Above, a military camouflage net protected the site from the prying eyes of satellites or surveillance aircraft. A lone guard sat in the middle of the camp, propped against a stack of plastic pails and tin jerry cans that held the chemicals needed for processing the drug. His AK-47 lay on the ground beside him, and his bored eyes were on the peasant workers in the clearing rather than on the jungle beyond.

"Shall we take them now?" a recruit whispered into the lieutenant's ear. "There are six of us and no more than a dozen of them. It will be easy."

The *teniente* considered the question thoughtfully. This was his first command, and he was trying to think like the *americano* training officer would think. He shook his head.

"No, these are only *peones*. We want their contact. And I do not think we have long to wait. Look."

He motioned toward the back of the wood and canvas structure, where two of the workers were transferring a stack of neat, white oblongs into backpacks. There must have been a hundred or more of the packages. "They are getting ready to move the drugs."

The unit settled in to wait, watching the peasant workers stir one last batch of raw paste into their witch's brew of chemicals. When the tubs had finished bubbling, the workers dumped the resulting white mass into the drying hammocks. The humid jungle air was heavy with the acrid fumes of sulfuric acid and ether.

Slapping noiselessly at a mosquito, the young *teniente* thought longingly of the canteen he hadn't thought worthwhile bringing on this morning's patrol. But he noted with pride that there wasn't so much as a rustle from the tangle of underbrush where his five subordinates lay hidden. His men were proving worthy of their training.

As the sun rose high above the jungle canopy, the guard slid down against a bright-orange pail for his afternoon siesta. Soon, half the workers joined him. The *teniente* was fighting a losing battle against his own heavy eyelids when his patience was finally rewarded. A shrill *r-r-rring* jolted him back to full alertness. His eyes widened as the guard rolled over reluctantly and hauled a briefcase-size satellite phone out from under a table. These *narcos* were moving up in the world!

The *teniente* heard nothing of the ensuing conversation, but the result of the call was to send the workers scrambling to scoop the latest batch of cocaine into one-kilo plastic bags. Adding these fresh packets to the load, they shouldered their backpacks and started off single-file down a narrow trail. The guard, with his AK-47 slung across his back, brought up the rear. The workers made no effort to keep quiet, which made it easy for the *teniente* and his men to tail them.

In less than thirty minutes, the trail opened onto a dirt track. A navy blue pickup idled at the trailhead, with one man behind the wheel and another crouched in the back, an AK-47 across his knees. As the line of *campesinos* stepped out onto the trail, the guard in the truck bed slung his weapon over his shoulder and jumped down to direct the loading.

The young lieutenant almost laughed out loud. He'd never expected this raid to be so easy. Visions of a swift promotion danced in his head as he signaled his men to move in.

Backpacks and weapons fell to the ground as the soldiers took control of the clearing. A pistol pressed against the pickup driver's right ear quickly convinced him to spill out what he knew about the drug's destination. Another bonus.

The delivery point for the cocaine turned out to be an airstrip at a hacienda only a few kilometers away. Better yet, the owner of the hacienda was flying in that very afternoon to pick up his latest shipment.

An hour later, the navy-blue pickup sat at the end of a gravel runway. Its distributor cap had been discreetly removed to discourage any last-minute heroics. The driver and the two disarmed guards watched from the cab in helpless fury as a small red-and-white Cessna touched down on the strip and taxied over. The *teniente* waited until the pilot climbed down and walked over to the truck before stepping out from behind a tree.

"*Alto!*" he barked as the man's hand slid under his suit coat. "Keep your hands where I can see them, or I'll blow them off."

The pilot sullenly raised his hands to the top of his head. Reaching under the man's suit coat, the *teniente* slid out a Hafdasa automatic pistol. "Going hunting?" he asked sarcastically.

A further search identified the pilot as Pablo Orejuela, a commercial agent with a street address in one of the more opulent neighborhoods of the province's capital city. The man himself was far less impressive than his address would suggest. Short and stocky, his body might have once been powerful. But that was before good living and alcohol had fleshed out his face and left his belly oozing over the confines of his belt. His expensive alpaca suit was totally inappropriate for both the weather and his build. Predictably, he blustered and stormed about his arrest.

"Yes, of course this is my *hacienda*. But I know nothing of these men nor this . . . this *cocaina*. If they were waiting for an aircraft, it was not mine. And you cannot prove otherwise. Is it any crime to see who these men are who dare to use my runway? As for the gun, these are dangerous times. How was I to know you were not *bandidos*? Did I not surrender as soon as I discovered that you were the law?

"It is you, *teniente,* who will regret this day's work." There was a sneer in his use of the young officer's title. "I have acquaintances in many high places, including among your own superiors. When I tell them of the brutality to which I have been subjected, you will be fortunate to have a position digging out the latrines in your army barracks."

The lieutenant began to wilt under Orejuela's diatribe. As a young junior officer, he knew only too well the truth of the angry landowner's assertions. It mattered little that he had caught Orejuela virtually red-handed. The landowner would still scream his innocence. And if Orejuela had the influence that he boasted, he would be heard and believed—certainly above an untried officer with minimal evidence beyond his own word and that of his men.

"*Teniente,* I think we may have found something." One of the recruits, who had been assigned to search the Cessna, walked up holding a briefcase. Orejuela lunged forward.

"Give me that, you little—! That is private property. I will break you if you touch it."

But the lieutenant was already inserting a knife blade into the lock. The briefcase snapped open, revealing a laptop computer and a small black ledger. Flipping through the pages of the ledger, the *teniente* began to smile.

"So! Numbered bank accounts in Panama and Miami. Deposits in cash. And so much cash! I think my *superiors*—he stressed the word with the same sneer that Orejuela had used—will find this of great interest."

"There is more, *teniente*." Another soldier stepped forward and held out his hand. Dust like white chalk clung to his fingertips. "He does not clean his plane very well."

Orejuela began to scream. "May the saint curse you. May your weapons blow up in your face. May your knives double up against you. May I see prison walls close forever around you."

The lieutenant looked at the portly man with contempt. "The

only prison walls you will see, Señor Orejuela, will be the ones around you."

With an exaggerated flourish he removed the radio from his belt and spoke at length into it, then turned to survey the prisoners. The peasant workers and the three men who had run the drug-processing operation stood stoically under the hot sun, barely acknowledging the presence of their captors. Orejuela slumped miserably in the shade of the Cessna, red-faced and perspiring in his crumpled suit. His sagging mouth was sullen.

"So! It would seem that you are as important as you say," the *teniente* said, ignoring Orejuela's angry glare. "Enough that the *americanos* themselves wish to speak to you. They are even now arranging a helicopter to pick you up."

He eyed the sweat trickling down the fat man's cheeks and added generously, "The helicopter will not be here for some hours. Why don't we remove you to the *hacienda* house where you can make yourself comfortable?"

Orejuela was livid. *That this . . . this insignificant cockroach should dare to offer me the hospitality of my own home!* But he was also frightened. *How could I have been so foolish as to bring those records along?* He'd planned to make a deposit on his way home, and who could have foreseen that the *antinarcóticos* would choose today of all days to raid his property? Where were the informants he had paid so well? Why had they not warned him?

Sagging into one of the comfortless wicker chairs in the hacienda's living room, Orejuela wiped a shaky sleeve across his damp face. There must be a way out of this mess, even now. He had the money. He only needed to reach the right people. Make the evidence disappear. He had seen it happen before. It could be done again.

If only the *americanos* were not involved. This was what frightened him the most. He'd heard the stories about these foreigners who had come to his country to interfere with the export of its most valuable product. It was said they could not be bought, unlike any decent politician. And they knew things it was impossible to know.

And worse, there were stories of tortures, and drugs that turned a man's mind inside out. He could not allow himself to fall into their hands. Orejuela glanced at the soldier standing guard in the doorway. *A judicious bribe, perhaps?*

But there was no time for that. Already—so quickly?—Orejuela could hear the steady *throp-throp* of a helicopter's rotors, and the scream of its engine as it swooped in low over the house. The screen door slammed open, and the *teniente* swaggered in, smiling. One look at his beaming face made it clear that any attempt at bribery would be fruitless.

"Move out the prisoner," the lieutenant snapped.

Orejuela began to tremble as two soldiers prodded him outside. The helicopter, long and sleek and gray, was settling into the dirt on the far side of the yard. It looked like the countless other UH-1 Hueys he had seen circling the skies of his city as part of the *americanos'* endless training missions. He clutched at his chest. This couldn't be happening! Not to him! Where was the luck that had carried him so long? The saint under whose protection he lived? Had he not burned candles? Recited the prayers?

But as the *teniente* impatiently urged him forward, a look of resignation settled across Orejuela's round face. He was a sleaze, and deep down he knew it. But even a sleaze has standards. If he must face ruin, at least let it be told to his wife and family that he had done so as a man and not a whimpering child. Straightening his shoulders with a dignity not totally incongruous to his plump, unprepossessing figure, Orejuela walked with unsteady steps toward the helicopter.

Hard hands pulled him aboard. Above the roar of the blades, he heard the angry voice of the *teniente* shouting, "You have orders only for Orejuela? And what of the other prisoners? How long must we wait for this truck?"

Orejuela was still groping for a seat when the helicopter lifted off—fast. Not until the ground had dropped a sickening distance below the open side door did he have a chance to notice the hard, unpitying faces of his escorts. His dark eyes opened wide with astonishment. Could it be that the saint had not failed him after all?

Then the bulky helmet of the pilot swiveled around. Orejuela gasped.

"You!"

CHAPTER ONE

The night sky was paling to dawn as the Boeing 757 luxury jet touched down at the international airport in La Paz, Bolivia. To Sara's surprise, it was snowing. She had always thought of South America as uniformly hot and humid, and she expressed her amazement aloud.

"*Querida*, where is your geography?" her husband murmured groggily into the thin pad of his airline pillow. "We're south of the equator here, remember? Yes, it's June, but that is the middle of winter." Yawning, he shifted to a more comfortable position and resumed his interrupted nap.

The two inches of fresh-fallen snow spread a rare, Christmas-card beauty over the flat, bleak landscape and low adobe buildings. But Sara was suddenly in no mood to enjoy her first glimpse of the small Andean republic. The plateau on which they had landed sat more than four thousand meters—almost fourteen thousand feet— above sea level. Sara had never been carsick in her life, but the sudden depressurization of the cabin, on top of an empty stomach and twenty-four hours of nonstop travel, produced a sensation she'd never before experienced—and never wanted to again!

"Uh, Nicky, could you reach me those motion tab—"

Sara stopped abruptly when she saw that her husband was fast asleep again. Around her, those passengers who were not continuing on to the lowland city of Santa Cruz were busy gathering their carry-ons from the overhead bins and making their way toward the front of the plane. But even the bustle of activity didn't disturb Nicolás's slow, even breathing. Sara's heart contracted as she watched his handsome profile. Really, it was ridiculous that after all these weeks her heart still turned over every time she looked at Nicolás. Leaning back in her seat, she closed her eyes and tried to ignore the combined effects of nausea and exhaustion. Finding the motion sickness tablets in the overhead bin wasn't worth waking him up.

"*Señorita?*"

Sara opened her eyes. A flight attendant was bending over her. Sitting up, she saw that only a handful of passengers remained onboard. A cleaning crew was preparing the cabin for the next leg of the flight. With a sympathetic smile, the stewardess handed Sara a Styrofoam cup brimming with a steaming green liquid.

"*Té de coca.* For the altitude. You will feel better."

Sara looked dubiously at the acrid-smelling tea, but accepted the cup with a smile of thanks. Curling up at the window, she sipped gingerly at the bitter green concoction.

Below, the ground crew, bundled in heavy ponchos and earmuffs, was unloading and loading luggage. As Sara watched a fuel truck ease up under the wing of the plane, she heard the crackle of a handheld radio nearby. Amid the rush of static-filled Spanish, she heard *"Llama a los agentes de narcóticos! Mándalos aquí!"*

A moment later, a flight attendant hurried up the aisle, returning shortly followed by a uniformed airline official. Although Sara could hear only a few words of their excited Spanish, she couldn't help noting their expressions of suppressed excitement and worry.

Sara turned her attention once again to the activity outside the window. The baggage handlers were now standing idly by while two soldiers in fatigues poked among the pile of suitcases on the baggage conveyor. Soon another soldier appeared, striding rapidly along the side of the plane, a large dog straining at its leash ahead of him. He was passing beneath Sara's window when the airline official who had been onboard the plane ducked out from under the wing to meet him. Just then came an announcement over the P.A. system:

"Would the passenger who left the package above row twenty-three please report to the front of the plane to claim his belongings!"

The announcement was repeated in English and Portuguese, but by then Sara had lost interest in the odd little scene. The tea, or whatever it was she had been drinking, had eased the headache brought on by the high altitude, but it had done nothing to soothe her empty stomach. As the new passengers began filing onboard, Sara closed her eyes and forced her mind to more pleasant thoughts. Like that fateful rainy night in Seattle when she had first met Nicolás Cortéz.

It had been almost ten o'clock when Sara left the University of Washington library to walk the nine blocks to her student apartment. Walking alone at night wasn't the best idea in that part of town, but her ancient sedan had sprung a radiator leak, and she still had to complete the research for her term paper. It wouldn't hurt to walk just this once. She'd hurry.

The night was vintage Seattle—half bluster, half drizzle. Sara walked with her head down, hood pulled close around her face, her gloveless hands thrust deep into fleece-lined pockets. She didn't realize she was being followed until a hand grasped her shoulder. She whirled around, praying that she'd been overtaken by a classmate. But she knew she hadn't.

With a sickening fear beginning to claw at the inside of her stomach, Sara looked up into the leering face of a holdover from the Seattle grunge music scene. Stringy blond hair drooped over the collar of a plaid flannel shirt that smelled of cigarettes and sour wine. The light from a nearby streetlamp glinted on a row of gold hoops lining both earlobes. Just then, a second man grabbed Sara's other arm. He wasn't much taller than Sara but was grossly overweight, with baggy, beltless jeans looped around his hips. The cloud of smoke he blew into her face was too sweet to be tobacco.

"She got anything we want?" he asked his companion.

Sara stood still and straight, not fighting against the grip on her arms. Neither of her assailants showed a weapon, but they didn't need one. There were two of them, and no one would respond to her screams in this part of Seattle. She slid her hand into her coat pocket and brought out her purse.

"Here, this is all I've got!" Her voice was just above a whisper but steadier than she had thought possible. "Just take it, and let me go!"

The two youths looked at each other. Something in the grin they exchanged made Sara's skin crawl. She took an involuntary step backward. Just then she heard quick footsteps coming down a dark side street. Both men quickly released her arms.

The man who stepped into the glow of the streetlamp was tall and broad-shouldered under his long coat and muffler. He paused when he caught sight of the strange trio blocking his way. Sara let out a breath she hadn't known she was holding. Sliding her purse back into her pocket, she stepped toward the well-dressed stranger.

"Oh, there you are!" Her voice was shaky with relief. "I thought I'd missed you!"

The stranger's glance slid quickly from the two street punks to regard Sara's pale, frightened face. He smiled—an utterly charming smile. "Sorry, dear!" he said without hesitation. "I got away a little late."

The smile and charm faded into cold steel as he stepped forward and spared the two thugs another glance.

"Did you want something?" he inquired with an icy arrogance, staring down the high bridge of his nose as though the two men had just crawled out from under a rock.

He didn't wait for a reply before turning his back. Draping Sara's quaking hand onto his arm, he said smoothly, "Shall we go?"

Sara cast an apprehensive glance at the two street punks, but they were already backing away into the shadows, and she had to scramble to keep up with the stranger's confident stride as he propelled her along the sidewalk. Sara tugged her hand loose as soon as they reached the corner.

"Thanks for rescuing me," she said breathlessly. "You saved my—well, maybe even my life."

"My pleasure!" The man's voice was deep and velvety with just the barest hint of an accent. "I've always wanted to play Prince Charming and rescue a princess."

"Well . . ." Sara hesitated. What was the proper protocol following a rescue? Should she shake his hand and watch him fade off into the night? Her eyes strained to see his shadowy features. It would at least be nice to be able to recognize her rescuer if she ever saw him again. "I . . . I guess I'd better be going. Thanks again for everything."

"Wait a minute!" he said with a laugh. "Do you think I'm going to let you walk off alone after all that? I'll walk you home. But first, would you join me for a cup of coffee or something? There's a place just around the corner."

Sara knew the place. It was only a few blocks from her apartment. She hesitated, knowing her roommate would be worried if she didn't get home soon. But maybe she could call.

Misunderstanding Sara's indecision, the man quickly added, "Look, I'm not trying to pick you up. But you're still shaking, and your hands are ice cold. A cup of coffee will do you good."

Taking her agreement for granted, he offered his arm once again. "So, what are you doing out here at this late hour?"

"Well, I was on my way home from the library . . ."

The stranger kept up a flow of lighthearted conversation as the two walked along the sidewalk. By the time they reached the all-night café, Sara was no longer shaking and had even managed to laugh about the night's adventure. "I was terrified you were going to say, 'Sorry, lady, you've got the wrong guy,' and walk on by," she told him as he guided her over to a corner table and helped her remove her coat. "And there you were—calm as a rock and not afraid at all."

"What was there to be afraid of?" The stranger dismissed her two assailants with a contemptuous gesture. He shrugged off his own coat and hat, and for the first time Sara saw him clearly. Her eyes widened. It really *was* Prince Charming! She stared in amazement at the best-looking man she had ever seen, then flushed scarlet when she saw that he was regarding her with a bemused smile on his face.

"So you really are a princess." He unself-consciously reached out to smooth a strand of her long, shining hair that had tumbled out when she pulled off her hood. "With hair like gold in the sunshine."

Dropping his hand, he pulled out a chair for her, then seated himself across the table. White teeth flashed as he offered another slow, irresistible smile. "So! You still haven't told me who I've had the pleasure of rescuing."

"Oh! S-Sara. Sara Connor." She found she was having a hard time breathing. *You're being silly!* she told herself fiercely. *You're a level-headed honor student, not some starry-eyed ingénue!*

"It's a beautiful name." He lifted a hand to signal the waitress. "Like its owner!"

Sara felt her cheeks grow warm. Leaning back in her seat, she studied her gallant rescuer surreptitiously as he ordered two cups of Colombian coffee. Nothing in his appearance or clothing suggested he was a foreigner, but there was something not quite American in the lazy grace of his body and the quick movements of his hands. The university had a large contingent of exchange students from around the world, so perhaps he was one of them. Sara's eyebrows came together as she tried to place the faint trace of an accent that showed itself more in an occasional turn of phrase than any mispronunciation of words.

"Spanish! That's it!" She didn't realize she'd spoken aloud until she saw the rueful expression on his face.

"My accent is that bad, is it?" He spread his hands in a gesture of mock defeat. "And I thought I had it licked!"

"Oh, no!" Sara was horrified. "Your English is perfect! It's just . . . well, I'm a Spanish major, and I thought . . . I mean, there was something—"

She stammered to a stop when she saw the twinkle of amusement in his eyes. Leaning forward, he said softly, "This is incredible! Not only are you beautiful, but you speak my language as well. How is it we haven't met before?"

Sara smiled faintly. "Well, I don't imagine you spend a lot of time hanging around the Spanish language lab, Señor . . ."

"Cortéz. Nicolás Cortéz—and very much at your service," he said with a smile as he reached across the table to shake her hand.

"Cortéz? You mean, like the guy who conquered Mexico?"

"Well, maybe a distant relative," Nicolás said, laughing.

When he showed no signs of letting go, Sara tugged her hand

away self-consciously, then covered her embarrassment with a question. "So, where are you from? Or am I wrong in assuming you're not from around here?"

"I'm finishing up my degree in business administration. A long ways, unfortunately, from the Spanish department. But I was born and raised in Bolivia. My father is a businessman there."

Sara never did call her roommate. She and Nicolás sat through another pot of coffee, and he complimented her by switching the conversation to his native tongue. Together they laughed over Sara's stumbling mistakes.

"It takes more than a class to teach a language!" he teased. "We'll practice together until you speak it like a true Bolivian!" Sara blushed when she realized the implications of his statement.

By the time he walked her home, it seemed incredible that they had never crossed paths before, and unthinkable that they might never have met. It was well past two when he finally dropped her off on the steps of her apartment building. He tried to pull her close as she thanked him again, but when she eluded his grasp, he didn't persist or take offense. Instead, he kissed her hand and made arrangements to see her the following evening.

✠

Nothing in Sara's orderly, well-disciplined life prepared her for the mad excitement and joy of the weeks that followed. She'd always believed that it was impossible to fall in love at first sight—only a complete fool would think otherwise—but now she knew better! Any rational observer would have seen that the dramatic circumstances that brought Nicolás into her life were tailor-made to promote just such an instantaneous attraction, but objectivity and reason were the furthest things from Sara's mind. She had no doubt that this was meant to be!

The two of them spent every free moment together—to the detriment of Sara's studies and part-time job. Fortunately, graduation arrived before her grades could drop too far or her boss lost his patience. Nicolás, who was on a student visa and therefore didn't work, found ample time to finish his courses while dedicating himself to Sara. He was romantic, charming, and considerate—everything she had ever dreamed of finding in a man. And he made her laugh.

He did crazy things like serenading under her window at midnight—

until the apartment manager threatened to have him arrested. He had an endless supply of flowers delivered to her apartment until she put a stop to it, protesting at the expense. He organized a mariachi band of Latin students for her birthday. He called her *querida* (beloved) and *corazón* (my heart). She called him Nicky. And she was wildly, deliriously happy.

The day before graduation, Nicolás told Sara that he would be returning to Bolivia. Sara's bubble of joy crashed in shards around her feet. "Can't you get a job around here?" she pleaded. "With your degree, you can surely find something a whole lot better than back there!"

Nicolás shook his head. "It has already been decided. My father is expecting me to work with him in his business. That's why he sent me here. I've got to go—and I want to! I haven't been home in two years."

She clung to him, allowing him to hold her closer than she ever had before. "I can't bear to have you go! I just know I'll never see you again!"

"Then come with me! Marry me! You know I love you. I can't live without you!" The urgency of his kisses made the trite phrases as profound as the first time a man in love had ever spoken them.

Sara pulled back from his embrace. She had researched Bolivia at the university library soon after she and Nicolás had met, and what she found hadn't been encouraging. Bolivia was the poorest country in South America, with a troubled history of military governments and one *coup d'état* after another. At the moment, the country was enjoying an experiment in democracy, but labor unrest and social violence—not to mention the growing drug traffic—dominated the news articles she read.

Nicolás brushed aside her fears impatiently. "You cannot base your opinion on what you read in the newspaper, *querida*. Bolivia is a beautiful country—quiet and peaceful. Sure, many of the people are poor, but the country is growing. There's a lot of opportunity and abundant natural resources: minerals, lumber, agriculture. They don't call us the treasure house of South America for nothing! You should see my own city of Santa Cruz. It's getting more modern all the time. And the people. They are warm and friendly, and they know how to have a good time in a way you Americans have forgotten. Every *gringo* who comes to our city falls in love with it—the music, the food, the people. You will too, I promise."

Nicolás caught her tightly against himself. "Sara, *corazón*, can't you see, I've got to go! And you have to come with me, because I don't know when I'll be back. If we get married right away, we'll have a couple of weeks to honeymoon before we have to leave."

"But that's so soon!" Sara gasped. "How could we possibly get ready? And your parents! What will they say?"

Nicky silenced her protest with a flurry of passionate kisses, sweeping aside any doubts she had—at least until her roommate got home.

"You're crazy!" Fran gasped. "Marrying a guy you hardly know from a country you've barely even heard of! Is this our sensible Sara talking? The one who's always trying to keep the rest of us out of trouble? I mean, really, Sara, at least wait until you know him a little better before you go flying off into the blue!"

"Franny, I love him!" Sara replied. "And we don't have time to wait any longer. If I don't marry him now, he'll be gone, and I'll probably never see him again! I'm not letting Nicky just walk out of my life!"

"Look, I can see why you've flipped," Fran said. "I mean, okay, he's the best-looking guy I've seen come along in years. But be honest, Sara! What do you really know about him, besides all that romantic Latin charm?"

"I know he's smart, and he's hardworking too," Sara said stubbornly. "Look at the way he's learned English! And you know how poor those Third World countries are. You've really got to have what it takes to get a scholarship to come all the way to the U.S. to study."

"Yeah, I've noticed how hardworking he is! I haven't noticed him holding a job—or doing much studying for that matter!"

"His student visa won't let him work." Sara threw her hands in the air. "And he stretched his courses over five years so he could see a little bit of America while he was here."

"You mean, have a roaring good time!"

Ignoring Fran's jibe, Sara continued, "He's loyal and self-sacrificing, too. You know how many exchange students just stay on in the U.S. when they get their degrees? I mean, you can't blame them. Any job here pays a lot more than back home, and life is a whole lot better, too. But Nicky—he's determined to go back! Doesn't that say what kind of a person he is? That he wants to help his own country and family, not just stay here and get rich?"

Fran shook her head doubtfully. "Boy, have you got it bad! Well, I really do hope it all works out. I mean, I like Nicky—he's charming enough. Maybe I'm just a little jealous. I just hope he doesn't let you down and leave you stuck in some awful foreign country where you don't have a soul to turn to!"

Sara laughed and said with earnest confidence, "That's not going to happen! He loves me too much for that."

A week later, Nicolás and Sara were married—a short, simple ceremony in Sara's church, witnessed by the half-dozen or so of Nicky's friends who were still in town after the end of school, Sara's roommate, several classmates, and around thirty of her friends from church. Sara's few remaining relatives were scattered across the Midwest and New England, and none of them could attend on such short notice.

After the wedding, Nicolás and Sara drove to Southern California for their honeymoon. It was everything Sara had ever dreamed of. They swam, sailed, and walked on the beach at sunset. Nicky was passionate and attentive and far more sophisticated than she was about such things as hotels, tips, restaurants, and travel arrangements. Sara adored him and took a shy pride in the way other women turned to look when he walked into a restaurant or along the beach. At the end of ten days she was, if possible, more in love than ever.

✠

"Ladies and gentlemen, the captain has turned on the 'fasten seat belt' sign in preparation for our arrival in Santa Cruz. At this time, we ask that you stow any carry-ons you may have taken out during the flight in the overhead bins or under the seat in front of you, and please make sure your seat belt is securely fastened. We will be on the ground in approximately fifteen minutes."

Sara watched eagerly as the tossing green of the jungle canopy rolled away under the triangular shadow of the wing. As the plane began its descent, a ribbon of water, sparkling gold under the brightening dawn, slowly faded into the muddy tones of a shallow river, meandering across the jungle like a torpid snake. Soon the jungle gave way to grassy plains and a scattered patchwork of cultivated fields.

The sight of palm trees dotting the grassy open spaces reminded her how far from home she was. And what a strange sight! Unlike the stately palms she had seen during their stopover in Miami—their gold-green fronds tossing proudly above straight, branchless trunks—the tops of these trees were bent at right angles toward the incoming plane, like a field of broken witches' brooms standing on end.

"It's the wind!" Warm breath tickled the back of her neck.

"What—!" Sara came to herself with a start. "Nicky, how did you know . . . ?"

"That's what you *gringos* always say!" Throwing an arm around her shoulders, Nicolás leaned across to look out the round port-hole. Mimicking a tourist from Texas, he drawled, "Would y'all take a look at those fuu-nny palm trees! Now, wha–at do you think makes them dooo that?" He gave Sara a mischievous grin.

Sara snuggled back against Nicolás's warm shoulder. On the ground below, the wind bent the tall grasses into one long, continuous curve and tossed the scattered clumps of uncleared scrub jungle like waves on a green sea. Sara shivered.

"*Corazón,* are you okay?" Nicolás murmured sleepily in her ear. "Is the motion still bothering you? You're awfully pale."

Sara smiled as his fingers slid up her cheek to tangle in her hair. It had been a long time since she'd had somebody worry about her, and it felt good! "I'm fine!" she repeated firmly. "It's just that wind. I've never seen anything like it. It looks so strong!"

Nicolás's concern relaxed into a grin. "You'll find out about our winds soon enough! They're enough to knock a little thing like you off your feet."

Sara lifted a hand to caress his cheek. Nicolás turned his head to press a kiss into her palm. But in the next instant, he caught her fingers and rubbed them hard along his jawbone where a dark, stubbly shadow indicated it was time for a shave. Sara snatched her hand away. "Ouch, that hurts!"

"Sorry!" Nicky's grin was unrepentant. "Here, let me kiss it better."

Sara's indignation evaporated as he caught her hand again and promptly raised it to his lips. How could anyone stay angry with a man like Nicky? As he lingeringly kissed her fingers, one by one, she studied him, heart in her eyes. Six feet of bronzed muscle. Dark curls styled ruthlessly back from a fine-cut profile of the type popu-larized by hundreds of movie stars, from Errol Flynn to Pierce Brosnan. Sooty eyelashes fringed eyes as blue as a mountain lake. And as if his looks weren't enough, he was romantic and charming and sweet-natured. Sara let out a sigh of pure happiness. He was almost too good to be true. And he was hers!

"What are you staring at?" Nicolás said softly. The long lashes had lifted, and he was watching her with amusement.

"You!" Sara answered simply. Then in a rush, "Oh, Nicky, I'm so lucky! I never dreamed anyone like you could happen to me. You're so . . . so beautiful!"

"Beautiful!" Nicolás growled. "I'll show you who's beautiful!" Slid-ing down a few inches in his seat, he nuzzled the soft spot below her right ear. "Do you realize how long it's been since you kissed me?"

"Sure, an hour!" Sara answered. "And you've been snoring the whole time!" A small flame curled in her stomach as she looked into his incredibly blue eyes. She forgot the alien landscape below as his mouth came down on hers. Her fingers slid around his neck.

"Sir, may I assist you in fastening your seat belt?" A flight attendant was peering down at the two of them.

Sara came down to earth with a crash. Hot with embarrassment, she pulled away from Nicolás. He muttered something rude under his breath as she hastily straightened her blouse. The landing light above them was blinking, and Sara realized that people all around them were tucking books and magazines into handbags and preparing for landing.

"Let me help you with this! The plane will soon be landing." The flight attendant was tall and attractive, with a full figure and abundant dark hair caught up under her perky cap. As she bent over Nicolás, the scent of her subtle perfume wafted over to Sara. Snapping his seat belt into place, the attendant pulled it tight—ever so slowly.

"That is better! We would not wish for you to be hurt!" She spoke in English, presumably for Sara's benefit, and her strong accent added a sultry undertone to her words.

Sara sighed. It wasn't Nicky's fault that women were always throwing themselves at him. He was just so . . . gorgeous! *Tall, dark, and handsome.* Trite or not, it sure described Nicolás. Sara stood up suddenly, ignoring the blinking seat belt light overhead. "Excuse me!" she said with pointed emphasis. "I'd like to freshen up before we land."

The flight attendant seemed startled, but she moved quickly aside to let Sara out.

The tiny washroom was unoccupied. Setting her handbag on the counter, Sara eyed her reflection with disfavor. She was still pale, and the faint blue streaks under her eyes told of a sleepless night. She pulled out her hairbrush. She couldn't do much about the sleep creases in her slacks and blouse, but she ran the brush through the tangles in her long hair and touched up her makeup. Frowning at the result, she leaned forward to study her face in the mirror. The wide-spaced eyes that looked gravely back at her were a brown that shifted with her moods from almost black to a clear, golden amber. Her fine, straight, waist-length hair was an unusual shade for an adult. *Towhead,* she thought disparagingly. But the silky eyebrows and long, curling lashes were dark enough to make less fortunate blondes gnash their teeth in envy. The light tan she had picked up on her honeymoon made the contrast between her hair and eyes even more striking.

Her heart-shaped face, ending in a small, pointed chin, was, if not plain, at least ordinary. The nose was OK, but her mouth was a little too wide and full to be called truly beautiful. Her figure, while nicely shaped, was a little bit thin after the whirlwind of the past few months.

A pang of misgiving struck her. Nicolás was so incredibly handsome—like the prince in a fairy tale! In her mind, he belonged next to one of those tall, elegant TV beauties. Maybe if she had the voluptuous figure and neat brunette hair of that flight attendant . . .

"But Nicolás loves me just the way I am," Sara reminded herself fiercely. And he adored the fine, straight gold hair she despised. He loved to bury his face in its sweet-smelling, shining length. She'd lost count of the number of times he'd told her she was beautiful since the night he had rescued her two months ago.

Sara gave the girl in the mirror one last look. The memories had curved the corners of her mouth into a lovely line, and the sheer joy that glowed from the amber eyes gave her a beauty that even she couldn't help but recognize. Snatching up her handbag, she wrinkled her nose at her reflection. "You'll do!"

When Sara returned to her seat, the flirtatious flight attendant was still hovering over Nicolás, laughing at something he had said. As Sara slid past her, the young woman straightened up reluctantly, managing to brush against Nicolás's shoulder in the process. Nicolás gave Sara a slow wink as the flight attendant threw him a last fluttering glance and scurried off to attend another passenger. Sara stifled a grin. She couldn't blame other women for trying to flirt. And even though Nicolás seemed a bit too willing to laugh and joke with them, Sara was confident that he only had eyes for her.

As Sara snapped her seat belt into place, a bell chimed overhead and the captain's voice came over the intercom: "We are now approaching Santa Cruz de la Sierra, elevation 437 meters. We will be landing at the international airport of Viru Viru. The temperature today is ten degrees Celsius—fifty Fahrenheit."

"There it is!" Nicolás leaned across Sara as the aircraft banked to the left. "*La bella Santa Cruz de la Sierra!* Have you ever seen anything more beautiful? Besides you, I mean," he added with a teasing grin.

Sara turned her head against his shoulder. The city spreading out below them wasn't at all what she had expected. In the center stood a nucleus of modern high-rise buildings, but most of the town consisted of tiny dwellings of adobe and brick, interspersed with patches of green, like clumps of uncut jungle. It was laid out, Nicolás had told her, in concentric rings with major avenues joining the city together like spokes on a wheel. In the spaces between the main rings and avenues, Sara could make out a tracing of paved and dirt streets that were connected like the web of a particularly unorganized spider. Accustomed to the skyscrapers and intersecting freeways of American cities, she couldn't see how the city below could possibly hold a population the size of Seattle's.

"Look at how it's grown!" Nicolás marveled as the plane curved around and dropped another one hundred feet. He pointed out a tall blue-green building that shimmered as though made of glass. "They've finished the new *Palacio de Justicia*. And they've added at least three new rings."

Sara smiled to herself. She was seeing a new facet of Nicky's personality. The boyish enthusiasm was a far cry from his usual polished sophistication. She suddenly realized that although Santa Cruz was an alien place to her, and one that compared poorly to Seattle, to Nicolás it was home.

I'm going to like it! she told herself firmly. *It's Nicky's hometown, and no matter what it's like, no matter how hard it gets, I'm going to like it.*

The plane banked away from the city and Sara could see that they were above the airport now. The terminal was a long, two-story building with a flat roof. From the roof, a crowd of people waved enthusiastically at the incoming plane. Alongside the terminal, a 727 passenger jet was readying for takeoff. The only other planes on the ground were a two-engine prop plane and a small, six-passenger Cessna parked in the far corner of the blacktop.

As the wheels touched down, a field dotted with witch-broom palms rushed by, each frond standing straight out in the wind. Up close, they seemed even more bizarre—like a painting Sara had once seen of a Viking woman walking along the sea cliffs, her hair streaming out behind her as she watched for her husband's ship. There was a roar as the powerful brakes slowed the jet. Then they were taxiing over to the terminal. All over the plane, passengers jumped to their feet and began collecting their hand luggage amid a babble of Spanish and other languages.

Sara had been fighting drowsiness since La Paz, but now she was wide awake, a mixture of nervousness and excitement squeezing at her stomach. This was it—the beginning of the new life she and Nicky would be making together. She'd show them—her roommate, her pastor, her friends—that she'd made the right decision.

She reached for her handbag, but Nicolás caught her hand. "Hey, we're in no hurry! Let everyone else do the pushing and shoving!"

Sara settled back into her husband's arms. It had been wonderful these last ten days to have Nicky all to herself. But, in just a few minutes, she would be shaking hands with her new family, the in-laws she had never met. She had a sudden premonition that once she and Nicky walked through the exit at the far end of the aisle, things would never be quite the same. *You're just being selfish!* she scolded herself. But she couldn't suppress a flicker of apprehension.

"Do you think your family will like me?" she asked abruptly.

"Of course they will!" Nicolás looked astonished at the question. "Why shouldn't they? You're my wife, aren't you?" He brushed a stray strand of hair away from her face. "Besides, look at you! You're beautiful, and intelligent, and loving. Boy, are you loving!" he added, burying his face in the hollow between her shoulder and neck.

"Nicky, you're tickling me!" Sara giggled. But her attempts to push him away were halfhearted. "Okay, okay, you've convinced me!"

Just then Sara's favorite flight attendant arrived, waving them toward the exit and clucking her disapproval as her gaze shifted from Sara's flushed cheeks to Nicolás's smug grin. Sara looked around and realized they were the only ones left in their seats. By the time they hurried down the aisle, all the other passengers had filed out, but the pilot and steward waiting for them at the exit showed no impatience. They looked Sara over with the approving smiles of a couple of connoisseurs, and as the pilot offered a farewell handshake to Nicolás, he muttered something in Spanish too soft and swift for Sara to hear. The three men laughed.

"What's so funny?" Sara stepped gingerly into the jetway connecting the plane with the terminal. The wind lashed at the thick canvas, shaking it as she hurried forward onto the firmer floor of the terminal. She swung around to face her husband. "What'd he say?"

Nicolás was still grinning. "He said, 'Your woman would make any man forget his responsibilities!'"

Sara blushed, but she replied indignantly, "Wait a second! What do you mean, 'your woman'? You make me sound like I'm a piece of property instead of a person in my own right! I'm your wife, not your 'woman'!"

"Maybe in America," Nicolás shrugged. "But you're in Bolivia now. And here you are my *mujer,* my woman. Even your name says it—*Sara Connor de Cortéz.* Sara Connor *of* Cortéz. You belong to *me* now." He quickened his steps along the walkway. "It's no big thing, *querida!* It's just the way the Spanish translates."

There was a brief delay at the end of the walkway while a clerk in a military uniform stamped their passports. The official barely glanced at the tourist card Sara had filled out on the plane, but when he flipped open the red Bolivian passport Nicolás handed him, his dark eyes widened a fraction.

"*Bienvenido a casa, Señor Cortéz,*" he said respectfully, stamping a blank page with a flourish. "Welcome home!"

"Hey, I think that man knows you!" Sara whispered as Nicolás took back his passport with the sketchiest of nods. "Who is he?"

Nicolás shrugged, tucking the passport back into the inside pocket of his leather jacket. "I haven't the slightest idea."

Sara glanced back. The immigration official was staring after them. But before Sara could say another word, Nicolás grasped her elbow and began hurrying her down a wide flight of stairs.

The broad staircase led to the baggage-claim area. The other passengers were already milling around a conveyor belt where the first of the luggage was beginning to appear. Sara looked with amazement at the glass security wall that separated the baggage area from the rest of the airport. On the other side, the crowd that had been on the roof now surged against the barrier, waving, calling, blowing kisses. The passengers were smiling and waving back as they snatched suitcases and boxes from the moving conveyor belt. Sara watched as two small boys escaped their parents and zeroed in on an older, elegantly dressed woman. As the woman pressed her hand to theirs through the glass, their shouts needed no translation. The expression on the woman's face brought a lump to Sara's throat.

When the passengers had secured their luggage, they began lining up at two long tables where customs officials snapped open suitcases and unzipped duffel bags. A pair of armed guards kept a careful watch over the proceedings. As each set of luggage was searched, the owner was waved through to the other side of the barrier. Sara watched the two small boys dash into their grandmother's arms. While Sara and Nicolás waited for their bags to appear, one passenger after another was swallowed up by a welcoming committee. Sara noticed how stylish and elegant all of the greeters were compared to the casual American dress code. The women were in dresses or smart pantsuits and high heels, and the men wore business suits. Even the children looked dressed for Easter Sunday. Sara brushed self-consciously at her own travel-creased outfit, wishing she'd thought to tuck a change of clothes into her flight bag. Where were all those poverty-stricken Bolivians she'd read about?

She glanced back at Nicolás in time to see him pointing out their suitcases to a pair of white-coated porters. Sara scanned the remaining crowd. Was anyone waving in their direction? She placed her hand on her husband's back. "Come on, Nicky, I'm dying of suspense! Where are your parents?"

Nicolás didn't even glance up from the baggage claims he was sorting. "Oh, didn't I tell you? They won't be able to meet us. We'll take a taxi home." He flashed her a brief smile. "You don't mind, do you? I was looking forward to having you to myself a little longer."

Sara smiled back at him, but she sensed that this wasn't the real reason. Then her hand flew up to cover her mouth, and she could have kicked herself for her insensitivity. Like a typical American, it hadn't even occurred to her that her in-laws might not have a vehicle of their own in which to pick them up.

"Of course I don't mind!" she assured him hastily. "I'd rather see Santa Cruz with you first, anyway."

The porters piled the last of their dozen or so bags on a pair of luggage carts. Only three were Sara's, along with two heavy boxes of books, favorite authors she couldn't bear to leave behind. "I swear you've packed your entire apartment—including the kitchen sink!" she teased Nicolás. "It'll take us hours to clear customs with all your stuff!"

Nicolás looked amused. "I'll make you a bet. Five minutes and we're out!" Nicolás flashed his ID under the nose of the customs official. Sara stared in amazement as the man nodded and waved them through the glass doors. *"Bienvenido a casa, Señor Cortéz."*

"And just how did you manage that?" Sara asked Nicolás as they followed the porters and their luggage across the vast tiled waiting area.

"It's called *muñeca.*" Nicolás tucked her hand into his arm. "And if you don't know what that means, you'll just have to wait and find out."

"I'm not sure I want to," Sara replied, glancing back at the lengthy line of less fortunate passengers who were still inching patiently forward. "It sounds like a bribe, or nepotism, or something illegal!"

"Only in North America," Nicolás grinned.

Sara's laughing response was snatched away by the wind as she stepped outside. The stiff breeze was like something alive, whipping her long hair around her face, cutting like an icy knife through her thin blouse. How in the world did all those well-dressed women she'd seen in the terminal maintain their hairdos in this wind?

"What did I tell you?" Nicolás shouted into her ear, holding her close against his side as they battled their way after the piled-up luggage carts. "Don't worry, it's not very far."

Their destination was a row of taxis parked along the curb only a few meters away. A mishmash of shapes and sizes, their only uniformity was a yellow-and-black checkered stripe along each side and a cardboard placard taped inside the windshield. The driver of the first car in line waved them over frantically. Sara crawled gratefully into the back seat while the porters and the cab driver wrestled with the luggage.

Even with two suitcases lashed to the roof, it quickly became evident that their luggage wouldn't fit in one vehicle. Nicolás motioned to the next taxi in line, a small white Toyota Corolla station wagon. Rubbing her hands up and down her bare arms, Sara watched as the rest of their belongings disappeared inside the second car. The driver's ragged clothing and dark, sullen features didn't strike her as particularly reassuring.

"Can we trust him?" she asked anxiously as Nicolás slid in beside her. "What if he drives off with our stuff?"

"He wouldn't dare!" Nicolás answered briefly. He leaned forward to give their driver directions before he noticed that Sara was shivering.

"I should have warned you to keep out a jacket," he said remorsefully, rubbing her cold hands between his own as the car moved away from the curb. "Our winters are mild compared to yours up north, but when the *sur* blows in—the south winds off the snowy peaks of Argentina—it can get pretty miserable. And it doesn't help that we don't heat our cars—or our houses for that matter—the way you do back in North America."

"Hey, it's okay, Nicky; really, it's not that cold," Sara reassured him through teeth she had to clamp together to keep from chattering. "It's my fault, anyway. I should have thought of a jacket myself after seeing the snow in La Paz. Besides, you were always saying you wanted to try out those arctic warming techniques they taught us in first aid, remember? The ones you said sounded, what was it—'intriguing'? So here's your chance! In fact," she added with mock reproof, "I'm not so sure you didn't plan all this, Nicolás Cortéz, just to keep me cuddled up close! Though how you managed the weather, I don't know!" Sara watched her husband's concern dissolve into laughter, and as she snuggled up under the soft leather of his jacket with his arm tight around her, she gradually stopped shivering and began to take more of an interest in the passing scenery.

At first, the city seemed much more modern than it had looked from the air. The highway leading in from the airport was wide and smooth; the billboards advertised IBM and Sony and Maytag, as well as a host of brand names she didn't recognize. Sara's spirits rose. The tall, glass-and-steel office buildings interspersed with an occasional development of gracious, hacienda-style homes didn't look much different than certain sections of Miami.

The traffic, however, was another matter altogether! Sara gasped as the sudden braking of the taxi threw her against Nicolás. The bus that had just cut in front of them roared away with a squeal of tires. The taxi driver honked angrily and promptly accelerated into the narrow space between the bus and the next lane of traffic.

A moment later, the bus slowed for a yellow light. Honking triumphantly, the taxi nipped around in front and accelerated across the intersection, making it to the other side just as the cross lanes of traffic began to move. Sara squeezed her eyes shut, then opened them again as the taxi slammed on its brakes for the next intersection. Here the light was already red, but cars and buses continued to race up beside them until the two lanes were crowded four and five abreast. Sara blinked as a horse-drawn cart plodded into the space between a brand-new Mitsubishi Montero and a thirty-year-old Volkswagen Beetle. Glancing back over her shoulder, she saw that the second taxi had, by some miracle, managed to keep up with them.

Nicolás laughed at the disbelief on her face. "A year from now, you'll be out here with the best of them." Sara wasn't convinced. She could never drive in this!

Eventually they turned off the wide, palm-lined avenue, and Sara began to feel as though she was moving back in history. Another ten minutes' drive took them through the center of the city, where the whitewashed walls and red-tiled roofs of colonial Spain still lined the narrow, cobbled streets. The taxi driver honked his way past a shady plaza patrolled by military police with automatic rifles slung over their shoulders, then through an open market where crowds in American-style clothing bargained with Indian vendors whose long, black braids and bright layered skirts proclaimed that they were Quechua, descendants of the ancient Inca.

As the two cabs came out on the opposite side of the city, Sara began to feel apprehensive once again. She had hoped that one of the gracious neighborhoods they had driven through might be their final destination. Even a development of respectable-looking townhouses sprouting up amid sprawling two-room cement-block homes roused her interest. *Those don't look so bad!*

But now the cobbled streets and colonial buildings of the old city were behind them, and they were driving through the maze of adobe and brick she'd seen from the air. The streets leading off from the main avenue were unpaved and strewn with garbage. An occasional respectable home, with graffiti-splattered walls topped with broken glass and barbed-wire, reared up above tiny adobe homes with tin or thatched roofs. *Surely Nicky's family doesn't live in one of these shacks!*

Nicolás had never talked much about finances—or about his family. Sara knew that both of his parents were still living and that he had at least one married sister, but that was about it. In fact, only now did she realize how many things they *hadn't* talked about in the two months they'd known each other. Somehow, she'd assumed that Nicky wasn't poor. He'd driven a second-hand car in Seattle, a re-stored 1967 Porsche convertible of which he'd been inordinately proud, considering its age. And though Sara had never been par-ticularly style-conscious, she knew good clothes when she saw them, and Nicky had never seemed to lack spending money. Still, these might have been the benefits of the exchange program that had brought him to the United States.

But, no! Nicolás had said that his father owned a business. Sara's heart lifted a little until she surveyed the shabby facades of the elec-trical repair and mechanic shops they were passing. Even these could be classified—if barely—as businesses. And if his parents couldn't even afford a car! Sara straightened her slim shoulders. *It doesn't matter how bad it gets!* she told herself fiercely. *We'll be together, and that's what counts!*

"About another five minutes." Nicolás's voice broke the silence, but his tone was pensive. Sara looked up at her husband. He was frowning, preoccupied. Nicolás, who usually had a joke or a clever phrase for every occasion, had said less and less as they drove through the city. Sara, who was busy with her own first impressions, had tried not to intrude on his thoughts. But now she reached up to kiss the corner of his mouth, which was tilted uncharacteristically down-ward. "Nicky, please don't worry! Whatever it is, I'll like it."

Nicolás raised a surprised eyebrow. His preoccupation relaxed into a smile. "I'm not worrying, *corazón*. Just calculating how much cash we have left."

Now it was Sara's turn to frown. Most of their wedding gifts had been checks or cash, because their friends had known they were leaving the country, and it was hardly practical to take along a profu-sion of toasters and towels. Sara and Nicolás had both cleaned out their checking accounts as well, and though the resulting sum had seemed huge to Sara, much had already been spent on their honey-moon. If they were to set up housekeeping, what was left wouldn't go far. Maybe she should have put her foot down a little more firmly about those extra days in California. But Nicolás hadn't wanted to leave a day earlier than necessary. Sara, who had never been so happy in her life, hadn't put up much of an argument.

Nicolás took out his wallet. "We've never talked about money," he said, echoing her thoughts. "But, here!" Pulling out a thick wad, he counted it out, shoved a few bills back into his wallet, and handed her the rest. "Put that in your purse."

"Oh, Nicky, no!" Sara pushed the money away. "I've still got a little. And we'll need everything we have to get set up."

"What are you talking about?" Nicolás laughed, shoving the roll into her hands. "This is just a little spending money. You'll want to do some shopping. Get yourself some nice clothes. What do you call it, your *trousseau*? I carried you off so fast that you didn't have time to get much together. And you're going to need a lot more than what you brought once we start entertaining. You can spend American dollars here as easily as *bolivianos*."

Sara riffled through the wad of $100 bills in her hand with disbelief. *There must be $2000 here! Doesn't he realize how much it costs to set up house? What if we have to buy furniture—and dishes? He can't think I'm going to spend all this on myself!*

Before Sara could make any further protest, Nicolás leaned forward to tap the cab driver on the shoulder. "Turn right up here."

The taxi slowed. They had just passed another small, open-air market and were now again on the outskirts of Santa Cruz. Across the road, an empty field stretched to the edges of another marginal-looking tin-roof neighborhood. On the near side, at the corner of the paved avenue and a dirt alley, stacks of lumber stood in an open lot fenced in by rude wooden posts and barbed wire. At the back of the lot, a half-dozen ragged children played merrily in front of the flimsiest shack Sara had ever seen. Sara caught her breath in dismay, but the taxi didn't turn in at the lumber yard or the alley. Slowing further, it rolled on alongside a high white wall. The wall stretched a full city block and was topped with a meter-high wrought-iron fence, with vicious-looking metal spikes that were definitely not ornamental. Beyond the stretch of wall, Sara caught a glimpse of a sawmill and a larger lumber yard.

It wasn't until the taxi bumped off the pavement and over a drainage canal that Sara realized they'd reached their destination. When the station wagon stopped in front of massive wooden doors, Sara's eyes grew wide. Rising high above the white walls, and completely out of place in its humble surroundings, was a house straight out of Hollywood. Sara was stunned! Swallowing hard, she said, "What is this place, Nicky? The presidential palace?"

Nicolás was already swinging his long legs out of the taxi, but he pulled his head and shoulders back inside long enough to toss a grin over his shoulder. "Of course, not, silly! It's our home!"

Sara sank back against the seat, her head spinning. *This—this mansion is Nicky's house?* Somehow the idea was a greater shock than her previous fear that she would be living in a shack. She recalled the speculative glance of the immigration official at the airport, the ease with which they'd sailed through customs, and the huge wad of bills that Nicky had pulled out of his wallet. Suddenly his teasing remarks about Prince Charming no longer seemed funny. She felt like a cottage-bred Sleeping Beauty who had just discovered her country swain's true identity—and she wasn't sure she liked it. *Who is Nicolás Cortéz?*

She leaned forward to watch through the windshield as Nicolás strode briskly over to a window that was set into a rounded abutment jutting out of the wall next to the gate. When he pressed a button near the window, a bored voice demanded over the intercom, "*Sí?* What do you want?"

Nicolás gave an impatient tap on the glass, and a dark face appeared in the window. The boredom changed abruptly into a delighted greeting: *"Don Nicolás!"* A moment later, the heavy mahogany gates swung ponderously inward. A short, stocky man in a khaki uniform, his broad features proclaiming his Inca ancestry, stepped forward to wave the taxi through the gate. With disbelief, Sara saw that he was wearing a hip holster. Two Doberman pinschers curled themselves around his legs.

By the time they had rolled inside and up the cobbled driveway, the second taxi was turning in through the gate. The two taxis came to a stop in front of the marble steps of the mansion. Climbing out slowly, Sara was torn between awed delight and a sinking realization that her travel-creased appearance didn't measure up to her new surroundings.

The house was even bigger than it had looked from the street, with a long, rectangular wing stretching back behind the main part of the house. Dormers jutted out on a half-dozen different levels. Stately pillars marched across the front of the house, reminiscent of a plantation mansion from the American South, but the balconies, with their wrought-iron grillwork, were pure Spanish. A squat stone tower just up the front steps reminded Sara of an English manor house, while an onion-bulb cupola straight out of the Arabian Nights topped a tall, slender folly in the back.

It should have been an architectural nightmare, but the cool white walls and burnt-red tile roof tied it all together in a harmony that was at least impressive. The high perimeter wall cut the chill of the wind, and flowers still nodded bravely in beds around the house. Vines trailed green leaves up the tower and over the front veranda. Citrus trees, palms, and ornamental pines punctuated the landscape, and a crystal blue pool sparkled in the distance. Despite her misgivings,

Sara was enchanted. Then, unbidden, the thought came: *If Nicky is accustomed to all this luxury, why did we have to take a* cab *home from the airport?*

"Well, do you like it?" Nicolás had chosen to walk up from the gate. Reaching her side, he threw an arm around her waist and drew her close.

"Like it?" Sara drew in a wondering breath. "I love it! It's incredible, like—like a palace!"

Nicolás looked pleased, but Sara sensed the same preoccupation, the same uncertainty she had noticed in the taxi. Something *was* bothering him. And it was obviously none of the things she'd been imagining. Could he possibly think she wouldn't be happy here? Pulling away from his embrace, she glanced around. "And your family? Where are they? I can hardly wait to meet them."

"Jorge is calling them now." Nicolás released her abruptly. "Sara, I—"

Just then, a man and two women emerged from the tall French doors that opened onto the pillared veranda. The man was an older, distinguished-looking version of Nicolás. Obviously his father. The two women were much alike: tall and brunette, with a Sophia Loren elegance that made Sara supremely conscious of every wrinkle in her blouse. *Nicky's mother and sister?*

"Nico!" The younger woman, who Sara could now see was about Sara's age, bounded gracefully down the steps, hands outstretched. "We expected you home a week ago! Why didn't you call?"

Sara glanced sharply up at Nicolás, unsure for a moment whether she'd understood the woman's quick Spanish correctly. Nicky had neglected to tell his parents which day they were arriving? No wonder they hadn't been picked up at the airport!

"Reina, *qué tal?*" Catching the young woman's hands, Nicky kissed her with affection on the cheek before turning to hug the older woman, whose descent had been a little more sedate. "*Mamá!*" Then his father was kissing him on each cheek in the customary Latin greeting. Sara stepped discreetly into the background, content to let Nicolás have this first moment with his family. Her throat tightened at their evident happiness. This was just the kind of warm family life she'd missed for so many years.

Sara lifted her head to find a pair of suspicious eyes studying her. Her neck prickled as she met the speculative gaze of the young woman Nicky had called Reina. The hostility in her eyes was instantly recognizable by any other female. Maybe this girl wasn't his sister after all.

Reina turned deliberately until her back was to Sara. Throwing her arms around Nicolás's neck, she planted a slow kiss on his lips. "And who is your little friend?" she asked in low, throaty Spanish.

Nicolás untangled Reina's clinging arms from around his neck. Holding a hand out to Sara, he flashed her a smile that made her forget the other woman's animosity. "*Querida,* I'd like you to meet my father, Don Luis Cortéz Velásquez de Salazar. My mother, Mimi. And this is my cousin, Reina Velásquez. Mamá, Papá, this is, uh . . . my, uh . . ." His words ran down to a stop.

With a quizzical look at her husband, Sara stepped forward, slipping her arm into his. Tilting her chin, she met Reina's antagonistic gaze straight on. She wasn't about to start married life quarreling with a member of Nicky's family, but neither would she let this kissing cousin get under her skin.

"What he's trying to say," she said, offering her other hand to Reina along with her friendliest smile, "is that I'm his wife, Sara."

The words dropped into a sudden silence like a boulder into the stillness of a pond. Reina stood like stone, ignoring Sara's outstretched hand. There was no mistaking the stunned disbelief on her face. "His wife!"

Sara's smile faltered as she realized that the other woman really hadn't known! Sara dropped her hand. "Yes, we were married almost two weeks ago."

She turned from Reina to her new in-laws, only to find the same stunned disbelief. And though she could not decipher her father-in-law's cool demeanor, his wife's proud features clearly mirrored Reina's hostility. Sara's heart went cold. There was something wrong here, all right, and she suddenly realized what it was! Not only had Nicky not told his family about his arrival, but he had said nothing about getting married. And the news was obviously far from welcome!

Sara's mother-in-law threw her hands up in the air. "Nico, what have you done?"

CHAPTER TWO

Sara looked up at her husband, her eyes wide with disbelief. "Why didn't you tell them, Nicky? Why didn't you at least tell *me* they didn't know?"

Nicolás's eyes darted down to his wife, then back up to look at his parents. "Look, I'm sorry! I just thought it would be easier this way! You know we didn't have much time."

"No time to tell your parents you were getting married?" Sara said.

Mimi Cortéz erupted in a stream of Spanish too rapid for Sara to follow, but she caught the gist. "How could you do this, Nico? Who is this girl? Why didn't you tell us? How could you keep this from your mamá?"

"Mamá, I am not the first one to come home with an American wife," Nicolás protested in a feeble attempt to cut across the flood.

"No, you are not. There was Rodrigo. And you remember what happened!" his mother snapped. Then, with unmistakable venom and a haughty toss of her head toward Sara, she added, *"She's* the one who would not let you tell us, isn't that true, my son? She would not risk losing such a fat prize. I know these little *gringas.*"

Up to this point, Sara had stood unflinching under the onslaught. In fact, she found herself sympathizing with Nicolás's mother. It couldn't be easy to have an unexpected daughter-in-law dropped in your lap—and a foreigner to boot. But Mimi's last statements sent red flooding to Sara's cheeks and an amber fire ignited in her eyes. Casting his bride a quick glance, Nicolás implored, "Mamá, please! She understands *español!*"

The torrent of words broke off immediately. Looking abashed, Mimi gave Sara a curt nod. Just then, Don Luis stepped forward and in one graceful motion lifted Sara's hand and kissed her gently on both cheeks. His eyes were cool, but the words he spoke were properly cordial. "Welcome, Sara, to our home." Though his English was accented, his voice was the same deep velvet as his son's. "Please forgive our discourtesy. You must understand that this has been a great surprise for us."

Sara, her hand grasped firmly in his, murmured a flustered reply. Her father-in-law's gaze narrowed as he studied her flushed face. "So! I see that this has been a shock for you too. You did not know that we were unaware of your marriage."

He threw Nicolás an unreadable look before adding with a slight smile, "I would ask that you forgive my rascal of a son. He can be very impulsive at times."

Sara smiled back. Grateful to find one member of Nicolás's family who didn't resent her existence, she put her whole heart into her smile. Don Luis blinked and glanced at his son before returning his attention to Sara. "I must say I understand his impetuousness. You are very beautiful! But come, let us go inside, and you shall be properly introduced to us."

He signaled the taxi drivers to unload the luggage and turned on his heel toward the house. His voice rose sharply. "Mimi, *amada! Reina!* Where are your manners? Are we not to welcome our son and his bride?"

Reina didn't move, and her eyes were pure poison, but Doña Mimi turned without another word and led the way up the steps. Sara felt the tension drain from Nicolás as he took her hand and they followed his parents through an arched doorway into the stone tower. With a relieved grin he whispered in English, "That went off pretty well, didn't it?"

By comparison, the rest of the day wasn't so bad. Reina said her good-byes almost immediately, flouncing out to her sports car with barely a nod to Sara. After Sara and Nicolás settled into their suite of rooms, they rejoined his parents in the drawing room. While a white-aproned maid served coffee and custard-filled pastries, Nicolás told his parents the story of how he and Sara had met. His storytelling was embellished with a natural flamboyance that made their first encounter sound a lot more exciting than it really had been, and by the time he finished, Doña Mimi's expression had softened slightly.

"You must have been very frightened, *hija*," she said to Sara. "It is a terrible thing, these people of the streets. Even here it is no longer safe at night."

After a few more minutes of polite conversation, Don Luis said something under his breath to Nicolás and the two men excused themselves and disappeared into Don Luis's office, while Mimi ushered Sara on a tour of the house.

Sara wasn't as impressed as a Bolivian might have been by the wall-to-wall carpeting, though it was the height of luxury in Santa Cruz's semi-tropical climate where mildew and dust storms made tile much more practical to clean. But she was suitably awed by the vaulted ceilings, sparkling chandeliers, and massive mahogany furniture.

One of the two dining rooms was cozy enough for family dining, but the other was banquet size. Sara gasped in astonishment when Mimi led her into a huge, vaulted room with tall, arched windows. *A real ballroom!* "Oh, this is beautiful!"

By the time her mother-in-law led her down a second-story hall past suite after suite of bedrooms, Sara had begun to feel that she had wandered into an exclusive hotel rather than a private home. Twice they encountered household servants vacuuming and dusting. Mimi sailed past them as though they didn't exist, and when Sara murmured a Spanish greeting, the women simply stared at her with blank faces.

Throughout their time together, Mimi kept up a polite flow of conversation, asking dozens of questions about Sara and her family. When Sara explained that her father had been an executive with a major American oil company, Mimi nodded grudging approval, as if to say that belonging to the upper management of an international corporation was an acceptable social stratum. Hearing that both of Sara's parents were deceased seemed to relieve Mimi more than anything else, much to Sara's indignation. *Is she worried that I'm going to flood them with a hoard of poor relations?*

They finished their tour in the vast drawing room where Nicolás and his father rejoined them. What Don Luis had met with him about, Sara wasn't told, but Nicky looked distinctly sulky. By then a parade of visitors had begun to arrive—Nicolás's two older sisters and their families, an elderly aunt, and an assortment of cousins and friends who had somehow heard that Nicolás was back in town. It wasn't until late in the evening that Sara had Nicolás all to herself.

✠

Sara studied her husband thoughtfully. He was slumped into his chair, a dark curl tumbling down over his forehead. He looked moody and tired—and younger, somehow, but still impossibly handsome. Her heart contracted. This wasn't how she had pictured their first evening in their new home, but she needed to understand a few things.

"Why didn't you tell them about getting married, Nicky?" she asked for the second time that day. "I mean, it's not like your family is living in one of those shacks out there with no phone. I even saw a fax machine down there!"

Nicolás shifted impatiently in his seat. "Look, I said I was sorry! But you don't know my father. If I'd called and told him I'd met a girl and wanted to get married, he'd have been on the next flight to Seattle to bring me home. And he would have made sure I never saw you again!"

He stretched out his hand toward Sara, who stood leaning against the open shutters, her hands twisted together behind her back. "Don't be angry with me, *corazón*. I know I should have told you, but I didn't want you to worry."

When Sara didn't move, he let his hand drop and his lips twisted into a crooked smile. "Okay, so maybe that wasn't the whole reason. The truth is, I was afraid you wouldn't marry me if you knew my parents didn't approve. It was hard enough to talk you into it without presenting complications!"

He looked across the room at Sara and said, *"Would* you have married me if I'd told you how my parents felt? Or would you have said, *'Hasta la vista, baby!'"*

"Oh, Nicky, of course I would have married you!" Rushing across the room, Sara knelt down next to Nicolás and lifted his hand to her cheek. "I love you! I couldn't bear never to see you again. But . . . I don't understand! Why would your parents disapprove of me so much? They don't even know me!"

"It isn't you," Nicolás said flatly. "My parents would disapprove of anyone they hadn't personally picked out for me. The way it works, you're supposed to come home from college, take your place in the family business, and find some nice Bolivian girl from a suitable family, preferably related."

"You mean, like Reina," Sara said in a small voice.

"Yes, like Reina," Nicolás admitted. "She's my second cousin, and it would have been—well, suitable. Not that I was ever interested in her that way. I mean, she was just a kid when I went off to college, and I've seen her only a few times since. But try telling Mamá that!"

"And what about this Rodrigo?" Sara asked. "Your mother said *he* married an American."

Nicolás looked startled. "You heard Mamá say that?"

Sara nodded. "So who is he? And what happened?"

Nicolás shrugged. "Rodrigo's my cousin, my mother's sister's son. He married some American tourist he met in a disco, but his wife never adjusted to life here. She was always whining about how things were different in America. Eventually, she moved back, taking her two daughters with her. Rodrigo got a divorce, but he still supports them—or rather, the family business does."

"So that's why your mother's so down on Americans," Sara said thoughtfully. "Well, I guess I can't really blame her. I'll just have to show her that all Americans aren't alike."

Nicolás slid his hand up from her cheek to thread his fingers in her shining hair. "So you see why this was the best way," he coaxed. "Now that we're married, there's nothing they can do. And once they get to know you, they'll adore you as I do. My father already thinks you are very beautiful!" he added persuasively.

Sara wasn't totally convinced, but she couldn't help smiling at his wheedling tone. She raised her head to look around at their spacious and luxurious suite. Waving her hand, she said, "And this? Why didn't you tell me about all this?"

"All this?" Nicolás glanced around as though seeing for the first time the thick carpeting, the canopied king-size bed, and the 25-inch TV. "What's wrong with it? Mamá gave us one of the nicest suites in the house."

"But that's just it! It's all so . . ." Sara struggled for words. "I . . . I thought you were poor."

"Poor!" Nicolás's face mirrored his astonishment. "What ever gave you that idea?"

"I . . . I don't know. I guess, everything I've read about Bolivia. I mean, it's the poorest country in South America, isn't it? And there's all those malnourished babies and . . . and people who work for hardly any pay, and all those wretched thatched huts we saw on our way in from the airport!"

"Would you really prefer that?" Nicolás was laughing now. "No, really, Sara, how in the world did you think my father managed to send his son off to an American university if he was one of those *campesinos* out there?"

"I thought you got a scholarship or something," Sara said defensively. "I mean, you never said anything. I just assumed—"

Nicolás shrugged. "I guess I never thought about it. I figured you'd know I wouldn't ask you to marry me if I couldn't support you in the style you were accustomed to. After all, your own father was quite an important man, wasn't he? You've told me that your home was very comfortable."

"Not like this!" Sara said. "This . . . this is like a palace! And to think I was bracing myself to live in that shack next door."

Nicolás looked at Sara as though he'd never seen anything quite like her before. "You really mean that?" he said slowly. "You really thought my family lived like those *indios* out there, and yet you were still willing to marry me?"

Nicolás stood up abruptly, pulled Sara to her feet, and enveloped her in a warm embrace. "I don't deserve you," he murmured against her lips. "You're more than I ever dreamed of!" Sara reached her arms up around his neck, answering him with a deep, passionate kiss.

✠

"Nicky? Are you still awake, honey?" Sara yawned and snuggled closer. Out of the corner of her eye, she saw the digital display on the bedside clock: 1:03 A.M.

"Hmmm?" Nicolás murmured, turning his head on the pillow. "Did you say something?"

"Tell me about your family," Sara said softly as she made herself more comfortable against his shoulder. "Your father. What does he do? I mean, is he a king, or the president, or just your ordinary, garden variety millionaire?"

Nicolás chuckled. "I already told you. He's a businessman."

"Hah!" Sara said skeptically. "The businessmen I know don't live in houses like this!"

"It's a big business," Nicolás said, with a tinge of pride in his voice. "My father is one of the biggest industrialists in Bolivia. Probably *the* biggest."

"So that's the reason for all the special treatment at the airport!" Sara was pleased to have one mystery explained. "They know your father?"

"*Everyone* knows Don Luis Cortéz Velásquez de Salazar. By reputation, if not by sight. It has its advantages," Nicolás added dryly.

Sara's curiosity was piqued. "So what exactly does he do? What kind of business is it?"

"A little of everything." Nicolás paused for a huge yawn. "Mainly import and export, but we own a few factories here and there. Fiberglass. Fine wines. Those native handicrafts the tourists go for. Even some boutique clothing, which you might like to check out. Papá believes in diversifying." His voice was slower now. "And sugar, of course. I'll take you on a tour sometime," he added with a yawn. "The main refinery is just . . ."

"Yes?" Sara prompted after a moment's silence. The only answer was a gentle snore. Nicolás was sound asleep, his mouth slightly open.

Sara rolled over. Slipping out of bed, she slid her silk nightgown over her head and padded across the carpet to the window. It had been a long, emotionally charged day, and she, like Nicolás, had been awake for most of the past forty-eight hours. But this was her first night in a strange country and she was too keyed up to fall asleep just yet.

Pushing open the tall wooden shutters, she stepped out onto the balcony. The *sur* had died down, but the air was still chilly. A whiff of wood smoke drifted down from somewhere—maybe their own chimneys—to mingle with the heady fragrance of the *franchipaniero* vine that twined over the edge of the balcony. Wrapping her arms tightly around herself to ward off the cold, Sara leaned over the wrought-iron railing. Their suite of rooms was on the third floor, and from the balcony Sara could see over the perimeter wall to the dim glow of scattered streetlights.

Overhead, the stars blazed in jeweled patterns from one end of the sky to the other. Sara gazed upward in wonder. You weren't supposed to be able to see stars like this in the city. The constellations were not the familiar ones of the northern hemisphere, but after a moment's search, she picked out the simple five-star pattern of the Southern Cross.

The night was not silent. It never was in Santa Cruz, she would soon discover. Not far away, a band was blasting out a Latin love song, heavy on the bass. From the branches of a flowering tree below the balcony, a cricket chirped along in perfect time. Across the wall, a dog barked with the hoarse, steady yap that informed the neighborhood he could keep this up all night. Next door, in the lumber yard, a gang of children kicked a soccer ball around despite the lateness of the hour. But it was a noisiness that spoke to Sara of warmth and laughter, and the fount of happiness that the circumstances of her arrival had briefly disturbed, bubbled up again inside her.

This big, restless city was now her home, and it was all so much more beautiful than she had ever dreamed. It didn't matter anymore that her welcome had not been what she'd envisioned. Nicky's family was *her* family now—and she would make them love her. Here, in this fairy-tale place, she and Nicky would build a home and a family of their own, and she would banish forever the feeling of rootlessness that had plagued her since childhood.

No one—not Nicolás, not even Sara herself—could guess just how passionate was Sara's longing for a home of her own. For just one place and person that belonged to her and her alone. For all the things that make up that feeling of warmth and security she only vaguely remembered from her own childhood.

Her mother had been that source of warmth and security. Her father had worked for AMACO, a large American oil company, and the nature of his job had been such that, by the time Sara was six, she had lived in five different countries on three separate continents. While her father by necessity had plunged into production estimates and local labor problems, it was her mother who had transformed each temporary apartment or company house into a home; it was her mother who'd curled up with Sara to watch cartoons, giggling harder than her small daughter at all the crazy characters; and it was her mother who'd helped Sara stir up cookies for Daddy's return and tucked her into bed at night, singing "Jesus Loves Me" in her husky, off-key voice.

"God told us to make a joyful noise to him," she'd tease when Sara clapped her hands over her ears. "He didn't say anything about being on tune!"

For years Sara had clung to those memories, replaying them over and over like a well-worn videotape. But the passage of time had dulled the memories, and now when she leafed through the old photo albums, her mother's face was almost that of a stranger. All that remained was an impression of laughter and happiness that had somehow faded into the cold gray pain of the "after" years.

When Sara was six, AMACO had moved the Connors to Bogotá, Colombia. There'd been a lull in the violence and turmoil of that troubled Caribbean republic, and American companies had once again been allowing their overseas personnel to bring along their families. The ups and downs of the political climate hadn't bothered young Sara, who'd learned her first Spanish from the small daughters and sons of her father's Colombian colleagues. If an armed security guard watched over their house day and night, and the unmarked company car that took Sara to a private American school routinely varied its route—wasn't that part of every child's life?

The Connors had lived in Bogotá for three full years, the most permanent home Sara had known. And in the end it wasn't a terrorist attack or a bomb that had shattered Sara's tranquil childhood—just a stupid truck driver who'd mixed a few joints with a bottle of Colombia's famous *aguardiente* and then had crossed all seven crowded lanes of one of Bogotá's elevated freeways and demolished the Connors' sedan.

Though her other memories had faded, Sara still vividly remembered the day the laughter and warmth had gone out of her life. She could still see her mother buckling Joshua, her four-year-old brother, into the back seat of the car before they left for the airport to pick up Grandma and Grandpa Hansen. The company car had arrived right at that moment to take Sara to school, and it was the last time she saw her mother and brother alive. The police later told her father that it had taken three days for the driver of the semi to sober up enough to realize he'd destroyed four lives.

Five, including Alan Connor's. Because he too had gone away that day, and to nine-year-old Sara, it had seemed that she'd lost a father as well as a mother, brother, and grandparents. There were no more three-way tickling matches when Daddy came home, no more wandering hand-in-hand through the long-ago splendors of Bogotá's fabulous Gold Museum, no more family vacations on Caribbean beaches.

Sara's father had requested an immediate transfer back to the United States, where he'd survived his grief by working longer and longer hours. He'd hired a housekeeper, arranged for summer camps, and paid for piano and tennis lessons, but Sara had sometimes felt that he'd completely forgotten a lonely little girl lost in her own world of grief.

But Sara had survived too. She'd been a good student and reasonably popular for a girl who changed schools at least once a year. When Sara was thirteen, her father, motivated by some twinge of conscience, had accepted a more permanent position in Seattle. There, she'd picked up Spanish again. She'd forgotten much of what she'd learned in Colombia by then, but a Cuba-born teacher and two trips to Mexico with her church youth group had expanded her classroom vocabulary into a reasonable fluency.

At the University of Washington, Sara had drifted naturally into Spanish as her major. She'd studied hard and had been a consistent member of the Dean's List, though at times she'd wondered whose approval she was trying to win. When her father died of a heart attack during her sophomore year of college, Sara had felt that she was saying good-bye to a casual acquaintance rather than her dad. But at least there'd been no financial worries. The proceeds from her father's life insurance policy had more than covered her remaining years of school.

She'd dated off and on throughout her university years—mostly fellow students from the large college-and-career church group she attended. But the guys had all seemed so young, still too caught up in the excitement of the present to be thinking of the future. And, consciously or not, Sara had been looking for marriage and children and a home. So she'd reached the last semester of college with her heart intact.

She hadn't been unhappy. Though life hadn't turned out the way her childhood fantasies had said it should, it hadn't been bad. With her GPA and fluency in Spanish, a teaching job for the fall had been almost a sure thing. And like any girl her age, she'd had an inner conviction that Prince Charming was out there somewhere. She had only to be patient.

Then Nicolás had walked into her life, and he'd been like no one she'd ever known before. Since the day she'd met him, the safe, even-keeled, *sensible* tenor of her life had been turned upside down. She'd been carried along in a current too swift to allow her time to think—and she hadn't wanted to think! Here was someone who adored her, who thought that she—ordinary Sara Connor—was beautiful, who loved her with a passionate love she'd never before experienced.

The swell of happiness was almost too great to bear. Sara lifted her face to the patiently blinking stars of the Southern Cross. Her hands tightened on the cold metal of the iron railing. "Oh, God, it's all so much more than I ever dreamed!" she whispered. "I just don't deserve all this! And Nicky is so wonderful! Please help me to be worthy of him."

She broke off suddenly when she realized what she was doing. How long had it been since she'd prayed like this? How long since she'd talked to God like a friend? It had to have been years!

The smile of reminiscence on Sara's lips suddenly tightened into a straight line. *The birthday party!* The cause of the argument she'd had with her mother right before her death. Sara couldn't remember which classmate's birthday it had been, but *everyone* who counted in her fourth-grade class had been invited. And then Sara's mother had said no. The party was to be held clear across Bogotá, and neither her parents nor the company car would be available to take her.

"There'll be other parties!" her mother had told her gently. But Sara had still been sulking when the company car picked her up for school the next morning. She'd turned her face away from her mother's good-bye kiss and hadn't even waved when her mother drove off to pick up Grandma and Grandpa.

For years Sara had thought she'd known why God had allowed her beautiful mother and little brother to be killed. He was punishing her for being so angry at her mother. At first she'd railed at God. *It was my fault! I'm the one who got mad! Why didn't you take me?* But when no answer came, something had frozen inside her and she'd simply turned her back on God.

Oh, not outwardly! She still attended church, obeyed her father and her teachers, and stayed away from the youthful follies that had pulled down so many of her classmates. She'd even prayed—perfunctory prayers at meals, at youth group, and before a tough exam—but there was no joy in her prayers or in her obedience, no more warm fellowship with a heavenly Father who was also a personal friend.

As Sara grew older, she'd come to recognize, of course, the foolishness of supposing that her childish temper tantrum had caused her mother's death. But that didn't make any difference. She knew the truth now. Sure, the Scriptures taught that "God so loved the world," but if he cared personally about the life of Sara Connor, if she was more than just a speck of excess lint in the midst of the universe, then he wouldn't have left her life so completely empty.

Then Nicolás had come into her life, and at long last the emptiness in her heart—that hollow place that needed so desperately to love and be loved—had been filled. Not with some nebulous "love of God," but with a love whose arms she could feel around her, a love that would keep her warm in bed at night, that would bring back the family circle she'd lost so long ago. How could life get any better?

A faint rustle broke into Sara's reverie. Startled, she glanced down. A dark form was moving silently through a bed of ornamental plants just below the balcony. *A burglar!* Sara was alarmed until she recognized the pair of four-legged shadows slinking along in front of the stocky figure. The Dobermans.

Two long, lean heads swung around to look up at the balcony, and one dog gave a low whine. Sara knew that the darkness of the unlit balcony hid the scantiness of her gown, but she stepped back hurriedly as the guard looked up, his features shadowed and alien in the faint gleam of a floodlight. A sudden chill settled over her happiness, and she hurried inside to bed.

CHAPTER THREE

An aging DC-3 flew low over the jungle canopy. Relaxing ever so slightly against the seat back, the pilot eased off the throttle as the tension of the past hour began to ebb. He glanced with satisfaction over his shoulder at the stripped-down interior of the two-engine plane, its belly almost visibly bulging with the weight of its cargo. He'd really done it! The last checkpoint was behind him. The invisible line in the middle of the jungle that marked the Brazilian border was now only a few minutes of flight time away. By this time tomorrow, he—and the men who owned the cargo—would be rich beyond their most extravagant fantasies.

He was safe now. *Safe and rich.*

If at first he didn't hear the hum of another aircraft, it was because he didn't want to. It just couldn't be! The rotors were first to emerge—gradually—above the treetops. Then came the body of the helicopter, long, sleek, and gray, its nose tilted slightly downward as it rose to hover directly in his flight path. The pilot of the DC-3 cursed viciously. *Militares.* How could they possibly have known?

The glare of the early morning sun on the helicopter's windshield hid the faces of the occupants. But there was no mistaking the arm in the olive-and-brown camouflage fatigues that thrust itself from a side window. Or the peremptory gesture.

Glancing downward, the pilot spotted a long, narrow gash in the foliage up ahead. A jungle airstrip. One that didn't appear on any chart *he* owned.

Reluctantly, the pilot banked his aircraft in the direction indicated, but his mind was seething as he reviewed his options. He knew that the helicopter was both faster and much less heavily loaded than his DC-3. But he'd also made it his business to discover a few details about his country's military that its commanders would prefer not be known. For one, the present economic crisis among the armed forces meant that its pursuit aircraft often flew unarmed. And fuel rationing had severely curtailed their cruising range. And with the border just ahead . . .

It was a gamble, certainly. But he wouldn't have to outrun the swifter aircraft, only keep from being headed off for a few more minutes. If he could just reach the border, no Bolivian military pilot would dare pursue him into Brazilian airspace. In any event, if it came down to a choice between taking on the air force or facing the angry owners of the cargo packed wall-to-wall behind his seat, it was an easy decision.

The helicopter was circling to take up a herding position on his wingtip when the pilot made his move, a sudden thrust of the throttle, left and down. Banking sharply, the DC-3 dove under the belly of the helicopter. The plane shuddered in protest under its heavy load, and for one sickening moment, the pilot felt the scrape of branches against the undercarriage. Then, by sheer willpower, he forced the plane to climb. Ahead lay a clear flight path.

The sharp *rat-tat-tat* of gunfire told him he'd lost the gamble even before his side window exploded inward. Shaking shards of safety glass from his hair and face, the pilot glanced out the shattered window to see the helicopter resume its position off his left wing. This time, it moved far enough forward that he could see through the open side panels. He cursed again, loudly. They were armed all right! And the powerful M-60 machine gun bolted to the helicopter's cabin floor had its sights carefully centered on the cockpit of the DC-3. With a defeated shrug, the pilot slumped into his seat, obeying without protest the gunner's angry gesture to turn back.

He was lining himself up with the landing strip when one of his engines caught, sputtered—and stopped. Thrusting his head gingerly out the broken window, the pilot swore steadily as he saw the flames flickering below his left wing and the liquid stream flowing away from a stitching of bullet holes along the fuel tank. Forget the fortune he was losing. He would be lucky to reach the ground alive!

The plane died just before the wheels touched the grass. Hitting the ground hard, the aircraft bounced twice, then barreled out of control down the runway. At the far end of the jungle strip, it crumpled its nose against a huge mahogany tree.

Groaning, the pilot straightened up from where the impact had slammed him against the wheel. Incredibly, he was still in one piece, even if his plane wasn't.

But there was no time for self-congratulation. Reaching behind the seat, he pulled out the Uzi machine pistol he kept there for just such an eventuality. He thrust the door open with a screech of tortured metal. At six inches, it jammed. An anguished glance revealed that a massive tree branch knocked loose by the crash had wedged against the door. It would take more than his strength to shove it loose. Cursing, he scrambled over the copilot's seat and clambered out the other door.

By the time his feet touched the ground, the helicopter was down and a handful of men in army fatigues were loping across the runway toward him. Swinging the Uzi up into firing position, he cut loose with a wild burst that hit nothing but had the satisfying result of dropping the soldiers to the ground. Still spraying randomly, the pilot backed toward the shelter of the jungle behind him. He was a step from cover when the Uzi clicked on empty air.

Casting aside the useless weapon, the pilot dove behind a tree trunk as the rattle of return fire sounded across the clearing. Cowering under the ensuing hailstorm of bullets, he wormed his way backward into a tangle of brush.

Then a shout rose above the gunfire, "Let him go!" The gunfire died instantly. "He's not worth the trouble," the leader called out. "We have work to do."

The pilot scuttled backward to a safer distance, but he did not immediately take the escape offered him. Every *centavo* he had in the world was riding on that cargo. Though unarmed, he had to at least make an attempt to salvage the situation. The *militares* were notoriously stupid. An opportunity would present itself.

Crawling under the cover of a tangle of ferns, he inched forward until he had a clear view of the airstrip. His mouth gaped open. These soldiers were behaving like no *antinarcóticos* he'd ever heard of. There was no inspecting the cargo, no searching for incriminating paperwork, no taking of pictures for their files. Working silently and swiftly, the handful of men in army fatigues were shifting the cargo from the plane to the helicopter, slinging the heavy bags into a neat stack around the M-60 with the ease of experience.

The pilot's eyes narrowed in fury. The explanation was simple and galling. These were no soldiers, military aircraft or not. They were *volteadores*—hijackers who lay in ambush, like vultures, to steal themselves an easy fortune after others had done all the work and taken all the risks. And unlike the *militares*, they were far too dangerous to be challenged or outwitted.

In a manner of minutes, the helicopter was loaded to capacity. Slamming the side door of the plane on the rest of the cargo, the *volteadores* scrambled into the chopper on top of their load. The rotors sprang to life and the heavy-laden pirate ship lifted off the ground.

The pilot waited until the rhythmic drone died away before crawling out of the brush. Wincing at the bruises and cuts that were just beginning to make themselves known, he limped back to the plane. Most of his payload was still intact, but it didn't take a mechanical genius to figure out that it wasn't going anywhere. Not in this plane, at least. Nor was there any point in trying to radio for assistance. The hijackers had made sure of that before they left. The pilot surveyed the bullet-shattered dashboard with despair.

There was only one thing left to do—cut his losses and walk away before the hijackers came back for another load. But how? He had no idea which direction through the trackless jungle led to civilization. He could wander for years without finding his way out. And that was only if he didn't starve first or get eaten by one of the jungle's more lethal inhabitants. Even if he made it out, his employers would not be as lenient as the *volteadores* had been.

Sinking down onto the doorstep of the DC-3, the pilot buried his face in his hands. After a moment, his shoulders began to shake. It wasn't until he heard the sound of the helicopter returning that he got up and stumbled into the jungle.

Sara stretched out a languid arm, reaching for the suntan oil. A cloudless sky arced overhead, and the heat radiating from the back of her legs told her she'd been outside too long. But she was feeling too lazy to move from the poolside into the shade of the *paraíso* trees that scattered rose and flame and peach petals over the tiled poolside.

Winter in the tropics! she sighed. The thermometer nailed to the bottle-shaped trunk of a nearby *toborochi* showed 27 degrees Centigrade—80 degrees Fahrenheit—and though the pool was still too chilly for Nicky's family, to Sara it was heaven.

She dabbled her hand over the edge of the pool, splashing the cooling water over her face and arms. It was incredible how easily she had adapted to her new life. She loved getting up in the morning without having to make her own bed; savoring a breakfast of fresh rolls, tropical fruit, and *café con leche* delivered to the sitting room; and lolling around the pool, sipping tall, cool glasses of pineapple juice instead of rushing off to classes or work.

And it was certainly nice having all the money she could spend. Not that Sara had ever been penniless. But with her father's death and the necessity of maintaining her own apartment and car, not to mention university bills, careful budgeting had been necessary. Now, at her mother-in-law's insistence, Sara spent countless hours shopping at exclusive boutiques, filling out her wardrobe with the newest American and European styles suitable to the upper echelons of Bolivian society.

As for married life, it couldn't be better. True, she had less time alone with Nicky than she'd like. Except for breakfast, they took meals with Don Luis and Mimi, and Nicky had almost immediately begun spending long hours with his father, learning the administration of Don Luis's far-flung business empire. Evenings were a series of welcoming parties, barbecues at other luxurious homes around Santa Cruz, and drop-in visits from friends who came to greet the returning Cortéz heir and meet his new bride.

But in the late night hours, when music blaring from some nearby party kept them awake, and the rising moon shone through the bars on the windows, casting a latticework of silver and shadow across the exquisite European bedspread, and cool night breezes wafted through the open balcony doors—the night hours were theirs.

She yawned and slathered more lotion on her arms and legs. Yes, it was all so wonderful and far more than she'd ever dreamed, but the truth was, she was just a bit bored. There was only so much shopping and sunbathing a girl could stand. Her mother-in-law seemed content with an unending round of high society teas and bridge parties, leavened by an occasional aerobics workout or racquetball game at the Las Palmas Country Club, but playing the role of society matron was hardly Sara's cup of tea!

At least Mimi had begun to thaw a little. Always formal, always exquisitely groomed, her mother-in-law had been horrified at first to find Sara sprawled with a book on the velvet cushions of the drawing-room sofa or sauntering off to town in jeans and a T-shirt. But when Sara meekly accepted—albeit through gritted teeth—Mimi's lectures on the proper behavior of a Cortéz bride, Mimi had declared herself quite pleased with her daughter-in-law's submissiveness and had even gone so far as to announce in Sara's hearing that the family could have done much worse. Sara, in turn, soon came to realize that Mimi's aloof demeanor was the inbred result of generations of patrician forebears and not a deliberate unfriendliness.

Nicky's two sisters had also extended a reasonably warm welcome to their sudden sister-in-law. Delores and Janéth were both married to men who worked for Don Luis. They had their own luxurious homes—though smaller than the Cortéz mansion—and a half-dozen small children between them, but nannies and servants gave them seemingly infinite freedom to be out and about or lounging around. They willingly included Sara in their shopping expeditions, visits to friends, and afternoon teas, and Sara had been greatly relieved to find that her own contemporaries among *Cruceño* society showed far more freedom of manners and dress than did her mother-in-law.

Sara rolled over onto her stomach. All in all, things were going far better than the consternation surrounding her first arrival had given her reason to hope. With daily use, her Spanish was improving by leaps and bounds, and if her new female relatives were not exactly kindred spirits, Sara enjoyed their company well enough.

Which left her father-in-law. Sara's fine brows came together. Though Don Luis had been the first to extend her a welcome, and he always treated her with exquisitely polite courtesy, somehow she never quite felt at ease in his presence. Maybe because he looked so much like—and yet unlike—his son. He had the same lithe movements and aristocratic good looks that would no doubt still have women's heads turning when Nicolás was seventy. But whereas Nicolás was open and easy-mannered with a ready laugh, Don Luis was a closed book, his handsome features giving no hint of his thoughts. The generous curve of Nicky's mouth was, in his father, a straight, thin line. And there was more steel in her father-in-law than in Nicolás. Though Sara had never seen Don Luis display anything less than smoothly good manners, she suspected that he was not one to be crossed.

"Aieeeee!" A splash of icy water on her scorching back banished her father-in-law from her mind. She rolled over, expecting to see one of her rascally young nephews.

"Just a little basting!" Nicolás grinned down at her, one hand tucked innocently behind his back. "You're starting to look like a fried lobster in back!"

Sara couldn't suppress a giggle. Although Nicky's English was impeccable, American idioms always sounded comical coming out of his mouth. He dropped an empty plastic cup next to Sara. "Sorry, I just couldn't resist." He backed away quickly when Sara cupped a hand in the water to retaliate. "Oh, no you don't! I'm dressed to go out, and you should be too."

Sara eyed his polo shirt, Bermuda shorts, and polarized sunglasses. Whatever appointment she'd forgotten, it was obviously nothing formal. "Go where? I thought you were going to the office to do inventory."

"And waste a perfect day like this? The next *sur* is plenty soon enough for inventory." Pulling a lawn chair from the shade of a mango tree, Nicolás stretched out, pushing his sunglasses onto his forehead.

"Go where?" Sara repeated.

"Have you forgotten your homeland already?" Nicolás teased. "Or don't you know what day this is?"

Sara sat up with an abrupt motion. "Fourth of July!"

Nicolás swung his long legs off the lawn chair. "One of my cousins— you remember Gabriela—called this morning to say that the American consulate is putting on a celebration at the American Co-op school. There's even going to be fireworks. You do want to go, don't you?"

Sara let Nicolás pull her to her feet. Walking her fingers slowly up his muscular chest, she gave a slow smile and mimicked the throaty, sultry voice she'd heard Reina use with practically every man. "And if I do, what's the hurry?"

Nicolás looked startled, then grinned as he captured her fingers in his own. "None at all, *querida*. No hurry at all."

✠

They picked up Gabriela on the way. It was a tight squeeze to get the three of them into Nicolás's sunny yellow Ferrari—a graduation gift from Don Luis—but Sara gladly folded herself into the crack between the seats. Though she'd only recently met Gabriela, Nicky's cousin was definitely her favorite Cortéz relative. Tall, thin, and somewhere past thirty, Gabriela was not really pretty, but her startling makeup and the casual grace with which she wore avant-garde fashions gave an illusion of elegance. When Sara first met her, Gabriela had promptly turned the conversation to world affairs, a welcome change from the endless recitation of servant problems, society events, and local gossip that seemed to consume the interest of every other Cortéz woman. Sara enjoyed the caustic wit with which Gabriela poked fun at both Bolivian and U.S. politicians, and she had been astounded to discover that Gabriela knew more than she did about American politics.

"Happy Fourth of July," Gabriela greeted Sara as Nicolás gunned the engine, his tires squealing out of the driveway. Her English was more stilted than Nicky's, but still very good. "Or is that the proper thing to say?"

"More or less," Sara assured her. "We say 'happy' for just about everything, other than Christmas." Her eyes were glued to the traffic. Although she trusted Nicky's driving ability, she could never quite relax as he zipped in between cars and pulled maneuvers that would have earned him a ticket in the United States. "Drive offensively" seemed to be the only rule of the road.

Nicolás slowed down at last, turning off the highway at a sign that read "Las Palmas Country Club." Unlike the area around the Cortéz estate, this neighborhood was a neatly laid-out development of elegant homes and larger mansions. Beyond the country club were the manicured lawns of an eighteen-hole golf course. A half-dozen yellow buses with "Santa Cruz Cooperative School" lettered on the sides marked the turnoff to the school driveway.

Sara looked around with interest as a guard waved them through the chain-link gate. The school was much like the American school she'd attended in Colombia, with classrooms opening directly onto wide, roofed verandas—a more sensible construction than a closed building in the heat of the tropics. There was a large sports complex and what looked to be a separate kindergarten and playground off to one side. Sara hadn't realized that Santa Cruz had a large enough English-speaking community to warrant a school this size. Nicolás jolted over a speed bump into the school driveway. The small parking lot was jammed full, and the grassy verge across from the school was lined with vehicles for several blocks, but Nicolás managed to find an open space, and the three of them walked back toward the school.

"Your big oil companies built all this," Gabriela told her. "There are not so many Americans in Santa Cruz anymore, but twenty years ago, there were thousands. Because of the oil, you know."

Sara knew all about the oil and mining companies that had swarmed into Latin America in the 1950s and 1960s to develop the vast untouched reserves of natural resources and reap healthy profits for their shareholders. Hadn't she been an oil kid herself? But by the 1980s, nationalization had burst the bubble, and most of the Americans had gone home.

"So who studies here now?" Sara asked, stopping to read an ad for scholarships to American universities on a glassed-in bulletin board. "Or is it all Spanish now?"

"No, the teachers are still American, hired in the United States and brought down," Gabriela said. "There may be few American students left, but there are many wealthy Bolivians who wish their children to go to the United States for university."

"Yeah, good old SCCS! Boy, does this place bring back the

memories." Nicolás was peering into a glass case filled with sports trophies. "Look, Gabriela, they've still got our trophy from the year we beat Tahuichi in the soccer championships. Remember that?"

"You mean, *you* went to this school?" Sara exclaimed with astonishment.

"Sure!" Nicolás lifted an eyebrow. "Anyone who's anybody in Santa Cruz studies here. Where did you think I learned to speak English?"

"I don't know," Sara admitted. She didn't know why she was so surprised. It was, after all, the most logical explanation. "I guess I just thought you'd studied really hard."

"Nico, *study?*" Gabriela hooted, giving her cousin a knowing look. "Nico wasn't exactly famous at SCCS for studying."

"And *you* were?" Nico grinned, not at all fazed by her sarcasm.

Gabriela shrugged. "Okay, so we weren't exactly model students. But at least I got decent grades. And you must admit, Nico, nobody else in the family was suspended so many times that they set a school record."

Nicolás winked down at Sara. "Just practical jokes. The principal didn't have much of a sense of humor. Besides, I graduated, didn't I?"

"Sure, by the skin of your teeth!"

"Hey, Gabriela, it's good to see you!" A cheerful greeting interrupted the amicable sparring. Gabriela's red-tipped hands flew into the air as she swung around. "Sam! Laura!"

Sara turned to see a couple in their late fifties approaching. Sam was a big bear of a man, with flaming red hair and beard; his wife was even shorter than Sara, and plump. Her slightly protruding, pale blue eyes reminded Sara at first glance of a mildly inquisitive fish. Laura was enthusiastically waving a small Union Jack, for reasons that became obvious as soon as she opened her mouth. "My, don't we look smashing today, Gabriela." She hugged Gabriela, then turned to arch her pale eyebrows at Nicolás and Sara.

Gabriela drew Sara forward. "Please, Sara, you must meet my very special friends, Sam and Laura Histed. They do very important work with the children of the streets. And Sam is the priest—no, no, how do you say it?—pastor?—of the American church here."

"*Pastor* is right," Laura Histed said with a comical glance at her husband. "He'd have to get rid of me if he were a priest, and I can tell you he'd never survive as a bachelor!"

Sara smiled politely at the joke, only too happy for the distraction. She hadn't appreciated Gabriela's implied criticism of her husband. Okay, so she'd only assumed that Nicky had been a serious student, and she'd wrongly concluded that he had come to the United States on a scholarship. But did it really matter what kind of shenanigans Nicky had pulled in his earlier years, or that his faultless English came from a lifetime of American schools and not years of hard study? *It's what Nicky is now that matters,* she told herself. Still, Gabriela's insinuations reminded Sara that just about everyone in Santa Cruz knew her husband better than she did, and she couldn't help wondering how many other surprises Nicolás was going to spring on her.

Sara pushed the thought away. She wasn't going to let anything so trivial spoil her enjoyment of the afternoon. "So your husband is the pastor of an American church here in the city?"

"Well, English-speaking, after a fashion," Laura laughed. "We're actually a pretty mixed crew—a few Brits like us, some Australians, Americans, Canadians, and several others who like to attend a church service in English. Why don't you and your husband join us? We meet right here in the school's dining hall every Sunday morning."

Sara glanced doubtfully at Nicolás. "I'd love that sometime," she said. Her first Sunday in Santa Cruz, she'd been eager to see how a Bolivian church service compared with her own church back home, but a pool party for the entire Cortéz clan had taken precedence. She'd understood, with Nicolás just back from a two-year absence, but in the weeks since, neither Nicolás nor his parents had suggested going to church. "Sunday is the only day the family has together," Nicky had said when she hesitantly brought it up. "Let's just give it a few weeks."

So Sara had dropped the subject. After all, her own church attendance had been pretty perfunctory since her father died. But somewhat to her surprise, she'd found that she really missed it—the stately hymns, the prayers, the peace and quiet of the sanctuary, even the somewhat lengthy and soporific sermons. The week just didn't seem complete without Sunday worship.

Sara tuned back in to hear Sam Histed talking about their work with the street children. "It's been five years since we came to Bolivia as missionaries, and it seems that every year the problem gets worse. I don't know if you've been here long enough to notice, but there are literally thousands of children in Santa Cruz who are earning their own living on the streets. A good number of them don't even have a shack to go home to at night."

Sara nodded her understanding. She'd already learned that she couldn't shop downtown without a half-dozen or more filthy children plucking at her clothes and demanding a handout. The more enterprising among them begged to shine her shoes or carry her bags. At every red light, a ragged throng of young boys jumped into the street with buckets and squeegees to wash windshields for a few cents. Both Nicolás and Mimi had warned Sara not to encourage them, but she felt guilty brushing them off like just so many flies.

"That's how we met Gabriela," Laura chimed in. "We were trying to get permission from the welfare department to hold some practical training courses for the adolescents. Carpentry, sewing, that sort of thing. With all the red tape piling up at every step, you'd think we were asking for a handout instead of offering some badly needed help."

Laura's pale blue eyes twinkled as she looked around the group. Sara could have sworn the woman had never heard of makeup, and she evidently hadn't updated her wardrobe in quite some time, yet there was something oddly appealing about her. Maybe it was her genuine interest in everything—the street children, Gabriela's work at city hall, meeting Sara—that bubbled up through the otherwise overwhelming cheerfulness. She reminded Sara of a diminutive footstove she had used in Seattle to heat her bedroom on frosty nights—old fashioned, but warm and round and infinitely cheering.

Laura was on a roll now. She reached out and grasped Gabriela's arm as she proudly proclaimed to the others, "Then Gabriela came along, took one look at the project, and all of a sudden, the paperwork was sailing through. Along the way, we became fast friends. It's been helpful having a little *muñeca* in the mayor's office."

Muñeca. Sara had learned the meaning of the word since the day she'd heard Nicky use it at the airport. The literal translation was "wrist," but it referred to anything that moved the hand of Latin society. Influence, clout, a family member in a key position, even cash slipped under the table was *muñeca*. *Muñeca* put politicians into office and greased paperwork through the Bolivian bureaucratic system. In fact, it was hard to get anywhere here without it.

Gabriela shrugged. "It was nothing. What Sam and Laura are doing for the children of our city—that is important."

Sara looked at Gabriela with a new respect. She hadn't realized that her flamboyant cousin-in-law involved herself in anything more than the usual social rounds favored by the other Cortéz women.

Nicolás shifted restlessly, and Sara could sense his impatience. Sara, who had grown up listening to missionaries speak at countless missions conferences and youth meetings, was actually enjoying herself. But it was easy to see that these weren't Nicky's kind of people, nor did he appear the least bit interested in the plight of Bolivia's unwashed homeless.

"If you'll excuse us," Sara broke in hastily, "Nicky has a friend he'd like to see." She wasn't entirely certain of the truth of her statement, but it was the best she could do on the spur of the moment.

"I'm sure he does." Sam beamed at Nicolás. "Cortéz isn't exactly an unknown name around here, is it?" His deep voice boomed out in a rumbling laugh. Laura added, "Please do forgive us for rambling. When we get to talking about our kids, we don't know when to stop."

"Not at all, it was very—uh, interesting!" Nicolás assured them politely. But there was a barely concealed note of boredom in his voice, and the relief as he turned away was obvious enough to draw a dirty look from Gabriela.

"We'll see you again sometime, I hope," Laura called after them. "And give some thought to Sunday. We've got a potluck after church."

Sara turned to respond with a noncommittal wave and smile, but Nicolás didn't even glance back. Quickening his pace, he steered Sara past the gymnasium and down a flight of steps before he let her slow down. "Phew, the friends Gabriela picks up," he said, wiping his forehead with an exaggerated gesture. "I thought we'd never get out of there."

"You don't think we hurt their feelings?" Sara asked anxiously.

"Of course not! People like that don't even know when they're boring you stiff." His ill-humor evaporating, Nicolás grabbed Sara by the hand. "Come on, let's go have some fun."

The steps opened out onto a lawn with a milling crowd of people. Patio tables set out under a large pavilion were full, and family groups spilled out across the grass. Small paper flags were everywhere— mostly American, of course, but Sara picked out another Union Jack, a Canadian maple leaf, and a fair scattering of Bolivia's red, yellow, and green. It appeared that others of the international community had come along to help their northern friends celebrate their Independence Day.

Out on the playing field, a baseball game was underway, with a mixture of children and adults. From one end of the pavilion the smell of melted butter and the rattle of popping corn teased the senses. Hamburger patties sizzled on a grill next to the popcorn machine, amid balloons, bunting, band music, and an underlying buzz of excited voices. Sara's spirits soared. Except for the palm trees along the perimeter of the school yard, it could be a Fourth of July back home.

"Boy, does that smell good!" Nicolás flared his nostrils appreciatively. "American hamburgers are one thing I miss from college. Come on! Let's get something to eat."

Their passage through the crowd resembled a triumphal procession. As Sam Histed had suggested, it seemed there were few, even among the expatriate community, who didn't know the Cortéz name. Sara saw nudges and whispers, and there were cries of "Nico!" from those who knew the Cortéz family personally. Before they'd advanced ten meters, they'd been stopped a dozen times with requests for Nicolás to introduce his beautiful bride.

Nicolás performed the introductions with obvious pride, and his friends were vocal in their admiration. By the time they reached the grill, Sara was flushed and happy. It wasn't that she took their extravagant compliments seriously. She knew that her blonde coloring was considered beautiful in this country of dark-haired women, but she was under no illusion that it was anything other than her position as the Cortéz bride that prompted all the flattering attention. Still, it did something for a girl's ego to find everyone so openly admiring, so eager to make her welcome.

No, not everyone! She had just accepted a burger from a tall, lanky American in a cowboy hat and boots when she became aware of a pair of cool gray eyes watching her. She looked more intently across the pavilion. The man leaning casually against one of the posts that held up the roof wasn't one who would stand out in a crowd, and Sara never would have noticed him if his piercing gaze had not, without question, been aimed in her direction. A gaze that held none of the warmth and approval she'd somehow come to expect, but speculation and—yes, criticism.

Why should he disapprove of me? Sara wondered, confused. She was sure she'd never seen him before. Then she saw that he wasn't watching her, but Nicolás, whose head at the moment was thrown back in laughter at some comment from the hamburger chef. *He doesn't like Nicky!* she realized with a shock.

Sara was suddenly angry. How dare this—this *person* criticize her husband! She looked him over with hostility. He was of average height and several years older than she was—maybe as old as thirty. His face was tanned almost as brown as his hair, making his eyes look oddly light. His short-cropped haircut and loose-fitting shirt and slacks had obviously been chosen for comfort rather than style. *He's not bad looking,* Sara admitted grudgingly, *in a rugged sort of way. But nothing like Nicky.*

The straight, uncompromising line of the man's mouth bent upward at one corner, and Sara suddenly realized that he was smiling at her with amusement. She tilted her chin haughtily and with great deliberation turned her back. Touching Nicolás on the arm, she whispered, "Nicky! There's a guy over there watching you. Do you know him?"

It took a moment to pull her husband's attention away from his conversation, but when he caught sight of the man Sara mentioned, his blue eyes narrowed instantly. He gave a low whistle. "Well, well, if it isn't Doug Bradford! Don't tell me he's still around. I thought they kicked him out a long time ago!"

"What do you mean?" Sara asked, but her question was drowned out as two loudspeakers perched precariously on a pair of tables switched over from country western to "The Star-Spangled Banner." The buzz of conversation ceased as everyone stood to their feet for the playing of the national anthem. Sara risked another glance at Bradford. He had turned to join in the singing, but Sara had the feeling that he was well aware of her eyes on him. She pulled her gaze hastily back to Nicolás, only to find that he too was watching Bradford, an enigmatic smile playing around his lips.

When the anthem ended, Nicolás grabbed two seats at a nearby table, next to a Bolivian couple and their two teenage sons. These turned out to be friends of the family, and there was a murmur of introductions as a young girl began reciting a patriotic poem over the loudspeaker. "Raul and Lidia Salvietti" was all Sara caught before someone at a nearby table hissed, "Shh!"

The ceremony was mercifully short, culminating in a brief speech from the American consul, a gray-haired lady who looked more like everyone's favorite grandmother than a government official. Nicolás was on his feet before she had finished reminding people not to forget the evening's fireworks. "If you'll excuse me. There's some-one I'd like to catch before he leaves."

Nicolás strolled across the pavilion toward where Doug Bradford was still leaning against the roof pillar, a surprisingly attractive smile lightening the sternness of his face as he bent his head to the chatter of the young girl who'd recited earlier. Not eager to be left with a group of strangers, Sara jumped up to follow Nicolás. Bradford straightened up when he saw them approaching. He murmured to the young girl, and she scampered away. A smile still curved his firm mouth as he turned to face Nicolás and Sara.

"Hello, Nicolás," he said cordially. "Back for good this time?" Sara noticed Bradford's amiable tone and wondered if perhaps she'd imagined his critical gaze.

"You can count on it, Bradford." Nicolás was at his most charming. "I must say I'm a little surprised to see you still hanging around. I thought you might be out of work by now!"

"It'll be a while yet," Bradford said dryly. He looked pointedly from Nicolás to Sara. Nicolás, catching the look, grinned. "You haven't yet met my wife. Sara, I'd like you to meet an *old* friend of the family, Doug Bradford."

Sara caught Nicolás's subtle emphasis on the word "old," and glanced up in time to notice a hint of malice in her husband's bright gaze. She murmured something polite as Doug Bradford shook her hand, but she had the distinct feeling she had inadvertently wandered into a fencing match. Nicolás slid his arm around her waist and pulled her possessively close. "Sara's an American like you, as I'm sure you've noticed. Not quite the same line of business, of course. And speaking of business . . ."

This time there was no mistaking the insolence in Nicolás's tone. "How *is* it going these days? No more of those little problems?"

Bradford's face was suddenly expressionless, his gray eyes cold and watchful. "It's got its ups and downs. I'm sure you've managed to stay informed," he said wryly.

"I sure have!"

A soft trill cut into Nicolás's cheerful reply. Unclipping a cellular phone from his belt, Doug Bradford flipped it open. *"Sí?"* He listened briefly, then spoke in fluent Spanish. "Give me a number and I'll call you back in five minutes."

Snapping the thin, oblong phone shut, he swung back to Nicolás. "If you'll excuse me, *work* is calling."

The two men looked at each other, one smiling, the other grim. Then Nicolás shrugged cheerfully. "Of course! We'll be seeing you around."

"I'm sure you will!" Bradford took a step away before pausing. "It was good to meet you," he said with a nod over his shoulder to Sara. But his tone held only formal politeness, and as he walked away, Sara felt that he'd already forgotten her existence.

I don't like that man at all! she told herself hotly.

"So, what was all that about?" Sara asked aloud as soon as Doug Bradford was out of earshot.

"Hmm?" Nicolás said absently. Sara thought he was looking extraordinarily pleased with himself.

"That guy, Doug Bradford!" she repeated with some impatience. "Who is he? What's he doing in Bolivia? What is this *business* you two were hinting about? And don't feed me that line about him being an old friend! He doesn't like you at all, and I didn't exactly get the impression he's your favorite *gringo!*"

"And you got all of that out of one two-minute conversation

between a couple of guys catching up on each other's news?" Nicolás teased. "Remind me not to play poker with you!" At Sara's exasperated sigh, he threw his hands up in mock terror. "Okay, okay, whatever you say!" Adopting a more serious tone, he continued, "Bradford's here with the American embassy. Well, not exactly with the embassy. With your American Drug Enforcement Administration. And you're right, he doesn't care for me at all—or anyone else in the Cortéz clan."

"You mean, Doug Bradford is a DEA agent?" Sara demanded, astonished. Her knowledge of the U.S. Drug Enforcement Administration was drawn largely from Tom Clancy novels and an occasional news article, but the man she'd just met didn't fit her mental picture of a guy who spent his days playing Rambo and shooting up drug traffickers. "What does he have against *you*?"

"We're wealthy," Nicolás said with a shrug as he steered Sara back toward their table. "That's all a guy like Bradford needs. If he had his way, he'd throw Papá and me—and every other Bolivian who's made a buck with their business ventures—behind bars."

"That's awful!" Sara gasped, appalled. "I mean, that's sheer prejudice! Your family has done so much to help this country. Can't you report it to the American embassy? Surely they'd want to know if one of their men is abusing his position like that."

"Oh, all these DEA types are the same," Nicolás laughed. "You know, 'the only honest Bolivian is a poor one,' and all that. But Bradford's as bad as they come. He even had Cortéz Industries raided a couple of years back."

"You mean, for drugs?" Sara asked incredulously.

"Oh, they didn't find anything," Nicolás assured her. "Of course!"

"I should think not!" Sara said indignantly. She turned to stare after the wide-shouldered figure still striding rapidly across the lawn. So she'd been right to dislike him!

"I was home from college at the time of the raid. That's when I met Bradford," Nicolás went on. "The whole thing was quite a show. Troops, dogs, helicopters, the works. Bradford's men did a lot of damage before they finally admitted there was nothing to be found. Papá estimates we lost about a million dollars in smashed-up merchandise and lost shipments."

Sara couldn't believe what she was hearing. *This is where our tax dollars are going? So American officials can throw their weight around overseas, bully innocent citizens, and destroy private property?* "So what happened? I hope the U.S. government had the decency to apologize and give you some restitution!"

"Hah!" Nicolás laughed. "The DEA doesn't make apologies. But even Papá felt the publicity was worth every penny. American drug forces overstepping their welcome on Bolivian soil and hounding the country's most prominent entrepreneur and philanthropist. The newspapers and TV stations ran the story for a week!" A malicious sparkle flashed in Nicolás's blue eyes. "Doug Bradford got into so much hot water, he hasn't dared to bother us since!" Arriving at the table, Nicolás pulled out the chair for Sara to sit down.

"Still talking about that raid, are we?" the father of the Salvietti family said as Nicolás grabbed a chair for himself. "Politics on such an afternoon, Nico? Is that any way to entertain a beautiful woman?" Sara didn't care for the bold way the man's eyes roamed up and down her figure, but neither Nicolás nor the man's wife seemed to notice, so she decided to ignore it.

"Just telling Sara about the kind of treatment prominent Bolivians can expect from the local representatives of our friendly neighbors up north."

"Yes, I saw Bradford, too." Salvietti bit into a hamburger, washing it down with a swallow of Coca-Cola. "So what's he doing here? I wouldn't have thought this was his scene. No peasants to torture or upstanding citizens to interrogate."

"At least he's American," Nicolás replied with amusement. "What's your excuse, Raul? I wouldn't have thought you'd be caught dead at a party where Coca-Cola is the strongest thing served."

"Business contacts." The man's wink included Sara. "You'd be surprised at the people you meet at things like this."

"Our children attend the Santa Cruz Cooperative School," Mrs. Salvietti informed Sara. "They have American friends here today, and for this reason they wished to attend. It is a good cultural experience for them as they will one day study in the United States." She glanced over at her husband. "But it is true that one sometimes meets useful contacts."

Both Salviettis spoke good, though strongly accented, English, which Sara realized they were keeping to out of consideration for her. She debated offering to switch to Spanish, but after three weeks of speaking little else, she was enjoying the freedom of a conversation in which she didn't have to grasp for every word.

Raul Salvietti, she soon learned, was third generation Italian, his grandparents having fled Italy on the eve of the Allied invasion in World War II (though exactly why, he didn't elucidate), eventually finding refuge here in Santa Cruz. When he talked, it was as much with his hands as with his voice.

His wife, Lidia, came from a family that had once owned much of the province before the agrarian reforms of the 1950s broke up their huge haciendas and parceled off much of their land to the peasants. Both were friendly and outgoing, and Sara found them fascinating. They, in turn, were eager to hear about the wedding and Sara's own background.

"You lucky devil, you!" Raul told Nicolás, slapping him on the back. "Why didn't you bring back a few more like her for the rest of us?"

Sara blushed, throwing a quick glance at Lidia. But if the other woman minded the suggestive leer her husband was now directing Sara's way, it didn't show. There were obviously some cultural differences here that Sara didn't understand. She was glad when talk drifted into more general channels.

"That raid was truly a scandal," Lidia was saying to Nicolás. "And it could have happened to any one of us. The Americans act as though they own our country!"

"Perhaps." Raul leaned back in his chair, his fat legs sprawled out wide in front of him. "But your father did us a good deed with that one, Nico. Those hotheaded *gringos* haven't dared bother honest businessmen since."

"What kind of business do you have?" Sara asked. She was beginning to feel at home with this warm, ebullient couple.

"Exports, mainly," Lidia told her. "Pottery, weaving, wood carvings, silverwork, leather goods, even paintings."

"Raul and Lidia buy up local Indian handicrafts and ship them to the states," Nicolás added in. "You remember that beautiful llama wool rug we saw in that tourist shop in Seattle?"

"You mean the one that cost $500?" Sara said dryly. "The one I wouldn't let you buy for me?"

"That's the one," Nicolás grinned. "And you were right. You can buy the same rug here for maybe $50. We'll check around for one next week."

Raul shook his head. "More like $200 these days, unfortunately. The Indians are getting greedy since they found out what kind of prices their goods bring overseas. And they're wanting to cut their own deals with the buyers. A few more years, there won't be any profits left. That's why we've decided to get out."

"You're selling out?" Nicolás arched his eyebrows. "That's a surprise! So what's next? Retirement in Europe? Or are you going to emigrate to the United States like half the country is doing?"

"Oh, no, we would never leave Santa Cruz." Lidia lifted her

shoulders emphatically. "This is our home. Perhaps our children may go the United States to study, but always they will return here."

"We are thinking of opening a new business right here in Santa Cruz," Raul added. "A big store, perhaps. Not a supermarket, as others have done. A store—what is it called in English?—like Wal-Mart in the United States."

"A department store, you mean." Sara's eyes shone with enthusiasm. "I think that would be a great idea! The one thing I hate about shopping in Santa Cruz is that you've got to go to a separate store for every pair of socks or shoes or even thread to mend a blouse. That or wander around those open-air markets for hours!"

"It sounds like a moneymaker," Nicolás agreed. "But you're looking at a big investment to get it off the ground. A building that size, and the merchandise . . ."—he shook his head—"I don't know! That's an awful lot of cash."

"Why cash?" Sara asked curiously. "Can't you take out a loan and make payments? That's what we'd do back home if we started a business."

"That's not the way things work here, Sara." Nicolás's blue eyes sparkled with amusement. "In Bolivia, people want cash on the barrelhead, as your American phrase goes. They just don't trust you not to bail out after the first payment."

Raul steered the discussion back to the subject at hand. "Eventually, we'd like to see a chain in La Paz, Cochabamba, every major city in the country. Maybe even branch out to Paraguay or Peru. Like a real Wal-Mart. But we figure we can get started here in Santa Cruz for about $20 million. That's all we can scrape together right now, anyway."

"Twenty million *cash?*" Sara gasped. "Wow! And you're telling me you can make that kind of profit selling Indian crafts? Maybe I'd better ship a few bundles of rugs and pottery back to my own friends!"

The silence was abrupt. The buzz of conversation from surrounding tables rang suddenly loud in Sara's ears. She looked around, bewildered. Raul and Lidia weren't meeting her eyes, but their faces were blank and all the friendly cheer had evaporated. Sara looked over at Nicolás, and his face was savage with anger. He stood up with a motion so violent that his chair clattered backward onto the concrete floor. "If you will excuse me," he said tightly. "I'll get back to you later."

Yanking Sara to her feet, he literally dragged her away from the table, his long fingers biting into her upper arm. Sara was too stunned to resist. Nicolás waited only until they were outside the pavilion and beyond the other family groups picnicking on the lawn before he stopped and hauled Sara around in front of him.

"What do you think you were doing back there?" he demanded furiously. "You practically accused them of making their money illegally. How could you be so rude?"

"What are you talking about?" Sara was pale with shock. Never had she seen Nicolás like this—or imagined that he could be. "I was just—just making conversation. It seemed so strange—and interesting!"

"You don't ever, *ever* question how people have made their money!" Nicolás punctuated each word with a shake. "Do you understand?"

Without waiting for an answer, Nicolás released her. Spinning on his heel, he stalked away. Sara stared after him, still pale with shock. She had no idea what she'd done wrong. But all her enjoyment of the afternoon was gone.

"You're right, you know!"

Sara whirled around to find Gabriela standing behind her, looking thoughtfully after her angry cousin. "What are you doing here?" Sara demanded breathlessly. "And how did you know?"

"I was sitting at the next table when you dropped your little bombshell. I followed you because I've had a little more experience with Nico's temper than I imagine you have. I thought you might need some help. I guess I was wrong."

"But what did I say?" Sara wailed. "Why was Nicky so angry?"

Gabriela looked at her with amazement. "Are you so naïve, Sara? Raul and Lidia didn't make that kind of money off Indian handicrafts, and Nico knows it. But you just don't say things like that out in the open." She made a gesture that encompassed the entire horizon. "Surely you know by now where this city's wealth comes from. You're going to have to wake up, Sara, if you want to last in Bolivian society."

"You mean—?" Since her arrival in Santa Cruz, Sara had completely pushed aside the darker things she'd read about this beautiful country. But suddenly all the magazine articles, news reports, and half-understood facts coalesced in her mind. She finished hesitantly, "—cocaine?"

Gabriela shrugged. "Of course. And the Salviettis are some of the most successful drug dealers in the country. Everybody knows that!"

Sinking down onto the edge of a large, round planter, Sara watched Nicolás rejoining his friends. His hands moved animatedly as he talked, and a moment later, she saw Raul Salvietti laugh. Smoothing things over for his *gringa* wife.

"I don't get it!" she said aloud. "How could the Salviettis be drug dealers? They're friends of Nicky's. And they're so nice!"

"Sure they're nice," Gabriela agreed without even a touch of irony. Joining Sara on the planter, she crossed her slim legs at the ankles. "Just a little touchy about how they made their money."

"But I didn't mean that! I just thought, wow, they've really got to be good businessmen. I mean, I'm not saying I know a lot about Bolivia, but all this talk about cocaine and drug dealing, you act like it's people we know!" Sara made a gesture toward the imposing roofline of Las Palmas. "Just because someone does well in their business doesn't make them a criminal! I mean, back home people are always starting some kind of company and striking it rich!"

"I didn't say there are not legitimate businesses," Gabriella replied. "Of course there are. The oil and gas that first brought the American companies to Santa Cruz, and the cattle and soybeans, and the sugar factories that Don Luis owns. But these do not bring great fortunes overnight. They require long years of hard work." Gabriela was speaking very patiently, as to a young child—and not a particularly intelligent one.

"You must remember, Sara, that I have lived here all my life. I knew the Salviettis when Santa Cruz was still a small town, not so many years ago. And other families, too, that are important in this city. But they were not always so wealthy. Oh, perhaps compared to the *campesino* in his *chozita,* but not as they once were with their huge haciendas and thousands of *peones.* My own family once owned much land in this province. My grandmother told us often of the balls, and the Arabian horses, and the dresses all the way from Paris, and the servants to pick up a handkerchief if it fell to the ground. The revolutions finished that for us."

Gabriela glanced ruefully over at Sara. "Yes, I know what you are thinking. And perhaps it was not right that only a few should enjoy the benefits of our country while the rest slaved and toiled. But it is not easy for those who had become accustomed to wealth as their birthright. I remember well the mending of old dresses and the selling of the grand piano from Germany and the crystal chandeliers from Milan. The leaks in the roof because there was no money for repairs. And always the lies so that others would not know how bad things were.

"And then, as a salvation to many, came the cocaine. The Americans wanted this little plant that had grown worthless for thousands of years. Why, no one understood. But the city began to grow and the mansions sprouted up, along with the businesses and the stores.

Friends who last year had no more than you, suddenly had millions in the bank."

"And no one arrested them?" Sara exclaimed. "But that's awful! I mean, if you've got people making millions overnight off of drugs and everyone knows about it, why hasn't someone picked them up? Where are the authorities? Or these DEA agents who've got all the time in the world to harass innocent people?"

"It is not as easy as that," Gabriela said. "First it has to be proven, and for those with enough power, nothing is ever proven. Besides, no one says, 'I am making a fortune in cocaine.' It is more what you call an 'open secret.' And it is all very respectable. When we get together at events such as this, people discuss their businesses and their haciendas, and brag about their new Mercedes Benz and their membership in the International Holiday Club, and how they took their children to Disney World for vacation.

"And no one asks how it is that a family who last year had not even the money to paint their ancestral home has suddenly profited millions of dollars from their few remaining cattle or from that car dealership with only fifty cars in the lot. And because, after all, the cocaine has brought prosperity to a country that badly needed it, it is easier to wink at it and not ask questions."

Sara was silent. She felt as stupid and naïve as Gabriela had called her. Of course, she'd known that Bolivia was one of the three principal producers of coca, the raw leaf that is processed into cocaine. But the information she had read back when she first met Nicolás had made far more of Bolivia's history of bloody revolutions and its present tottering economy than its largest cash crop.

She had been pleasantly surprised to find Santa Cruz far more prosperous than she had expected. There were still the beggars and adobe huts, of course, but there were also supermarkets and boutiques, and import stores and luxury cars, for those with enough money. Until now, it hadn't occurred to Sara to wonder where the affluence came from, or who was pocketing the profits from Bolivia's cocaine trade, in a country where a schoolteacher made less than $100 a month. If she'd thought about the matter at all, it was to decide that the problem was grossly exaggerated. After all, she'd never seen any sign of the violence and crime that the American media associated with the drug war. She said as much to Gabriela.

"You haven't been in the right parts of town," Gabriela said dryly. "But you're right. We in Bolivia have kept our drug trade civilized. None of the assassinations and guerrillas of Colombia and Peru. Just business."

"Just business!" Sara repeated. She glanced over at the pavilion, where Nicolás was on his feet, smiling as he leaned over to kiss Lidia on the cheek. "So why are you telling me all this? What does any of this have to do with me?"

Gabriela gave Sara an odd look before she shrugged. "I like you, and I do not like to see trouble between you and Nico. These are things you should know if you are to live in Santa Cruz. That rascal of a cousin of mine should have told you himself instead of blaming you. At least when you meet the Salviettis again, you will not put your foot in your mouth, as you Americans say."

"The Salviettis!" Sara exclaimed indignantly. "You don't think I'd have anything to do with them after this! That's the one thing I don't understand at all. How can people just *mix* with these—these drug dealers—like they've done nothing wrong?"

Gabriela shrugged her shoulders again. "The Salviettis have been friends with the Cortéz family for generations. If you are going to refuse to associate with anyone suspected of having profited from cocaine, you will have to cut relationships with a substantial part of Bolivian society. And the Cortéz family is a very influential part of that society. If you do not want more trouble with your husband and his family, I would suggest you learn to do as the rest of us have done. Just keep your mouth shut and don't ask difficult questions."

"Is that what you do?" Sara demanded, incensed.

"I don't have to," Gabriela said simply. "I am a lawyer with the *alcaldía,* the mayor's office. My income is $300 a month. My husband is a pediatrician. He makes less than $1,000 a month—but all of it legally. We drive a ten-year-old car and live in a small apartment on the other side of town. We live well enough compared to most Bolivians, but to the Cortéz clan we are poor relations. Sometimes my relatives invite me to a barbecue—or a Fourth of July celebration—but otherwise, we do not participate much in your circles."

Sara wasn't satisfied, but Nicolás was now striding back across the lawn toward them. His smile was gone, and one glance told Sara that he was still angry. "Let's go!" he snapped as he reached the two women. Sara jumped hastily to her feet.

"And the Salviettis?" Gabriela asked sweetly, standing to her feet with a leisurely stretch.

"I've smoothed things over," Nicolás said curtly. Not waiting for any further conversation, he led the way to the car with long, angry strides.

The ride home was completed in silence. Sara held back her own anger until she could be alone with Nicolás. But instead of taking Gabriela home first, Nicolás dropped Sara at the front gate of the Cortéz mansion, hardly letting her get out of the car before he took off again with a squeal of tires.

✠

The helicopter sank slowly past red roof tiles and whitewashed walls, settling only meters from the old colonial mansion. Even before the rotors stopped turning, huge mahogany doors slammed open, and a half-dozen *peones* spilled out onto the veranda that ran around the base of the big, square building. Hurrying toward the helicopter, they began unloading the illicit cargo.

Leaving the rest of his crew to supervise, the leader of the *volteadores* climbed down from the pilot's seat. As he strode toward the veranda, he ran a practiced eye over his surroundings. Beyond the helicopter, a lawn smooth as any golf course stretched quiet and empty to a gravel airstrip. In the middle of the lawn, some twenty meters from the house, a massive satellite dish, topped by the needle point of a radio antenna, raised its steel-bright solar panels to the sky. Closer to the house, an armed security guard walked his Doberman pinscher alongside neatly groomed flower beds. A second guard lounged on the veranda, lazily watching his peasant charges heft the heavy sacks.

Were it not for the solid expanse of jungle that formed a wall of green around the perimeter, it might have been any rich man's estate. Certainly there was nothing to indicate that more than a hundred kilometers of tropical rain forest lay between these manicured grounds and the nearest town.

The guard jumped to attention as the leader of the *volteadores* reached the veranda, hurrying to thrust open the heavy front doors. Inside, the *volteador* crossed a wide tiled foyer. Pushing open ornate mahogany doors as massive as the first set, he entered the old ballroom, his boots echoing hollowly on the scuffed wooden floorboards. A pair of aproned workers glanced up at the noise, but under the man's cold gaze, they quickly averted their eyes.

Ignoring the bustle of activity, the *volteador* strode down the center of the long room. At the far end, he paused in front of another door. This one was neither mahogany nor ornate, but solid-core steel—and recently installed, judging by the fresh plaster around the door jamb. At his knock, a sharp voice called, "Come in."

The cool hiss of air-conditioning welcomed the *volteador* as he stepped inside. If the old mansion was incongruent with its jungle surroundings, the room in which he now stood wouldn't have been out of place on Wall Street. Ankle-deep carpet, leather chairs, a wide desk of polished mahogany, and above the desk a painting in an ornate gilt frame that an expert would have attributed to one of the eighteenth century's finer religious artists. The only contrary note was the harsh but energy-efficient fluorescent lighting, a necessity when fuel for the electric generating plant had to be flown in.

Behind the desk, a man lowered his newspaper. "Well?"

The *volteador* permitted himself a thin smile. "He came just as your information said he would, *jefe*. We have it all. Three full tons."

"Ahh!" The exhaled breath was sharp with satisfaction. The man's long fingers played idly with a small object on the polished desktop. Nodding his approval, he said, "It is not enough, but it is a start. Good fortune is indeed with us."

"Good fortune is with us," the *volteador* repeated mechanically. His cold gaze dropped to the gleam under his boss's hand. "Orejuela's, no?" It was a statement, not a question.

The long fingers closed sharply. "No—mine." Glancing at a calendar on the wall, the man behind the desk returned brusquely to the subject at hand. "Go then. Tell the workers to make ready this first load. We have lost far too much time already."

CHAPTER FOUR

What does Chavarría have this time? Doug wondered, speeding his Land Rover onto one of the broad avenues that circled Santa Cruz. *It better be good!*

To be honest, he wasn't totally disappointed to cut short the day's celebration. It was good to visit with the American friends who he seldom had time to see, but all those cheerful families only brought home his own solitary status. There'd been a time . . .

He forced his mind back to current events; memory lane wasn't a place he wanted to visit right now. He might as well turn the afternoon to some use, if at all possible. With Chavarría, you never knew. More than once he'd kept Doug dangling, only to hand over a tidbit of information that wasn't worth one cent of the American taxpayers' hard-earned dollars. This time, though, he'd insisted that he had something really valuable. Something big was going down, and he had a friend who was willing to talk—for a price.

Pulling up outside a high stucco wall, Doug gave a long blast on the horn. The response was not at all like what he'd seen at the U.S. Marine Corps base where he'd received his training. Peeling himself lazily from the weathered side of the guardhouse, a uniformed policeman lifted an M-16 machine gun in a friendly wave. Meanwhile, his partner sauntered from beneath the shade of a spreading *paraíso* tree and pressed a buzzer on the wall. A moment later, a black metal gate rolled open, its steel joints groaning. Doug, who personally had detested the spit-and-polish of that Marine base, snapped the guards a cheerful salute as he drove inside.

Though the faded wall was topped with a particularly lethal-looking set of black spikes, there was nothing otherwise to indicate that the three-story white plaster building was one of the United States Justice Department's most crucial outposts in its war against the international drug traffic. No discreet sign, no American flag— even the presence of guards was not unusual. Their counterparts could be found outside every bank or major jewelry store in the city.

The facility was just one more walled compound on an avenue lined with gated homes and businesses. Unlike their fellow government employees in embassies or consulates, the agents of the U.S. Drug Enforcement Administration didn't care to advertise their whereabouts to an unfriendly world.

Parking the Land Rover at the rear of the office building, Doug let himself in the back door. The hall was quiet and unlit, and Doug thought he was alone until he caught a whiff of freshly brewed coffee mingling with the metallic odor of the air-conditioning. So Kyle was in, and he'd broken out his supply of Mocha Java. Doug checked his watch—still twenty minutes before Chavarría was due. More than enough time for a cup of coffee.

Halfway down the hall, a sliver of light showed under the door of the research office. Muted voices and static from a UHF radio filtered out into the hall. Doug tapped lightly on the door, pushed it open, and poked his head inside. Yes, there was Kyle, playing with one of his precious computers. Looking over his shoulder was Ramon Gutierrez, the office's newest recruit.

"Mind if I swipe a cup of your Java?" Doug asked.

The two men didn't even look up. "Feel free," Kyle mumbled without taking his attention from the recording he was playing.

Angry voices could be heard through the static on the radio. Ramon hooked a nearby stool with his ankle and pulled it forward. "Hey, Doug, grab a seat. We've got a live one for you."

"Just for a minute. I've got a new guy coming in." Crossing the room, Doug looked at the computer screen where the two men had evidently been translating the radio transmission into English. "What are you two doing here, anyway? It's supposed to be a holiday, you know."

Kyle and Ramon turned to look at each other solemnly, then swiveled to face Doug. "Well, you see, that's the problem with *narcos*," they intoned in unison. "They have no consideration for other people's schedules."

Recognizing the paraphrase from a popular spy movie, Doug grinned. The truth was that, both men being single and in love with their jobs, the two agents couldn't stand to be away from the office anymore than they had to. For a couple of polar opposites, they made quite a pair.

Kyle Martin didn't fit the physical profile of a DEA agent at all. Well over six feet tall, he was thin to the point of emaciation—mainly because he couldn't be torn away from his computers long enough to eat. His entire wardrobe consisted of T-shirts and jeans, and he wore an earring in his left ear and his hair tied back in an unkempt blonde ponytail—not as a social statement, but because it fit his mental image of what an intelligence analyst should look like.

By contrast, Ramon Gutierrez was a model of neatness, precision, and professionalism. A Californian of Mexican descent, with dark hair and eyes and a wiry build, his thin, expressive face masked a driving ambition. Though he had been in Bolivia less than a month, he was no rookie. After four years in the military with Special Forces, where he had also earned his G.E.D., he had gone on to college for a degree in criminal psychology. After graduation, he had applied to the DEA, and as soon as he could, put in for overseas duty.

Kyle was one of those guys who would have done his job for free. He'd been in Santa Cruz for about a year and still couldn't quite believe that he was being paid a good salary to play with some of the best computer and surveillance equipment Uncle Sam had to offer. Tucked away behind the office were a couple of powerful satellite dishes that allowed him to tap into the world's most complete databases on criminal activity or drug trafficking, and pull up information on an informant or suspect. He could contact other DEA offices, keep track of agents in the field, or listen to a radio or cell-phone broadcast half a country away. All in all, it was more exhilarating than any of the complex strategy games he'd once tried his hand at designing, and he wouldn't have traded his job for ten million dollars and the presidency of Microsoft.

Ramon had made his own mark when he'd managed to convince a major Colombian dealer that he was the new liaison to a particularly nasty street gang that controlled the distribution of drugs in South Central Los Angeles. Doug had seen the surveillance tape where an almost unrecognizable Ramon appeared as the archetypal "Paco," complete with greased-back hair, black leather, and gold earring. For such a nice guy, he could sink himself into the role of a bad guy with almost frightening ease, and the Colombian's admissions on that tape had resulted in L.A.'s biggest DEA bust in years, along with Ramon's promotion to overseas service after only two years of street duty.

When the recording came to an end, Kyle punched a button to return it to the beginning. A printed transcript was sitting on top of the sound system, but Kyle knew that Doug, whose Spanish had been perfected during his childhood on the Arizona-Mexico border and four years in Bolivia, preferred to hear the actual tone of voice rather than read a printout.

"You've got to hear this, Douglas. It's killing," Kyle said with a chuckle.

Doug reached for the transcript to follow along. "So you're telling me this thing is so important it couldn't wait until office hours tomorrow?" he asked skeptically.

"Maybe not." Ramon shrugged. "But it's funny. You remember Operación El Lobo last week?"

Doug winced at the memory of that botched-up raid, though this time it hadn't been his fault. Radio chatter had indicated that a two-engine DC-3 loaded with three tons of Bolivian cocaine was headed for the Brazilian border and a clandestine airstrip carved into the jungle just on the other side. For once, they had all the details—description, destination, even the plane's call number.

More than one drug dealer had been astonished to land a plane on a lonely strip to unload a shipment of cocaine, only to find himself surrounded by local anti-narcotics troops and their DEA advisors. It wasn't that the narcos were so foolish as to overlook the possibility that their radio or cell-phone conversations might be monitored. In fact, they took great care in how they phrased any messages on the open air. Yet time and again they would put together a deal that they thought was absolutely secret, only to walk into an ambush at the delivery point. How did the *gringos* do it? *"Magic,"* the superstitious muttered; but there was no magic, only patience and painstaking investigation.

The El Lobo case had started six months earlier when one of the local communications intelligence operatives was monitoring the cell-phone frequency of a suspected drug dealer. This particular phone call wasn't especially interesting—just an invitation to a certain René to fly his plane down to the alleged dealer's *estancia* for a birthday party. The odds were that it was perfectly innocent, but along with the usual summary of the day's phone log, the operative had dutifully noted the name "René" with the annotation "pilot" as a possible connection with drugs.

René was never again mentioned on that frequency, but more than a month later, a report of private aircraft traffic at the old Trompillo airport listed a self-employed pilot named René asking permission to land his DC-3. As a matter of routine, the call numbers and description of the plane were added to the earlier annotation.

René's name cropped up again during a random sweep of unauthorized radio frequencies. Once again, it could have been innocent. Many Bolivians never bothered with the weighty process of registering

—or paying for—a particular radio frequency. But an obscure reference to a "delivery" alerted the listening operative, who also noted that the person on the other end of the transmission spoke Spanish with a Brazilian accent. The possibilities were intriguing enough to warrant programming that particular frequency into the computer for constant monitoring.

It took more than a month of wading through lengthy computer printouts, including the tedious conversations of a rural Guarani village that had also logged onto this frequency to communicate with the outside world, before anything else of interest turned up. But this time they hit pay dirt. A lost pilot radioed on the monitored frequency, asking for directions. A man with a Brazilian accent was on the other end. Upon investigation, the coordinates he gave turned out to be a little-used airstrip a half-hour's flying time from a small border town called El Lobo.

Now that a drug-smuggling operation was more than a possibility, a full-time operative was assigned to listen live to that frequency. They now had the pilot's name, the call letters and description of the plane, and the landing coordinates. So when, late one night, René announced, "I have three large packages ready to deliver," and the man with the Brazilian accent, secure in the knowledge that he was giving away no crucial information, responded, "The usual place. Tuesday," the DEA was ready to move. The Santa Cruz agents contacted their Brazilian counterparts, and well before the plane was due to arrive, the underbrush around the strip was bristling with a joint force of Bolivian and Brazilian anti-narcotic troops and their DEA advisors.

The operation had been a showcase of flawless investigation and planning. There was only one hitch. The plane never arrived. The troops had sweltered in one hundred degree heat for two days, unable to break cover even for a good scratch, before a small Cessna finally flew in for a landing. Neither the description nor the call numbers were the same, but the troops were tired and frustrated. Besides, who else but a drug dealer would land his plane this far from civilization? They'd ransacked the plane and roughed up the pilot before discovering he was a jungle missionary with engine trouble. The missionary had been forgiving, but the whole incident had been embarrassing and an enormous waste of time and resources.

"Yeah, I remember El Lobo," Doug nodded. "Not exactly one of our success stories."

Kyle started the recording. "Well, now we know why they never showed!"

Doug listened as the two angry voices were played back for him. It quickly became clear what had caught Kyle's and Ramon's attention. One of the voices was accusing the other of absconding with more than ten million dollars worth of his merchandise. The pilot was defending himself. It wasn't his fault. His plane had been forced down, he insisted, by a military helicopter. Bolivian, from the markings. He'd been shot at, made to land on a jungle strip twenty kilometers shy of the Brazilian border, and his load and plane had been confiscated. It had taken him two days to walk out of the jungle to Puerto Suarez.

"And they did not arrest you?" his skeptical boss demanded. Doug strained to make out the man's exact words. The static was bad and getting worse. "Do you take me for a fool?"

"They did not care about me!" the frantic pilot insisted. "They were not truly military, I swear, but *volteadores*—hijackers. They have taken our shipment for themselves! What are we to do?"

"It is not what *we* are to do, but what *you* are to do!" the authoritative voice informed him. "The problem is yours. But I will tell you this. The Brazilians are even less forgiving than the Colombians. You had better replace the shipment—and soon."

"How am I supposed to do that?" the pilot screamed through the static. "All my funds were in that load. I have nothing left. And it is not my fault—"

The transmission ended abruptly and Kyle snapped off the tape player.

"Can you imagine? Ten million bucks," Ramon said. "And worth ten times that by the time it hits the streets!" Even after two years, Ramon couldn't get over the casual references to that kind of money. Ten million was more than his own inner-city neighborhood would see in ten years. "I'll bet he's going to wish we *had* caught him by the time those Brazilians get finished with him."

"He got cut off in midsentence." Kyle tapped the dash on the screen. "I wonder what happened. Maybe the Brazilians walked in right in the middle of his transmission."

"Yeah, and before he could even finish the sen—"

"The static probably just got too bad to hear," Doug cut dampeningly into the other two agents' budding Hollywood script. He grabbed the English translation from the top of the sound system. "It's that military helicopter that interests me. It looks to me like the hijackers have friends in high places."

"Well, it certainly wasn't a real bust." Ramon tipped his chair back thoughtfully. "Unless the FELCN have stopped sending information our way."

"Three tons?" Doug shook his head. "No way! That would be the biggest bust since the *narco* plane that took four tons out of La Paz a couple of years back. And that went down in Peru, not here. If the FELCN had stumbled over anything that big, we'd be all over the place by now. No, the pilot's right. This was hijackers. And hijackers with connections. That helicopter—what are the odds it was a Huey?"

Ramon's chair crashed down as he sat up straight. "You're thinking the Orejuela case?"

"A mysterious helicopter popping up out of blue sky? Sounds like a common denominator to me," Doug quipped. "And what can a military chopper spell around here but a Huey?"

Kyle abandoned his keyboard and swiveled around. "Orejuela? Mysterious choppers? You mind letting me in on this, guys?"

"You never heard about that one? Well, it wasn't really our show." Doug dropped the computer printout back onto the stack. "Some *campesino* farmer down in the Chapare started pulling dead fish from his local fishing hole. One of the *Leopardo* units I worked with last summer was on patrol in the area and went in to check it out. Sure enough, they found a lab dumping into the lake. They traced the lab back to a local landowner, a Pablo Orejuela. The guy actually lives—or lived, I should say—right here in Santa Cruz. Had a few minor business ventures around town with a profit margin that didn't quite add up to his lifestyle. Anyway, they caught him cold coming in to pick up his latest shipment. Colonel Torres and I flew down to take him into custody. But when we got there, he'd already been picked up. By another Huey."

"Another Huey?" Kyle repeated blankly. "But then—where is he?"

"Precisely," Doug said. "He was never seen again. And none of the Hueys in the air that day admitted to making an extra run out that way."

"So you think these *volteadores* are Orejuela back in operation?" Ramon put in thoughtfully.

"Maybe," Doug answered. "But the big question is that chopper."

Ramon nodded. "Yep. Sounds like we've got a bad egg somewhere."

"What do you mean?" Kyle demanded.

"It's simple," Doug explained. "The pilot said that the chopper looked like military—which can only mean one thing: It was a Huey. And the only Hueys around these parts are the ones we—our government, I mean—donated to the local anti-narcotics effort. So if there's one flying around loose out there, it sounds like they've got someone on the inside taking out one of our choppers for an occasional joyride."

"Well, that should be easy enough to check out," Kyle commented.

Doug shook his head. "Not necessarily, as we found out with Orejuela. But we'll sure give it our best shot. Ramon, if you're just lazing around here today, why don't you get on that? Start with last week's flight schedules over at Trompillo. See if anyone was flying a Huey out that direction. And have them keep an eye peeled for a ditched DC-3 with those call numbers. Maybe we'll get lucky and trace that load before it crosses the border."

"Aye, aye, captain," Ramon replied sarcastically, snapping Doug a crisp salute. But he was already on his feet and heading out the door. With a grin, Doug waggled his fingers at the intel analyst as he followed. "I'd better grab that Java while I've got a chance. Chavarría's on his way over."

Kyle's snort echoed his own feelings on that.

At least something was salvaged out of the El Lobo mess, Doug thought as he strode down the hall. *Maybe this new lead will tie into an even bigger operation.* That was the way it went in this business. You won some, you lost some. And missions seldom turned out the way you planned. Unlike the Hollywood depiction of DEA agents living a glamorous life, more often than not it was just hard work and frustration.

He walked into the kitchen and was surprised to find his boss lifting a mug from the microwave. Doug raised his eyebrows. "I thought you were taking the day off. Isn't anyone around here feeling patriotic?"

"Angie and Michael flew stateside to spend Fourth of July with the twins. I figured I might as well get some things done." Resident Agent-in-Charge Grant Major cautiously sipped the brew in his cup, grimaced, then placed it back in the microwave and punched in another sixty seconds.

Doug sniffed the air with a wrinkled nose. "It smells like my grandpa's ranch in here. Damp fields, cows dripping slobbery cud, rotting straw. What *is* that stuff?"

"Alfalfa tea." Grant enviously eyed the fragrant stream of coffee Doug was pouring. "Doc says it's good for—well, for something!"

Doug threw him a satirical look. "Sure, if you're a cow!" Grabbing a day-old donut from an open box on the counter, he told Grant about the radio transmission Kyle was running through. Then he added casually, "Nicolás Cortéz is back in town. Brought an American wife with him."

Grant set his cup down so hard that tea sloshed onto the counter.

"You're not starting that again, Doug," he said sharply. "We don't need any more problems."

Doug didn't answer. Grant looked at his best agent's stubborn jaw and sighed. Doug Bradford was steady and dependable, and occasionally brilliant, with a flair for piecing together incomplete data into a coherent whole and an ability to communicate with their Bolivian colleagues that went far beyond his fluent Spanish. But he did have this bee in his bonnet about the Cortezes and certain other prominent Bolivian families. "You leave Cortéz alone," he ordered. "He's as clean as a whistle—at least as far as we can prove, and that's all that counts."

Without a word, Doug raised his mug in a gesture that could have been assent or dismissal, and started back down the hall.

"I mean it about Cortéz, Douglas," Grant Major called after him. "Just forget him."

The problem was, Doug couldn't forget. It had been two years, but he remembered the details as though it had all happened yesterday. The informant had come out of the blue, an employee who'd said he had stumbled over his employer's illegal activity and wanted to do the right thing. The corroborating details were astounding—names, dates, smuggling methods. The man even had samples of contaminated merchandise. To Doug, it had looked like an agent's opportunity of a lifetime. One of the most powerful and respected men in Bolivia caught dabbling in crime, and he'd be the one to bring him down. But Doug hadn't let his enthusiasm overrule the caution that five hard years in the business had instilled in him. A good agent always proceeded under the assumption that an informant might be lying, and Doug had begun the tedious task of checking out every detail of the employee's story.

There'd been nothing spur-of-the-moment about the operation. The research and planning had taken weeks, and for once everything had checked out—names, places, dates—everything. Two other witnesses were found. The case was solid. Maybe too solid—too easy, Doug thought now. But he didn't see how he could have proceeded any other way.

Grant Major had reviewed all the evidence, and though the political implications that attended the Cortéz name had given him pause, he had agreed that the potential rewards outweighed the risks. The raid had been authorized, the go-ahead given by the requisite Bolivian authorities, and each of the Cortéz factories and businesses had been hit simultaneously one hour before opening time.

And then—nothing! The search hadn't come up with so much as a milligram of cocaine in any branch of the Cortéz business empire. Doug had been frantic, unwilling to give up. But finally he'd had to admit that there was no shred of evidence of any illegal activity—other than the immense wealth that the family flaunted so publicly. He still might have been able to put together some sort of case—if his three informants hadn't disappeared. Without their testimony, there was no case against the Cortezes. The cocaine-filled merchandise that he had seen as the final measure of proof could have come from anywhere.

The whole thing had been a field day for the Bolivian press. Police brutality. American interference with Bolivian sovereignty. Persecution of prominent citizens. The controversy had bounced from the newspapers to the television news to the talk shows. Doug's name had even made the news, and only an eleventh-hour intervention by Grant Major with the powers-that-be in Washington had kept him from being shipped ignominiously back north—or drummed out of the agency altogether. Doug had, after all, done everything by the book, and Resident Agent-in-Charge Major had authorized the operation.

The news reports had all been grossly exaggerated, of course. Some merchandise was broken open for drug testing. Doug made no apology for that. And there had been a brief scuffle when the employees at one of the Cortéz warehouses refused to cooperate. But nothing like the carnage reported in the news. Doug knew each of the NIFC soldiers who had made the hit. Each one was well-trained and professional, and they had followed their orders to the letter: Take samples, make as little disturbance as possible while searching, and show extreme politeness in dealing with disgruntled employees.

The troops of the Narcotics Intelligence Fusion Center, or NIFC, were the DEA's closest allies in the war against drugs in Bolivia. An elite force of Bolivian anti-narcotics police, they had each been carefully selected, investigated, and trained in surveillance techniques, tactics, and modern weapons, until they now reached—and occasionally even surpassed—the DEA's own standards for professionalism. They were also paid well enough to remove the most urgent reason for corruption within the grossly undersalaried Bolivian police force—simple economic survival.

The quasi-military FELCN, or *Fuerzas Especiales Contra el Narcotráfico,* of which the NIFC was a small branch, was a different story. A far larger group of anti-narcotics forces, employing thousands, perhaps tens of thousands, of operatives around the country, the FELCN—along with their rural cousins the UMOPAR, and the Special Forces *Leopardos*—had proved invaluable in providing personnel for roadblocks, vehicle searches, raids on jungle labs, and a growing percentage of the actual seizures and arrests that made up the bulk of the anti-narcotics effort. But they were simply too numerous to guarantee freedom from the corruption and drug dealing that had filtered through every level of Bolivian society. When you considered that the salary of a FELCN colonel was less than $200 a month, was it any surprise that he might be tempted by a narco who offered ten times as much for a simple tip-off to the next raid?

It had been a few overzealous FELCN troops who had lost their tempers when a group of Cortéz employees had refused them entrance. Instead of simply taking the required samples, they had proceeded to shoot up an entire shipment of liquor. And it was there, in the midst of that chaos, that Doug had first met Luis Cortéz and his son, Nicolás, who was home from college for a few months. Don Luis's right hand man, Julio Vargas, had been screaming at the young FELCN troops, but Nicolás and his father had been smiling.

Probably thinking of the publicity bonanza, Doug told himself with some bitterness. *I wouldn't put it past those two to have planned the whole thing, just to smear egg all over the DEA.* No, now he was indulging in wishful thinking. Doug shook the thought from his head. Grant was right. Cortéz had been found clean, the affair was long over, and there was little profit in brooding on the past.

On a sudden impulse, he poked his head back inside the research office. Ramon had left for Trompillo, but Kyle was busy analyzing another printout. "Hey, Kyle, do me a favor, will you?" he called across the room. "Check out a name for me. Sara Cortéz. American. Just married to the Cortéz kid, Nicolás."

Glancing up from his work, Kyle gave Doug a sharp look. He hadn't been around for the Cortéz debacle, but he'd heard stories. He opened his mouth to comment, but took one look at Doug's face and thought better of it. "Is that all you've got?" he demanded instead. "Just her married name? That's not going to be in the computer—not unless she's been arrested since the wedding. Come on, man, I've gotta have some info!"

"So use your imagination," Doug said impatiently, wishing now he could withdraw his impulsive request. "You're always bragging about what those machines of yours can do!"

"Well, let me think." Kyle's fingers went instinctively to the computer keyboard. "I could check recent marriage licenses in Seattle. That's where Cortéz was studying, right? And student transcripts at UW. They might have met there. And, of course, if she applied for a visa to get into the country, there's got to be a photocopy of her passport somewhere over at Immigration. Not to mention fingerprints . . ."

Doug watched with some amusement as his colleague's long, thin fingers started moving over the keys, slowly at first, then picking up speed until they were a blur of motion. He cleared his throat just loud enough to penetrate the intelligence officer's concentration. "Yo, Kyle, I've got to be going now. Just let me know if you find anything. And thanks!"

Kyle lifted a hand, his eyes still on the screen. "No problemo."

✠

Resident Agent-in-Charge Grant Major shook his head as he climbed the stairs to his office. Doug Bradford was a good agent, and the Cortéz debacle had been in no way his fault. But there was no denying that the whole thing had been a political embarrassment, and the entire DEA operation in Bolivia was still suffering the repercussions. Although the Bolivian anti-narcotics forces had the authority to investigate and even search the businesses and homes of prominent citizens—regardless of social status—who showed a sudden expansion in wealth, they were increasingly reluctant to do so. Without their support, the DEA, in Bolivia ostensibly in an *advisory* role, could do little.

The upstairs was dark, the other offices empty. Setting his mug and two doughnuts—he could still eat those—on the mahogany desk, whose ample dimensions supposedly emphasized his importance to this establishment, Grant sat down heavily. The brief meeting with Bradford had soured his mood, and only now did he realize that Doug had given him no firm promise to stay away from the Cortezes. Maybe he should have sent him back stateside. The Santa Cruz field office couldn't afford any more scandals right now.

Grant pushed the doughnuts away, his appetite gone. What rankled him was that Doug was undoubtedly right. If not the Cortezes, then certainly plenty of others among Santa Cruz's upper crust had profited from the cocaine trade. When Grant had first visited Bolivia in the late 1970s, Santa Cruz had been a sleepy cattle town of eighty thousand, its upper classes still reeling from the loss of their haciendas in the agrarian reforms, and then from the crash in the international market for tin, Bolivia's principal cash export.

He'd returned fifteen years later to find a city that had grown to a population of one million, with many of the same families that had suffered such devastating setbacks now living in brand-new mansions and operating businesses whose start-up capital seemed to have sprung from thin air. There were more BMWs and Mercedes on the streets here than in the capital city of his home state, and block after block of stores filled with big-screen TVs, Pentium computers, and other luxury items. In a Third World country where even the urban population earned little more than $100 a month, on average, there was only one possible source for that kind of income—and everyone knew what it was.

So why didn't the authorities just go in and arrest the whole bunch? most Americans might ask. But what the average American failed to appreciate—and even top agents like Doug Bradford hated to admit—was that the United States Justice Department's Drug Enforcement Administration had no actual jurisdiction in countries like Bolivia. Technically, their mission was to gather intelligence regarding cocaine shipments to the United States and to train the locals in anti-narcotics techniques. They couldn't actually make an arrest or fire a weapon, except in self-defense. It was all part of a deal cut by the U.S. government with drug exporting countries in return for substantial economic aid and funding for their anti-drug efforts. If, in practice, a fair percentage of the operations that made their way into the local news were actually planned and carried out by the DEA in cooperation with their NIFC colleagues, the restrictions were nevertheless in force.

To make it more complicated, U.S. laws didn't apply here. In the United States, if a bad guy exhibited a sudden increase in unexplained wealth, you could dig into his financial records. If he couldn't come up with a plausible explanation for the additional cash, you nailed him. Not so in Bolivia. Their entire anti-narcotics policy could be summed up in one little law called the *Ley de Posesión*, which in practical terms meant you had to catch the guy in the act with his hands on the white stuff in order to arrest him. But if he did what a lot of *narcos* had done—got in, made his pile of cash, and got out, then he was safe forever. Once that money was laundered into a respectable business—a car dealership, an import store—no one could touch him.

As a former prosecuting attorney, Grant didn't like letting criminals off. But cleaning up the corruption that infested the Third World countries south of the Rio Grande wasn't really any of his business or that of the DEA. If the Bolivians themselves weren't interested in punishing the *pez gordos*—the "fat fish" who'd gotten rich off the white gold—that was their problem. His job was to prevent today's shipments of poison from reaching America. And on that score, the stake was personal. He had two beautiful, golden-skinned daughters back in the United States, eagerly preparing for their first year of college. His only son, Michael, would be graduating from high school in a couple of years and heading north to join his sisters. What he could do to make America safer for them, he would.

Grant stared down at his coffee-brown reflection dancing across the green surface of his tea. It would be easier if he knew that anything he was doing was making one whit of difference. But it was like stamping on a colony of ants. No matter how many you smashed, there were that many more that skittered away. At one time, he'd thought that bursting the powerful Colombian and Mexican cartels would end—or at least put a major dent in—the flow of narcotics into the United States. But it wasn't just the cartels anymore. Now there were dozens—maybe hundreds—of smaller operations. As fast as you wiped out one group, someone else moved into the vacuum.

And the inventiveness of these people! Grant had seen cocaine disguised as cold capsules and orthopedic soles, hidden inside hollowed-out statues and the double-binding of mail-order books, injected into sardine cans and Colombian beer. It crossed borders between the thighs of little old grannies or stuffed up the body cavities of athletes. And for every "mule" you caught, another ten offered to make the run, lured by the easiest money they'd ever earn.

That was the problem. "White gold" was worth far more on the streets of America or Europe or Hong Kong than all the gold mankind had dug out of the ground in the last few millennia. Who wouldn't be tempted, despite the risks, when a single run could set a man up for life?

Grant Major was an optimist. You *had* to be in this line of work. But sometimes he looked at the reality of the situation and quailed. With all the hard work, all the risks his special agents took, the best technology in the world, the occasional letter to the family of a dead agent, the fact remained that their efforts were stopping only five percent—ten, if they were lucky—of the flood of illegal drugs pouring over the borders of his country.

And even if they could stamp out every kilo of cocaine in the world, there was still heroin, inhalants, hallucinogens, PCP, THC, LSD, MDA, and dozens more. Not to mention the new designer drugs whose ingredients could be bought in any drugstore and processed in any basement in America. If American kids were determined to poison themselves, they'd find a way. Was it worth the struggle? Was any of it worth the life of one of his men?

Grant lifted the lukewarm alfalfa tea to his lips. Well, he had a job to do, and too much analysis didn't make it easier. Maybe the job *was* hopeless. It was certainly thankless. But for the thousands rotting in jail thanks to the DEA's continued presence in this country—and Bolivian jails made the Louisiana State Penitentiary look like the New York Marriot—the program was successful enough. And despite his occasional doubts, he knew deep down where it counted just how vital his task was.

If he could just keep hot-headed agents like Doug Bradford focused on what they could do and not what they couldn't. Grant gagged, spewing green liquid across the report he'd just finished. Why had he let that quack doctor talk him into trying this garbage? Indigestion might just be better!

✠

Special Agent Doug Bradford didn't bother with analysis. Before he'd joined the DEA, he'd been a cop, and to him it was simple. Drug dealers were criminals, just like murderers and thieves and men who molested little girls. And what you did with criminals was put them behind bars. If you started worrying about how many bad guys were still out there before arresting the ones you had at hand, there'd be no respect for the law anywhere. If all he did was provide a deterrent, put the fear of God—and the United States Justice Department—into these people so they'd at least think twice before messing with his country, then that was enough. A man had to do his own job and let the rest of the world take care of itself.

In his office, Doug scooped half-a-dozen MRE rations from his desk to make room for his coffee mug among the stacks of paperwork. Dumping the ready-to-eat meal packets onto a nearby pile of smoke grenades and flares not yet returned to inventory after the last raid, he removed the black jacket with DEA printed boldly across the back from the seat of his swivel chair. Leaning back in his chair, he propped his feet up on the scuffed finish of his desktop. Maybe the place was a little disorderly, as the Administration Officer, a motherly woman in her late forties who actually tried to get the men to pick up after themselves, had pointed out strongly on several occasions, but it suited Doug just fine. He knew where everything was and could put his hand on it in an instant, and that was all that mattered.

Reaching for his coffee, Doug glanced at the clock on the wall. Chavarría was late—as usual—which was something Doug had learned to be philosophical about. The locals referred to punctuality as *hora gringa,* or "American time," and had as little to do with it as possible. If Doug had a dollar for every minute he'd spent waiting for informants to show up, he'd be as rich as the drug lords he was after.

Rrrr-inng! Doug grabbed for the phone sitting on a corner of his desk. But it wasn't Chavarría, just a female member of the expatriate community, wondering why the single members of the embassy staff hadn't shown up at the Fourth of July celebration. Doug punched a button on the intercom. "Kyle, it's your girlfriend on line six. I know you're still over there, so pick it up."

He waited until he heard Kyle's annoyed voice, then hung up, grinning to himself. The aforementioned female was single, over thirty, plain, and bored. Somehow, she'd managed to get the DEA office's unlisted number and had been making Kyle's and Ramon's lives miserable with her constant suggestions on how to spend their free time.

Well, he might as well put his own time to good use. Picking up a report he'd left unfinished the night before, Doug scanned the first line.

On the morning of July 3, Special Agents Doug Bradford and Ramon Gutierrez met with the informant Arturo Guzmán.

Doug grimaced as he reached for his pen. More than all the high-tech gadgets this building contained, it was "snitches" like Chavarría and this Arturo Guzmán who made his work possible. Doug had spent more time than he cared to remember just talking with them, listening to their problems, analyzing their reports, tracking down facts to see if they were telling the truth. It eventually paid off, but that didn't make the job a pleasant one. There were times after an interview when Doug felt like taking a bath just to scrub away the slime.

Some informants were honest citizens, of course—a rancher who reported a strange plane with foreign tail numbers landing on his ranch, a bank manager who called about a client who had just received a million dollars in wire transfers from the United States, even an occasional reformed drug dealer who had seen the error of his ways and genuinely wanted to help—but most of these guys were scumbags. The majority were themselves implicated in drug traffic, and their reasons for turning were legion. A Cessna pilot who'd been caught in a shoot-out, narrowly escaping with his life, and wanted out. A "mule" who had successfully smuggled a kilo or two of cocaine, then been cheated out of her wages by the drug dealer. Others simply wanted money. Or revenge. Or, like Chavarría, both.

Doug had first met Chavarría when the informant called to report that his brother-in-law, whom he hated, was supplying drugs to the neighborhood teens. For a small reward, he'd happily spilled the when and where, and the brother-in-law was now languishing in an overcrowded cell at the local prison of Palmasola. Since then, Chavarría had called Doug at least every two weeks, hinting that he had further information of value. So far, he'd come up with nothing but a few unsubstantiated rumors.

Personally, Doug detested the man, but you didn't get to choose your snitches any more than you could choose your relatives, and playing best buddy with these lowlifes, no matter how obnoxious, was something that went with the territory. Like a shrink or a priest, you held their hands, soothed them, cajoled, wheedled, and generally made them think you were the only guy in the world in whom they could confide. But you always watched your back with them. After all, what kind of man would turn in his own brother-in-law?

Bzz-z-z-z. Doug's palm-size Motorola walkie-talkie interrupted his thoughts. He yanked the unit from his belt. *It's about time!* But the guard made it clear that he wasn't calling about Chavarría.

"Please, Señor Bradford, could you come? We have a problem here!" Doug could hear angry voices in the background. Slamming open the top drawer of his desk, he grabbed his Glock-17 pistol and punched in a fresh clip. Ramon Gutierrez was walking down the hall as Doug bolted from his office. "Some trouble outside, Ramon. Let's go." The two agents took off at a run.

CHAPTER FIVE

Sara leaned her elbows on the wrought-iron rail of the balcony, cupping her face in her hands. Evening was falling with the swift twilight characteristic of latitudes close to the equator. A rose flame still tinged the bank of clouds piled high on the horizon, but the sky above was paling to green, and the first stars were emerging from their daily hibernation. The gardener and his apprentice passed beneath the balcony, carrying their tools to storage, but they were oblivious to Sara's presence. She hadn't bothered to turn on the light, and she was almost invisible against the blackness of the open doors. Was it only three weeks since she'd stood in this same spot, breathing a prayer of thankfulness to God? Had he even heard her prayer, or had it risen no higher than those clouds?

From inside the room, she heard a knock at the door, and a maid's timid voice announcing that supper was being served. Sara ignored the summons. She wasn't hungry, and she couldn't bear to spend the next hour making polite conversation with her in-laws. Where was Nicky? Why hadn't he come home?

The knock came again, but Sara stood unmoving as the sky darkened to night and the lights of the city blinked on one by one to twinkle back at the stars. The scene was as achingly beautiful as ever, but tonight her eyes didn't see it. These last ecstatic weeks had been the happiest in her life, but now the Cinderella bubble had burst, and it seemed that things would never be the same again. She knew that all honeymoons must come to an end, but this was too soon, too sudden.

Our first fight, she thought dully. *And over what?* Despite Gabriela's facile explanations, she still didn't understand how she had angered Nicolás. It all seemed so stupid, no matter how many times she turned the events of the afternoon over in her mind.

A sudden shiver caused her elbow to slip from the balcony rail. With the sun's heat chased by the coming of night, the temperature had dropped dramatically, reminding Sara that it was still winter. Straightening, she wrapped her hands around her upper arms but made no move to return indoors or fetch a sweater. Her heart was even colder than her hands.

The flick of a switch spilled a rectangle of light through the open balcony doors, casting Sara's slim shadow across the lawn below. A taller shadow moved up beside her. Sara swallowed back tears, but didn't say anything. She couldn't. Then a warm arm slid around her shoulders, and a voice of velvet whispered the words she'd been longing to hear. "*Querida,* please forgive me. I know I've been a beast."

"Oh, Nicky!" Turning convulsively, Sara buried her face in her husband's shirt, the two shadows on the grass blending into one. "I thought you were angry with me. I'm so sorry!"

"I'm the one who should be sorry." Nicolás looked contrite as he rubbed his thumbs over the bruises that were clearly visible where his hands had gripped her. "Gabriela chewed me out good for the way I treated you. It was just a little social blunder, and I had no right to get so angry."

A little social blunder? To Sara, it was considerably more than that, but she was too happy to have her husband's arms around her again to press the subject. She tilted her head back. Nicolás laughed as he gave her a quick kiss. "Come inside, *corazón.* I think we have an audience."

Sara glanced blankly at the dozens of windows beyond the perimeter wall, then allowed Nicolás to pull her into the room. As he shut and locked the balcony doors, she stopped in surprise. Sitting on a small, round table between the two armchairs was a supper tray. There was a fragrant odor of hot food, and Sara suddenly realized she was hungry.

"Nicky, what a sweetheart!" Sara lifted the silver cover of the tray. There was an egg-spinach soufflé, still hot with cheese melting on top, a bowl of diced papaya and mango, and a flan custard. It was all served on fine china, and there was even a single red rose in a crystal vase, just like the roses Nicky had sent her by the dozen during their courtship.

The flower was the crowning touch that melted the last crystals of ice in Sara's heart. *He really is sorry!* Winding her arms around his neck, she whispered, "It looks beautiful. I love you, Nicolás Cortéz."

Nicolás flung himself into a chair and pulled Sara down onto his lap. "Oh, don't thank me," he said carelessly. "Mamá had the cook send that up. She thought if you had a headache, it would go down easier than the *picante de pollo* we had."

He nibbled a tender earlobe. "Let's forget food. I can think of better things to do."

So the rose wasn't Nicky's idea of an apology! And while she'd been up here alone, imagining all kinds of accidents and disasters, Nicolás had gone in to supper with his parents without so much as a word to her. To top it off, he'd obviously given them the idea that she was ill as an excuse for her absence.

Sara bit back her disappointment, forcing herself to smile. Even if the thoughtful gesture had been her mother-in-law's and not her husband's, at least Nicky was back, repentant and no longer angry. It was time to put this first awful misunderstanding behind them. Pulling away from his hold, she said gaily, "That's easy for you to say with your belly full of chicken. I'm starved!"

But later she asked, hesitantly, for the first time unsure of her husband, "Nicky, I know the Salviettis are friends of your family. But don't you think . . . I mean if you know they're—well, how can you just laugh and joke with them like that?"

Nicolás was stretched full-length on the bed, his arms propped up behind his head watching Argentina and Brazil play an elimination game for the next World Cup on the TV angled above the bed. "If I know they're what?" he said impatiently.

"Well, Gabriela said . . ." Sara trailed off, not sure how to approach the subject. But his cousin's name dragged Nicolás's attention from the goal Argentina had just kicked in. Cutting off the cheers with a click of the remote control, he rolled over. "What do you mean? What did Gabriela tell you?"

Sara told him. Nicolás was swearing under his breath before she finished, and when she did, he exploded, "That busybody!"

Sitting up, he tossed the remote control onto the floor. "Let's get something straight right now. No one has *ever*—not now, not in the past—proved that the Salviettis are into cocaine. Sure, they made a lot of money fast. So have a lot of others. But isn't it your own American justice system that says a man's innocent until he's proven guilty? The Salviettis are good people with a good reputation. They've donated land for a soccer field and built at least two schools I know of, and their business has brought a lot of money into Santa Cruz. It's people like the Salviettis who are making this city grow, and that's what counts as far as I'm concerned, not a lot of malicious rumors about how they did it!"

"You mean, none of that stuff Gabriela said was true?" Sara asked with relief. "I thought it seemed a little exaggerated."

"I didn't say that." Nicolás ran an exasperated hand through his hair, ruining the perfect styling, a sign that told Sara more than anything else how perturbed he was. "I mean, it's no secret that there are a lot of people in cocaine. Maybe even people we know. The *gringos* are always telling us that Santa Cruz is filthy rich with drug money, and I guess they ought to know.

"But what do they think we're supposed to do about it? Tell people, 'Sorry, you made your money too fast, you can't come to our parties anymore unless you can show us a business audit and a bank statement for the last five years'? You've seen how our life is here. Foreigners always think we're snobs because we don't mix with what you call the 'lower classes'—oh, you do too, Sara, so don't look at me like that!" Nicolás's exasperation lifted for an instant as he slanted a grin at Sara. "I've seen your face when Mamá is giving orders to the maids. And maybe that's true. Personally, I've never found I have a lot in common with an *indio* in his mud hut.

"At any rate, we *cruceños* are a pretty tight society, and we all know each other. We attend the same schools, marry within the right families until it's a wonder we're not all idiots"—another slanted smile—"and if you go back far enough, most of us are related some-where along the family tree. That doesn't make it so easy to go around accusing people of being *narcos* just because they've done a little too well in their business. So around here, until a judge says otherwise, you just accept people as they are and don't ask stupid questions!"

Sara flushed, and Nicolás added quickly, "Look, I didn't mean to bring that up again. But face it, Sara, these are the people we've got to live with. We do business together. Our kids are going to grow up with their kids."

"But that's just it!" Sara protested. "I don't *want* my kids growing up with criminals, and I can't believe you would either, no matter how much money they're bringing into Santa Cruz—*or* if they're your distant relatives."

"Criminals!" Swinging his feet over the side of the bed, Nicolás rose to his full six feet. "Look, Sara, we're not talking your American Mafia here. Put aside your American prejudices for a minute and look at things from our point of view. My people—well, the *indios,* anyway—have been growing the coca plant for hundreds, maybe thou-sands, of years. And they've probably been chewing it that long too! It's never hurt them any, and you can't expect them to look at this cocaine thing the way you Americans do. To them it's just a crop, a crop someone all of a sudden wants to pay good money for."

Sara, a little chilled now that he was gone from beside her, drew her knees up to her chin, tucking her feet under her nightgown. "But I thought—I mean, don't people get addicted to coca? Isn't that why it's so bad for you? At least that's what I've always heard."

"That's because people don't know the facts! For the poorer Bolivian, the coca leaf is a lifesaver. You chew it and you don't feel hunger and you don't feel the cold. You can work longer hours without being tired. It's no wonder the *indios* call the coca their sacred leaf. It lets you drive all night without falling asleep, and study too—better than ten cups of coffee. I'd never have made it through exam week at SCCS without a bit of coca, and it was the one thing I missed in college. And you've seen for yourself that coca tea is the best medicine for high altitude sickness there is."

Sara didn't understand what he was talking about until she suddenly remembered that cup of bitter tea on the airplane. "You mean, that was coca leaves I was drinking?" She grimaced. "I'm not impressed. That stuff was horrid."

"Maybe, but it works. It's the trace of cocaine in the leaves that helps your lungs absorb more oxygen from the air, which is what you need up there. And that isn't the only legitimate use for cocaine. It was developed as an anesthetic right here in Bolivia, and it's used in other medicines too. And even as a recreational drug, it's not all *that* bad! Oh, sure, it's got some bad effects if you overdo it, but it's not like it blows your mind like LSD or heroin. I've never taken it myself, but my grandfather used to take a pinch with his beer, and he swore it was the best sober-upper there was."

Nicolás was now pacing up and down beside the bed. He was wearing only a pair of black silk boxer shorts, and he looked both magnificent and angry. Chin on her knees, Sara admired the play of the lamplight across the tight muscles of his shoulders and long legs. Who said a woman couldn't enjoy the physical perfection of a man as much as a man enjoyed a woman's beauty? But she didn't allow herself to get distracted. She hadn't brought up this sordid subject, and she'd done her best to keep it out of her life. But if this was something that was going to touch her family and even her own future children, then maybe it was time she learned as much about it as possible.

"Our coca growers feel they have a legitimate crop that could do the world a lot of good if they were allowed to market it properly. So if a little involvement in passing that crop on to the buyers puts an honest, upstanding family or two back on their feet financially, well, you can't expect people to get that excited. Okay, so it's not the best way to do it, but they're certainly not common criminals. It's not like they've killed anyone, or stolen, or even hurt anyone, really."

Sara listened, troubled. More than anything, she wanted to understand her husband's point of view and to please Nicolás by agreeing with him. But he was going against everything Sara had ever been taught.

"But it's illegal!" she put in as Nicolás paused to draw a breath. "You can't get around that! And how can you say they're not hurting anyone? Maybe cocaine does have some legitimate uses, but that's not how most of it ends up, and you know it. You've seen how many kids back home are addicted to drugs. A lot of them even die! And if they don't, they spend the rest of their lives as . . . as zombies! How can you say these people aren't criminals when they're selling a product that hurts people that much?"

Nicolás swung around angrily. "It's illegal only because the American government says it is. Their people can't handle drugs properly, so they pressure the rest of the world into making cocaine use a crime. And who are they to talk? Do they care if people die as long as it puts money in their own bank accounts? You want to talk criminal, let me tell you about criminal!"

Sara let out a silent sigh. It was getting late, and her neck was starting to ache from following Nicolás's pacing. But she'd never seen her husband so serious, and this was obviously something that mattered a lot to him. She patted the bed next to her invitingly. "Okay, Nicky, but can you sit down? You're making me dizzy."

Nicolás stopped pacing. Looking a little sheepish, he plumped a pillow against the backboard of the bed and sat back down. "I'm sorry, it's just that I wrote my final economics paper on the subject, and the total hypocrisy really gets to me. Your country is so self-righteous, always telling other countries what they may or may not do. But you don't see them worrying about people dying from their products. How many alcoholics do you have in your country? I know! I've seen the statistics. And tobacco. Your media is always moaning about smoking-related diseases. But does your government make tobacco or alcohol illegal? Of course not! And why not? Because Americans make billions of dollars on alcohol and tobacco, and of course, the government doesn't want to lose its cut in taxes. A cousin of my father's is the Bolivian ambassador to Washington, D.C. He's told us about the big tobacco lobbies. They spend millions of dollars to keep nicotine legal, and yet it's a drug as addictive as cocaine. People know the risks, they say, and if they want to indulge, it's their choice.

"Don't make it illegal," he mimicked an imaginary government official sarcastically. "Just teach people about the dangers and let them make an 'informed decision.'" Then in his normal voice, "Well, they've got a point there, I guess. I mean, you know I like a beer myself now and then."

Yes, Sara knew. It had been another one of Nicky's surprises. Always with the memories of her mother's death to haunt her, Sara had made it clear at the beginning of their relationship that she didn't care for alcohol. Nicolás hadn't pushed the point, and because they'd seldom been in a situation where alcohol was served during their time in Seattle, she'd assumed he shared her sentiments—until she saw him back in the social whirl of his own world. At least he'd shown no signs of overdoing it, something she couldn't say for other members of his family. She'd already had one slobbering-drunk uncle paw at her when Nicolás wasn't looking, and the heavy drinking was the one thing she disliked about Cortéz social events.

"People have a right to decide if they want to drink, though, personally, I can take it or leave it. Too hard on the physical training." Nicolás surveyed his own physical condition with some satisfaction before he went on, "And to smoke, too, I guess, if they want to kill themselves. But the same argument goes for cocaine and other recreational drugs. And when American kids pick up their first snort of coke, at least they're well aware of how dangerous it is. The kids down here who are killing themselves on American cigarettes don't have that privilege."

"What do you mean by that?" The scorn in Nicolás's voice stung Sara into defending her country. "The U.S. government has always required the cigarette companies to warn about the dangers of smoking."

"Sure, if you're American!" Nicolás retorted. "You've got all those little warning tags and health classes and cute little TV commercials to tell you smoking is bad for your health. But do you think the U.S. government cares how many Third World kids grow up to die of lung cancer or emphysema as long as they still get their cut of the taxes?"

Nicolás twisted a length of Sara's hair around his fingers as he went on, "No, all those warning labels stop at the U.S. border. You see, all that anti-smoking stuff is working. Every year there's fewer Americans smoking. And that's left your poor tobacco growers with quite a problem. This great big crop, and people getting too smart to smoke it! Not so different from our coca growers here.

"Only your tobacco farmers have the all-powerful American government on their side, and if Americans are too smart to smoke, well, there are plenty of other people in the world to poison. That's the deal your government cut with the tobacco companies. Cooperate with our public health campaigns, and you can do anything you want outside U.S. borders. Take off the warning labels, increase the nicotine, whatever. The tobacco companies still get their money, the U.S. government gets its tax dollars, and the American people spend less on tobacco-related diseases. Everyone wins.

"Except, of course, all these Third World peasants who are spending more and more of their budget supporting a nicotine habit. I mean, when you're making $100 a month, a pack or two of cigarettes a day is as expensive as a coke habit in the U.S. And the Bolivian *campesino* can't just trot down to the local hospital when he comes down with lung cancer.

"So getting back to those kids!" Nicky's fingers tightened on Sara's hair until she winced. "Oops, sorry. It's just you Americans are so . . . so hypocritical! Your media and your government love to spout off about the poor American teenagers and all those nasty *latinos* pushing drugs on them. Well, let me tell you, a lot of these countries didn't even know what cigarettes were until the American tobacco companies moved in. And just how do you think they made a market for themselves? It isn't so easy to hook an adult on smoking, which means, if they want to get rid of that tobacco surplus, they've got to target the younger crowd.

"They capitalize on the fact that every Third World kid thinks America is the Promised Land. If you smoke, you'll be rich and famous like the *gringos* on TV—blah, blah. Kids here know Joe Camel before they know Donald Duck. And just to make sure they get hooked before it's too late, your thoughtful tobacco companies put pretty girls out on the street corners to hand out free cigarettes to those underprivileged children who can't scrape up enough cash to try them."

"But that's awful!" Sara was aghast. Now that she thought about it, she *had* seen a lot more cigarette ads here, and without the familiar warning labels. But this! "I can't believe—"

"It's true," Nicolás cut in. "I saw it myself last year when I was down in Argentina and here as well. They know, you see, that if they can get the kids past their first two or three cigarettes, they'll have a customer for life. Not a lot different than your neighborhood pusher, don't you think?"

Sara didn't question that Nicolás had his basic facts straight, but she knew her country better than Nicolás did. "Look, I'm sorry if American citizens are doing things to hurt your country. But I can't believe that American tobacco growers have any idea people are doing that, and there's no way our government would approve of selling cigarettes to kids, in the U.S. or anywhere else. I mean, you can't hold the farmers and the Congress responsible for what a few greedy companies are doing overseas."

Nicolás shrugged his bare shoulders. "Don't kid yourself; they know all right! And even if they don't necessarily approve, they are doing nothing to stop it. Their attitude is: as long as you don't kill *our* kids, we don't care what happens to anyone else. I mean, be honest. If the American government applied the kind of sanctions against their own tobacco companies that they do against countries like Bolivia, there'd be an end to it in no time. But, of course, that would cut into American income and American taxes, and they wouldn't want that!

"So there it is. If America can't take moral responsibility for its own actions, how can they blame our *campesinos* for growing what is, after all, a perfectly legal crop here? And if certain of my country-men make some money shipping a product that has been part of our culture for centuries, a product that is to them no different than your tobacco, who are we to judge them so harshly? The *gringos* say it's wrong, yes, but they still don't own Bolivia, even though they think they do. Invading our country with their soldiers and their helicopters and their busy-body agents!

"Personally, I figure that as long as the U.S. is fattening its bank accounts exporting tobacco to Third World countries, they have no right to complain about those same countries profiting from co-caine. If they put half as much effort into stamping out drug use in their own country as they do into terrorizing ours, they wouldn't have a cocaine problem. I mean, who are they to tell us what to do when they can't even control their own citizens? Let them start by putting their own affairs in order instead of messing in ours!"

Releasing the curl he'd made in her hair, Nicolás caught Sara's chin in his hand. His voice held a coaxing note, but he was looking very sure of himself, like a man who knows he's won an argument. "And *that* brings us back to the Salviettis. So, say they did take the easy route—and I'm not saying that's true—are they any more re-sponsible for a bunch of spoiled American kids choosing to abuse a perfectly good product than the tobacco growers are for millions of deaths in Third World countries? You wouldn't have any problem socializing with a tobacco company executive. So why be so hard on people like the Salviettis?"

Sara was silent for a moment. One of her strong points—and perhaps a weakness at times—had always been an ability to see things from another person's perspective, and she couldn't help recognizing a certain logic and justice in what Nicolás was saying. But two wrongs didn't make a right. Her mother had taught her that at a very young age, and though she dreaded a return of Nicky's earlier coldness, she couldn't let this go. She shook her head, her long hair spilling over her shoulders.

"I'm sorry, but I can't take it that casually, Nicky. I lost a good part of my family because some idiot had too much marijuana and alcohol in his bloodstream. I can understand how you feel, but it's still wrong to break the law, and it's wrong to profit off other people's weaknesses—I don't care if you're American or Bolivian!"

Nicolás dropped his hand, the smile vanishing from his blue eyes. His voice hardened. "I'm not asking that you approve of it, Sara. I don't either, of course. I'm just asking that you be polite to the Salviettis. And keep off the subject in public—for my sake and the sake of my family. You can understand that much, can't you?"

Sara nodded a reluctant agreement. The last thing she wanted was to quarrel with Nicky again. And after all, it wasn't her responsibility to start a drug consciousness campaign here. No one could make her approve of these people, but she'd keep her opinions discreet if that's what it took to keep peace in her new family.

The tension left Nicolás's shoulders, and he pulled her into his arms. But as he reached overhead for the lamp switch, Sara couldn't resist one last question. Taking a deep breath, she asked what she'd been longing and dreading to ask all evening. "Nicky, the Cortezes—all those relatives of yours—you weren't talking about any of them, were you?"

Nicolás looked blank. Then he chuckled. "Of course not, silly!" He turned off the light.

✠

It wasn't Chavarría, Doug saw immediately, taking a precautionary glance through the peephole set in the door that led to the street. And he wouldn't need the gun. Shoving the pistol into his waistband, he opened the door and stepped out to meet a very angry young man. The guards had their weapons raised and ready; they looked worried, and the young man was obviously unimpressed by their authority.

"I must speak to the *americanos*," he was shouting. "You call them right now! And do not tell me there is no one! I saw them go in."

Ramon gave Doug a wry look. "That must have been me. I take it this kid hasn't heard of office hours?"

The boy whirled around as the two agents approached, and he threw himself in their direction. "Where is my father? What have you done with him?"

The guards instantly stepped in the way, blocking the young man with their weapons. One of the guards said to Doug, "I told him that this is an American holiday and the office is shut. But he insisted on speaking with one of you. He was very abusive."

Doug studied the young man more closely. He couldn't have been more than sixteen or seventeen, and though he was dark, with a *mestizo* cast of features, the designer sportswear and Nike Air sports shoes he was wearing distinguished him from Bolivia's poverty-stricken masses. The red Mitsubishi Montero pulled up against the curb confirmed that the youth was a member of Santa Cruz's younger jet set.

A spoiled rich kid who figures he only has to raise a finger for everyone to jump, Doug surmised. But there was hurt and bewilderment mixed with the anger in the boy's dark eyes, and Doug made an intuitive decision to hear what he had to say. He raised his hand. "It's okay, Juan, I'll take him."

The guards reluctantly allowed the boy to pass. Without looking back to see whether the kid was following, Doug led the way across the concrete courtyard to the office building. He knew without checking that Ramon would be bringing up the rear.

"Hey, Ramon," he called back over his shoulder, "what did you find out at Trompillo?"

"Not a whole lot," Ramon said with a shrug. "Well, actually zip, zero, zilch! In fact, nobody knew anything, saw anything, or had any hopes of finding out what's been going on."

"What about flight schedules yesterday? Surely they have some idea which aircraft were out yesterday and who might have been doing maneuvers in that area." Doug stopped in front of a gray metal door and fished in his pocket for his keys. "I mean, even in Bolivia it's a little hard for a military helicopter to go AWOL without *someone* knowing!"

"Yeah, well, like you said, maybe someone's got powerful friends in high places. The colonel down there did say they'd do some checking, but he sure didn't sound very optimistic." Ramon glanced from Doug to the boy, whose uncomprehending expression showed that he didn't understand English.

Unlocking the door, Doug motioned for the boy to go inside. The sparsely furnished room was one of several used to interview informants, allowing for private conversations without permitting visitors access to the main building. The DEA was leery about potential bad guys checking out their work space.

The young Bolivian stepped slowly into the room, his black eyes darting around as though he expected to find torture instruments or a gang of thugs inside.

"Do you need any help here?" Ramon asked Doug. The question was rhetorical, because any interview with an informant—or even a walk-in like this teenager—required at least two DEA agents to be present. Like the never-ending series of reports the agents were required to complete, this regulation was designed as a protection—not just against physical threats, but against legal liability, in case a complaint was later filed, charging abuse or other wrongdoing.

"Sure, if you've got nothing better to do," Doug said casually, then looked thoughtfully at Ramon. "How are you at interviewing teenagers?"

"Never come my way," Ramon admitted. "But how hard can it be? I mean, we're not talking Colombian drug cartel here!"

"Yeah, well, now's your chance to find out." With a mischievous grin, Doug stepped aside, waving Ramon in front of him. "The kid's all yours."

Ramon stared suspiciously at Doug's amused expression, then sat down at the table, motioning the boy toward a chair on the other side. He'd never turned down a challenge before, and he wasn't going to start now.

The teenager stood stiffly for a moment, then slid with obvious reluctance into the chair offered to him. Doug elected to stand beside the door, where he could see the faces of the other two. He stifled another grin as he took in the angry profile and arrogant posture of their unexpected visitor. So Ramon figured an irate teenager would be an easier sell than a Colombian drug lord. Well, it would make a good test of their newest agent's abilities. Doug settled himself against the doorjamb. *Okay, Gutierrez, let's see what you've got.*

Ramon started out simply enough. "Okay, son, what is it you want from us? Maybe you can start by telling us your name."

The boy had been staring sullenly at the tabletop, but at the sound of Ramon's voice, his head shot up. Eyeing the DEA agent warily, he said, "Ricardo." Then in an angry burst, he added, "Where is my father? I know that you have him!"

"Yeah, well, it'd help if we knew just who your father is," Ramon drawled.

Ricardo bristled at the hint of boredom in the agent's tone. "His name is Pablo Orejuela," he said defiantly. "You do know of him, is that not so?"

Pablo Orejuela! The two DEA agents exchanged a quick glance.

Ramon leaned forward, his dark eyes narrowing. "You're saying your father is the *narco* who pulled that helicopter escape a couple months back?"

"No, no, that was never true!" Ricardo exclaimed. "My father has not escaped. If he were free, we would have heard. He would have contacted us, I know it. He knows how concerned we are. He would never leave my mother and sisters to weep themselves to sleep every night." The teenager looked close to tears himself, and he was obviously convinced of what he was saying. "No, my uncle says the whole story of the escape is a lie. The helicopter that came belonged to the *militares*. The television news even said so. But it was not the *antinarcóticos* who took him. They know nothing. They think he has escaped and cannot be found. And I know they are not lying, because—"

The boy bit his lip. Doug didn't shift from his casual stance beside the door, but his gaze sharpened. So, this kid had a contact in the FELCN. Perhaps the same one who'd broadcast the news of Orejuela's arrest even before the DEA was notified. Well, they'd know soon enough, if Ramon played his cards right. Doug hated dirty cops, and it would be a pleasure to nail this one.

The boy blinked rapidly, then glared across the table, his back stiffening with new anger. "No, it is you *americanos* who have taken him! The helicopter. The search by the police. It was all lies so you could make my father disappear and no one would ask what happened to him. But we are not peasants to disappear just like that"—he snapped his fingers—"with no questions to be asked! My family has powerful friends, and you will be very sorry if you do not return my father at once!"

"Now, just a minute!" Ramon slapped his hands flat on the table. "What are you getting at here, Orejuela? That *we* kidnapped your father? Sure! Like we'd go to the trouble of rigging some phony escape when all we had to do was walk in there and haul your father's fat carcass off to jail. Kid, you've been watching too much TV!"

Pushing his chair back abruptly, Ramon stood up. "We're wasting our time here, Doug. There's no mystery about what happened to Orejuela." His sharp features hard, he swung around to face the boy. "Face the facts, kid, your father wasn't exactly a model citizen! He got his pals to spring him, and then he skipped town. If he hasn't called home, I guess he figures it's just too risky. He's probably got another woman somewhere and figured it was time to cash out. Start a new life with no excess baggage. My guess is, unless we catch him, you'll never see him again!"

"That is lies! All lies!" The boy was on his feet, his black eyes glittering hatefully. He hissed an obscenity. "My father would never leave us. He loves us! No, my uncle is right. The DEA has taken him, and that is why we have heard nothing. You wish to get information from him without the interference of the police and the powerful friends that my father has. I have heard how you torture and use drugs that destroy the mind and steal away families to force your prisoners to cooperate. . . ."

The boy's voice was rising, but his defiance was shading to fear, as though he had just realized he was in a closed room with the very men of whom he'd heard such terrible things. Ramon looked over at Doug, his almost imperceptible shrug admitting his helplessness in the situation. Doug stepped forward.

"Sit down," he ordered, placing one hand on Ricardo's shoulder and pushing him into his chair.

Ricardo took one glance at the Glock-17 protruding from Doug's waistband and slumped back into his seat. Doug swung a chair around backward and straddled it, leaning his arms on the back and rubbing his chin with his right hand. This kid had guts coming in here if he really believed all the old witch tales perpetuated in the Bolivian media. If the DEA carried out even half the tortures, rapes, and other heinous crimes of which they were routinely accused, mayhem would be a full-time job for every special agent in the country.

"Those stories aren't true, Ricardo," Doug said gently. "We are here as guests of your country, invited by your own government to train your police to combat the *narcotraficantes*. We have no power or authority in your country, nor does your government permit us to arrest or interrogate your citizens, only to advise. Do you really think we could hold a prisoner without your government finding out? Impossible!"

Doug caught Ramon's ironic glance as the other agent flopped back into his own chair. What he was saying was true enough, as far as it went. The DEA had no legal jurisdiction on Bolivian soil. But the political weight of the U.S. presence in Bolivia was considerable, and both agents knew that if they really wanted a say in anything, including the interrogation of one overweight *narco*, the locals were unlikely to deny them. The difference, which this boy wasn't likely to appreciate, wasn't what they *couldn't* do, but what they *wouldn't* do. The DEA had standards, and they didn't include torture or any of the other funny business that occasionally went on in Third World countries south of the U.S. border.

"We have no knowledge of your father's whereabouts," Doug

said firmly. "Search this building yourself if you don't believe us. You'll see soon enough that we're not holding your father."

Doug had no intention of allowing the youth anywhere past this room, but the offer seemed to pacify Ricardo. Still eyeing the pistol, he said scornfully, "Do you believe I'm so foolish as to think you would keep him here?" But doubt was replacing the anger and fear in his eyes, and he sounded more like a troubled child than an angry teen as he added, "But if you don't have him, then who does? And where is he now?"

Doug frowned. Colonel Torres was satisfied that Orejuela was the *pez gordo*, the "fat fish" of Operation Motacusal. Torres had picked up a dozen of Orejuela's employees without looking any further and was congratulating himself for having taken down a major organization. Doug wasn't so sure. He'd known too many *narco* bosses, and Orejuela didn't fit the profile. In his experience, the real bosses didn't do the dirty work. They sat behind fancy desks and let someone else take the risks. And that's why they usually got off scot-free while their underlings went to jail.

A thought was pushing its way up from Doug's subconscious. When Orejuela had skipped the coop, the assumption had been that he'd somehow managed to contact part of his organization still at large, who'd promptly blazed in to rescue him. But if this boy was telling the truth, and even his own family had no idea who'd mounted that rescue, that put a different construction on things. Someone had certainly arranged for Orejuela's escape. But what if that someone had been, not a faithful employee, but his boss?

The pieces were starting to fit together like one of those mystery puzzles that comes without a picture, giving you only a vague idea of what the puzzle is about until you piece together that first key bit. What if Orejuela's escape had been arranged by a superior? No Brazilian buyer was going to cross the border just to break his supplier out of jail. The risk was too great, and the threat posed by Orejuela's arrest was too small. Orejuela wasn't likely to have known the buyer's true identity anyway, and the big fish would know he was safe enough across international borders. As for the lost cargo, there were always other dealers eager to fill the vacuum left by a drug runner's arrest.

No, if Orejuela had a boss, it had to be someone local—a Bolivian. Someone with the connections to reach into the FELCN and the resources to put together a rescue mission at a moment's notice. Someone who was afraid he might be implicated if Orejuela was interrogated.

Doug was suddenly certain that Pablo Orejuela would never be seen again. Not alive, anyway. He looked at the boy. "Have you considered," he suggested delicately, "that perhaps your father hasn't made contact with you because he can't? You say you don't know what happened to your father after his arrest. Neither do we. All we know is that someone went to a lot of trouble to come after him. If you really haven't heard from him since, is it possible he was taken by an enemy rather than a friend?" Looking the boy squarely in the eye, he continued, "I don't want to alarm you, Ricardo, but I think you need to face the possibility that he's being held somewhere—or even worse!"

Ricardo didn't answer, but the look on his face told Doug that the thought wasn't an entirely new one.

"That's right," Ramon chimed in. "Drug dealing is a dangerous business. A man like your father, I'll bet he has a lot of enemies. Maybe a business partner who was afraid he'd squeal. If that's who came after Orejuela and broke him loose, he's probably six feet under by now."

Doug, seeing the storm clouds building on the boy's dark face, intervened hastily. "Ricardo, we want to find your father as much as you do. I realize you have no reason to trust us, but if he's being held somewhere against his will, then he may be in serious danger."

Doug had the kid's attention now, and he followed it up by saying persuasively, "Maybe we can help each other here. My friend here and I"—Doug hooked a thumb toward Ramon—"have means of investigating these things that others don't. But we need information that only you can give us. Perhaps together we can find your father. I know you don't want to see him back under arrest, but at least with the police, he'd still be alive. And we'd make sure he got fair treatment, I promise." He put out his right hand. "Is it a deal?"

Ricardo looked at Doug's hand, then slowly stretched out his own. "Okay, a deal! And if I find that someone has hurt my father," he added fiercely, his hand clenching into a fist as Doug released it, "I will kill that man myself!"

Doug ignored this remark and with a glance turned the interview back over to Ramon. The younger agent for some reason had a burr under his saddle, but he quickly reorganized his scowl to look as benign and inoffensive as his streetwise features would allow. "Great, kid!" Ramon pulled a notebook and pen from his shirt pocket. "Let's start with your family friend in the FELCN."

Ricardo's eyes narrowed. He hadn't forgiven the special agent's earlier comments about his father. His answers were grudging and brief, and he addressed them to Doug, ignoring Ramon as if he weren't in the room. Ramon tolerated this rudeness for only a few minutes before he slammed his notebook down on the table. "Look, kid, you came to us, not the other way around. If you want our help, you'd better start cooperating, or I'll throw you out that door myself!"

Like a toddler refusing to eat his spinach, Ricardo tightened his lips in a straight line and glared at Ramon across the table. Finally, Ramon threw up his hands and strode over to lean against the doorjamb.

"You take the little—so-and-so," he told Doug in English. "I don't have to put up with this."

Without a word, Doug spun his chair around, pulled out his pen, and took over the interview. It turned out that Ricardo knew little of use. His contact within the FELCN was an underling paid by Orejuela to inform him if his name cropped up in any investigation. The man hadn't known about Orejuela's arrest or escape until it was all over. Ricardo knew nothing of his father's business contacts, and of the list of employees he reeled off, most had already been picked up by the FELCN. He could think of no one who might be considered a business partner, and he was sure his father reported to no one as boss.

After a few more minutes, Doug set down his pen and leaned back in his chair. "Well, see what you can find out about your father's business contacts," he said. "And we'll do what we can here." He gripped the boy's shoulder as they got to their feet. "Don't worry, Ricardo. We'll find him one way or another. Let's go. We'll escort you to the gate."

"Good job, by the way," Doug told Ramon dryly as they let Ricardo out. "A little lacking in diplomacy, maybe, but an interesting technique. Is that what you used on the Colombian?"

"Okay, so hotshot punks aren't my line." Ramon had the grace to look a little shamefaced. "It's just—well, kids like that really get me! Flashy clothes, new wheels, acting like the rest of the world is dirt under their feet. We had our share in the barrios back home. And for what? Because they're so much better? No, just 'cuz their old man's got money—and dirty money at that! This kid's no different. His dad's a drug dealer, for Pete's sake, and he's got the nerve to come waltzing in here, whining for sympathy like he's filing some missing-person's report!"

"You're not paid to like him." Doug checked his watch. Apparently Chavarría wasn't going to show up.

"Yeah, well, we're not paid to nursemaid him either!" Ramon

retorted. "Why did you put us on the line to help him? Tracking down his old man isn't our job. And if Orejuela's dead, like he probably is, well, I for one am not going to cry over one less creep in the world."

"Information." Doug started rapidly toward the garage. "And if you don't know that, maybe you're in the wrong business."

"Yeah, a lot of information we got out of him!" Ramon was at Doug's heels, his sharp features scornful. Then he paused, and his angry expression turned thoughtful. "Information," he repeated. "You mean, like maybe Orejuela's only the tip of a bigger operation? Like he was working for someone real high up in society or he'd never have settled for second place? Maybe someone local who can put together an op real quick and who's got enough influence to have connections with the FELCN?"

Doug stopped long enough to slap Ramon on the back. "I knew there was a reason we kept you around."

"Thank you, *sir!*" Clicking his heels at attention, Ramon snapped a salute worthy of his Special Forces days. "Speaking of information, we'd better let Torres know he's got a clerk to fire."

The tires of the red Mitsubishi squealed as Ricardo sped away from the DEA office. He was still angry—with the DEA because they'd brought down his father, but now with others as well.

He hadn't known about the drugs. His father had told him only that he had successful business dealings, and in Santa Cruz you didn't ask questions about such things. But he wasn't stupid, even if he was only seventeen. Though he wouldn't admit it to those *gringos,* he knew they were telling the truth. His father was a *narcotraficante.* But so what? He was still his father, no matter what he'd done— which wasn't a big deal anyway. After all, everyone did it who was anything in this city. And as long as you weren't caught, no one pointed a finger, even if you showed up at school with a $45,000 Mitsubishi Montero for your seventeenth birthday, as he himself had. It was only when you got caught that fingers started pointing. You hadn't been clever enough. Even then, if you protested your innocence loudly enough, insisted that the *gringos* had framed you, your friends and social peers found it a whole lot easier to believe you—or at least pretend they did. Ricardo hadn't suffered socially for his father's arrest. He was still welcome at parties, the girls begging for a ride in his new car.

Of course, it made a difference that the money was still there, and Ricardo wasn't too young to recognize that. Like others, his father had registered most of his property in the name of his wife and first-born son, and even some distant relatives—a fictitious bit of paperwork that was all local law required to keep the FELCN from confiscating the goods of a presumed drug dealer. Thanks to his father's foresight, the Orejuela family would go on as they always had.

But what if the *gringo* was right, and his father was working for someone else? Someone who had planned that helicopter escape, then betrayed him. But why? And who? His father had always prided himself on being his own boss. Ricardo didn't know of anyone who would fit into the category of *jefe,* or boss. Where could he go for help?

Wait! There was one man. A man his father respected above all others. The man who was *padrino* to all the Orejuela offspring. It wasn't that he was a close friend. His family was in too different a social class for that. But there was some connection between the two families. It had something to do with the good fortune that had attended the Orejuelas all these years. Until now. Ricardo had never understood exactly what the relationship was, but his father had always been proud of his distant kinship to this prominent family. Who else would his father turn to for help? He would find his *padrino* and ask if his father had contacted him.

Ricardo pushed his right foot to the floor. Whatever he found out, he had no intention of sharing with the *gringos.* If his father turned up alive, so much the better. But if someone had betrayed him, Ricardo would take care of the matter himself. Family honor demanded as much.

CHAPTER SIX

Stretching out on a lawn chair, Sara languidly turned the page of her novel. Breakfast was over, and another leisurely day stretched ahead. *At least Don Luis hasn't announced any plans for the evening. Maybe Nicky and I can slip out alone together—if there's anyplace we can be alone in a city where everyone knows my husband!*

Sara sighed, turning another unread page. In the days since the Fourth of July incident, it seemed she'd seen Nicolás even less than usual. Not that there was any lingering coldness between them. In fact, the day after their argument, a florist had delivered a dozen red roses, a wordless apology that had gone a long way toward helping Sara forget the troubling glimpse she'd had of her husband's temper. Since then, he'd been as tender and passionate as she'd ever known him. And if Sara, usually forthright in her opinions and convictions, found herself extending to Nicolás some of the same caution she used with her in-laws, this too would surely pass as they got to know each other.

Which would be easier if they had more time together! Don Luis had put Nicolás to work in the family business within twenty-four hours of his arrival in Bolivia, and aside from the *siesta* break, when they returned home for the usual midday meal, father and son were out of the house from early morning until seven or later at night. Even when the men were home, more often than not they were closeted in Don Luis's office near the downstairs drawing room.

"Papá's been waiting for me for two years," Nicolás had explained. "After all, I am his heir, and he paid for a North American university education so that I could come back and put what I learned to use in the plant. It won't always be this way. Just be patient."

Sara was willing to be patient about the long work-related absences, but she was beginning to resent the constant social whirl that took Nicolás's attention away from her as much as when they were physically apart. Barbecues, dances, restaurant parties—they all blurred together. At first it had been exciting, but now it was just too much. And on evenings when there were no guests expected or social activities to attend, both Nicolás and his parents seemed to take it for granted that the young couple would sit and visit downstairs until bedtime.

Sara slammed her book shut and sat up, grimacing at the memory of her conversation with Nicolás the night before.

"Nicky, don't you think maybe it's time we rented a house of our own?"

"Hmmm? What makes you say that?"

"Because I hardly ever see you! If you're not with Don Luis, we're with someone else. Your parents and sisters and cousins and . . . and friends! We've had four parties this week alone. It just seems that we're hardly ever alone anymore!"

"We're alone right now!" Nicolás leered.

Sara swatted his hand away. "That's not what I meant. Come on, I'm serious! It's not that I don't love your family, Nicky. It's been great to get to know them. But I married you, not them, and I just thought, well—maybe it would help things to have our own home. I don't care if it's small."

"Well, I do!" Nicolás said, rolling onto his back. "What is it you want me to say? This is my home. Someday it'll all be mine—and my son's after me. Why should I live anywhere else?"

"That's someday," Sara argued. "Right now it's your parents' home, and I'm sure they'd understand that we're ready to be on our own. I mean, look at your sisters. They've both got homes of their own."

"They aren't Cortezes," Nicolás answered impatiently. "Delores and Janéth belong to their husbands' families. Of course they live elsewhere. But it's different for us. I am Papá's heir. And they have willingly given me up for five years already. How could I even suggest moving out? My parents would be very disappointed and hurt, and I wouldn't blame them."

Sara had to admit she didn't get it. At twenty-three and married, it seemed only natural to her that Nicolás would want to be independent of his parents. Apparently this was another one of those cultural differences it would take her time to understand, and it would gain her nothing to force the issue. The home she'd always dreamed of would have to wait, but maybe soon Nicolás would begin to see her need for greater privacy as a couple.

Footsteps tapped across the tiles of the veranda. *"Querida?"*

Sara looked up with surprise and delight as Nicolás sauntered across the patio, looking more handsome than ever in the light sport coat and tie that he always wore when accompanying his father to the office.

"Nicky, you're back already!" Sara glanced at the gold Rolex he had given her to celebrate their first month together as a married couple soon after they'd arrived in Bolivia. Ten o'clock. "Is something wrong?" She hadn't expected to see him before lunchtime.

"No, of course not." Pulling off his tie, Nicolás flipped it onto the lounge chair. "Papá flew out to the hacienda this morning, and he won't be back until this afternoon. So I thought—what's your saying up north?"—his blue eyes gleamed with mischief—"'When the cat's away, the mice will play'? I've got to be back at the office this afternoon, but this morning I could take you on that tour you're always on me about."

"Really? You mean, just the two of us?" Sara's face lit up. "Oh, Nicky, I'd love it!" Swinging her feet over the edge of the lawn chair, she added with a mock frown, "And what do you mean, I'm always 'on' you? You make me sound like a nagging wife!"

"Well, aren't you?" Nicolás ignored Sara's squeal of outrage. Dodging the paperback she threw at his head, he pulled her to her feet and caught her close. "A woman as beautiful as you can nag me any time you want!" he murmured against her ear.

Sara smiled but refused to rise to his bait. Not when the reward for her weeks of forbearance was a whole day—or at least half a day—alone with Nicky. "You're sure Don Luis won't mind?"

"Of course not! In fact, it was his idea. He thinks—and I quote—it is time my bride acquaints herself with the Cortéz family business."

Nicolás helped her into the Ferrari with supreme care, and soon they were zooming through the streets of Santa Cruz. Despite his quick dismissal of her complaint the night before, it seemed that Nicolás had taken it to heart. He put himself out to entertain her, teasing her for her patent interest in anything bearing the Cortéz name, but answering each of her eager questions with easy good manners and charm.

Sara, in turn, listened with rapt attention, her amber eyes glowing with such happiness that Nicolás couldn't keep his admiring gaze off of her—which earned him a few incensed honks from fellow motorists.

Industrias Cortéz was more than just a business, Sara soon found out. She was far more impressed than she'd expected to be with the sheer extent of the Cortéz holdings. There was a pharmacy and a small factory where leather workers and other artisans produced the tooled leather bags, and wool wall hangings, and etched pewter that delighted the tourists. Downtown, near the central plaza, was a travel agency and an expensive boutique where Sara herself had shopped unknowingly a few days earlier. A five-story retail store displayed the latest in computers, sound systems, big-screen TVs, cellular phones, fax machines, and video cameras.

Who buys all this stuff? she wondered, thinking of the poverty of the crowds that thronged the streets outside. She remembered Gabriela's comments with unease, then quickly pushed the thought away. People like the Cortezes and their friends, no doubt.

They ate at *La Parilla,* one of two four-star restaurants owned by Don Luis. The thatched roof and rustic wood furnishings were an affectation meant to appeal to the tourist trade, but Sara was new enough to enjoy the mock-rural ambiance and the breeze through the open sides of the dining area. Nicolás ordered the "plate of the house," which included the largest steak Sara had ever seen. She shook her head with amazement.

"Why you guys don't all die of heart attacks, I just don't know!" she said gaily. "I can already feel the cholesterol clogging up my arteries!"

Nicolás grinned at her. "We in Bolivia don't suffer from the obsession you Americans have with your diet."

"Yeah? Well, you're going to end up with a fat wife if you don't stop feeding me like this!" Sara replied, pushing away her half-finished steak with a sigh of contentment. The light-hearted banter made her feel more in harmony with Nicolás than she had in days. So much so that she was encouraged to broach a subject she had been hesitating to discuss with him. Blotting her lips with her napkin, she blurted out, "Nicky, do you think Don Luis would give me a job?"

"A job?" Nicolás frowned. "Why do you need a job? My wife doesn't need to work."

"I know that," Sara said patiently. "But it's not as if there's anything for me to do at home. We've been here for over a month now, and I haven't lifted a finger yet! Mimi has the house running like clockwork, and there are so many servants she won't even let me clean our rooms. It's been a wonderful vacation, but I'm used to being busy. You know that. I just feel so—so useless!" Not to mention bored, but she didn't say that. "My degree's in Spanish, but I do have secretarial skills. The job I had in college was mainly typing and filing and that sort of thing. I just thought—well, if Don Luis, or even you, had some secretarial work that needed to be done, that would keep me busy, and I'd get to see more of you, too."

"That's out of the question!" Nicolás snapped. The response

was so sharp that Sara blinked in surprise. Noticing her reaction, Nicolás added more mildly, "Papá has never expected the women of this family to worry their heads about business. Besides, do you know how much a secretary makes here? A hundred bucks, maybe one-fifty a month. That's not even pocket money for you."

"Oh, I wouldn't expect to be paid!" Sara protested. "I just want to be with you!"

"And take a job away from someone who really needs it? I can't believe you'd want to do that!" The brilliant blue of Nicolás's eyes deepened as he smiled persuasively at Sara. "No, really, *corazón mía*, I'd love to have you at the office with me, of course. But I can tell you now that Papá will never consent for you to become involved in Cortéz Industries. Maybe he's a little old-fashioned, but that's the way it is, and I don't think you're going to change his mind."

Sara didn't press the point. Her father-in-law had never been less than cordial with her, but she'd seen enough of how he dealt with others—including his wife and son—to know that arguing with Don Luis was like hammering bare fists on a steel door. Though the door would remain unmoved, the hammerer was liable to go away bruised.

"What about teaching, then?" Sara's eye caught a glimpse of a half-dozen scruffy youngsters loitering outside the restaurant. "I took a lot of education courses with my Spanish major, and if that isn't enough to teach here, I'm sure one of the poorer schools would appreciate a volunteer to work with the kids a few hours a day."

Nicolás turned his head to follow her gaze. "Like those little beggars?" he said ironically. "Can you imagine what kind of diseases they might be carrying?"

"There are ways of getting around that!" Sara's suggestion had been an impulsive one, but the more she considered it, the more the idea began to appeal to her. "Teaching children like those would meet a real need, a lot more than working for your father would, now that you mention it. And it would give me something to do all day while you're gone."

"The government pays people to teach those kids." Nicolás was still smiling, but Sara could hear the exasperation creeping into his tone. "I don't understand why you're so anxious to fill your hours with work. Mamá and my sisters find plenty to keep them busy. Why can't you do what they do? Most women would be happy to have the kind of life I've given you."

"Oh, Nicky, of course I'm happy! Don't you see, that's just it!" Sara pleaded. "You've given me so much! And then I look around and see people like those children, who have so little. I feel guilty just sitting here with all these leftovers on my plate when those kids probably haven't had a square meal all day! I guess I'd just like to give a little something back—do more with my life than laze around the way I've been doing, pleasing no one but myself."

"You're pleasing me, isn't that important?" Nicolás reached for Sara's hand, his voice softening. "*Querida*, your tender heart is one of the things I love about you. But you don't have any reason to feel guilty. You've worked hard all these years since your father passed away, may he rest in peace. All I want is for you to enjoy yourself for a while. At least take a few months off, then we'll talk again. And if you really want some volunteer work, Mamá is on all kinds of committees. I'm sure she'd be happy to get you involved."

Sara stifled a sigh. She couldn't tell Nicolás that his mother's idea of volunteer work wasn't quite what she had in mind. Mimi chaired the country club social committee and excelled in planning bridge parties and society teas. Her main volunteer outlet was the National Federation of Women's Organizations, where she was president of the local chapter—an honor, she'd impressed upon her daughter-in-law, open only to women from the most prominent families in the nation.

"We work to help the downtrodden women of Bolivia," she'd informed Sara. "There are so many things our women lack—literacy programs, maternity care."

Surprised and impressed at this unexpected civic concern in her mother-in-law, Sara had looked forward to attending her first meeting. But when she went to a luncheon with Mimi, Delores, and Janéth, it soon became apparent that the elegantly dressed and impeccably coiffed women of the NFWO were more interested in discussing the plight of the lower classes—over plates filled with deviled quail's eggs, cream puffs, and broiled prawns—than in actually doing anything to help them.

It's not enough to hear and gasp and exclaim, Sara told herself now. *You've got to get your hands dirty.*

"Come, we'd better go." Nicolás broke into Sara's thoughts. He was already on his feet. "Papá will be waiting."

Sara stopped the head waiter on the way out. "Please, if you wouldn't mind, we have quite a few leftovers at our table. Could you please give them to those little boys who are watching the cars outside?"

The man's thin-bridged nose flared at the suggestion, but when Nicolás added a curt order of his own, the waiter reluctantly clapped his hands for a subordinate. By the time the shiny yellow sports car accelerated out of the parking lot, a pack of hungry children crowded around a metal basin heaped with scraps.

"It looks like I've married a social revolutionary," Nicolás remarked as they drove away. "I thought Alfredo was going to have a heart attack when you ordered him to waste prime Argentine beef on a horde of beggars." He turned the Ferrari onto the main boulevard heading east out of the city. "Just don't make it a habit, or we'll have every street kid in the city camped out in front of our restaurant. Which won't do a whole lot for business!"

Sara hadn't considered that consequence of her impulsive generosity. "Oh, dear! I guess maybe that wasn't the best idea. Poor Alfredo!"

The thought of Alfredo's discomfort seemed to afford Nicolás more amusement than concern. "Don't worry about it," he assured Sara carelessly. "Taking Cortéz orders is what he gets paid for."

Gunning the engine, Nicolás darted around a lumbering gravel truck, pulling back into his own lane in time to avoid an oncoming bus. "So, are you ready to see Cortéz Industries?"

Sara was happy enough to change the subject. "Isn't that what I've been doing?"

Nicolás made a dismissive gesture. "All you've seen this morning are businesses Papá has added since I left for the university five years ago. What you'll see now is the *real* Cortéz Industries. It's still the heart of everything we possess, the original *Industrias Cortéz* that restored our family to the greatness of its past."

"Oh, . . . really?" Taken aback by the intensity of his statement, Sara began scanning the industrial buildings and warehouses that were pushing the city limits out into the scrub jungle. "So which one is it? And what, exactly, do you produce?"

"Oh, it's none of these!" Nicolás said with a disparaging glance at the cinder-block factories they were passing. "*Industrias Cortéz* is twenty kilometers outside the city limits. As to what we produce, it's a sugar refinery. I thought I'd told you."

"Well, come to think of it, I guess you started to . . ." Sara smiled impishly, suddenly remembering that first evening. "But you were snoring long before you got into the details."

"Well, there you have it." Nicolás waved a careless hand toward the windshield. Sara turned her head to look. The wide boulevard had given way to a narrow two-lane highway, and on both sides of the road, as far as she could see, fields of sugar cane, mixed with intermittent patches of scrub jungle, tossed their tasseled heads.

"We process a good part of the sugar cane you see around here," Nicolás explained.

Another fifteen minutes passed before they came to a break in the sea of sugar cane. A chain-link fence topped with nasty-looking spikes and coils of barbed wire ran along the side of the highway. Behind the fence, a vast expanse of manicured lawn swept up to a modern glass-and-brick office building. A complex of smaller buildings spread out around it. Rising above it all were steel towers, glinting silver in the afternoon sun like something from a futuristic science fiction movie.

The Ferrari slowed, and Sara could see a wide set of gates flanked by security guards dressed in olive green. Like the guard at the Cortéz mansion, they were armed with pistols, and from their hips hung long, white batons like those used by the U.S. National Guard for crowd control. The guards snapped to attention as Nicolás swung off the highway, and one man ran to open the gates. Sara's mouth dropped open as the realization hit her. "*This* is your sugar refinery?"

"You like it?" Nicolás looked both amused and pleased at her reaction, just as he had at her first glimpse of the Cortéz mansion.

"*Like* it?" Sara struggled for words. "It's . . . it's fantastic! And so modern—just like back home!"

"The most modern manufacturing complex in Bolivia. And the first to be completely computerized with all the latest North American technology." As the Ferrari slowed to ease over a cattle grating, Nicolás pointed out a large warehouse to one side of the main administrative building. "This is where we do our shipping for several of the businesses you saw in town. Actually, it would be a lot more efficient to allow each of our enterprises to ship directly, but Papá likes to keep a tight control on our exports."

"And all of this belongs to your father?" Sara's voice was tinged with a mixture of awe and some dismay. Would she have dared marry Nicky if she'd known just how wealthy he truly was?

"Well, it belongs to Cortéz Industries. My father is CEO, of course, and still owns the lion's share of the stock. But every aunt and uncle and cousin in the family has a share in the business."

"It's all so much bigger than I dreamed!" Sara raised her eyes to gaze at the towers, which at close range she recognized as enormous stainless steel holding tanks. In the center of each tower was a large, stylized *C* with a crown just above the letter, its three spikes topped by little gold balls. Sara had seen the same symbol on the gates, but here the words *Industrias Cortéz* had been added, the ornate letters circling the crowned *C* to form a sort of emblem. "I can see why the people of Santa Cruz think so much of your family. You must provide a lot of jobs around here."

"We've had our successes," Nicolás conceded. "I can't believe myself how quickly the place has grown." He looked with affectionate pride at the tall cylinders and stretches of metallic tubing. "It doesn't seem that long ago that this was all jungle. I was only four or five, but I can still remember Papá bringing me out here to watch the bulldozers clearing out the brush. My cousins and I used to drive the builders crazy, playing space explorer in and out of all that tubing."

The image of a younger, mischievous Nicolás made Sara smile, but a sudden thought gave her pause. "Nicky, you said that this sugar factory was the very first business your family owned. But if you can remember all this being built, then that means Cortéz Industries is less than twenty years old. What was your father doing before then? You must have had some kind of business with that beautiful house and . . ."

Sara stopped abruptly when she realized that her questions were leading into forbidden territory, but Nicolás answered readily. "Oh, we had our hacienda and some rental properties. Papá sold them off when he started Cortéz Industries. And, of course, we didn't live where we are now. That came a couple years later when I was maybe six or seven. Before that, we lived near the plaza in this big old colonial mansion that's been in the Cortéz family for at least a couple of hundred years."

Nicolás grinned at Sara. "Just be glad I didn't take you there! It was—still is—the most gloomy, mildewed place you ever saw. Not to mention, the roof leaked in so many places it wasn't worth even trying to keep up with repairs. After we moved out, the government took it over for an immigration office or something like that. We were perfectly happy to let them have it!"

The Ferrari had now reached the administrative building, but Nicolás made a sharp left turn and drove another thirty meters before braking with a flourish in front of the refinery complex's largest building. This was a multistoried, modernistic structure with tubing and chimneys, and the rumblings and groanings of heavy machinery that proclaimed it to be some sort of processing plant.

"I thought you'd like to see the sugar before Papá gets back. We still have another half-hour before he's due. And that's if the flight's on time." Throwing an arm around Sara's shoulders, Nicolás turned her chin to where she could see through the Ferrari's windshield a long, narrow strip of pavement beyond the processing plant. At one end was a small control tower.

Sara stared. "You're telling me you've got your own airport too?"

Next to the control tower stood an open hangar with aluminum siding. Inside, Sara could see two single-engine prop planes and a larger two-engine plane. Unlike everything else she'd seen, the aircraft didn't have the Cortéz emblem on them. "You said Don Luis flew out to some hacienda, but you didn't say it was your own plane!"

"Hey, it's not that big a deal. Everyone around here who's anyone flies their own plane. I only need a few more hours myself to renew my license," Nicolás explained carelessly.

"What!" Sara said incredulously. "You never told me you could fly a plane."

"Sure. I'll take you up as soon as I get my credentials back."

"That sounds great!" Sara's eyes sparkled gold with anticipation. "My dad used to take me up in a Cessna when I was a kid. I'd love to go again. Maybe we could fly down to that hacienda. You haven't shown me any of the countryside yet."

Nicolás snorted. "If you did, it'd be a first! Mamá and the girls won't go near a place without cable TV and room service." He grabbed her hand. "Enough about that. Let's go see some sugar."

Sara found the next half-hour fascinating. Nicolás showed her the giant silos where raw sugar was stored. She sampled the frothy green sugarcane juice and inspected the newly crystallized sugar being spun in a series of centrifugal machines. She tasted a piece of still-warm lump sugar and watched an immense funnel pour the finished snow-white crystals into five-kilo bags. The scurrying workers wore white coats like doctors or scientists, and everything was modern and sparkling clean.

"Molasses, powdered sugar, brown—if it's made out of sugar, we produce it," Nicolás boasted. He stopped beside a vat of dark syrup that smelled like vanilla with a hint of maple. "We're even experimenting with our own pancake syrups for the *gringos.*"

Next, Nicolás next led Sara past some huge holding tanks which permeated the air with an acrid odor that wrinkled her nose. "Isn't that—?"

"One hundred percent pure alcohol," Nicolás supplied. He lifted a one-liter plastic jug from a shelf and handed it to Sara. "We supply a good part of Bolivia's pharmacies from here—including our own, of course. We've even started shipping some to Brazil. A lot of their cars are now fueled by alcohol, you might have heard, instead of gas."

"Wow, that's fascinating," Sara said as she passed the liter jug back to Nicolás. "I guess I didn't realize it really worked."

"It sure does. If the world runs out of gas someday, they can always plant a few million more hectares of sugar cane."

Glancing at his watch, Nicolás suddenly exclaimed, "Aieee! We'd better go, or we're going to be late! Papá doesn't like to be kept waiting." He quickened his steps and Sara had to scramble to avoid being left behind. She was almost completely out of breath by the time they emerged from the plant to find the airstrip still empty. Nicolás slowed at once, and Sara breathed a sigh of relief.

At a stroll now, they climbed the marble steps of the administrative building. A security guard, who had been lolling against the wall, jumped to attention and hurried to open the wide glass doors. Nicolás strode past him without so much as a nod, but Sara murmured a polite *"Gracias."* Tipping his olive-green cap in response, the guard spun around on his heels, his back straight and the wooden stalk of his rifle now at a sharp, professional angle across his shoulder as he scanned the horizon for intruders. *At least until we're out of sight,* thought Sara with amusement, watching him through the glass.

The foyer was big enough for square dancing, its pale walls bright with modern art paintings. A faint whir drew her attention upward. A security camera had pivoted to film their progress across the floor.

"Buenas tardes, Don Nicolás." Two receptionists jumped up from behind a large desk, beaming with delight at the sight of Nicolás. Nicolás didn't slow his pace, but he gave the young women a wink and a careless greeting as he steered Sara past a metal sculpture that looked to her as though a kindergarten class had been turned loose in an auto-wrecking yard.

"Don Nicolás!" one of the women called after him. "Your father is not yet here, but *el señor* Vargas said to tell you that he is awaiting you in your father's office."

Nicolás raised a hand without looking back as another guard hurried to push swinging doors open onto a long hall. Nicolás walked through without a glance at the guard, so Sara paused to make up for her husband's oversight, offering her warmest smile. But the smile froze on her lips as her eyes fell to the words lettered in bronze across the man's shirt pocket. *Policía Nacional.*

National Police? This man and the others she'd seen patrolling outside were not just security guards; they were policemen! Sara waited only until the doors swung shut behind them before she clutched at Nicolás's arm. "That man out there is a policeman!" she whispered. "And those other guards—they're policemen too, aren't they?"

Nicolás shrugged. "Yes, of course they are! Why?"

"I knew it! Something's wrong, isn't it? There's something you haven't been telling me. I should have guessed from that guard and all those dogs at home." Wild possibilities began racing through Sara's mind. Weren't there guerrillas in these Latin American countries who specialized in kidnapping prominent citizens for ransom or political bargaining? Sara's fingers contracted on her husband's forearm. "Nicky, you've got to tell me the truth! Is your family in some kind of danger?"

"Danger?" Nicolás looked blank for a moment. Then, as the meaning of her question sank in, he threw back his head in a shout of laughter.

Sara blushed, casting a self-conscious glance around. "Don't laugh at me!" she hissed, hurt at Nicky's reaction to her concern. "What's so funny, anyway?"

"I'm sorry, *querida*." Nicolás wiped the smile from his face, but his blue eyes danced as he pushed the "up" button on the elevator. "Were you really so worried about us, my silly *princesa*? Of course there's nothing wrong! Why shouldn't the police be here? That's what they're for!"

As they entered the elevator and he pressed the button for the fourth floor, Nicolás explained the situation to Sara. "Here in Bolivia, much of the government, including the police department, suffers from a lack of funding. To keep the department afloat, the police routinely hire out a large percentage of their personnel as security guards for the more affluent businesses and banks in the city. Of course, they don't have the kind of training your American police have, but the uniforms are usually enough to scare off petty criminals."

The elevator doors slid open. "So, what about all the ordinary people?" Sara demanded indignantly as they stepped out into another hallway. "I suppose it doesn't matter if *they* get robbed or mugged or something while the police are all guarding the rich people's businesses?"

Nicolás shrugged. "What do they have worth stealing?"

"Nico!" A man with a cellular phone plastered to one ear stepped out of one of the executive offices. "Nico, where have you been?" he demanded in Spanish, placing one hand over the mouthpiece of the phone. Behind him, the office door swung shut, locking with a click. "I was expecting you some time ago. Where are those papers for the meeting?"

Sara caught the look of annoyance on her husband's face. The other man's casual address told her that he was someone with considerably more rank than the employees she'd met until now, but Nicolás made no move to introduce her as he would have for a family member or social equal.

"Julio," he said, without answering the man's question, "where is my father?"

"One moment." Julio listened intently to the person on the other end of his phone call. He took his hand off the mouthpiece. "Yes, put him on. I will wait."

There was a pause, then he snapped, "Vargas here."

Julio Vargas! So this was the man the receptionist had mentioned downstairs. It wasn't the first time Sara had heard the name. Her father-in-law had mentioned Vargas on occasion in conversations with Nicolás at mealtimes. Julio Vargas was Don Luis's personal assistant and the head of security at Cortéz Industries. While Vargas carried on his low-voiced conversation and Nicolás tapped his foot impatiently, Sara studied the security chief with interest.

He was slim and only a few inches taller than she was, but then most Bolivian men were short compared to Americans, and he carried himself with a straight-backed posture that made him seem taller than he was. His jet-black hair was slicked back and tied in a ponytail at the base of his neck. He wore an open-neck silk shirt tucked into close-fitting pants and a lightweight, tailored sport coat. All black. The sunlight slanting through the window glinted off a series of gold chains around his neck, and his left earlobe held two small gold hoops.

He looked so much like a stereotypical Hollywood rendition of a drug dealer that Sara had to turn a giggle into a cough. But all her mirth vanished when Vargas's eyes flickered in her direction. They were the flattest, coldest eyes Sara had ever seen. Like slate.

"Yes, I'll be right there." Snapping the phone shut, Vargas turned to Nicolás. "That was the tower. The Cessna ran into bad weather over Monteagudo, but they made it through the storm safely and are landing now."

"Then go pick him up," Nicolás cut him off sharply. "Papá does not like to be kept waiting, and neither do I."

Sara saw a smolder of fire spring into the security chief's cold eyes at the curt command, but he said smoothly. "That was my intent, *señor*. If you will please excuse me."

He had taken a step toward the elevator when Nicolás reminded him softly, "The door."

There was no visible expression on Julio Vargas's chiseled features as he turned back and quickly punched a series of numbers into a control panel beside the door. He stepped aside as the door opened with a click, but he waited for Nicolás's nod of dismissal before striding toward the elevator.

"I don't think he liked that!" Sara commented as the elevator doors slid shut. "And though I hate to judge anyone too quickly, I don't think he cares a whole lot for you either!"

"Oh, he'll be okay," Nicolás assured her airily. "You just have to let him know who's boss. Vargas was a colonel in the army before he came here, and he just can't get it through his head that it isn't his place to be throwing out orders anymore."

Sara didn't say anything more, but as she followed Nicolás through the open door, her face was troubled. With her, Nicky was always loving and tender—except for the Fourth of July incident, of course. And he was considerate of her wants—well, most of the time. She pushed aside the fleeting thought that *she* was the one who gave in whenever there was a difference of opinion. He was affectionate with his mother and sisters, and vastly popular with his contemporaries in Bolivian society. But Sara couldn't help noticing that Nicky's thoughtfulness and concern didn't extend much beyond his own tight little circle.

It wasn't that he was rude or tyrannical with the employees or servants. It was more that he took their services for granted. As though the workers and officials who jumped to attention every time he walked by were not people in their own right but part of the furniture or surroundings. And he didn't seem to notice any incongruity in the vast gap between his own enormous wealth and the grinding poverty that existed everywhere outside the high, guarded walls of the privileged upper class.

Well, what can you expect? Sara told herself. *After all, he's been treated like the crown prince since he was born. He's probably never lifted so much as a handkerchief off the floor! Maybe I can help him to see things differently, and then maybe together we can use some of this to help these people.*

The executive suite on the top floor of the Cortéz Industries building was as richly appointed as any American Fortune 500 offices might be. In the reception area, a young woman sat behind a computer at an L-shaped work island, her red-tipped fingers flying gingerly over the keys. She glanced up briefly and smiled at Nicolás. Behind her, a fax machine sat atop a row of file cabinets made from a dark, burnished wood. A well-stuffed leather couch and three matching chairs offered comfort to waiting visitors. On a coffee table lay the day's paper and the latest issues of *Visión* and *Selecciones*.

"Papá's secretary," Nicolás said, gesturing with his hand turned palm-side up. "But she takes care of me too, don't you, Dolores? At least until I get a secretary of my own."

He grinned at Dolores, and her smile widened to show pearly teeth. "Papá should be here any moment, but first"—Nicolás waved in the direction of a door on the far side of the reception area—"let me show you what I do all day when I'm not daydreaming of the most beautiful blonde in Santa Cruz."

Sara blushed as Nicolás put his arm around her shoulder and ushered her toward his office. He flung open the door with a flourish and said, "Here is where Papá keeps me slaving."

Apart from a mahogany desk and a work table piled high with folders and ledgers, the room had an unfinished look about it, the walls freshly painted and empty. Sara picked up a framed picture from the desk. It was a snapshot of Nicolás and her on the beach in California on their honeymoon. The two of them were posed smiling against the backdrop of the Pacific. Sara was holding her wind-tossed hair back from a face that was sunburned and eager and unmistakably in love.

"Tío Gualberto, one of Papá's cousins, had this office until I got back. But he's been kicked down the hall, and I've taken over his position as vice-president of business administration." Nicolás waved a hand at the walls. "As you can see, I haven't gotten around to decorating. Now, maybe *that's* a job you'd like."

"Hey! Sounds like fun," Sara agreed eagerly. She was no professional decorator, but brightening up this drab office shouldn't be too hard, and it would keep her busy for a few days at least. Setting down the snapshot, she looked around with new interest. "That must have been awfully hard on your cousin after so many years. Getting kicked out of his office, I mean. Didn't he mind?"

Nicolás raised a surprised eyebrow. "Why should he mind? Gualberto knew that this office was his only until I was old enough to fill it."

He grinned at her. "If you're worrying that he's lost his job, don't! We don't fire family, and I'll still have plenty of use for him as my assistant. Papá hasn't even reduced his salary to match his new position. We know how to be generous with our employees."

Without giving Sara a chance to comment, Nicolás steered her out of his office and over to a third door behind Dolores's work area. "And *this* . . . this is Papá's office!"

Sara's eyes were wide with astonishment as the heavy wooden door swung slowly open. Don Luis had the most ostentatious office she'd ever seen.

The room was easily as big as her entire student apartment had been back in Seattle. The carpet, a blend of golds and browns, was so thick that the pile came up over the tops of her flat sandals. There were paintings on the walls and sculptures of bronze and porcelain on pedestals, and a sitting area the size of the average

American living room, furnished in the same red leather accessories as the outer office. Matching drapes framed the back wall, which was a gigantic floor-to-ceiling picture window, its polarized glass filtering out the sun while affording the room's occupants a spectacular view of Cortéz Industries and the Andes mountains, smoky-green in the distance.

"Takes your breath away, doesn't it?" Nicolás was watching Sara's response with satisfaction. "Papá had this all redone since I was home last. Now that he's the biggest businessman in the country, he's got to live up to his image."

Sara drifted over to the window. At the far end of the property, where the lawn edged into sugarcane fields, a miniature-looking riding mower was cutting fresh swaths through the grass. On the airstrip, Sara saw that a single-engine plane was now parked near the hangar, with three people clustered beside it. As she watched, a gray Mercedes pulled up to the edge of the runway and a black-clad figure emerged and walked briskly toward the plane. Above the horizon, a cloudless sky stretched deep and blue, the usual brassy tinge added by the tropical sun, filtered out by the polarized glass. The view was so clear, it was hard to believe that anyone looking up from below couldn't see her.

Behind Sara, Nicolás wandered restlessly around the office. He stopped to type a few words on the computer, frowned at the screen, then threw himself into his father's chair. "What's taking so long?" he grumbled. Picking up a pewter letter opener, he ran it back and forth between his fingers. "Papá has a fit if I'm not right here when he wants me, but *he's* got all the time in the world! Well, I've got things to do, even if he doesn't!"

"It looks like he's talking to the pilot or someone," Sara told him over her shoulder. "Mr. Vargas just pulled up. There, now they're walking away from the plane. No, they've stopped by the hangar."

Nicolás dropped the letter opener and picked up a pewter pen holder. Shaped like a German beer stein without the lid, it was engraved on each side with the Cortéz emblem. Dumping the handful of pens and pencils onto the blotter, Nicolás poked them into a random pattern with short, irritated jabs of the letter opener. With his left hand, he continued to fidget with the pewter container.

"Papá has an important conference call scheduled for later this afternoon. He told me to have some shipping invoices ready, but then he leaves this morning without giving me the numbers. And now he's so late I'll never get them finished in time. If I could have gotten into his computer files, I could have finished those invoices myself. But no, I can't be trusted with his password. He lets Vargas have access to his private files, but not me—his own son! When is he going to learn that I'm just as capable as anyone of making hard business decisions? After all, I've had a whole lot more business training than he ever did! Why did he send me to the U.S. to study if he's going to keep treating me like a child?"

Sara turned around. Nicolás was wearing his sulky look again. Leaving the window, she slid her arms around his neck, her fingers slipping under his collar to rub the tense muscles of his neck. "Give him time, Nicky. It's not easy for fathers to admit their sons have grown up. When he sees what a great job you're doing, he'll start trusting your judgment more."

Kissing the top of his dark hair, she added, "Would it help if I just took a taxi home? It's been great, but I've taken enough of your time today."

His sullen expression lifted a little. Mollified, Nicolás said, "Of course I don't want you to go. You haven't even seen the warehouse yet. But—well, it *would* be a big help if . . . Would you mind if Dolores showed you the rest? Then maybe I can finish that report once Papá gets here."

"No, of course I don—" Sara broke off as Nicolás sat bolt upright in the chair. "What—?"

Nicolás lifted a hand for silence. Placing the pen holder he'd been fiddling with close to his ear, he shook it. Now Sara heard the sound, too, something between a clunk and a rattle in what should have been an empty container. Nicolás turned the pewter container upside down, shook it again, then looked inside.

"Well, well, if this thing isn't at least two inches short in there!" He grinned at Sara, the sulkiness gone. "Shall we see what Papá has hidden here?"

Sara shook her head doubtfully. "I don't think Don Luis . . ."

But Nicolás was already running his fingers over the engraving on the outside of the pen holder. "I've seen something like this before. Ah!" There was a sudden click, and the entire bottom of the pewter container popped open. Setting it down, Nicolás picked up the object that had fallen out onto the blotter. Sara gasped when she saw what was dangling from his fingers.

CHAPTER SEVEN

Nicolás held up a cross attached to a gold chain. A little more than two inches long, it was wide and oddly flattened in proportion to its height, the four arms of equal length, like a Maltese cross, and slightly flared at the ends. Small green stones were set at the end of each arm, unfaceted but gleaming softly in the light of the window, and ornate scrolling twisted across the gold. In the center, set like a cameo in the space created by the junction of the four arms—a *painting?*

Sara stepped around the massive desk chair to take a closer look as Nicolás laid the beautiful necklace on the desk. "Are those real emeralds?" she asked with awe, touching one with a forefinger.

"Would they be anything but?" Nicolás picked up the cross by its chain and dropped it into Sara's hand. Snapping shut the bottom of the pen holder, he began straightening up the mess he'd made on the desk. "That, *mi querida,* is the cross of Cortéz. I never even knew it was still around."

"The cross of Cortéz?" Sara echoed, the upswing in her voice making it a question. The shining ornament was unexpectedly heavy in the palm of her hand, and she didn't need to be told that this was no gilded piece of costume jewelry. It was definitely solid gold. The chain was also heavy, each link flat and thick with swirls of etching across the surface. The whole thing looked at once fresh and untarnished and incredibly ancient.

Sara tilted the cross so that the light fell full on the inset in the center. It *was* a painting, no bigger than the locket she had worn as a child, but by some incredible artistry, each tiny figure was so distinct that she could read the expressions on their faces, the colors as bright and vivid as though painted last week. There was a knight in shining armor, with a red cloak, mounted on a white charger. His face was ablaze with triumph, and under the rearing hoofs of his horse lay the coiled, thrashing body of a dragon. The knight's spear was buried in its red-gold belly, and a snarl of defeat was on its serpentine snout. In the background, a fair maiden stood in sky-blue robe and white wimple, her eyes raised piously to heaven, but a coy smile playing about her mouth.

"It's a family heirloom. Look!" Flipping the cross over in Sara's hand, Nicolás pointed out a tiny stylized *C* engraved in the flat hammered gold on the back of the ornament. Taking the cross back from Sara, Nicolás pointed to the painting. "That little fellow on the horse is *San Jorge*. He made a career of rescuing gorgeous virgins from dragons. Not a bad life!

"I don't know that it's all that valuable," Nicolás went on. "At least not compared to most of Mamá's jewelry. But it's been in the family a long time. Come on, I'll show you." Getting to his feet, Nicolás slipped the heavy gold chain around his neck. Grabbing Sara's hand, he led her over to one of the paintings on the wall of the office. The portrait was a classic example of pre-Simón Bolivar Latin-American religious art, dark and gloomy with an ornate gilt frame. The man in the picture wore the dark robes of a priest, and sure enough, the same cross now around Nicky's neck gleamed against the blackness of the rich material.

"My great-great-great uncle. I'm not sure just how many 'greats,' but he and his brother were the first of the family to cross over from Spain. They say he was quite a guy. He came over as a Jesuit missionary not long after Pizarro, baptized thousands of Indians—of course that was when you had a choice of getting baptized or having your head cut off—and settled down to make himself a real power in these parts. The story goes that he had the cross and chain made out of confiscated Inca artifacts. The artist was the same painter who did this picture and a couple of others we have hanging around. Family history has it that he was some court painter who managed to displease the king of Spain—painted too realistic a portrait or something—so he decided to throw in his luck with Pizarro's army. My ancestor here took him under his wing and set him to converting his share of Inca gold into images more appropriate for a priest. This cross is the only one that was handed down. It's supposed to bestow God's protection on the man who wears it—good luck and all that."

Sara gave the man in the picture a closer look. He was undoubtedly a Cortéz, with the same proud, aristocratic features as Nicolás and his father, and the same brilliant blue eyes. But his mouth was the thin, almost invisible line that marked Don Luis, not Nicolás's open, laughing expression. *Like a steel trap,* she thought. She could easily imagine this man forcing thousands of frightened Indians into a river for a rite that should have been precious with spiritual symbolism, but which his captives wouldn't even have comprehended.

"So what happened to him?" Sara asked, looking back over at Nicolás.

"Well, I'm afraid that cross didn't do him a lot of good in the end," Nicolás admitted. "He was shot on one of his missionary trips by some ungrateful converts who didn't appreciate all he was doing for them. That's when the cross passed to his brother, my umpteenth great-grandfather. He's the one who got all the good luck. He accepted a position as an officer in Pizarro's army and eventually carved out a nice little personal kingdom here in Bolivia."

Sara followed Nicolás across the room to another portrait. This one showed a young man, who bore a startling resemblance to Nicolás, dressed in riding clothes and standing next to a horse. The cross wasn't visible around his neck, but then Sara spotted it wrapped around the pommel of the young man's Arabian stallion.

"The cross of Cortéz shows up in several of these old paintings," Nicolás said. "Religious merit, supposedly. But this one of my great-grandfather was the last. I figured it had been sold like a lot of other family heirlooms when things got tight a generation or so back. And to think Papá's had it all this time!"

Nicolás weighed the cross in his hand. "Maybe I should keep it on. A little extra protection never hurt anyone."

Sara couldn't believe she was hearing right. "Come on, Nicky, you don't really think a piece of jewelry is going to give good luck or God's protection?" she said skeptically. "That's just superstition!"

"Sure I do! St. George is the saint of protection, everyone knows that," Nicolás argued. "Okay, so we don't go to church much anymore, but that doesn't mean we're pagans. We still believe in miracles and pray to the saints and all that. And this cross was blessed by a priest. Not just any priest, either. A bishop of Rome itself that my dear great-uncle over there paid to bring over after he'd gotten his cathedral built. Just look at all the good luck this has already brought our family over the years."

Nicolás had never put his tie back on after removing it at the house, and he'd unbuttoned the top buttons of his shirt in the heat of the early afternoon. Now he reached under his collar and pulled out the thin gold chain he always wore. Stripping it off over his head, he dropped the Cortéz cross into its place. Striking a pose for Sara, he said triumphantly, "St. George is now back where he belongs. How does it look?"

"It's beautiful," Sara admitted. "But are you sure you should just be taking it like this? After all, if your father had it hidden—"

"Why should he care?" Nicolás cut in. "It's not like he's using it himself. And it's just a trinket. The emeralds are small, and Mamá wears more gold than this around her neck at any of her society teas. The only real value it has is sentimental—and that good luck. I can tell you this. If it was so important to Papá, he wouldn't be stashing it in a pen holder on his desk. He'd have it in the safe with the rest of the Cortéz family jewelry. He's probably had it in there so long he's forgotten it's there."

"Well, just so long as you tell him you were the one who took it," Sara conceded. "I'd hate for Dolores or someone to get accused of stealing it. Maybe it isn't much to you millionaires, but to us ordinary working folk, it looks pretty valuable."

"As if you could ever be ordinary." Tucking the chain inside his shirt, Nicolás pulled Sara close, his fingers threading through her hair as his mouth hovered tantalizingly close to hers. "But don't you worry your honest little head. I'll tell Papá I've got it."

His lips had barely touched hers when the door of the office slammed open. Nicolás and Sara jumped apart. Don Luis strode into the room, Julio Vargas at his heels. Sara's father-in-law was frowning, his eyes on his watch as he walked around his desk and punched some keys on the computer keyboard. He looked up. "Nicolás, you're here. Good! I am expecting the call from Amsterdam at four. The new import company, you remember! Do you have those shipping invoices ready?"

"Not yet, Papá, but I can have them in half an hour if you'll—"

"What do you mean 'not yet'?" Don Luis straightened up from the computer, his blue eyes flashing anger. "Didn't you finish them before you took off this morning? How could you be so careless!"

"You didn't leave me the shipping codes of the marked merchandise. I wasn't able to get into the com—"

Don Luis cut Nicolás off with a sharp hand gesture. "Nico, I told you this was important! If you needed information from the computer, you should ask Julio. How can you expect to take over my place one day if you do not show responsibility?"

Nicolás flushed angrily, darting a glance at his father's assistant, and Sara didn't need to be told that he would rather risk Don Luis's displeasure than ask for help from Julio Vargas. The security chief now stood impassively watching the confrontation between father and son, but there was a glitter in his black eyes that told Sara he was enjoying Nicolás's humiliation. With a scowl marring his good looks, Nicolás muttered, "Yes, Papá, I'll do it right away."

Sara let out a silent sigh. She knew it wasn't her fault that Nicolás had failed to finish those stupid invoices. But she couldn't help feeling guilty for having kept him away from the office all day. She was also angry at Don Luis for raking Nicolás down in front of Julio Vargas.

The relationship between Nicolás and his father was one more thing she didn't understand. Back at school in Seattle, Nicolás had always seemed so sophisticated and self-confident, older than his years. Even today she'd seen that same assurance in the air of command he adopted with Cortéz Industries employees. But when he was with Don Luis, he seemed different, younger, almost boyishly anxious to please. Maybe if Nicky would stand up to his father a little more. Make it clear that he was no longer a child and that he expected to be accorded the respect and authority he deserved as the Cortéz heir and vice-president of this corporation. The idea of the vice-president of business administration, or whatever Nicky's new title was, having to beg his father's assistant for access to the computer! It was so absurd, it was incredible!

But then, maybe it wasn't so easy for someone who'd spent his entire life dominated by his father's iron-willed personality to make a declaration of independence. Sara had to confess to being more than a little nervous of Don Luis herself. She'd certainly take Nicky's easygoing charm over her father-in-law's dictatorial disposition any day. Still . . .

"I'd better go," Sara murmured to Nicolás. "Are you sure your father won't mind if I borrow Dolores? Maybe I'd better just go home."

"No, no, you must finish your tour, Sara, *hija*." Sara could have sworn Don Luis hadn't even noticed her presence in the room, but now he glanced up from the computer keyboard. "I regret that I am in need of the services of my secretary. And your husband too. But Julio will be delighted to escort you."

He snapped his fingers, and his assistant stepped forward, clicking his heels together in a way that made Sara suppress a sudden giggle. "Of course! It will be my pleasure." Sara could see no pleasure or any other expression on the man's darkly chiseled features. Nor did she care for the way his cold black eyes swept over her—not in the openly admiring stare she was growing accustomed to from Latin men, but as though . . . *as though I were some sort of security risk instead of Nicky's wife,* she thought, her amusement turning to indignation. She wasn't so sure she wanted to continue with this tour. Not if she couldn't go with Nicolás, or at least the friendly secretary she'd met in the outer office. She opened her mouth to decline the invitation, then snapped it shut as Don Luis beckoned Nicolás over with an imperious wave. Tapping out a series of numbers on the computer keyboard, he ordered impatiently, "Make speed, Nico, they will be calling in only ten minutes."

It was a definite dismissal. Nicolás hurried to join his father at the computer. Wrinkling her nose expressively, Sara trailed Julio Vargas across the wide expanse of oriental carpet. At least she could keep the security chief off her husband's back while he worked things out with his father.

"One moment." The command stopped them at the door. Straightening up from the desk, Don Luis permitted himself a small, thin smile. "Sara, *hija,* I wish you to have a souvenir of your visit today. Julio, you will allow my daughter-in-law to choose anything that she would like."

Sara thanked him politely but without pleasure and stepped through the door that the security chief was holding open for her. Dolores didn't glance up to smile this time as they crossed the outer office, but cast an apprehensive glance toward Vargas before bending industriously over her keyboard.

She's afraid of him, Sara said to herself as she eyed the tight black ponytail and glittering earlobe bobbing along in front of her. Then she scolded herself for her snap judgment. The security of a complex this large could be no easy job, and maybe a good security chief needed to inspire a degree of intimidation in those around him.

Vargas bowed slightly from the waist as he paused to type the door code into the control panel. "*Señora* Cortéz, if you will tell me what you have not yet seen, I will guide you there."

The tone of his voice held nothing but polite servility, and Sara, ashamed of her earlier thoughts, responded with her warmest smile. What kind of person was she, anyway, to take such an instant aversion to two different men in the span of one week? Of course, that underhanded DEA agent who'd caused so much trouble for the Cortezes deserved it. But what had Julio Vargas done to her? Nothing. And Don Luis trusted the man implicitly. Was all this attention she'd been receiving since her arrival in Santa Cruz going to her head so much that she resented any man who didn't fall over his feet with admiration?

"I think I've seen most of it," she confided in her careful Spanish. "Nicolás showed me the businesses you have in the city and the sugar processing plant. Would you mind if I cut the rest short and just went home? I'm really a little tired."

Vargas was silent for a moment, then nodded. "We will go then directly to the warehouse. Don Luis will wish to know that you have selected your gift. When you have chosen, I myself will direct the limousine to drive you where you wish."

The warehouse was well worth seeing, Sara admitted, despite her taciturn companion. To make up for her initial aversion to Vargas, Sara was at her friendliest as Vargas ushered her into the gray

Mercedes and drove past the processing plant to the shipping center, where a fleet of trucks was being loaded with the latest shipment of Cortéz products. She attempted to make polite conversation, but the security chief's answers were terse, and the only information she was able to elicit was that he had no wife or family and that he'd been with *Industrias Cortéz* for three years.

The huge warehouse covered more than an acre of floor space, and to Sara's unaccustomed eyes it was a madhouse of confusion. Forklifts and flatbed carts piled high with cardboard boxes and wooden crates crisscrossed the vast floor with no seeming pattern, a chaos that resulted in lots of rapid braking, much hand waving, and a profusion of shouted curses among the workers.

"It's so much!" Sara exclaimed, taking a hasty step backward as a truck pulled up uncomfortably close and a pair of brawny men began loading a stack of carved mahogany tables.

The security chief's dark eyes roved the warehouse, looking for any sign of trouble. Along the back wall of the warehouse, workers were packing leather goods and native handicrafts into padded cardboard boxes. Julio Vargas moved in that direction, gesturing for Sara to follow. Trailing behind him, Sara threaded her way past two supervisors who were arguing over the contents of a stack of sealed crates. It seemed odd that Don Luis would truck all these goods clear out here from the city only to turn around and ship them somewhere else. It certainly would seem more efficient—not to mention create a lot less chance for mix-ups—if each Cortéz enterprise were to ship its own products from its own factory.

Julio stopped beside a collection of tooled-leather purses and bags. He gestured along the row of tables. "You may select anything here that pleases you. If you will then inform me of your choices so that the supervisor may note—"

He broke off his instructions with an annoyed exclamation. Sara turned to see what had caught his attention. A forklift was bearing down on them, its load of cardboard boxes weaving erratically from side to side. Sara spotted the problem at once. The operator had simply been too ambitious and had lifted far more boxes than the fork could comfortably handle.

"Those boxes do not come here!" Vargas snapped. "What is he doing?" Then, as the forklift swung even more precariously to one side, Vargas snarled, "The fool! He is going to lose that load."

He started angrily forward, shouting for the operator to stop the engine. As the load of boxes weaved to a halt, Sara turned back to the row of tables. The workers here were women, their fingers deftly wrapping each handcrafted item in old newspapers and laying them carefully into boxes. Each box bore the crowned emblem of *Industrias Cortéz* carefully centered on each side. The women—most of them hardly more than girls—seemed to know who she was, because they giggled and poked each other as she passed. Sara heard whispers of "*de Don Nicolás,* "*La señora Cortéz,*" and "*qué bella!*" ("how beautiful"). She smiled at them as she moved along the tables, and they responded with shy smiles of their own. More than one smile revealed missing front teeth, the result of a lifetime of chewing sugar cane and poor dental care.

Sara decided against the tooled-leather purses. They were beautiful, but she had just bought a new bag downtown last week. Pausing at the next table to finger a glazed plaque incised with the starburst face of Viracocha, the Inca sun god, she glanced over to where Julio was still berating the forklift operator. Someone had been careless with the stamp, she noted idly, taking in Julio's gesticulating hands and the forklift operator's sulky face. Instead of being nicely centered, the emblem on these boxes was set almost up to the top left-hand corner.

The forklift was backing up now. Julio's gestures made it clear that he was ordering the load back to its original location. Sara followed with fascination the struggle of the fork's prongs to maintain control of its outsized cargo. The pressure was indenting the tops of the boxes and had made the center of the stack bulge outward. It was going to be touch-and-go to get that load back before—

Crash!

Like a watermelon seed spurting from between two fingers, the outermost box separated itself from the others. The force of its ejection was enough to make it bounce and roll over twice before skidding to a stop at Sara's feet. Behind it, the rest of the boxes were already tumbling to the concrete floor.

"You fool!" Julio hurried toward the forklift, his dark face livid with anger. "You! You are fired! Get out of here! Out! Out!"

The hapless forklift operator scrambled down from the driver's seat. Already, Julio was ordering nearby workers to help pile up the tumbled boxes. Sara checked the box at her feet. The crash had burst it open, and its contents were spilling out onto the floor—tightly rolled cylinders of a soft material. She bent over to pick one up.

"Here, let me help."

The soft voice belonged to one of the young women Sara had seen giggling behind the leather goods table. She had the high cheekbones, flattened nostrils, and milk-chocolate coloring of a full-blooded highland Indian, but her simple cotton dress was urban in style, and the traditional black braids had been cropped into a modern shag. It had been some time since this girl had left her highland village for the city. She quickly set down an empty packing box identical in size to the one that had broken open. Taking the cylinder from Sara's hand, she unrolled it with one quick wrist motion, revealing a woven wall hanging. Shaking it free of any dust it might have picked up from the concrete floor, she deftly rolled it back up and placed it in the padded box she had brought with her. She worked with such practiced speed that in less than a minute she had dusted and re-rolled a half-dozen cylinders, which were now lying in the bottom of the new box. Sara reached down to her feet and grabbed for the closest loose cylinder. Taking hold of the exposed end, she let gravity unroll the soft material as she had seen the young woman do. It was the first chance she'd had to take a good look at the tapestries, and she caught her breath with delight.

The wall hangings were of llama wool, hand-dyed in browns and greens and blues and woven into scenes of the Bolivian highlands. The one in Sara's hands showed a Quechua woman in flared skirts and poncho urging three reluctant llamas up the narrow cobblestone street of an Andean village. The last llama in line, woven in blacks with a broad, white stripe down its nose, was glaring over its shoulder at the sharpened stick in the woman's hand, the expression of wounded dignity on its woolly face remarkably clear in the broad details of the weaving. Overlooking the Indian woman and her small herd was the bell tower of an old adobe church. The burnt-orange of the tile roof, the ivory of the adobe walls, and the varied blues of the Andean sky were so realistic that Sara was enchanted.

"Now this is what I'd like!" she exclaimed. "It's gorgeous! I wonder if anyone would mind if I took this one as a souvenir."

At that very instant, the tapestry was twitched from her hands. Sara whirled around.

"I am sorry, Señora Cortéz, but these are not available." Julio Vargas deftly rolled up the wall hanging and thrust the cylinder back into the original broken box. "You will understand that they have already been counted and invoiced for shipping."

The words were as smooth and courteous as befitted any subordinate speaking to his employer's wife, but Sara took in the glitter in Vargas's black eyes and the flare of his thin nostrils, and realized with a shock that the head of security was furiously angry. Spinning on his heel away from Sara, he snapped a brief phrase at the young Inca woman. Sara didn't recognize the language—an Indian dialect, she guessed, Quechua, or maybe Aymara. But she didn't have to understand the words to read the menace in Vargas's cold tones and the sudden apprehension on the face of the young worker. The young woman was shaking as she dropped the weaving in her hands. *What's going on here?*

"What is going on here?" Sara repeated aloud.

Julio Vargas ignored Sara as though she weren't there. Grabbing the half-filled box of freshly rolled hangings, he dumped its contents onto the concrete. Kicking the offending box across the floor, he snapped out another incomprehensible phrase, its unmistakable tone of command accompanied by a brusque jerk of his head toward the open door at the rear of the warehouse. The young worker wailed her dismay and turned away.

That does it! Sara hadn't spent the last month learning to be *la señora Cortéz* for nothing. Putting out a hand to keep the young woman from leaving, she drew herself up to her full height. "Señor Vargas, I demand to know what is the difficulty here!"

Now she had his attention. "This woman is fired," the head of security informed her coldly. "She will leave immediately before I ask the police to have her arrested."

"What?" Sara exclaimed, aghast. "What do you mean, she's fired? She wasn't doing anything wrong, just helping me clean up this mess!"

Hearing her defense, the young woman clutched at Sara's hand, crying, and Sara realized for the first time how young she was. Certainly no more than eighteen, possibly even younger. "Please, Señora Cortéz, do not let him fire me. I meant no harm. Please, I need this job. My father is gone. My mother—she has the young ones. They depend on me."

Sara put her arms around the sobbing girl. "Of course no one is going to fire you just for trying to help!" She glared at Vargas. "This is a lot of fuss about nothing," she said firmly. "The girl was working for me, and it's not like she's done any harm. If there's any problem, I'll speak to Don Luis myself."

Once again, she caught a glitter of rage in Vargas's eyes, but then his eyelids drooped and when he raised them again, the anger was gone and his slate-black eyes displayed no emotion. "Of course, Señora Cortéz," he said urbanely. "But it is by order of Don Luis himself that this woman is fired."

"I don't believe that!" Sara replied hotly. "Why in the world would Don Luis fire a perfectly good, hardworking employee just because she happened to help pick up a broken box of wall hangings?"

Julio's narrow mouth thinned at the rebuke, but he explained with no less cordiality, "It is the order of Don Luis that no one touch the boxes once they have been sealed and made ready for shipping. Only those whose job it is to move them to the trucks. This box was sealed. The young woman was removing its contents. I have no choice but to fire her. She is only fortunate I do not have her arrested as a thief."

"This is absolutely ridiculous!" Sara cut in. She was beginning to feel as though she were losing control of the situation. Glancing around, she saw that everyone within earshot had stopped working to stare at them, but she was too angry to care if she was overheard. "Señor Vargas, you know good and well this girl wasn't trying to steal anything. You should be thanking her for being so helpful, not trying to fire her!"

"What is the meaning of this?"

Sara whirled around with a gasp of relief. Don Luis and Nicolás were coming toward them across the warehouse floor, and for once Sara was delighted to see her father-in-law. Don Luis frowned at the employees who had stopped working to watch the argument between Sara and Julio Vargas. Clapping his hands together, he ordered sharply, "Back to work now!"

"Oh, Nicky!" Sara hastened to her husband's side. "I'm so glad you're here!" she said breathlessly in English. "That horrible security chief of yours is trying to fire this poor girl just for trying to help me."

Switching to Spanish for the benefit of her father-in-law, Sara spilled out her version of the events just passed. "You won't let him fire her," she finished, "will you, Don Luis?"

Don Luis didn't answer. Instead, he stepped aside and began a low-voiced conversation with Julio Vargas, who was bundling up the spilled wall hangings and stuffing them into a spare box, without consideration for dust or careful folding.

"Come on, *querida*. Papá will take care of it now." Nicolás slid an arm around Sara's waist, the pressure of his hand on her back urging her toward an open door in the rear wall of the warehouse.

Sara moved away with reluctance. Taking a quick glance back over her shoulder, she saw that the young worker had scurried back to her original work site and was busily filling another box, her hands moving with their accustomed speed. Sara gave her an encouraging wave. The Indian girl managed a tremulous smile in response. Then her frightened gaze shifted back to the two men who were deciding her future.

"Don Luis *will* make sure she's okay?" Sara asked Nicolás urgently. "That poor girl really needs this job. Her father's gone, and she has to help support her mother and younger brothers and sisters."

Nicky's blue eyes sparkled with laughter. "My little revolutionary," he teased. "First a street brat, now a careless employee. What's next on your list—one of those beggars in the plaza? When are you ever going to stop trying to take on everyone's problems?"

"I just feel responsible," Sara said defensively. "The only reason she got in trouble was because she was trying to help me. I can't believe Julio actually tried to have her fired for that!"

"Well, that *is* his job," Nicolás pointed out. "Julio's responsible for security measures around here, and he's got a right to fire anyone who breaks them."

Sara stopped dead in her tracks, her brown eyes flashing, and Nicolás hastily added, "Now, just a minute, Sara. The reputation of Cortéz Industries depends on our customers getting exactly the amount of merchandise listed on their invoice. And the first rule every employee learns is that once a box has been sealed and invoiced, *no one* goes near it without authorization. In fact, no one touches *any* goods except what they're supposed to be packing. Breaking that rule means automatic dismissal, and they all know it. Maybe that seems harsh to you, but in America you don't have our problems with petty thievery. This is the only way to keep theft under control."

"But that box *wasn't* sealed," Sara protested. "It was broken open and spilled all over the ground. And *I'm* the one who started picking it all up. Like I told you, she just came over because she saw I could use some help."

"Well, if that's the case, I'm sure Julio will be reasonable," Nicolás assured her carelessly. "Don't worry your head about it anymore."

Sara, remembering that look of fury on the security chief's face, wasn't so sure. No matter how you looked at it, the man's reaction had been extreme, to say the least. She stopped again as they reached the outer door of the warehouse. "You'll check on it for me, won't you? Just to make sure he doesn't go firing her as soon as Don Luis's back is turned?"

Nicolás let out his breath with exasperation. Placing his hand on his chest in a parody of a school yard vow, he swore dramatically, "Cross my heart and hope to die. I will make sure your little *campesino* friend gets to keep on supporting that horde of siblings. Now stop worrying, and let's get out of here before Papá finds something else for me to do!"

✠

Doug snatched up the phone on the first ring. His NIFC team was well overdue returning from the morning's raid, and he was anxious to hear how it had gone.

"Chavarría on line one," Ellen Stevens informed him sweetly.

Doug frowned as he punched the button to pick up the call. He hadn't heard from Chavarría since that abortive Fourth of July meeting almost two weeks ago. *What does the little weasel want now?*

"Bradford," Doug said flatly.

The flood of excited Spanish that spilled from the other end of the line was definitely Chavarría. The no-show wasn't his fault, he whined. His friend had panicked at the last minute. It was the location that was the problem. The man had adamantly refused to come anywhere near the DEA offices.

Doug could understand that. Most new informants—and some not so new—were skittish about being seen around the *americanos*. He murmured appropriately soothing noises as Chavarría rushed on. His friend was still anxious to talk. If Señor Bradford would just give him one more chance, meet them in some neutral location, he swore that the *americanos* wouldn't be sorry. He was putting his own life in danger to deliver this information, and it was only his feelings of friendship that had induced him to get involved in anything so explosive.

Yeah, that and a nice cash bonus, Doug tacked on cynically, correctly interpreting the distraught note in Chavarría's voice. Chavarría was more worried about a potential reward slipping through his fingers than whatever information he had to offer.

Doug didn't debate long. There was a fine line sometimes between wasting time and cutting off a potentially valuable contact, and Doug preferred to err on the side of time-wasting—at least his own. You could just about bet that the one time you decided "enough is enough," that would be the time when you missed something vital.

"Fine." He cut Chavarría off in midsentence. "I'll meet you and your pal. But my choice, not yours. You bring your friend around to the Hostal Real in a hour. Room 107. And, Chavarría? You stand me up this time, and I don't want to see your face around here again. *Comprende?*"

"*Sí, señor.* One hour."

Doug walked briskly down the hall and nudged open Ramon's office door. The younger agent was sitting behind a desk as tidy and well-dusted as Doug's was a mess. Doug shook his head in wonder at the sight of Ramon's dark head bent diligently over a batch of forms stacked precisely in the center of the blotter. *This kid actually likes paperwork!*

"Hey, *amigo,* you want to dump the pencil-pushing?" Doug offered. "Chavarría says he's got something big going down. I could use some back-up."

"Yeah, like sitting around listening to Chavarría blow smoke ranks

higher on my entertainment list than filling out DEA-6 forms!"
Ramon snorted, but he was already sliding back his chair. "Just let
me sign off this interview, and I'll be right with you."

   The Hostal Real, located well off the beaten tourist track, was
just sleazy enough that no one would be asking any questions—perfect
for occasions such as this. While Ramon swept out a collection of
dusty wrappers and beer bottles left behind by the last occupant,
Doug brought in some folding chairs. A tray of refreshments was set
prominently on a small wooden table, now polished and clean. A
notepad and mini-cassette recorder would come out later.
   The two men settled in to wait.
   And they waited.
   Scratching at one of the residents of the bed's straw mattress,
Doug checked his watch for the umpteenth time. Well past lunchtime. He glanced over at Ramon's tight expression. "Okay, you don't
have to say it. Let's pack it in. And next time Chavarría calls, remind
me I'm not available."
   Doug was reaching for the shoulder holster that he'd placed
discreetly out of sight when the knock came. Chavarría strutted in
as though he were ten minutes early—rather than four hours late.
Releasing him from the hearty *abrazo* of greeting—handshake, pat
on the back, handshake—Doug wiped his right hand surreptitiously
on his jeans. He always forgot between contacts just how oily the
man was!
   It wasn't just the slicked back hair and the shiny face, or the ring
of lard that lapped over his belt. It was his manner—obsequious and
fawning and as slippery as a spot of grease on the kitchen floor.
   Doug's irritation faded with his first good look at the man who
was slinking in on Chavarría's heels. Sometime not too long ago,
he'd been youngish, fit, and good-looking. Now he was haggard and
aged, his haunted eyes sunk deep into black circles that told of tor-
mented dreams. This guy was scared out of his wits.
   Doug exchanged a meaningful glance with Ramon. This wouldn't
be another wasted morning, after all! Not with Chavarría oozing the
self-satisfaction of a man who knows he's got an ace in his hand.
   Doug's ears perked up when Chavarría introduced his companion
as "René," but the first order of business was to put their visitors at
ease—especially René, who looked ready to bolt out the door at any
moment.

As though they were hosting an ordinary social gathering, Doug busied himself serving drinks, while Ramon passed around a dry assortment of sandwiches and cakes.

Interviewing a new contact was like a courtship in a lot of ways—and Doug had played through the ritual dozens of times. The new contact was usually both wary and eager, doing his best to sell himself and his information as honest and trustworthy.

For his part, the agent had to convince the snitch that this wasn't a trap. If the would-be informant—like so many—had been involved in the drug trade, he would want assurances that he wouldn't be arrested for some past deed. At the same time, the agent had to be sure that the contact wasn't just taking him for a ride.

Back and forth it went, both parties doing their best to impress the other with the sincerity of their intentions. Eventually, enough rapport and trust would be established to begin the transfer of information. If the contact was serious about working with the DEA, arrangements would be made for passing on information, and a small retainer paid, if necessary. But the first step was just winning the guy's confidence—which wasn't proving easy in René's case. The man was terrified. And it was a toss-up whether he was more afraid of Doug and the DEA or whatever enemy that had frightened him into coming forward.

Under Chavarría's impatient prodding, René told his story—slowly at first, then with the words tumbling out, stopping only long enough to moisten his dry and cracking lips with large gulps of the imported Chilean beer he'd requested. By the end of the first minute, it was all Doug could do to maintain the impassive expression he'd cultivated for such interviews. Who would have dreamed that Chavarría's elusive acquaintance would turn out to be the erstwhile pilot of that equally elusive DC-3?

The story he told was much the same as Doug and Ramon had heard on the fourth of July. The DC-3 had been forced down by a military helicopter, definitely a Huey, by the description. René had managed to escape into the jungle, but he'd hung around long enough to see a crew of men from the helicopter off-loading his cargo. Then he'd set off on foot to try to make his way back to civilization. The horrors of that march were still in his eyes as he talked. A chance encounter with a hunting party of Ayoreo Indians—sufficiently exposed to the outside world to speak to the ragged madman they found roaming their territory, instead of spearing him—was the only thing that had allowed him to escape with his life. They had delivered him to a Guarani village, and the Guaranis had helped him get back to Santa Cruz.

The two agents listened attentively, without giving any indication that they knew more about René than they were hearing. And it soon become apparent what had convinced the pilot to come forward. Not money, like his buddy Chavarría was seeking, but protection. The Brazilians wanted their lost shipment. And if they couldn't have it, they'd take their ten million dollars out of René's hide. One slow, painful inch at a time.

By this point, the pilot was such a shivering basket-case that Chavarría had to take over the negotiations. A more unlikely partnership Doug had seldom seen. Apart from his corpulent girth, Chavarría was not a big man, reaching barely to Doug's shoulder, with the stunted, barrel-chested build so prevalent among Bolivian *campesinos,* whose early years included too much heavy labor and too little nutrition.

René, on the other hand, was no *campesino.* The quality of his clothes and the educated lilt of his speech placed him in a considerably different social class than Chavarría. He was as tall as Doug, though slimmer, and his fine features were predominantly southern European rather than Indian.

"A friend," Chavarría had called him, but Doug had his doubts about that! Men like René didn't have friends like Chavarría. A business acquaintance was more likely. And that posed an interesting question. For someone supposedly on the right side of the drug business, Chavarría knew just a few too many of the wrong people.

Nevertheless, the scumbag—for once!—had earned his reward fair and square. And René had more than earned a trip into Argentina with a new identity and a stake to start a new life. This was going to make for some very unhappy people. Maybe even some of those Brazilians, if the DEA office across the border was able to pursue René's nebulous identification.

On the down side, Doug resigned himself to the fact that the three tons of pure cocaine hydrochloride were long gone. The next place it would surface would be on the school yards and street corners of the United States of America.

Unless some miracle intervened.

The tension left Ricardo's shoulders as he spotted an upright, distinguished figure in a quiet corner of Michelangelo's upstairs balcony. It had taken more than a week to get through the net of secretaries and underlings that surrounded his *padrino,* and even though the distinguished gentleman had been the one to suggest the small Italian restaurant, Ricardo hadn't been so sure his *padrino* would really keep the appointment.

The older man glanced up as Rodrigo hesitantly approached the table. "Ahh, you have made it." He held up his hand as Ricardo opened his mouth. "No, first sit and share a glass of Italian wine with me. Then we will talk."

Ricardo gulped the wine and pushed back the glass. Sipping at his own, his *padrino* listened with flattering interest as Ricardo poured out his suspicions and worries, including all that the *americanos* had told him.

"I thought you might have heard from my father," Ricardo choked out. "I don't know who else to go to. None of my family knows anything."

"No, no, of course you were right to come to me," his *padrino* assured him gently. "I only wish I had better news for you. But I have not heard from your father since his arrest. I would have helped him, you understand, sent my own lawyer if need be. But your father was too much of a man to call for me. He did not want his own troubles to touch his friends. And then came his escape—if that is what it can be called."

To Ricardo's shock, it soon became evident that his *padrino* took much the same view of the situation as the *gringos.* "We do not judge these things as harshly as the *americanos,*" the older gentleman said, "and no matter what he has done, I will still count your father as my friend. But there is no denying that he had cause to make powerful enemies. It has been rumored that he was dealing with both the Colombians and the Brazilians, and you know how easily they turn to *asesinato.* They are not like our people, peaceful and loving of mankind. They hold life cheap. Nor do they like informers. They would not risk your father speaking of something that could destroy their operation."

Ricardo's godfather had heard rumors that a Brazilian *capo* had engineered the snatch. "And you know that I have ears everywhere. If there were other word, I would have heard."

Ricardo couldn't argue with that. With the wealth and the influence his *padrino* wielded, there was little he couldn't find out on either side of the law.

"There is no other solution to what has happened to your father. I have heard from excellent sources that most of your father's associates were arrested by the *gringos.* You must know that there were

not enough left to bring about his escape. And as you say, Pablo
Orejuela was a good man. He would have come home if he could.
No, you must be brave and accept the truth. Your father is dead."

The finality of the gentleman's brief statement convinced Ricardo
of the truth in a way the *americanos'* assurances hadn't. To his shame,
he found his eyes blurring. "I'll kill them!" he growled between
clenched teeth. "I'll hunt them down myself and kill them!"

"And where will you find them? The Brazilians do not stay in
our country to be found. No, they are long gone. Already they have
found others to deal with. And they are more dangerous than you
can imagine. Do you wish to put your mother, your young sisters, at
risk? No, it is time to put this behind you, to go on with your life."

The older man held Ricardo's eyes with his own. Commiseration
and sternness mingled in his compelling gaze. "Ricardo, I know that
this is very painful for you. A son loves his father, of course. But
someday you may see that this is perhaps the best for your family.
No more will your mother suffer the shame of her husband's arrest.
And without your father, there can be no case against him. This will
all blow over, and your life will go on as before. Your father has
provided well for you. For the sake of the blood ties between your
family and mine, I urge you: do not let fruitless revenge throw it all
away."

Ricardo nodded. Maybe his *padrino* was right. The very worst of
Bolivia's appalling prison accommodations were reserved for drug
dealers. Wouldn't his father perhaps prefer death to a lifetime of
such shameful imprisonment?

For Ricardo was well aware, deep down where he didn't have to
admit it to his waking thoughts, that his father had neither the
political pull nor the influence of family to buy his way out of his
fate as others more fortunate had done.

Ricardo would miss his father, naturally, but already he was
accepting the inevitability of his death. He would, of course, have
liked revenge. But he was practical enough to see how impossible
this would be.

He reached for the wine carafe and poured himself another glass.
No, he would do as his *padrino* had advised. He would let it go.

CHAPTER EIGHT

The first streaks of daylight stained the eastern sky, though stars still glittered on the western reaches of the horizon, and a tired moon edged its way down toward the distant foothills. The ebullient, noisy life of Santa Cruz was at its lowest ebb. The drums were silent, the children next door still huddled together on their sleeping mats like puppies, and the neighborhood dogs had surrendered to an exhausted slumber with the proud satisfaction of having done their duty to warn away intruders throughout the night. Even the roosters had not yet raised their morning song.

Sara buried her nose in the night-blooming jasmine that had snaked its way over the frangipani and onto the balcony, its honey perfume still heavy in the air, though the blossoms were beginning to fold up with the coming of day. She loved this quiet hour when the rest of the world was asleep, and the tapestry of colors in the Cortéz gardens brightened slowly into focus below the small platform of wood and wrought-iron that had become her own special sanctuary. Leaning over the railing, her unbound hair sweeping across the black filigree, she felt like a princess surveying her kingdom. Rapunzel, maybe.

Her gaze drifted upward to the onion bulb of the minaret looming black against the paling sky. No, more like a sultan's wife out of *The Arabian Nights,* with white robe and bare feet. *And a harem where she's kept neatly out of the way until the sultan has time for her.*

She pushed that last unbidden thought away. It was all so beautiful here, so peaceful. And she had everything she'd ever wanted, didn't she? A husband who was the envy of every other woman, the family she'd longed for, a fabulous home. So why wasn't this peace and beauty around her reflected in her heart? Why did she feel so restless—as though something were still missing?

Sara yawned and stretched, dismissing the faint cloud of depression from her mind as she swept a long tangle of hair back from her face. *I'm just a little tired, that's all! That wretched party last night—*

At the sound of footsteps from inside the half-open shutters, she swung around, startled. Nicky was not a morning person, and last night's party had been late. She hadn't expected him up for hours yet. Not on a Sunday morning.

A thud from inside the room was followed by a crash. Sara winced as she heard a muffled curse. A stubbed toe wasn't likely to improve Nicky's mood at this hour of the morning. Padding across the balcony, she pushed open the shutters. Her husband was still hopping around the room, clutching one foot. Half the contents of his closet drawers appeared to be on the floor, but he was wearing only a pair of slacks.

"Where are my gray socks?" he demanded when he saw Sara.

Silently crossing the carpet, Sara dug the socks from the one drawer he hadn't opened. Her eyebrows came together as he ducked back into the closet and yanked out an alpaca sweater that was far too warm for the morning. "You're sure up early! Are you going somewhere?"

"Papá wants me to fly out to the hacienda this morning." Nicolás was rifling through a row of neatly ironed shirts on his side of the double closet. "What happened to that Van Heusen with the brown and gray stripes?"

Sara unearthed the missing shirt from a section Nicolás had already searched. The airplane flight explained the alpaca sweater. The cockpit of the Cessna was unheated, and it flew high enough to require some kind of overgarment, even on the hottest of days.

"On Sunday?" Sara asked, trying to keep the disappointment out of her voice. She'd been hoping that they might actually make it to church this morning. Laura Histed had called again during the week to invite them to the services of the English church. Embarrassed to keep making excuses, Sara had told her they'd do their best to come. "Oh, Nicky, do you really have to go today?"

"It's the first time Papá has trusted me to handle things out there without looking over my shoulder. I'm not turning down the chance." His shirt flapping open, Nicolás padded into the bathroom. "Where's my electric razor?" he demanded irritably. "Isn't anything kept in the right place around here? I've got to be at the airstrip in half an hour!"

Sara uncovered the razor in the drawer where the maid had stored it. Her spirits rose when she realized that Don Luis wasn't going along. If she couldn't get to church, a Cessna flight with Nicky sounded like a lot of fun. Sara hadn't been in a small plane since she was a little girl in Colombia, when her father had sometimes allowed her to accompany him on inspection trips to the oil fields. She still remembered the exhilaration of sitting only inches from the open air, with the world unfolding right beneath the wings in a way that couldn't be duplicated in a high-flying jet.

Handing Nicolás the razor, she slid her arms around his waist. "Mind some company? I'd love to see some of the countryside. Do you realize I haven't been outside of Santa Cruz since we got here?"

Nicolás shook his head as he applied the razor to his frowning face. "Not today. This is men's business. Besides,"—he paused to run the blade over his upper lip—"the way you feel about Vargas, I didn't figure you'd want to spend the whole day in his company."

"Julio's going along?" Sara released him with a grimace as he reached for a towel. "Well, you're right about that! Tagging along all day after Julio Vargas sounds about as much fun as . . . as . . ."

"As last night's party?" Tossing the towel aside, Nicolás looked sideways at her in the mirror. "I was too tired when we got home to say anything, but you sure weren't exactly sparkling with fun!"

Sara sighed. She *hadn't* enjoyed last night's party, but she thought she'd done a better job of hiding it. For Nicky's sake, she was doing her best to fit in with his friends, but she had to admit she was finding herself increasingly uncomfortable with the hard drinking and seductive dancing that seemed to be the only entertainment at most of these social events.

It wasn't that she was so narrow that she categorically condemned all forms of dancing. In fact, she'd always loved the old-fashioned square dances, complete with callers and fiddlers, that the church she'd attended during her college years had sponsored in their huge gymnasium. But that was a far cry from the frankly sensual styles that were popular with Nicky's friends and younger relatives. So far, she'd managed to avoid embarrassment by pleading her ignorance of the intricate Latin steps, and Nicolás had laughingly backed her up, informing his buddies that he wasn't ready to share his wife with anyone. He'd seemed content enough to stay at her side, showing off his bride to all his old friends. Until last night!

Reina had hosted a poolside barbecue at her house—a welcome-home celebration for Nicky and his closest circle of friends. Right from the beginning, Nicky had been the life of the party, displaying the same gaiety and easy charm that had won Sara's heart back in Seattle. Reina hadn't exactly welcomed Sara, but she'd shown no overt rudeness either.

At first, everyone had been content to soak up the sun around the pool, but as darkness fell and the cases of *Ducal* beer began to empty, the party had grown wilder. Even Nicolás was seldom without a beer can in his hand, and when Reina undulated up to him in rhythm to the Latin rock blasting out of the speakers above the pool, he'd jumped to his feet and matched her movements with a practiced ease that showed he'd danced with her more than once before.

She was wearing an outfit that looked to Sara like a tutu a ballerina or an ice skater might wear, but with little more than a string bikini underneath. When the music shifted suddenly to a new tune with a catchy beat, Reina set the skirt to whirling in a manner that was somehow more revealing than the skimpy swimsuit she'd been wearing earlier. Though everyone else seemed to take it for granted, Sara found herself blushing and furious at the way Reina pressed herself close to Nicky. There were calls of *"sopa de caracol,"* and Sara was soon left standing awkwardly alone while the other party guests paired up to join the two cousins.

The dance that followed had nothing to do with "snail soup," which was its literal translation, but consisted of the male dancer gyrating his pelvis, hands on hips, while his scantily clad partner went through a series of motions that were nothing short of suggestive. To Sara's dismay, it was obvious that Nicolás was thoroughly enjoying himself, and it was some time before he noticed her absence and came to find her. She had curled up in a lawn chair to keep out of the way. He'd been laughing and flushed with excitement and beer and had shown only impatience when she refused to let him draw her into the dance. Only when she'd pleaded a crashing headache had he consented to take her home.

"Reina was pretty put out about us taking off just when things were heating up last night," he said now as he headed back into the bedroom, buttoning up his shirt as he went. "After all, she planned that party just for us."

You mean, just for you! Sara sniped under her breath, but aloud she said contritely, while trailing him into the room, "I'm sorry, sweetie. I really did have an awful headache. But I didn't mean to embarrass you in front of your friends or anything—or cut your fun short. You should have just let me call a taxi. I told you I wouldn't mind!"

"Yeah, and that would have looked really good—sending my sick wife home in a taxi while I stayed to party," Nicolás scoffed. "No, I made our excuses—newlyweds are supposed to be a little crazy, anyway. Besides, I didn't really mind leaving early—not with the flight this morning. One more beer, and I'd have had to cancel the whole thing. That would have made Papá *really* happy!"

He rummaged through a pile of clothes on the floor. "Where's my belt?"

Sara found the belt, which had been kicked under the bed. Taking it, Nicolás went on, "It's not just the headache. Or leaving early. You weren't having fun a long time before that! Okay, so you don't drink. Fine! But do you have to act like you're smelling something rotten every time someone offers you a beer or tries to get you to dance? Gustavo was asking me last night if I had an ice-cube for a wife! And making *that* kind of excuse *is* embarrassing."

Sara was dumbfounded. And hurt. Nicky's rebuke was so unfair! When she thought of how polite she'd been, even with that old boozer of an uncle, Don Santiago! And any refusals she'd made had always been accompanied with her warmest smile. She'd never tried to force her opinions or standards of conduct on anyone. Was it wrong to expect to receive the same courtesy? As for that creep Gustavo—!

"I'm sorry," she said again, quietly but with some sarcasm. "I didn't realize you were expecting me to keep your friends entertained. But you're right, I *don't* feel comfortable with all this partying. Not the kind I saw last night anyway. That . . . that *sopa de caracol,* or whatever you call it!"

"*Sopa de caracol?*" Nicolás looked genuinely surprised. "What's wrong with that? It's one of the most popular dances in the country! In fact, *sopa de caracol* is one of the dances that's putting Bolivia on the map. I've even seen it in your country."

"Well, I sure haven't!" Sara retorted.

"That's because you never went anywhere!" Nicolás said impatiently. Pausing in front of the large, ornate mirror over the dresser, he brushed his dark hair back into a windswept style that looked natural but took time and gel to accomplish. "Look, I don't have time for this. So that church of yours doesn't approve of anything but those cutesy little folk dances. Well, you're not there anymore! This is Santa Cruz. You've got to learn to let loose a little, have some fun, drink a beer or two. We don't want people thinking you're a fanatic!"

"Fanatic!" Sara was incensed now. "Those girls were half-naked! And Reina—she was all over you! Is that really what you want? You'd really like me to show everything off for the other guys the way that cousin of yours does? It's . . . it's indecent!"

She'd said more than she meant to, but instead of getting angry, Nicolás began to smile. "So that's it! You're jealous!" Nicolás lowered the brush. To Sara's annoyance, he was now looking downright pleased with himself. "Hey, you've got nothing to be jealous about!

Reina's a fabulous dancer and a lot of fun, but you're—wow!" He snaked out his arm and pulled her close.

Sara's cheeks warmed, her flash of temper fading, but even as she snuggled against him, she persisted. "I just can't dress or act like some of those girls were last night. And I can't believe you'd really expect me to. Maybe I wouldn't mind if it was with you, and if we were by ourselves. But to be letting other men hold me the way those girls were doing, men I don't even know—well, I just couldn't!"

Nicolás dropped his glance to linger on the thin white robe that outlined Sara's slim figure. "Maybe you've got a point," he admitted. "I rather like the idea of being the only one who knows what's under there. And it's for sure I wouldn't put up with other men looking at my wife the way they were looking at Reina last night."

He covered Sara's mouth with a deep kiss, but then pushed her gently away with a rueful grin. "I'd better get out of here, or I'm going to have to file another flight plan." Picking up the alpaca sweater, he slung it over his shoulder. "All I'm saying is, lighten up a bit. Start thinking for yourself instead of letting that church of yours do it for you. There's nothing wrong with having a little fun. Reina always did go to extremes, but you don't have to go to the other. Live and let live—that's *my* motto."

With a careless wave, he started for the door. "Don't wait up for me. I don't know when I'll be back. Maybe not until tomorrow if the weather turns bad. Hey, and when I do, maybe I'll teach you the *sopa de caracol* myself. That way you won't feel so out of it at the next party."

"But I don't *want*—"

He was already gone. With troubled eyes, Sara watched the door swing shut behind him. At least a quarrel had been averted, and for that she should be thankful. Nicolás was charming, romantic, easy-going—as long as things went smoothly. But Sara was learning how easily his anger could be aroused when things didn't go his way. Because she loved her husband, she'd made it her responsibility to make sure that things *did* run smoothly. But it wasn't easy. Sara had a temper of her own, and there were times when she had to bite her tongue until she was certain it must be bleeding.

If only there wasn't such a gap between their views of life! She'd never dreamed that Nicky's standards—and those of his family—could be so different from what she was used to. But then, how could she have guessed otherwise? In the few weeks they'd known each other before the wedding, Nicolás had been in *her* world. He'd attended church with her and had never once suggested he was bored or disinterested. He'd been happy enough just to be with her.

"That church of yours," he'd said just now. *As though he wasn't a Christian himself!*

The realization struck her like a palpable force. For the first time, she admitted to herself that Nicky *wasn't* a Christian. Not, at least, the way she understood it: a personal relationship with a personal God. She remembered now how she had brushed off her pastor's concern before the wedding. After all, Nicolás had told her that his family had their own church back in Bolivia. That had been enough for her.

She knew now—and underneath it all, maybe she'd known all along—that she'd been fooling herself. The Cortezes' Christianity was a nominal thing at best, a social affair that was part of their culture but held no claim on their daily lives beyond an occasional holiday festival and a few superstitious ideas.

Like that Saint George business of Nicky's, and other things she'd noticed since then, such as the icons that Mimi kept a candle burning in front of at all times and seemed to put more faith in than God Himself. And the centuries-old religious paintings, affixed with costly stamps and seals by no less than a cardinal, which her mother-in-law had assured her would guarantee the Cortezes a position in heaven.

It wasn't that Nicolás had lied to her. He honestly thought he was a Christian—because he'd been born on a so-called Christian continent, and the church was as much a part of his ethnic background as soccer. No, it was Sara who had lied to herself—because she loved Nicolás so much, because she'd wanted so badly to marry him. *Because I was afraid to be alone again!*

Sara wandered restlessly back out onto the balcony. Did it really matter so much? After all, she'd be the first to admit that her faith hadn't counted for much in her life for a long time now.

And yet, it did matter! Maybe in the past few years she hadn't done much praying or reading the Bible, but she still believed that God's way was the best and only way to run the universe. Some things were just plain right and others wrong! And it seemed that every argument she'd had with Nicky hinged on just such a question.

Well, it was too late for second-guessing now. She'd made her bed, and for the most part she wouldn't trade it for any other. She loved Nicky, and he loved her, and that was surely enough to make up for their differences. All young couples had to make adjustments. She and Nicolás just needed some time to talk these things out, to come to some kind of compromise. After all, her husband loved her too much to want her to be anything other than what she was. And maybe she needed to learn to bend a little. In time, Nicolás would understand what it meant to be a real Christian.

Yeah, like you really know! a voice inside her jeered. Sara rested her elbows on the railing. The guard was out making his early-morning rounds with the Dobermans. Sara looked across the high, whitewashed wall to the distant green haze that was the foothills of the Andes. *Oh, God, are you out there somewhere? Are you listening?*

Catching the speculative eye of the guard, she suddenly realized that the dawn had spread its way across the sky and her skimpy robe was no longer appropriate attire. She hurried inside to change. Maybe she could still go to church on her own. She didn't know Laura Histed very well, but she'd enjoyed what little she'd seen of the bubbly older woman, and it would be a relief to hear some English for a change—even with a British accent.

The big house was quiet as Sara made her way downstairs. Sunday was the servants' day off, and even the live-in maid who had brought Sara her morning *café con leche* and croissant had already taken off for her home village a short distance outside of Santa Cruz. Mimi was a late riser any morning, and who knew where Don Luis was!

Sara stopped to use the phone in the hall outside the drawing room. She hadn't yet gotten up the nerve to try driving in Santa Cruz's rat race of traffic, but a radio taxi was almost as convenient and a whole lot easier when it came to parking. The service was cheap enough here in Santa Cruz—at least by U.S. standards—to use for everything from picking up a load of groceries to filling a doctor's prescription at the pharmacy. *"Radiomóvil Cortéz!"* a feminine voice announced on the other end of the line. As might be expected, Don Luis owned his own company. Sara gave her address in her slow Spanish, then listened while the switchboard operator paged the network of taxis.

"Number twenty-four! Are you there? Number seventy! Number eighty-four! Is anyone free for the *casa Cortéz?*"

The operator came back on the line. "I'm sorry, señora. I'll send a taxi as soon as there is one free," she was saying when Sara heard a man's voice break through the static of the CB radio in the background. "Number twenty-four here. Tell the señora twenty minutes. I have another passenger to drop off."

"Señora Cortéz?" the operator came back on the line, with relief in her voice. "I have a taxi for you. He says he can be there in ten minutes."

Smiling to herself, Sara mentally revised the time estimate up to half-an-hour and walked outside to warn the guard, who was now back in his guard shack, that a taxi would be arriving to pick her up.

Jorge was eating his breakfast, perched high on a stool with one eye on the window that overlooked the street as he juggled a *salteña* and a steaming tin cup. He placed these hastily on a shelf when Sara knocked, wiping coffee from his mouth and almost stumbling over the dogs at his feet as he jumped to attention. He didn't look at all pleased at the interruption, and after nodding an unsmiling agreement, he reminded her with pointed emphasis that all she had to do was pick up the phone and page him on the intercom.

Really! Sara thought with exasperation as she returned to the house to get her purse and dig out her Bible from a box of books in the closet. Even after all these weeks, the guard still treated her with suspicion.

✠

It was well past 9:30 by the time Sara hurried down the corridor at the American school, but she could still see a substantial group of people laughing and talking at the far end. Maybe she wasn't so late after all. It seemed that even the English-speaking community had adjusted itself to *hora boliviana*—Bolivian time.

Catching up to the other stragglers, Sara waited patiently as a young couple in front of her paused to chat in the doorway. A baby chuckled at her over the man's shoulder. Sara was chuckling back when they moved on, leaving her a clear view of the man who was handing out church bulletins in the doorway. Sara stiffened with surprise.

Isn't that . . .?

It was! Sara stopped dead in the doorway. What was Doug Bradford, DEA agent and avowed enemy of her husband's family, doing here? And greeting worshippers just as though he were some ordinary human being?

It was too late to back away. Bradford had already seen her, and it was obvious that he recognized her. His smile faded, and Sara caught a flicker of surprise that mirrored her own before his gray eyes became unreadable. He held out his hand. "Señora Cortéz. Welcome to this morning's worship service."

Sara suspected mockery behind Bradford's bland tones and snatched her hand away before she realized he was only trying to hand her a bulletin. Blushing scarlet, she took the folded sheet with a murmured thanks. Bradford showed no signs of noticing her discomfort. He had already turned away and was greeting the people behind her, the warmth returning to his voice. Sara took a hasty step into the room, feeling suddenly lost and alone. Why had she decided to come here? She didn't know any of these people, they didn't know her, and for two cents she'd turn around right now and leave!

But before her thoughts could translate into action, Laura Histed bustled up to her side. "Oh, Sara, it's so good to see you!" Her pleasant features beamed with genuine delight, and Sara felt her reluctance evaporate as she submitted to the older woman's enthusiastic hug.

"I'm so glad you could make it!" Laura bubbled on. "Come, let me introduce you to a few of the others." Catching Sara's surprised glance at her watch, she laughed. "Oh, I know, it's past nine-thirty. I guess we've become a little *too* used to the culture around here. We tend to get started whenever it looks like most of the people have arrived."

The sanctuary turned out to be the school cafeteria. The dining tables had been stacked against the far wall to make room for rows of blue plastic chairs. A huge canvas screen attempted to hide the cafeteria's service window, and in front of the screen was set a small wooden pulpit.

Laura Histed led the way across the back of the room, chattering all the while and stopping every few steps to introduce Sara. Sara was astonished at the wide variety of people and nationalities represented in this "English" church. She met an exchange student from India, a pair of geologists from Australia, an elderly couple from New Zealand, a photographer from Holland, and an assortment of missionaries and oil personnel from the United States and Canada. A Bolivian doctor, whom Sara vaguely remembered meeting at one of the social gatherings Nicolás had dragged her to, appeared surprised and a little uncomfortable at the introduction. Sara felt a burning resentment welling within her. *Is it really so remarkable that a member of the Cortéz family would attend church?*

"The earth is the Lord's and the fullness thereof," intoned Sam Histed as he called the worship service to order. Laura excused herself and hurried to the front of the room, while Sara threaded her way to a seat in the back row.

"And now, if you will stand and turn in your hymnbook to hymn number 167," Laura announced as her husband finished the psalm. An electric piano thundered out the introductory chords to "Onward, Christian Soldiers." The exchange student from India passed Sara a hymnbook. She took it with a smile of thanks, and as the familiar words of the hymn swept over her, she felt the tension and restlessness that had plagued her all morning ease away. Yes, this was where she belonged. These were the kind of people she felt at home with. All except . . .

Sara glanced back toward the doorway, where Doug Bradford was offering a smiling welcome to a latecomer. This was a problem that Sara hadn't counted on! The international community in any foreign city was a small circle, she knew from her own childhood, and you never knew when you might run into a fellow expatriate. But who would have expected someone like Doug Bradford to show up here? Attending something as ordinary and reverent as a worship service, much less actually participating, just seemed out of character for a man who was known in this city for abusing the power and authority invested in him by the U.S. government.

Well, she would have to ask Laura about him afterward. If this was a regular habit of his, there was no way she'd ever talk Nicolás into attending this church. But for now, there was an easy enough solution. She would just ignore his existence—as he apparently had hers—and enjoy the service.

A state of affairs that lasted until the sermon.

"Now if you will turn with me to the book of Habakkuk, chapter three, verses seventeen and eighteen," Pastor Sam Histed said.

The Scripture passage was unfamiliar to Sara. She scrabbled hastily through the last half of the Old Testament as Sam read aloud:

"Though the fig tree does not bud, and there are no grapes on the vines,

Though the olive crop fails, and the fields produce no food,

Though there are no sheep in the pen and no cattle in the stalls,

Yet I will rejoice in the Lord, I will be joyful in God my Savior."

Sam laid his Bible down, and his eyes roved the faces of the assembled worshipers. "Quite a list of disasters, isn't it?" he said. "But then, Habakkuk knew what it was to face disaster. A prophet who had the dubious honor of serving God during the last days of Israel's existence as a nation, he was one of those who foresaw the coming of the Babylonians and the final destruction of his people. He saw the famine that would sweep across his land, the children left starving in the streets as the land was laid waste and the cattle carried away by marauding soldiers. It certainly wasn't a pretty picture! And yet, in the midst of all that, he was able to say victoriously, 'I *will* rejoice in the Lord.'

"Of course it was different for Habakkuk, right? After all, he was one of God's greatest servants. He even has a book of the Bible named after him! He was famous, a prophet of God. Easy enough for someone like him to talk about handling disaster and still come up rejoicing! After all, men like Habakkuk didn't battle the discouragement and doubt that we go through, did they?

"Don't you believe it! Oh, sure, Habakkuk preached the very unpleasant message that God gave him for his people. But that doesn't mean he was happy about it. In fact, he spends a good part of the book arguing with God about the way God is handling things. Like any of us, like you and like me, Habakkuk knew anger and bitterness. When his own people turned on him for preaching God's message, he begged God to punish them. But when God revealed his plan to send the Babylonians to chastise Israel for their sin, Habakkuk raged at what he saw as God's injustice. After all, weren't the Babylonians even more sinful than the Israelites? This great prophet of Jehovah questioned God right to his face, shouting out at God in his anger, hurt and pain. Does any of this sound familiar?

"And yet in the end, with his world falling to pieces around him and the enemy pounding at the city gates, Habakkuk could bow his head in submission and give us this incredible prayer: *Though the fig tree does not bud . . . though the fields produce no food . . . I will be joyful in God my Savior.*"

The burly pastor leaned so far over the flimsy lectern that Sara thought for one hysterical moment it would crash under his weight. "What about you?" he asked solemnly. "Are you facing troublesome times right now? Financial problems? A crisis in your marriage or in your job? Sickness? Despair so great, you don't know where to turn?"

Sara stirred restlessly. She hadn't come here for—actually, she wasn't sure *what* she'd come for, but it wasn't to hear a doomsday sermon. Still, there probably were people here with serious problems, people who really needed this kind of preaching. She should just be thankful she didn't have to worry about such things.

Closing her eyes, she let the words flow over her. Sam Histed's preaching voice was both melodic and soothing, and last night had been short and troubled. Her thoughts were drifting toward somnolence, when a piercing question reached out and grabbed at her heartstrings.

"Do you remember the joy you felt when you first knew God?" the pastor was saying.

Sara went rigid. How had he gotten onto this subject? Somehow, she'd missed the transition.

"Do you remember his first whispering to your heart that he loved you? That he had chosen you to be his child forever? Do you remember when the happiness bubbled up in you so strong that you just had to share it with everyone you met? When you couldn't wait to get alone and talk to God and read his Word—like two friends meeting for lunch?"

Yeah, remember, God? Remember when we were best friends? Remember when I thought you could do anything?

Sara tried to make herself relax into the rounded plastic back of the chair, but the spasm of homesickness that twisted inside her was so strong, she thought for an instant she would cry aloud. Homesickness, not for a place, but for a time. A time when she'd loved God so much, she'd thought her heart would burst with sheer happiness. A time when she'd never doubted that God was only a whispered prayer away. Where had it all gone?

"Do you wonder now where it all went?" Sam Histed was saying.

Is he reading my mind? Sara thought with a start.

"Does God seem so distant right now that you feel as though you can't reach him no matter how loud you shout? Do you find yourself asking whether he cares any more about you and your specific needs and problems? Or whether he ever really did?"

Memories that Sara had carefully repressed for years pushed their way unwanted to the surface of her mind. She remembered when she was just a small girl, giggling with God over a hilarious mishap at the embassy school. Then, when she was slightly older, kneeling with her mother beside her bed to pray for her father's safety as he traveled to an oil field in a remote area of Colombia, where the threat of Marxist guerrillas lurked behind every bush.

And the time her new kitten—Mozart—had disappeared somewhere into the megatropolis of Bogotá. She'd prayed and prayed for him to come home. Her parents had tried to prepare her for the unlikelihood of that happening. But one day, two weeks later, Mozart had shown up on their doorstep, only slightly underfed and with a ragged pink ribbon around his neck. Wherever her kitty had been, Sara had known with absolute certainty that God had answered her prayer.

Sara's fists clenched against the sudden sting of tears behind her eyelids. *You were the one who left me, God. I didn't leave you!*

"No, God hasn't abandoned you," Sam continued as though he could hear Sara's thoughts. "His promise in Joshua 1:5 is that 'I will never leave you nor forsake you.' If anyone walked away from the relationship, it was you. Ask yourself this morning, what was it that came between you and that first love you shared with God? Maybe those troublesome times we were talking about? Maybe something you thought God should do that he didn't do? Or maybe something you thought he shouldn't do and he did?"

Yeah, like you could have saved my mother! Like maybe you didn't have to destroy my entire family!

"Can you say, like Habakkuk in the midst of disaster, 'Yet I will rejoice in the Lord, I will be joyful in God my Savior'? Or have you walked away from God? Maybe because you didn't like the way he was handling your life? And now you've let bitterness and anger and hurt build up a wall between you and your heavenly Father? And you wish you could pull it down, but you can't?"

I won't listen! Sara told herself fiercely. *That was all over a long time ago. I've got everything you took away now. A family, someone of my own, all the love I need—with or without you, God.*

Despite Sara's resolve to close her ears, the pastor's gentle phrases kept hammering into her mind. "You see, that's where people get it wrong. God never told us that life would always be easy. He gave mankind free will, and unfortunately, we often have to reap the consequences of what mankind has done to this earth with that free will. But what God has promised is that we will never have to go through the hardships *or* the good times of this life alone. God is still waiting, right where you left him, longing like a father for his child to turn back to him and come home. Maybe this morning could be that time for you. Why don't you close your eyes with me and make this familiar song a prayer."

Sara sat rigidly in her chair as the electric piano swelled into a soft melody, and Sam Histed began to sing a hymn that Sara had known from childhood:

"I come to the garden alone while the dew is still on the roses.

"And the voice I hear, falling on my ear, the Son of God discloses."

The tears were threatening to overflow, and Sara had to dig her nails into the palms of her hands to keep from completely dissolving into a torrent of sadness.

Sam Histed's rich tenor rose triumphantly into the chorus: "And he walks with me, and he talks with me, and he tells me I am his own. And the joy we share as we tarry there none other has ever known."

I won't make a fool of myself in front of all these people! Sara insisted. Running a surreptitious finger over her eyelashes to catch the one traitorous drop that had managed to slip through, Sara cast a covert glance along the back row. Doug Bradford's cool, gray eyes met hers. Sara was certain she saw amusement in his gaze, and it was enough to dry up any further tears. Tilting her chin to fasten her gaze on the embroidered runner that hung down from the pulpit, Sara began a mental recitation of the multiplication tables, an old technique that had proved useful over the years to block out unwanted thoughts or lectures. She didn't stop until the last notes of the hymn had died away and Laura Histed was signaling for the congregation to rise for the final prayer.

✠

Doug knew spiritual anguish when he saw it. He'd gone through enough of it himself. Those months after . . .

He studied Sara's averted profile under lowered eyelashes. What could be so troubling to a bride of a little more than a month? Doug knew the exact date now, just as he knew many other facts about Sara Cortéz, Kyle having come through with his usual competence. And if those facts were accurate, then the one-time Sara Connor was exactly what she appeared to be—a nice girl, of good background, with an admirable scholastic history and not so much as a parking ticket on her record.

In other words, of no professional concern to Doug Bradford, Special Agent, U.S. Drug Enforcement Administration. But any fellow human being in trouble concerned him. Bowing his head, Doug offered up a quick prayer for this young girl who just happened to have married into the richest and most powerful family in Bolivia.

CHAPTER NINE

"Well now, honey, how did you enjoy the service?"

The accent was American. Texan, to be precise. Sara turned to see a tall woman, her good-natured features made up expertly enough to take a decade off the forty-odd years Sara guessed her to be. Her arms were full of books and sheet music, and Sara suddenly realized that she'd seen her earlier playing the piano. The woman paused to give Sara a searching scrutiny. "We haven't met before, have we?"

Shifting her books onto one arm, she held out her right hand. "Hi, I'm Ellen Stevens. Didn't you just love Pastor Sam? His messages always hit me right where I need them. And isn't this a great idea, doing something practical to help out? I just feel *so* guilty when I think about how much we have. Too much, really, you know, when you stop to realize it. And then you see something like—well, at least we can do a little bit. Those poor little babies!"

Sara blinked at the onslaught of words, but Ellen Stevens continued without hardly taking a breath. "You *are* coming with us, aren't you? You really don't want to miss it. We always have such a good time. Well, maybe not good, if you know what I mean, but educational, anyway. Those poor little kids!" she repeated.

"Uh, I . . ." Sara was lost. She had been so intent on making her escape that she'd paid little attention to the announcements that had followed the final hymn. She vaguely recalled hearing something to do with a children's home that the church was sponsoring. But what that had been about, she hadn't the foggiest idea. "I don't think . . . I really just need to call a taxi. If you could just tell me where I could find a phone—"

"Oh, you need a ride? No problem!" Sara's new acquaintance brushed aside her objections before she could formulate them. "Just about everyone will be going. There's Laura Histed right over there. They've got room. I know she and Sam would be glad to take you. Hey, Laura, yoo-hoo!"

Stretching to tip-toe, Ellen waved wildly at a knot of women chatting near a commercial-size coffee pot, but she continued talking to Sara without a break. "Now, what did you say your name was, honey? I'm sorry, I'm just so lousy with names. Well, never mind, Laura here will take care of you. I'd give you a ride myself, but I've got to get things organized and turn the grill on. The potluck, you know. Some of the guys are bringing *surubí* and *jochi* to barbecue. So delicious! Oh, there's Barb! I've got to catch her before she leaves. See you in a jiffy."

Then she was gone, leaving Sara feeling as though she'd just had a close encounter with a particularly benevolent tornado.

"Sara dear, did you need a ride?" Laura Histed said warmly at her elbow. "We'd love to have you, of course. But don't let Ellen stampede you into coming along if you have other plans. She's a wonderful person, but she can be a little overwhelming until you get to know her."

"Come where?" Sara shook her head, completely bewildered now. "I'm really sorry, but I guess I wasn't listening too well earlier. Did she say something about kids? And a potluck?"

"Oh, did I forget to tell you about that? I'm sorry, I meant to tell you when I called yesterday. Yes, we always have a potluck on the last Sunday of the month—sometimes here at the school, sometimes at different homes. Today we're doing something a little different. For some time now, our church has helped support one of the children's homes here in Santa Cruz. So before the potluck, we're all going out there to throw the children a collective birthday party. You can imagine that not too many of those come their way. We'd love to have you come along."

"No, really, I couldn't!" Sara said hastily, grabbing at the excuse offered her. "I mean, I didn't bring any food or anything."

"Oh, don't worry about food," Laura reassured her with a twinkle. "There's always more than enough. Today especially. A couple of the men were on safari last week and they're going to grill us some of the game they brought home. That's always a lot of fun. Besides, you might find the children's home of real interest. After all, it was Gabriela who got us involved there."

"You mean . . . Nicky's cousin?" Sara's interest was piqued.

"That's right. I think I mentioned before how Gabriela helped us through some of the red tape we've run into with our street-kids ministry. You wouldn't believe the bureaucracy involved! Anyway, one problem we've had with these kids is figuring out what to do with them once we get them off the street. Gabriela, in her official capacity in the *alcaldía*—the mayor's office—interceded for us with the child welfare department. They finally agreed to take our kids into some of their homes for children. But when we started checking out the situation—talk about an eye opener!

"I must admit, I've been pretty critical of the child welfare system here in Bolivia and the way they've handled this whole problem of street kids and orphans. But when we actually went out there and saw what they had to work with—well, that's when we decided to get involved as a church. We've kind of adopted the *Hogar de Infantes,* which houses all the littlest ones. We collect a monthly offering, as well as secondhand clothes and toys, and several of our women do volunteer work out there in their spare time. And every once in a while, we like to take the whole church out there—or anyone we can talk into it. Working for the oil companies or the embassy, as most of our congregation does, they have little contact with the real Bolivia. It's good for them to get out of their secure, access-controlled, Americanized neighborhoods once in a while and see how a good part of the rest of our world has to live. I really do wish you'd come with us, Sara. It will help you appreciate how much you have!"

Laura broke off, her pleasant features suddenly flustered. "Oh my, now I'm the one pressuring you. I do understand if you have other plans. I suppose that handsome husband of yours is just waiting for you to get home. And I'm sure you never counted on anything like this for your first visit here. We'd love to have you, of course, but please don't feel you have to come, unless you really want to."

If Laura had pushed at all, Sara would have gone straight home. But the older woman's apology disarmed her. Now that the spell of Sam's preaching was broken, she could see how silly it had been to take his sermon personally. Everyone here had been extremely kind and friendly—except for that DEA agent, and surely he wouldn't take any interest in an orphanage—and it would be nice to make some friends of her own nationality, or at least her own language. Besides, why should she hurry home? Nicolás wouldn't be back before nightfall at the earliest, and she was definitely not in the mood for an afternoon of her mother-in-law's company. "I'd love to come," she said sincerely.

✠

The *Hogar de Infantes* was in the oldest part of Santa Cruz, a few blocks from the central plaza. Sara glanced around with interest as she trailed the Histeds through huge, arched doors studded with rusty spiked nails almost a handbreadth across. Nicolás had said he'd been born into one of these old mansions. Maybe even this very one.

And thinking of Nicolás . . .

A quick look around as they stepped into a wide entryway reassured Sara that Doug Bradford was not among the group. Not that she'd expected the government agent to show up at a place like this, but it would be a lot easier to talk Nicolás into coming to church if she could assure him he wouldn't have to deal with a member of the DEA on a social basis.

"If we can get your attention up here!" Sam Histed's booming request silenced the noisy chatter and Sara noticed for the first time that a woman was standing next to the pastor. She was slight, no longer young, and wore a harried expression. A stained white apron protected the front of her print dress. Behind her, an open door looked in on what might once have been a gracious receiving salon but now appeared to serve as the institution's office area. File cabinets and desks lined the walls, and boxes and sacks were piled in every available corner.

Sam raised his hand to maintain the silence as the woman murmured something in low, rapid Spanish. "Okay, everyone!" he said. "Doña Inez tells me that the kids have something ready for us. So we'll go on in now, then come back to unload the party stuff. By the way, for those of you who haven't been here before, Doña Inez is the director of the *Hogar de Infantes*. She doesn't speak any English, I'm afraid, but she's asked me to express her gratitude to all of you for your support of this institution. Now, if you will just follow this way."

He turned and walked with Doña Inez through another set of arched portals. As Sam pushed open the heavy doors, Sara heard a muted roar reminiscent of a distant football game. When she followed the others into a large courtyard, the reason for the racket—and for the director's harried appearance—became immediately obvious. The courtyard was jammed with small children jumping and hopping and playing leapfrog, or simply racing around in circles with voices at full-throated volume. In one corner, a pack of small boys kicked a deflated soccer ball, the only toy that Sara could see. There must have been hundreds of children in the courtyard, and not one beyond six years old.

Cheers and excited shouts of *"Los gringos"* broke out as the children spotted the visitors. Sara soon found herself in the middle of a pushing, jostling mob that tugged at her clothes and reached up to touch her long hair. She was in imminent danger of losing her skirt before the director blew a shrill whistle blast. An impressive silence followed—for about two seconds. Then the children scrambled to the far end of the courtyard, and a pair of teenage girls rounded up the stragglers. In a surprisingly short time, the whole mob was lined up in uneven rows from the smallest—who looked to be about three—to the tallest. Knowing that this was a state-run orphanage, Sara had expected to see uniforms; but instead, the kids were wearing a mismatched collection of tattered clothes that looked as though they should have been consigned to a rag bag long ago.

The director inspected the children with a stern eye, nodded approval to her assistants, then turned to her visitors. "Please! The children wish to show their gratitude for what you have done for them. They have prepared a song."

At her signal, the children shrilled into an enthusiastic chorus that might have held a melody, had it not been sung in a half-dozen different keys. Sara, shaking her skirt back into position, gave up trying to decipher the words and studied her surroundings instead. Like many of the old Spanish colonial mansions, the house had been built as a hollow square facing in on a central courtyard. The remnants of its former elegance were still evident. Fluted columns held up a wide second-story balcony that ran around all four sides of the square. Ornate hand-carved banisters curved up either side of the courtyard to the balcony. A colorful mosaic of chipped tile adorned a dry fountain that had once burbled merrily in the center of the plaza. Huge planters stood empty along the perimeter.

Only a few of the ceramic tiles that had once paved the courtyard remained. The rest of the floor was an ugly gray expanse of rough concrete. There were gaps in the burnt-red roof where scraps of wood and tin had been nailed over leaks and missing tiles, and the breeze that whistled through the courtyard no longer carried the perfume of citrus or roses but of old urine and too many unwashed little bodies in too small of an area.

When the song was finished, the children marched away in creditable order for such tiny tots, the hands of each child placed squarely on the shoulders of the one in front. Sara followed the group into a long, narrow salon lined with row upon row of makeshift tables. Soon she was ferrying birthday cake and glasses of Kool-Aid to the eagerly awaiting children.

The orphans didn't seem to notice the dinginess of their surroundings. Their black eyes shone and their little bodies wriggled with excitement as Sara handed out pieces of cake as fast as her hands could move. She wondered how in the world the few workers she had seen could deal with so many sticky faces—and so many crumbs. And where did all these kids sleep? This place might have been ample for the family of a Spanish conquistador, but not for hundreds of children. What did they do, sleep them in shifts?

Sara was pouring refills on Kool-Aid when Laura tapped her shoulder. "Sara, dearie, Doña Inez has offered to show our newcomers around. Would you be interested?"

Sara glanced doubtfully from the pitcher in her hand to the row of empty plastic cups. "The children . . ."

Laura lifted the pitcher from her hand. "Oh, go on! You can trust me to keep the Kool-Aid flowing."

Sara joined Doña Inez and two couples from the church who had gathered for the tour. None of the others spoke more than minimal Spanish, and Sara soon found herself nominated group translator by default.

"As you can see, the house is very old," the director said, pointing out the exquisite handcarving on a row of doors that led off the balcony into the second-story rooms. "For many generations, it belonged to the Cortéz family. Perhaps you have heard of them? They are one of the most prestigious families in our country."

So this really *had* been Nicky's home! Sara turned wonderingly to survey again the remnants of beauty and graciousness. Her husband had actually raced along these very corridors as a child, kicked a ball down in that courtyard, maybe even slid down those same wooden banisters. It was certainly a coincidence! Or maybe it wasn't such a coincidence. Hadn't Laura said that Gabriela was somehow involved in securing this children's home?

The answer came with the director's next statement. "It was a member of the Cortéz family, Gabriela Cortéz de Oropeza, who graciously arranged our use of this facility for the *Hogar de Infantes*. She is a member of the *alcaldía*, and it was to the city council that the Cortéz family sold this building when they built their new home. Perhaps you have seen that as well? They say it is one of the finest examples of Bolivian architecture in Santa Cruz."

Now, wait a minute! Sara's mind began to churn as she translated for the others. Was Doña Inez saying that the Cortezes *sold* this place to the city council? *I thought Nicolás said they'd donated their old home to the city.*

Sara suddenly realized that she had missed a sentence or two, and the others were looking at her curiously. "Oops, sorry," she said with an apologetic smile. She decided not to pursue the director's error. It would only serve to embarrass their guide, and it wasn't as though it really mattered whether her in-laws had sold or donated the place. She caught up with Doña Inez's next statement and returned to her translation as the director led them from the balcony into a short passageway.

"The *alcaldía* had offices in this building for many years until its condition became too poor to be an adequate representation of our beautiful city. Then they in turn decided to sell it, but *la señora de Oropeza* convinced them to turn it over to the child welfare department. We are so grateful to have such a spacious place for the children. We are now able to house more than five hundred here in the *Hogar de Infantes,* whereas before, many had to be turned away. Now, here is one of the dormitories where the children sleep."

Spacious indeed, Sara thought ironically, following the director through the door. The room was quite large, with the same high ceilings they'd seen in the rest of the old mansion, but bunks lining each wall were built so close together that the mattresses were touching, giving the appearance of one long, double-decker bed. Another double row of bunks filled the center of the room. There was no sign of closets or drawers, and Sara wondered if the tattered clothing she'd seen the children wearing was all they possessed. Her nostrils flared as Doña Inez led the group along a narrow walkway between the bunks. Like the courtyard below, the room smelled of urine and sweat, only here the stench mingled with the harsh odor of bleach, as though at least some effort was made to maintain a standard of hygiene. *Mimi would cringe to see what they've made of her old home!*

"This dormitory is for children from eighteen months until they turn three," Doña Inez said as they reached the far end of the dormitory. "After their third birthday, they will move to the other side of the patio with the older children. The children may stay here at the *Hogar de Infantes* until they are six. Then they must go to the Girl's Home or the Boy's Home, where they will learn to work and earn their own living. It is difficult for us to send the children away, because conditions are not as healthy at these other homes. Because our own children are too young to work much, we receive more help and nurses and supplies than the other homes. Unfortunately, we have no choice but to send them, or there will be no room for the new little ones. At these other homes, they may stay until they are sixteen—or even eighteen, if there is room."

One of the men in the group plucked at Sara's sleeve. "What is she talking about, earning their own living? Ask her what kind of work these young kids could possibly do."

"They may shine shoes, or carry shoppers' bags at the market," Doña Inez answered as they crossed another corridor. "Some wash the windshields of cars at intersections or sell newspapers. The older boys may work in carpentry or building, and the girls work as maids. They will bring back what they earn to the home. And all have daily tasks to do in exchange for their room and clothing."

"But that's child labor!" the man who had asked the question blustered. "Where are the child protection laws? This is outrageous!"

"It is not so bad," Doña Inez reassured him after Sara had translated his outburst into more diplomatic language. "The children go to school. The younger ones work in the morning and study in the afternoons. The older ones may study at night to complete their education. It is not, of course, what we would wish, but we have no choice! If the children do not work, they will not eat."

The director pushed open the door in front of her. "We are a poor country, you see, and our government does not always have the funds to keep these homes running. It has been three months since we have received our promised allotment for food. It is more than a year since we have received an allowance for the children's clothing. And conditions are even more difficult in the homes for older children. This is why we are so grateful for all that you people have done. Without your help, even our little ones here would not have food to eat. And the milk—these babies will grow healthy and strong because of you. Come! Come! I will show you."

Doña Inez beckoned them to enter the room. Sara took a step inside, then stopped short, her translation catching in her throat. It didn't matter. The others, trailing in behind her, seemed bound by the same spontaneous silence.

The room had the same vast dimensions as every other one they had seen so far in this place. But here the expanse of tiled floor was lined with decrepit cribs rather than bunks, with rusted metal showing through the chipped paint and thin vinyl pads serving as mattresses. In each crib, lying sideways three and four to a mattress, were bundles, which proved upon closer inspection to be infants, their limbs bound tightly to their sides with strips of cloth much like the traditional swaddling clothes found in Christmas manger scenes.

In some of the cribs, older babies had managed to squirm free from their bindings and had pulled themselves to a sitting position from which they watched the newcomers through the bars with incurious stares. Other young toddlers sat on the hard floor, a few battered toy blocks at their feet, which offered the first blotches of color Sara had yet seen in this bleak place. One of the youngsters had pulled himself up on the edge of a crib and was doggedly practicing his first staggering steps.

"I saw something like this once in Romania," the same man muttered beside Sara.

"The place looks like a baby factory!" his wife, who was quite obviously expecting a child of her own, added in horrified awe. "Where did they all come from?" She nudged Sara's arm. "Excuse me, but could you ask if these are all orphans?"

Sara translated the question into Spanish.

Doña Inez glanced around at the rows of cribs. "Some are orphans, yes, with no living relative that may be asked to feed them. Others have been abandoned, and we do not know who their families are to return them. And many have been brought here because their mothers are too poor to feed them. Or they simply do not wish to. Without our care, they would be left to starve."

"Oh, that's just awful," the pregnant woman said, throwing her hand over her mouth.

Several of the babies chose that moment to break into sorrowful wails, and soon the entire nursery was in an uproar. Abandoning her efforts to speak above the noise, Sara reached into the nearest crib and lifted out a squalling bundle. The ripe odor at one end told her the problem.

"Oops!" Sara held the infant away from her Sunday dress. "Can we get a change job for this one?" Then, catching the chagrined expression on the director's face, she regretted her impulsive action.

"Yes, of course, I am sorry," Doña Inez apologized, her hands fluttering into the air with her distress. "It is true that the babies need more attention. Unfortunately, we have eighty infants here and only four helpers to attend to their needs. It is impossible to pick them up every time a child begins to cry. But we will take care of this now. If you will allow me . . ."

She lifted the baby from Sara's arms. "María!"

A teenage girl who had been feeding the older babies straightened up, a bottle still in her hand. She looked hot and harried, and Sara wished she'd never opened her mouth. The last thing she'd meant to do was to cause these busy attendants more work!

"No, please! Why don't you let me do this? Really, I didn't mean to interrupt your schedule. If you would just show me—"

Sara broke off in startled recognition. There were hundreds—maybe thousands—of Indian girls in the city with that same thick, black hair and round faces similar enough to pass for the Doublemint Twins. But surely she had seen this one before, hurrying forward with just such a cheerful, tired smile. Of course! At the Cortéz warehouse hardly more than a week ago.

"Why, hello, María," she said with pleasure, recalling the name Doña Inez had used. "It's good to see you again!"

The response was hardly what she'd expected. As she picked Sara out of the group, María stopped cold, her smile fading and her black eyes widening with apprehension. Only at a curt order from the director did she come forward, her eyes refusing to meet Sara's as she took the crying baby. Sara stared after her, bewildered. The girl certainly had every right to hold a grudge after the trouble Sara had caused her, but she hadn't seemed the type. And what was she doing here in the *Hogar de Infantes*? A weekend job? Or . . .

With decisive quickness, Sara lifted another wailing infant from a crib and turned to Doña Inez. "Please, I really would like to help. Would you mind if I changed this one?"

Others in the tour group were already following her example, lifting crying bundles from the cribs and looking around for the means to comfort them. Following María over to the changing table, Sara smiled with determined friendliness at the Indian girl as she laid her own bundle down beside the other baby.

"I really am glad to see you again, María. That is your name, isn't it? I never did get a chance to thank you for your help the other day. I'm sorry it caused so much trouble for you."

María didn't look up, though she slid Sara a sullen glance. Sara searched for the right words as she reached for one of the pieces of muslin that was all there was for a diaper. "I must say I'm surprised to see you here at the children's home. Do you come here on weekends? Or . . ."

The unwelcome suspicion her first sight of the Indian girl had roused thrust itself to the surface of her mind. "There hasn't been any problem with your job at Cortéz Industries, has there?"

The flash of anger in María's black eyes, before they were hastily lowered, confirmed Sara's suspicions. Her indignation boiled over. "Then he did fire you, didn't he? Why, that absolute creep!" No wonder the girl had been hostile! She must have thought Sara had forgotten her promise—or had never had any intention of keeping it. "I just *knew* Julio Vargas wasn't to be trusted! I'll bet he did this just as soon as Nicolás and Don Luis turned their backs. He'd never figure on us ever running into you again!"

Sara brought her indignation under control as the tiny form under her hands broke into a fresh wail. It wasn't until she caught sight of María's uncomprehending gaze that Sara realized her explosion had been in English. Switching to Spanish, she said remorsefully, "Look, I'm really sorry about this, María! I had no idea you'd lost your job for helping me, I swear. But don't worry, I'll make sure you get it back. Julio Vargas had no right to fire you, and Don Luis is going to be very displeased when he hears about it!"

Tucking the diaper under the baby, she fumbled with the pins. "Let's see, I'm afraid my husband is out of town at the moment, and I haven't the slightest idea where Don Luis is, so it could be a day or two. But I'll speak with them just as soon as they get back. If you'll give me a phone number or something so I can reach you. Or maybe you'd rather I came back here."

"No! No! No!" The Indian girl was shaking her head with agitation. She showed none of the delight or gratitude Sara had anticipated. Sara broke off in confusion. "I don't understand! No, I'm pinning this diaper all wrong? Or no, you don't want your job back?"

María was silent for so long that Sara thought she wasn't going to answer. Plucking the bunched-up diaper from under Sara's infant, she refolded it and deftly fitted in the pins. Then she muttered, "No, it was not *el señor* Vargas who fired me. It was the *patrón*, Don Luis, and the son of the *patrón*, your husband, Don Nicolás."

✠

Sara watched the empty Sunday afternoon streets flow past the windows of the Histeds' elderly minivan, her brown eyes dark with trouble. She couldn't get the faces of the children out of her mind. Yes, Bolivia was a poor country, as Doña Inez had said. But too poor to feed its own children? Memories of the previous night's poolside barbecue flashed in her mind. How much wealth had been represented in that laughing, abandoned crowd? Surely enough to meet these children's meager needs! Her own monthly allowance that Nicolás had allotted with such careless generosity would keep most of those babies in milk and diapers.

And the girl, María! She'd managed to convince Sara that she didn't want her old job back. It hadn't been so easy for Sara to convince María that there'd been some kind of mistake. Well, there was nothing Sara could do to clear up that misunderstanding until Nicolás and Don Luis got home. But she wasn't just going to drop it. At the least, the girl deserved some compensation for all the hardship she'd endured. And Don Luis needed to know the kinds of things his head of security did when his back was turned!

"You do remember her? Our church pianist?" Laura Histed's cheerful tone rose to a question mark and stopped before Sara realized that the pastor's wife had been talking for some time. Grabbing a name from the air, she responded hurriedly, "Oh, Ellen Stevens? I don't think I saw her at the children's home."

"No, she stayed back to get things ready for the rest of us," Laura went on without missing a beat. "But you'll have a chance to visit more this afternoon. She's such a nice person and a gracious hostess. So busy too, but always ready to help out when we have our little social gatherings. I'm sure you'll enjoy getting to know her and the rest of our small congregation as well."

They were back in Las Palmas now. The golf course went by and then the American Co-op school before Sam slowed to turn into a narrow residential street that was choked on both sides with cars. Sam drove slowly down the narrow passage before pulling up in front of a house halfway down the block. This was so different from the stately residences on either side, that Sara forgot her somber thoughts in an exclamation of delight.

The house was two stories high and fronted with stone, its steeply pitched roof a soft forest-green instead of the customary red tile. It had jutting gables and vines of frangipani crawling up the stone walls and, except for the high security wall, looked more like a product of a New England village than a Bolivian upper-class neighborhood. The security wall, too, lacked the usual white plaster and row of deadly iron spikes. These had been traded for a facing of flat, water-smoothed stones, a security breach remedied by the presence of a guard shack next to the front gate. But even this grim reminder of street crime and petty thievery had been painted a soft green to match the roof.

"What a gorgeous house!" Sara said wistfully, admiring the hibiscus and roses that were climbing their colorful way over the wall. It couldn't be compared, of course, to the palatial Cortéz mansion, but it had its own charm and was just the kind of house that Sara might have fallen in love with had she and Nicolás been looking for a home of their own. She looked over at Laura, who was leaning forward to point out a parking spot for her husband. "So, this Ellen Stevens who's hosting the potluck. You probably already mentioned it, but is she living here alone, or does she have family here in the country?"

"She's here alone, as far as I know," Laura replied. "I did hear something about some grown children back in the states, but I haven't really asked. We tend not to talk a lot about our families back home since it's unlikely anyone here will ever meet them. What do you think, Sam? Has Ellen ever had any family down to visit?"

Sam only grunted. The parking space Laura had pointed out was an extremely tight one, which was probably why it was still vacant. The side of the minivan nudged the back bumper of the Land Rover in front of them before a last twist of the wheel left them safely parked but so close to the sports car behind them that Sara didn't see how they could possibly get back out again.

Setting the hand brake, Sam turned off the engine with a flourish. "Well, ladies, we made it! Now let's get inside while there's something left to eat. If they've cleaned out all the *surubí*—!"

As Sara stepped onto the sidewalk, a guard detached himself from the stone wall. Behind him, she could see another guard leaning out the window of the guard shack. Her steps slowed. Sara was still not used to seeing armed men on guard in residential neighborhoods, and the man strolling toward her was more intimidating than most. He was dressed in full camouflage, instead of the olive-green worn by the police guards at Cortéz Industries, and there was something in the way he carried himself—more like a professional soldier than the guards Sara had seen until now. And though she knew little about guns, she was certain that was a machine gun he cradled carelessly in his hands.

"Names, please?" the guard asked courteously.

As Sam gave their names, the first guard glanced over at his partner, who was running a finger down a clipboard. He nodded toward the Histeds. "These two may pass. But the Cortéz woman is not listed."

"She's with us," Sam explained. "She visited the English church for the first time this morning, and she's joining us for our meal."

Sara shifted impatiently. Though she didn't like it, she had come to understand that residential guards were a necessary substitute for an adequate local police force. But weren't two a little excessive for a one-person dwelling, even in Las Palmas? And this business of names and lists. Cortéz Industries didn't even have security this tight! As for the way the guard had positioned himself between the three visitors and the gate—*like we might be smuggling in a bomb or something!*

"Look, if there's a problem—" Sara started to say.

"No, no, it is no problem," the guard denied quickly. "But I will have to consult."

Taking a step away from them, he lifted a hand radio from his belt and spoke into it in Spanish, too low and rapid for Sara to follow. As the radio crackled in response, the guard returned it to his belt and reached up to push a button set into the stone wall. A metal door beside the guard shack swung open. The guard stepped back. "You may proceed."

A cobblestone path led up a flight of steps to the front door. Sam didn't bother knocking before pushing the door open. Inside, it was noisy and crowded. To the right, steps led down to a sunken living room with sofas and chairs grouped around a stone fireplace. Beyond the living room lay an open dining area, where food had been arranged buffet-style on a long oval table.

"Hey, Pastor," someone called, "you're going to have to hurry if you're wanting any of that *surubí!*"

Straight ahead, beyond a more informal den, sliding glass doors looked out onto a tile patio, and a stretch of green lawn slanted down to a small swimming pool. Sara could see several children splashing around. The sizzle of cooking meat from the patio grill reminded Sara that she'd had only a single cup of coffee and a croissant for breakfast.

"A lot of the men like to hunt," Sam said, steering his wife and Sara in the direction of the barbecue. "Especially those who've lived long-term around here. One or two have haciendas outside of Santa Cruz, and every once in a while they'll get up a safari and invite a few friends. It's not at all like hunting in the United Kingdom—or the U.S., from what I hear. All jungle and terribly hard to get through on foot, not to mention all the mud and rain. But they seem to think it's fun. There are no game laws, so they can shoot anything that moves. They'll come back with jaguar and puma and tapir and *jochi* and even iguana, if they get one big enough. Those aren't half bad—kind of like chicken. In fact, for myself, I think they're all pretty tasty, once you get past where they've been."

"There's Ellen right now with a load fresh off the grill," Laura interrupted her husband. "Hey, Ellen! Oh, and there's Doug too. You've already met him, haven't you, Sara, dearie? Doug Bradford? You'll just love his *jochi*. I don't know what he does, but anything he brings home comes out so tender. I'm so glad he got to go hunting this past week. He works so hard, the poor boy!"

Sara recognized the wide shoulders and uncompromising profile bent over the grill. She hung back as Sam and Laura hurried across the patio. *Not him again!* Though why she'd assumed that just because Doug Bradford hadn't shown at the orphanage she'd seen the last of these awkward meetings, she didn't know. Maybe because, like church attendance, her preconceptions of a DEA agent hadn't included relaxing and eating with friends like any normal person. To tell the truth, it had never occurred to her to wonder—or care—what they did in their off-duty hours.

"Sam, Laura! It's about time you two showed up." Ellen Stevens freed up a hand to wave back, then had to grab at the platter to keep its contents from sliding to the ground. "Hey, watch it there, Doug! You add any more to this pile, and you're going to be wearing it!"

Straightening up, the DEA agent lifted the platter out of her hands. "Glad you could make it, Pastor, Laura," he said smiling. "I've saved some *surubi* for you over here, though I had to fight like you wouldn't believe to keep Ellen out of it. And you might want to try some of this *jochi*. Ellen seasoned it herself, and it's really not too bad!"

Picking a small piece of meat from the edge of the platter, he chewed it thoughtfully. "A little too much on the pepper, maybe. I'm still working with her on that."

"Why, you!" Ellen Stevens exclaimed. Grabbing a pair of tongs from the grill, the tall brunette waved them threateningly. "Just see where I am the next time you come crawling to me for help!"

"Okay, okay, I'm sorry!" Doug Bradford staggered back in mock alarm. He was laughing, Sara saw, and it made him look a lot younger and more human than she'd thought before. "You're my right hand man—pardon me, woman—I'll admit, and I don't know what I'd do without you!"

"And my cooking?" The church pianist hadn't lowered the tongs by an inch. "Come on, spit it out! I can cook circles around you any day, and you know it!"

"Sure, sure, you're a great cook," the DEA agent said soothingly. "And I really do appreciate your help today. Now, have I groveled enough, or are you going to make me beg the next time I need you to bail me out of a mess?"

Mollified, Ellen dropped the tongs back onto the grill. "I'll think about it! Now let me get you two some plates while our *comedian* here"—she gave Doug a withering look—"keeps the rest of this from burning." She glanced around. "Now where's that little friend of yours? I thought I saw her come in with you. I did hope she'd get to join us today."

Sara had already edged back inside the glass doors of the den. Paying her respects to the hostess was going to have to wait until Doug Bradford wasn't standing right there, even if it meant going hungry a little longer. Wandering over toward a burst of laughter at the other end of the den, Sara slid into an armchair. When Laura finally caught up to her, Sara was engrossed in a safari story as outrageous and improbable as anything she'd ever heard in North America.

"So here's where you disappeared to," the pastor's wife said cheerfully, handing her a Styrofoam plate. "I didn't know your tastes, but I grabbed you the last of the *surubí* before Sam could get it all, and a bit of everything else. If anything looks too exotic for you, don't hesitate to dump it. Not everyone cares for wild meat."

"Oh, no, Laura, it looks delicious! Thanks, you're a sweetheart." Gratefully taking the plate, Sara discovered that *surubí* was a fish fillet that rivaled salmon in flavor, and the *jochi* tasted like pork. A piece of white meat in a triangular piece of shell turned out to be armadillo, which was surprisingly good after the first cautious bite.

Laura laughed at her enthusiasm. "Hey, don't stop there! We have a whole table of salads and casseroles in the other room. Come on, I'll show you."

Trailing Laura back into the dining area, Sara took the opportunity for a more leisurely look around. The interior decorating echoed the same pleasing combination of northern and southern influences. There was a jaguar pelt over the back of one sofa and another, of alpaca fur, flung over the other. A bearskin rug brooded in front of the fireplace, glass eyes glaring yellow rage as though these noisy intruders were the ones who had dragged him so far from his arctic forest home. A waist-high replica of an Inca monolith stood by the front door. A few weavings adorned the walls. A collection of fencing swords were displayed over the fireplace, and an assortment of native bows and arrows covered the wall separating the living room from the den.

Sara drew in a deep breath of satisfaction. The place was a far cry from the elegance of the Cortéz mansion, but it had something her father-in-law's opulent residence lacked—the warmth and coziness that make a house a home. Though it did seem surprisingly stark and almost masculine for a hostess who struck Sara as more likely to go for frills and knickknacks.

"If Nicky and I ever move out on our own, we'll definitely have to check out this neighborhood," she told Laura, spooning a portion of casserole onto an already overflowing plate. "I'll have to ask Ellen if she knows of any more houses like this one. Though the security end does seem a little extreme. Two guards for one person! Even my in-laws aren't that careful. And all that business of having your name approved from a checklist. I'd think it'd drive you crazy to go through that every time you want to visit a friend! Is that standard procedure for all the expatriates?"

Laura chuckled. "Oh, no! The only guards we have at our house are a couple of aging German shepherds. And they'd be more likely to hand a flashlight to a thief than try to stop one! Some of the others have neighborhood watchmen, of course, but they certainly don't have anti-narcotics troops standing guard outside. That's just your American Drug Enforcement Administration personnel. Maybe your other embassy people too, I don't know. I've never met any of them. You Americans always do take security more seriously than any of the other embassies. Though I guess they do have to be careful with all this drug business."

The serving spoon stopped halfway between Sara's plate and the casserole dish. "Ellen Stevens is with the DEA?" she asked incredulously. "Are you sure?"

"You didn't know? I'm sorry, I keep forgetting how new you are here." Laura turned to smile as one of the couples who had toured the children's home with Sara approached the table. "Maybe I shouldn't have told you. I do talk too much, I know. They don't really like having their occupations broadcast all over the city. Security again, you know. But everyone here at the English church knows Ellen and Doug and what they do. Not that Ellen's an agent like Doug. I think she's an administration officer or something like that."

So those were *soldiers out there! But Ellen Stevens with the DEA? That's not possible!* Sara set the serving spoon down a bit too hard. All the resentment that had first been stirred by Doug Bradford's callous actions toward her husband's family rose up hot within her. *Why can't I get away from these people?*

Looking around, this time with a more critical eye, she estimated the probable rental value of this gracious home, and the cost of the entertainment center along the far wall. The pool in the back yard. Two full-time security guards—and soldiers, no less—out front. And all for one person!

"So this is where all our tax money goes!" she said caustically. "They certainly do pretty well for themselves, don't they? I'll bet the average American would love to see how our representatives live overseas!"

Laura looked surprised at her vehemence, but she swallowed her words when a cool voice addressed Sara from behind. "And exactly how do you think we should live, Mrs. Cortéz? In a two-room apartment? Or perhaps a mud hut."

CHAPTER TEN

Sara turned around slowly to find Doug Bradford regarding her with a look that was one part amusement and two parts pure annoyance. Reaching his arm past her, he picked up a stalk of celery from a platter of raw vegetables and crunched it between his front teeth. "You seem to be a strange one to talk about living off the hard work of others," he added, but his casual tone belied the bite of his words.

Sara drew herself up to her full height, which didn't amount to much next to his broad frame. "*I'm* not living off the taxpayer!" she snapped with all the coldness she could muster.

Bradford arched an eyebrow. "Oh, no?"

Before Sara could begin to decipher his cryptic reply, he went on, waving the uneaten end of the celery stalk as though he were a police instructor enlightening a new recruit. "It might interest you to know, Mrs. Cortéz, that the embassy chooses our homes for security, not luxury. In an overseas post, we happen to need high walls. Easily defended perimeters. A line of retreat in case of attack. Something you don't find in the average mud hut, in case you hadn't noticed. As I'm certain you can attest, there are a lot of people around here who don't like us."

"I wonder why!" Sara muttered under her breath.

A flicker in Bradford's gray eyes showed he'd caught her remark, but he continued as evenly as though he hadn't heard. "As for the rest, call it a perk for working a few thousand miles from home. You seem to be laboring under a misapprehension, Mrs. Cortéz. The DEA is not a welfare agency asking for handouts from the American taxpayers. The agents who work for the Drug Enforcement Administration, both overseas and back home, are highly trained professionals who happen to do a dirty and often very dangerous job. We earn every cent of our salaries, which, in case you're interested, amount to considerably less than the earnings of most of the oil executives and overseas businessmen you see here today." He waved the remains of his celery stalk in the direction of a group of men standing near the fireplace.

Sara's cheeks were burning by the end of his lecture. The worst part was, she knew he was right! She had no business making those critical comments. From all she'd seen, Ellen Stevens was a very nice person, and Sara was ashamed that she'd allowed her distaste for the woman's profession to goad her into such unaccustomed rudeness. Illogically or not, she blamed the man standing in front of her. It was his treatment of her husband's family that had provoked her into bad manners.

"You're right, of course," she managed to say through lips stiff with resentment. "I apologize. Ellen has made a beautiful home here, and how she lives her life is certainly none of my business."

"Ellen?" Bradford's eyebrow shot up again as he threw a glance around the open living area. "I'm glad you approve, but this place isn't Ellen's. It's mine."

"Yours!" Sara choked, then tried to cover it up with a cough. *Of course!* The masculine decor, the animal skins, the weapons hanging on the walls—it all made sense now, even as she stammered, "But Ellen . . . I thought she was the hostess. I mean, the potluck . . . she invited me here."

"Yes, Ellen very graciously volunteered to be my hostess here today," Bradford answered blandly, but Sara was sure she detected a twinkle in his eyes. *He's laughing at me again,* she thought angrily.

"She's so used to keeping us all in order in the office, she figures it's her duty to help us single agents out in the entertainment area as well."

It didn't surprise Sara to hear that he was single. The wonder would be that anyone would ever marry him! She looked wildly around for any excuse to escape his gaze. Her eyes lit on the animal pelts thrown in front of the fireplace and over the back of the couch.

"Nice furs," she commented with deceptive innocence. "Is hunting animals on the endangered list another one of those necessary security things for the DEA?"

"As a matter of fact, that bearskin rug was handed down to me from my grandfather, who shot it only after it slaughtered two of his best sheepdogs and a fair crop of lambs. That was back when public opinion was still on the side of the farmer and rancher, of course. As for the jaguar, I killed that myself—just after it got one of my men on a TDY in the Beni last year."

"Oh, that's quite interesting," Laura Histed interjected cheerily. She seemed oblivious to the tension between Doug Bradford and Sara.

But Bradford's mild answer didn't improve Sara's disposition. Her appetite suddenly gone, she put her plate down on the table—with considerably more force than necessary. *Bother!* Scooping a landslide of casserole back onto her plate, she grabbed a napkin to wipe the spot she'd left on the tablecloth. *What is it about this guy that just sets my teeth on edge?*

"Here, don't worry about that." Bradford lifted the napkin from her hand. "It'll wash."

Ignoring him, Sara turned to Laura. "Look, I really need to be going. Is there somewhere I could call a radio taxi?"

"Oh, Sara, but you just got here!" Laura protested, distressed. "You've hardly even touched your plate yet!" Glancing from Sara's stormy face to Doug's sardonic expression, she broke off, flustered. "Of course, dear, if you really have to get home. Come along with me, and I'll show you where the phone is. You don't mind if we borrow it, do you, Doug?"

Doug's outstretched arm stopped her. "That won't be necessary, Laura," he said gently. "I'll be glad to drive Mrs. Cortéz home. If you'll just let Ellen know, I'll be back shortly."

"Oh, would you, Doug?" Laura exclaimed. "I do hate sending her home in a cab—if you can even get one on a Sunday afternoon."

"I don't—" Sara started indignantly, but she changed her tone when she saw Laura's eager look. "I don't know how to thank you," she finished weakly. Giving the pastor's wife a hug, she said, "Thank you so much, Laura, for inviting me and for all your kindness. I really did enjoy the service."

"It's been such a pleasure to have you," Laura beamed. "And I do hope you come back next week. And tell your husband that we'd love to see him, too."

Leaving the house was a lot easier than entering. When the soldier on guard saw Doug Bradford, he simply raised his gun in a salute. His partner didn't even stick his head out of the guard box.

"I'll be back as soon as I take the *señora* home," Bradford informed the soldier in Spanish. "If there are any problems, call." He tapped a black, palm-sized apparatus on his belt that Sara hadn't noticed before. It was a smaller, more streamlined version of the foot-tall handheld radio the guard was carrying.

"*Sí, señor!*" The guard brought his weapon up to his forehead again, then hurried over to open the driver's door of the Land Rover that Sam Histed had squeezed his van in behind. *No need to lock your car when you've got two soldiers to keep an eye on it,* Sara thought sardonically as she followed the guard around to the passenger side. Opening the door, the guard ushered her inside. The windows of the Land Rover were polarized, and the interior felt suddenly chilly and dark after the brightness of the sun outside.

Bradford waited until the guard had slammed the door shut before climbing in himself.

"Thank you for the ride," she said stiffly as he put on his seat belt. "I live over on—"

"I know where you live," he cut in. He nodded over her shoulder. "There's another seat belt there. I know it isn't the law here, but I don't like to take chances with my passengers."

Sara cast him a sideways glance as she pulled her seat belt tight. He was looking straight ahead, a frown between his brows. Trying to figure out how he was going to get out of this impossibly small space without having everyone move their cars, no doubt!

But it only took a few deft turns of the steering wheel before the Land Rover was moving quickly down the street. Bradford relaxed against the seat back and looked over at Sara. "So, how did you enjoy the service?" His voice was cordial, almost friendly, with no hint of the tension that had marked their earlier conversation.

Sara dragged her gaze away from the side window. If he was willing to make polite conversation, so was she. "It was good to hear some English again," she said briefly. "Your pastor and his wife seem very friendly."

"Yes, Sam and Laura are great, aren't they? I really admire the work they've done with those street kids and the orphanage. And Pastor Sam's sermons—they always seem to hit home right where I need them. Today's message was especially good, don't you think?" The car reached the outskirts of Las Palmas and the elegant mansions gave way abruptly to dusty truck yards and a ramshackle mechanic shop.

Sara flushed, remembering his eyes on her at the end of the service. *Is he amusing himself again?* A quick glance at the DEA agent revealed nothing but polite courtesy. *You've got to stop looking for a double meaning in everything he says,* Sara told herself sternly.

"I guess we've all been through times when God seems a universe away," Bradford said as he merged into the frenzied traffic of the third ring with the ease of long practice. "And yet, like Pastor Sam said, it's really us who do the running. Kind of like a poem I started to memorize a few years back when I was going through a rough patch. *The Hound of Heaven,* by Francis Thompson; do you know it? 'I fled Him, down the nights and down the days; I fled Him, down the arches of the years; I fled Him down the labyrinthian ways of my own mind; and in the mist of tears I hid from Him. . . .'

"It's an old poem, a classic really, but far too long-winded for most of us today. The whole thing talks about God's relentless pursuing of man, kind of like a tracking hound, wooing us back to himself. It's the ending that Pastor Sam's sermon made me think of—when the guy finally turns around at the end of his messed-up life and sees who he's been running from all that time, and God says basically, 'You poor, foolish child, can't you see I'm the one you've really been seeking all this time? I'm the only one who can love you the way you really are. You were driving away love when you were driving me away.' It does seem, sometimes, that we spend our whole lives running frantically around, searching for meaning and love, when if we'd just turn around, we'd see God standing right behind us, holding out his love in both hands."

Sara eyed him suspiciously. What a surprising man! Quoting poetry—Christian poetry, at that—with all the fervor of real faith. And yet this same man could hound Nicolás and his family as relentlessly as the poem he'd just quoted! It was plain hypocrisy.

She turned back to the window. The intersection, like many others within the first few rings of the city, was built around a circular green, the traffic flowing around the circle in a more or less orderly left-to-right pattern.

As the Land Rover slowed to a stop, a slight figure emerged from the shadow of a few meager palms and hurried toward the line of cars, one hand crooked in the universal appeal for money. Despite the heat of the afternoon sun, a heavy poncho hung in folds across her back. As the woman reached out her hand toward the car window, Sara could see movement in the folds of the poncho. *Why, there's a baby in there!*

With the memory of the hapless infants in the orphanage still vivid in her mind, Sara fumbled for her purse. Here at least was something she could do. Grabbing the first bill that came to her hand, she lowered the power window. Seeing the motion, the woman hurried to the passenger side of the car. But before the money could change hands, the window rolled back up.

"No, you don't want to do that," Bradford said firmly.

The light turned green before Sara could protest, and a cacophony of honks sent the beggar woman dodging back to the sidewalk. As the Land Rover moved away, Sara saw the woman shake her fist after them. Sara turned indignantly to Bradford. "I can't believe you did that! What was that for?"

"I don't believe in encouraging beggars—at least perfectly healthy ones like that woman back there." With firm hands on the wheel, he negotiated a narrow opening between a bus and a cattle truck before glancing over to catch Sara's look of indignation. "Look, if it makes you feel any better, that woman most likely has both a family and a home. These Aymara have been coming down in truckloads from the highlands around La Paz. You'll find them all over town. The men work in the sugar factories. The women beg."

"How can you blame them when they're that poor?" Sara argued. "I mean, a few *bolivianos* wouldn't have made any difference to me, but it might at least have bought some milk for that baby."

"It's a pity so many tourists agree with you." Bradford accelerated into another gap, ignoring the irate honk of the taxi that had tried to cut in front of him. "Look, I appreciate your compassion for these people, Mrs. Cortéz, but a handout just isn't the answer. It may ease our consciences to drop a little of our overabundance through a car window. But it's ruining these people. The Aymara highlanders managed for centuries without the tourist trade. Maybe they didn't have much, but they were hard-working and self-sufficient with their little plots of potatoes and flocks of llamas and goats."

He slowed at the next intersection, where a handful of Aymara women—some with dutiful children in tow—were working the line of vehicles. *"Limosna! Limosna!"* they cried, thrusting the children forward to garner more sympathy. Bradford waved an impatient hand.

"Now look at them—a bunch of extremely dirty beggars! And the money they're making likely won't even end up in their own pockets. According to police reports, this whole movement of people down here from the highlands is part of an organized racket. And you can bet that whoever is setting them up to beg is skimming off a good part of anything you give them."

There was a knock at Doug's window. One of the Aymara women thrust a small mesh bag of lemons at the glass. Rolling it down, Bradford took the bag and tossed her a ten boliviano note, twice what the lemons were worth.

"See, I don't mind if they're selling something. At least they're working. But we're not doing anyone any good—least of all them—when we start handing out freebies to people perfectly capable of putting in a day's work. The failure of our own welfare system back in the states should teach us that much. So if you want to feel sorry for someone, save it for the genuinely needy—the blind and the lame. There's a few like that down at the plaza."

Sara threw Bradford a curious glance. Maybe he wasn't as lacking in compassion as she'd assumed. He was certainly right about the American welfare system, but she'd never considered that the same principle applied here in Bolivia. Catching Sara's eye, Doug smiled, a slow, companionable grin that transformed his stern features and drew a glimmer of a smile from Sara despite her reservations. "Or better yet, toss your spare change to that children's home you visited today. They could use the help a lot more than a bunch of perfectly healthy highland Indians."

"Oh, I know, isn't it awful?" Sara agreed fervently. "I never dreamed anyone lived like that—especially kids! And those poor babies!" Distress darkened her amber eyes. "How can they possibly grow up normal, jammed in there like sardines? And with no one to love them or make them feel like they're more than just a . . . a face in the crowd!"

"It's a lot better today than it used to be," Doug assured her. "And at least with Doña Inez you can be sure she's not trying to feather her own nest. Which is more than you can say for some of the institutions around here. So if you're really looking for a charitable organization to benefit, that's not a bad option. Talk to that cousin of yours, and see if she doesn't back me up."

"You mean Gabriela?" Sara's ears perked up. "You know her?"

"Not socially. I met her a couple of times when I was helping Pastor Sam through some of the red tape that was strangling that street-kid's ministry. That's a good example of what I was talking about. The top man in Juvenile was demanding a sizable chunk of the ministry's assets in return for permission to help those kids. To line his own pockets, of course. Until Gabriela stepped in. All she had to do was flash the family tree, and the permits were through the next day. For once, use of the Cortéz name resulted in something worthwhile!"

He stopped speaking abruptly when Sara stiffened. "Excuse me, I didn't mean that in a negative way. As a matter of fact, I have a lot of respect for your cousin. She's the only Cortéz I know—"

"Who isn't involved in drug dealing?" Sara finished angrily. *Of all the nerve!* She'd almost been in danger of forgetting who this man was.

"Who's involved in social work, I was going to say." Doug let out a low whistle between his teeth. "So that's it! You know, I've been wondering all day what I've done to offend you. As far as I can recall, we've only met on one other occasion, and I don't remember having committed any grave errors of etiquette then. And yet it's been obvious since I laid eyes on you this morning that you have it in for me. But maybe it isn't me. Maybe it's my job? You have a problem with what the DEA is doing here? Is that what all that was about back there at the house?"

Sara had carefully kept her resolve to be polite to this man, but if Doug Bradford was going to drag it out into the open, then it was time that *someone* let him know what an honest American citizen thought about U.S. government employees who abused their authority on foreign soil.

"It's the way you do things that I have a problem with! Nicky's told me about how the DEA hounds every successful Bolivian in the country, about how you use the power of the U.S. government as a hammer over their heads, badgering innocent businessmen and spying on them so they can hardly function and smashing up their businesses in search of drugs that were never there. You'd think there were enough real drug dealers out there to keep you busy, instead of harassing the very people who are trying to turn this country around!"

Sara trailed off into dead silence. Even the rush of traffic sounded suddenly distant. She stole a glance at Bradford. The DEA agent was watching the car in front of him as though his only thought was negotiating traffic, but the straight line of his mouth and the tightness of his jaw warned Sara of an anger being kept rigidly in check. She felt a small thrill of fear. Maybe she'd gone too far. After all, she was alone in the car with this man, and he was looking as though he'd like to murder someone!

When Bradford finally spoke, however, his voice was even, and Sara found herself reluctantly admiring his self-control. "I take it you're referring to our raid on Cortéz Industries."

"You know I am!" For an instant, Sara regretted the return to hostilities, but she rushed on. "Nicky told me how you raided their offices and destroyed millions of dollars worth of merchandise on some supposed drug search. And how you refused to pay them any compensation. You owed them that much, at least!"

"It sounds like Nicky told you a lot of things. Look, Mrs. Cortéz—"

"And stop calling me Mrs. Cortéz!"

Bradford's eyebrows rose. "Excuse me?"

"My name is Sara," she said sharply. "You don't need to keep calling me 'Mrs. Cortéz' as though I were fifty years old or my mother-in-law or something. Especially with that nasty emphasis you always put on the last name, like it tastes bad in your mouth!"

A twitch at the corner of Bradford's mouth relieved the rigidity of his jaw. "Okay, Sara it is," he agreed almost mildly. "And maybe you can go ahead and call me Doug. I don't know what all your husband's told you, but I'm afraid neither he nor you have your facts straight. For your information, we did pay a very adequate compensation. I signed the vouchers myself. And it wasn't in the millions of dollars—just a few broken whiskey bottles. As for the rest, I'm not making any apologies for doing my job. Our reasons seemed adequate enough at the time, and if the incident was unfortunate—well, it's long past now and best forgotten."

"But it *isn't* forgotten!" Sara insisted. "Not by Nicky—not by you! I saw the way you looked at him the other day! You still think he's involved in cocaine traffic, don't you? You just can't conceive of a Bolivian having the brains to build his own business empire without drug money, can you?"

Doug's breath went out in an audible sound. "Look, Mrs. Cortéz!"

"Sara!"

"Sara. Let me ask you something, Sara. How long have you been married?"

Sara eyed him warily, but she couldn't see any catch in the question, so she admitted, "Almost two months."

"And how long did you know your husband before you married him?"

Sara saw now where he was going, and she didn't like it. "A month. But that doesn't mean I didn't know him well, if that's what you're getting at. At least, well—"

"So you've known him—what, three months? And you've known your in-laws for half that, right? Well, Sara, I'm not going to debate the pros and cons of what we do here in Bolivia. It would take too long, and it's clear you've already got your mind made up. But I *am* going to tell you a little story. A story of a family that was accustomed to having things pretty much their own way."

They were approaching the second ring now. The Land Rover slowed to a crawl to accommodate the sudden increase in traffic. Up ahead, the intersection was jammed, with taxis and trucks and private cars pushing so far into the line of cross-traffic that vehicles moving on a green light were reduced to one lane. Buses on a tight schedule were taking to the shoulder, bumping over the dirt ruts to inch their way to the front of the line.

"There's a World Cup elimination game letting out from Tahuichi stadium," Doug said with a nod toward the congestion. "It's going to take awhile, so you might as well sit back and relax."

Following his own suggestion, he leaned back in his seat, his fingers tapping idly against the steering wheel. "Let me see now; where shall we start? Maybe back when this family first came to Bolivia. They were right on the heels of Pizarro's conquering army, some of the first to exploit the remains of the Inca empire." Doug glanced over at Sara. "Not that I hold any grief for the Incas. They were a brutal lot, with a penchant for human sacrifice, who got exactly what they'd meted out to plenty of others. But their Indian slaves didn't get a much better deal when they traded their Inca masters for the Spanish.

"Anyway, this family prospered. They had their land grants and their shares in the silver and tin mines, not to mention a few thousand Inca serfs—now called Quechua—to wait on them hand and foot. Things went on just fine for a few hundred years. Bolivia became a nation, and this family managed to insinuate its way into every aspect of public life. More than one *presidente* and *generalísimo* were close relatives."

The Land Rover inched forward. "Then something terrible happened! The peasants started revolting. For some reason they were lacking in appreciation for the benefits of Western civilization brought to them by their benefactors. Such luxuries as allowing them a mud hut to live in, a garden in which to grow a bit of food after working all day in the landlord's fields, and the privilege of viewing—from the outside, of course—the fine Spanish architecture being raised on their aching backs. Then, in one bloodier-than-usual revolution fifty years or so back, a dastardly piece of legislation was signed into law, called the Agrarian Reform Act. By the time things had quieted down, this privileged family had lost ninety percent of the family estates to these same unappreciative peasants, who promptly showed their ingratitude by bending their efforts to growing their own crops instead of enriching their former landlords.

"Still, this family had its shares in the tin mines—silver was running dry by then—and though they missed their Indian *peones,* they managed to keep going without curtailing their standard of living by too much."

Sara listened with unwilling fascination. It hadn't taken her long to recognize who "this family" was. Despite Doug Bradford's obvious sarcasm, his story was essentially the same as the Cortéz family history she'd heard with such pride from Mimi and with careless indifference from Nicolás.

"Until that horrible day about twenty years back when the price of tin plummeted. The United States, you may or may not know, financed the biggest tin strike in history—in Malaysia! Overnight, Bolivian tin was no longer worth the cost of digging it out of the ground. Our friends were broke, and they didn't like that one bit. After all, hadn't they made this country what it was? Weren't they entitled to a reasonable share of its wealth? For the next several years, they limped along, selling off family heirlooms and jewels, and their last bits of property, until it became obvious that even this wouldn't keep the roof over their family mansion in downtown Santa Cruz. And then, one day, just as suddenly as they'd lost everything, this family was wealthy again."

Bradford's conclusion was all the more dramatic for being delivered in the same even tone as the rest of the story. He wasn't looking angry anymore. *In fact, he looks tickled to death with his little lecture,* Sara thought with resentment. She itched to wipe that complacent expression off his face.

"So get to the point," she said coldly. "If you're wanting to tell me how they did it, I can't stop you—not without jumping out of the car."

Doug shrugged his shoulders. "I thought maybe you could tell me."

Sara bit her lip. "Maybe they had a good year. They still had the hacienda and . . . and their sugar fields. Maybe that's when they started exporting things—how am I supposed to know? I wasn't there!"

"Precisely," Doug said dryly. "Within a year, they'd built that mansion you live in and laid the foundation for the finest industrial complex this country has ever known. Where did they get that kind of capital? Certainly not from other family members. They were all in the same boat—and most of them have profited from the same sudden prosperity as your in-laws. Do you understand what I'm saying, Mrs. Cortéz?"

"Sara!" Sara corrected automatically. She lifted her chin as high as it would go. "What I understand is that you're obsessed! You already investigated them, didn't you? And what did you find? Nothing! And you never will find anything, no matter how many times you smash up their business. Nicky told me himself that none of his family has ever been involved in drug traffic. Do you think he wouldn't know if they were?"

"Your husband—" Doug broke off, then said carefully, "There's more than one explanation for coming up dry on an investigation."

"And I don't have to listen to it!" Sara clamped her hands over her ears, but the point had been made. *If only he wasn't asking the same questions I've been asking myself!*

No, she wasn't going to allow Doug Bradford's insinuations to poison her mind. She knew her husband, and she knew his family. Delores and Janéth, idle and extravagant, but outgoing and affectionate. Doña Mimi, stiff with family pride, but slowly warming to her new daughter-in-law. The aunts and uncles who'd embraced her and made much ado over her. Nicky's many cousins and friends, genial and passionate and fun-loving and—except for Reina—more than willing to accept a stranger and foreigner into their circle. Okay, so maybe they had different standards than she felt comfortable with! But would any of them stoop to criminal activity? Ridiculous!

And yet, there was some validity to Doug's arguments, and Sara was too honest not to recognize it. Slowly, she lowered her hands.

"Look, I'm sorry," she said carefully. "Maybe you really are just trying to do your job. But you've got it all wrong! Okay, so I'm not familiar with the family's financial background. But I know the Cortezes a lot better than you do. They're not these Mafia types you're getting at. They're nice people!"

"I never said these guys couldn't be likable."

Sara swept on, ignoring Doug's comment. "But . . . but even say you're right and . . . well, maybe some of the money *did* come from cocaine. That's what you're getting at, isn't it? I'm not admitting that that's where it came from, but . . . well, I'm not stupid! I know where a lot of the money around here comes from, and . . . and I suppose it's just possible that some acquaintance or—I don't know, maybe even a relative or someone—could have been involved with cocaine and maybe lent them the money. Laundering or whatever you call it. That's just hypothetical, of course, because I'm sure they have a perfectly good explanation for their money. Maybe an international bank lent it to them, for all I know."

Her sentences were tumbling out faster now and disjointed as she marshaled arguments to convince herself as well as Doug Bradford. If she could just make him understand!

"But even if it *was* true, that's a long way from saying the Cortezes were involved in drug trafficking," she continued. "Or even that they knew where the money came from! Besides, you . . . you've got to remember that people here don't look at cocaine the same way we do. I mean, to us it's this big crime! To them it's just this crop they've been growing for thousands of years. They don't think of it as any different than . . . than Americans growing tobacco. I mean, who are we to talk? We let tobacco companies ship cigarettes to Third World countries that are so broke their people can't possibly afford to smoke. We give away cigarettes to poor little street kids just to get them hooked, and we don't even tell them it'll give them cancer. I mean, really, what's the difference between that and peddling cocaine? And yet no one back home would think twice about a businessman taking a loan that came from tobacco profits. It . . . it's just plain hypocritical!"

"I suppose you got all that from Nicolás!" Doug cut in caustically. "You don't need to go on. I've heard the whole spiel often enough. That old tobacco-coca argument has been a favorite justification for drug-dealing around here for years. Compare the whole cocaine problem to the tobacco industry! Blame it all on the U.S.!"

"Well, it's true, isn't it?" Sara argued. They were through the intersection now, and traffic was speeding up. In ten minutes she'd be home. "At least the Bolivians out there are growing coca to keep their families from starving. What's our excuse? American tobacco growers *know* what nicotine can do. They've heard it all their lives. So why do they keep growing it? Because it's making a lot of money for them, that's why!"

Doug shrugged. "Hey, I'm not going to argue the point. So the U.S. has its problems too! But two wrongs don't make a right. And no matter how you cut it, there's one major difference between your American tobacco farmer and your average coke peddler. Growing tobacco's legal. Dealing in cocaine is a crime—even in Bolivia!"

"Only because the U.S. decided it was a crime *and* used their influence to make it one," Sara countered swiftly, even as she wondered at herself. *I can't believe this! I'm sounding just like Nicky! And he's using my own arguments back on me!* "I'm not saying cocaine isn't bad. Of course it is! I'm just saying you have to look at it from their point of view. They've been chewing coca for thousands of years. After all, it's their sacred leaf, isn't it? And it's never really hurt them. It's even got a lot of medicinal uses."

Sara faltered. The DEA agent was listening but with an increasingly forbidding expression. He was angry again, she realized with a sinking heart. She pressed doggedly on. "So . . . so you can see why they don't really understand that it's wrong to sell it—except that some foreign government is telling them it is! It's not like they're going to see a lot of drug addicts on the news and all the way we would! Most of them probably don't have any idea what cocaine actually does. They . . . they just see it as this byproduct of their sacred leaf that . . . that's all of a sudden bringing a lot of needed cash into the country. The way they see it, they can't be expected to feel responsible if a lot of foreigners in a far-off country decide to take the stuff and do something stupid with it. I mean, really, should they be blamed because a lot of spoiled American teenagers insist on poisoning themselves with the stuff?"

The Land Rover braked hard and Sara was thrown full-force into the shoulder strap of the seat belt. They were almost through another circle intersection, this one without a traffic light. But by yanking a hard left on the steering wheel, Doug managed to miss the divider in the middle of the boulevard by a few inches and bring the Land Rover around in a U-turn that left him speeding in the opposite direction. Sara slid herself back into her seat, indignant and genuinely frightened for the first time. "Where are you taking me?"

"To give you an education!" the DEA agent said grimly. He raised a hand when Sara opened her mouth. "No, you've had your say. Now you listen to me! I've put up with your defending drug dealers and criminals, because I wanted to see what kind of a line the Cortezes have been feeding you. Well, it's the usual one, and it's obvious you've bought it hook, line, and sinker. So now you can just listen to a few hard facts on the other side."

They were back where the traffic jam had been, but the throng of soccer fans had thinned out, and the Land Rover sped through the green light without even slowing down. "To start with, this cigarette thing you've gotten off on! Okay, I'm not saying the U.S. has nothing to answer for—although there *are* those who are trying to bring about more ethical changes for marketing overseas. But the Bolivians aren't exactly guiltless in the situation. Or maybe you're not aware of the experimental tobacco plantations right here in Santa Cruz province that are working on developing a crop that will match the quality of the top American brands."

"I don't believe it!" Sara gasped in dismay.

"It's true. Okay, so maybe the Cortezes aren't into that. They prefer products that have already proven themselves profitable. But plenty of their friends are. And I can tell you this: They aren't objecting to America's overseas marketing techniques out of any concern for Bolivian children, but because those companies are competing for their own market. As for that 'sacred leaf' hogwash of yours, that's just one more favorite excuse around here to keep expanding coca production. The truth is, they're quite well aware that 95 percent or more of it is already ending up on the streets as cocaine."

A thunk against the windshield interrupted his tirade, and Doug slowed momentarily for a pack of small boys who were squatting on the meridian, tossing twigs at the cars going by. "For your information," he continued, "far from being a staple of life for the Inca, coca was mainly used for ceremonial reasons and little else. That is, until the Spanish came along—the ancestors of your in-laws, for example—and your friendly *conquistadors* found out what it could do. Pretty useful stuff it turned out to be, especially when they found out where the Incas were getting their silver from. You could send a Quechua miner down into those tiny dark shafts to mine silver or tin for two or three days at a stretch—as long as you kept him well supplied with his pouch of coca and a bit of ash to leach it. No need to feed him or let him rest between shifts. The fact that your miner would be burnt out and dead by age forty didn't matter much. After all, there were plenty more Indians where that one came from."

"I don't believe it!" Sara gasped again, this time with even less conviction. "I thought . . . Nicky said . . . I mean, I thought chewing coca leaf was like a high-powered No Doz!"

"Oh, maybe for a while. But your body has the same needs whether you dull your senses or not. Once the effects wear off, you've got to pay for that lack of sleep or food or water. And in the long run, it does permanent damage to your brain and even affects the intelligence of your children after you. After the Agrarian Reform, coca use actually began to drop as health workers and the *campesinos—*the peasants—started learning what it could do to their bodies. Until the big cocaine craze came along. Then all of a sudden it was everyone's sacred leaf!"

Doug swung the Land Rover around another intersection, this time curving all the way around the circular green to bring them out on the opposite side of the boulevard, where a wide canal bordered the second ring. "Now you've been doing a lot of talking here about how our average neighborhood cocaine dealer is really rather naïve and ignorant of the problems he's causing; that, in actuality, he's doing his level best to work in the best interests of his country."

"That's not what I meant!"

"Let me finish!"

The sharp authority in his voice compelled Sara to obey despite herself. She clamped her mouth shut.

"Okay, I can understand where you're coming from," Doug continued without looking at her. "These are your friends, the people you've gotten to know here, and it's obvious you've picked up some kind of romanticized view of the whole thing. Like they're a bunch of Robin Hoods, stealing from the rich—the Americans—and giving to the poor!"

But they're not my friends! Sara wailed to herself. *I hate all this as much as you do! I was just trying to explain!*

"Well, for your information, these guys couldn't give a hoot about the poor! They're in it for the money, and as long as they get a good share, they couldn't care less if the rest of their country goes right down the drain. Or did you think they volunteer to pay taxes on their ill-gotten gains? If you believe that, take a look at the neighborhoods around most of these fancy mansions. Not even so much as sewers and electricity! As for knowing what kind of harm they're doing, well, you tell me!"

Doug slammed on the brakes, a little more cautiously this time, pulling over to the shoulder as he did so. Climbing out, he strode around to yank open the passenger side of the Land Rover. Unwilling and bewildered, her head still reeling with the hammering of his lecture, Sara stepped down. They were in one of the better parts of Santa Cruz, with pavement everywhere and walled houses and little of the garbage that strewed most of the city's streets. Straight across the canal from where Doug had parked the car was a condominium development, and the brick-and-glass facade and elegant gardens of *El Banquete,* one of the city's finer restaurants.

"Nice neighborhood," Sara said with sarcastic emphasis. "Is there a point I'm missing here?"

"Not up there!" Doug beckoned her over to the rail that edged the canal. "Down here!"

At first, Sara didn't see what Doug found so interesting down in the canal, a V-shaped concrete sluice wide enough and deep enough to hold an entire river of water during the rainy season, but reduced at this time of year to a few inches of sludge. Then she noticed movement in one of the huge drainage outlets that brought the city's runoff into the canal. She stared. *That's a child down there!*

The boy—if it was a boy; the child was too dirty and thin to really tell—couldn't have been more than ten or twelve years old. Curled up in the entrance of the culvert, he appeared to be asleep and unaware of the smoking taper in one of his outflung hands. As Sara watched, the taper must have burned too low because he awoke with a start and a cry of pain. Scrambling to a sitting position, he switched the taper to his other hand then raised it to his mouth while rubbing his burned fingers against the ragged pair of shorts that was all he wore.

A few yards away, a pair of teenagers, gaunt and red-eyed and only slightly better dressed than their neighbor, dangled their legs from the edge of another pipe. They too were smoking, their hands moving in idle conversation as they pulled in long drags of whatever their homemade cigarettes contained. Looking along the canal, Sara realized that all the drainage outlets held human life—young life! Most looked to be teenagers, but some had to be as young as seven or eight. They were stretched out or sitting listlessly against the curved sides of the drain pipes, alone or in groups of two or three. Some held paper bags in which they buried their faces at frequent intervals.

"Who are they?" Sara asked, too appalled to remember that she wasn't on speaking terms with the man next to her. "What are they doing down there?"

"Just a small part of your non-existent Bolivian drug problem," Doug said laconically. "As to what they're doing, they live down there."

When Sara bent over the rail for a closer look, she saw with horror that there were blankets in each of the drains, bunched up into makeshift beds, and backpacks and other meager belongings. In some of the culverts, cardboard boxes were folded flat to give some protection against the chill concrete of the pipe. *What in the world do they do when the rain brings water swirling into the pipes?*

Doug Bradford leaned his forearms on the railing beside her. "What a waste of human life," Sara heard him mutter under his breath. Pulling her eyes away from the canal, she saw that the DEA agent was watching the dismal scene below with an intensity equal to her own, his face somber and with a bitter twist to his mouth. *Why . . . why, he really cares!* she realized with astonishment.

Glancing down and noticing her troubled gaze, Doug relaxed his bleak expression to a half-smile. "Makes those kids at the orphanage look pretty well off, doesn't it?"

Then, seriously, with none of the disapproving undertones she'd felt from him until now, he went on, "Actually, you weren't wrong about one thing. Twenty years ago, people around here *didn't* know much about what cocaine could do. But they're finding out—thanks to the easy availability of the stuff these days! There are thousands of these kids in Santa Cruz now, sleeping in the drains and on park benches, pickpocketing or worse to stay alive and get a high. The stuff those kids over there are smoking is probably cocaine paste— half-processed cocaine that's still laced with kerosene and acetone and who knows what else. You can imagine what their life expectancy is like!"

He gestured toward one of the drains where a pre-teen was sniffing a plastic bag. "And for those who can't afford the few *bolivianos*— which is all the paste costs around here—industrial glue will make them forget their misery for a while."

Sara didn't answer. She couldn't. Across the canal, a skeletal figure staggered to the mouth of one of the drainage pipes. He glanced with glazed, unseeing eyes across the canal, then leaned over and retched. Sara stepped hurriedly back despite the distance that separated her from the dreadful, nauseating splash. Doug straightened up from the railing. "So, do you still think our friendly cocaine dealers have no idea of the damage they're causing?"

Sara swallowed, tried to speak, and swallowed again. But when she finally got her question out, it wasn't any of the ones she'd wanted to ask. "If . . . if you disapprove of my family so much, why did you bother giving me a ride home?"

"I've been asking myself the same thing," Bradford said. "Curiosity, maybe. You're not what I would have expected Nicolás Cortéz to bring home."

"And what did you expect him to *bring home?*" Sara tried for sarcasm, but it didn't come out that way. "No, don't tell me, I know! Another drug-dealer like the rest of the family! That's what you think of me, don't you?"

"No, I don't!" Doug said unexpectedly. The stern line of his mouth softened a little. "I think you're a nice girl caught up in something far too serious for you to comprehend. You have no idea what you're messing with, Sara, and if I thought you'd listen, I'd suggest strongly that you head right back home to North America—and take that husband of yours with you, if you could get him to go!"

Doug hesitated, then reached into his pocket and took out his wallet. Pulling out a card, he scribbled on it. "Look, I know you're not too happy with me right now, and maybe I have said too much. But, well—if you ever have a problem or need help, I just want you to know that you can give me a call—any time. Here's my cell-phone number."

He held out the card. Sara took it gingerly, as though it were something that might bite. In the left-hand corner was a gold seal like a police badge with an eagle on top. In the middle was Doug Bradford's name, and in Spanish underneath was the declaration: *Agente Especial. Embajada de los Estados Unidos.* Across the bottom was scrawled a phone number. Sara looked at the bold, black numbers for a long moment. Then, deliberately, she ripped the card into quarters, tossing the pieces over the rail and watching them float down into the canal.

"I don't need your help," she said stiffly. "My husband is quite capable of taking care of any problem I might have. Now, if you'll excuse me, this has all been very educational, but I think I've had enough of your propaganda for one day." Turning hard on her heel, she walked away so fast that she almost tripped over her high heels. Or maybe it was the tears that for the second time that day insisted on blurring her vision.

"Hey, now just a minute!"

Ignoring the call from behind her, Sara waved frantically at an oncoming taxi. It wasn't until the white Toyota Corolla station wagon screeched to a halt beside her that she saw the Radiomóvil Cortéz sticker on the windshield. The driver wasn't one she'd seen before, but it was evident that he recognized her.

"Señora Cortéz!" he greeted her with ill-concealed surprise. His black eyes roved from Sara to the four-wheel-drive vehicle pulled up beside the canal to the man striding toward them. Yanking open the back door, Sara scrambled in. "Take me home, please," she ordered breathlessly. "Hurry!"

"*Sí, señora!*" Obediently, the driver accelerated away from the side of the road, leaving Doug Bradford standing in a shower of gravel.

Boy, you sure made a mess of that! Doug brushed the dust and small pieces of gravel from his clothes as he watched the taxi disappear into the flow of traffic. He could have kicked himself for letting it end this way. *Wouldn't Ramon laugh if he could see the lack of finesse I just displayed with* this *interview!*

Doug strode resolutely back to the Land Rover. Better get back to his guests, who were probably wondering what had happened to their host.

The offer to drive Sara Cortéz home had been an impulse, as much to ease Laura's concern as anything, and he hadn't intended to be gone so long. He still wasn't sure why he'd bothered. Until today, he had scrupulously followed Grant Major's orders to leave the whole Cortéz thing alone—except for his equally impulsive request of Kyle Martin to run a background check on Sara. But even when Kyle had wordlessly handed him an impressively comprehensive intelligence sheet, Doug had tossed the report aside with no more than a fleeting thought about Nicolás Cortéz's impeccable taste in women.

He'd been surprised to see Sara in the worship service this morning—his acquaintance with the Cortezes hadn't led him to believe that church attendance played any part of their agenda—but not duly interested. Yet the distress she had tried so hard to conceal during Pastor Sam's message had aroused both his sympathy and professional curiosity. And when she'd started spouting that secondhand mixture of half-truths and misinformation they'd been feeding her, he'd experienced an overwhelming urge to shake some sense into her.

Which is precisely what I didn't manage to do! Doug admitted ruefully, putting the Land Rover in gear and pulling away from the canal. Sara Cortéz was as stubborn as his own Julie had been when it came to conceding she was wrong.

In fact, she reminded him of his wife in more ways than one.

Not in appearance, of course! Julie had been a long-legged brunette. But this Sara had that same spark of temper, called forth by a
perceived injustice or unkindness. That same fierce, loyal defense of
those she loved—regardless of the facts, Doug remembered with a
wry twist of his lips. And that same deep compassion his wife had
displayed for anything weak, small, or oppressed.

Julie! The familiar pain was there, but for once Doug accepted it,
let it flow over him for the sweetness of the memories it brought.
The rock in the turbulent sea of his daily life. The assurance, after
dealing with scumbags and filth until it seemed the whole world was
one seething sore, that there was still warmth and love and tenderness worth fighting for.

His wife had never liked the danger that Doug faced on the job
every day, but she'd accepted it with the same cheerful resignation
with which she had accepted all the vagaries of life. She hadn't even
objected when he'd decided to leave the Miami PD to buck for a
position with the DEA, though by then they'd been expecting their
first child. Her faith had always been the deeper of the two, and
she'd been able to release Doug to God's protection each morning
with a serenity that astonished those who knew only her outer
effervescence.

That danger might strike her instead of him never occurred to
either of them.

Doug had been on a stakeout when headquarters called. And
Julie, his rock, his love, had been gone long before he ever made it
to the hospital—along with the tiny son they'd so eagerly awaited,
still two months short of his due date.

And his daughter! Little Esther Rose, named for another beauty
who'd lived thousands of years earlier. A bubbling imp, with her
mother's thick, dark curls and mischievous grin, she'd known—even
at age two—how tightly her daddy's heart was wrapped around her
finger. Two years! That's all the life she'd known before a trio of
joyriding teenagers collided with the Bradfords' car, scraping Esther's
car seat out of the front seat and her father's heart out of his breast.

No, that hurts too much! Doug's hands tightened convulsively on
the wheel as he willed away the memory of that diminutive, laughing
face. There was a pain in losing a child that was like no other. That
your parents should go before you, or even a beloved wife, was a
natural, though grievous, part of the flow of life. But that a child
should leave a parent behind, that the very flesh of his flesh and bone
of his bone should lie broken, her fingers flaccid and unresponsing
in her father's desperate grip—surely God never intended this to be!

Doug had never imagined the bottom could be so far down. He couldn't even find release in hating the boys who'd destroyed the center of his universe. They were suffering their own private hell, their own young lives haunted by a single lighthearted decision they would regret for the rest of their years. Instead, he'd put in for overseas duty. It didn't matter where as long as it was far away from the white-framed house where every corner held memories of a little girl, where the sudden glimpse of a tall, long-legged figure would send him racing to follow a complete stranger down the street. Better to go where the children would be chattering in another language, where a sudden "Daddy" overheard on the streets wouldn't wrench at his heartstrings.

So he'd come to Bolivia. It had been four years, and though he'd once told Pastor Sam he'd never forget, it had grown easier with time. The early anger had given way to a deepened faith that drove him to his knees when the pain became too much to bear. If he still didn't understand why God hadn't chosen to intervene, then he'd at least learned to accept it. He had friends—good ones who accepted what little he could give them and demanded no more—and a job that needed to be done, and for now that was enough.

This Sara Cortéz knew what it was like to go through such loss, Doug mused, turning onto his own street. The similarity of their circumstances had struck him even as he'd tossed aside Kyle's report, and maybe it was the knowledge that she was alone in the world, outside of that Cortéz bunch he wouldn't trust the length of his arm, that had prompted him to that indiscreet offer of help. Not that it had done any good! He'd only managed to alienate the girl, who was doubtless on her way home to tell hubby all about it. Which just might bring Nicolás Cortéz screaming down on the DEA office, with a justification this time that would have Grant Major nailing Doug's hide to the wall.

And yet he couldn't regret the warning, because the instinct that had failed him only once with these very same people persisted in telling him she might need it. He just hoped that this time he was wrong!

CHAPTER ELEVEN

Sara sat tense and straight in the middle of the back seat as the taxi sped down the road. She was shaking with anger, shock, and confusion. She clenched her hands in her lap. How could that man suggest that she might need help against her own husband? And just when she'd been willing to forgive all the other awful things he'd said!

She tried to arouse her former indignation against the DEA agent, but she managed only a momentary flare. The somber concern she'd seen on his face back there at the canal was too fresh in her mind. Justice compelled her to admit that the man seemed to genuinely care about his job and the people affected by the drug traffic he was trying to stamp out. And though it seemed disloyal to admit he could be right, Sara had to acknowledge that much of what he'd said tallied with what she'd heard from Gabriela and others.

But not about Nicky! There he was wrong, wrong, wrong! Okay, so maybe there were people like the Salviettis who really were all those things he'd said. But not the Cortezes! Doug Bradford had started out with a preconceived idea, that was all there was to it, and then tried to force all the facts to fit it without even considering other, more innocent, interpretations.

Rrrr-inng! It took Sara several seconds to realize that the shrill signal was coming from her own purse. Unearthing her cell phone, she fumbled with the keypad. Another first for Sara, Nicolás had ordered the phone for her just last week and insisted she carry it everywhere.

When a final stab lit up the screen, she raised the small oblong to her ear. "Yes?"

"Sara?" The word was as clear as though it came from the front seat of the taxi.

"Nicky!" Only now, when she heard his voice, did Sara realize just how much she wanted to see her husband. To have him laugh and tease and kiss away all her doubts and questions. "Oh, Nicky, you're back! Where are you right now?"

"Certainly not anywhere you're thinking!" he answered with amusement. "I'm out at the hacienda."

"At the hacienda? But—" Sara bit back her disappointment. "You have a phone at the hacienda? I thought it was out in the jungle!"

"Hey, we're in the age of modern communications. Who needs a phone? Anyway, I'm just calling to let you know I won't be home for a couple more days. Things are pretty busy here right now." Nicolás was clearly in a good mood, his voice high with elation.

"I take it everything's going well?" Sara said.

"You'd better believe it! Papá is going to be impressed with this one! Maybe now he'll see that I can get the job done as well as Vargas." Belatedly, Nicolás added, "So what have you been up to?"

"Well, I went to church this morning. And guess where else? Your old home." Sara went on to tell him briefly of the orphanage. "They told me it used to belong to your family."

"So that's what they've done with that place!" Nicolás answered carelessly. "And what did you think? Quite a dump, isn't it? It was falling apart even when I was a kid. The best thing Papá ever did was to unload that place off onto the *alcaldía*. For top dollar, too, since his uncle was mayor at the time."

And that, Sara told herself, was the obvious answer to Doug Bradford's most unsettling insinuation—the source of the capital needed to launch *Industrias Cortéz*. She'd simply misunderstood Nicolás earlier. He'd said that they'd turned the place over to the *alcaldía*. She'd assumed he was referring to a gift. Still, that left one other troubling question.

Sara hesitated, not wanting to upset her husband's good mood. But her disquiet was too great. Taking a deep breath, she said, "Guess who else I saw at the orphanage? That girl from the warehouse—María."

"María." Nicky's tone was blank.

"You know, the one who got in trouble with Julio Vargas for helping me with those hangings?" Sara couldn't keep a quaver out of her voice. "Nicky, she says you fired her—you and Don Luis. After I left that afternoon. Nicky, you . . . you didn't!" Then, doubtfully, "Did you?"

Nicolás's annoyance came right across the airwaves. "Look, I'm sorry!" he said defensively. "Okay, so I promised I'd take care of it. But there was nothing I could do. When it comes right down to it,

Vargas is a lot more valuable to Cortéz Industries than one little *cholita*. To make him lose face by rescinding her dismissal would undermine his authority with the workers. Surely even you can see that much! Besides, she did know the rules and she did break them, no matter what kind of an excuse she tries to offer. We can't maintain discipline if we're going to start allowing exceptions. Papá backed Vargas all the way."

"He would!" Sara said, but under her breath. "You could have told me the truth, Nicky," she said to her husband, adding with a hint of bitterness, "instead of letting me assume that a request of mine actually carried any weight over there!"

"I didn't tell you because I knew you'd be upset," Nicolás said impatiently. "And what's the big deal, anyway? You said she's already got another job!"

Before Sara could respond, he added, "Look, I've got to go. Vargas is waiting for me. See you in a couple days."

Then he was gone, the irritating tone of a dead line replacing his voice. Slowly Sara folded the cell phone and returned it to her purse. What a horrible day this had turned out to be! And now Nicolás wouldn't be home for two whole days.

Nor could she so easily dismiss María's firing. Maybe Nicky's reasoning made sense from a business viewpoint, but it still wasn't right, and it angered and frustrated Sara that Julio Vargas had won the battle of wills.

Leaning back against the seat, Sara wearily closed her eyes. She didn't want to think about broken promises and angry DEA agents and treacherous employees. Her mind went instead to the things she'd seen that day—those lost, unloved, *young* faces. How could she be so concerned with her own petty problems when there were so many others out there who were hurting so much more?

Wait a minute!

Sara's eyes flew open. Hadn't she said she wanted a job? Well, here was one staring her in the face. Laura had mentioned that Doña Inez needed volunteers. And even Nicolás couldn't object to her helping out a few hours a week at that orphanage. Sara sat up straight, eagerness banishing her despondency. She'd check it out first thing tomorrow.

Lounging against the tailgate of the army truck slanted across the road, Doug watched Ramon steer a small black mongrel around the rear of a donkey cart. The sun was just lightening to dawn above the jungle canopy, awakening a roosting flock of macaws that took off abruptly with a thunder of wings, their raucous screams drowning out the sudden vociferous barking of the dog. Doug took a deep breath of the damp sweetness that would become a cloying sauna later in the day. It had been a week since he and Ramon had left Santa Cruz for temporary duty—TDY—in the Chapare, and he had yet to miss the air-conditioning and padded seat of his office.

His mood soured a little as his gaze fell on a clearing beside the road, just becoming visible in the growing light. The vegetation dotting the terrain was heavy and green. Doug's gray eyes grew bleak. The Chapare was one of the prettiest spots he'd ever seen, with its luxurious rain forest, exotic orchids, and soil rich enough to grow any variety of crops. Too bad it also had to be the best soil in the world for growing coca. As a result, what could have been one of the most productive agricultural regions of Bolivia had become little more than a vast cocaine lab, its jungle marred by coca plantings, its streams and ground water increasingly poisoned by the deadly runoff of maceration pits and production sites.

"Hey, Doug!" Handing the canine's leash off to one of the *Leopardo* troops, Ramon walked over from the roadblock. Wearing the same camouflage fatigues and floppy-brimmed hat as the soldiers, the wiry Latino was indistinguishable from the other men, an advantage Doug, with his bigger frame and light hair and eyes, could envy. "Take a look at what Blackie picked up."

Doug took the sardine tin with a smothered yawn. The two agents and the *Leopardo* unit had been staking out this lonely jungle track since the early hours of the morning, part of Ramon's introduction to the Chapare, center of Bolivia's coca and cocaine production, as well as a training exercise for these latest recruits. The *Leopardo*s were the Special Forces branch of UMOPAR, FELCN's country cousins, and Doug, a Ranger graduate from Fort Benning, had long been involved in their training. He'd chosen this particular location because of rumors—which could be every bit as accurate as the finest DEA intelligence—that the newly finished dirt road, built with U.S. aid to the region, was becoming a favorite new bypass for the FELCN drug checks on the main highway.

And it seemed the rumors had been correct. Doug turned the sardine tin over. The slit along the edge of the lid would have been barely perceptible if Ramon hadn't pried it up to display the solid white cake underneath. The younger agent dropped down onto the tailgate beside Doug.

"How he got that in there without touching the lid is really something. Must have sucked out the fish and pumped the stuff in liquid. We'd never have caught it if it hadn't been for our canine pal. What these guys will think up next!"

Doug nodded absently, his attention drawn to a Nissan Safari that was pulling up to the roadblock. It was a nice rig, absolutely gleaming with the perfection of its paint job—a deep navy blue that would have been indistinguishable against the night sky an hour earlier. The driver's face was shaded by a tipped-down sombrero, but Doug could see the man's fingers drumming against the door. A nervous reaction that probably meant nothing. He'd be skeptical of anyone who *didn't* show unease when a band of soldiers pulled him to the side of the road.

Doug cut into Ramon's explanation. "I'll be right back."

Striding over to the roadblock, he sauntered leisurely around the Safari as the *Leopardos* performed their usual thorough shakedown—tires, seats, the odds and ends strewn about the back. The search turned up no suspiciously thick walls, no compartments whose interior size didn't measure up to their exterior, no unexplained weapons, not so much as a whine from their K-9 patrol. The soldiers were just dropping the rope across the road when Doug stopped them with a gesture. Walking around to the back of the Safari, he studied the interior. It too had been freshly painted.

Doug crawled inside. Pulling a knife from a pocket on the side of his boot, he ran it along one of the stitched seams of the ceiling lining, one eye on the driver, who was morosely watching the search from between two guards. When alarm flickered across the man's defiant expression, Doug plunged the razor-sharp blade into the padded material, making two swift cuts. The driver surged forward against the sudden grip of the guards. "You can't do that! You are destroying private property!"

"Can't I?" Doug answered grimly. Ripping back a triangular piece of fabric, he carefully worked free a plastic-wrapped white package the size of a small manila envelope and not more than a half-inch thick. Tossing the packet to the nearest *Leopardo*, he clambered back out of the Safari. "It's all yours, boys."

The driver cursed and screamed as the *Leopardos* peeled off the rest of the ceiling liner and went on to the wall panels. He had reason to be distraught. The entire interior was one solid layer of cocaine, not more than a half-inch thick anywhere and virtually undetectable under the false paneling. It was one of the best jobs of concealment Doug had ever seen.

"So how did you know it was there?" Ramon demanded with chagrin as the two agents took advantage of a break in traffic to eat breakfast. "I didn't see a thing."

"Experience, my dear boy," Doug told him loftily, slitting open a couple of MRE rations and tossing one to the younger agent. "It takes a special nose, see? A sixth sense, you might say. Kind of like that canine over there. You keep working at it, and in another twenty years you might be just about as good as I was five years back."

Doug fended off a plastic fork that came flying at his head, then the cardboard box that had contained Ramon's loaf of bread. "Okay! Okay! It was the fresh paint job. No one in these parts would waste money painting a car like that unless they had something to hide. He should have dirtied it up and added a scratch or two."

This last comment was offered in a raised voice, and in Spanish. The glare it drew from their prisoner was pure poison.

Ramon watched with a sardonic eye as the *Leopardos* led the prisoner away. "Never thought I'd see the day when Ramon 'the Snake' Gutierrez was reduced to baby-sitting raw recruits!" he complained, only half-joking. "Not that I haven't appreciated the jungle tour. But I left L.A. to get a bigger piece of the action, not to stand around in the back, handing out advice and playing it safe. Seems that's all we do around here!"

"Oh, I don't know about that." Doug stirred a package of juice powder into his canteen. The grape flavor wasn't improved by the chemically purified water he was carrying, but Doug no longer noticed.

"We get our share of action here. It's just a different kind. Like— well, you might say you've graduated from street hockey to chess. Except that you get to be the chess master instead of the pawn. Going after a gang that you *know* is bringing dope into your streets. Only these are no neighborhood pushers. You've finally got a chance to stop the 'big fish' at the source. Piecing together the puzzle until you've got that last bit of intel. Building your strategy until you can take down the whole rat's nest in one shot. Then—springing the trap. Now *that's* what I call fun! For an adrenaline rush, it beats taking out a bad guy on your own any day. And, every once in a while, you might even find out you've made a difference!"

The two agents mirrored the same savage grin. "Yeah, maybe!" Ramon admitted.

A sudden shrill ring sent both agents groping for their cell phones. Doug flipped his open, then raised his eyebrows at Ramon. "Speaking of action—!"

✠

Doug kicked at the charred tire. It was the same modus operandi all right. The crumpled shell of a crash-landed plane, this one a four-engine DC-6 rather than René's DC-3. The stitching of machine gun fire across the fuselage. The landing marks of a helicopter trampled into the grass of the airstrip. Traces of a large load of coke in the back.

Only these guys hadn't been as lucky as René.

Blanking his mind to the stench of burnt flesh, Doug walked slowly around the blistered fuselage. The fuel tank, leaking from a half-dozen bullet holes, had burst into flames upon contact with the ground. Traces of CO_2 foam in the cargo hold explained why the entire plane hadn't been consumed, but it had evidently arrived too late for the blackened shapes in the cockpit that had once been men. Or perhaps the firefighters had simply been more interested in saving the plane's cargo than its human occupants.

Leaving Ramon scraping and bagging samples with the Leopardo troops, Doug hunkered down to study the broken grass stems and rotor-scattered dirt of the helicopter's landing. Definitely military in size, judging by the length and position of the landing runners. He touched an indentation in the soft ground. Wasn't that a tire mark? Yes, there was more of the pattern. Not from the DC-6 either. More like that of a smaller Cessna.

Doug walked slowly along the grass strip. The signs were easy enough to read for the experienced eye. The Cessna had landed further down the airstrip, then taxied over to the burned-out plane to take on a load of its own. So, the rogue Huey wasn't alone in this operation. But was this new addition a superior or an employee?

The Leopardo unit was finishing its preliminary investigation. The fire damage had been enough to render the DC-6 inoperable, but it hadn't touched the registration numbers or more than scorched the contents of the two dead men's wallets. That was one scant blessing, anyway. Identification just might lead to the band of narcos who'd put together this sizable haul in the first place.

But Doug was frowning as he climbed back into the Huey that had ferried them from the roadblock. It was those volteadores he'd really like to ID. That they were Orejuela's rescuers—or kidnappers—was a given. But just who were they? Not Orejuela himself, he'd stake his pension on that. The hit was too smooth for that lowlife's bumbling operation. No, this one was someone a whole lot smarter than Orejuela. And someone who, along with the obvious military link, had major connections within the underworld of drug trafficking to know just where to hit two of the biggest cocaine shipments Doug had ever seen. The sheer quantity staggered the imagination.

The DC-6 was slightly larger than a DC-3, and judging by the signs, it had held close to five tons. Add three tons from the other hijacking. That was eight tons in a matter of weeks! Hundreds of millions of dollars when sold on the streets of the United States or Europe. Of course, moving that much cocaine across the border was the hard part. What were they planning? Another attempted flight into Colombia or Brazil? Piecemeal smuggling? Or were those tons already out of the country?

Doug found no answers as he watched the blackened remains of the aircraft drop away below him. But he had no intention of letting it stop here. Bringing down the owner of that DC-6 might put a temporary dent in the country's drug flow. But if they could get their hands on those *volteadores* and their eight tons, they'd have the biggest bust in the history of the DEA in Bolivia.

Chapter Twelve

The maid's quiet knock brought Sara to the bedroom door. *"Teléfono, señora."*

"Thank you, Carmelita. I'll be right there." Sara finished brushing her hair with a few quick strokes and hurried down the stairs to the phone.

"Hello? Oh, good morning, Doña Inez."

"Good morning, Sara." The director sounded exhausted and desperate. "I know you were not planning to come to the home today, but I wonder if you would be available to help us for only a few hours. Several of our helpers have come down with this flu that is going around, and ten of the younger children are also sick. I don't know how we're going to care for everyone today."

Sara took a quick mental inventory of her plans for the day. There was the fiesta scheduled for tonight, of course, but Mimi had arrangements for the party well under control and had made it clear that she neither needed nor welcomed help. *Actually, it might be better if I'm out of the way,* Sara decided, *and I'll be back in plenty of time before Nicky gets home from work.* "Yes, Doña Inez, I can come in. I'll be there just as soon as I can."

As soon as she hung up the phone, Sara picked up the receiver again and dialed the now familiar number for Radiomóvil Cortéz. Ninety minutes later, she was elbow deep in soiled linens as she changed an unending line of soggy toddlers.

Sara didn't allow her heart to play favorites among the small scraps of humanity she cared for at *Hogar de Infantes,* but if she had a favorite, it might have been Carina, a tousle-headed little girl named after the ice-cream store in front of which she'd been abandoned at a scant six weeks of age. When Carina's turn on the changing table came, Sara was pleasantly surprised to find a dry diaper. She used the extra seconds to tickle the little girl's toes, trying to coax out one of the shy smiles with which Carina had finally begun to reward her attentions. But the toddler seemed listless, and Sara suddenly realized that the tiny body under her hands was dangerously warm; her skin was paper-dry. When Sara pinched a fold of skin, the imprints of her fingers remained in the toddler's flesh, an even more definite sign of dehydration than the dry diaper.

Sara wasn't immediately concerned. A fair scattering of the children had already come down with the same strain of flu that had debilitated their keepers. She coaxed the toddler into swallowing a teaspoonful of infant Tylenol, tucked a digital thermometer under her arm, and sent María to call the home nurse.

The thermometer beeped its readiness, and Carina chose that exact moment to heave up the Tylenol along with her lunch. Grabbing for a clean diaper to swab at her blouse, Sara glanced at the digital readout. *Forty-one Centigrade. That's 106 degrees!* She hardly had time to panic before Carina lapsed into convulsions.

Sara had never felt so helpless in her life. Carina's eyes were rolled back in her head, and her limbs quivered so uncontrollably that Sara had to hold her down on the changing table. Sara's remaining helper was a mere teenager, and she was more panic-stricken than Sara—wringing her hands and wailing even as Sara shouted at her to help. By now, Sara could no longer detect a breath through the toddler's lips, which were rapidly turning cyanosis-blue. This baby was dying in front of her very eyes, and if anything were to be done, Sara would have to do it herself. Dredging up memories of the first-aid course she'd taken as part of her teacher's training, Sara snatched the toddler up in her arms and raced for the nearest source of water, a faucet at the bottom of the outside staircase where buckets were filled for cleaning.

The little girl's body was limp by the time Sara reached the patio, and she was afraid it was too late even as she turned the faucet on full blast and thrust the toddler under the cool spray. But when she checked for a pulse, it was there, and though the child remained unconscious, her breathing grew easier and the frightening blue color left her lips as the cool water lowered her body temperature to a less deadly level. Sara held the toddler under the faucet for a full ten minutes, getting thoroughly soaked in the process, and when María finally showed up to say there was no nurse available, Sara sent her off to find Doña Inez and call for medical assistance. But here she ran into a snag. Doña Inez had stepped out to take care of some paperwork over at the children's welfare office, and it seemed that none of the remaining helpers had the authority even to call a doctor.

"Then call a taxi," Sara said decisively. "I'm taking this baby to the hospital." Wrapping Carina's tiny form in a dry towel, Sara went to the front door to wait for the cab. When the Toyota station wagon pulled up in front, Sara jumped into the back seat and gave the driver directions to the exclusive private clinic used by members of the Cortéz family. Here again, she ran into unexpected difficulties.

Taking one look at Sara's damp, vomit-stained clothes and the towel-wrapped baby in her arms, the receptionist sniffed disdainfully.

"I'm sorry, señora, but we cannot accept this child for treatment unless the fees have been paid in full in advance."

Sara rummaged in her purse, looking for her wallet, but she had bought a load of powdered milk for the children on her way to the orphanage, and there was little more than another taxi fare left. "Look," she said imploringly, "my name is Sara de Cortéz. My husband, Nicolás Cortéz, will guarantee payment for whatever needs to be done. His company has an account here. *Industrias Cortéz.* You must have heard of it."

The receptionist thawed measurably. "You have identification that will show that Nicolás Cortéz is your husband?"

"Well, of course his name isn't on my papers, but you can see from my driver's license that my married name is Cortéz." As the receptionist hesitated, Sara reached into her purse and slapped a credit card on the counter beside her ID. "Look, take my Visa card if you want, but this little girl is going to die unless you treat her immediately!"

By the time Sara finally lifted Carina onto the examining table, the little girl's fever was soaring again, her wet clothes steaming dry on her thin little body. By now she had regained consciousness and was screaming with terror at the strange, sterile environment, the bright lights and exploring hands, the needles probing for blood samples. She scrambled, sobbing, into Sara's arms. Sara was relieved that the girl had recognized her.

That has *to be a good sign.*

The emergency intern nodded approval when Sara explained her rough first aid. Her quick action in lowering the toddler's lethally dangerous body temperature had certainly saved her from permanent brain damage, possibly even death.

Sara stayed by Carina's side until Doña Inez rushed in several hours later, horrified, yet grateful, to find the young orphan girl in such luxurious surroundings. The ibuprofen the intern had injected had taken effect, and Carina's fever was dropping. Even so, Sara made arrangements to have the little girl admitted for the night.

Then, exhausted, she dialed the number for Radiomóvil Cortéz to order a taxi to take her home.

It wasn't until the cab neared the Cortéz mansion that Sara remembered the *fiesta*. A line of parked cars extended the full length of the outside wall, curving around the corners to fill the alleys on either side. More crowded the driveway as the taxi jounced over the drainage canal and through the open gate—sleek, new Mitsubishi Monteros, Nissan Patrols, Toyota Landcruisers, and a variety of other all-terrain vehicles, the status symbols of a society where even the wealthy had to contend with rutted roads and muddy, unpaved streets.

"Just drop me here." Sara handed a bill over the back of the front seat. Clambering out, she checked her watch as the taxi backed away. The grounds were bright with extra floodlights added for the occasion and strings of colored bulbs threaded through the trees, and Sara had no problem reading the position of the tiny gold hands on her Rolex. She groaned inwardly. *Nine-thirty!* Unacceptably tardy, even here where the better-class restaurants didn't open until eight or eight-thirty at night. *Nicolás is going to kill me!*

A few strolling couples turned to stare curiously as Sara hurried up the drive, and an acquaintance, whose name she couldn't remember, hailed her from the veranda. Sara, self-consciously aware of her disheveled appearance, pretended not to hear the summons as she ran breathlessly up the cobbled steps. The door into the stone turret was standing open, attended by a white-aproned maid. Her dark eyes opened wide when she saw Sara, but she immediately schooled her chocolate-brown features back to their customary impassive expression.

Sara realized too late that if she'd wanted to make an unobtrusive entrance, she should have taken the longer route through one of the side doors where she could have escaped upstairs unseen. The vast drawing room to her left was crowded with glittering party frocks and dinner jackets and the white coats of waiters who moved among the guests with trays of appetizers and drinks. Down the wide, portrait-lined hall, the double doors of the ballroom stood open. An overflow from the dance floor had spilled out into the hall, chattering and laughing and sipping from long-stemmed crystal goblets like a flock of vividly colored macaws from the jungle outside Santa Cruz.

Sara threaded her way through the throng as quickly as she could, acknowledging the raised eyebrows and surprised greetings with a faint, apologetic smile and tilted chin. As she passed the first set of double doors, Sara glanced inside the ballroom, where a live band in black tuxedos was belting out the latest hit song from Mexico.

She quickened her steps when she glimpsed her sister-in-law Janéth swinging her ample hips in the frenetic steps of the *macarena* only meters away. *If I can just reach the stairs without running into a member of the family* . . .

As Sara came abreast of the second set of ballroom doors, a pair of dancers whirled out into the hall. Sara had to move quickly to avoid tripping over their fancy footwork, and she was just murmuring an apology when she realized who the couple was. Nicolás—looking incredibly handsome in a dark-blue tuxedo that captured the brilliance of his eyes, his head tossed back in laughter—and Reina!

Nicky's cousin was the first to notice Sara. Stopping her dance partner with a hand on his chest, she remarked sweetly, "Why Sara, *querida,* we thought you'd decided not to show tonight."

Nicolás whirled around, the laughter draining from his face as he caught sight of Sara. Releasing Reina, he took a step toward his wife. "Sara, where in the world have you been?" The question was that of a concerned husband, but the glitter in his eyes and the flare of his nostrils told Sara, who was beginning to recognize the signs, that he was in a towering rage. "Have you any idea what time it is?"

"Don't scold her, Nico, *querido!*" Reina slipped her arm around her cousin's back, pressing herself close to his side, her green eyes flickering from Nicolás to Sara with avid interest. She was looking her best in a black-sequined spandex mini-dress that left her shoulders bare and clung to her curves in a way that left little to the imagination. Her perfectly applied makeup and piled-up hairdo, combined with Nicolás's casual elegance, left Sara even more conscious of her own disarray. "Can't you see she's had a hard day? Your little orphans, was it not?"

Nicolás took stock of Sara's appearance for the first time and his lips tightened into a thin line. "Sara, what have you been doing to yourself?" Extricating himself from Reina's grasp, he spun Sara around and propelled her down the hall. "If you'll excuse us, Reina," he said pointedly over his shoulder.

"Hurry back, Nico," Reina murmured throatily. "I'm saving the next dance for you."

Nicky's only response was an impatient flick of his fingers. *That girl watches too many American movies,* Sara thought wryly but without any real jealousy, watching Reina saunter away with a wink over one bare shoulder, even as Nicolás grabbed Sara by the arm. Much as she resented the other girl's blatant flirting, she knew how little it meant to Nicolás, who took his cousin's attentions for granted as he did all the women who flattered him, hung on him, and fell in love with him at the drop of a hat. *Like I did!*

Just around the corner, Nicolás pulled Sara to a stop. The foyer wasn't completely empty, but Nicolás ignored the couple cuddling in one corner as he repeated in a low, hard voice, "Where have you been, Sara? I want an answer—now!" He looked her up and down with disgust. "And what in the world have you done to yourself? You smell like—like vomit!"

Glancing into the mirror behind Nicolás, Sara saw herself for the first time. Her fine cornsilk hair lay tousled and limp, complementing her wrinkled skirt and blouse with the damp stains she had tried so hard to wash out. The paleness of exhaustion showed on her face under her light tan, and her eyes were rimmed with black smudges from the combination of tears and her supposedly waterproof mascara. She pushed the tangle of hair back from her face and forced a smile. "I'm sorry, Nicky. We had an emergency at the children's home. I honestly forgot about the party until I came in just now."

She raised her eyes, hoping for a glimmer of forgiveness or a hint of understanding. But Nicolás's eyes were remote and unforgiving. "You weren't at the children's home. I called there several times."

"I was at the hospital," Sara explained wearily. "One of the babies was sick. I know I should have called, but—well, things got a little later than we planned. I came home as soon as I could get away. I'm really sorry I was late for your party."

"I'm sorry, too!" Nicolás responded in the same hard voice. "Sorry you thought some beggar brat was more important than being here with me. Now hurry up and get changed before anyone else sees you like this!"

Sara felt the glare of her husband's disapproval on her back as she hurried up the stairs. She didn't blame him for being irritated. She felt terrible about her tardiness herself. This evening's *fiesta* wasn't the first social event the Cortezes had hosted since Nicolás's return from college, but it was the biggest, and she should have been here to greet their guests. It wasn't entirely her fault, but Nicky hadn't even given her a chance to explain.

Not that it would have done much good if she had. It seemed to take less and less these days to trigger her husband's explosive anger. And though they always made up later—Sara apologizing, Nicolás brushing off the incident as though it had never happened—the repeated conflict was causing a tension and uncertainty in their relationship.

Dampness stung Sara's eyes. Sometimes it seemed that everything had gone straight downhill ever since that ill-starred visit to the English church three weeks ago. She just didn't understand!

Nicky, on his return from the hacienda, had given his full approval to her volunteer work at the *Hogar de Infantes*. True, that had only been after her mother-in-law, who had no idea what Sara actually did over there, approved it as a suitable charity. And even Mimi had been clicking her tongue lately over the hours Sara was putting in. But Sara had been careful to arrange her schedule so that it conflicted as little as possible with any time Nicolás might have to spend with her. This was the first time she had ever been out into the evening.

And that was what bothered her. How many times in the last two months had she waited for hours on Nicolás because he'd gotten caught up in something at the office? Or eaten dinner with only Mimi for company? Or sat alone in their suite in the evening, not even knowing where her husband was, only that he was presumably on company business with Don Luis or Julio Vargas?

Never once had she complained. And yet, if Nicolás came home unexpectedly to find her at the children's home, even though she kept him well posted on her volunteer schedule, she could expect an evening of recriminations and sulky silences. Oddly enough, she could be out shopping or with a friend, and he didn't seem to mind that at all!

Sara paused on the third landing just outside their bedroom suite to rub her fingertips across her forehead. These last hours had been terrifying and exhausting and thoroughly unpleasant, and the only thing that warmed her was the knowledge that a tousle-headed little girl was alive and lying in a clean hospital bed because she'd taken action in time. It would have been nice to be caressed a little, told that she was a heroine, and offered a shoulder on which to shed a few relieved tears.

"Sara?" A hand on her shoulder caused Sara to whirl around, startled.

Her hand flew to her throat. Then she saw Nicolás. She had been so deep in thought, she hadn't heard his footsteps coming up behind her. She relaxed, but only a fraction, her heart still beating in double time. "You scared me! What's the matter?"

"Nothing's the matter." Nicolás reached past her to push open the door to their suite. "I just figured I'd make sure you were coming back down. Knowing you, you'd be stricken with another sudden headache and not show up at all!"

Sara stiffened and pulled away. Only once had she ever used that excuse—and then, as it would be now, it had been genuine. She *did* have a headache, and if Nicolás had exhibited the slightest sympathy, she might have admitted it. Instead, she reminded herself again that he had every reason to be irritated, squared her slim shoulders, and slipped past him into the suite.

"You really don't have to wait for me," she told him quietly, shaking out a couple of Tylenol from a bottle on the dresser before heading for the shower. "I promise I won't try to escape."

"No, I'll wait," Nicolás answered curtly. "Just hurry up."

Throwing himself into an armchair, he picked up the remote control from the coffee table. When Sara came out of the bathroom less than five minutes later, he was channel surfing. He had undone the top three buttons of his ruffled shirt and loosened his collar, and Sara could see the gleam of gold against the bronze of his throat. True to his word, he'd worn the Cortéz cross since the day they'd found it, not removing it even in the shower.

"So what was the deal with the kid?" Nicolás asked belatedly as Sara began running her blow-dryer down her long hair.

Sara briefly recounted the events of the day, but if she was hoping to soften her husband's mood, it didn't work. Nicolás sat upright, his eyes darkening to storm warnings even before she finished. "You what? You took that kid to our clinic? What did you do that for? These institutions have their own doctors, you know, not to mention the state children's hospital, for cases like this. Why didn't you take the kid over there? Or send someone else and come home? It's not like it was your responsibility. And if you looked like you did just now when you went in there, I can't imagine what they must have thought of you. I just hope you didn't bring the Cortéz name into it!"

Sara didn't answer that. "Have you been to the state children's hospital?" she asked wearily, trying to ignore the pounding in her temples. "Well, I have, and I wouldn't send my dog over there! They don't have medicine or proper nursing care—or even clean sheets half the time. And you can lay around all day, waiting for a doctor to pay you any attention! Last time I was there, they were all on strike."

"These people aren't used to fancy care," Nicolás assured her impatiently. "They wouldn't even feel comfortable in a decent clinic. Or a clean one, either, for that matter. Speaking of which, who paid for all this, anyway? Not your children's home, I'll bet!"

"I did." Sara's hands shook slightly as she lifted out the dress she'd chosen to wear. "I didn't think you'd mind. It didn't cost all that much. Less than this dress. And I'll take it out of my own allowance."

"Your allowance!" Nicolás said angrily. "I didn't give you that allowance so you could turn it over to the state welfare department! You think Cortéz Industries doesn't pay enough taxes already? I gave you that allowance so you could have some fun and do some shopping, dress yourself as my woman should. And speaking of dress . . .'"

Striding across the room, he snatched the dress she had chosen from her hands. It was a soft chiffon in one of the pastel colors that Sara favored, with a full skirt that swirled around her calves and a halter-style bodice that was two widths of material crisscrossing over the shoulder to end in a soft tie at the back of her neck. Sara had fallen in love with it the moment she'd glimpsed it in the boutique window, but Nicolás now tossed it aside in disgust. "Can't you find anything better than this?"

Rooting around in the closet, he pulled out a black frock with a very short hemline and spaghetti straps that he himself had picked out on a shopping spree, but which Sara had never worn. "Here, put this on."

He rummaged around in her jewelry box and grabbed a pair of long, dangling earrings of chunky *bolivianita,* a semiprecious stone native to the country that looked as though nature had swirled together topaz and amethyst. "And these. And do something a little more spectacular with your makeup. My friends expect my woman to look a little less like a grade school teacher and more like—"

"—Reina?" Sara was struggling hard to hold on to her temper. The dress he'd shoved at her was a close facsimile to the one Reina was wearing tonight, and Sara had loathed it ever since she'd first tried it on, though Nicolás had insisted she looked sensational in it. In Sara's opinion, the dress made her look like a pale imitation of Reina's flaunting sensuality, and if she hadn't been too tired to face another argument, she'd have given in to her first impulse, which was to throw the dress on the floor and stomp on it. Instead, she dropped her bathrobe and reluctantly pulled the outfit over her head.

"Yeah, like Reina, for one. Okay, so you girls haven't exactly hit it off. I'm not blind to that. But there's some lessons you could learn from her. Like how to have a good time, swing a little, get some fun out of life."

Nicolás lounged on the bed, taking no heed of what it did to his formal attire, as Sara wriggled the hated dress down over her hips. "I just don't get you, Sara! You've got girls like Reina beat hands-down for looks—when you want to use it! And you can be a lot of fun—when you want to! You sure never had any problem back in Seattle. You were always smiling and laughing and ready for any kind of a good time. Now look at you! You act like you're going to a funeral instead of a party. Boy, have you changed!"

Sara drew her breath in sharply. His complaint stung even more because it carried so little truth. She saw little change in herself since their marriage, apart from the initial blossoming into self-confidence that had come with the happiness of being loved. It was true that with Nicolás she'd discovered a capacity for having fun and letting her hair down that her college friends would have found astonishing. But she had always been an essentially serious person, looking at the perplexities of human life through interested but sober eyes. And if Nicolás had ever thought otherwise, if he really expected something like Reina Velásquez from his bride, then it showed how little he really knew her.

"I know what's doing it, too," Nicolás pursued his argument in an aggrieved tone as he flicked irritably past ESPN, ECO—the Spanish news channel—and C-SPAN. "It's all this volunteer work. If working with these kids is going to have you so depressed that you can't put on a smile for your husband and friends, then it's time you put a stop to this craziness. I'd never have let you get involved with that children's home in the first place if I'd known you were going to take it so seriously. Like this thing today. I mean, really, Sara! There's nothing wrong with a little charity, but you've gone way overboard, and that's the truth! The next thing we know, you're going to be bringing home some infectious disease."

"What are you saying, Nicky?" Sara swung around as she fastened the back to one of the bolivianite earrings. "You . . . you aren't asking me to quit the *Hogar de Infantes,* are you?" She faced him, taut and slim and anxious, one earring still clutched in her hand. "Please, Nicky, don't ask me to quit. I . . . I *like* working out there, and the kids aren't getting me down. Really, I promise! It's important to me, don't you see?"

The TV channel clicked on to CNN, and Sara heard a polished voice announce, with just that perfect touch of solemnity, "And on the domestic front, the burning of a black church in Alabama signals new race problems; an unusual drug seizure in Miami shows the incredible ingenuity of the cartels in getting their product to your streets; and, in Chicago, a man murders his wife over custody of . . . their pet parrot?"

Nicky impatiently tossed aside the remote control. "No, I don't see! I don't see at all! What are these kids to you, anyway? You'd never heard of them a month ago. Okay, so you feel sorry for them! So hire a couple of extra nursemaids or whatever it is they need over there. I'll even foot the bill if it's that important to you. But you're a Cortéz now, not some servant girl to be changing their

diapers and scrubbing their floors and cleaning up their puke! I
didn't get married so my woman could wear herself out for a bunch
of beggar brats!"

My woman. There was that phrase again. *"Mi mujer."* When she'd
first heard it at the Santa Cruz airport, it had been a joke. Now it
seemed more ominous. Was that really all Nicolás wanted of her?
To be a decorative appendage for him? To have no thoughts or
opinions or aspirations of her own? To be satisfied with sunbathing
around the pool and spending hours on her hair, makeup, and
clothes, and attending an occasional bridge party or those interminable society teas, while she waited for her husband to come home
each night?

Sara sat down slowly on the edge of the bed. She couldn't believe that this was anything as simple as a basic difference between
Bolivian and American cultures. Gabriela's husband, after all, encouraged both her professional career and her involvement in the
community. But it certainly seemed, in the Cortéz circle of friends
and acquaintances, that the women were expected to do little more
than spend the money their menfolk earned and be agreeable, ornamental complements to their husbands' success in life and business.
Why couldn't Nicolás see that this wasn't enough?

Sara leaned forward, her second earring clasped tightly between
her hands in her lap. She looked at Nicolás with earnest eyes that
were glowing a deep amber. "You're right, Nicky. I could just hire
some more help over there! In fact, maybe I will, if you're really
serious about it. But don't you see? I want to do something myself to
help other people! Not . . . not just throw money at someone else
to do it for me. It would be different if I was doing something here
at home or at the office. But Mimi doesn't need me, and neither do
you—at the office. And . . . and . . . you know I love you, Nicky,
and I love having fun with you, of course I do! But I can't just sit
around all the time, taking and taking and never giving anything
back! I need to do something useful with my life!"

"And keeping me happy isn't useful enough for you?" Nicolás
demanded. His glance flickered over from the TV screen, and his
icy demeanor thawed a bit when he noticed her eager, heart-shaped
features and the shining, smooth fall of her hair across her shoulders.
He modified his tone from irritated to merely peevish as he went
on. "I just don't get it, Sara! Most girls would love to be in your
shoes! You've got everything you could possibly want—all the money
you could spend, freedom to do whatever you want . . . something
I'd think you'd appreciate after the way you were slaving back in

Seattle. You're respected and honored in this city—no, in the whole country—as my wife. So why can't you just enjoy it? Sunbathe. Go shopping. Visit your friends. Go to all those little teas the way Delores and Janéth and Reina and the rest of the Cortéz women do. They're perfectly happy with that kind of life. So why can't you be? Why do you always have to be *doing* something?"

Sara didn't know whether to laugh or cry. "Because I'm *not* Delores or Janéth or Reina—or any of the rest of your 'Cortéz women,'" she said as evenly as she could. "And I don't want to be! Can't you understand that?"

She started to cross her legs, tugging fruitlessly at the black dress to bring it a little further down over her thighs, then abandoned the attempt as it slid scandalously high. "You say I've changed, but I don't agree. I never was the social butterfly you're making me out to be! I don't drink, I don't smoke, and I don't dance *sopa de caracol*—and I never did! I've always studied hard and worked hard—and I like it! And I can't make lying out in the sun and having a good time the whole substance of my life!"

Sara could no longer keep the hurt from her voice. "If anyone's changed, Nicky, it's you! You used to like the things I liked. You . . . you never asked me to party or drink or . . . or be any different from what I am. You even went to church with me. You said you loved me just the way I was. You were—" *You were polished and sophisticated and complimentary and—oh, so gorgeous! Like a prince in a fairy tale, and just as real!*

Sara suppressed a sigh as her gaze rested on the handsome, sulky features turned away from her to look at the TV screen. "Maybe . . . maybe the truth is that neither of us has changed. Maybe that's the problem. Maybe we've both been seeing each other as what we wanted, not who we really are. That romantic way we met—like something out of a story. I guess it's kind of colored everything we've ever thought about each other."

"What the—?" Nicolás jerked to an upright position, swinging his feet off the bed with a phrase that burned Sara's ears. She stared at Nicky with astonishment, shocked at the violence of his reaction, until she realized that he wasn't even looking at her. He was staring at the television as though he hadn't heard a thing she'd just said. The CNN reporter's commentary fell into the breach between them.

"In downtown Miami . . . a reputable gallery of native arts . . . exquisite wall hangings woven from native llama wool . . . from the Andean highlands . . . each one impregnated with half a kilo of pure cocaine."

Sara twisted herself around to face the screen. Despite the commentator's claims, the gallery shown on the screen looked like little more than a souvenir shop. Around the periphery of the wide-angle shot, garish, second-rate Cuban-American watercolors clashed with Native American wall hangings displayed above a haphazard assortment of Mexican pottery and South American wood carvings.

Two uniformed officers walked past the camera, escorting a woman between them. She wasn't handcuffed, but she was obviously crying, with one arm raised to shield her face from the prying lens. A pair of black windbreakers disappeared through a door at the back of the gallery, the foot-high white letters on their backs announcing to the world that this case belonged to the DEA.

As the voice-over report continued to describe the scene inside the shop, the camera zoomed in to show a large table filled with colorful tapestries. They were just such scenes of Andean country life as the one that hung now at the head of her bed, brought home by Nicolás as a replacement for the one that Julio Vargas had refused to let her keep. Hand-woven on looms that were no more than the lashing together of sticks, the hangings were one of the Quechua handicrafts most popular with tourists.

Sara tuned in to what the reporter was saying.

". . . This unique smuggling method was discovered when an unnamed buyer spilled a can of 7-Up on his purchase and noticed a white residue oozing out of the wool. Police forensics experts say the hangings were most likely soaked in a liquid version of cocaine, then dried. Reprocessed to remove the alkaloid, any one of these hangings, sold in this shop for a few hundred dollars, would be worth at least $25,000 on the streets of Miami. The twenty hangings found here alone have an estimated value of half a million dollars. Gallery owners deny that the shipment was intended for them, but police sources say that the business has been suspected in the past of being a receiver of stolen goods. . . ."

Beside her, Nicolás was watching the TV screen with an intensity that astonished Sara. She herself found the newsclip of minimal interest, and it hurt that her husband could find some meaningless news broadcast so much more fascinating than this vital discussion of their own relationship.

Impatiently, she reached for the remote control, but she was still fumbling for the power button when the camera zoomed in on the pile of wall hangings. Sara froze, the remote falling from her fingers. She knew that tapestry!

Somehow, she found herself on her feet and taking a step forward as the image slowly expanded to fill the entire screen with living, vibrant color. Yes, there was the cobblestone street and the adobe church with its bell tower and burnt-orange tile roof. And if she might confuse it with another, similar scene, she couldn't mistake that haughty black llama glaring down its white-striped nose at the Quechua herdswoman who was prodding him up the street.

Sara groped for the post that held up the canopied roof of the bed, dizzy with shock and horror. Her head whirled as the implications of what she had just seen began to sink in. The clearest and most awful was that Doug Bradford had been right all along. There *was* drug trafficking going on within Cortéz Industries!

But with that initial shock came almost instant relief. If the DEA agent had been right about Cortéz Industries, he hadn't been so right about Nicolás or his family.

Sharp, angry features rose onto the screen of her mind. The box of tapestries broken open on the warehouse floor, the cowering Indian girl, and looming over it all in an explosion of rage, Don Luis's head of security. *Julio Vargas!*

Sara stared blindly at the screen as the pieces of the puzzle clicked into place with appalling clarity. That load that had spilled. Those ridiculous orders about firing anyone who so much as touched a sealed box. That inordinate burst of anger. Julio's summary dismissal of María. It all made sense now. She even knew—or was fairly sure she did—how the security chief had managed to set up an operation like this right under the nose of the Cortéz family itself.

The Miami gallery was fading into another story in another state. With another angry oath, Nicolás grabbed for the remote and clicked off the TV. Then he glanced over to where Sara stood motionless, staring at the empty screen, wide-eyed and white-faced. "Sara, what's got into you?" His eyes fell to the earring dangling forgotten from her fingers, then dropped again to her bare feet. "Are you still not dressed? I've got to get back downstairs!"

Sara came to herself with a shiver that cleared her head. Rushing over to where Nicolás was sitting at the end of the bed, she dropped to her knees beside him. "That doesn't matter now," she said urgently, wrapping her arms around his waist with no thought of their earlier disagreement. "Nicky, those hangings! I know who shipped that cocaine to the United States."

"What the—?" She felt him go rigid under her arms. "Sara, what are you talking about?"

"That tapestry they were showing. I recognized it! It was in that box of hangings that broke open at the warehouse that day. The one your father's head of security went and fired María over. Don't you see? That cocaine came from Cortéz Industries! And I know who did it, too! Julio Vargas!"

"What?" Nicolás pushed Sara's arms away. "I know you don't like Julio Vargas, but to be accusing him of dealing in cocaine—you must be out of your mind!"

"It's not ridiculous, I swear! Listen to me!" Suddenly cold, she wrapped her hands around her bare arms, her eyes still wide and shaken. She had to get him to see! "Remember when Don Luis said I could have any souvenir I wanted? Well, that hanging they were showing on the TV was the exact one I picked out of that box to bring home. I'd know that herd of llamas and that church anywhere! And it's not like I didn't get a good look. I was holding it in my own two hands when Julio Vargas grabbed it away and threw that raving fit where he fired that poor girl!"

Sara hurriedly recounted everything that had happened that afternoon before Nicolás and Don Luis had shown up. "Don't you see? I couldn't understand why he was so rabid about that girl touching those hangings. Even if there *was* some stupid rule, his reaction was clearly out of line. But now it all makes sense! He was afraid she would notice something unusual about those hangings. She'd handled enough of them to spot anything different, if anyone would. Even I noticed how dusty my hands got—though it didn't mean anything to me until now. And that's why he's so strict about firing anyone who even gets near one of those sealed boxes. It's not just to keep people from stealing. It's because they've got cocaine in them. Or at least some of them."

Nicolás looked more impatient than impressed. "Don't you think you're overreacting a little, Sara? I mean, this is crazy! Those hangings on the television could have come from anywhere. You can't even be sure it was the same one you saw."

Sara started to protest, but he cut her off with a sharp gesture. "No, wait! I'm not saying you didn't see that hanging—or one just like it. But these Indian weavers find a pattern that's popular with the tourists and they make dozens, maybe hundreds of the things. And this box that fell off and broke in front of you. Sara, have you any idea how many thousands of boxes go through our warehouse in a week or even a day? And every one looks almost exactly the same. And yet you say Julio Vargas took one look at this particular box from halfway across the warehouse and recognized it as being part of this, uh—coke shipment or whatever? There's no way!"

"But that's just it!" Sara countered urgently. "There *is* a way.

That's why I'm so sure it was Julio. You know how all the boxes you ship out have that emblem stamped in the middle of each side? That curly-cue *C* with the crown on top like you have on the gate? Well, on that box with the hangings, the stamps weren't in the middle. They were all way off-center, kind of up in the top left-hand corner. And not just on that one box either. That whole load on the forklift was the same way. I was just telling myself that someone was getting pretty careless with the stamp when the whole thing crashed and that box flew out and landed at my feet.

"Anyway, I don't think those stamps were an accident. I think that's how Vargas marks the boxes that have cocaine in them so he knows which ones are his. And so whoever his contact is on the other end can separate them from the others. Oh, Nicky, don't you see how it all fits together? And that would explain why the DEA came sniffing around. They must have gotten wind of what Julio Vargas was doing."

"Aren't you forgetting something here?" Nicolás interrupted sarcastically. "Bradford and company didn't find anything, remember?"

"So maybe Julio isn't doing it all the time! After all, you and Don Luis might start noticing if he got too big. Maybe he just does it once in a while to bring in some extra income. If you can call a half-million dollars or more extra income!"

Sara paused, her brows knitting together. "That souvenir shop, though. That doesn't make sense. There's no way those people knew there was cocaine in those hangings, or they wouldn't have been selling them to just anyone walking in off the street. That had to be some kind of a mistake. Maybe . . . well, the police *said* the place was suspected of receiving stolen merchandise! So what if maybe one of those boxes got stolen somehow before the real contact could get his hands on it? Those people who ran the gallery could have been selling the merchandise without having any idea of what those tapestries were really worth."

Nicolás was giving her his full attention now. He sat curiously still as she finished her reasoning, his blue eyes bright and speculative. "And you're telling me you figured all this out just now while you were staring at that news broadcast?" he said slowly when she was done. "I guess I never realized just what an intelligent woman you are, Sara!"

The glow that warmed her at his words was interrupted by the crackle of an intercom on the wall. "Nico, Sara, where in the name of heaven are you two? Have you forgotten that you have guests down here?"

Nicolás walked over to push a button. "We'll be right down, Papá! Something's come up here that you'd better hear about."

"Oh, no! And I'm still not ready!" Sara scrambled to her feet. "Oh, Nicky, I'm sorry! It'll just take me a minute to get my makeup on."

"No, it's too late for that now!" Nicolás said sharply. "Do you realize how long we've been sitting up here? If you're not ready yet, I'll just have to go ahead on my own!" Sara felt the sting of his words, but he sounded preoccupied and distant rather than angry. Switching off the intercom, he stood for a moment, drumming his fingers in an indecisive rhythm against the side of his leg, before his gaze dropped to her face, anxious and pale against the black of her dress. He frowned. "You really don't look so hot. Maybe you'd better just stay here. Just go on to bed, and I'll tell everyone you've got a headache or something. Anyone who saw you come in will believe that!"

He brushed past her and headed for the door. Sara ran after him, catching at his arm. "But what are you going to do? About Julio, I mean? You . . . you do think Don Luis will believe me, don't you? Because if he doesn't . . ." A shiver ran down her neck. "If they trace those hangings back to Cortéz Industries . . . well, those DEA people already have crazy ideas about the Cortéz family. They might even think it was Don Luis who was smuggling cocaine. Or . . . or you, Nicky!"

Nicolás was looking grimmer than she'd ever seen him before, but he managed a short laugh as he released himself from her clasp. "Oh, he'll believe you, all right!" He gave her a slight nudge. "Now go on to bed and stop worrying your head about Julio Vargas or Cortéz Industries. Papá and I will take care of everything."

Nicolás closed the door behind him, then popped it open again and thrust his head back into the room. "I don't have to tell you not to blab about this to anyone, do I?"

"Of course not!" Sara said indignantly. As though she didn't have enough sense not to prattle about what she'd discovered before the police and the DEA had time to do their investigations and make arrests! "You think I want Julio Vargas hearing about this before the police have a chance to get to him?"

"Good! You just keep it that way!"

CHAPTER THIRTEEN

As soon as the door shut behind Nicolás again, Sara gratefully stripped off the black dress and crawled under the covers. She was exhausted, but her mind was awash with everything that had just transpired, and sleep didn't come easily. What was happening downstairs right now? How was Don Luis reacting to Nicky's news? What steps were they planning to take? Maybe even tonight!

The appalling realization that illegal drugs really were flowing through Cortéz Industries—that Doug Bradford had been right all the time, at least in part—still had her shaken and aghast. That one box alone had carried a half-million dollars of cocaine. There'd been maybe a dozen more boxes on that forklift. How many kids could that much cocaine poison? It had to be stopped, even if it meant some embarrassment for Cortéz Industries.

That it was going to be an embarrassment for Cortéz Industries, Sara had no doubt, and it troubled her. Both Nicolás and Don Luis had been loud and vehement in their disapproval of the DEA and its efforts to stem the flow of cocaine from Bolivia. The raid on their business still rankled, and they—or at least Don Luis—had used it to stir up considerable local sentiment against the American anti-narcotics efforts. Her father-in-law certainly wasn't going to be happy about having to disclose to those same DEA agents that one of his most trusted employees was a drug trafficker. Not that Sara knew how these things worked, but surely the Americans would have to be called in at some point, especially since the drugs were being shipped to the United States. *I just hope whoever's in charge over there has enough good sense not to send in Doug Bradford again. Nicolás would be absolutely furious if he had to deal with the very same agent who conducted that raid.*

Yes, the whole thing was bound to be a mess, even if it proved possible to avoid a lot of negative publicity, and for one brief instant, Sara wondered if it wouldn't have been easier just to keep her mouth shut. But only for an instant, because the only two alternatives she could see were even more appalling. One, that the shipment already in the hands of the Miami police could be traced back to Cortéz Industries in a way that would implicate its owners and not the employee responsible. Or, an even more ghastly possibility was that it would *not* be traced back, leaving a pipeline of drugs flooding into the streets and schools of her own country. Because, as she'd told Nicolás, there was no reason to believe that this was the first time Julio Vargas had pulled something like this. Nor would it be the last, if he wasn't checked.

Julio Vargas! Had he too seen that CNN news clip? Did he have any inkling yet that something had gone wrong with his plans?

Rolling over, Sara permitted herself a small feeling of gratification. The first time she'd met the security chief, she'd thought him the perfect candidate to play a *Miami Vice* drug dealer, and for once it seemed that her instincts hadn't played her false. She still burned with indignation, recalling the hostility that had crackled between them at that last confrontation. She'd thought she'd won that round. He'd known she hadn't. And the instant her back was turned, he'd gone right back to what he was doing. The man was cruel and sneaky and underhanded, and it wasn't going to hurt her feelings to see him arrested for drug dealing.

But is he truly guilty? Sara sat up and restlessly smoothed the sheets. Stuffing a pillow behind her head, she reexamined, one by one, the links in her chain of reasoning. Was it possible, as Nicolás had suggested, that she was letting her personal dislike for Vargas lead her to build a case of circumstantial evidence on unsubstantiated facts?

No! If there was cocaine in those tapestries—and there didn't seem to be any question that there was—then it was already there when that box fell at her feet. There was no way that anyone could have taken out those wall hangings, soaked them in cocaine, and put them back after that box left the warehouse. Julio Vargas himself had explained the security precautions that kept export goods from being tampered with from the time they were catalogued and sealed until they reached their final destination.

As for Vargas, the dark fury on his narrow features, the angry clenching and unclenching of his hands at his sides, his screaming mouth almost foaming with rage, were as clear in her memory as yesterday. *No, he knew what was in that box, all right! There was too much emotion there for any other explanation.*

There was, too, Nicolás's own reaction to show that she wasn't absolutely crazy. In the end, he had taken her seriously, with a grimness that made Sara wonder if he hadn't perhaps entertained his own suspicions about Vargas. At any rate, he'd believed her and had promised to take care of the matter.

With that assurance, Sara turned her thoughts back to her own problem: Nicolás himself! The pain from his earlier comments welled up again to squeeze at Sara's stomach and heart. Her husband found her physically attractive, she knew that, but so much else seemed to irritate him! The self-confidence she had so painstakingly built up under Nicolás's admiration and approval now crumbled under a storm of doubts and fears. How could she ever have thought herself exciting enough, stimulating enough, for someone like Nicolás, who had the whole world at his feet?

But then he'd never asked her to be exciting. He'd only asked her to love him!

Sara found herself twisted up in the top sheet so tightly she couldn't move. Unwrapping herself from the strangling folds, she stared desperately, hopelessly, at the ceiling. The harsh white light from the extra floodlights outside filtered through the slats of the balcony doors and left alternating bars of light and dark on the textured plaster above the bed.

If only there were some way to go back—just two short months— to that state of perfect happiness at the beginning of their marriage. Back to those days when Nicolás had looked at her as though she were something infinitely precious and wonderful. When it had been enough just to be in the same room together, to catch each other's eye across a sea of heads. If only they'd stayed there, in Seattle, far away from all this luxury and wealth and fawning attention that was Nicky's real world. Maybe then he wouldn't have changed so drastically. Maybe he wouldn't be demanding that she change!

The bars on the ceiling wavered suddenly, as though seen from underwater. Sara closed her eyes against the sudden sting at the back of her throat and nose. Sometimes it seemed that it was all slipping away from her—the dream she'd cherished just a few short months before of a family, a home of her own. . . .

You're being ridiculous! Sara scolded herself sternly. *You're doing exactly what you said you'd never do, turning into one of those hysterical women who get themselves worked up every time their husband has a bad day or glances at another woman! Nicky loves you, you know he does. This is just one of those ups and downs everyone has with marriage. Now get to sleep!*

But the hours dragged on, and still sleep eluded her. Then,

abruptly, the music outside her window stopped, replaced a few moments later by honking horns and the roar of departing sport utility vehicles. Stumbling footsteps and voices slurred with drowsiness and alcohol passed by her door on their way to the guest suites down the hall. Sara waited, tense, unhappy, her ears straining for the sound of footsteps at her own door. The floodlights blinked out, casting her bedroom into inky darkness. Silence fell over the big house. Still Nicolás didn't come.

Suddenly, she couldn't wait alone another minute. She had to see him, hold him, reassure herself that all was well, or she'd never be able to rest. Sara slid her feet over the side of the bed. Groping around for her bathrobe, she slipped it on and padded to the door. The hall outside was dark except for a night light left burning over the stairwell. Quietly clicking the door shut behind her, she eased her way down the two flights of stairs, her bare feet silently negotiating the polished treads.

The main floor of the big house was as silent as the corridors above. Sara paused at the door of the ballroom. The vast room looked ghostly and abandoned. The dim light filtering in through the tall, narrow windows cast mysterious shadows across the dance floor.

As she stood there, a sudden movement startled her. It was only a mouse in search of a cake crumb, but she shuddered and hurried on, her breath coming more quickly in the eeriness of the silent house. She was beginning to feel a little foolish and had decided to return to bed, when she saw a slit of light up ahead—under the door of the one room she'd never entered in this part of the house. Don Luis's personal study.

The door was cracked open several inches, laying a slim pencil of light across the hall and down the steps into the drawing room. The familiar sound of her husband's voice, sharp with irritation, told her that her search had been rewarded.

". . . sheer bad luck! What do we do now?" she heard him say.

Don Luis responded, but Sara caught only a few words of his reply.

". . . damage control . . . the police report."

She might have guessed they would still be dealing with the bomb-shell news about Julio Vargas and the cocaine shipment. At least Don Luis appeared to be taking her seriously. Sara put her hand on the door. She could make her presence known, at any rate, even stay for a while if the two men didn't mind.

". . . not our packaging, may the saints be praised . . ."

The apologetic phrase, rising for just a moment, arrested Sara just as she was about to push open the door. So Nicolás and Don

Luis were not alone. Sara snatched her hand away, vaguely aware of something familiar about the respectful tone, so different from the authoritative, staccato voices of Don Luis and Nicolás, but even more aware of the scanty material that made up her bathrobe. Taking a hasty step backward, Sara turned and fled upstairs.

CHAPTER FOURTEEN

ello, Sara! Read the paper yet? Pretty big day for you Yanks, what?"

The familiar British accent drew Sara's attention away from the lentils she was spooning into Carina's mouth. Laura Histed bustled across the toddlers' ward, waving a doubled-up newspaper. Plopping the newspaper down on an empty highchair, she stooped to tickle Carina under the chin.

"She's looking well, aren't you, dearie?" she crooned. The toddler's mouth widened to show a mass of chewed food. "That's right, give auntie a grin here! You're just the most gorgeous little girl, and we're going to have you all better in no time."

Actually, Carina was looking far from well or beautiful. She had lost weight, her dark curls were matted, and her tiny face was pinched and sallow. But the expensive antibiotics Sara had paid for were beginning to take effect, and Sara felt amply compensated by a spark of animation in the girl's long-lashed eyes. To her relief, Nicolás had said nothing further about dropping her volunteer work at the children's home. Sara didn't know whether that was because he'd changed his mind or simply because he hadn't been around enough in the last few days to notice what she was doing.

Pulling up a chair, Laura grabbed up the newspaper again, stabbing at the front page with her finger. "So, aren't you just wild? I know I would be. Or haven't you seen the paper today? Here then, take a look!"

Lifting the spoon from Sara's hand, the older woman shoved the newspaper in her direction. "I'll feed this little sweetie."

Sara grabbed up the newspaper with a mixture of excitement and dread. It had been four days since she'd seen the CNN newsclip, and every morning since, she'd expected headlines linking the Miami arrests to Julio Vargas and Cortéz Industries. Instead, there had been silence. Not only from the press, but from Nicolás and Don Luis as well.

Sara still didn't know when Nicolás had slept the night of that broadcast. He hadn't come to bed before she dropped off into an uneasy sleep, and when she'd awakened the next morning, he and Don Luis had already left for the sugar refinery. He'd stopped by the house that afternoon, but only long enough to pick up a change of clothing and inform Sara that he was flying with his father out to the hacienda. They'd been gone overnight, and on their return had flown directly to the refinery. When Nicolás had finally called late that afternoon, it was to ask Sara to pack him an overnight bag for a late-night flight to Miami on Lloyd Aereo Boliviano, the national airline. Then he had sent the limousine over to pick up the suitcase. Sara's suggestion that she deliver the case to the airport had been strongly vetoed. There was too much going on right now for personal farewells. He'd see her when he got back.

She'd seen even less of Don Luis, and when she'd carefully probed Mimi concerning his whereabouts, her mother-in-law had informed her that she left it to his secretary to keep track of his schedule. Not that Sara would have dared ask Don Luis any questions. Even after two months, she still found herself treading warily around her formidable father-in-law.

As for the rest of the family, no one had shown any awareness of anything out of the ordinary, and though Sara had watched the news and scrutinized *El Deber* daily, there'd been no hint of any scandal or arrest connected to Cortéz Industries. If it hadn't been for Nicolás's and Don Luis's frenetic activity over the past few days, she would have begun to wonder whether she'd imagined the whole thing.

Well, Nicolás was due back this afternoon, and this time Sara was going to insist on some answers. In the meantime, there was the newspaper Laura had so excitedly shoved at her. Shaking out the heavy pages of print, Sara scanned the headlines eagerly. Inch-high letters blazed back at her: "U.S. Vice President to Meet with Mayor of Santa Cruz."

"What's this?"

"What's this?" Laura threw Sara a scandalized look. "Your vice president is coming into town today, and you ask 'what's this?' Why, I figured you Yanks would be going crazy with excitement! Or haven't you been following the news?"

"Oh, yes, of course," Sara said lamely. "I knew he was coming. I . . . I was just expecting something else."

She feigned interest as she glanced over the columns of print under the headline. She'd known, of course, about the impending visit of the American vice president. After all, it had been years since anyone so close to the Oval Office had made an official tour of Bolivia, and the media had been making the most of the upcoming event. But for the past few days, at least, Sara had been too preoccupied scanning for any reference to Cortéz Industries to give much attention to any other news story.

"He isn't actually leaving the airport," Laura informed Sara, as though she weren't reading the newspaper article for herself. "Just laying over on his way to La Paz. But the mayor will be going out to meet him. And I suppose all you Yanks will be out at the gate waving those little striped flags of yours. I know how we Britons would be if the Prince of Wales made it all the way here to Santa Cruz."

Sara made appropriate murmurs of interest as she abandoned the front page for the police section, but her lack of genuine enthusiasm finally sunk in to the pastor's wife. Shoveling the last bit of lentils into Carina's mouth, she shot Sara a sharp glance. "You don't look overwhelmed with excitement. You *are* planning on going out, aren't you?"

The police section mentioned only a couple of minor drug seizures, nothing more than a few kilos, and both were in Puerto Suarez over on the Brazilian border. Sara folded up the newspaper. "I hadn't even thought about it," she answered honestly.

"You haven't thought about it!" Laura looked scandalized again. "That's just what Ellen Stevens said when I asked her. What is it with you Yanks? If that was our royalty showing up out there, every British citizen in the country would be lining the road, cheering them in."

"Oh, I don't know." Sara stood up and lifted Carina down. With an affectionate swat on the little girl's diapered rear, she sent her off into the pack of toddlers. "I guess we Americans have a different relationship with our leaders than you do with your royalty. Maybe because they don't stick around long enough for us to get quite so attached to them."

"Well, maybe," Laura admitted, her pleasant face crestfallen. "I guess this means you won't be interested in my other news, either. I know Ellen wasn't!"

"Oh, no, of course I would!" Sara assured her hastily. She hadn't meant to snub her friend. Though she'd never returned to the English church, she'd run into Laura on a fairly regular basis when their volunteer hours at the children's home coincided, and with every encounter, her admiration and respect for the pastor's wife had grown. She especially appreciated the tact with which Laura refrained from pressing her with invitations to church.

"I understand, dearie," she'd told Sara with warm sympathy after her one stammering explanation that Nicolás didn't approve. "It isn't easy when your husband doesn't share your faith. We'll just be praying that God will change his mind and heart." Sara hadn't known whether to be grateful or indignant.

"So, tell me what you have!" Sara encouraged Laura now with more eagerness than she actually felt as she wiped down the highchair. "Is there something else going on? Or someone else arriving in town?"

"Well, it's really all part of the same thing," Laura said apologetically. "But it's not in the paper. Our church got an invitation from the consulate. I didn't know if you had too." Rummaging around in her big black handbag, she pulled out a crumpled sheet of paper. "It's those people who are here to set up the security for your vice president. They're staying on this evening to offer some kind of security seminar for all the Americans and any other English speakers who might want to attend. Over at the Co-op school. I thought it looked rather fascinating myself."

Sara glanced over the bulletin, indifferently at first, then with growing interest as she read through the list of discussion topics: kidnapping, burglary, political revolution, as well as a hands-on self-defense workshop. This certainly sounded more interesting than waving a flag from behind a chain-link fence. She could get a better look at the vice president on TV. But how often did you actually get to meet an honest-to-goodness Secret Service agent?

"Laura, this is great! I'd love to go!" she exclaimed. Laura beamed, while Sara continued to scan the sheet looking for the date and time. "Oh, no! That's this evening! And Nicolás is flying in from Miami this afternoon. In fact, I'm leaving from here to pick him up. I don't think he'd be too happy about me leaving him on his first night back. And I wouldn't want to. I haven't seen him in days."

"So why don't you bring him along?"

"I don't think so!" Sara shook her head emphatically as she lifted another toddler into the highchair. She could just imagine Nicolás's reaction to a seminar that suggested, rightly or wrongly, that expatriates might find themselves in danger in his country. "But thanks for the invite. I really do appreciate it, and I'd love to go if I could."

"Well, you do what you must, dearie." Shoving the bulletin back into her bag, Laura fielded a toddler of her own. "Oh, and I've got another bit of news for you. I think we have a family who just might be interested in adopting Carina. If we can just track down her next-of-kin to sign the relinquishment papers . . ."

Leaving the toddlers' ward, Sara rooted around in her purse for her cell phone. Calling up the menu, she keyed in the number for *Radiomóvil Cortéz*.

This time the wait was short. She had just stepped out the huge, arched doorway of the old mansion when a white Toyota Corolla station wagon with the Cortéz crown on its side pulled up to the curb. The driver was one Sara knew.

"*Buenas tardes,* Don Adolfo," Sara greeted the driver as he jumped out to usher her into the back seat. After asking him to drive her to the airport, she inquired, "And how is your youngest son doing? Did he pass that biology exam?"

Mimi would be horrified at her easy conversation with a taxi driver and her use of the honorific "Don," but Sara was equally appalled by the idea of treating the people who served her as social inferiors to be addressed only with direct orders. She listened with genuine interest to the driver's hopes of a professional career for his university-age children before she keyed in the phone number that would bypass the downstairs switchboard at Cortéz Industries.

"Has Nicky's flight been confirmed?" she asked when she heard her father-in-law's secretary on the other end. "I'm just leaving for Viru Viru now to pick him up."

"The flight is due in at any moment," Dolores informed her. "But there is no need for you to drive to the airport, Señora Cortéz. Don Luis has already dispatched the limousine to pick Don Nicolás up."

"What?" Sara sat up straight, incensed. "What do you mean, he sent the limousine? I called this morning to let him know I was going to pick Nicky up. Didn't you give him my message?"

"Yes, of course I did, Señora Cortéz. But Don Luis wishes him to come here and not to the house. There is to be a meeting, I think. He left a message for you." Sara heard a rustle of paper. "It says to tell you that it is not necessary for you to go to the airport. Nicolás is to come straight here, and he will be very busy this afternoon. He does not know when Nicolás will be home. It will not be necessary for you to wait up for him."

Despite Dolores's softening of the message, Sara could imagine exactly the brusque tones in which Don Luis had given those orders—and *orders* is what they amounted to! "This is ridiculous!" she fumed. "It's like there's some conspiracy to keep me from seeing my own husband!"

"I am sorry, Señora Cortéz. Your father-in-law's instructions were very clear. But if there is any way in which I can serve you . . ." The apology in Dolores's voice was tinged with reproach as she added, "I did try to reach you earlier. But you were not available at any number I could call."

That was Sara's own fault. She had faithfully obeyed Nicky's instructions to keep her cell phone with her at all times, but the unfamiliar beep-beep of an incoming call always startled the babies —and more than once had turned a quiet nursery into an epidemic of wails. So Sara had gotten into the habit of switching the phone off while she was at the orphanage.

"Yes, I know; I'm sorry too," Sara apologized, resisting her inclination to argue further. It would do no good anyway, and Dolores already sounded flustered enough. She was just following orders, after all. "Look, don't worry about it anymore. But could you at least have Nicky give me a call when he gets to the office? I should be home by then. Thanks."

Punching *End* with a little more force than necessary, Sara shoved the cell phone into her purse and leaned over the front seat to ask Adolfo to take her home. If the phone conversation had aroused his curiosity, he was too professional to show it, and he turned the taxi around without comment. A half-hour later, the taxi drew up outside the high white wall of the Cortéz estate. At Adolfo's honk, Jorge, the surly guard, thrust his head out of his window. He scowled when he saw Sara, then meandered around to open the gate.

Adolfo honked again, impatient at the delay. "Your guard does not do his job properly," he told Sara as the gate creaked open. "And he is insolent. I would get rid of him quick."

Sara only smiled as she added a generous tip to the fare. She could just imagine herself demanding that Don Luis dismiss his faithful watchdog. Still, she *was* tired of the guard's attitude. How long did it take to be accepted as a member of the family around here?

The house was quiet. Sara passed only a lone servant girl as she made her way along the long halls and up the stairs to her room. Mimi, she remembered, was at an NFWO committee meeting this afternoon. *Really, this place is absurdly huge for so few people,* she thought caustically, then caught herself. *Boy, aren't you in a bad mood!*

It was just that she'd been looking forward to having Nicky home and to herself again! Shedding her handbag, Sara stripped off the jeans and T-shirt she'd worn to the orphanage. Her nose wrinkled up at the faint odor of ammonia, stale urine, and burpy babies that always seemed to permeate her clothing and hair. Maybe it was just as well she hadn't picked up Nicolás. She padded into the bathroom and turned on the shower.

She was just toweling her hair when the phone rang. The one

beside her bed, not her cellular. Dropping her towel, Sara snatched
it up.

"Sara," Nicolás acknowledged her breathless greeting without
any preamble. "Dolores said you needed to speak to me. What is it
you want?"

"Want!" Sara wailed with all the pent-up frustration of the past
four days. "I want *you!* Do you realize I haven't seen you or . . . or
even really talked to you—well, not since that party! You haven't even
called!" Then, quickly, lest Nicolás think she was accusing him, she
added, "It's just that I've missed you! When are you coming home?
You *will* be here for supper, won't you? I don't care how late Don
Luis keeps you. I'll wait up."

A sparkle began to lighten her amber eyes as she expanded on
the thought. "Mimi ordered some real T-bones and American sour
cream for baked potatoes. I was thinking I'd ask the kitchen to send
ours up here. How does that sound? A candle-lit dinner for two?
Then a soak in the Jacuzzi? I picked up a new bikini while you were
gone—for your eyes only!" she tempted slyly. "And you can tell me all
about your trip to Miami. Speaking of which—" She lowered her
voice instinctively, even though she was alone in the room. "What's
going on? With Julio Vargas, I mean? I haven't heard a thing since
you left! Not on the news or anywhere else. Haven't they arrested
him yet? And what about Miami? Did they ever trace that cocaine
back here to the warehouse? I know you're busy, Nicky, but I've
been going crazy to hear! If you could just tell me the bare bones."

An exasperated sigh came down the line. "Sara, I can't talk about
this now! I've got other people here. Why do you always have so
many questions, anyway? It's all under control, and that's all you
need to know! As for supper, I'm afraid I'll have to take a rain check."
Nicolás sounded more impatient than regretful. "I'm in a meeting
right now, then Papá wants me to fly out to the hacienda."

"The hacienda!" Sara exclaimed with astonishment and dismay.
"But—you were just out there! Honestly, can't Don Luis even give
you one night home? I mean, what's so important on some country
farm that it can't wait until morning? Besides, I . . . I thought you
were working on this thing with Julio Vargas. What does the hacienda
have to do with anything?"

"It's just something I have to do, okay?" Nicolás snapped. "I
should be back in the morning. If I'm not, I'll let you know—or
Dolores will give you a call. Now, if you don't have anything more
urgent, I have to go."

"Wait!" Sara pleaded before he could hang up. "Look, if you

have to go, can't you at least take me with you? I could be out there at the airstrip by the time you've finished your meeting. It won't take me a minute to pack. *Please*, Nicky! I . . . I just want to be with you! To talk to you! I promise I won't get in your way, whatever it is you're doing."

Nicolás didn't even hesitate. "Sorry, not this time." His voice faded again. When it came back, it was a little more placating. "Look, Sara, things are a little crazy right now. I wouldn't get to see anything of you if you did come along. So be a good girl and just do what you're told, okay? And next month, when things calm down, I'll take you up in the Cessna myself, I promise—out to the hacienda or any place else you want to go."

"But—!"

The phone went dead in her ear. Then Sara heard a dial tone. Disappointment and anger stung her eyes. She'd been only half-joking when she'd told Dolores that she felt there was a conspiracy to keep her from seeing her husband. She didn't feel like joking anymore. But if there was such a conspiracy, it wasn't just Don Luis. It was being ably abetted by Nicolás himself.

Sara slammed the receiver onto its cradle. She didn't buy for a minute his story about being too busy to take her with him. Two months ago, he wouldn't have let wild horses keep her from his side—not after four days apart. And at least he could have called! The idea that he couldn't find ten minutes in the last four days to pick up his cell phone and talk to her—*really* talk to her, not just that brief, impersonal exchange—was ridiculous. It was like . . . like he was deliberately avoiding her!

The phone jangled under her hand. Sara snatched it up eagerly. Maybe Nicolás had changed his mind. But the voice on the other end was sharp and autocratic—and very female. "Allo? Allo? Who is this?" Mimi demanded without making any effort to identify herself.

Sara stifled a small sigh. "Hello, Mimi. This is Sara here. How did your meeting go?"

"The meeting was fine. I would like to speak to my son. Has he returned yet?"

"Yes, he's back, but I haven't seen him yet. Don Luis asked him to go straight out to the refinery. He's there now in a meeting, then he'll be flying down to the hacienda. He . . . won't be back until tomorrow." Sara cleared her throat to disguise a sudden wobble in her voice. If her mother-in-law thought something was wrong, she'd pick up on it in an instant. "If you call the office, you should be able speak to him before he leaves."

"The hacienda! What do you mean, the hacienda?" Mimi snapped as though she'd heard nothing else. "But this is ridiculous! The men were just down there this weekend. And what about the *aniversario* tomorrow evening?"

"The *aniversario?*" Sara repeated blankly. Then she slapped the palm of her hand against her forehead. The twentieth anniversary of Cortéz Industries! One more thing she'd forgotten about in her single-minded preoccupation with Julio Vargas. Half the city—and certainly all of its upper crust—would be at the refinery to celebrate. *Oh, great! And I haven't even bought my dress yet!*

"Really, this is most inconsiderate!" Mimi was fuming. "Nico must be here tomorrow! He is to be presented as the next in command after his father. That he should be flying off to the hacienda at a time like this . . ." Her voice sharpened further to suspicion. "Have you been quarreling with my Nico, Sara, *hija?*"

"No, of course not!" Sara responded indignantly. Whether that was strictly the truth, she wasn't entirely certain. But in any case, it was none of her mother-in-law's concern and certainly had nothing to do with Nicky's trip.

"He . . . he said it was business."

"Business!" A disbelieving sniff came down the line. "Really, child! Can you not tell an excuse when you see one? Why should my son have to concern himself personally with the business of one small country estate? Do we not have employees for that?"

My question exactly! Sara agreed silently.

"No, no, you must understand that this talk of 'business' is their polite little fiction when the men wish to get away from the office and their women. They go to the hacienda to do the safari, to fish and hunt. But that my son should go down there now? And without even coming home to see his mamá and his wife? This is too much! Sara, *hija,* you must work to keep your husband closer by your side if you do not wish his eyes to begin to wander elsewhere."

The statement was so outrageous that Sara was left speechless. So this was somehow supposed to be her fault! Her temper, none too even after her frustrating phone conversation with Nicolás, simmered dangerously close to a boil, and she found herself gripping the receiver until her knuckles turned white. *I will not fight with my mother-in-law. I will not fight with my mother-in-law,* she recited silently before she got out in a carefully controlled voice, "I'll keep that in mind, Mimi. But it wasn't exactly my idea that Nicky go without me. I asked if I could go along—"

"And he said no," Mimi broke in impatiently. "But of course!

Have I not just said that the hacienda is for the men? You will learn as you grow wiser in the ways of men, Sara, *hija*, that they need their little pleasures away from the women. It is not wise to interfere. If I do not demand to see this hacienda in the ten years or more that my husband flies down there, then why should you? If our men wish us to accompany them, then they will make the arrangements."

"But . . ." Sara couldn't believe what she was hearing. "Are you telling me that you've never been out to this hacienda of yours in ten years?"

There was another sniff on the line. "Do I have time to visit all the properties my husband owns? I do not even know in which direction it lies. Nor do I have any interest in the matter. It is enough to know that it is far out into the jungle. So far out that one must fly there. One can only imagine the commodities such a place must have. Let the men have their safari and show themselves *macho* living like *campesinos*. What woman of good family would lower herself to such conditions?"

Sara, who had enjoyed her fair share of camping and hiking expeditions during her growing-up years, didn't bother to enlighten her. She shifted impatiently from one foot to the other as her mother-in-law swept on, fretfully, more to herself than to Sara.

"Really, it does seem strange that Nico should fly down there when he knows that there is the *aniversario* tomorrow night. So perhaps you are right, and it is business—papers or something. I do not understand these things. Still, if this is so, then why does Luis not send Julio Vargas instead of my Nico? It is he who takes care of matters at the hacienda."

"Julio Vargas?" The name was out of Sara's mouth before she could think. "You mean, the head of security out at the refinery? What does he have to do with this hacienda?"

"He is in charge of security for *Industrias Cortéz*, not just the refinery," Mimi informed her reprovingly. "But it is for my husband to say what his duties include. Vargas is a pilot, like my husband and my son, and so it is easy for him to fly down to make sure that the place is ready and to bring back the beef that we need. It has been useful for Luis not to have to hire another pilot."

"Julio Vargas is a pilot," Sara mumbled.

"Of course, did I not just say so? This man Vargas was once an officer in our military. Did you not know? He flew their planes and helicopters. And he learned there many other things that are useful to *Industrias Cortéz*. That is why my husband chose him."

Mimi didn't wait for a response from Sara. "*Bueno,* if my Nico is not there, then I must go. There is to be a farewell tea for a dear friend of mine, who is moving to Miami. Sara, *hija,* you will call the kitchen and tell them to cancel the dinner plans. I will call Luis to let him know that he must go to La Parilla for his dinner. And I will ask him about this ridiculous business of flying to the hacienda again and again. How are we ever to have a new Cortéz heir if he is forever sending my Nico from your side?"

Sara wasn't sure whether to laugh or pull her hair out at Mimi's parting shot. So much for her mother-in-law's concern over Nicky's absences and their marriage relationship! She just wanted to make sure the two of them were spending enough time together to produce a grandchild without any unnecessary delay.

And what about these absurd assertions of Mimi's about the hacienda? Sara hung up the phone, then stood staring down at it. Or were they so absurd? She would hate to think that Nicolás might have been less than open with her—again! But there was no denying that Mimi would know a little more about her husband's and son's habits than Sara. And if the hacienda really was the Cortéz men's private getaway, then it was logical enough that Don Luis—and Nicolás—would choose to supervise the place personally rather than push it off on a subordinate, even if that supervision was motivated more by recreational considerations than actual urgency.

"He could have just told me he wanted a couple days off!" Sara informed the wall in front of her. "I wouldn't have minded."

Sometimes she despaired of ever understanding these people! It all seemed so immature, pretending you were doing one thing while the women knew good and well you were doing something else. And yet Mimi seemed to take it for granted. Just as Delores and Janéth took it for granted that their husbands spent far more leisure time partying with their male colleagues and friends than with their own wives and children. Not that taking it for granted stopped her sisters-in-law from complaining about it! Was this one more thing she was going to have to resign herself to as she and Nicolás left the honeymoon months behind?

Still, even if Mimi was right and Nicky's flying trip with Julio Vargas last month had been more of a macho safari than business, Sara knew something that apparently Mimi did not. With this Julio Vargas situation, there was no way that Nicolás was simply popping down to some country hacienda for a day of hunting or fishing—or to get away from his wife!

But why *was* he flying down there? And twice in as many days? For that matter, Don Luis had gone down with him this weekend. And it was Don Luis who was sending Nicolás down there now.

"Business" didn't seem much more likely a reason than Mimi's suggestion of R&R. As her mother-in-law had said, Cortéz Industries had more than enough executives and assistants to handle anything that might come up at some jungle property, without Don Luis and Nicolás having to fly out there personally. Certainly not at a time like this. There was just no sense to it! Unless . . .

Unless the hacienda is somehow connected to this whole Julio Vargas thing. The thought went off in Sara's mind like one of those cartoon lightbulbs that supposedly symbolize a brilliant idea.

Could that be what this is all about? Mimi had just told her that Vargas was always flying down there. And . . . well, Sara didn't know much about how drug trafficking was handled, but Vargas had to be getting that cocaine he was smuggling from somewhere. And where better to run a smuggling operation than on some remote corner of a country property that his employers visited only at intervals? A place to which he had access by plane to ferry the stuff out?

And if that isn't what this is all about, I'll eat my bolivianitas! Nicky and Don Luis must have figured out what Julio's been doing, and they've been down there checking it out! Maybe even with the DEA!

But Sara's satisfaction with the logic of her reasoning faded as her thoughts drifted back to the telephone conversation she'd had with Nicolás. Even if her suspicions about the hacienda were true, it didn't explain why Nicky had been so evasive with her. Why hadn't he called or made any effort to see her in four days? Was he still mad at her about the party Friday night?

Sara rejected that idea even as it occurred to her. As angry as she'd seen Nicolás, it never took long before the easygoing, charming side of his personality reasserted itself. No, she knew how he sounded when he was angry—and it wasn't anger she'd picked up over the phone. It was wariness. And she remembered exactly when that wary note had crept into his voice. *"Sara, I can't talk about this now! I've got other people here."* A prevarication that was more than could be explained by the presence of other people in the room. The truth was, he didn't like her asking questions about Julio Vargas. It was that simple!

Sara sighed unhappily. Maybe she did ask too many questions. Nicolás certainly complained often enough. But after all, *she'd* been the one to stumble over what Julio Vargas was doing at Cortéz Industries. Wasn't it only natural that she would want to know what was happening? Or was this simply another example of that "Cortéz women don't need to know anything about business affairs" attitude she'd run into before? Or . . .

This time the thought came reluctantly. *Or is it because Nicolás knows I wouldn't like the answers he'd give?* Because something was going on over there that he knew she wouldn't approve of. And to dodge the subject, he was dodging her!

Impulsively, Sara reached for the phone again and dialed Don Luis's office. Maybe there was another way to get some answers.

"*Buenas tardes,* Señora Cortéz." Dolores couldn't quite hide her surprise under the trained courtesy in her voice. "Don Luis and Don Nicolás have already entered the meeting. Do you wish me to have one of them paged?"

"That won't be necessary," Sara assured her hastily. "I know how busy they are right now." She hesitated. "Is . . . is Julio Vargas in the meeting as well?"

"Oh, no!" Sara could almost hear Dolores shaking her sleek, dark head on the other end of the line. "Señor Vargas is not here now. He has left *Industrias Cortéz.*"

Sara's relief took the stiffness out of her shoulders. "Yes, of course, I knew that. You . . . you wouldn't happen to know where he went, would you? And when?" *Like, did you see the police come and haul him away? Or maybe just some plainclothes North American invited him for a spin?*

"I'm sorry. *El señor* Vargas does not leave me with that kind of information. But Don Luis will know, I am certain. Señor Vargas met with him this morning."

"*What?* This morning? Are . . . are you sure?" Sara demanded, then realized she'd put far too much urgency in her voice for a query that was supposed to be casual. "I . . . I just needed to ask him a question."

"Yes, of course I am certain. It was just after Don Nicolás called from Miami. Don Luis asked to speak to *el señor* Vargas. After their meeting, *el señor* Vargas left, as I have said. I know only that it was on a business trip for Don Luis. If it is urgent to find his whereabouts, I can inquire of *el patrón.* Or perhaps I could help you with this question . . . ?"

The upswing at the end of Dolores's sentence changed the statement into a question.

"Oh, no, really, it wasn't that important. I'll just wait until he gets back." Sara hesitated again. "Do you know when that's supposed to be?"

"No, I do not have that information either, Señora Cortéz," the secretary said patiently. "But Don Luis will know. Perhaps you wish for me to have him paged so that you may speak to him directly?"

And you can be responsible for your father-in-law hitting the fan at the interruption! Sara tacked on mentally with some amusement. At the same time, she was saying, "No, really, I don't want to bother him. It doesn't matter. Thanks, Dolores—and forgive me the disturbance." She added the polite Spanish phrase that no other Cortéz would have bothered with.

"It was nothing." This time Dolores let her surprise slip through, and with genuine warmth she added, "It is always my pleasure to serve you, Señora Cortéz."

Any amusement Sara was feeling evaporated as soon as the secretary rang off. So Julio Vargas had been at the refinery as late as this morning! Whatever information she'd been expecting from Dolores, it hadn't been that! Sara sank down slowly onto the side of the bed, the receiver forgotten in her hand. A cold suspicion was tightening in her stomach. Could it be . . . ?

No, it wasn't possible! But . . .

Sara's head whirled as she went back over what she had just learned. Yesterday Nicolás had arrived in Miami. This morning he had called his father. Right after that, Don Luis had called in Julio Vargas for a private conversation. And now the security chief was gone. Not led off in handcuffs—just gone! What this was adding up to, Sara didn't like at all. And what it *didn't* add up to—at least as far as she could see—was Julio Vargas's arrest for drug trafficking!

Maybe . . . maybe they're working undercover with the police. They're laying some trap for Vargas . . . and that's why he was still there.

But even as she made the excuse, Sara was already rejecting it. These last days of silence from both Nicolás and Don Luis. That overheard mention of "damage control" and "not our packaging" that now took on a different significance. And most disturbing—why hadn't she thought of this before?—was the fact that she herself had never been contacted by the authorities. After all, Sara was the only one who could positively identify that hanging. And yet she'd never even been asked to tell her story.

Now that the suspicion was there, the facts slipped too easily into place. Nicolás and Don Luis hadn't called in the police—*or* the DEA! They had decided to deal with Julio Vargas themselves!

Sara twisted the phone cord absently around her fingers. When that bombshell newscast had dropped into her lap four days ago, her biggest concern had been that Nicolás, and more importantly, Don Luis, take her seriously. She'd more than half expected her father-in-law to dismiss the whole thing as some hysterical exaggeration —after all, Julio Vargas had been his trusted associate for years—and Sara had braced herself to go to bat for what she'd seen. She'd been surprised when Don Luis hadn't even asked to speak to her, but the midnight conversation she'd overheard and the burst of activity that followed, had reassured Sara that both men had taken her story seriously. It had never occurred to her to question exactly what they were doing about it. As an American, raised to think of drug dealers as only one step higher than a Nazi or a child molester, she'd assumed that Nicolás and Don Luis would simply call in the police or the DEA, and it hadn't even entered her mind that her husband and his father might think differently.

Until now.

And yet it should have! To assume that Nicolás—much less, Don Luis—would be operating according to an American ideal of civic responsibility had been naive, to say the least. Scraps of past conversations played through Sara's mind. Nicky's easy tolerance of the Salviettis and their known connection with drug dealing. His complete indifference to what Bolivia's chief export was doing around the world. His grievance against Doug Bradford, the DEA, and the anti-narcotic forces of his own country.

And where had he gotten those ideas? From his father, Don Luis Cortéz Velásquez de Salazar, who rubbed shoulders with these drug lords, had them as friends and business associates—and employees; whose grudge against the Bolivian police and American DEA was even greater than Nicky's; who was accustomed to lifting only a finger to have people jump to his orders; and who had spent a lifetime arranging events—and life itself—to be exactly what he wanted it to be!

Even after three months, Sara still didn't claim to understand her aloof and autocratic father-in-law. But if there was anything she'd learned about Don Luis, it was his vast pride in the Cortéz name—and in *Industrias Cortéz*, the conglomerate of businesses that had restored his family's social image, wealth, and political stature. To call in the police, to admit to the despised North Americans that he needed their help, would be galling and humiliating for this proud patriarch. Sara had considered that and felt sorry for him. What she hadn't considered—and should have—was that he simply wouldn't call in the law if he didn't have to! Handling matters himself was far more in character, and she'd have seen that if she hadn't been thinking so much like a *gringa*.

Looking at the events of the past few days from this new perspective—and with all she'd just learned from Dolores—everything now made sense. Once Nicolás had passed on to Don Luis what Sara had told him about the tapestries, the two men must have taken time to check out both the warehouse and the hacienda. That would explain the first hectic day, which had ended with Nicky's overnight trip to the hacienda. Sara could only speculate as to what they'd found there. But she didn't have to guess about the next part. Nicolás had been dispatched to Miami to check out the situation there and to find out whether the U.S. authorities had connected the confiscated wall hangings with Cortéz Industries.

In the meantime, Julio Vargas had been left undisturbed in his job at the refinery. Dolores's statements had made that clear. Again, Sara could only speculate about her father-in-law's reasoning. If the tapestries had indeed been traced back to Cortéz Industries, she had no doubt that the head of security would immediately have been tossed to the wolves to save the company's good name.

But what if no link had been established? What if the trail had come to a dead end with the hapless owners of that art gallery/fencing operation?

Try as she might, Sara could see no other conclusion that fit the morning's events. Nicolás had called his father before leaving Miami, presumably to give him the good news. And in response, Julio Vargas had been sent away. Not on a trip, she was sure, despite what Dolores had said. But not arrested either. That left one alternative. The security chief had been fired—F-I-R-E-D—thereby removing the problem from Cortéz Industries without dragging the proud family name through the mud or the courts. And now, no doubt, Nicolás was flying back down to the hacienda to take care of that end of the clean-up operation before anyone found out that they'd had a cocaine lab on their land.

The irate beep-beep of a phone too long off the hook finally penetrated Sara's deliberations. She stared at the receiver, then dropped it onto its cradle, her mind still swirling.

All this was well and good for Nicolás, Don Luis, and Cortéz Industries. And Julio Vargas, of course. It sidestepped any legal and political difficulties, and saved the business and the family from embarrassment. There was only one problem. It was just plain wrong!

There were kids out there poisoning themselves—and even dying—from the cocaine that Julio Vargas was selling. Maybe shutting down his access to Cortéz Industries would put a temporary crimp in his operation. But couldn't Don Luis—and Nicolás—see that he'd just go elsewhere and start over again? So long as Julio Vargas was out there on the loose, people's lives would be at risk. Maybe Don Luis, who had never been out of Bolivia, couldn't see the implications of letting Vargas go free. Besides, he'd been conditioned to see drug dealing as more of a social embarrassment than anything actually wrong. But Nicolás, who'd spent the last five years in the United States, should at least know better.

Oh, Nicky, how could you? I trusted you with this! Sara whispered into her empty hands. But, as always, her mind was already leaping ahead to defend him. This wasn't really Nicky's fault! Sara had no doubt whose idea it was to keep this matter from the authorities, and she didn't imagine her husband had been given much say in the matter. Don Luis was such an overpowering personality! How could she really expect Nicolás to stand up to him now when he never had in the past? She could understand why he had been avoiding her these past few days. Torn between his father's orders and the way he knew she felt about drugs and drug dealers, it was just like Nicolás to evade more trouble by staying away until it was all over.

Jumping to her feet, Sara paced restlessly, her bathrobe flapping around her ankles so that she had to slap it out of the way. It wasn't enough to say she understood. Assuming that her logic was correct and that she hadn't just added two plus two and come up with five—what was she going to do about it?

She knew what would be easiest. To kiss her husband when he got home tomorrow, accept his assurances that everything was taken care of, and let life get back to normal. But she just couldn't do that. After all, she was the one who had stumbled over the cocaine smuggling operation, and she couldn't help feeling some responsibility. And, unlike Nicolás and Don Luis, her loyalties were not just to Cortéz Industries. She felt she owed something to those kids whose lives were being affected by Julio Vargas and his greed.

Another quick lap took Sara to the door and back to the bedside table. There was no question what she had to do. She didn't like the idea, but she was going to have to confront Nicolás when he got home tomorrow. Don Luis too, if necessary. Insist on knowing exactly what was going on. And if what she feared was true, then for once she was going to have to put her foot down with these Cortéz men. Make them see that stopping Julio Vargas was more important than their personal convenience and expedience. To some extent, she could understand her father-in-law's reluctance to call in the law. If he had indeed discovered that Julio Vargas was using Cortéz property to process cocaine and ship it out, it must look to him as though a finger could easily be pointed in his direction. But Sara had more faith in the justice system than that. Besides, wasn't Nicolás always boasting about how much influence Don Luis had in high places?

As for the Americans, if the Cortezes went to the DEA voluntarily, surely they would be fair. Maybe they'd even be willing to keep the whole thing out of the media in return for cooperation from the

Cortezes. Didn't the police make deals like that sometimes? Either way, there had to be some way this could be worked out.

Sara stopped pacing. And if Nicolás refused? Or more importantly, Don Luis? She took a deep breath. Well, then, she'd have to give them an ultimatum. Either they reported it, or she would!

Apprehension squeezed at her stomach even as she made the decision. Things had been difficult enough lately in her relationship with Nicolás without adding this. He might not speak to her for a month this time! But she just couldn't live with her conscience if she stood by and let Julio Vargas walk away free and clear to start over again somewhere else. Not if she could do something to stop it. And surely, when Nicolás stopped sulking, he'd see that too.

Well, there was nothing more she could do about it tonight! Sara walked over to the intercom. She would be the only family member in for supper, she informed the servant who answered her summons. Would the kitchen please send up a tray with something light—and a cup of coffee? Switching off the intercom, she went to the closet and pulled out the first blouse she came across and a corduroy skirt. Now that her decision was made, there was no point in sitting around brooding. She'd eat her supper, then take in that security seminar at the Co-op school. That would not only please Laura Histed, but it would help fill the hours of waiting.

But as soon as Nicky got home tomorrow, there would be a showdown. Enough time had been wasted already. Ex-army officer, ex-security chief, and present-day drug trafficker Julio Vargas wasn't going to walk away from this one. Even if she had to drop a hint to the DEA herself!

Chapter Fifteen

Sara was running five minutes late for the security seminar, but when she arrived at the Co-op school's library, only a handful of people were milling about the big room. Laura Histed hurried over to greet her. "Why, Sara, you made it! Didn't your husband get in after all?"

"Yes, but he had to leave again." Sara didn't explain further. She glanced around. The library's few bookshelves were set flat against the walls, creating a central open area that was usually filled with study tables, but tonight was crowded with rows of plastic chairs—enough to seat about a hundred people. "I won't even ask if I'm late! Bolivian time, right?"

"Yes," Laura sighed. "You wouldn't think so for something like this. But even us *gringos* tend to get into bad habits after we've been here awhile." Laura gestured ruefully toward the front of the room, "I don't think your security people are very happy about it!"

Sara's eyes followed the direction of Laura's wave. At the front of the rows of chairs an easel stood with a huge pad of blank paper on its rack, larger than any Sara had ever seen. A tall, thin man with graying brown hair and glasses stood beside the easel, studying a notepad in his hand. He looked more like one of Sara's college professors than a security officer, an impression reinforced by his buttoned-up shirt and tie, which were considered the height of formality in this hot climate. He didn't seem particularly impatient, but as Sara watched, he glanced down at his wrist before walking over to speak to another man, who was lounging in the front row.

This second man was as slim as the first, but there the resemblance ended. He was a good twenty years younger and wore a collared T-shirt and slacks. His sharp, copper-toned features showed considerable irritation as he glanced around at the empty chairs. He made a comment that was inaudible from where Sara was standing, and then the first man walked back to the easel.

"Well, folks," he announced in a crisp, clear voice that cut across the buzz of chatter. "We're a little behind schedule here, so let's get started."

The dozen or so participants meandered over and scattered themselves among the available seats. Laura beckoned Sara to join her and Sam. "And, of course, with the whole place to choose from, they've got to leave the front rows completely empty!" Laura commented over her shoulder to Sara as they threaded their way after the burly pastor. "Just like in church! What is it with people? Do they feel naked or something without a seat in front of them to protect them from the speaker? Or are they afraid someone's going to ask them a question?" She tapped her husband on the back. "Hey, Sam, where are you going? They've left all the best seats for us!"

Sam groaned as his wife advanced with determination toward the center of the front row. "Now just a minute, sweetheart. I rather sympathize with those back-rowers myself. I was thinking more on the lines of that far back corner."

"The back corner!" Laura turned back, but she protested, "We won't even be able to see back there! Much less get involved in the discussion."

"Just my point," Sam agreed with a wink at Sara. "I'm off duty, remember? I want to sit back and listen—just be a member of the congregation for a change. And I don't want to have to be answering questions, either!"

"Oh, Sam, no one's going to make you answer any questions!" Hands on her hips, the plump little pastor's wife frowned up at her husband. "Honestly! Men! Take them to a new place, and all they want to do is hide. Well, maybe we should let Sara decide."

"Oh, no!" Sara threw up her hands with a laugh. "I'm not getting involved. You two settle it between yourselves."

She listened with amusement and some envy as the couple compromised amiably on the third row from the front, just off center from the easel. If she and Nicolás could settle their arguments like that! The thought furrowed a crease across her forehead. She hurriedly pushed it away and turned her attention to the security officer—or whatever he was called—who was sketching onto his pad a rough representation of the concentric rings and connecting spokes that made up the Santa Cruz city plan. Dropping the marker into a shallow trough, he turned to face his scant audience.

"It's a pleasure to see this good group out tonight," he said with no apparent attempt at irony. "Welcome to our seminar for Americans abroad. My name is Nathan McKinley. I work for the Mobile Security Division, and if you're wondering what that is, we're the branch of the Bureau of Diplomatic Security that provides security for embassies and American diplomatic personnel around the world."

"Also with us here tonight is Ramon Gutierrez. He'll be helping me later on with a little demonstration of self-defense techniques." McKinley motioned toward the dark-haired man in the front row, who acknowledged the introduction with an unsmiling nod. Unlike McKinley, he hadn't flown in from the United States for the occasion, but was stationed right here in Santa Cruz. His job had something to do with the embassy, but Sara, who was busily digging a pen and a small notebook from her purse to take notes, didn't quite catch what the younger man's responsibilities were.

Taking a long step away from the easel, Nathan McKinley peered over his glasses at his small audience like a teacher asking a trick question. "Okay. You are an oil executive working in a Latin American country. You've just received a vague warning that you may be the target of a kidnapping attempt. The motive: your company is financing oil exploration in the territory of a well-known insurgent group. The threat isn't definite enough to warrant evacuation, but neither does it pay to take it lightly. What should you do?"

A middle-aged man in the back of the room took a stab at the question, and the discussion was off and running.

"A kidnapper or a terrorist will try to hit you at what we call a 'choke point,'" McKinley explained. "This is a place that you *must* travel every day. Analyze the routes you normally take. Routes you *have* to take. Kidnappers are going to pick a choke point with cover, concealment, and a way to escape. Know what those points are. Be prepared when you pass them."

Sara scooted her knees over as a latecomer squeezed in beside her. It was all well worth coming for, even if she hadn't needed the distraction. The ex-Secret Service agent might be a bit unprepossessing in appearance, but what he had to say was both interesting and practical, and it was just too bad, after all the effort he'd put into offering the seminar, that so few of the city's large expatriate community had taken advantage of it. She glanced around—and opened her eyes wide with surprise. Her new seatmate hadn't been the only late arrival while she'd been listening with fascination to the discussion. The seats behind her were no longer empty. In fact, the room was almost full. *Hora boliviana,* she thought with a grin. Bolivian time.

The crowd was a varied one. Sara recognized a family of Canadian oil people she'd met at the English church, as well as others she knew to be Americans. She scanned a group of adolescents in the row behind her, and two of the faces also looked familiar: a teenage boy and girl with identical dark curls and olive complexions, and features that were enough alike to mark them as brother and sister.

Now where have I seen them before?

Then it came back to her. The Fourth of July picnic. Nicky's explosion of temper. *What are the Salvietti kids doing at something like this?* Judging by the boy's bored expression, it wasn't fascination with the subject matter. If she remembered correctly, the teenagers did attend the Co-op school, so maybe one of their teachers had made the seminar a class project. The girl and her friends looked interested enough, whispering and giggling as they craned their necks to inspect Mr. McKinley's younger companion.

The object of their scrutiny showed no sign of noticing their giggles and stares. He sat slid forward in his seat, shoulders resting comfortably against the back, his dark eyes fastened unblinking on the speaker. And yet, as Sara watched him for a moment to see what was drawing the girls' attention, she sensed somehow that he was well aware of everything in the room and was, in fact, about as relaxed as—what was that trite old phrase?

"A coiled spring" jumped to mind. What, exactly, did this slight young man do for the embassy? A clerk here at the Santa Cruz consulate? Somehow, that didn't seem to fit. A security officer like Mr. McKinley?

Sara's eyes were drawn back to the easel by the sound of tearing paper, as Nathan McKinley ripped his city plan from the pad. On a fresh page, he outlined a small square. "Your simple awareness of possible danger is the first and best defense against that danger," the security officer continued. "Too many people walk through life without ever being aware of what's going on around them." McKinley began rapidly blocking in other squares below the first. "A man named Cooper invented a code that assigns colors to describe the levels of awareness with which people face a given situation. We call it, logically enough"—a brief smile teased the corners of his mouth as he scrawled the words across the top of the sheet—"Cooper's Color Code."

His attempt at humor hardly warranted the explosion of giggles and noisy rustles that ensued from the row of adolescents behind Sara. Sara glanced back as their excited murmurs rose loud enough to become annoying.

Talk about rude! Where are their teachers? But her frown froze on her lips as she realized what had aroused the teens' sudden interest. Not the lecture, but the latecomer who was threading his way quietly between the bookshelves and rows of seats.

Doug Bradford, United States Drug Enforcement Administration.

Sliding into a seat next to the young man Nathan McKinley had introduced as Ramon Gutierrez, his gaze scanned the crowd, his eyes slightly narrowed.

Looking for all the world as though he's checking out a lineup of the usual suspects, Sara thought irreverently, knowing now where she'd seen his seatmate's air of relaxed alertness. And where she'd heard the euphemism "working for the embassy." The two men were even dressed alike, though Bradford's collared T-shirt and casual slacks were khaki rather than black. *Embassy, my eye! I'd bet anything that Ramon Gutierrez works for the DEA just like Bradford!*

"The first level in Cooper's Code is *white*." McKinley didn't miss a beat in his presentation, but he glanced momentarily at Bradford as the DEA agent sat down. Bradford lifted his hand halfway in salute, and McKinley acknowledged the greeting with a slight nod before turning back to the easel.

So they're together, Sara deduced. *Does that mean Doug Bradford is involved in this seminar as well?*

The black marker lines against the paper made the first square a creamy color. In bold letters next to it, Nathan McKinley printed W-H-I-T-E. "When you're in *white* mode, you're completely unaware. You're getting along with your spouse. The house is painted. The bills are paid. The birds are chirping. And you're not paying any attention. Your head is down. You're not noticing what is happening around you. These are the people who get pickpocketed and mugged, because they're such easy targets."

Sara scribbled a few words in her notebook. But despite her genuine interest in the material, she couldn't keep her mind—and her eyes—from drifting across the room to the two men seated so quietly at the far end of the front row. It had been three weeks since Sara had left Doug Bradford standing amid the spun-up gravel of her getaway taxi, and she had been less than thrilled to see him walk in tonight.

Not that she still clung to any of her earlier animosity. She was actually developing a grudging respect for the DEA agent—not only because he'd proved himself right in so many areas, but because of the kind of man she'd glimpsed him to be under that unbending surface. There had been compassion there, and even kindness, along with that uncompromising zeal for the job he'd been chosen to do, and he was really just the sort of person, Sara considered with some wistfulness, that under other circumstances she might have enjoyed having as a friend. But she cringed to think of the poor opinion he must have of her after the way she'd stormed away from their last encounter, and the thought of facing him here again tonight was not a comfortable one.

"The next level of awareness is *yellow*." Nathan McKinley traded his black marker for a yellow one and began filling in the next square. "Here you recognize some threat, some element of potential danger, and so you're in a minimal stage of awareness. For example, you're walking down a dark alley. You're not worried, but it's a bad part of town, so you keep an eye out around you—to make sure no one is following you. You can be in *yellow* all the time. You automatically check the area when you leave the house. You notice if there is someone loitering who could be surveying the place. When you're going through a danger area, you're on alert and paying attention to everything going on around you. This is the normal stage for security personnel or policemen."

Or DEA agents, Sara thought wryly. She was suddenly very tired. Julio Vargas and the responsibility she felt to see him brought to justice had haunted her waking hours—and even her dreams—these past few days, and only now did she realize how much of a strain the watching and waiting had been. What a relief it would be to unburden her mind and lay the whole dilemma on somebody else's shoulders. Someone she could trust to do something about it! She glanced reflexively at Doug Bradford, then shook her head and pushed the thought away.

Nicolás—and Don Luis—might still have a satisfactory explanation for all this. Maybe . . . maybe she wasn't giving them enough credit. Perhaps even now they were working out some way to hand Julio Vargas over to the authorities without jeopardizing their own position or that of Cortéz Industries. And even if they weren't . . .

"*Orange* takes us a step higher," McKinley was saying. "You now recognize a serious potential for danger in the situation and must develop a plan. This level takes energy, puts stress on your body. For instance, you're at the entrance to that dark alley. You're already in *yellow*, so you notice a pair of questionable characters watching you from the other end of the alley. You begin to get worried. Now, you don't know that they're dangerous. They could simply be out for an evening stroll. But the potential of danger is considerably higher than it was a moment ago. You now have the opportunity to decide what to do before you get into the situation. That's *orange*. You can continue on, but now you're cautious of a possible attack. Or you can choose to turn around and remove yourself from the situation."

Sara bent over her notebook. *Remove yourself from the situation.* If only it were that easy! She had removed herself from the situation these past few days—deliberately or not—and what had been the result? Sometimes you can't just walk away! Sometimes you have to go forward and face the situation head on.

"That's exactly right!" McKinley's enthusiastic response to a comment from a person in the audience drew Sara's attention back to the presentation. "*Red* is under attack. Those punks in the alley are coming after you. You need to do something, get away, execute that plan you formulated in *orange*."

Sara realized she'd missed part of the discussion, and McKinley was now filling in the last square. "What you must avoid at all costs is *black* here. *Black* is the unfortunate result"—the security officer tapped the first square at the top of the pad—"of spending your life up here in *white*. When you're aware—you're in *yellow* or *orange* mode—and you come under attack, at least you're thinking. You've got some kind of plan. You're able to react, however effectively. But when you're completely unaware—in *white*—and you're attacked, your body just can't handle the stress. Instead of reacting to the threat, you freeze. You can't think. You can't move. You just park there, paralyzed by shock and terror, while those precious first seconds tick by. We call this an inappropriate response to stimuli. You are always better off doing *something*. You may not be sure it's the right thing, but if you don't get moving, you're dead!"

Do something. Formulate a plan. And execute it. Well, that was exactly what Sara had made up her mind to do. But not tonight, she decided with some regret as she sketched in the last points. She was serious about going to the DEA if she had to. But she owed Nicolás a chance to explain first—and she still hoped he'd make his own decision to do the right thing.

Besides, she hadn't forgotten Doug Bradford's insinuations about the Cortezes. It would be one thing for Nicolás and Don Luis, with or without her insistence, to go to the DEA themselves and cooperate voluntarily. But if she told Doug Bradford what she knew—or rather, suspected—it would simply confirm his belief that the Cortezes were some kind of desperate criminals. And though she didn't want Julio Vargas to get away, neither did she want her new family to get into trouble. No, talking to the DEA would have to wait until she'd talked first to Nicolás.

Laying down her pen, Sara straightened her back. But maybe if she could ask just a few discreet questions . . .

Her gaze wandered again through the gap between two sets of shoulders in front of her—and locked with a pair of cool, gray eyes.

He couldn't really have overheard her mental debate. Sara knew that. He'd simply turned his head and caught her staring. But it gave her a jolt, and for a moment she couldn't pull her eyes away. He didn't look away either, but gave one of those slight nods that acknowledges unexpected eye contact across a room. And then—as though he had a different memory of their last meeting than she did—he smiled.

It was a nice smile, a friendly smile. It barely touched the corners of his mouth but crinkled the corners of his watchful eyes with a warmth that she'd seen him express to others, but never to her. She could find none of the amusement and mockery she was accustomed to reading into his every expression, and for the first time in their admittedly limited acquaintance, Sara felt that Doug Bradford, DEA agent, was actually seeing her—Sara Connor de Cortéz—as a fellow human being and not a job-related problem. Briefly, the curve of her own mouth tilted upward in response.

But only for an instant. Then she blushed, the wave of color rising from her neck in a surge of embarrassment and guilt that she could feel burning all the way to her hairline. Embarrassment for how she had stormed away from their last encounter, and guilt for the information she was withholding. Wasn't there a law against failing to report a crime? If Doug Bradford really could read her mind, he wouldn't be smiling at her right now.

Snatching her eyes away, Sara buried them in her notebook. So much for asking discreet questions. She couldn't even look at the man without giving herself away!

Across the room, Doug Bradford misinterpreted Sara's averted eyes and blushing cheeks. His mouth twisted wryly as he looked away. So the girl was still harboring those silly prejudices. That was too bad. Personally, he liked the girl. More, he approved of her, and not just because she reminded him of Julie.

The line of his jaw relaxed a fraction as his last image of Sara Cortéz popped into his mind, not storming angrily away, but bent over a sobbing child—those same features he'd seen stubborn and angry and proud softened to a tenderness and distress that had touched something inside him. The girl had class and character. And, in his opinion, she was too good for the Cortéz clan. He just hoped that young Nicky-boy had the sense to appreciate what he'd gotten in a wife.

Yes, he approved of Sara Cortéz. That he also felt sorry for her and—in some strange way—responsible, made no sense at all. Granted, she was a long way from home and had been dealt some tough breaks in life. But she seemed to have found her feet well enough here in Santa Cruz. This crazy concern for her well-being was undoubtedly the result of all that snooping into her file, and was a sure sign that he was getting too personally involved in his work.

And yet, all Doug's logic couldn't rid him of the feeling that Sara Cortéz needed a friend. A friend outside the circles in which her husband and his family moved. Just in case . . .

Well, he was the last to qualify for that job. It was only too clear that she hadn't forgiven him for the facts about her new family that he'd hammered at her on their last encounter. Not that he blamed her. He'd been tactless and bullheaded. Still, he was glad to see her here with Laura and Sam. Maybe it was just a lingering trace of his own distrust for anything to do with the Cortezes, but illogical or not, he'd sleep better knowing she had someone she could turn to whom he trusted.

Doug took a quick peek at his watch. He hoped this class wasn't going to run too late. He still had to go out tonight. An unwise druggie had crossed the wrong set of people, and Doug was going to do him a favor by taking in a NIFC team to bust his rear end before the Colombians managed to track him down.

Ramon nudged Doug, and he returned his attention to the seminar in time to hear Nathan McKinley say, "And speaking of 'doing something,' I'm going to turn the rest of the evening over to Doug Bradford and Ramon Gutierrez, members of our U.S. embassy staff here in Santa Cruz. I'm sure you will find their advice on self-defense techniques quite valuable." His eyes twinkled behind his glasses. "I can tell you this! I watched the two of them work out last night, and I can't think of anyone I'd rather have on my side in that dark alley we were talking about."

Doug and Ramon exchanged glances as they got up, but they offered no disclaimer for McKinley's praise. Neither did they waste any time on introductions. Ramon set the easel back against the wall while Doug stepped out in front of the audience.

"I'd like to make one thing clear before we start. When we talk about self-defense techniques, we're not talking about what you see on television or in a martial arts tournament. We're talking simple survival. You're not out there to be a hero, or catch a bad guy, or win a fight. That's the job of the police. Nor are you out to kill— unless there is absolutely no other solution. When it comes to self-defense, you've got one aim: to distract or disable your opponent long enough to get you—and anyone with you—away from the scene of the attack to where you can get help."

Doug nodded to his partner and Ramon picked up the discussion. "Anything that you can lay your hands on to cut, stab, blind, distract, jab, strangle, trip—whatever—can give you the edge to survive." Ramon unbuckled his belt and pulled it off, wrapping it around his hand as he continued, "A belt, for example, can be used as a whip."

Without warning, he whirled around, lashing the belt out toward Doug so fast that it cracked in the air like a snapping branch. There were gasps and exclamations from the audience. Doug managed not to flinch, though the buckle had come close enough to graze his shirt. He resumed the lecture calmly as Ramon slid his belt back on.

"As you can see, there are things all around us that can aid in a self-defense situation. It's just a matter of taking advantage of them. We'll be handing out a sheet in a moment with a list of common items that can be used as defensive weapons. You may have other suggestions you'd like to add yourselves. These items can be used by anyone and don't require special skill or hours of training."

Doug began emptying the contents of his pockets onto the easel as he spoke. "What they *do* require is a willingness to act—and to act first and fast." Picking up his pen, he made a downward jabbing motion. "Use your pen to stab an attacker. Aim for the neck or the eyes."

Slipping the pen back into his breast pocket, he took up his key ring. Spreading the keys apart, he slid them upward between his fingers, then made a fist around the ring. "Your keys can be used like a set of brass knuckles." He demonstrated the technique, grazing Ramon's chin, before pocketing his keys and picking up his wallet and comb. "Use your ID card to jab into the assailant's face and eyes. The teeth edges of a comb can be used as a razor. Grip it tightly, teeth out. Again, slash it across the eyes or the neck."

Ramon took over while Doug returned his belongings to his pockets. "You've got to learn to look around and assess what you see as a possible weapon. You can throw bleach or paint into the attacker's face. Spray deodorant or bug poison. Beat him over the head with a bat or a crowbar. Stab him with a pair of scissors or screwdriver or fork. Fend him off with a chair or a garbage can lid or a hub cap."

"How about a chain saw?" somebody offered from the audience.

Ramon smiled for the first time. "A chain saw—now that's really hard to defend against. The point is, you've got to reach for something, and you've got to do it fast!"

From nowhere, an empty soda can appeared in Ramon's hand.

Placing it upright on his right palm, he gripped the sides with his fingers. Holding his other hand out in front of him, he punched the can at it as though he were doing a shot put. The crunch of aluminum could be heard halfway across the library. The crumpled can fell to the floor. "Just imagine that was someone's face!"

"Of course, you may not always have access even to such simple weapons as these," Doug went on easily as Ramon bent to pick up his object lesson. "But your own body can be a formidable weapon, even without training, if you can get past your own reluctance to strike another person. Go for the eyes or the groin. Those are two of the most vulnerable—"

Ramon came off the floor in a blur of motion, the pop can scooped up in his left hand, his right shooting out stiff-fingered toward Doug's face with the swiftness of a striking snake. This time Doug did move. He whipped his arm up to knock Ramon's jabbing fingers away from his eyes, while at the same instant he lashed out with his foot, hooking one of his partner's ankles and giving an upward jerk. Ramon hit the ground, but not alone. He twisted his leg before Doug could pull his foot away, using the momentum of his fall to send Doug flying over his head. Doug turned the fall into a somersault, coming back to his feet in a smooth roll. The audience was cheering and clapping.

"Hey, cool!" a boyish voice exclaimed from several rows back. "Did you see how fast they are? Ninja!"

Doug lifted a hand to the audience, smiling as though this had all been part of the planned presentation. "And that"—he announced matter-of-factly—"was an example of an eye jab. The trick is to make sure your opponent doesn't know it's coming." Dusting off his khaki slacks, he bent to pick up the easel, which had crashed to the ground, punctuating their display. "Wasn't that a little dramatic?" he muttered to Ramon. "You just about put my eyes out!"

Ramon grinned unrepentantly. "I would have stopped in time. You should have trusted me! Besides, they loved it. Listen to them!"

"Yeah, well, stick to the script from now on. I've got a job tonight, and I don't have time to stop by the infirmary."

The rest of the presentation proceeded routinely as the two agents demonstrated the various hits and vulnerable spots that could be exploited even by an untrained victim. Sara watched and listened, as fascinated as anyone else in the group. She'd never thought of Doug Bradford as a particularly athletic individual, and his younger companion had seemed even less so, especially when compared with

Nicolás's carefully sculpted physique. Now she saw that both men were, in fact, superbly fit.

Upon request, the two agents obligingly repeated each maneuver in an exaggerated slow motion. A palm strike to the head. A side kick to the knee. A head smack into the face. They made it all look so easy, but when Doug called for the group to stack their chairs against the wall and pair up to try the moves on each other, Sara quickly discovered that it was harder than it looked. She wasn't sure why she was so surprised. But then, nothing so far had been what she'd anticipated.

Sara knew she must have had contact with U.S. embassy personnel during her time in Bogotá as a child. Maybe some had even been DEA. But once her father had moved her back to the United States, her only exposure to diplomats, government agents, and the hundreds of other men and women who served their country overseas, had been on the movie screen and in the pages of political suspense novels. CIA, FBI, Special Forces, Secret Service—these were legendary heroes, the cowboys of the modern era—alternately vilified and glorified, but always larger than life.

Sara had too much sense to judge the world by Hollywood standards. Still, she'd expected—well, she wasn't really sure what she'd expected, but it had been quite a surprise to find out how normal— even ordinary—these people were in real life. Gregarious, sociable Ellen Stevens. Doug Bradford the church usher. Mr. McKinley, with his receding hairline and slightly stooped shoulders and glasses. None of them fit the preconception she'd had of a "government agent." They were just—people!

Now, as she laughingly fended off the elbow that Laura Histed was pretending to rake across her face, Sara found herself revising her first estimate. Not only because of the unexpected martial arts skills that Ramon and Doug had demonstrated. There was something about these men—yes, even gray-haired, balding Mr. McKinley— something that went beyond appearances and made the Hollywood version seem like an overplayed caricature of the real thing. Something in the way they walked and the clarity of their gaze; something in the habit of authority that was unmistakable under all the affability, and the unobtrusive but completely self-possessed air of competence. An unyielding quality she'd noted first in Doug Bradford that wasn't so much a hardness as an awareness that life wasn't always safe and easy and good—and that, when a bad guy drew a line in the dust, they were the ones who might have to step over it. And if they wore their occupations with a certain casualness, unlike their cinematic counterparts, maybe it was because they were too busy doing their jobs to concern themselves with creating an image.

And if that isn't being corny, I don't know what is! Sara told herself as she joined in the applause that signaled the end of the seminar.

The audience spread out into chattering knots that filled the open area where the rows of chairs had been. Sara spotted Nathan McKinley over by the easel, talking to a handful of oil executives and their wives. The two DEA agents were surrounded by a mob of teenagers. Doug was patiently answering their questions, and Ramon Gutierrez actually seemed to be enjoying himself.

Sara threaded her way toward the door from the back of the library, where she and Laura had ended up during the one-on-one drill. She took her time, eyeing rather wistfully the animated clusters of people who all seemed to know each other. She had no reason to hurry home, and she wouldn't have minded staying around a little longer to chew over the seminar as so many of the others seemed to be doing. But Laura and Sam had already said their good-byes, and though Sara recognized a few other faces, she didn't know any of them well enough to sit around and chat.

She was almost to the door when she realized that the two DEA agents had disentangled themselves from their eager fan club and were heading through the crowd directly toward her. Her first impulse was to lengthen her steps, but as she reached the door, she hesitated. She had recovered from that earlier flush of embarrassment, and the questions she'd been holding in all evening still burned on her tongue. Now that Doug Bradford was actually crossing her path . . .

Lifting her chin, she turned to face the approaching DEA agents. They were talking to each other and didn't even glance in her direction. Sara's courage and the words she'd quickly rehearsed died in her throat. She stepped back hastily as an elderly woman shuffled into the doorway, her walker inching slowly ahead of her. The two agents also stopped to allow the woman to pass. Sara didn't dare raise her eyes. She was feeling all the awkwardness that attends a chance encounter with someone with whom you haven't been on the best of terms. As much as she wanted answers, she couldn't bring herself to start a conversation.

She didn't have to.

"Good evening, Mrs. Cortéz." The formal greeting came from above her head.

Sara swung around. "Sara!" she corrected automatically, then gave herself a mental kick. Now, why had she started that again?

"Sara," Doug agreed with a suspicious meekness that told her that he too was remembering the last time they'd held this conversation. Sara looked up at him doubtfully. He was smiling again, a half-grin that held some of the same friendliness that had startled her earlier. His gray eyes crinkled at the corners with an amusement that wasn't so much laughing at her as inviting her to share in the joke. Her spirit unfolded wings. Maybe he wasn't thinking so badly of her after all!

"I . . . I really enjoyed your presentation," she gathered up the courage to say, a shy smile extending her appreciation to include Ramon Gutierrez. "And Mr. McKinley's too, of course. It was"—she hesitated, searching for the right word—"impressive."

"Thank you!" The DEA agent looked surprised at the compliment. "I'm glad you enjoyed it. I just hope it was of some practical use."

"Oh, it was practical, all right!" Sara responded with feeling, remembering with an inward shudder a dark city street almost four months in the past. "I just wish someone had taught me some of those things before now!"

"That's what everyone says after the fact," Doug agreed seriously. "It's one reason seminars like McKinley's are so valuable. Not that they're really enough. It takes time and practice to react quickly to aggression, and you can't get that in one evening. Personally, if I had my way, I'd make it a requirement for every U.S. citizen to take a full training in self-defense. Especially women. Maybe you'll never need it, but it's better to be prepared than sorry when you do. And statistically, it's downright scary how many people are likely to be a victim of aggression at some time in their lives. I can tell you, there'd be a lot less work for the policeman on the street if the average criminal wasn't so much better prepared than the average citizen. I've—"

Ramon's pointed cough interrupted Doug's commentary. He'd heard this particular lecture before. Doug glanced at his partner and recognized the appreciative gleam with which Ramon was eyeing Sara. Doug's lips twitched. His friend, he'd already learned, had a thing for blondes. He turned back to Sara. "Sara, I'd like to introduce you to one of my colleagues, Ramon Gutierrez. Ramon, Sara de Cortéz."

"Cortéz. Not—" Ramon shot a glance at Doug, received a warning shake of the head, and turned his exclamation into another cough. He extended his hand, the frank appreciation in his dark eyes toned down to a more decorous level. "It's a pleasure to make your acquaintance."

"Ra-muun! Ramon. Oh, there you are! Honey, you boys were great tonight!" Both men winced at the enthusiastic and strident female voice.

Ramon dropped Sara's hand and stepped hastily away, his narrow features taking on a hunted expression as a tall, thin woman bore down on him. "Uh, it was good meeting you, Sara," he said apologetically over his shoulder. "But if you'll excuse me . . ."

Doug's grin broadened as he watched his friend make an unsuccessful bid for escape. Ramon's and Kyle Martin's "favorite expatriate" headed him off at the pass and launched into a spirited monologue. She had finally quit phoning the office, but only because the DEA's administrative officer, Ellen Stevens, who saw no humor in the woman's relentless pursuit of every unmarried agent assigned to the Santa Cruz office, flatly refused to put through any more of her calls. How she'd known Ramon would be at the security seminar tonight was anyone's guess, but she was one determined woman!

Without a twinge of sympathy, Doug turned back to Sara. Her cheeks were dimpled and her amber eyes danced as she watched Ramon's back stiffen with protest, while the woman carried on obliviously, her colorful bracelets flashing in animated discourse. "I take it that's someone your friend isn't too anxious to meet," Sara smiled.

"The lady is determined to find a husband," Doug answered bluntly. "Preferably, American." Then he checked himself, looking down at Sara with one eyebrow raised high. "I'm sorry. I can't believe I said that!" The curve of his mouth grew rueful. "I guess I feel like I've known you longer than I really have. If you meet her socially, please don't pass along my opinion."

Sara dimpled again. "No, of course I won't. I don't even know who she is." With a start, she realized that she was actually having her first friendly conversation with Doug Bradford. She knew what he meant, too. It didn't seem possible that their entire past acquaintance had been one rather acrimonious discussion. There was nothing like giving—and getting—a good chewing-out to break down social barriers. She wracked her brain for some other innocuous topic of conversation that would hold the mood of the moment. "I . . . I didn't see your friend Ellen Stevens here tonight."

"Ellen?" Doug said carelessly. "No, she wouldn't come to something like this. Our diplomatic staff receive these kinds of briefings before they ever come to places like Bolivia."

Sara saw his glance slide to his watch before he added, "I was glad to see you've gotten involved in the *Hogar de Infantes*. You're doing a good job there. Doña Inez has really appreciated the help you've given her."

"Why, thank you!" It was Sara's turn to be surprised. "How did you know about that?" Her smile faded abruptly as she recognized the absurdity of the question. Had she forgotten she was talking to the man who'd made a career out of investigating the Cortezes? He probably knew what she'd had for supper tonight!

Doug followed the change of expression on her face. "No, I wasn't spying on you!" he informed her dryly. "As a matter of fact, I stopped by the children's home the other day to drop off a load of clothes some of the families in our office had put together. You were playing games with the little ones in the patio there. When I walked in, you had some kid bleeding all down the front of your shirt. I'd have volunteered first aid, but you seemed to have things well under control."

Sara reddened at the mixture of approval and exasperation in his tone. "Oh!" she said in a small voice. She remembered the occasion, though she hadn't noticed him at the time. "That must have been when Juan Carlos hit his head on the fountain. It wasn't as bad as it looked, though he sure thought so. Poor little guy! I just wish . . ." Sara trailed off as she saw Doug's gaze flicker past her to the doorway before returning to her face.

"Yes?" he prompted, but the syllable was preoccupied, and Sara could sense his attention straining away from her. The social requirements had been fulfilled and only good manners were still holding him by her side. Sara drew a deep breath, her heart suddenly racing, indecision catching at her throat. It was time to stop beating around the bush. If she had anything else to say, this was her last opportunity.

"Look, Sara, it was good to see you here tonight." Doug glanced at his watch again, this time openly. "But if you'll excuse me, I'm afraid I'm going to have to run or I'll be late for an appointment."

His nod was one of polite dismissal, but he made eye contact long enough for her to say good-bye. In another moment he would be walking out the door. Sara hadn't even consciously made up her mind to speak before the words were bursting out.

"About . . . about that drug bust in Miami. Those Bolivian tapestries they found in the gallery? Did they ever find out where they came from? Or who put the cocaine in them?"

Her words caught the DEA agent in midstride. It was almost comical the way he finished setting his foot down, then turned slowly around. Sara had his full attention again.

"What did you say?"

"I was just—"

Before she could get anything else out, Doug was back at her side.

"No, not here." He glanced swiftly around the library, then took Sara by the arm. "If you would care to walk with me for a moment, Mrs. Cortéz?"

He didn't give her a choice. Steering Sara to the door, he propelled her out onto the wide, roofed veranda that ran along the full length of the library wing. Most of the evening's audience was still in the library—but a few curious glances were thrown in their direction. Beyond the veranda, where a dark rectangle of lawn swept across to the unlighted bulk of the gym, adolescent laughter rose from the black shadows of a clump of *toborochi* trees. Doug jerked his head to the left, toward the far end of the corridor. "Over there. I want to talk to you. In private."

Sara had to almost run to keep up with Doug's long strides, but after one glance up at his face, she bit back any protests.

At the corner, Doug turned left again. Another veranda ran along the back side of the library wing, and this one was unlit and empty. It was also very dark, and Sara was beginning to wonder what she'd let herself in for when, high above the school, a scattering of clouds separated, revealing an almost-full moon; its soft beam angled under the wide roof of the veranda and shone a dim light across the polished tile floor.

Sara's forced march came to a halt halfway down the corridor. Swinging her around to face him, Doug released her and took a step back. "Now, tell me," he said sternly, "what do *you* know about the gallery in Miami? And about where those hangings came from?"

"I . . . I . . ."

The DEA agent shifted impatiently at the hesitation, bringing the rugged planes of his face into sharp relief against the pale light of the moon. Staring up at him, Sara swallowed a momentary panic. The gray eyes that had smiled at her just a few minutes before were again watchful and hard. Sara lowered her eyelids. "I was just asking a question," she finished feebly.

"You were just asking a question!" Doug echoed loudly. "And since when did you start taking such an interest in the DEA and its cases? Come on, Sara! You know and I know you didn't ask those questions without a reason." He studied her lowered eyes with hard speculation. "Now, what is it you're not telling me? For one thing, how did you know those hangings came from Bolivia?"

"Why, I saw it on the news!" Sara's eyes flew up, her genuine surprise at the question dispelling her alarm. "Weren't they?"

"The news!" Doug muttered something under his breath that Sara didn't catch. He leaned back against the wall, his shoulders rubbing against the ceramic tiles. "So you're telling me this is all just idle curiosity. You just happened to catch a newsclip on CNN and figured, 'Hey, there's something for casual conversation next time I run into someone from the DEA.' And I'm all wet thinking you're hiding something from me in that little head of yours."

Try as she might, Sara couldn't keep the telltale color that always betrayed her from creeping up her face. Doug's shrewd gaze watched its progress. A low whistle escaped his teeth. "Well, well!" he exclaimed with satisfaction. "So that's what all the guilty blushing in there was all about!"

Sara felt her color deepen even more. A hand flew to her hot cheeks. "I don't know what you mean!" she protested, not sounding convincing even to herself. "What . . . what makes you think I'm hiding something?"

Doug folded his arms across his chest. "Because you're about as easy to read as the front-page headlines," he informed her silkily. "If you're going to start lying to me, Sara Cortéz, you're going to have to learn to keep it out of your face."

"I wasn't lying!" Sara said angrily. "I didn't say anything." She broke off. This was *not* how she'd planned for this to go. "Look, it's not what you think!"

She fell silent for a moment. Doug waited, arms across his chest, his eyes steady on her face. Then she asked hesitantly, "What if . . . well, what if you suspected someone you knew might be involved in a crime? I mean, you weren't sure, but you had good reason to believe that maybe he was! Only . . . only if you said something, you might get a lot of innocent people in trouble—"

"If they're innocent," Doug cut in implacably, "you don't need to worry about getting them in trouble."

"That's not true, and you know it!" Sara argued. "You're always hearing about innocent people ending up in jail. If there's evidence that points the wrong way, or someone lies about them—"

"Don't kid yourself." Doug's tone was dry. "With the legal system —and lawyers—the way they are these days, loaded ten to one on the side of the criminal, there's not one chance in a million of ending up in jail unless you're as guilty as sin! Not for drugs, anyway! Certainly not in this country. In fact, half of those who should be there aren't!"

Unfolding his arms abruptly, he straightened up from the wall. "That *is* what you're talking about, isn't it? Cocaine? And those innocent friends of yours—that would be the Cortezes? Oh, don't try to fool me, Sara! You wouldn't be scrambling so hard to protect anyone else. Is that what you're trying to hide? That your in-laws had something to do with those tapestries in Miami?"

"I . . . I . . . Of course not!" Sara felt like stamping her foot with frustration. She'd been right! She never should have allowed Doug Bradford within a mile of her. "Oooh—honestly! All I did was ask a question! Why can't you just answer me, or . . . or leave me alone?"

"And what, exactly, was your question? I seem to have lost track." The DEA agent sounded anything but encouraging.

"I told you!" Sara cried. "I just wanted to know if they'd found out where that shipment came from. And who put the cocaine in those hangings. It was no big deal. It's not like I'm asking for classified information! I mean, if you're with the DEA, you should at least know if they found out anything!"

"And you're not going to tell me why you want to know." When she didn't answer, Doug ran his fingers through his hair in a gesture that was pure exasperation. "What do you expect me to say, Sara? You're asking for information dealing with a crime. I couldn't give out that kind of intel, even if I *did* have it!"

"In other words, you don't!" Sara said in a low voice. "I . . . I was afraid of that."

She turned quickly away and walked over to the edge of the veranda. Wrapping an arm around one of the pillars that held up the roof, she rested her head against the rough stucco, her eyes unseeing. If he would just go away now so that she could think.

"Well, I'm sorry I bothered you. I won't take up any more of your time."

"And I'm supposed to just let it go like that!" Doug crossed the few feet that separated them in one swift motion. He was suddenly very angry. With her and with himself. Why was he letting this girl get under his skin? He had a job to do tonight, and he didn't need this distraction!

"Look, I don't pretend to know what this is all about. But if there's something you should be telling me, just spill it out instead of all this hinting around! You talk about getting innocent people in trouble. Well, maybe you need to trust us on that. We don't exactly get our kicks from arresting the wrong guys. But if you've got information—or even suspect—that someone you know might be dealing in cocaine, then you've got a responsibility to tell me about it. Or did your sense of civic duty go out the window when you married into the Cortéz clan?"

Sara just shook her head. Doug had to restrain himself from shaking her. Finally, she straightened up from the pillar, her eyes coming back from the distance to his face. They were dark and unhappy and wide with emotion. Doug found his anger softening despite his irritation. He gentled the roughness of his tone.

"Look, you're a nice girl, Sara, and I can't really blame you for trying to protect your family." He held up his hand to stop her reply. "No, don't try to tell me that isn't what this is all about! I won't believe you. Okay, so you think the Cortezes are as white as driven snow. I don't, but I can't prove it. That's beside the point. And maybe you're right, and I've been wrong all along. For your sake, I really do hope so. Either way, I told you once before that if you ever needed help, I was available. I suppose if I give you my card again, you'll just tear it up, but—well, I just want you to know that if you're ever in need of a friend, that offer still stands."

A fleeting smile touched the straight line of his mouth. "And if you change your mind about talking, don't wait too long. These people don't play around! I'd hate to see you fall through that thin ice you're on."

The sudden kindness caught Sara by surprise. She felt tears begin to sting her eyes, and she looked away quickly. She could feel Doug's steady gaze on her face as though he was willing her to speak. Again, she felt a sense of time running away from her, and the impulse to pour it all out was so strong that she had to bite her lip to keep it in. Then Doug let out an exasperated sigh. "Well, Sara Cortéz, if you have nothing to say, I really do have to go! I've still got work to do tonight—making sure at least some of this country's garbage doesn't make it to American soil!"

Stepping off the veranda, he strode briskly across the playground —not back toward the library, but on a trajectory that would take him toward the parking lot.

"Wait!"

Sara's quiet voice stopped Doug before he had taken a half-dozen strides. He swung around on his heel. Sara stepped down from the veranda onto the grass. "Look, I really can't tell you much. I . . . I don't know much right now! But—well, do you know a man named Julio Vargas?"

Doug made no move to return to the veranda. "Enlighten me."

"He's the head of security for Cortéz Industries." Sara stepped back up onto the veranda even as she got the words out. "That's all I can say right now. Just . . . just check him out." And with another step backward across the polished tile, she turned and fled.

CHAPTER SIXTEEN

Sara glanced back after her first few hasty steps. The DEA agent had made no effort to follow her. He was standing in the middle of the school yard, his face a white blur in the moonlight. Whirling back around, she stretched her slim legs to a faster pace. As she rounded the corner of the building, she ran smack into a teenage boy who was loitering just out of sight. Recovering her balance, she backed off with a murmured apology, then her eyes went wide with surprise when she realized who it was. *The Salvietti boy.* The hostility and suspicion in his eyes told Sara that he'd recognized her as well.

Well, I don't care for you a whole lot either! she said to herself as she pushed past him and sped toward the beckoning fluorescent glow of the library.

✠

Doug watched Sara disappear around the corner. *Confound that girl!* What was it that possessed otherwise decent human beings to withhold information from the law? Well, the answer to that was easy enough! She felt it was her duty to protect someone, and it wasn't hard to guess who. Unfortunately, there was no law that said she had to volunteer anything. Not without a subpoena. And he could just see a judge granting a subpoena for a member of the Cortéz clan.

Pivoting on his heel, Doug continued across the grass toward the parking lot. He had half a mind to go after Sara de Cortéz and shake the information out of her, if he had to. But he had a raid going down in a couple of hours, and last minute details to attend to. The Cortezes would have to keep.

But as he sped toward the DEA office through the dark and almost empty streets of Santa Cruz, an anxious young face kept intruding on his thoughts. Finally, he pushed his plans for the raid to a back burner and gave his mind over for a few minutes to this new puzzle. What had gotten Sara de Cortéz so worked up that she would come to him, of all people, with her questions and that totally unconvincing story of interest in a news broadcast? Uncooperative as she had been, there were certain facts that he could fit together. She'd seen or overheard something that had her worried. That much was evident! Equally evident from her guilty reaction was the fact that it had something to do with the gallery case in Miami.

Doug knew about the tapestries, of course. The details of the case had been forwarded to the Santa Cruz DEA office, as was standard with any case that had possible connections on their end. But there hadn't been much information to go on. The tapestries in question had ended up at the gallery as stolen goods and hadn't been in their original shipping container. And despite the news reports that had mentioned Bolivia, the authorities hadn't been able to prove yet the country of origin. The tapestries were the handiwork of native Quechua highlanders, who were widely dispersed throughout Ecuador and Peru, as well as Bolivia. Similar woven scenes could be found in the tourist markets of any one of these countries, all three of which were major players in the international distribution of cocaine. So until the actual weaver could be identified—and Grant Major had already assigned a man to sniff out the local artisan markets—tracing their passage to U.S. soil would be next to impossible.

Not that there was any further doubt in Doug's mind about where those wall hangings had come from! More, he'd wager whose name had been stamped on the shipping container that had never turned up. What other "innocent people" besides the Cortezes would Sara be so anxious to protect? Whatever she was hiding, it had to be tied in somehow with Cortéz Industries. And just when he'd given up on anything new ever surfacing in that case! Was this the break he'd been waiting for?

And what about this Julio Vargas, whose name she'd thrown at him as though conferring some priceless gift? Where did he fit in? And what was his connection with the shipment of Quechua tapestries? What did Sara de Cortéz expect him to do with nothing more than a name? He needed more information!

Well, he'd started investigations before with little more. Successful ones, too. Offhand, he couldn't say that the name Julio Vargas jangled anything in the back of his mind. But that was no big deal considering the hundreds—even thousands—of informants and suspects he'd dealt with over the years. There were agents who claimed that they never forgot a name or a face. But for himself, unless it was a current case, all those Latino names tended to blur together after a while. If the man was head of security at Cortéz Industries, he was sure to be in the files somewhere. That was a start.

The high outer wall of the DEA complex was bleached white in the ghostly flicker of the street lamps. Doug pulled up to the gate, using his walkie-talkie to request entrance instead of the customary honk. The yellow glow of the guard shack's open doorway darkened as the soldier on duty stepped out to identify his late-night visitor. Rolling down his window, Doug left low-voiced instructions for the guard to call him when his NIFC squad arrived, then drove through as the gate slid open. It was a hassle to park inside when he'd only be there a few minutes, but the sight of an American DEA agent and half-a-dozen NIFC troops loading arms and equipment into the Land Rover wasn't exactly what he wanted to show any midnight strollers.

The soft whir of the air-conditioner was the only sound that followed Doug as he strode down the hall to his office. No one else was working late. Yanking a Kevlar vest and a black DEA jacket from their hangers in the supply closet, he tossed them onto a chair. Then he crossed the room and unlocked the weapons cabinet, lifting out an M-16 and adding a half-dozen magazines for the automatic rifle and a couple of extra nineteen-shot clips for his Glock-17 pistol to the pile.

His personal preparations finished, he dropped into his swivel chair and reached for a pad of paper. The night's mission had its humorous side, if anything about a drug bust could be humorous. Propping his feet up on the corner of his desk, Doug reviewed the information his hysterical informant had brought him earlier in the evening.

Informant #30578 was an accountant by training and corrupt and greedy by inclination. Perhaps because of this, he'd been chosen to be the money man linking a minor Colombian narcotics network with the small-time local supplier Doug was about to visit. He'd made a dozen runs, delivering twenty-kilo shipments of cocaine and bringing back extravagant quantities of cash. But with each trip, he'd grown progressively more nervous. He was the most vulnerable link in the chain, both coming and going, and he was smart enough to know that, sooner or later, he was going to get caught. And he wasn't even being paid enough to underwrite his family's dream of migrating to beautiful Argentina, which to the average Bolivian was as much the land of opportunity as the United States was to Mexicans.

A close call at his last border crossing had convinced #30578 to get out before his luck ran dry, and a streetwise relative had convinced him to enlist the *americanos* in his move back to the right side of the law. Like most informers, #30578 wasn't a stellar citizen, but the DEA had agreed to help him relocate on the condition that he make one more run, allowing them to catch the Colombians in possession of the goods before taking down the dealer on this end. They'd still been working out the details when #30578 had come screaming into the office just as Doug was heading out for a quick dinner before McKinley's seminar. News had just come down the line that the Colombians were not satisfied with his last delivery. In fact, they were hopping mad! It would seem that #30578's boss, not content with the huge sums he was pulling in, had decided to quadruple his profits—at the Colombians' expense. If a wrought-up #30578 could be believed, the Colombians had been repackaging the haul for its trip north when one of the less intelligent members of the organization decided to try a sample snort. A snort that proved suspiciously sweet in his sinuses.

"I cannot believe he was so stupid!" #30578 had screamed to Doug. "I told him they would find out if it was not pure! Now they want my head! And his too, of course." So now they were having to scratch the Colombian end of the operation and make an immediate grab for the supplier.

Doug shook his head in disbelief as he scribbled out his deployment plans for the raid. This wasn't the first case he'd come across of Bolivian narcos adding filler to their cocaine to increase profits. Mannitol, a sugar product used in baby food, was in its pure form a close enough twin to cocaine hydrochloride to fool any casual observer, and if they weren't too greedy, they could have gotten away with some judicious mixing—for a while. But five kilos of cocaine and fifteen kilos of mannitol? That was just plain stupid! And dangerous. Not to mention bad business. But it was certainly typical of the corruption that permeated this culture that they'd try to cheat even the drug cartels they depended on for their illicit income. Rumors were circulating that some of the bigger Brazilian cartels were actually refusing to deal with Bolivian suppliers, because of their propensity for dishonesty. And now, in an ironic turn of events that maybe wasn't so humorous after all, Doug was probably saving this sorry little creep's neck by going after him tonight! The Colombians didn't like being cheated.

Doug finished his deployment plans, then checked them over twice. He didn't like surprises, especially when his own neck was on the line, and even though the map put together by the NIFC surveillance team of the hit site was explicit in detail, he'd reconnoitered the place himself last night. There was one particularly obnoxious dog next door that would have to be taken out if they were to have any hope of surprising the supplier. A tranquilizer should do it. And a neighbor, whose return home from the late shift they'd have to avoid if they didn't want him mistaking the dark figures slipping through the next yard for burglars and raising the alarm.

Satisfied there was nothing more he could do to prepare, Doug flipped the pad of paper onto the desk with an expert twist of the wrist that missed the computer and landed it in his "out" basket. He'd go over the plans again with the men when they arrived, and incorporate their input and suggested changes. In the meantime, he had a few moments to spare. He didn't plan to hit the supplier's house until two in the morning, when the occupants would most likely be in their deepest sleep. The NIFC squad he'd chosen for the raid wasn't due to meet him until midnight—still fifteen minutes away. Doug folded his arms behind his head, stretched back in the swivel chair to an almost prone position, and reached again for the puzzle that Sara de Cortéz had left him.

Julio Vargas. Both names were as common in Spanish-speaking countries as Smith or Jones in English. And yet there was something about the name that nagged at Doug, now that he was free to think about it. Something it seemed he should know. Something completely unrelated to this present complication. With sudden decisiveness, Doug lowered his feet from the desk, sat up, and reached for a switch that lit up the blank glass of the computer monitor on his desk.

Five minutes later, he clicked the mouse on "Close." The file entry on Julio Vargas, head of security at the Cortéz refinery, had been disappointingly brief. He'd been a relatively new employee at the time of the raid two years ago, the one time Doug had really had the manpower or the authority to do any intensive investigation. In fact, he'd succeeded to his position as security chief just weeks before the raid, which was the only reason Doug had any real information on the man at all. Thirty-nine years old. Native of Santa Cruz province. Married and divorced. No children.

The only item of any real interest in Vargas's file was his military background. He'd been a colonel in the military police until he'd resigned three years ago and taken employment with *Industrias Cortéz.* That wasn't unusual in itself. Military or police experience was always a plus in the field of security. No reason for his change of jobs was mentioned in the file. Economics, perhaps. Major corporations offered higher salaries than government payrolls, here as well as in the United States.

There *had* been one odd note in the file, however. A clipping of a news story dealing with the death of Vargas's immediate superior —a rather gruesome homicide committed in the execution of a burglary, according to the police. They'd never caught the thief. Interesting! Was there some connection the informant who'd written up the report had been trying to convey? Or was the clipping just a surplus bit of data? At any rate, this Vargas was disappointingly clean, at least according to his file. And yet, there'd been something!

Leaning forward, Doug jiggled the mouse to banish the screen saver. Calling up the Vargas file again, he waited impatiently until the scant paragraphs of information reappeared on the screen. Yes, there it was! The item he'd read two years ago, amid a stack of such reports, and discarded as irrelevant at the time. Julio Vargas's military service had included pilot training. Cessnas. DC-3s. And helicopters.

Doug switched off the computer. A small flame of excitement was beginning to burn away his exasperation. But it had nothing to do with the unsolved case involving stolen Quechua tapestries. He was thinking of a lonely grass airstrip and the skid tracks of a military chopper. Pilots were a dime a dozen in Bolivia, but those with helicopter experience were considerably less common. Helicopters were still rare in Bolivia, mostly surplus Hueys donated by the United States for the drug war. Since those two hijackings, he'd had Ramon investigate the ranks of Air Force and FELCN helicopter pilots. But unless the *Fuerza Aérea Boliviana* was lying from the commander right down to the mechanics, every pilot and chopper had been accounted for at the appropriate times.

And now, here was a wild card staring him in the face.

A red button on his desk lit up. His NIFC team had arrived. "Let them into the conference room," Doug told the guard. Getting up, he considered the mound of equipment on his desk, then decided to leave it until after the briefing. That Kevlar vest chafed too much at the armpits to wear a minute longer than necessary. Collecting the map and the pad of paper, he stood for a moment while one thought slid into another.

A guilty expression on a transparent, heart-shaped face. A shipment of native tapestries impregnated with a half-million dollars of cocaine. An ex-colonel with military chopper experience. Huey landing tracks on a jungle airstrip. And, after a long dry spell, the inclusion of a name Doug had ample reason to dislike and distrust. Was it wishful thinking to see some tenuous linkage between all these assorted puzzle pieces?

Yes it probably was, Doug admitted. For the moment. There were holes in his database so big he couldn't even begin to convince himself. Still, stranger things had happened. There was little else he could do unless Sara de Cortéz chose to divulge some more information, but he'd turn the name of Julio Vargas over to Kyle and see what that eccentric genius could dig up. In the meantime, he had a job to do. Doug closed his mental files on Sara de Cortéz and Julio Vargas as neatly as he'd reached over to switch off the computer.

Sara lingered in the bright refuge of the library until she was sure Doug Bradford would be long gone. The crowd was thinning out, and though Nathan McKinley was still patiently answering questions, the other agent, Ramon Gutierrez, had made his escape. The tall, thin, bleach-bottle blonde who had cornered him was now wandering around from group to group as though she didn't know what to do with herself. Sara watched her for a moment with half understanding, half pity. She knew what it was to be hungry for human love and companionship, though she couldn't recommend the woman's strategy. When the woman caught Sara looking and started in her direction, Sara decided it was time for her own departure.

She expected to have to hike out to the main avenue to catch a taxi home, but when she reached the parking lot, she found the Histeds still there, standing by their van, chatting with another couple. When Laura saw Sara crossing the pavement, she hailed her in a cheery voice. "Sara, dearie, can we give you a ride? Or are you here in your own car?"

"I'd love a ride, if you're sure it isn't too far out of your way," Sara accepted gratefully. "But I thought you two left ages ago!"

"Well, you know how it is." Laura let out a mock sigh. "Someone traps you in the parking lot, and you just can't get away."

"Who trapped *whom* is the question!" her burly husband muttered a bit too audibly.

Laura gave him an indignant nudge. "You've been visiting as hard as I have!"

Sara found herself smiling as she listened to the married couple's comfortable banter. As long as there were people like this in the world, it couldn't be all bad! Giving into Laura's urging to crowd with them into the front seat, she allowed the Histeds to pull her into a spirited review of the evening's seminar.

But Sara's smile faded as soon as she waved good-bye to her friends outside the Cortéz estate. She'd made a fool of herself—again! Rummaging around in her purse for the key, she unlocked the small side door that bypassed the massive main gates. The dark glimmer of a face showed briefly through the unlit glass of the guard window as she slipped inside, but Jorge didn't show himself. The two Dobermans emerged momentarily to sniff her over suspiciously before a low whistle called them back inside the guardhouse.

Yes, she'd made a fool of herself. But even though she'd completely fallen apart under Doug Bradford's third-degree treatment and had ended up giving away more information than she'd received, his reaction to her query had left her with the answers she'd been after. The DEA agent was well aware of what had happened in that Miami gallery. That was evident in his own terse questions. But it was equally evident that the name Julio Vargas had meant nothing to him and that he had no notion of any connection between Cortéz Industries and that shipment of cocaine-laden tapestries. Whatever Nicolás and Don Luis were doing about Julio Vargas, they hadn't gone to the authorities. She couldn't delude herself anymore about that.

Sara walked slowly up the driveway, her sandals scuffing softly against the gravel. There was no sign yet of Mimi's compact Mercedes or Don Luis's limousine. That was just fine, because she didn't feel like facing either of them right now. This had been a lousy ending to a long and disappointing day. And tomorrow didn't promise to be any better. She'd hoped against all logic and evidence some explanation would prove her suspicions wrong. Now that last hope was gone, and in its place was anger and disappointment, and more than a little apprehension.

Skirting around the house through the gardens, Sara entered the side door behind the pool and climbed the wide stairs. It had seemed so simple, in the first flush of determination that afternoon—when she still had hope that she might be wrong—to talk about confronting Nicolás and Don Luis and convincing them to do the right thing. It didn't seem so easy now that she was faced with actually doing it. Every time she and Nicolás had argued in the past, she had been the one who had ended up backing down and making peace. What made her think this time would be any different?

And what about Don Luis? At least she *knew* Nicolás. She knew the warmth and generosity and sweetness that had characterized her husband when she'd first fallen for him back in Seattle—and of which she still saw glimpses when they were alone. Maybe he hadn't been raised with the same ideas of right and wrong that she had, but when it came right down to it, he would surely never deliberately hurt anyone or take his own pleasure at the expense of someone else. If she could just make him see, as she had, the desolate faces of those young addicts that Doug Bradford had shown her.

But with Don Luis, she couldn't be so sure. He could be ruthless when it came to Cortéz Industries; she'd already seen that. However courteous he might be to Sara in his distant way, she hadn't forgotten María and the way her father-in-law had allowed the girl to be tossed aside just to save face for this same Julio Vargas. So how willing would he be to consider the welfare of a bunch of nameless Americans over his own convenience and the success of his business empire?

And even if she managed to convince Nicolás, would he back her up with his father? Could she do it on her own if she had to? Much as it had irritated—and hurt—her that Nicolás hadn't made more of an effort to build a separate life for himself—for them—away from the constant presence of her in-laws, she had to admit that she was as overawed as Nicky was by her formidable father-in-law. He just wasn't the type of person you argued with, and the more that she considered asking—no, demanding—that Don Luis go to the authorities, the colder the feeling that squeezed at her stomach.

Please let him see reason! Please don't let him be too angry! The plea became a prayer, though she wasn't sure which 'him' she was referring to. Either way, tomorrow promised to be—well, unpleasant, at the least.

"Don't be such a wimp!" she said aloud, pushing the door open to her empty suite and tossing her purse onto a chair. "It's not like they're going to bite!"

With that reassurance, Sara busied herself with getting ready for bed. Pulling on a nightgown, she brushed her teeth, then considered the numbers blinking from the alarm clock on the bedside table. Tomorrow was almost here. She really should try to get some sleep, but she knew she'd just end up tossing and turning if she went to bed now. Crossing the room, she unlatched the tall wooden shutters that led onto the balcony.

The night was still warm, a sign that Santa Cruz's brief winter was coming to an end. High overhead, clouds were racing across the night sky, gray against black, indicating strong winds higher in the troposphere. But down below, in the black waters of the pool, a golden ball smiled its placid reflection at the almost perfect circle of the moon. Sara leaned her arms on the rail, the moonlight transmuting her nightgown and the silky strands spilling down over her shoulders to the same silvery-pale as the blossoms whose vines curled up onto the balcony to release their perfume. This place had been special to her since the very first night she'd looked out over the beauty of her new home. But tonight it brought no solace.

All I want is for this to be over! No more drug dealers, no more problems, no misunderstandings. Just . . . just Nicky—the way he was! Is that too much to ask?

The moon blinked down at her with stony indifference.

God, are you even up there?

As though in answer, a cloud bank skittered across the surface of the moon, swallowing up its light and making the world a gray-shadowed place whose sudden chill had nothing to do with the temperature of the air. Sara hurried inside, slamming the shutters to keep out the night. Crawling into bed, she pulled the covers up over her head in the manner of a small child hiding from the shadows on the wall.

✠

She was walking through a jungle, vines dripping down into her face, brilliant-green growth curling up around her ankles. There was no sound in her world—no cawing of parrots or chattering of monkeys, not even her own soft breathing or the tap-tap of her footsteps. But she wasn't conscious of the anomaly. All her concentration was up ahead on something that lay around the next curve of the path. What it was, she had no idea. She knew only that she had to reach the curve and find out. And yet at the same time, she was strangely reluctant to round the bend in the path.

How long she'd been walking before she realized that she had a companion was hazy, in the manner of dreams. But there was no reason that the sudden revelation should bring such consternation. She stopped, her heart beating faster with an unfathomable fear. If this wasn't a dream, her hands would be clammy, her extremities cold. As it was, she felt nothing—not the jungle path under her feet, not the vines hanging into her face, just that senseless fear.

Her companion stopped with her, in the same midstep, as though they were connected by some invisible string or bond. It was a man, that much she knew, but he was of no particular height or shape. Then his head turned, and it was Nicolás. No, it wasn't Nicolás! This face was older, harder. Then she recognized her father-in-law, Don Luis.

The aristocratic features dissolved into new lines: Julio Vargas, with his slicked-back hair and his face twisted with rage and spite. Then the face shifted again, becoming that of a stranger who was somehow all three faces in one. There was nothing particularly alarming about this new visage, yet somehow, Sara knew that it represented something horrible and frightening. Lifting a hand, the stranger reached toward her. Sara tried to move, to run. She *couldn't* let that thing touch her. But it was like struggling in quicksand to move her arms and legs.

The hand grasped her shoulder, lifting her off her feet, shaking her, as a dog would shake a rat before finishing the job. Her shoulder ached with the force of it. The stranger's mouth opened in a ghastly parody of Nicky's charming smile, moving only its lips, but with the rest of that familiar yet unfamiliar face appearing as though it were carved in stone. Sara hung in midair, too frozen in terror to struggle. Either she had shrunk or the man-figure had grown much larger. The smile spread wider, the gaping mouth swelling into a fathomless, blood-red pit that was pulsating and utterly loathsome. It swallowed up the jungle green and would soon swallow her up as well. Sara's mouth opened in a scream that produced no sound.

Then the mouth spoke, the words incongruently quiet and ordinary. "Sara, wake up!"

Sara sat up in bed with a start. She gasped with relief as that terrible maw dissolved into the night shadows of her bedroom. Then she caught her breath again, in fright, as a black form loomed above her and hard fingers clamped down on her shoulder. A small scream escaped her throat.

"Sara! What is it with you? Wake up!" The hand released her shoulder. The mattress creaked as a weight lowered itself down beside her. A shadow in the shape of an arm reached for the bedside lamp. Sara blinked under the sudden assault of light, then relaxed as she recognized Nicolás, sitting on the edge of the bed dressed in jeans and a V-necked polo shirt, his hair tousled as by wind or sleep.

"Nicky!" Throwing her arms around him, Sara buried her face against his chest. Under her cheek, she could feel the knobby outline of the Cortéz cross. She moved her head to find a more comfortable resting place. Her heart was still pounding as though she'd been in a race. "Oh, Nicky, I'm so glad it's you! I thought . . . I was having a horrible nightmare!"

When he didn't lift his arms to comfort her, she raised her head from his chest. She stiffened as she caught sight of his face in the quiet light of the lamp. This wasn't Nicky! It was his father—those incredible blue eyes as icy as a glacier-fed lake, the full-lipped mouth thinned to a narrow slit. Sara shook her head to clear it. No, of course it wasn't Don Luis. That had been her dream. "What . . . what's the matter, Nicky?"

Only now was she awake enough to wonder at his presence. She hadn't expected him back before midmorning, but the night beyond the slatted shutters was still pitch black. Her eyes darted to the digital alarm clock blinking on the dresser: 2:30 A.M. "What are you doing here? It's the middle of the night! I thought you were out at the hacienda!"

"I flew back. I had to see you." The words should have gladdened Sara's heart, but there was nothing lover-like in the hard tone. Or in his expression. "You flew back?" she asked blankly. "But . . . isn't that dangerous? I thought you didn't fly the Cessna after dark."

"Well, it wasn't any joyride, that's for sure! At least we had a moon, but we had to wait for the clouds to break open to land. Otherwise, I'd have been here an hour ago." Unpeeling her arms from around him, Nicolás placed them in her lap and moved away from her on the bed. "But then, we didn't have a whole lot of choice, did we?" His voice hardened further. "What have you been up to, Sara?"

"Up to?" Sara's astonishment outweighed her hurt at his rejection of her embrace. Was she still dreaming? She blinked at him, owl-like. "What are you talking about, Nicky? You're the one who's been away for days! I haven't done anything but wait for you to get home!"

"Don't act innocent with me, Sara," Nicolás said icily. "You were seen at the Co-op tonight. Do you know how humiliating it is to have someone call Papá and tell him that my wife is hobnobbing with the DEA while I'm gone? About as humiliating as it was for me to have Papá order me home just to talk some sense into my wife!"

"What?" Sara was wide awake now. "Are you telling me someone was spying on me at the seminar? And then they had the nerve to call Don Luis? I don't believe this!"

Scooting back into the tangle of bedclothes so that she could fold her legs cross-legged underneath her, she said angrily, "Okay, yes, I did go to the Co-op. The U.S. embassy was advertising a seminar for Americans abroad. When you didn't come home, I didn't see any reason I shouldn't go. It was really interesting, too! And yes, the DEA were there. Two of them. In fact, you know one of them. Doug Bradford. You introduced me to him at the Fourth of July picnic. They were helping with part of the seminar. And, yes, I did talk to them for a few minutes. So did a lot of other people. I didn't realize it was some kind of crime!"

The glacial blue of his eyes didn't thaw by so much as a degree.

"You were doing more than talking to them," he said deliberately. "You went off alone with Doug Bradford. Why? And don't try to deny it. You were seen!"

Sara couldn't believe she was hearing this. Who had been watching her so closely in that crowd? And who would care enough to want to make trouble for her? She'd hardly known anyone there! "Then whoever saw me can tell you that I wasn't outside with him for more than five minutes, max! Are you telling me Don Luis made you fly all the way up here in the middle of the night just because I was asking Doug Bradford a couple of questions? I suppose that's what your *spy* was talking about! That's incredible! I was going to tell you about it in the morning anyway."

Nicolás ignored her indignation. "A couple of questions?" he demanded with icy disbelief. "That won't wash, Sara! You were over-heard mentioning Julio Vargas to the guy. And you weren't asking questions, either! What did you tell Bradford about him?"

"Julio Vargas!" Sara repeated blankly. *How could anyone have known about that?* Then, as she suddenly remembered a lurking figure just meters away from where she and Doug Bradford had been talking, and a boyish face filled with hostility and suspicion, she gasped with outrage. "So that's your spy! The Salvietti boy! Of all the little sneaks! Well, if you're going to listen to someone like him . . ."

"He isn't a spy," Nicolás said coldly. "He's a friend of the family, and he was just doing his duty. Which is more than I can say of you! He was rightfully concerned over what he saw and reported it to his father. Raul owes Papá a few favors, so he called him right away. Fortunately! Now, answer me! What did Bradford want from you? Did you tell him about that shipment from the warehouse?"

"No, of course not!" Sara said indignantly. "I wouldn't do that without talking to you first. Look, I didn't mean to upset you. I was just trying—" She stopped, stifling an inward sigh. This was exactly what she'd dreaded for tomorrow. Nicolás in an icy rage, she already apologizing. Why couldn't this have at least waited until morning, when they could discuss things more reasonably. It was the middle of the night! She was tired, and so was he.

Well, this was hardly the place or time she'd have chosen. But now that Nicolás was insisting on bringing up the subject, she might as well get it over with. Shifting her legs, which were starting to fall asleep, Sara drew a deep breath, gathering up her courage. "Nicky, I have to tell you. I know what you've been trying to hide from me these last few days. I talked to Dolores, and I found out that Julio was still there at the refinery this morning. And Doug Bradford too, when I talked to him. He hadn't even heard of Julio Vargas. You and Don Luis never did call the police, did you?"

Sara faltered under the storm clouds that were darkening her husband's handsome features. This was going to be even worse than she feared. But she couldn't back down now. "Look, I know it's not your fault, Nicky. Don Luis wouldn't let you do it, would he? And I do understand why he doesn't want to call the police. He doesn't want any trouble for Cortéz Industries, and so he'd rather just let Vargas walk away. But that's wrong, and you should know that, even if he doesn't. There's kids out there who are ruining their lives because of that cocaine Julio Vargas is selling them. We can't just let him walk away with—ow!"

She broke off with a cry of pain as Nicolás reached out and grabbed her by the upper arms. "What . . . did . . . you . . . tell . . . him?" he gritted between his teeth, punctuating every word with a shake. His fingers bit deep into the soft flesh just below her armpits, and she had to bite back tears.

"Nicky, please! You're hurting me!"

Nicolás stopped shaking her, but he didn't release his grip. "Now, you tell me every word you said to him," he ordered harshly. "And every word he said to you."

"I . . . I told you! I just asked him a couple of questions." Bewilderment and distress stung at Sara's eyes. "Nicky, please! Why are you doing this?"

Nicolás ignored her plea. "What questions?"

"I just asked him if he'd heard anything about those tapestries in Miami . . . and if they knew yet how they'd gotten from Bolivia to the States and . . . and who'd put the cocaine in them. That's all, really, I promise!" she said louder as his grip tightened. "He wouldn't answer me, anyway! He said it was DEA business."

"And Julio Vargas? Where did he come into this conversation?"

"Well, I . . . I did ask him about Julio Vargas. Just if he knew him. I thought something was strange, the way you were avoiding me, and . . . and after what Dolores said, I just wanted to see if you'd talked to the DEA at all. I didn't tell him why or what I saw at the warehouse. I wanted to talk to you first. But—I did tell him to check Vargas out." Sara's voice dwindled to a thread at the look on her husband's face. She had to swallow before she could go on. "I . . . I thought maybe he could find something in the police computers—"

"You what?" Sara flinched as his grip tightened again, but instead of shaking her, Nicky released her, flinging her back against her pillow and storming savagely to his feet. A steady stream of curses poured from his mouth, first in English, then Spanish—vile phrases whose meaning Sara could only guess at. For the first time, she felt fear mixing with her bewilderment. She'd never seen even her father-in-law this furious. Had Nicky been drinking?

But there was no lack of sobriety in the sarcastic interrogatives he was spitting out. "So all you did was ask a couple of questions? First you ask Bradford about the tapestries and the cocaine. You think he isn't going to wonder why my wife is so interested in the subject that she's got to ask a DEA agent about it? When he knows how we feel about them? And all the time, if I know you, you're acting guilty and blushing and showing you know more than you're telling! Then you tell him to check up on Vargas. You think Bradford isn't smart enough to put two and two together and come up with Cortéz Industries? You stupid little fool!"

Sara couldn't deny the accusations. Doug Bradford had indeed drawn those very conclusions in almost those same words. Struggling back to a sitting position, she wrapped her arms around herself, her hands rubbing her upper arms where Nicky's painful grip had left them sore and tender. "Does it really matter so much?" she pleaded. "Look, I'm sorry. I didn't mean to cause trouble for you or Don Luis."

Again, she caught herself. What was she doing hanging her head like a guilty child under a scolding? *She* wasn't the one who'd been caught in wrongdoing! Straightening up further in her cocoon of sheets and blankets, she squared her slim shoulders, gathering up the shreds of her dignity. "I really *am* sorry that you're so upset, Nicky," she said quietly. "But I have to tell you that I was going to tell the DEA everything tomorrow—" She glanced over at the alarm clock. "I mean, today. Anyway, I was just waiting to talk to you first."

Drawing another deep breath, she tried again. "Look, Nicky, I know Julio Vargas is a friend of your father's and . . . and maybe you don't want to cause trouble for him or for Cortéz Industries. But I can't go along with what you're doing. No matter how people argue down here, smuggling cocaine is a crime! And Julio Vargas is a criminal! There's kids out there whose lives are being ruined because of him; people are even dying. Do you think he won't just start over again somewhere else if you let him go? I can't believe you'd want to live with that on your conscience, Nicky!"

She rushed to a finish. "Well, anyway, I can't! I didn't tell that DEA agent what I saw that day because I wanted to give you and Don Luis the chance to tell them yourselves. But . . . but if you won't tell them, then I will! I'm sorry if you're angry, but you've got to see how important this is to me. I'm the one who found out about Julio Vargas, and I couldn't live with myself if I just walked away from it. I'll talk to Don Luis myself in the morning, and . . . and I hope you'll be on my side. But even if you won't, I'm not going to change my mind. Either you or Don Luis go to the DEA in the morning, or . . . or I'll have to go myself!"

For a long moment, as her challenge hung in the air between them, the room was as silent as the jungle of her dream. Sara raised her eyes to her husband. He was staring down at her, his blue eyes bright and hard and unreadable. Then he said softly, his voice as chilling and implacable as anything she'd ever heard from her father-in-law, "Oh, no, you won't! You're not doing any more damage than you already have!"

He walked away from the bed to the intercom, punching in a series of numbers. "Papá?"

There was a crackle of static. *"Sí? Don Nicolás?"* The disembodied voice was respectful and vaguely familiar.

"Julio? Is that you?" Nicolás responded shortly. "Is Papá with you? Tell him we've got a problem here, all right. But it isn't as bad as you thought. I'm bringing her down."

Sara listened with astonishment. "Julio! You can't mean . . . ?" Her voice trailed off to a whisper as the awful realization hit her. "Oh, no! That's who it was in the office the other night! It was Julio Vargas! No wonder he sounded so familiar! He . . . he was saying something about not finding the hangings in your packaging. But that means . . . no, that's impossible!"

Nicolás spun around with the same cold rage as he switched off the intercom. "And to think I told Papá you wouldn't be any trouble! Even with this Miami mess, I told him I could count on you to keep quiet. Who could you talk to, anyway? You didn't know anyone dangerous! I could handle you without Papá getting involved. And now look what you've done! Less than a month to go before deliveries are completed, and you've got to get Doug Bradford stirred up again. And after all that work I did to get that weaver where they won't find her, and calm things down in Miami. You can bet Papá will blame me too! 'A real man can control his wife,'" he mimicked. "He should be married to a squeamish little *gringa!*"

Striding back to the bed, he said harshly, "Well, you're going to do what I say this time! Get up and get your clothes on! Papá wants to speak with you!"

His command hardly registered. Sara gripped the edge of the bedclothes tight in her hands. Her mind was oddly blank now, unable —unwilling—to add up what she was hearing. "What are you saying,

Nicky? That . . . that you and Don Luis knew all along that Julio Vargas was using Cortéz Industries to ship cocaine? That you were helping him or . . ."—she had to swallow to force the words out of her throat—". . . or working for him?"

"Working for Vargas?" Nicolás let out an incredulous snort. "A Cortéz working for some second-rate *coronel*?" Then, as though the absurdity of the joke had tempered his anger, he actually cracked a short laugh, the set lines of his face relaxing into his more habitual good humor—which was suddenly more frightening to Sara than his rage.

"Come on, Sara, don't act so shocked! Look, I never meant you to find out like this! Or find out at all. But it's your own fault, always asking questions and sticking your nose where it doesn't belong. If you'd be more like Mamá and the other women of this family and just enjoy what we give you instead of worrying your head over where it comes from, or all these *campesinos* that are none of your concern, you'd never have known about it until it was all over."

"No! No!" Sara was back in the grip of her nightmare, her head whirling, her stomach doing crazy somersaults. This couldn't be real! This wasn't her Nicky standing here saying those incredible things. It was a stranger wearing her husband's face. It had to be! "Please, Nicky!" she whispered. "Tell me I'm not understanding you! Please tell me you're not dealing drugs."

"Only eight tons worth." Nicolás shrugged. With sarcasm, he added, "And Papá is going to be real happy when he finds out you've brought the DEA crawling all over the place again!"

CHAPTER SEVENTEEN

It couldn't be true!

Even after Nicolás repeated his impatient order for her to get up and get dressed, Sara sat stunned, unable to move. It had been hard enough to accept that Nicky and Don Luis might be shielding Julio Vargas in order to protect their family and Cortéz Industries. But this? That her father-in-law was the head of a drug-smuggling operation that measured in the tons of cocaine? That her own husband was in it up to his neck? It *had* to be part of the nightmare!

And yet, even as her mind whirled in a vain effort at denial, Sara could not help but recognize the unmistakable ring of truth in what she'd just heard. The signs had all been there, after all, if she'd only opened her eyes to see them. Doug Bradford had spelled them out for her step by step. And so had Gabriela.

"What does this have to do with *me?*" Sara had asked Gabriela when she'd explained the source of her city's new prosperity.

Only now did Sara understand the strange look her husband's cousin had given her in response. Gabriela had been too loyal—or something—to compare the Salviettis directly to the Cortezes. But she'd known, all right! The discrepancies between what Don Luis could have gotten for his crumbling ancestral properties and the millions it must have taken to build that shining, state-of-the-art refinery. Why hadn't Sara seen that? The extravagance with which the entire Cortéz clan lived—except Gabriela, again—and Gabriela's refusal to take advantage of the family's good fortune, should have been another clue.

Even the evidence Sara had used to pass judgment on Julio Vargas pointed so obviously at the head of Cortéz Industries, now that she was faced with the truth. After all, who controlled all shipping and destinations for *Industrias Cortéz?* Who had the international business contacts and could arrange for someone halfway across the world to separate and deliver one discreetly marked shipment from a ware-house of goods? Not Julio Vargas! But she'd been in such a hurry to convict him, she hadn't even stopped to consider that he might be working for someone else. Or who that someone else would have to be.

"*Nico!*" Don Luis's autocratic voice crackled over the intercom. "What's taking so long? Get the girl down here!"

"*Sí, Papá!*" Nicolás stalked over from the intercom to the bed. "What is it with you, Sara? Would you hurry up? You know how Papá is about being kept waiting."

He ripped back the blankets and sheets, leaving Sara exposed in her scanty nightgown. "You've got to the count of three, or you're going as you are! I'm sure Vargas will appreciate the sight!"

The threat goaded Sara into scrambling out of bed. For the second time that week, she found herself pulling on her clothes with hasty and trembling hands. She shivered as she stripped the nightgown over her head, more from misery and shock than from the night air, which was still balmy. No, it was true, all right, the whole of Nicky's horrifying revelation. It had, in fact, been staring her in the face all the time! How was it that she, a reasonably intelligent person who had always prided herself on seeing the world through wide-open eyes, had fought so hard against believing any of it?

The answer came easily. Because things like this didn't happen with people you knew! Because she'd loved her husband and had believed him when he'd told her his family wasn't involved in drug trafficking. Because Sara, as she'd accused Doug Bradford of doing, had started out with a preconceived idea—that the handsome, laughing man she'd married could do no real wrong. And so every clue that had come her way had been forced into the framework of that idea. Until now, at last, it had come tumbling down under the weight of its own inconsistencies.

Reaching for a brush to run through her sleep-tousled hair, Sara glanced over at Nicolás, who was waiting impatiently in the doorway to the sitting room, his long frame taut with irritation. *Because I didn't want to believe! Because I deliberately buried my head in the sand to keep from believing!*

"Would you skip the primping!" With an oath, Nicolás left the doorway, crossing the room to snatch the brush from her hand. "No one down there's going to care what you look like! Now let's get out of here!"

Tossing the brush onto the dresser, he stalked back toward the sitting room, so assured of her cooperation that he didn't even glance back.

Sara didn't follow. She couldn't! The shock of the past few minutes suddenly hit her full force, a wave of terror that rooted her feet to the floor. She *couldn't* go down those stairs to whatever dreadful secrets were waiting below! What did her father-in-law want with her, anyway? What did drug dealers do with people who found them out?

She swayed, dizzy with the thought—paralyzed, floating. It was her dream all over again! If she could just shut her eyes, surely she'd wake up from this too . . .

"For crying out—" Coming back to the bedroom door, Nicolás impatiently snapped his fingers. "Come on, Sara, don't make this harder than it is! You just do what Papá says, and we won't have any problem."

The normality of his tone released her. What had she been thinking? This was her husband, whom she knew and loved, not the monstrous stranger of her dream! She flew across the room, clutching Nicolás by the arm and placing herself in front of him before he could open the door into the hall. Wrapping her arms around his waist, she pressed herself close to him in desperate appeal.

"Nicky, please, you don't have to do this! We don't have to go down there! I know this isn't really you! You'd never want to hurt anyone—not me, not anyone! It's Don Luis who's making you do this, isn't it? Well, you don't have to, can't you see that? I know he's your father, but you're not a child anymore! He can't tell you what to do or think! If he wants to do something criminal, then let him! But . . . but that doesn't mean that you—we—have to go along with it."

The eyes she lifted were dark with pleading. "Please, Nicky, let's just get out of here! We could leave right now before Don Luis would ever know. Out the side door. Back to the States. You've got your business degree. I can teach. We can make our own home there. Maybe . . . maybe we won't live as well as this, but . . ."

Sara glanced with sudden revulsion around the suite with its rich carpet and furnishings, the open closet she could see through the bedroom door with its rows of expensive dresses. ". . . I wouldn't want anything bought with drug money, anyway."

Nicky was stiff and unresponsive under her embrace. Pushing her arms away as he had earlier, Nicolás demanded irritably, "What are you talking about, Sara? This *is* my home! Do you really think I'd ever leave all this for some stupid entry-level job in North America? As for Papá, he isn't forcing me to do anything. I'm just pleased that he finally realizes I'm man enough to help him with more than fiddling with reports and shipping invoices. To have him trust some-one like Julio Vargas over his own son—"

An impatient buzz from the intercom cut him off. Sara's pleas

died in her throat. Despite her habit of making excuses for her husband, she could no longer fool herself. Nicolás was involved in this
by his own free will. And he hadn't shown the slightest guilt or compunction. Like a sleepwalker, she let him lead her through the unlit
hall, down the wide staircase, and past the empty ballroom. His arm
around her shoulders might have been almost affectionate were it
not for the tightness of his grip.

But by the time they reached the front of the house and Nicolás
pushed open the solid hardwood door of Don Luis's office, a curl of
anger was beginning to burn away the shock and terror that held
Sara captive. Nicolás had lied to her! They'd all lied to her! All of
this—the luxury, the beauty, her new life and family, her marriage—
it had all been a sham from the beginning. She didn't know these
people! She'd only thought she did! Her sudden anger stiffened her
spine, and it was with almost steady steps that she stepped through
the open door.

Sara had never been inside this room before. She glanced around,
if only to put off looking at the two men in front of her. It was well
lit and almost too bright after the dark passageway outside, but the
overall effect was somber, gloomy, and expensive, with lots of plush
red leather and polished hardwood. The atmosphere was absurdly
like something off a movie set. Don Luis sat behind a huge mahogany
desk, his light alpaca suit and personal grooming as unrumpled as
though he'd just come from the hands of a makeup artist instead of
a long day at the office. Julio Vargas stood behind him and slightly
to the right, wearing the same all-black clothing Sara had seen him
in before, though without the suit coat, his hair pulled back in a
ponytail, the earrings glinting in his left earlobe. His bearing suggested that he ought to be wearing a military uniform—his shoulders
ramrod straight, feet slightly apart like a sentry on duty—and Sara
was reminded that Mimi had said that the security chief had once
been an officer in the Bolivian armed forces.

Sara lifted her chin as Nicolás dropped his hand from her shoulder
to the hollow of her back and propelled her forward across the
carpet, but Don Luis gave no sign of noticing her gesture of defiance.
He waited without speaking, drumming his long fingers on the edge
of the desk blotter. Gone was the gleam of admiration and the thin-
lipped smile with which he usually greeted his daughter-in-law. And
Sara, scanning his aristocratic features—that were so much like
Nicky's—for any hint of encouragement, saw only the face of a
stranger, implacable and without emotion. Sara couldn't suppress a
sudden shiver, and her last bit of courage drained away.

Don Luis let the silence drag out several endless seconds longer before addressing himself to his son. "Well? What did the girl have to say?"

Just like that, Sara was no longer his daughter-in-law with a name of her own. Just a girl! A girl who'd caused him some trouble. Like María, the Quechua girl at the warehouse who had been cast aside when she got in the way. Don Luis didn't even glance at Sara. In fact, neither he nor Julio Vargas had so much as acknowledged her presence in the room.

"Oh, I got it all out of her!" Nicolás boasted. "I told you Salvietti was overreacting! All she did was ask Bradford a couple of questions." Dropping his hand from Sara's waist, Nicolás threw himself into a leather armchair. "I can't believe you dragged me all the way up here just for that!" He let out a derisive snort. "Would you believe she thought she was doing us a favor? She figured Bradford might be working with us on the case. It'd almost be funny, if the man was as dumb as he looks!"

Don Luis didn't respond to his son's attempted humor. "What questions?"

This time he did look at Sara, who'd been left standing alone in the middle of the floor like a prisoner at the bar, and she felt the power of his arctic gaze commanding an answer. But Sara was not one of Don Luis's native employees, trained by centuries of subservience to the Cortéz name. She glared back at him, white with misery, but with her head held high, hating the man in front of her with an intensity that burned her stomach. Never in her life had she loathed anyone as much as she did Don Luis at that moment. Maybe Nicky *had* chosen this . . . this awful thing by his own free will! But she knew where the real blame lay. It was Don Luis who had raised his son with his own twisted ideas of right and wrong, his own egotistical belief that wealth and privilege were his by right of birth. It was Don Luis who had brainwashed Nicolás into believing that drug smuggling was an acceptable means of achieving their goals. It was Don Luis who was no more than a common criminal instead of the progressive industrialist that everyone—including Nicolás—seemed so proud of. But if he thought he was going to get any cooperation out of her . . . !

Gathering up the shreds of her courage, she tilted her chin and narrowed her eyes. Amber sparks clashed with glacier ice across the massive desk. But Don Luis didn't waste time trying to force Sara to talk. He turned his cool gaze to his son. "Nico, you will tell me exactly what she has said. I wish to hear every word."

"Sure!" Nicolás settled himself more comfortably against the red leather of the armchair, crossing his legs at the ankles. "But like I said, there wasn't much! Okay, I was concerned myself, and I gave it to her good for talking to Bradford in the first place. But now that I've seen what he got from her, I don't think it's going to throw us any problem we can't handle. In fact, if Salvietti and your security-minded *coronel* over there"—he threw Julio Vargas a darkling glance—"hadn't all panicked, my wife still wouldn't know what was going on here, and none of this would be necessary."

The narrow line of Vargas's mouth compressed at the gibe, but he made no response. Nicolás went on with his recital. Like the other two men, he ignored Sara as he spoke, talking as though she wasn't even there. Sara stared straight ahead in stony silence. There was a comfortable-looking sofa only a few feet away, and she'd have given almost anything to walk over and sink down on it. But no one had bothered to suggest that she take a seat, and she wasn't going to give these men (already, she realized with a jolt, she was counting Nicolás in with the other two) the satisfaction of knowing how frightened and exhausted she was. So she kept her head high, her eyes fastened on the wall just to the left of Don Luis, and focused her concentration on keeping her legs from trembling.

Don Luis listened in silence, leaning back in his chair, one well-manicured hand stroking his chin. Noticing his thoughtful gaze moving to her face, Sara quickly raised her eyes to a painting on the wall. But even there, she couldn't escape the hard blue stare. The portrait was of one of the Cortéz ancestors, but, except for the out-dated clothing, it might have been a painting of Don Luis himself. There was the same mouth thinned with self-will and temper, the same stamp of arrogance and ruthless determination, the same hard gaze that brooked no opposition. This was the same man, Sara remembered, who had carved out the first Cortéz kingdom over the bodies of thousands of Indian serfs. Studying the singular resemblance to the man at the desk in front of her, Sara was no longer astonished at the lengths Don Luis seemed willing to go to ensure his own future. She averted her eyes from the painting to her husband. Would he, too, look like that in another twenty-five years?

". . . so that was it," Nicolás was finishing. "I really don't think it's such a big deal! Okay, so Bradford might decide to do some poking around. But there's nothing they can find right now, and it's not like Vargas has any record they can dig up. She didn't tell him about the mess-up at the warehouse or anything we've been doing the last few days. She says she wouldn't do that without talking to me first!" he added with a satiric inflection that made Sara flush. And then, in a sudden change of mood, as though his recital had chased away his earlier fury, he uncrossed his ankles, leaning forward to take Sara's hand in his own. "A loyal wife, like I told you, Papá. Aren't you, *querida?*"

Nicky's blue eyes laughed up at her through incredible dark eyelashes in that half-teasing, half-tender way that had made her heart flop over ever since she'd first laid eyes on him. Sara hated him at that moment as much as she hated Don Luis. How dare he smile that way, as though there had been no hurt and anger and hard words between them? As though he hadn't terrified her more than she'd ever been in her life? As though this were nothing but some minor difference of opinion they were talking about instead of a crime?

Snatching her hand away, she rounded on him, stung into speaking aloud for the first time. "I wish I *had* told him! I would have, too, if I'd known what you were really doing here! Oh, Nicky!" Her voice shook with all the disappointment and disillusionment of the past few days. "How could you? I trusted you!"

Her outburst hit home. Nicky's smile congealed on his lips, then vanished. Don Luis clapped his hands together imperatively. "We do not have time to quarrel. We must see now what is to be done. Nico, it was not necessary to criticize Raul or Julio for their precaution. Since we did not know what the girl had said, they were correct to be concerned. But you too are right. It is not as bad as we feared. Even if the *americano* concerns himself with what the girl has said, there is nothing to be found now on that trail. We will no longer use this Miami contact, and they will find nothing there that can be traced to us. As for this man Bradford, he has been well discredited. Not even his superiors will listen to him if he tries to harass us again. However, it is best to be cautious."

He raised his hand in a gesture that brought Julio Vargas hurrying over to his side. "You, Vargas, will fly back down to the hacienda immediately. You will tell them to do nothing more until I have given the word. It is not that I have great concern. The man Bradford can have nothing but speculations, and he will soon lose interest in a young girl's chatter when he finds that the trail leads nowhere. But I prefer to take no chances. Another week will not matter so much. By then, my sources will inform us about whether the *americanos* are snooping around. As for you, Vargas, you will stay at the hacienda and away from the city until all of this is finished. It is a great inconvenience that the girl mentioned your name, because we have need of your services right now. But if you are not here, they cannot interrogate you." He turned a stern look toward his son.

"Nico and my daughters' husbands will have to take over your respon-sibilities. And if the *americanos* do come looking for you, we will tell them that you are no longer in our employ. As for the girl . . ."

The hooded eyes shifted from Nicolás to Sara. There was no inflection in his voice to give a hint to his emotions as he added, "She now knows too much. She will have to be taken care of."

Sara had been bracing herself for this moment since she'd en-tered the office, but that didn't keep her from paling, the blood draining from her face with a swiftness that left her dizzy and swaying. Nicolás bolted upright in his chair. "Papá!"

Don Luis raised a hand to silence his protest. "Do not be in such a hurry, *hijo*. The girl will be confined to this property until all is finished. After that, it will not matter what she says or where she goes. Nico, I leave her in your charge. If she must go anywhere, it must be in your company. And no phone calls, no speaking to any-one. You know what must be done. Do not fail me. Oh, yes, and her cell phone. You will bring it down, Nico, immediately."

Dismissing Nicolás with a curt wave of the hand, he swiveled his chair around to confer with Julio Vargas. And that was it, much to Sara's astonishment and relief. She said as much to Nicolás as he escorted her back upstairs. His response was every bit as surprising. Stopping dead in his tracks on the landing, he threw his head back in a hearty laugh. "And what did you think we were going to do? Murder you?"

He caught her change of expression. "You really did, didn't you?" He hooted again as though he'd forgotten his own instinctive protest. "Oh, Sara, you don't really think I'd let them hurt you. You're my wife!"

Still laughing, he pulled her into his arms, his kiss landing on her neck as she twisted her face away. "Besides, there's no need for anything like that! You do as you're told, and we won't have any problem. It'd be different, maybe, if you could do any real damage. But it's like Papá says. All we've got to do is keep you from talking to anyone until we get those eight tons of cocaine moved. Once that's gone, you can shout it all over the streets if you want."

Sara separated herself from his arms with a shudder of revulsion. How could he think she'd want his affection now? "And that doesn't bother you?" she asked bitterly. "You're so sure no one would believe the word of some *gringa* over a Cortéz?"

Letting her go with a shrug, Nicolás reached past her to push open the door into their suite. "It doesn't matter if they do or not! That's what you still don't get, Sara. This isn't the United States, with all your computers and people snooping into your finances and having to account for every penny you make. I studied all that in my business courses. No one around here could care less how we make our money—not unless we're stupid enough to get caught with the coke on our hands. And we're not stupid! Once this shipment goes, we're getting out—permanently. And once we're out, we're clean. A month from now, it won't matter what your DEA pal knows. He'll never be able to prove a thing. And as for us"—with a grin, he waved Sara past him into the sitting room—"everything will go back to normal, except we'll be a few hundred million dollars richer. And maybe we'll even have some time for just the two of us. How does a Caribbean cruise sound? Or a month on the Riviera to make up for being stuck in the house these next few weeks?"

That was the worst of it! The way Nicolás was acting as though this was all normal. It was as though his recent aloofness and the cold anger that had frightened her earlier had evaporated with the need to hide things from her. Throwing himself down on the sofa, he ordered Sara to hand over her cell phone. Then, as she rummaged through her purse, he began telling her about his trip to Miami, as cheerfully and matter-of-factly as though he were any ordinary husband—instead of a criminal!—sharing the events of his day with his wife.

There, she'd admitted it! Her handsome young husband, whom she'd loved and trusted and believed in, was just a common criminal, like her father-in-law and Julio Vargas. No, not common! Very successful criminals.

"The police never did find the rest of the boxes," Nicolás was saying. "They never even knew there were more. So at least the shipment wasn't a total loss—though we had to make up half-a-million dollars on the bundle that ended up at that gallery. It was stupid, really, what happened! Our man there had already separated the marked boxes from the rest of the shipments at the warehouse, and he was on his way to deliver them, when his van got jumped at a red light by a Cuban street gang. The idiot hadn't even bothered to take a back-up with him. And in downtown Miami, of all places!"

Sara sank down into a chair, her purse on her lap and her cell phone in her hand, unwillingly caught up in the story as Nicolás blithely continued his narration.

"Of course, he couldn't yell for the cops. But fortunately, the punks were amateurs. All they were carrying were knives. When Sanchez pulled his automatic out from under the seat, they grabbed the nearest box and took off. At least they had the brains to get rid of the shipping container before they fenced the tapestries."

"So where does Julio come into this—if he's not the one running the cocaine," Sara asked wearily. "And the hacienda? That *is* where you have your cocaine lab, isn't it?"

"Oh, we don't make our own cocaine," Nicolás answered carelessly. "Papá won't touch that end of things. It's too risky. You just have to read the papers and see how many labs the *anti-narcóticos* turn up every month to know that! No, Papá had a relative—of sorts—who took care of the actual production, until his operation was busted a couple months back. All we do is just what you saw at the warehouse. We take the coke and mix it with some of our own products—not just the tapestries, but all kinds of things. Wine. Shampoo. Pottery. Sugar. Just about anything we make and export. Which is where Julio comes in. It would look a little odd if Papá and I were flying down for a *campo* rest cure every other week. So Julio flies the goods down—he's put together a security force from some of his old army unit to keep an eye on the workers—then flies back to pick the stuff up when it's ready. Then it just goes out with our regular shipments."

"And you've never been caught?" Sara asked incredulously. "That's what I can't get over! How can you sneak millions of dollars of drugs past who knows how many customs officials without anyone ever noticing? It's crazy!"

"But that's the beauty of Papá's plan. These other guys—they all get caught because they get too greedy and too big. But a box or two of tapestries, or a case of Bolivian wine, mixed in with a hundred others—do you know how much stuff goes through a shipping port every day? They can't even start to check it all out! Papá doesn't try shipping it all through one port, either. He's got it spread out all over the world, to every country where we ship legitimately. That way—well, if he loses one link in the chain, like this Miami thing, he just cuts his losses and shifts the next shipment elsewhere."

Nicolás yawned hugely, a reminder that he had not yet been to sleep that night. "That's what we were doing down at the hacienda this weekend. Cutting losses. Papá made us get rid of every bit of coke we had stashed there, including a full load of products we had ready to ship. Just in case that lost shipment was traced to *Industrias Cortéz* and the Americans started sniffing around our properties again."

His careless statement brought Sara's head up sharply. "You mean, the cocaine—the eight tons—it's gone? You got rid of it?"

Nicolás snorted. "Of course not, don't be foolish. You think we're stupid enough to keep that much coke lying around the property? No, all we lost was one load—maybe two hundred kilos. And even that seemed a little unnecessary. It's not like the hacienda's registered in our name, and not too many people even know where it is. But Papá doesn't believe in taking chances. And I guess he's right. The less contact we have with the stuff, the safer we are. Back when we still had that supplier, Papá used to make him keep the stuff until we were ready to process it. And even he never knew where it was going. Julio would take the chopper or DC-3 and meet the guy on some dirt strip. A few days later—a week at the most—the load would be gone, shipped out, and it wouldn't matter if anyone stumbled over the place or not. Not until the next time. In fact, if it wasn't for this last big shipment Papá has been planning, and that we can't afford to have the Americans snooping around right now, it wouldn't have been necessary to—"

He broke off abruptly. "Anyway, our trip down tonight was to take a fresh load of coke and goods so the workers could get back to work. Now, thanks to you, we're going to have to tell them to hold off all over again!"

Sara was no longer listening. She was still mulling over one of the details from Nicky's narrative. "The *chopper?*" she blurted out. "You mean, a helicopter? I didn't know you had a helicopter. I've never seen it at the airport."

"Sure, we have a helicopter!" Nicolás let out a bark of laughter. "In fact, boy, do we have a helicopter! Though I guess, technically, you'd say it isn't really ours. Vargas brought it with him when he started working for Papá. And don't ask me where he got it. Nowhere legal, I'm sure. And you'd know why if you saw the thing. That's why we keep it out at the hacienda. It's had its uses, but it's not the sort of thing you want landing or taking off in full sight of all Santa Cruz."

Nicolás chuckled again, his eyes bright with remembered excitement. "I'll say this about Julio. I can't stand the guy. He's arrogant and doesn't know his place, and when this is all over, I'm going to push Papá to phase him out, even if it means paying him a fortune to get him off our backs. But he's good at what he does! Remember that time I went flying with him last month?"

Sara remembered all right! He'd refused to take her along, and she'd gone instead to the English church, a chain of events that had led to the orphanage and her quarrel with Doug Bradford and, eventually, to the predicament in which she found herself right now.

"Well, I guess it won't hurt now to tell you what we were really doing. I told you Papá's supplier was busted a few months back? Well, you can imagine, Papá wasn't too happy about having his production end closed down. Not this close to getting out, and with this last shipment already committed. But Papá has his ways of getting information, and somehow he found out about a couple big planeloads of coke heading to Brazil. Julio took me along the second time, and I just laughed at the way he had those pilots thinking he was the Bolivian Air Force. We didn't have so much as a shot fired at us. He's better at strategy than Papá or I could hope to be. All that military training, I guess. But then, that's why Papá hired him. The way he suckered Doug Bradford into that raid he pulled . . ."

Sara was lost! She had no idea what Nicolás was talking about, and she was too tired to try to figure it out or ask him to explain. Instead, she grabbed on to the one thing that did make sense. "What do you mean, Julio suckered Doug Bradford? What are you saying, Nicky? That you knew ahead of time that the DEA was going to raid Cortéz Industries? That you planned it? But—I don't get it! You were so upset about that raid. All those things you said about the DEA and Doug Bradford! And all the trouble he got into—you said he almost got kicked out of the country! And now you're saying that was all a lie too? Oh, Nicky, that poor man! How could you?"

Nicolás raised his hands, laughing, palms outward. "Hey, whoa! It wasn't my idea! In fact, I blamed Bradford as much as anyone else—until I started in on that side of the business, and Papá told me what a sucker he'd made of the guy. It was actually Julio's idea—the first job he ever did for Papá. He'd heard from his FELCN buddies that the *gringos* were snooping around *Industrias Cortéz*. Which wasn't that big of a deal, because the only time they would ever find anything was during those few hours when a shipment was passing through the warehouse. Otherwise, they could search up and down and not find a thing. But Papá figured if the *americanos* were going to pull something, we might as well get it over with and use it to our own advantage.

"So Julio dangled the bait. And when the DEA took it and pulled that raid, Julio arranged for his FELCN buddies to smash up the depot. It just about killed Papá to waste that good Cuban rum, but it was worth it just for the stink it made in the press. The *gringos* have been afraid to touch us ever since, and thanks to that, Papá has been able to move more cocaine through the warehouse in the past two years than in the last twenty. That's why it was so funny to see Bradford acting so high and mighty at that Fourth of July thing, as though we hadn't made a total fool of him. If he had any idea what that raid was really all about—"

"Wait!" Pushing the purse from her lap, Sara left her chair to kneel beside the sofa. In all of Nicolás's careless narrative, there was only one point that really mattered to her now. "That raid—you said you didn't know about it," she said in a voice only slightly above a whisper. "That your father hadn't let you in on that side of the business. So, you didn't know back then that Don Luis was dealing cocaine? When . . . when you married me, you didn't know?"

This was the hardest point for Sara to grapple with. That the same Nicolás who had walked so wondrously into her life—almost four months ago now—and wooed her with such passion, and loved her with such tenderness, and charmed all her friends, and even sat in church with her and listened with all attentiveness to her pastor's rather dry sermons—that he had all the time been a knowing accomplice in criminal activity. She just couldn't reconcile the two! But if he hadn't known! Not that it really made any difference now, but it would seem like less of a betrayal.

Nicolás reached a lazy arm to lift the cell phone from Sara's hand. "Don't be silly, Sara! Of course I knew! I'm not stupid! Oh, maybe when I was little, I just accepted that we were rich again. But you think by the time I was in high school, I didn't have a pretty good idea how Papá had managed to come up with enough cash to buy everyone in the family—down to the last aunt—a brand-new four-wheel-drive vehicle? Not likely! Not that Papá ever came right out and said that's what he was doing, but we all knew—Delores, Janéth, even Mamá, though she'd never admit it. Of course, it wasn't until now that Papá has trusted me to handle any of that side of the business. But even back then—well, you take that offset seal. That was my idea when production picked up just after the raid. They were having all kinds of trouble keeping track of the shipping numbers and invoices. Of course, Papá didn't come right out and tell me he was having problems getting his coke shipments mixed in with his regular ones. He just mentioned that they were having trouble distinguishing special consignments. But I knew what he meant, and he knew that I knew. And it worked. Papá said it was the first use he'd seen for all that business training he'd been paying for."

Sara stood up and walked away from him, unable to bear any longer the sight of that complacent grin. "Then . . . all these weeks . . . these months," she said with infinite sadness and weariness. "You've been lying to me the whole time! I . . . I just can't believe it! And when I asked you if any of the Cortéz family were involved in drug-dealing—"

"Well, what was I supposed to do?" Nicolás asked reasonably. "You'd made it pretty clear whose side you were on. Look, Sara, you're acting like we're a bunch of criminals. Okay, so we've passed along a few kilos of cocaine to a bunch of spoiled brats who'd just get their kicks from someone else if they didn't get it from us. But, was that really so bad? Is it really so different from selling rum or cigarettes? Come on, Sara! No one's forcing them to buy from us! It shouldn't even be a crime to start with! And look what we've done with it. You may not like how we did it, but you've got to admit *Industrias Cortéz* is one of the best things that ever happened to this country. Do you know how many jobs we supply or how much money we put into the economy here? You talk about people dying. There are kids who were probably starving until we started creating jobs for their families. Isn't that worth moving along a load or two of coke that would have gotten shipped anyway, with or without us?"

"We've already had this argument, Nicky," Sara said tiredly over her shoulder. "No, it's not worth it. To get rich off of other people's suffering—well, maybe there are people who do it legally, but it's still wrong. Dead wrong! And as for you . . ." She turned around slowly to face him. "You *are* a bunch of criminals, no matter how you want to argue it! And I can't believe you really think you're going to get away with this!" she added, but even in her own ears it carried no conviction.

Nicolás moved restlessly under the accusation in her eyes, but he managed an incredulous laugh. "And who do you think is going to stop us? Sara, I don't think you realize just what the name of Don Luis Cortéz Velásquez de Salazar means here in Santa Cruz. Papá is one of the most powerful men in this city, maybe *the* most powerful. He's got people everywhere—in the city government, the police, the customs, the border patrol, even in the FELCN. How do you think we know to take measures every time they start snooping around us? Not to mention the *narcos,* though they have no idea who they're reporting back to."

Getting lazily to his feet, he crossed over to where Sara was staring at the closed balcony shutters and pulled her close, adding softly and slyly, close to her ear, "So if you're thinking of making a run for it, *querida,* don't kid yourself. Even if you could get past our people, there's nowhere you could go in this country that someone wouldn't see you and report back to Papá. Especially the way you stand out in a crowd."

Sara shivered at the caressing fingers that ran through the blonde hair spilling down her back. Misinterpreting it, Nicolás pulled her closer. "Do you know how gorgeous you are, *corazón?*" he muttered thickly, ignoring the stiffness of her response. "If Papá wasn't waiting for me . . ." He abruptly released her and went whistling back downstairs, taking the cell phone with him.

A long time later, Sara moved away from the shutters. Stripping back into her nightgown, she crawled into bed. But not to sleep. With a sense of déjà vu, she tossed and turned the remaining hours of the night away. The arguments, the tears, the sense of events beyond her control—even that late-night trip through dark halls to Don Luis's office. It was as though time were repeating itself! Only this time she couldn't hope that time itself would be a solution. This wasn't going to go away in the morning.

What do I do now? What do I do now? The refrain ran over and over through her mind. Then—*Oh, God, what do I do now?*

CHAPTER EIGHTEEN

Spring was coming to Santa Cruz. The *toborochi* and *paraíso* trees had finished dropping their rainbow pods, but there were other trees blooming, and flower-laden vines crawling over the barbed wire fence across the highway.

Beyond the fence, a herd of cows, newborn calves at their side, munched as placidly as though they weren't in the middle of a city of a million people. A mother goat scrambled over a brick pile to reach a tuft of grass, ignoring the two frisky kids who somehow managed to cling to her bulging udders. And just inside the open gate of the Cortéz estate, a family of ducklings was demolishing a border of tulips with noisy indifference to the sanctity of Mimi's flower beds.

Sara, watching the farm parade from inside the French doors of the drawing room, saw neither the delightfulness nor the humor of the scene. She was waiting for Nicolás. Something she'd done often enough before, with joy and anticipation and impatience as well. She'd never have dreamed then that the day would come when she'd actually be dreading her husband's arrival.

Pushing open the French doors, she walked out onto the veranda. It would have been easier to watch for the Ferrari from her balcony, but the thought of waiting there, where she'd dreamed so many naïve fantasies of happiness and home, had her shuddering in revulsion. So she'd come down to this spot that held no special meaning or happy memories for her.

An angry quacking rose from the tulip beds as Jorge, the surly guard, finally bestirred himself to chase the ducks out the gate. It was Jorge who had called up to the house with the message that Nicolás was on his way home from the refinery, and that Sara was to be awaiting his arrival. Sara hadn't seen Nicolás since he'd left to take the cell phone down to Don Luis. Though she'd tossed sleepless until the gray hours of dawn, he had never returned, and when she finally dragged herself, dull-eyed and still exhausted, out of bed, the Ferrari had been gone from its parking slot.

Since then, she'd heard nothing—not from Nicolás, not from Don Luis, not even Mimi, who was surely somewhere on the property. Only Nicolás's impersonal, secondhand order to present herself dressed and waiting, as though she were some truant schoolgirl.

The ducks flapped squawking across the canal. A spark of curiosity made its way past Sara's listlessness to wonder why Jorge had opened the gates now instead of waiting until he heard the honk of the Ferrari, as he usually did. Was the guard trying to tempt her into making a bid to leave the property? She'd already approached the gate once that morning, only to have him block her way, one hand on his outdated service revolver, the Dobermans no longer sniffing her suspiciously, but pressing close to his sides with low, bared-teeth growls. He'd probably love for her to try to escape so he could use that gun on her!

No, now she was being melodramatic. Or was she? After last night, she could believe just about anything!

Restlessly, Sara paced along the veranda. She should have been at the orphanage by now, but she hadn't even been able to give Doña Inez a call to let her know she wouldn't be coming. When she'd tried, she'd found that Don Luis had been as good as his word. The line to her bedroom had been disconnected, and when she'd come down to the hall to use the phone there, a servant had appeared out of nowhere to remove the receiver from her hand. He'd murmured something apologetic and insincere about *el patrón* having to approve all calls, but the usual deference had been missing, and none of her protests that she was just trying to cancel an appointment had availed.

Nor had he been the only one. Every time she turned around, it seemed there was someone standing behind her, or a suspicious gaze following her movements. And she had no doubt that they would stop her if she tried to go anywhere. Despite the lack of any visible restraints, she was just as much a prisoner as if Don Luis had thrown her into a dungeon.

A honk interrupted her thoughts. The bright yellow Ferrari was turning in at the gate. As it swept up the driveway, Jorge hurried to shut the heavy wooden portals. The car squealed to a stop in front of the stone tower, and Nicolás unfolded himself from the driver's seat. Spotting Sara on the veranda, he strode toward her, looking cheerful and wide awake and not in the least affected by his sleepless night.

How does he do it? Sara wondered resentfully. This was, after all, his second all-nighter in a week, and he'd had two Cessna trips last night on top of it all. Still, if Nicky could stay up all night to party the way he did, why not to commit a crime!

Glancing back at Jorge, who was still watching from the driveway, Nicolás gave a jerk of the head. "Come on, Sara. I need to talk to you—alone." He led her around the side of the house toward the pool.

"I've got some news for you," he told her as soon as they were out of sight of the guard. "Your DEA friend Bradford—you want to know how he spent the night? He just turned in a big bust this morning. A local with fifty kilos right in his own house—the idiot! Papá knows the man—not personally, just through some business contacts—and the only surprise is that it's taken the guy so long to go down. Like I said, these *gringos* are a little slow!"

Pulling a lawn chair out from under the *paraísos* into the morning sun, Nicolás glanced around the pool area. The closest person was the gardener's young assistant, who was digging in a flower bed twenty meters away. Stretching out on the lawn chair, Nicolás yawned. "At any rate, it doesn't sound like Bradford spent the night worrying over anything you said. We're going to have to wait a few more days to see if he starts poking around and asking questions, but I think it's going to be all right. Now, if you'd told him about the warehouse or that offset seal we've been using—well, that could have really set us back. We'd have had to scratch our whole system of delivery. And with eight tons of coke sitting around the property . . ."

Nicolás looked over at Sara, his tone suddenly serious. "For what it's worth, Sara, I'm beginning to think you're right—and so does Papá, really."

Perching herself reluctantly on the edge of the next lawn chair, Sara studied her husband incredulously. Was this supposed to be some kind of apology?

"The truth is, this cocaine business is getting dirtier—and more dangerous—all the time," Nicolás went on, folding his arms behind his head. "The Americans aren't all dumb, and they're starting to get a lot more cooperation. Even what we're doing—well, I know we're safe enough, but when I think of all the coke we've got sitting around right now, I'll admit I feel like I'm sitting on a keg of gunpowder. Besides, there's just too many lowlifes in it these days. It's giving Bolivia a bad name! We get tired of having the international news paint us as nothing but a bunch of *narcos* down here."

The irony of the statement seemed to escape him.

"It's not as though we really had much choice in any of this—not if we wanted to get the family back on its feet and give *Industrias Cortéz* the start it needed. But all things come to an end, and it's definitely time to put an end to this whole coca thing and start cleaning up this country! And Papá agrees with me. That's why this shipment is the last. Then we're getting out. So, . . ."—he yawned again, closing his eyes—"if it eases your tender little conscience any, a month from now, when we—and *Industrias Cortéz*—are in the clear, your DEA pals are welcome to cut down every coca plant in the country and every dealer, too. For that matter, we might even help them do it!"

"And I suppose that makes everything you've done all right," Sara said wearily. If he'd only show the slightest compunction for the *people* involved, not just his precious image on the international scene! Then, as she'd made up her mind to do in those sleepless hours of the early morning, she pleaded once more with Nicolás to leave.

"Oh, Nicky, please, we were so happy back in Seattle! And we could be again if we could just get away from all this! You . . . you used to say that I was all you really needed, that you just couldn't live without me. If you meant that, if you love me at all, then . . ."—she faltered as she saw his face harden—"then show it by coming away with me. *Please*, Nicky!"

Nicolás sat up in his chair with a violent motion. "If *you* really loved *me*, you wouldn't be asking me to go!" he said sharply. "What do you want me to say, Sara? I'm a Cortéz! This is my home, my inheritance—which I've shared with you rather generously. And instead of appreciating everything I've worked to give you, you're asking me to throw it all up for some nine-to-five job in some second-rate American corporation that doesn't even appreciate what the name Cortéz means. And for what? Because my wife can't face reality?"

"Reality!" Sara cried. "I'm not the one who's up to my neck in drug-dealing and trying to pretend it's another day at the office." She looked down at Nicky's obdurate, chiseled features as he stretched back out in the lawn chair and sighed. "Why did you ever marry me, Nicky, really? I'm . . . I'm so different from all the other girls you seem to like!"

Nicolás was silent for a moment, as though considering her words. Then he answered slowly, "I guess maybe that's why. You *were* different than the other women I've known. You weren't always throwing yourself at my head like the girls here or trying to attract the other men. I liked that! When I met you that night, it was like—oh, I don't know!

Like you'd walked out of one of those fairy tales they used to read to us at the Co-op. All that hair like spun gold, and those big eyes begging me to save you, that innocent, untouched look in them. Like one of the *Vírgenes* in the cathedral. Or the Sleeping Beauty in your children's story. It was exciting that a girl would want to save herself for me! Especially such a beautiful one. I guess I wanted to be the one to wake you up."

Sara listened with astonishment. There was a reminiscent tone in Nicolás's voice and a softer expression on his face than she'd seen there in a long time. But then he made an impatient gesture, and his voice hardened. "The problem was, you never really woke up! I should have guessed you'd turn out to be some religious nut after seeing that church you went to. All that 'do this' and 'don't do that,' and praying and reading the Bible! I put up with it because I thought you'd loosen up once I got you away from there. How was I to know you took your religion so seriously?"

The accusation took Sara aback. Taking her religion too seriously? Personally, she'd thought she'd fallen down badly at taking her faith seriously at all! She shook her head. "I don't understand you, Nicky. You believe in God. Or you say you do. And you wear this . . ."—she leaned forward to touch the outline of the Cortéz cross under his polo shirt—"because it means something special to you. So how can you deliberately go out and do things you know are evil—criminal? Doesn't it bother you—or even scare you a little—to know there's a God up there watching everything you do?"

Nicolás brushed her finger away as though it had burned him. Recovering, he said sharply, "Don't be a fool, Sara. Of course I believe in God. But religion is religion, and business is business! We've learned not to mix the two. And you'd get along a lot better if you'd learn to do the same and not be so judgmental."

He reached over to push a buzzer imbedded into the trunk of a *toborochi* tree. "I don't want to hear any more about this, Sara! There's no need for this! I'm not leaving Santa Cruz, and there's no reason for you to be talking about it either. I mean, this is crazy! If I hadn't happened to turn on that newscast—or if you'd just kept your nose out of things like a woman should!—you'd have never known anything about this anyway. In a few weeks it would have all been over, and then we'd have settled down to married life with no difference you'd have noticed, except that we'd have never had to worry about finances again. Well, we can still do that! All you have to do is forget any of this ever happened and keep your eyes—and your mouth—shut for a few weeks. Then we can get on with our lives!"

He broke off as a servant girl appeared beside the lawn chair, wiping her hands on a white apron. *"Sí, señor?"* Her black eyes flickered to Sara as she spoke, and Sara was taken aback by the blatant hostility she read there before the girl lowered her eyes with a respectful, "You called? In what way may I serve you?"

The servant girl was still in her teens, with the long, black braids of the *campesino* and a rounded body under her maid's uniform that would in a few years be misshapen with hard work and too many children, but which was at the moment pretty enough. Nicolás lost his angry look and turned on the engaging grin that every attractive woman had elicited from him since he was old enough to understand its effect.

"Bring me a beer, Teresa . . . you are Teresa, aren't you? No, make that two. I could really use them right now!" He slanted a mocking look at Sara. "And a *limonada* for the *señora*. She doesn't care for beer."

"Sí, señor! Right away, *señor!"* The servant girl responded with a dimpled smile and a respectful bob of the head. Then she directed another hostile glance at Sara before scurrying off. Sara watched her disappear through the door that led to the kitchen, momentarily diverted from the painfulness of her argument with Nicolás. Was this just another female who resented Sara because she had a crush on Sara's handsome husband? Or was there something more?

"Why is she looking at me like that?" she asked abruptly. "Just like Jorge earlier. I mean, he's never liked me, but he glares at me now like I'm some kind of leper! And the others. The way they all follow me around and make sure I don't get near the phone or the gate. Are they *all* in on what you're doing? The drugs and everything? And if they are, why"—she added deliberately in an effort to sting Nicolás from his complacency—"do they act as though I'm the criminal instead of you?"

Nicolás refused to rise to her provocation. "No, of course they don't know! You think we'd trust all these loose tongues? There aren't more than a handful of people who know anything about our . . . ah, *other* business. And, except for Julio Vargas and Papá's people out at the hacienda—and he doesn't exactly let them go wandering around—they're all family. Like I said, Papá doesn't believe in taking any chances. But don't think that's going to make it any easier to talk your way off the property! I'm afraid you're not very popular around here right now! Because, you see," he added blandly, *"I* am!"

Sara stared at her husband as though he'd suddenly grown two heads. "What in the world are you talking about?"

"Well, if you really want to know . . ." Nicolás slanted another mocking look at her. "We had to have some way to keep an eye on you. So Papá told the staff you'd been caught cheating on your husband—me! So now you're in disgrace and are not to be allowed off the property. They understand that sort of thing here, no matter how free women might be to run around on their husbands in your country. And since the staff happens to appreciate me—especially the females—they're going to make good and sure that Papá's orders are carried out. Not to mention, there's a big reward out for anyone who catches you trying to leave the property or to make contact with your lover."

"There's *what?*" Sara had thought she'd heard too much to be shocked again. But this was beyond anything she could have imagined! And that her own husband was sitting there telling her as calmly as—

"You mean, Jorge believes . . . no wonder he—and Teresa . . . ?" Sara was suddenly more furious than she'd ever been in her life. And that made it easier to say what she had to say next. "And you really expect me to stay here in this house? When . . . when they're all going to be thinking for the rest of my life that I'm some kind of cheap—"

Sara was up off the edge of her chair, almost stamping her foot in her fury. "I can't believe you could do this to me, Nicolás! Well, that's it! You're going to have to choose between me and . . . and all this." She waved an angry hand around the grounds with its stately house and gardens and placid swimming pool. "Because I'm leaving here just as soon as I can get away. And if you won't leave with me, then I'll go by myself."

Nicolás was not taking her seriously, she saw at once. He was openly laughing, his blue eyes, alight with mirth, roving appreciatively up her slim figure, taut with defiance, to the heart-shaped features, no longer pale but flushed with angry color. "Oh, come on, Sara, you're making too much of this." Grabbing at her hand, he tugged her down onto the lawn chair beside him. "Who cares what a bunch of servants think? Besides, they'll forget soon enough about this 'lover' of yours once this is all over. Especially when they see how crazy you really are about me. Mmm! You taste good!"

Sara jerked away from him. "Don't you touch me! I mean it, Nicky! Maybe you're right, and you guys really are going to get away with all this. Maybe your laws are really so corrupt that you can buy off the whole country! But I won't go along with it. I can't condone a crime, no matter how much you try to whitewash it. And I won't live with a criminal! You can set your guards on me and keep me locked up, but just as soon as I get a chance, I'm going! And I won't be back!"

Releasing her, Nicolás raised his hands into the air. "Fine! You do what you want. You've got a month or so to think about it. When you can't cause us any more problems, well then you can make up your own mind about what you want to do. But I think you'll come around," he added with the confidence of someone who has never been denied anything he wanted. "You've been too in love with me to just walk away. Besides, what do you have to go back to? You don't have a home there anymore, or a family. If you think I'm going to believe you'd really choose that old apartment and a part-time job over me and all of this . . ." He lifted his shoulders in a Latin shrug. "And if you don't come around, there's plenty of other women available who know how to have a good time! Like Reina, maybe?"

Nicky's blue eyes were hard on Sara's face, but though her mouth quivered at the jibe, she didn't respond. Swinging his legs over the side of the lawn chair, Nicolás stood up. "Well, I'm off. Tell Teresa to keep the beer—the little incompetent! How long does it take to get to the kitchen and back, anyway?"

He started toward the house, then turned back. "I never did get a chance to tell you why I came home. Papá told me to see if you needed anything for the party tonight. Mamá told him you hadn't gotten your dress yet, and he thought you might need an escort downtown. But in the mood you're in, I don't think I'd trust you outside the gate! Besides, you've still got the dress you never wore for the last party, don't you?" he taunted.

"The party?" Sara had no idea at first what he was talking about. Then she remembered with a shock what day this was. "You mean, the anniversary? That . . . that's still going on? No, of course I don't want to go shopping! As if I'd spend another penny of your family's filthy money. But you can't really be expecting me to go to that! Aren't I supposed to be under this—house arrest, or whatever you want to call it?" she demanded with heavy sarcasm.

"Oh, you're going, all right!" Nicolás assured her. "You don't think we want to advertise to the whole world the problems we're having with our newest family member! You'll be up there on the platform with everyone else, and I can tell you Papá is expecting you to do the family proud. After all"—the corner of his mouth curled disagreeably—"whatever else you are, you're decorative enough."

His blue eyes roved up and down her again, but this time there was more calculation than appreciation in his gaze. "I'll be here to get you at eight. And don't keep me waiting. I told Reina we'd pick her up on the way. She *knows*, by the way!" he added mockingly.

"She knows *what*?" Sara demanded. "The truth or the lie?"

"Oh, the lie, of course," Nicolás said coolly. "Though she can't understand how any woman could want a man other than me. So you can figure she'll be keeping a close eye on you tonight."

With that, he turned on his heel and strolled away. Sara watched him go as though he were a stranger. And that was exactly what he was, she knew now. A devastatingly handsome stranger, but a stranger nonetheless. The Nicky she'd fallen in love with had never existed— and she'd have seen that long before this if only she hadn't been so determined to shore up every crack that appeared in his pedestal. He was no more than a cut-out paper doll, a fairy-tale prince that she'd invented and pasted up and defended despite all evidence to the contrary.

Sara's eyes burned with anger and grief and humiliation. How was it that life had put her in this situation? No, how had she put *herself* in this situation, she admitted with sudden bitter honesty. It wasn't as though she'd had no warning! Her pastor had warned her. And so had her friends. But she'd been so head-over-heels in love that she'd refused to listen. A wry grimace stung Sara's eyes with tears as she remembered the final argument she'd had with Franny, and her own confident defense.

How little she'd known! Her husband's noble self-sacrifice in returning to Bolivia had turned out instead to be the natural choice of a rich kid returning home to a lifestyle that no entry-level position in the United States could offer him. His studies had been paid for in full by his father, who had, in fact, been quite vocal over the subject of his final grades. And the fluency of his English, which she'd found so impressive in a foreign student, was only natural considering his attendance since kindergarten at the Co-op school.

Even the fearlessness with which Nicky had chased away her two assailants that night he'd come to her rescue, was no great feat of courage, Sara saw now. It was simply the supreme arrogance of someone who had never had anyone question his orders. It would never occur to Nicolás Cortéz, any more than to his father, that a pair of low-bred street thugs would dare defy him.

As for the casual charm and laughing tenderness with which he'd won her heart those first wonderful weeks, she'd been a fool to think that she was the only woman who called that from him. He used the same technique on every woman he found attractive—as she'd witnessed just now with Teresa. He just couldn't help it. But the truth was that there was only one really important person in the life of the man she'd married, and that was—and always had been—Nicolás Cortéz.

A late-clinging *toborochi* pod released its grip and dropped into the pool, disturbing the placid surface. Sara watched the concentric rings chase each other until they dissolved again into stillness. Did she still love Nicolás? She didn't know. She'd loved the Nicky who had existed in her mind. Loved him passionately and desperately as she'd loved no one since her childhood had ripped away everyone she cared for. But this stranger who had just walked away from her with a careless laugh and egotistical complacency, as though Sara Connor was simply one more starstruck girl who couldn't possibly resist him? This—this *criminal* who displayed not the slightest remorse at battening on the misery of others?

Teresa appeared, carrying a tray of drinks. Sara waved her away, ignoring the speculative sideways glances, and sank down again on the edge of the lawn chair. She didn't want to think about Nicolás and his refusal to go back to the United States with her, and the difference this would make in her future. She was too hurt and angry and terribly alone. More alone than she'd ever been, even after her mother died and her father retreated to the refuge of work. What she wanted desperately right now was to run home, as she'd been able to do those long years ago when some childhood trouble came, and sob out her grief and bitterness on the shoulder of someone who would care. But Nicolás was right. She had no home to go back to, now that her tiny student apartment had been cleared out and rented to someone else. And now that her college friends had scattered back to the winds from which they'd come, there was no one in Seattle who really cared about her, either.

A pleasant, cheerful face rose into Sara's mind. Yes, maybe Laura Histed cared a little. She was a good person and had been kind and welcoming. If only Sara could pick up the phone and spill out her hurt and confusion to one person who was sane and whole and not part of this nightmare! But she couldn't, and Laura would never know why her new acquaintance had dropped so suddenly out of sight.

That thought brought to mind another face, stern and masculine, with observant gray eyes that saw too much. Doug Bradford had also been kind—kinder than she'd given him credit for being. He'd pledged to help her and had even offered his friendship. But how much of that he'd meant, she would never know, because he was as far out of her reach as Laura Histed. Would he wonder when Sara dropped out of the orphanage and the Santa Cruz scene? Or had he, as Nicolás had intimated, already forgotten her fumbling questions that had aroused such sharp interest just last night?

Sara drew a deep breath that didn't alleviate the hard lump in her chest. If only she could pray, as her mother had once taught her to do in times of trouble. Others seemed to find comfort from it. But the bitter years had taught her how much good that did. *God, I know you're out there somewhere! But while you're busy keeping this whole huge galaxy turning on its axis, do you even know I exist down here? Do you care?*

There was no more answer than she'd expected. No, no one was going to help her out of this. She was on her own. And tears and self-pity weren't going to help her. Brushing a quick hand across her eyelashes, Sara straightened her back and braced her shoulders, as though the act would give her the courage she needed. All she could do now was take one hour at a time. And wait. Though for what, she had no idea!

When the time came to dress for the anniversary party, Sara did put on the previous week's unworn party dress—but not the skin-tight black one that Nicolás had intended. Instead, she chose the soft chiffon dress he had so disdainfully cast aside. That small act of defiance improved her spirits enough that she was able to ignore Reina's pointed comments and scarcely veiled attitude of triumph as she crowded between Nicolás and Sara in the cramped front seat of the Ferrari. Sara contented herself with staring out the window at the city lights while the two cousins laughed and talked as though she weren't even there.

But when they reached the refinery, Reina had no choice but to take a back seat. As the Ferrari crawled up the driveway behind a procession of cars all looking for parking, Sara could see that the grounds of *Industrias Cortéz* had been transformed for the evening's celebration. Bunting and balloons hung from every available wire, and small Chinese lanterns sparkled among the branches of the *toborochi* trees that lined the drive. A band playing raucous Latin pop-rock had set up next to the bas-relief of the Cortéz emblem. On both sides of the drive, concession stands offered free beer and soda. And everywhere, spilling out across the vast lawn, people were drinking and dancing and chattering.

In addition to the well-dressed acquaintances of the Cortezes, there were tradesmen who supplied Cortéz contracts and technicians who repaired their equipment. And lower still on the social scale, the store clerks and assembly line workers and other employees of the Cortéz business empire were openly enjoying this one night when they were the invited guests of one of the country's most powerful men.

There were also far more security guards, in their olive-green uniforms, than Sara had seen the last time she'd been here. One guard from the *Policía Nacional* strolled by as the Ferrari inched forward another few feet. Recognizing the occupants of the car, he raised a hand to his cap with a respectful "Señor Nicolás" before continuing on. His services would no doubt be needed in a few hours, judging by the number of beer cans already littering the lawn.

As long as that was the only reason he was here.

Leaning across Reina, who was grumbling about the slowness of their progress, Sara asked Nicolás in English, which she knew Reina didn't understand, "All these police—what did you tell them about me? Or are they all on Don Luis's payroll?" she added bitterly, remembering Nicolás's earlier comment about Cortéz connections within the city government.

The look Nicolás shot her was comprehending and malicious. "I'm afraid even we can't buy off the entire police force! And no, Papá didn't think it was necessary to complicate things by giving them any—ah, *other*—instructions. But if you're thinking of doing something stupid, don't! There'll be other eyes on you out there that aren't dressed in green."

Which answered the question she hadn't dared ask. Sara settled back against the seat, but without relaxing. There were far more people here than she'd expected, and the door handle was only inches away. If she jumped out while they were crawling along like this . . .

Nicolás gave her another sharp glance, then moved his left hand down from the steering wheel. There was a sudden *click,* and Sara didn't need to reach for the door to know she'd just been locked in. They inched along another ten feet before Nicolás slammed the palm of his hand against the steering wheel. "This is ridiculous! Why should I have to sit here in line like some—?"

Giving the steering wheel a sudden sharp twist, he edged the Ferrari out of the line and onto the shoulder of the gravel drive while his other hand hit the horn. People walking under the trees scrambled to get out of his way as he accelerated up the edge of the driveway past the queue of cars waiting patiently to turn into the improvised parking area. Sara held her breath for fear that someone would be run over, but no one else seemed bothered by Nicolás's maneuver, and many were even waving and cheering as they recognized the yellow Ferrari.

I'll never understand these people, Sara told herself silently. It was a more convincing display of Cortéz power and influence than even the subservience of the household employees.

At the end of the driveway, the cars were being directed into a designated parking area at the foot of the syrup tanks. As Nicolás kept a hand on the horn, a gap opened between two cars. Accelerating between them, Nicolás skidded across the gravel to brake with a flourish at the front steps of the main administration building. There was another *click* as the doors unlocked. Then Nicolás climbed out, tossing his keys up the steps to one of the security guards, who had hurried forward. "Take this over with the rest of the cars. And be careful! I don't want a scratch on it!"

Their arrival hadn't gone unnoticed. The semicircle of gravel in front of the administration building was already crowded with party-goers, and there were craned necks and excited murmurs as Nicolás strode around the car to the passenger door. He was smiling now, and it was with great care that he helped Sara out. His blue eyes were appreciative as he looked her over, then drew her to his side with an affectionate gesture that brought another approving murmur from the bystanders. "You look just like a bride should—innocent and beautiful," he purred. "Papá should be happy. Now let's hurry up. We're already late."

"So what is new!" Reina gave Sara a black look as she clambered out after her, jerking angrily at her short dress as it slid dangerously far up her thighs. The security guard who'd been ordered to move the car dashed around to offer his help, but Reina brushed him away with a sharp rebuff. It was so typical of Nicolás, Sara thought with resignation, to flirt with his cousin the whole way there and now ignore her entirely. Nor did his sudden solicitousness toward Sara herself mean anything. It was show time, and she was part of the production the Cortezes were mounting tonight.

Above a temporary platform, bright with bunting, a banner proclaimed, "HAPPY TWENTIETH ANNIVERSARY, CORTÉZ INDUSTRIES." Don Luis and Mimi and other family members and dignitaries were already taking their seats behind the podium.

Placing his hand on her waist, Nicolás led Sara toward the dais, with Reina trailing a sulky step or two behind. She was looking spectacular, as always, with her dark hair piled high in a magnificent creation atop her head, and her dress—spangled silver this time instead of black, but just as skimpy—clinging to her generous curves. But the sultriness of her good looks was marred by the sullenness of her expression.

She's jealous! Sara realized with a flash of sympathy as well as amusement. Reina was used to being the center of attention wherever she went. But tonight the eyes of the crowd were on Sara. Sara and Nicolás. The young Cortéz heir, fresh home from college, and his lovely *extranjera* bride—that was what people had come to see. Were it not for the circumstances, Sara would have been exhilarated by the turning heads and murmurs of admiration.

She slid a quick look upward at Nicolás's chiseled profile. They *did* make an attractive couple, she admitted wistfully. Nicolás was looking handsome enough to bring a pang to her heart, his cream-colored summer suit making him appear even taller and leaner. And even if she couldn't compete with Reina's brunette sensuality, Sara had taken special care tonight with her own appearance. The warm glow of her new tan and the long-lashed amber of her eyes, made larger by careful makeup, formed a striking contrast to her northern fairness.

Not that she really cared what these people thought of her, but the knowledge that she was looking her best gave her the armor she needed to step onto the dais with her head held high and a bright smile. And to face the angry glares and open contempt that her mother-in-law and Delores and Janéth turned on her as Nicolás steered her to a seat. Sara's heart sank. It hadn't occurred to her that Don Luis and Nicolás would feed the Cortéz women the same false story they'd spun for the servants and Reina.

It doesn't matter! None of it matters! You've just got to wait it out!

Sara held that thought firmly in place as the ceremonies dragged on. She sat primly between Nicolás and the mayor of Santa Cruz, her back straight and her chin up, and the same bright smile glued on her face until it ached. Speech followed speech. The mayor presented Don Luis with a plaque recognizing his services to the economic well-being of the city. Don Luis duly presented his son as the new vice-president and heir of *Industrias Cortéz.*

Then Sara caught Mimi's frown and realized that she was being motioned to the front of the dais. Nicolás drew her close as she stepped to his side, smiling and waving to the crowd with his usual ease, and if Sara couldn't muster up equal enthusiasm, that was put down to the appropriate shyness of a new bride. It was evident from the roars of approval that the crowd had been well deceived into seeing the young couple as adoring newlyweds.

If they only knew!

Sara played with a wild impulse to grab the microphone from her father-in-law and scream out that she was being held prisoner against her will. And that the man they were honoring was really a cocaine smuggler who was planning on using this very facility to ship eight tons of coke overseas in the next few weeks. But the impulse waned as quickly as it had come. She would be stopped before she got two words out of her mouth. And her stunt would be followed, no doubt, by some discreet announcement that she'd taken sick or gone insane!

Still, what if she just dashed off the dais and down those steps into the crowd? Were there really eyes out there, spying on her, guarding her, as Nicolás had claimed? Sara looked down from the edge of the stage. There she met Reina's long-lashed gaze, narrowed with antipathy. The other girl had been forced to leave Nicolás and Sara at the steps to the platform, which she'd done with ill-grace and a rude comment about how she was more a member of the family than Sara. Now she stood—there were no seats—at the front of the crowd that extended from the dais clear back into the dark of the trees, her glare implacably fixed on Sara. Yes, there was at least one person out there watching her with ill-will, Sara reluctantly conceded. And who knew how many others that she wouldn't even recognize until they stopped her.

If the ceremonies had seemed interminable, the receiving line was even longer. Sara found herself shaking hands with every person she could possibly have ever met in Santa Cruz, and hundreds more who didn't mind standing in an endless line for the privilege of greeting the country's leading industrialist, and his son with his new bride. By the end of the first hour, she was ready to go on strike. Her hand was limp. Her cheeks felt as though they'd been washed by so many kisses. And if she had to smile at one more person as though she were really a happy bride and daughter-in-law . . .

And why should I? she thought with a sudden frown that startled the city dignitary holding her hand into dropping it and scurrying on. Don Luis and Mimi were still doing their duty on the other side of her, but Delores and Janéth and their husbands had escaped long ago. So what was she doing standing here, helping people she despised make a good impression?

Beside her, Nicolás was looking patently bored. He'd had more than his usual limit of alcohol—glasses of champagne and imported German beer that circulating waiters were discreetly reserving for the more privileged guests—and between that and the warmth of the evening, he'd finally removed his jacket and tie, handing them to one of the hovering waiters. Now he was reaching to unbutton the top two buttons of his patterned silk shirt, leaving the bronzed column of his throat bare to the slight breeze. The perfect styling of his hair had been disarranged by that same breeze, and there was the barest hint of dampness at his armpits.

"Another five minutes, and I'm out of here!" he muttered to Sara as one of his great-aunts finally released his hand. Sara bent her head as the tiny old lady stood on tiptoe to brush her papery cheek against Sara's. This elderly relative had been kind to her, and Sara gave her a hug and her first genuine smile of the evening.

"It is good to see our Nico so happy," the old lady told Sara with evident delight.

Murmuring something noncommittal, Sara turned to see who was next. The line was finally dwindling down. Coming through now was a good-looking boy in his late teens who greeted Don Luis with every evidence of pleasure, received a short nod from Doña Mimi and a glance without recognition from Nicolás. Which meant, Sara could deduce by now, that the boy wasn't among their own social circle. But he was well-dressed and obviously affluent, and showed some of the Cortezes' own easy arrogance as he extended a well-manicured hand to Nicolás. *Nouveau riche,* Sara surmised.

"*Buenas noches,* Don Nicolás." Affluent or not, there was deference in the young man's greeting. "I know you do not remember me, but your father is my godfather and that of my sisters. He has been very good to me and my family, and though my sisters and my mother are not able to be here tonight, they wish to add their own sincere congratulations to my own for the success of *Industrias Cortéz* and for your marriage."

The boy finished abruptly. Nicolás, who hadn't even pretended an interest in the teenager's rehearsed little speech, muttered something marginally polite and glanced past him to the next in line, an open indication that his visitor could move along. But the young man wasn't taking the hint, Sara saw as she waited to offer her own hand—and cheek. He had stopped smack in the middle of the receiving line, and his black eyes were fastened on Nicolás with such narrow-eyed intensity that Sara glanced automatically upward. Then she realized that it wasn't Nicolás who was drawing the boy's interest, but the jeweled cross that had worked its way out of the open neck of her husband's shirt and lay gleaming gold and emerald against the soft fabric.

The boy raised a hand as though to touch the piece of jewelry, then snatched it back. "Where did you get that?" he demanded sharply.

Nicolás brought his attention back from the distance. He glanced down, surprised. "What, this? It's just an old family heirloom."

"How long have you had it?" The boy's question was insistent and no longer deferential. Nicolás looked annoyed.

"Long enough!" he snapped. Tucking the cross back inside his shirt, he turned his back on the boy. "Come on, Sara, we've done our share. Let's get out of here!"

The boy made no attempt to detain them. Lifting another glass of beer from a passing tray, Nicolás stalked away. Sara followed, not because she particularly wanted to, but because she had nowhere else to go. But she glanced back as she went, then turned sharply to look again, caught by the expression on the teenager's face as he stared after them.

He was looking at Nicolás as though he'd seen a ghost.

Chapter Nineteen

"You know, if I had a wife, she'd never put up with this kind of hours." Kyle Martin belched, tossing aside the box his McDonald's Big Mac had come in. The Golden Arches had recently come to Santa Cruz, and while it wasn't exactly fine dining, it was one of the few places in the city you could get cooked food quickly and at any hour. Which happened to be almost midnight, at the moment.

Doug Bradford set his coffee cup down hard enough to splash its contents onto a pile of communication intercepts. "If I had a wife, I wouldn't be working this kind of hours."

Kyle winced, cursing himself for being such an insensitive fool. He knew Bradford's story as well as he knew the file on every man in this office.

But Doug's face showed nothing but mild interest in the readout he'd picked up to compare with the report in his other hand. He skimmed through the two recorded cell-phone conversations, then dropped both readouts onto the rest of the stack with a yawn. "Well, I don't see anything here that couldn't have waited until tomorrow. I'm heading out. And don't expect me any too early in the morning. I was up to all hours last night too."

Removing his feet from the top of Kyle's desk, he stood up and stretched. Kyle reached out a lanky arm to start gearing down his computers. "Yeah, I'm heading off too. Enough is enough. If I hadn't promised to check those Brazilian Interpol records for Ramon, I'd have been off hours ago. What we really need around here is another one of me!" But his complacent glance around the research office, spotlessly neat except for the disarray of reports that Doug had left on a chair, showed strong doubt that the U.S. government could come up with another of him. Besides, if anyone back in Washington thought he'd allow just any numskull who called himself an intelligence analyst into his territory . . .

Kyle suddenly slapped his forehead with the palm of his hand.

"Oh, great, I forgot all about that Vargas name you asked me to run through this morning!"

Doug yawned again, hugely. "Hey, don't worry about it. Tomorrow will be soon enough. It's probably nothing, anyway."

"No, that's what I forgot to tell you. I had that done before I started on Ramon's. You want it before you go?" His fingers were already dancing over the keyboard, calling a file onto the screen.

"Sure, why not." Grabbing a chair, Doug pulled it close to the computer. "Anything there?"

"I don't know. You tell me." A newspaper headline was coming onto the screen now with two neat columns of print underneath. Kyle swiveled his desk chair around to face Doug.

"There wasn't much to go on," he said apologetically. "The guy's file is squeaky clean—at least as far as drugs go. But I tracked down that informant who did the initial report two years ago. Just on the phone, but he remembered Vargas just fine, and he came up with some stuff that he'd left out of the file—because there was no drug connection, and it wasn't really anything you could prove either. But it was enough to make you start asking if this Vargas is such a solid citizen after all. For example, did you know he was in the military before he joined up with Luis Cortéz? Yeah, sure you did. That was in the file we had. *Policía Militar.* Only thing was, he was living a whole lot better than you could account for on what the military here pays their colonels. He was in charge of the recovery of stolen property, and I'd say a lot of it ended up in his pocket instead of back with its owners. I'm surprised your informant didn't jump on that when he was checking into Cortéz Industries."

Doug smothered another yawn. The thought of that king-size waterbed he'd brought with him from the States was becoming more irresistible with every minute, and he sure hoped this was going somewhere more exciting than what he was hearing so far. Kyle tended to get a little overenthusiastic at times.

"Simple," Doug informed the intelligence analyst. "If we took the time to investigate every official we turn up who used their position to line their own pockets, we'd never get around to doing what we came for. That's one of the perks of government service around here, remember? Besides, we were looking for someone with a known drug connection. Vargas didn't have one, and he was new over there at the time, anyway. He just didn't look too interesting."

"Yeah? Well, that's what I thought. Then I started digging a little further. This Vargas fellow was sitting pretty over there at the *Policía Militar*—big house, new car—until, all of a sudden, he got the boot.

Well, actually, he resigned, but it was that *or else.* According to our informant, scuttlebutt had it that he'd gotten greedy and was cutting into his boss's share, and that's why he got the chop. Then he gets slapped with a corruption charge—filed by that same boss. He buys his way out of that, but it leaves him broke and probably not too happy. A month or so later, said boss ends up dead with a knife in his throat. They put it down to a burglary, but it kind of makes you wonder, doesn't it? I went over that police report myself, and the only thing stolen was a bit of cash in the guy's wallet. Like I said, not much—not what you were looking for, anyway. There just wasn't any more info to grab. The guy's been working for Cortéz Industries ever since, but I didn't figure you'd want me calling out there for references. Still, I didn't want to just drop it, either. So I figured I'd run a name search—just check the newspapers and anything else we had on file to see if that name has popped up anywhere else in the last few years."

The casual note of triumph in his voice brought Doug out of his slouch. So there *was* a point to all this! "And you found something," Doug said flatly. It was a statement, not a question.

Kyle used a ballpoint pen to tap the computer screen. "*El Deber.* Almost three years ago. Just about the time Vargas left the military."

Doug leaned over to skim the newspaper article on the screen. Then he read it again more slowly, his right eyebrow arching high. "You're telling me this Julio Vargas crashed one of our Hueys on a training exercise?"

The helicopter in question was one of the many Vietnam leftovers donated to the Bolivian government for peacekeeping duties. The largest number were utilized by the anti-narcotics forces, but a few had ended up in the possession of other branches of the military. At the time of the crash, this particular helicopter was serving a turn at flight training. The newspaper clipping described the incident as an unfortunate accident—a combination of a sudden tropical storm and human error by an inexperienced young pilot. The name of the trainee responsible for the crash wasn't listed in the article. But the instructor was. *Coronel* Julio Vargas of the Military Police. Straightening up from the screen, Doug gave Kyle a sharp look. "I take it there's more."

"You're not kidding there's more! They had to investigate the crash, right? It was in the middle of the jungle, and the gas tank exploded, and the chopper was completely unsalvageable, okay? The only reason Vargas and the kid got out was some big heroics on Vargas's part—you saw that in the article. So I figure I'll talk to someone who saw all this. I called over to the *Policía Militar* to see what I could find out—there's a Colonel Sanchez over there who's helped me out on some other intel. Anyway, he did some checking around, and would you believe he couldn't find a single person who'd actually eyeballed the crash site? Not one! Like, where was the investigation team that checked this all out? I couldn't even get the name of this trainee who's supposed to have caused the accident. And no pictures—not in the papers or in the accident report Colonel Sanchez dug up. As for the *comandante* who signed the report—well, he isn't there anymore, either! He left the same time Vargas did."

Doug let a low whistle out between his teeth. "What are you saying? That maybe our Huey here wasn't so crashed after all?"

Kyle hunched his bony shoulders. "I don't know! But you've got a military helicopter that's been flying around out there, hijacking cocaine shipments. And now here's one whose final destination seems to be a little fuzzy. Besides, that's not all. I sort of wondered about this *comandante* who took off so conveniently right after he filed that report. So I ran his name through the computer search. And—you're not going to believe this! The guy transferred over to the FELCN. I found his name listed in a news report—from that raid you pulled on Cortéz Industries a couple years back. He was in charge of those FELCN troops that smashed up the warehouse and gave you all the bad PR. So then, I cross-referenced the rest of the files on that raid—just to see if maybe there was some other connection to Vargas there. And *voilà!* One of the informants—the one who disappeared on you—well, he just happened to have served in the same PM unit with this Julio Vargas."

Doug was sitting so still that Kyle paused to demand, "Hey, wake up, man! Isn't any of this ringing any bells?"

Doug came to himself, his gray eyes bright and hard. "Mean anything? It means I've been played for a sucker, big time! Why those little—!"

He got abruptly to his feet, pacing around the small space left by the computers and other equipment. "Vargas is dirty, all right. And so are the Cortezes. I knew it! That whole raid was a set-up."

The pieces were all coming together in his mind. "Ten to one Vargas planned the whole thing. And all this time, we've been sitting around with our hands tied while they—"

He slammed his fist down on Kyle's desk, then winced—not at the discomfort it had caused his hand but at the visible dent he'd left in the polished wood. "Sorry, Kyle. You've done a great job. Thanks." He controlled his anger long enough to clap the intelligence analyst on the shoulder. "Anyone ever tell you you're a genius?"

"Not often enough!" Kyle informed him smugly. "So what are you going to do about it?"

"I'll have to think. Tonight, nothing. But I'm going to push to get this case reopened, no matter what those people's connections are."

Doug's cell phone beeped, signaling an incoming call. He yanked the phone from his belt and placed it to his ear. *"Sí?"*

"Doug, is that you?" The voice was distant and broken by static but still recognizable.

"Ramon! Where are you? I thought you were on a stakeout."

"I was. I am." Ramon's voice kept fading in and out of the static. "Doug, I could use some backup, *pronto*. The bad guys we were watching loaded up maybe a hundred kilos. We've been following them—about fifteen kilometers, so far. It's a dirt road—nothing out here, no airstrip, nothing—so we were figuring a land meet or a safehouse. But it's a plane! A Cessna-206 with registration number PTX-TM, . . . you got that? Two-oh-six . . . PTX-TM."

"Yeah, I got it." Doug was scrabbling through a pile of printouts as he listened.

"They landed right on the road, okay?—using the headlights of the truck we were following. Only they misjudged things, and now they've got the plane run under some trees and stuck. We caught them trying to pull the plane out. Got the pickup and the dope and one driver. But the rest are holed up in the plane—five or six, I'd say—and they're armed. We can keep them buttoned down, but we don't have the firepower to smoke them out. So if you're not doing anything else this evening and wouldn't mind getting your butt down here and bailing us out . . ."

Doug had it now. A report forwarded from the Brazil DEA office. A Cessna-206 with registration number PTX-TM. Registered as hijacked in Brazil just two days before. "Okay, Ramon. We've got something on the plane. They're Brazilians, so watch your back. And calm down. We'll be there just as soon as you give me some directions I can follow."

So much for that waterbed.

✠

Ricardo Orejuela walked away, but not far. He was stunned, then thoughtful, then murderously angry. The *americanos* had been right! His father had been betrayed. They had all been betrayed. He'd seen the proof with his own eyes. And now what was he to do?

Honor demanded that he do something. But what? He had no weapon with him, and even if he had, he wasn't sure he had the strength of will to use it.

Should he go to the *americanos*? They had promised help—of course only because they wished to use him for their own schemes. But perhaps, in the same way, he could use them. It was maybe not the most satisfactory revenge, but in some ways it might prove even better. With any luck, the *americanos* would deal with Don Nicolás as harshly as he had once feared they had dealt with his father.

From the shadow of a *toborochi*, he watched his father's murderer with eyes narrowed with hate. He would go now. But he knew what he would do. And if that was not enough, then he would find something else. He might be young, but he would show these people that he knew how to avenge the honor of his father and his family. He would not rest until Don Nicolás and all of his family were humbled in the dust.

Don Luis Cortéz followed the direction of Ricardo's angry glare with thoughtful eyes. What had upset the boy so badly? Perhaps it was nothing, but on the other hand . . .

He waved away the people who were still pressing in around him—his time was no longer theirs—and walked over into the shadow of the tree. "Ricardo?"

The soft, autocratic tone whirled the boy around. It was his godfather. The man he'd respected and revered above all others. And now he too had betrayed him, lied to him! Despite the cloaking shadows, he felt his godfather's eyes on his face as though the man could read straight through to his mind to the burning hate that was there. "What is it, *hijo*?"

"What is it?" Ricardo spat out. "You lied to me! You told me the Brazilians killed my father!"

"Shh!" With satisfaction, Ricardo saw that he had actually startled his godfather. "Lower your voice, young man. What are you saying?"

"You lied to me! That's what I'm saying." Ricardo's voice rose even higher. Wisdom dictated that he turn and walk away right now. But that would be to show cowardice before this man. With a bravado born partly of genuine courage and burning rage and partly of the half-dozen beers he'd consumed that evening, he rounded on his godfather.

"I know who killed my father! And it wasn't the Brazilians!"

Nearby, heads began to turn. Don Luis shot out a hand and gripped Ricardo by the arm. "Enough! I have no idea what you are speaking of. But if we must discuss this again, we will do so in private where we will not make a circus for the whole world. Come!"

Ricardo shrugged to loosen his arm, and was shocked to find that he couldn't. A security guard approached. "Is there a problem, *patrón?*"

"No, the boy is just coming with me."

Ricardo went. What was there to worry about, after all? His godfather was taller and broader than he. But he was an old man, and Ricardo was a sturdy youth who prided himself on his athletic prowess. He was not afraid to be alone with him. Besides, there were questions he wanted to ask. He had never been inside this building before, nor, despite his own family's prosperity, had he ever been in such rooms as the office suite through which Don Luis now led him. But any awe he felt was banished as soon as he saw the lavish gilt-framed paintings on the walls around him.

Don Luis waved him to a seat before leaning back in his own custom-made chair. Taking no notice of Ricardo's murderous glare, he looked at him contemplatively, without expression. His voice was gentle when he spoke. "And now, *hijo,* what is your difficulty? Who is this that you imagine has killed your father?"

"Imagine?" Ricardo cried out in fury. "I don't imagine. I know! It was your son who killed my father. I've seen the proof myself."

"My son?" His godfather's eyebrows went up in mild surprise. "But my son wasn't even in the country when your father disappeared. What is this 'proof' that would make you think my son could be guilty of harming your father?"

"You can't fool me!" Ricardo spat. "The proof is right there on your own walls. See? In that painting. The cross of the Cortéz. My grandfather received it from yours, the only inheritance his father ever gave him. My father told me about it. It was such a small thing to your grandfather—he had finer and more costly jewels!" Ricardo said with bitterness. "He didn't need the Saint anymore. He had enough protection, enough good luck. Let San Jorge protect instead this son who was too low-born to be acknowledged. Then his conscience would be free. A bone thrown to a dog! But to my grandfather and my father, it was priceless. The proof that they too were Cortezes, even if they would never bear the name."

His godfather was now looking bored. "Your great-grandmother was a maid in my grandfather's house. Your grandfather was born. You and your family have reaped generously the rewards of our distant relationship. And what does this have to do with my son?"

"My father was wearing the cross the day he was taken by the *anti-narcóticos,* as he had worn it every day since his own father passed away," Ricardo said furiously, losing any control he had left. "And now your son has the cross of my father hanging around his neck!

So do not think I will believe anymore your stories about the Brazilians. If your son has the Cortéz cross, then he took it from my father's neck. And that can mean only one thing: that my father is dead and your son is his murderer."

For the first time, Ricardo saw a crack in his godfather's composure. Reaching across the desk, Don Luis snatched up a pen holder. It was a fat-bellied thing, like a silver beer stein, but without the lid. Ricardo watched with mystified annoyance as his godfather dumped out the contents, then did something to the ornate scrolling on one side. There was a soft *click,* and the bottom of the container popped open. Ricardo stared at the empty cavity, uncomprehending. Then it registered.

"You had it in there! You didn't know it was gone! But that means . . ." Ricardo shivered from a sudden chill. It felt as though the temperature had dropped ten degrees in the room. Still he wasn't afraid. He was stronger and fitter than the man across the desk, and he could be out the door before the older man could come anywhere near him. But he still had to swallow to finish his sentence through dry lips. "It was *you* who killed my father!"

Don Luis's hand shot under the desk. Ricardo spun around at the sudden soft grating sound behind him, just in time to see the heavy mahogany door that divided the office suite from the rest of the building shut firmly. He was locked in. He whirled back around when he heard the sound of a drawer sliding open, and blinked at the weapon that suddenly appeared across the desk from him.

Don Luis's face was implacable. With his free hand, he reached for the phone. "I really am sorry," he told his godson gently. "But you must understand that it was necessary."

The jangle of a ringing phone was barely distinguishable above the music blasting from a loudspeaker mounted in the crook of a tree a few meters away. But it said something about the social station of this particular group in this Third World country that everyone instantly looked to their belts. Except Sara, of course, and Reina, who dug into her purse instead. The two young women were the only females among the knot of acquaintances that Nicolás had chosen to escape his duties as host. Reina had regained all her usual complacency at the completion of the evening's ceremonies, and when Nicolás and Sara had joined her, she was patently enjoying herself as the lone woman in a circle of admiring men. But as soon as she'd seen Nicolás, she'd abandoned her admirers and thrown her arms around his neck as though she hadn't seen him in days, rather than an hour or so, kissing him in a most uncousinly way. Since then, to the open annoyance of her other male companions, she hadn't detached herself from his side.

The jangling cell phone sounded again.

"It's yours, Nico," Reina informed her cousin, sliding a bare arm around his waist to lift the instrument from his belt.

Nicolás let out an oath as he grabbed the phone from Reina's hand. Sara, eyeing his flushed face, hoped the call was something that would take them away from here soon. In the past twenty-four hours, she had gone from terror to anger to apathy as she realized how little she could do about her situation. Now a new surge of rebellion was raising its head. It was bad enough that she'd had to spend the evening pretending everything was roses and cream in the Cortéz clan. But having to make lighthearted conversation while putting up with Reina's hostile glances and blatant flirting was too much! Wasn't Nicolás at all worried that she might blurt out something to one of these other people?

But no! He was so confident that she'd play the role of dewy-eyed Cortéz bride, that he'd hardly spared her a glance. In fact, he was enjoying himself so much that Sara suspected he was no longer completely sober. His friends definitely weren't. All but Sara had a glass or a beer can in their hands, and their hilarity was progressively more uncontrolled, the jokes more ribald. As for Reina, she was now openly hanging on to Nicolás's other arm.

"*Sí?*" Nicolás drawled, waving impatiently with his beer can for his friends to quiet down. But as he listened intently to the phone pressed against his ear, Sara saw the impatience and remaining mirth drain from his face. Shaking Reina free, he put a hand over his other ear to block out the noise. "Sí, Papá. Yes, I—no, I didn't know. . . . How was I to know? . . . Yes, I'll be right there. . . . Yes, of course Sara is with me. . . . No, I won't leave her alone."

Putting his hand over the receiver, Nicolás glanced down at Sara, his handsome face flushed and angry. "I've got to go. Papá's all shook up about something. He is sending the limousine home with Mamá and the girls. You're to go with them. If I can find them!"

He swung around to scan the crowd, swearing under his breath. Sara could see why. The celebration was in full swing, and there were people everywhere. The receiving line was scattered now, the dais empty, and the lighting so intermittent that it was impossible to pick out individual faces more than a few meters away. None of the Cortéz family members was anywhere in sight.

The cell phone crackled again with an urgency that even Sara could hear. "Yes, I'm coming now, Papá!" Nicolás slammed the phone shut. Catching the curious glances from his circle of friends, he explained with a shrug, "Papá is worse than the *gringos*. Everything is now! He needs me for some piece of business that cannot wait for morning. But he's concerned that I don't leave my wife alone in all this crowd."

"Hey, don't worry, Nico, *amigo*." It was Gustavo, one of Nicolás's friends, whom Sara already had ample reason to dislike. He was even more unsteady than the rest, and he leered unpleasantly at Sara as he offered, "I'll be happy to keep an eye on your lovely wife. Just tell her to warm up a little."

Nicolás ignored the comment, looking annoyed as he scanned the jostling mob of people around them. He swore again. "How am I supposed to do this?" he complained to Sara in English. "Papá doesn't want me to leave you until I've made sure someone's got an eye on you. But I'm supposed to be upstairs yesterday! And for what? This is supposed to be a party! I don't know why he's got to get into such a stew tonight! Reina?"

Swinging around to his cousin, he switched back into Spanish. "I don't have time for this! You take Sara and find Mamá or the girls. And don't leave her alone until you do. And don't let her stop to talk to anyone, understand? You have your phone? Fine! Then I will give you a call from Papá's office, to make sure she got there. *Comprende?*"

Reina looked far from pleased at his curt orders, but she nodded grudgingly and shot a malicious glance at Sara. Draining his beer can, Nicolás shoved it at Sara, then spun around on his heel and stalked away toward the administration building, followed by some openly curious looks from his friends. "Your husband is overprotective of you, *Sarita*," Gustavo smirked. "Does he fear that we will run away with you?" He glanced slyly at Reina. "Who would have believed our Nico would settle down to be such a family man, eh, Reina?"

Reina turned her back on him. "You're a drunken fool, Gustavo!" she told him over her shoulder, then snapped at Sara, "*Vamos!* Let us leave this *idiota* to find a woman who will appreciate his wit!"

Sara went with her, if only because the alternative was to stay with Gustavo and her husband's other half-sloshed friends. Besides, going home with Mimi and her sisters-in-law, hostile though they might be right now, was vastly preferable to staying here.

As the two women worked their way through the crowd, Reina suddenly stopped, her exquisite features openly gloating as she turned on Sara. "I don't know what this is all about," she told Sara with a sneer. "But Nico has told me how foolish you have been. To be caught so soon—how indiscreet! Now I have some advice for you, *gringa*. Go back to your own country. You don't belong here. And you're not wanted any longer. Not by Nico. Not by his family. Don't think that you can make things right and remain here. Nico was mine before you came, and he will be mine after you are gone!"

So, war was being declared! Sara met Reina's triumphant smirk coolly. "Going back to my own country is precisely what I have in mind. Just as fast as I can get away from here!"

"Good!" Reina inclined her head regally. "We understand each other. Then let's go."

But finding her female in-laws didn't prove so easy. They just weren't there, though Sara and Reina threaded through the crowd from one end to the other. Depositing Nicolás's beer can in a garbage receptacle as they hurried by, Sara toyed again with the idea of making a run for it. But the thought was brief. Grudging or not, Reina was sticking to her side like a leech.

Her next thought was even briefer. What if she told Reina the truth? That there was no "lover," and that her cousin and the head of her family clan were dealing in drugs? That Sara was being held against her will?

No, even if Reina believed her, she wouldn't listen to a plea for help. She hated Sara—and more than likely shared the Cortezes' attitude toward drug dealing. Besides, even if she did get away from Reina, what was she to do then? She was more than twenty kilometers out in the country here with no purse, no money, and no transportation. And if she could get back to the city, then what? She couldn't get out of the country without her passport. And that was locked up for safekeeping in Don Luis's office safe. Nor did she have enough cash to buy a plane ticket, even assuming the Cortezes would allow her on a flight to Miami without trying to stop her.

And if she did make a run for it now and was stopped—she wasn't forgetting what Nicolás had said about other eyes watching her—she could be sure that controls would be tightened to where it might be impossible to try again. Sara wasn't as intimidated as the Cortezes seemed to think. But if she did try something, it would have to be with a plan and a better chance of success. In the meantime, she'd act just as docile and cooperative as they evidently thought she was! It was her meek suggestion that finally took the two girls back through the crowd to the parking lot. The limousine was there and so was its chauffeur, but there was no sign of Mimi, Delores, or Janéth.

Great! Sara told herself with a small resurgence of humor. *Here's the prisoner trying to give herself up, and I can't even find my jailers!*

"I saw the car of *la señora* Delores leave a short time ago," the chauffeur explained obligingly. "But I do not know if the other two *señoras* went with her." Nor had he received any instructions from Don Luis. "But if you and the *señorita* Reina would like for me to take you home, I will, of course, be pleased to do so."

"That won't be necessary!" Reina told him sharply. She was showing the effects of their fast-paced search. Her tight mini-dress and her spiked heels were not particularly suited for walking. Reina was limping badly, there was a sheen of perspiration on her powdered cheeks, and her pulled-up hairdo was beginning to come down. She was also livid with anger. Her long fingernails dug into Sara's arm as she pulled her a short distance from the limousine.

"This is *ridículo!*" she spat out. "I have better things to do than lead you around as though I were your jailer! Why should I care where you go, or who you speak to? If you wish to run away to see this lover of yours, does Nico really think I would wish to stop you? No, I would be glad to have you gone!"

She was digging furiously through her purse as she spoke. Pulling out her cell phone, she thrust it into Sara's hands. "Here, I am finished with you. If Nico wishes to call to see where you have gone, then let him speak to you. Or you may call your lover and leave this place. I do not care! I only wish for you to be gone from my life and Nico's."

With that she stormed away, her high heels teetering as she went. Sara watched her go with mixed incredulity and a sudden desire to laugh. This was unbelievable! She was supposed to be a prisoner, wasn't she? At least that's how she'd been thinking of herself all day and half the night! A prisoner of an international drug trafficker and his powerful and ruthless organization. Despite the defiance she'd tried to muster up, she'd pretty much resigned herself to waiting out the weeks of confinement until this was all over, then meekly departing the country, leaving the Cortezes and Julio Vargas as winners all around.

Only now, the lie that Don Luis had concocted had backfired in a way that her husband, at least, should have foreseen. And because of that, and because Nicolás had been in a hurry, and because the women in the family had gotten tired of mingling in such low company— and who knew what other compounding errors—Sara was now standing here in the middle of this dark parking lot, not only free, but with the cell phone they'd been so anxious to deny her. It just seemed so—so *amateur!* Like a scene from a B-grade movie, complete with the "other woman" throwing a scene and storming off.

With that thought, much of the strain Sara that had been under lifted. These people weren't so all-powerful! She'd been dramatizing, making more of them than they really were. After all, this wasn't Colombia or Peru—or even Miami, with killings and cartels. What had Nicolás said? Here in Bolivia, drug-dealing was just business. A business that "everyone" did and got away with. And perhaps because it was just business, they weren't used to violence. Don Luis hadn't tried to hurt her, had he? They didn't even seem to know how to hold someone prisoner. And so, like amateurs do, they'd made mistakes.

The chauffeur was still watching her, perhaps wondering why Reina had left her behind. Had he too been informed of her "disgrace"? If so, he didn't seem inclined to act on it. Still, it would be best if she at least appeared to be following at Reina's heels. Sara closed her hand on the cell phone. It was the latest model, a downsized, flip-out affair, remarkably similar to the space-age communicators on the original *Star Trek* shows, and small enough to fit into the palm of her hand. Reina had stormed back toward the main administration building, so Sara headed in the same direction. Once she was out of sight of the chauffeur, she could lose herself in the noisy, surging multitude and go any direction she wanted.

And then what?

What do I do now? The question was no longer a hopeless refrain. As Sara reached the edge of the crowd, she looked around in the dim lighting. There were no faces she recognized. In fact, all she could see were the darker features of Quechua and other lowland natives. It appeared that the Cortezes' peer group had drifted off as the evening wore on, leaving the celebration to the lower echelons of *Industrias Cortéz* employees. So she was free—at least until the phone in her hand rang, and Nicolás realized that Reina hadn't carried out his orders. That thought made her flip open the phone and push the power button. She didn't need this thing going off to attract anyone's attention.

On second thought, the ring of the phone would let her know if someone was starting to think about her. And it wasn't as though she had to answer it. She changed her mind and turned the power back on. She was no longer taking seriously her husband's hints about "other eyes." If she could just make it to the gate—Nicolás had said the guards had no orders to stop her. That would be her first goal. What to do once she got outside on the highway, she wouldn't even think about now. Maybe hitchhike?

And if she did make it back to the city? She had a phone now, and though she didn't have Laura Histed's phone number, she could get it by calling Doña Inez at the children's home. She had no doubt that her kindly British friend would be willing to give her shelter. Of course, that still left her facing the same dilemma: No passport, no money. And the first place Don Luis would look for her would be the friends she'd made during her few months here. Especially the foreigners.

But, wait! She did have one asset! Information. The existence of eight tons of cocaine, for instance. The worldwide shipping system Don Luis was using to move his drug shipments overseas. The processing lab at the hacienda. She knew it all. Laura would know how to contact someone from the DEA. And if she gave them that information, surely they would be willing to help her in return. They were representatives of the American government and, by all accounts, could do just about anything they wanted. They could get her new documents and fly her out of this terrible country back to her own home soil. As for the Cortezes . . .

Sara stopped in her tracks, her fingers tightening on the cell phone, frozen in a sudden agony of indecision as the enormity of what she possessed hit her. In her mind and this small instrument in her hand, she now held the potential to bring down the entire Cortéz operation and the family itself. And they certainly deserved it! Don Luis was a criminal who had made countless millions on drug trafficking. Nicolás and Delores's and Janéth's husbands, and who knew how many others in the family, were willing accomplices, uncaring and without conscience.

But they were also people she'd lived with, counted as family and friends. Could she really help to put them under arrest? Her own husband? Every principle she'd ever held true screamed that this was the right thing to do. But how could she? A vision rose before her eyes against the dark shapes of the *toborochis* that lined the driveway. A handsome face she'd once desperately loved, no longer laughing but old and gaunt and seen through steel bars. No matter how much he'd hurt her or how bitterly angry she was with him, she couldn't help put Nicolás in jail! She just *couldn't!*

Sara started walking again, quickly, drawing in deep breaths to calm herself down. Think now! Did she really have enough to put Nicolás—or Don Luis—behind bars? Oh, sure, she could tell the DEA about the off-center seal and the way contaminated goods came in and out of the warehouse. But Nicolás had said the warehouse was clean right now. A DEA raid on *Industrias Cortéz* would end up being as much of an embarrassment as the last one, with nothing to show for it. As for the hacienda and the eight tons of cocaine—she could tell them about it, but she had no idea where they were. An hour or two of flight time covered a lot of territory. And Nicolás had said that the property hadn't even been purchased under the Cortéz name.

So what would be the result if she got out of here tonight and went to the DEA and told them everything she knew?

A surge of excitement rose in Sara as she took one thought and added another and then another. Of course! Even if her information wasn't enough to get the Cortezes arrested, it was certainly enough to stop what they were doing. After all, wasn't that why Don Luis was hesitating right now? Why he'd sent Julio Vargas down to put their whole operation on hold? Don Luis was a cautious man who took no chances; that was what Nicolás had said. Why, he'd told her last night that his father had been on the verge of destroying the whole eight tons for fear of what she might have told the DEA. Not that she'd known much, but her spilling of that offset stamp alone would have been enough to force him to scrap his whole system of delivery. How much more so with what she knew now?

And Don Luis had already made his decision to get out. Nicolás had said this was to be their last shipment, that the drug trafficking was getting too dangerous. Once they knew that Sara had gone to the DEA, they would never dare to start up again. Not with the DEA breathing down their necks in the future and customs officials scrutinizing their shipments in every port where their goods arrived. And unlike Julio Vargas, the Cortezes couldn't just pick up and move somewhere else to start over again. Their very position and prominence worked against them.

Sara quickened her pace with the first real lightening of her spirits since Nicolás had awakened her from that nightmare almost twenty-four hours before. She had made such a mess of things, and happiness now seemed something so distant that she would never find her way to it again. But here at least was something she could do that counted before she slunk back to the United States and tried to pick up the broken pieces of her life and her dreams. Maybe it wasn't much, but eight tons of cocaine erased from the back alleys and schoolyards of her country—not to mention permanently closing down that pipeline of poison—was at least something to balance the mistakes she'd made and the fool she'd been. All she had to do was make her way through the dark shadows of the trees that lined the drive to the front gate. Once she was safely on the outside, she would call Doña Inez. That was one number she had memorized. And from there—

"*Señora Sara!*"

Sara whirled around, her throat catching in shock and dismay. It didn't help when she saw who it was moving out from the overhanging branches of the *toborochis*. The short, thick figure and flat features were those of Jorge, the guard who had closed the gate to the Cortéz mansion behind her and Nicolás not so many hours earlier. Sara gaped at him, knowing that she was gaping yet not able to stop herself, as she frantically wracked her brain for some excuse, some plausible explanation.

"What . . . what are you doing here, Jorge?" was all she could manage. "Who's watching the gate?"

"I have a replacement. Don Luis requested that I help here tonight."

Nicky's "eyes," Sara thought hollowly. They really had been there! The guard peered around suspiciously. He wasn't in his usual khaki uniform, which might explain why she hadn't noticed him until now. "You are alone. Why did the *señorita* Reina leave you? And where is Don Nicolás?"

Sara didn't know what to say. Her prospects of escape had been dashed so suddenly that her mind was left blank. So she told the truth—or part of it. "Reina went off to find some friends. She was bored with my company. Nicolás had some business with Don Luis. I think they're in his office."

She glanced up at the top floor of the administration building. The heavy curtains were drawn, but a gleam of light at the edges showed that the office was being used. Jorge grunted, his suspicions somewhat mollified. "Then I will take you there. You cannot stay here alone."

He motioned for Sara to precede him, but she didn't move immediately. Instead, she studied Jorge consideringly. Don Luis had miscalculated once tonight. Was there a chance she could use that same mistake again? Taking a step toward the guard and putting all the sincerity she could into her voice, she pleaded, "Look, Jorge, you must know that what they're saying about me isn't true. You've been there when I get home every day. You know how often I've been out at night, and except for last night when I came home with the Histeds, it's always been with Nicolás. Please, you've got to believe me! This is all a big mistake. If you could just—"

Sara broke off as a sound came from the guard's throat. It was like nothing she had ever heard from a human, and it made every hair on her arms stand up. He sounded like one of his Dobermans growling at her—low, menacing, deadly! Sara took a hasty step backward. "Okay, so you don't believe me! Fine! No problem!"

Spinning around, she started hastily toward the administration building. Jorge was instantly on her heels, so close that she could feel the dank heat of his breath on the back of her head. She didn't try to stall anymore, but walked quickly, anxious to get the guard off her case. She kept her right hand down at her side, concealed in the folds of her dress. How long had Jorge been watching her? Had he seen Reina thrust the phone on her, or had the lack of lighting in the parking area been her ally? No, he couldn't have seen the exchange or he would have said something, and she had no doubt that he would confiscate the instrument if he knew she had it. If she could keep him from noticing . . .

The front reception area of the administration building was lit up and still full of activity. This had been the staging area for the waiters serving refreshments to the dignitaries involved in the celebration and other special guests, and though the partygoers were mostly gone, the caterers were still packing up the leftovers. The two security guards at the big glass entrance had orders to keep the general public out, but they recognized the flaxen-haired *señora* of their *patrón's* son, and one of them jumped forward to open the door. Sara had hoped that Jorge would leave her once she went inside, but he trailed hard on her heels through the reception area and down the hall. At the elevator, he punched in the buttons for the third floor, demonstrating that this wasn't the first time he'd been there. The most Sara could do was maneuver his position away from the side where she was hiding the cell phone in her skirt.

When the elevator doors slid open onto the third-floor hall, Jorge stayed close on Sara's heels all the way to the heavy door that led into Don Luis's office suite. The door was shut and locked, the only light coming from the glow of the control panel on the wall and the red dot near the ceiling that showed that the surveillance camera was in operation. Sara could hear voices on the other side, faintly because the suite was well sound-proofed, but enough to know that there was more than one person inside. Before Jorge could reach for the intercom, Sara reasserted herself, quickly keying in the combination that would unlock the door. Three sets of six numbers. The date of Don Luis's wedding. Then Nicolás's birth date. And finally, the date when the first shovel of dirt had been lifted for the foundations of *Industrias Cortéz*.

The information readout at the top of the control panel blinked *INCORRECTO*. With a disgusted sigh, Sara remembered that, in Spanish, dates are typed day/month/year rather than month/day/year as they are in America. Her fingers flew as she typed them in again.

The door unlocked with an audible click and swung a few inches outward. The voices inside the office increased in volume. Slipping through the narrow opening, Sara pushed the red button on the inside control panel. "*Gracias,* Jorge," she whispered sweetly as the door swung shut on his scowling face.

Well, so much for that! With resignation, Sara turned from the door. She was standing in the big square reception area where Dolores worked. The room was unlit, but not so dark that she couldn't see as her eyes adjusted to the gloom, because the door at the far end leading into Don Luis's brightly lit office was standing open.

From her position by the door, Sara could see clearly everything that was happening in the other room, and it puzzled her that no one there had reacted to her entrance until she realized that anyone looking out would see only a rectangle of black. As for any sound her entrance had made, the voices of the men in the other room—in rapid and angry Spanish—had more than covered it.

There were five of them. Don Luis was sitting at his desk, facing Sara. Behind him stood Nicolás. Or rather, Nicolás was pacing back and forth from one side of the desk to the other, his steps angry and impatient. Don Luis snapped a quick order and he stopped pacing, coming to a halt at his father's right hand. Facing father and son, their backs to Sara, stood her two brothers-in-law. *So that's where they went!*

There was someone else there, too, sitting in a chair that had been pulled away from the wall into the center of the carpet. The chair was slanted at an angle so that it was almost sideways to Sara, but she couldn't see who was seated there, because her two brothers-in-law were standing on either side of it. Delores's husband, Diego, had what looked to be a friendly hand resting on the shoulder of the person in the chair.

Don Luis was speaking now, his cold, even tones too low for Sara to make out. It looked like they were having a business meeting, and her mind was already considering how she could turn this to her advantage. If the men hadn't noticed her entry, maybe there was still some way she could get away. Maybe slip into some quiet corner and wait for the others to leave? Or at least use the time to make a phone call.

Moving as quietly as possible out of the line of sight of the open office door, Sara silently turned the knob on the door that led to the conference room. To her dismay, it was locked. So was her husband's office door on the other side of the reception area. She glanced around the dim room. The desk? A table? Where could she hide?

This was getting ridiculous! She could just see those men coming out of their meeting to find her huddled under Dolores's desk, talking on a phone she wasn't supposed to have. Besides, there was still Jorge. Assuming he was still on guard outside that door—and knowing him, he would be!—he would sound the alarm in an instant if they came out without her. No, she was back where she'd started.

Sara was discouraged, but her spirits couldn't quite sink to their earlier levels. After all, she'd already seen that these men weren't as careful or invincible as they thought. There'd be other chances! And she still had the cell phone. If she couldn't use it now, there was always later, when she could find some opportunity to be alone. That is, if Reina didn't come looking for it too soon. Her next move had better be to get that precious communication device out of sight.

Sara wasn't carrying a handbag, but the pastel chiffon she was wearing was cut generously in the front, with wide strips of soft material crisscrossing her bodice and blousing loosely from a tight elastic waistband. Tucking the phone down the front of her dress, she checked to make sure it couldn't be seen. The rectangular outline against the fabric just below her ribs seemed terribly obvious, but it was the best she could do for now.

Okay, what next? Was she better off making her presence known? Or should she wait unnoticed as long as she could? *That's a no brainer,* Sara decided. Don Luis was still talking, and neither he nor Nicolás would appreciate an interruption. Besides, there was always the chance that their meeting might go on long enough for her to risk slipping back out into the hall again, and it wasn't as though she had any interest in their sleazy business affairs anyway!

She was groping in the dark for a chair when all that changed.

"Was it not enough to take him from the *americanos*?" she heard from within the office. "Did you have to kill him as well?"

The fury and the high pitch in the angry voice startled Sara. *What in the world?* She moved back across Dolores's work area until she could see once again through the open door. The occupant of the chair in the middle of the floor was leaning forward now, and for the first time Sara could see his face. He was young, like his voice had suggested. And though she didn't immediately recognize him, as she caught the anger, his face became familiar. This was the boy who had come through the receiving line. The boy who had looked at Nicolás as though he had seen a ghost.

"The police are not entirely incompetent," Don Luis said coldly and evenly. "Neither are the *gringos*. Sooner or later, they would have found him. Was I to allow one man's stupidity to bring down my own family? Your family? Even you must see there was no choice, *hijo*."

There was no answer from the youth. Don Luis sighed. "What is it that you want from us, Ricardo? Money? A cut in the business?"

The boy spat furiously, but he was well out of range of the man behind the desk. "I want nothing! Nothing you can give me! Only to see you pay for what you have done! And you will pay! Do you think that others have not seen what your son has been wearing? What is on these very walls for all to see? Do you think they will not ask how the cross that was around my father's neck when he disappeared is now around the neck of your son?"

There was another murmur from Don Luis, and then Nicolás erupted with a loud, defensive, and petulant outburst. "How was I supposed to know? If you'd told me what was going on instead of hiding the thing!"

He was not looking his best, his hair in disarray and his face reddened with anger and alcohol. His silk shirt was still wide open at the neck, but the gold chain was no longer in evidence.

Don Luis turned his head and said something sharp to his son. Sara was drawn closer to the open door as she strained to translate the rapid flow of Spanish words. *The cross!* That's what this meeting was about! The Cortéz heirloom that was painted into so many portraits around this room and that Nicolás had taken from the pewter container on his father's desk. She glanced quickly at the huge mahogany desktop and saw the pen holder lying on its side in front of Don Luis with its false bottom slid open.

But what–? Sara took another step closer.

"Could they find Orejuela?" Diego asked tersely. He took a step away from the armchair where the boy was sitting, and now Sara could see that her other brother-in-law also had his hand on the boy's shoulder and that it was not a friendly grip. They were holding the boy down!

"No, they will not find him," Don Luis assured him coolly. "And if they did, there would be nothing to say how he died. The beasts of the jungle have made sure of that."

There was a scream of rage from Ricardo. "I will kill you for this! You killed my father, and I will kill you! I swear it!"

He lunged forward so that the two men beside him had to yank him back hard. Though short and stocky and with the beginning of paunches from too much beer and good living, her brothers-in-law were still strong men, and they easily pinned the boy back against the leather chair. Twisting fruitlessly against the strength of their grip, the boy raged on.

"Worse, I will destroy you! I will humble your house to the ground!

I will see you in prison, as was the fate of my father and his men. You will not like that, you proud Cortéz! To lie and rot in the stone cells of Chonchocorro with the air freezing every night, a bucket for a toilet, and food fit not even for the pigs that clean the streets! And don't think I cannot do so! You think you have hidden yourselves so cleverly. Well, I know what others do not! I know where to find your *hacienda*. The *hacienda* where you always took the goods my father delivered to you. And if the *americanos* drop with their helicopters into this place of yours, what will they find there?"

The silence as he finished was so complete that Sara could hear the sound of her own heart, which was pounding far louder and faster than it should have been. She had no idea what they were talking about, but the inference was clear. These men, whom she'd begun to dismiss so lightly and even with some contempt, had been involved in . . . in *murder*? She'd discounted so thoroughly the possibility of violence that her mind didn't want to process what she was hearing. But they weren't even trying to deny it! And with that realization, the cold terror that she had been fighting to keep under control all day squeezed again at her stomach. What more were these men capable of? And what would they do if they found her here, listening?

I've got to get out of here! she thought frantically.

But even discounting Jorge, who would still be waiting outside, something held Sara where she was. Not just the need to know what was going on, but the boy. Whatever his father had been involved in with the Cortezes, this Ricardo, as Don Luis had called him, was only a kid, not more than sixteen or seventeen years old. What she could do to help, Sara couldn't begin to imagine. But she couldn't just walk away and leave him.

Inside the office, the boy laughed as he caught the glances the four men were exchanging. The sound was triumphant and hysterical. "I knew it! Even without my father, you have still been dealing in the white gold. And tonight when the *americanos* come on you, where will you be then?"

"Why, you little—!" Nicolás took a long step toward the boy.

"No, wait!" Don Luis raised his hand.

"But, Papá, he's right!" Nicolás protested. "If he's really sicced the DEA on us, we're finished!"

"Wait," Don Luis repeated calmly. As Nicolás backed off, his father addressed himself to the boy. "You have been talking to the *americanos* again? Since last we spoke?" His hooded eyes studied the boy, then he nodded with satisfaction. "No, you have not spoken to the *americanos*. Not yet! But what is this about the *hacienda*? Your father did not know where it lies. So how could it be that you should know? You are lying!"

"I am not lying!"

The boy should have shut up, but his rage and that peculiarly adolescent sense that mortality is something that only strikes others—which makes teenage soldiers the easiest to send into harm's way—were carrying him far beyond the bounds of discretion.

"My father knew where your *hacienda* lay. He did not tell you, but he knew! It was a challenge to him to find out. He told me how you would make him land his plane, and then you would transfer the deliveries he had for you into your own plane. He did not tell me then what these deliveries were. 'Sugar,' he would say. 'Sugar for our noble relations, the Cortéz.' And he would laugh. But I know now what these goods were. The *americanos* told me. And my father did not laugh when he would say, 'These Cortéz think that we are only good enough to wash their feet. They make us land in the jungle because they are too proud to welcome their lowbred cousins onto their land.'

"But the blood of the Cortéz runs in the veins of the Orejuela as it does in yours, and if my father was not an educated man, as you are and I am, he wasn't stupid! He set himself to find this hacienda of yours—to amuse himself, no more. All the places that you made him land, he placed on a map. And he drew a circle in the center. 'It is in here that their hacienda lies,' he told me. And then he took the plane your own pilot taught him to fly. And he found it. Just before the *americanos* came and took him captive, he found it. He didn't tell anyone but me. Nor did he ever do more than fly overhead. It was enough to have done what you told him he could not do. It was a joke to him, you understand, and he did not wish you to be angry, because he respected you above all other men.

"And when he was gone, I did not tell you either, because I too respected you and counted you a friend to my family! And perhaps, too, because I thought my father was foolish to care so much about the name he bore. To be an Orejuela is enough for me, and if I did not know what my father was doing, I knew that it was you who made possible the life my father gave us. And so, when I guessed what it was that my father was delivering in his little plane, I did not say anything to the *americanos* because I was grateful. And because I knew that if my father had gone to you, he would have received your aid."

The boy's voice rose with an anger that held both pain and

betrayal. Sara, listening without even breathing, understood completely.

"But now I see that I have been as foolish as my father to have ever trusted you. I spit on the name Cortéz!" He spat again, this time twisting his head so that the spittle landed somewhere on the shirt of Raymundo, Janéth's husband. "And I swear that anything I can do to hurt you, this I will do! On the honor of my family, I swear!"

There was a sharp *smack!* as Nicolás stepped forward and slapped Ricardo across the face. "You show respect when you talk to your betters!" he said viciously. "As for hurting us, you'll never get the chance!"

The boy touched the back of one hand to his mouth. It came away red. Sara saw the hate in the glare he directed at her husband. Diego, tightening his grip on the boy's shoulder, interrupted the silence that had fallen over the room.

"Do you hear what the boy is saying? Orejuela had the coordinates of the *hacienda!*" Sara's brother-in-law sounded appalled. "And that was right while we were processing that last shipment of his. If Orejuela had talked to the *americanos* before Julio picked him up—!" He shook his head. "Nico is right. This is getting too dangerous. We must finish this and be out before anything else happens."

"But what are we going to do now?" Raymundo interjected. "We cannot keep this boy quiet and hidden as the girl. Not for so much time. His family is now wealthy and known. There will be questions. And if he talks—that is a great loss if we must destroy all that we have been doing. And it won't be so easy to do this a second time."

"What are you talking about?" Nicolás demanded, his handsome face still twisted with fury. "Who's speaking of destroying anything? You heard my father! The boy hasn't talked to the *americanos* yet."

He spun around to face Don Luis. "Papá, this is three hundred *million* American dollars we're talking about here! You're not thinking of letting this . . . this *campesino* spawn of your grandfather get away with making threats against our family! And when we're so close to putting an end to all of this! Do you realize what it would take to start over now? The DEA would be all over us!"

Don Luis looked consideringly at his son. "And what do you propose?"

They were talking, as they had with Sara, as though Ricardo Orejuela wasn't in the room. The boy had fallen silent, perhaps because of the pain of his mouth, perhaps because he too wanted to hear Nicolás's reply. He was sitting straighter now, his head turning from one to the other, his hands gripping the arms of the chair in a way that made it evident that he would be on his feet were it not for the two pairs of hands holding him down.

"You didn't have any problem taking care of his father!"

Nicolás's words hung in the air as though they were tangible. The boy gave a strangled sound that was cut off as Raymundo clapped a hand over his mouth. The two Cortéz sons-in-law looked at each other quickly, but Don Luis said mildly, "Come, son, do you really think I would sully my own hands with such things? Vargas took care of his father. And he is not here anymore."

"Vargas!" Nicolás exploded. "Always Vargas! Why do we need him? Do you think your own son is not man enough to do anything that Vargas can do?"

There was no expression on Don Luis's face as he looked at his son. Sara took a step toward the light and then another as she waited for her father-in-law's answer.

"And you think that you are?" Don Luis inquired softly.

Father and son stared at each other for an endless instant. Then . . .

"Yes, I am!" Nicolás snarled.

If he hadn't been in such a rage, fueled as much by his resentment of Julio Vargas as the number of beers he'd consumed that evening, he might have hesitated. As it was, Nicolás reached over to the desk and snatched up a pistol without a blink of his eyes.

Sara caught her breath as she saw the gun—black and shiny and deadly looking, with a round cylinder around the front of the barrel that made the whole thing look unwieldy and overbalanced, more like a child's toy than anything real.

But this wasn't a toy. Sara was in the doorway now, and her mouth opened, but no sound came out, and it wouldn't have mattered if it had. Nicolás was already firing, point-blank, into the chest of the boy in front of him. Once, twice, three times, rapid-fire, he pulled the trigger. For an instant, Ricardo jerked up straight. Then he sagged.

Sara had to cling to the doorjamb to keep from falling. It had all been so fast! And so quiet. The boy was slumped back in the chair, his head resting against the leather upholstery, his left hand hanging loosely through the space between the padded arm of the chair and the seat. His face was untouched, and his eyes were open; Sara, who knew nothing about the workings of a silencer, thought for one hopeful moment that the gun hadn't gone off.

But there was something about that limp figure that was different from a human being sitting at ease. Then she saw something dark trickle down the boy's slack hand and drip in soft, soundless splotches on the carpet. Bile rose in her throat. She didn't know that she'd made a sound until her husband's head shot up. For a long instant, their eyes met—the slim, white-faced girl in the doorway and the handsome young man with a gun in his hand and a killing rage on his face. The fury slowly drained from his face as they stared at each other, and Sara saw shock and shame and some of the horror that was mirrored on her own.

"Could this not have waited?" Sara heard her father-in-law through a roaring in her ears. He sounded angrier than Sara had ever heard him as he looked pointedly at the pool of red that was forming on the pale beige of his very expensive carpet. "It was not necessary to do this here and now!"

As though his father's rebuke had brought him to his senses, something changed behind Nicolás's eyes, and Sara's horror increased as she saw cold determination and something so ugly that it caused her to recoil. "Papá, she saw us. And this time we can't keep her quiet!"

Don Luis turned his head, his hooded eyes narrowing slightly as he saw Sara standing frozen in the dark doorway. For that one instant, she couldn't tell the two men apart as they looked at her and then at each other. Then Don Luis snapped an ice-cold order. "Get her!"

Nicolás took a purposeful step forward, the pistol grip hard in his hand. Sara turned and fled into the dark.

CHAPTER TWENTY

She knew it was futile even as she fled through the darkened reception area, blind and stumbling, her hands stretched out in front of her. There were men behind her and a hostile guard outside, and after the light of the office her eyes were no longer adjusted to the dimness, so that she knocked into a coffee table and tripped over something on the floor.

But that very darkness saved her, because the men behind her were even less adjusted to the lack of light, and they were bumping into each other and cursing. Then she was at the door and slapping a button, guided by the phosphorescent glow of the control panel. Just as someone hit the light switch, the door made its quiet click and swung open. Sara scrambled out into the hall and slammed the heavy mahogany door shut behind her.

At first glance, the hall was empty. But before Sara had time to consider her good fortune, she saw Jorge down at the far end. He stood at the window overlooking the back of the administration building, peering down at the huge coils of piping that led from the tanks and silos to the different processing areas of the refinery. He swung around as Sara stumbled down the hallway. His hand instinctively went to his hip before he realized that he was out of uniform and his old army pistol wasn't there. With an ugly shout, he broke into a run.

Sara didn't hesitate. She knew only one way out of this place, and the same terror that had earlier rooted her feet to the floor now gave her the impetus to move faster than she ever had in her life. Her hand was pounding the down button on the elevator before Jorge had covered a third of the distance down the hall. She waited an agonizing second as the door creaked open, then she fell inside.

She was scrambling for the controls even before she whirled around. When she did, she saw the office door open again and Nicolás and his two brothers-in-law came tumbling out. Nicolás still held the weapon he had used to shoot Ricardo, and when he saw

Sara standing frozen beyond the open elevator door, he raised it and shouted, "Wait! Sara! Stop!"

Sara saw that last second with preternatural clarity. The guard pounding toward her only a few meters away now to her right, the anger of his snarl tinged with chagrin as he recognized that she was getting away. Diego and Raymundo a pace behind Nicolás, their plump faces showing something of her own bewilderment and confusion at the rapidity with which everything was happening. And Nicolás, raising that gun with pitiless blue eyes, as though she were a complete stranger, his fine features so convulsed with frustrated rage that he'd lost all semblance of good looks.

They were all moving so slowly, and the elevator door inching its way shut was slower still. Then Sara heard a small *pfftt* and something smacked into the wall behind her. She spun around to see a small hole in the wood paneling of the elevator wall. It was at the height of her head, and there were tiny cracks radiating from around it.

He shot at me! she realized with a shock. Then the door clanged shut, she was alone, and the elevator plunged downward.

Sara clung to the bar that ran along the elevator wall. The numbers above the door were shifting with excruciating slowness. Surely something was wrong! Maybe the elevator had stopped between floors. Then, with another clang, the doors slid open, and Sara was running down the hallway on the first floor. Pushing her way through the swinging wooden doors, she raced toward the entrance, ignoring the curious stares of the catering personnel who had watched her come in just a few minutes earlier.

The two security guards gave her an inquiring glance as she shoved open the glass doors, but they didn't try to stop her. Their job was to check people going into the building, not coming out, and if it occurred to them that their boss's pretty daughter-in-law was in an awful hurry, it wasn't their business to question what any member of the Cortéz family might be doing.

Then she was down the front steps and into the crowd that was still dancing and laughing as though terrible things hadn't just happened behind the lighted window three stories above their heads. She paid no attention to the turned heads and the ripples of excited comment as she pushed frantically past. Her aim now wasn't stealth but speed. She didn't know how long it would take for the elevator to return to the third floor and come back down, but her head start was a small one, at best. And now it wasn't just getting away that was at stake, but her very life!

It was this certainty that drove Sara on with such panicked haste.

They had killed Ricardo Orejuela. And his father. Because they had posed a threat to their way of life. And because of three hundred million dollars, a sum of money so vast as to be beyond belief. Nor would they hesitate to kill her if they caught up with her—she had seen it in their eyes. Seen it in Nicky's eyes!

That was what her mind refused to take in. Her husband had snuffed out the life of a man—a boy—without hesitation or compunction. And he had shot at her! But she couldn't stop to think about that. She had to keep running. There would be no second chances now. She had to get away. If only she could lose herself in the welcome anonymity of the crowd, she might still find a way off the property or at least a place to hide or . . . or . . .

Sara glanced back over her shoulder, and her heart stopped.

Diego, Raymundo, and Jorge were already running down the steps of the administration building, while Nicolás paused at the top to scan the sea of people below him. There must have been another exit from the third floor that Sara didn't know about. A flight of stairs, maybe, that they had taken rather than waiting for the elevator to return.

The gun was no longer in evidence—but then, it wouldn't be— but the four men were no longer bothering with any pretense of normality. Nicolás must have already spotted her pale head among the darker ones around her because he was waving a hand to the others with a whistle shrill enough for her to hear above the dance music.

Then he was racing down the steps, and Sara couldn't see him anymore because she was too busy running for her life, dodging around knots of people and through the darkness under the trees, putting as much distance as she could between herself and her pursuers.

But there was no real anonymity in that crowd. Not for her. Not with her light Caucasian features and flaxen-pale hair flying around her face. She was attracting too many astonished stares, an astonishment that heightened as people looked past her to see the swirl in the crowd where Nicolás and his companions were shoving their way through. And though people were moving out of Sara's way as they recognized her, allowing her to increase her pace, a frantic glance over her shoulder told her that the crowd was also making way for the men coming after her. She could no longer see Jorge or her two brothers-in-law, but Nicolás was a full head taller than the stocky Quechua around him, and he was much closer than he had been.

Off to her right, a security guard, his interest aroused by the agitation in the crowd, was leaving his position by the tailgate of one of the *Cerveza Ducal* trucks and heading in her direction to investigate. Sara saw him glance behind her, then break into a trot. Calling on every remaining reserve of strength, she increased her speed.

But there was no place left for her to run. The four men behind her had successfully headed Sara away from the heavy concentrations of people to the very edge of the evening's entertainment. The band, still beating out its strident rhythms, was behind her now. So was the bas-relief emblem with its three-pronged Cortéz crown. The crowd was thinning out rapidly, and all that still lay between her and the perimeter fence was a smooth expanse of lawn, empty except for an occasional couple who had wandered away from the music and re-freshments, and the last fifty-meter stretch of gravel driveway leading out to the front gate.

Sara's breath was coming now in short, quick pants of terror and exhaustion. She had managed to dodge her pursuers in the crowd, but there was no chance she could outrun them on a straight-away, hampered as she was by skirts and heels that were not made for racing.

Sheer stubbornness was all that kept her fleeing onward across the grass. But she was finished, and she knew it. They would catch her and they would kill her. Maybe not here and now, but they would do it for sure when they got her away from all these questioning eyes.

Unless a miracle intervened.

And then, because Sara only knew one source of miracles, and because there was nothing else under heaven that she could do, she cried out with all the panic and fear and despair that was in her, "God, help me! Oh, God, please help me!" *Oh, God—!*

Yet even as her cry went upward, the fleeting thought came that her mother might have prayed these same words when she had seen that massive truck bearing down on her all those years ago. God hadn't provided a miracle then. So why should He now?

That's when it happened.

The miracle came in the shape of a small white Toyota Corolla station wagon. There were thousands of other small white Toyota Corolla station wagons all over Santa Cruz, but this one had a Cortéz emblem on the side and the yellow-and-black checks of a taxi cab, and it was inching its way down the driveway, honking at the partygoers to move out of its path. It reached the thinning edge of the crowd and started to pick up speed for the remaining stretch of driveway to the open gate just as Sara's last mad dash carried her out onto the road and straight into its path. With a scream of brakes, it skidded to a stop, its angry horn blaring.

Then an astonished face thrust itself out an open window. "*Señora Cortéz?* What—?"

But Sara had already recognized the driver. And the possibilities. Scrambling around to the side of the taxi, she saw to her dismay that the car was full. Adolfo was taking the evening off from his job at Radiomóvil Cortéz to attend the celebration, and much of his family had come with him. There was an older woman in the front seat beside him, with a small boy and a smaller girl on her lap. In the back seat was a young couple with two more kids crammed in with them, while at least one more adult and several other children were squatted down behind them in the luggage compartment. But there wasn't time to question the respite she had just been offered. Yanking open the passenger door behind the driver, Sara squeezed into the back seat. An indignant grunt greeted her as she landed on someone's lap.

"Go, Adolfo," she gasped, slamming the door shut behind her. "Quickly!"

She turned back to the window just in time to see Nicolás and his three accomplices emerge from the edge of the crowd. They sprinted across the stretch of lawn she had just evacuated.

The men hesitated when they saw that their prey seemed to have vanished into thin air. Then Nicolás spotted the car and Sara's terrified face behind the glass. With a shout, he started running again. He was only a dozen meters away now and closing fast. Wrenching her eyes away, Sara saw that Adolfo had not yet reacted to her order but was gaping over his shoulder at his unexpected passenger.

"Adolfo, now!" she snapped, her panic making her voice sharp. "Hurry!"

She knew she was being terribly rude, but there wasn't any avoiding it. And the sharpness of her tone had its effect as a lifetime of subservience induced Adolfo to stamp down on the gas pedal even before his head whipped back around to face the road. The little station wagon leaped ahead. Sara shifted her position as the astonished occupants of the back seat scooted over to make room for her. Then she leaned forward to touch the driver on the shoulder.

"Thank you for picking me up, Adolfo," she said more quietly. "But please do hurry. I . . . I have an emergency in town."

She glanced over her shoulder. Her pursuers were in the road now, racing after the car. But already they were falling far behind as Adolfo obediently roared down the driveway. There were no lights strung between the entertainment area and the front gate, and within seconds she couldn't make out their individual shapes—only that one was much taller than the others. Excited murmurs from behind her told Sara that the kids in the back were not blind to the men racing after them. But they kept their curiosity to themselves and their faces respectfully averted from their distinguished passenger.

Twenty yards. Ten yards. The station wagon slowed to bump over the cattle guard at the end of the driveway. A security policeman stooped to shine a flashlight into the car, his black eyes widening a fraction as he caught sight of Sara. But he straightened up without comment, waving them on with a salute and click of his heels. The station wagon rolled through the gate and past the guardhouse. Sara let out a breath she hadn't even known she was holding—only to catch it again in renewed terror as angry shouts rose behind them.

Twisting frantically around in her seat, Sara saw a man in an olive-green uniform hurrying after the station wagon, the beam of his flashlight bobbing up and down in front of him. Behind him, a handful of other shapes, indistinct in the dim illumination offered by the one streetlight high above the guardhouse, clattered over the cattle guard. Nicolás and the others had gained on her while the station wagon was slowing to clear the gate. Now they raced forward, with Nicolás calling orders that had the security police scrambling away from the comfort of their guardhouse.

But they were too late! The station wagon was already jolting up over the verge and onto the asphalt highway. Adolfo picked up speed, leaving their pursuers standing frustrated on the edge of the road.

Sara was free.

✠

Don Luis settled back into the contours of his customized armchair. He was alone except for the bloodstained corpse of his godson that still lay sprawled on the chair where he had died. How had it come to this?

Contrary to the shadowy reputation that had proved so useful in the drug underworld—where his anonymity had served to fuel the fear that others had for him—Don Luis Cortéz Velásquez de Salazar did not consider himself a violent man. Not like the first ancestor on the wall opposite him, who had thought nothing of running down a disobedient *peon* with his horse or wiping an entire Indian village off the map.

Times had been different then, of course, and such things had been accepted as the ways of conquerors. But over the centuries, the descendants of that *conquistador* had become more civilized, and wanton violence troubled Don Luis as much as it would any man. Fortunately, his countrymen were a passive people, and it had always been enough to pay well to keep his own hands clean of the white powder. Only once in twenty years had he been forced to have a man killed to protect his name and his family.

This boy's father.

How different the events of this night might have been had Don Luis and Julio Vargas not been at the hacienda when word came in of Orejuela's arrest. The interception had been simple. Their position was closer to Orejuela's country estate than FELCN headquarters, and one Huey is much like another. Don Luis's own first thought had been to sequester Orejuela at the hacienda. After all, he was family, however remote. It had been Julio who had murmured that Orejuela was a liability they couldn't afford at this late stage. Already the man was whining to rejoin his family. The *gringos* would have him inside of a week.

Vargas had been right, of course. The life of one stupid bungler could not be allowed to weigh against the safety and honor of his own family. The *coronel* had taken Orejuela for a stroll in the jungle, returning alone an hour later with no more comment than the jingle of the man's good-luck piece as he dropped it onto Don Luis's desk. And that had ended the matter.

Or so they'd assumed.

The habitual impassivity of his aristocratic features twisted in a momentary spasm of grief and regret that would have astonished any of Don Luis's underlings. He'd really liked the boy! Had hoped to use him as he had his father. But what else could he have done? Was it his fault that the tide of history had turned against him and his family?

It was *la Veta Madre*—the Mother Lode—that had first drawn the Cortezes from the courts of Spain to Bolivia. The ancestor on the far wall had been like so many other *conquistadors,* younger sons with nothing at home but a proud name that would not allow them to stoop to work a trade or other mundane occupations. Their swords had been their only hope of a future. And so they came to swell the ranks of Pizarro's army and the armies that came after him, drawn by rumors of the great Mother Lode and riches beyond imagination.

They found those riches in the soil of Bolivia.

The first Mother Lode had been gold and silver and land. But especially silver. The cone-shaped mountain of Potosí, 14,000 feet up in the Andean highlands, was a solid lump of it. On its proceeds, the Cortezes and their fellow Spanish aristocrats settled down happily to their elaborate mansions and huge haciendas and thousands of Quechua *peones*. It was a good life and well worth leaving behind the culture and refinement of Spain.

By the end of the nineteenth century, the *Veta Madre* was petering out, the gold gone, the silver found in increasingly deep and inaccessible pockets. Fortunately, by then another Mother Lode had been discovered—tin.

The wealth of the tin mines was more than enough to maintain the descendants of the *conquistadors* through the agrarian reform and the loss of their huge estates to the ungrateful peasants who had tilled them. If anyone troubled his mind over Bolivia's dependence on one cash export, it wasn't for long. After all, it was the only spot on the face of the globe where tin came out of the ground in such abundance. Everyone had to come to them, even the *americanos*, whose political and economic influence in this Third World country was becoming an increasing force to reckon with.

And then it had all ended, with betrayal by these same *americanos*.

Even while Don Luis's own father, high in the ranks of COMIBOL, the state mining company that had replaced the private holdings of earlier decades, was negotiating higher profits with their major American trading partners, the news hit the streets. The *americanos* had been secretly prospecting for tin of their own. In some unheard of place around the globe called Malaysia. And they had found it. In abundance. Overnight, the price of tin dropped to less than it cost the Bolivians to take it out of the ground.

Don Luis remembered that time vividly. So vividly that it canceled out any regret for the things that he'd had to do later. The lies when social acquaintances asked how things were going—acquaintances who were lying just as much. The loss of his Arabian horses and the reduction of his fleet of vehicles to one elderly Toyota jeep. The pawning of the paintings on these walls. The dismissal, one by one, of their remaining servants.

By this time, Don Luis was head of the Cortéz family, his father not having survived the loss of everything he held important. Not that there'd been much left by then of his inheritance—a crumbling family mansion and one country estate. And his family. Lots of family. Brothers, sisters, cousins. All expecting the head of the family to bail them out of their own financial difficulties.

He hadn't failed them. If he'd lost his cash flow, he was still a Cortéz with the political and social weight that name carried. He'd found them jobs in the city government and immigration and the police bureaucracy—all places where a steady flow of *propinas* (it would be unseemly to call them bribes) could be counted on to supplement their tiny government stipend. The best plum he'd saved for himself—a high-up position in the customs department, where grateful importers gladly paid an extra commission to expedite their goods before they mildewed in their containers.

And he'd dug in to survive. After all, even though the Cortezes had been reduced in stature, everyone else was in the same boat. That they were actually very fortunate never crossed his mind. Depression had hit more than the ruling class. The country was awash with unemployed miners, and hunger, malnutrition, and disease were everywhere. If he'd given it a second thought, he would have dismissed it with the judgment that the *campesinos* were well used to their poverty, hunger, and disease.

It wasn't until a pilot whose salary he'd once paid built a brand-new mansion and invited him to the housewarming that Don Luis woke up to the changing world around him. He'd accepted the invitation, somewhat to his own surprise. He, Luis Cortéz Velásquez de Salazar, who had never in his life graced such a plebeian social gathering. And what he'd seen had shocked and alarmed him. There were people here he knew! People who had been no more than the fringes around his own social class. Lawyers and politicians and technicians and owners of trucking lines and merchants—all members of that thin layer of society that provided the technical support that maintained his own class and cushioned them from the vast peasant sea that made up most of Bolivia's population.

And they'd had money such as he had not seen since the Mother Lode failed. Nor had they shown him the deference to which he was accustomed.

He'd known, of course, where their money came from. Even back when tin was still the Mother Lode, there had been rumbles about foreigners—mainly Colombians—buying up a larger and larger percentage of the country's traditional coca crop. American youths were moving from marijuana to broader fields in search of something to bring purpose to their self-indulgent lifestyles, and it seemed that cocaine was their new drug of choice.

Don Luis had come away more than a little concerned. These people were no *campesinos*. They had education and technical skills. And now they had money. The only thing they lacked was social and political clout. And with the kind of money they were flashing around, a shifting power base wasn't out of the realm of possibility. Where would that leave the traditional ruling class? Was it right that these inferiors, who had nothing of tradition, blood, or honor, should usurp the place in society that was properly his?

He'd thought hard, but not very long. Already several of his own friends were beginning to show signs of renewed wealth. One, who three months earlier had been struggling to pay his children's private school bills, had just flown to Miami and returned with, among other things, a wide selection of the most expensive and up-to-date electronic toys for his two boys. Even as Don Luis pocketed his *propina* for waving the toys through, he knew he had only two choices. He could jump on the bandwagon with everyone else and turn it to his own profit. Or he could get left behind, and before long the Cortéz name would be nothing more than a memory.

Don Luis had no real moral feelings about cocaine. It was a part of his culture, a homegrown drug that had been around as long as he could remember. The leaf had proved vastly useful to his own ancestors. The drug itself had remained a cheap and popular anesthetic in the Andes well into his own childhood, and was still an active ingredient in many a local home remedy. His own father had often used a discreet pinch as an antidote for drunkenness. As for the *gringos,* everyone knew theirs was a decadent culture. If they chose to abuse their use of the drug, was that his problem? Even the drug's illegality was only a nominal thing, pushed through by the *americanos* flexing their political muscle over smaller and weaker countries like his own.

So he'd made his decision.

It had all seemed an easy matter at first. It hadn't even been necessary to get his hands dirty. A friend—the same one whose children were now enjoying their Apple computer and remote-control race cars while his own children played with worn-out toys—had whispered to him that there were fortunes to be made in lending money. Four . . . five . . . even six percent monthly interest! That there was only one business in Bolivia that brought in that kind of return didn't even have to be discussed. He'd sold the hacienda and the family mansion—at top dollar too, considering its crumbling condition —and invested the proceeds.

That had been the start. He'd been able to move his family into a newer home and pay off his outstanding bills. Then he'd branched out. The favors he'd done for his mob of relatives now came back to him. He had connections everywhere, and for a price he could arrange for a plane laden with cocaine to slip "unseen" through airport control, or a truck to go unsearched at the border, or a spot of jungle to go unpatrolled by the military.

Within two years, Don Luis had amassed enough capital to lay the foundation for the most modern sugar refinery Bolivia had ever seen. Then he'd branched out again as the new upwardly mobile traffickers bought their mansions and their cars and began to wonder what to do with the rest of their cash. Don Luis took their money—for a cut, of course—and invested it in car dealerships and import stores, travel agencies and supermarkets, businesses whose proceeds were now squeaky clean. With men like Luis Cortéz as financiers and organizers behind the scenes, Bolivian drug trafficking moved from amateur and haphazard to big business; it began challenging the Colombians' stranglehold on the market.

Those had been the good years. The years when Bolivia had gotten rich—at least the people who counted. The years when a *narco* could stalk with his bodyguards into a restaurant and order everyone out for his own private party. The years when cocaine and cash could—and often did—exchange hands in broad daylight. *La Gran Veta Blanca*, they called it, the Great White Mother Lode, for the snowlike consistency of the cocaine crystals. And it was only poetic justice that this bountiful new source of income had come through the very *gringos* who had taken away their former base of wealth.

Yes, everything had been going beautifully. Until the *americanos* struck back.

There had always been arrests, of course. Small fry. Tokens to the technical illegality of the drug. People stupid enough to be caught red-handed with their product. But now the *americanos* were pouring aid and massive resources for an anti-narcotics war into the country. And in return, they expected some results. There were people in government—those who had not been smart enough to cash in on the drug profits and some who genuinely believed that the trafficking was bad for their country and its image—who were actively cooperating with the foreigners.

Some of Don Luis's own friends were among the first to read the writing on the wall. Few, after all, had ever really wanted to get involved in criminal activity. They'd simply wanted their due—a life of wealth and luxury and the reaffirmation of their traditional place in society. Now that this was secured, they were more than willing to get out.

One major victory over the *americanos* had been the Bolivian government's refusal to enact any serious illegal-gains legislation. There were historic reasons for this. Drug trafficking wasn't the only way to amass wealth that couldn't be accounted for. In a country where the under-the-table *propina* was accepted practice and more goods came into the country on the black market than through customs, there were few government officials who would vote for a law that required accounting for every cent of their income.

And that made it easy for those who wanted to put their involvement with drug trafficking behind them. One by one, they took their profits and invested them in legitimate businesses and settled down to live on the proceeds. And once they'd gone "respectable," as it was termed, they were home free, according to Bolivian law.

More, they were proving surprisingly cooperative to these foreigners who were so determined to stamp out the flow of Bolivia's chief export to their shores. They hadn't minded making money—and lots of it—off their ancestral product, but they weren't blind to what the easy availability of cocaine was now doing to their own society. Bolivian cities were filling up with crime and vagrants and vicious street gangs. Not to mention a growing pool of addicts who could no longer contribute their hard labor to society.

Besides, the whole thing was becoming an embarrassment, as their beautiful country, once synonymous with its wealth of mineral resources, became synonymous in international circles with the trafficking of drugs. The Bolivians were a proud people, and it wasn't pleasant to be vacationing in Miami or the Riviera only to catch the curious glances and covert speculation every time their country of origin became known. So now they were willing enough take the money these *gringos* were eager to pour into their country and in return point them toward the low-class scum who were taking their places in the drug business. The *americanos* might take all the credit for the increase in drug arrests in recent years. But the Bolivians knew otherwise!

Don Luis had hoped to emulate his friends' example. He didn't like this new feeling of vulnerability. When Jorge Roca Suarez, Bolivia's most renowned drug *capo* and a personal family friend, was arrested during a quiet trip to the United States, and his uncle Roberto condemned to begin a lengthy prison sentence in a Bolivian jail, he could see that the days of immunity for even the most rich and powerful were numbered.

But Don Luis had two problems that his friends with their small ambitions and their car dealerships and their import businesses didn't have. One was his family. His very large family. All of whom had grown accustomed to their fancy homes and brand-new cars and the huge salaries that were less a reflection of their job value as business executives or "consultants" in his new company than their cut of his less legitimate enterprises.

Then there was *Industrias Cortéz* itself. If he was to build the state-of-the-art modern facility he envisioned, he needed huge sums of capital. The benefits of such a project more than justified the means. Not just to him and his family. To his country. It would provide needed jobs and show the world what Bolivian businesses could do.

So he'd decided to stay in. Just for a while. And there'd have to be some changes. No more would he sell his influence to others or lend them his money or launder their profits. That was too dangerous. Sooner or later, one of them would get caught and point a finger in his direction. And with the new laws and the pressure of the *americanos,* even his family's position could not guarantee his immunity. Besides, the cuts he'd been receiving of others' dealings just wasn't enough. He needed something bigger if he was to amass enough capital to leave it all behind once and for all. He disliked getting involved in the actual marketing of cocaine, but it was there that the profits lay. And the risks, of course. But those could be minimized by a man of intelligence like himself.

And indeed, the scheme he'd come up with had a subtlety that had allowed *Industrias Cortéz* to prosper and expand for more than ten years now. The acquisition of the hacienda shortly after he'd started had minimized the risk at his most vulnerable point—the actual preparation of the cocaine for shipping. This wasn't the rural cattle ranch his wife assumed it to be, though there was one of those too somewhere on *Industrias Cortéz's* list of properties.

No, this place had belonged to one of Bolivia's earliest and more eccentric drug *capos,* who had chosen—whether because he thought its remoteness would give him protection or because it suited his image and impressed his friends—to build a Spanish colonial mansion in the middle of the jungle a hundred kilometers from the nearest town. He'd spent vast sums—sums large enough to make Don Luis realize how minor-league his own business attempts still were—carving a track through the jungle to the nearest passable road and ferrying out construction materials and workmen and the most luxurious of furnishings.

Don Luis had been out there just once in the early years, when he'd still been dependent on the goodwill of these men. It was the drug lord's birthday, and he'd expected all who had dealings with him to pay their respects. Don Luis had touched down under cover of night, his Cessna guided in by a radio beacon the *narco* had set to allow his associates with planes to find the exact spot in the trackless jungle. Even in the dark, the place had astounded him with its remoteness and incongruous luxury, and the guards armed with automatic weapons. Like a Mafia boss out of an *americano* movie, he had thought at the time.

Don Luis had intended only to pay the necessary respects and get out of there. And so he was furious when his host insisted on showing him around. Fifty rooms. Twenty bedrooms, each with its own shower and bathroom, TV and VCR. All occupied by people he didn't want to meet. Most were like his host, the hard-drinking, high-living *nouveau riche* of those early drug cartels, partying with a care-free openness made possible by the political climate of the time. But he'd also caught a glimpse of more than one acquaintance of his own class before making his hasty escape, and they were no more anxious to be recognized than he was.

Well, that man was gone now, languishing in an American jail, having badly miscalculated the climate of change. And Don Luis had acquired his jungle estate, more by squatter's rights than any-thing. It was long abandoned by the time he claimed it for his own use, the track covered over by the fast-encroaching growth of the jungle. It had, in fact, taken three days of random flying before he'd stumbled onto the right opening in the canopy of trees.

He'd never bothered to clear the track. Its inaccessibility suited him just fine. Anything he'd needed, he'd brought in by air. But he'd needed surprisingly little, because even the expensive furnish-ings had been abandoned upon the owner's unexpected arrest. At first, Don Luis had done his own processing with the help of his two sons-in-law. Then Julio Vargas had come along. And his Huey. It had been Raul Salvietti—who himself had benefited from Vargas's talents when the *coronel* was still in the military—who had suggested that Don Luis might find some use for the unemployed *coronel* at *Industrias Cortéz*. And he'd been right. Vargas turned out to be a genius at security and tactics—as evidenced by the FELCN raid setup and the two successful hijackings.

With Julio on board, they'd been able to expand operations. Security guards. A handful of workers. Even a couple of university-trained chemists. All willing to remain in that isolated spot in return for flown-in comforts and generous salaries. From their first simple mixing of cocaine into liquid exports and sugar products, they had branched out to impregnating it into clothing and native handicrafts and a growing variety of other Cortéz products.

He'd worried little about discovery. Few of those who had once partied on the hacienda were now anxious to boast of their friend-ship with the former owner, and even fewer could have hazarded a guess as to its location after all these years. The jungle was vast, its endless sea of trees deceiving, without exact coordinates.

Yes, things had gone surprisingly well to date. Too well, the su-perstitious might say. True, it had taken longer to get out than Don

Luis had expected. Several times he'd approached his goal, only to find costs of doing business and revised expectations pushing it upward. But now at last he was close. The *americanos* had backed off after that raid two years ago, allowing the Cortezes to increase the pace of their shipments.

Even Pablo Orejuela's arrest had not proved the disaster Don Luis had feared. The two hijacked cargoes he'd brought in were more than enough to offset his loss. Eight tons. Three hundred million dollars on the streets of the countries for which they were destined. Even deducting the considerable costs, that sum would put him over his goal of one billion American dollars, safely divided among a dozen unnumbered bank accounts from Switzerland to Panama.

All he needed was another month.

And now this!

Don Luis sighed, running a weary hand over his face, as he considered the newest complication that had just run terrified from his presence. He had entertained no intentions of harming his daughter-in-law, any more than he'd wanted to hurt his godson. The girl was a pretty little thing, perhaps rather naïve as to the realities of life, but that was no great fault in a woman. While it was true he couldn't afford any scrutiny right now, it had been enough to order the girl watched and confined to the house. A month from now, she could say what she liked. The evidence would be long gone, and who would believe the word of a foreigner over a Cortéz?

But now things were different. There was no statute of limitations on murder. And it was clear from the shock and horror he'd seen in her transparent young face that the girl would not keep silent, not even for the man she had married. It was imperative that she be found immediately.

Don Luis looked reflectively at the body of young Ricardo, slumped sideways in the armchair, blood dripping down one slack arm to a pool on the floor. His eyes narrowed, the grief and regret gone as though they had never been. He had an idea that might take care of both of his problems. He picked up the phone.

CHAPTER TWENTY-ONE

Sara relaxed slightly against the vinyl back seat of the little Toyota Corolla station wagon. Only then did she realize she was pressing heavily against someone else's plump flesh. With a murmured apology, she scooted closer against the door. The woman beside her said nothing, but she moved her arm away, her eyes flickering in the dimness of the car toward Sara and then away. Sara's conscience smote her again as she saw how cramped together the family was beside her. But what choice had there been?

The car was quiet, abnormally so, with none of the usual chatter of family and children. Her presence was casting a damper on their holiday fun. Even in the gloom of the taxi's interior, she could see that they were all wearing their finest outfits. The men and boys all wore button-up white shirts and dark slacks. Adolfo's wife in the front seat had the traditional braids and flared skirts that most older Quechua women still wore. The younger woman sitting next to Sara was of the new generation, with a sleeveless cotton dress and her hair cropped short and permed into a frizz, and she smelled strongly of cheap perfume. Sara had to resist the impulse to roll down the window. After all, *she* was the intruder here, and the last thing she needed was to exhibit any further bad manners.

Oh, well! They'd be reaching the outskirts of the city in another fifteen minutes. She'd have Adolfo drop her off there. Then they would be free again to gossip and laugh about the strange *extranjera* who had forced her way so rudely into their midst. Sara would rather have requested a ride clear to the Histeds, but she'd never been to the British couple's home and wasn't even sure of the neighborhood. Besides, it was better if Adolfo didn't know her destination. She liked the taxi driver, but she couldn't expect him not to report back to his employer.

Sara's fingers tightened around the cell phone that she'd somehow managed to hold onto during the chase. The best thing would be to lose the taxi once she was within the city limits, then call

Laura and ask the pastor's wife to come and pick her up. At least with Adolfo, she didn't have to worry about her lack of funds. She'd just have the taxi driver charge the fare to the family account at *Radiomóvil Cortéz*, as she'd done before when caught short of change. Her in-laws owed her that much!

The taxi topped a rise in the road, offering a glimpse of the scattered lights that marked the outskirts of the city. They were still so small and distant. Adolfo grunted as they dropped again into the trough between the sugar cane fields and uncut brush. Sara realized that she was pressing her feet into the back of his seat as though to urge the car to greater speed. Hastily removing her feet, she leaned back into her corner. But she couldn't relax. She wasn't going to feel that she'd escaped until she was off this road and safe with that kindly British couple.

"Atención! Radiomóviles Cortéz! Informen a toda unidad!"

The sudden sputter of static and excited Spanish brought Sara upright with a jolt. It took a disoriented moment to trace the noise to the CB radio on the dashboard. By then the small black box was spitting out another rush of words. The Spanish was too rapid and garbled by static for Sara to follow, but she couldn't miss the word "Cortéz" repeated once and again. Nor the astonished murmur that rippled across the car and the curious glances that not even politeness could suppress.

Adolfo snatched up the CB mike. *"Sí?* Number 89 here. I have *la señora* with me here."

Sara's heart chilled. She should have considered this possibility. Nicolás had seen her escape in a Cortéz radio taxi. He'd had his own cell phone with him. How long did it take to call the central office and have the dispatcher broadcast a general message on the company's CB frequency?

Adolfo was already slowing. *"Señora,* it would seem there has been some confusion. The *central* is asking that I return you to *Industrias Cortéz."*

Sara leaned forward urgently, her tongue faltering in her haste over the Spanish phrases. "No, *por favor,* Adolfo, don't stop. There has been no mistake. It is only that the *central* does not understand the situation. I must get to the city right away. I . . . I have an emergency there."

But Adolfo was shaking his head even as he slowed further, hugging tightly to the shoulder of the highway at the hollow blare of a truck horn demanding to pass. "I am sorry, *señora.* But it is by orders of Don Luis himself that I am to take you back."

"No, please, I don't want to go back!" Sara tried to speak calmly, but she could hear the panic creeping into her voice. Her hand groped for the door handle. "Just let me out here, then. I'll find my own way if you won't take me."

"I cannot do that, *señora*." There was reproof now in the taxi driver's drawling, uneducated Spanish. "Don Luis would be very displeased. Besides, it would not be right to leave such a young girl here in the darkness alone."

He glanced over his shoulder and took in Sara's strained features, pale in the headlights of an oncoming car, and his tone became kind, almost fatherly, as he jounced down off the highway to where a T-junction, formed by an unpaved side road intersecting with the asphalt, offered a space wide enough to turn the taxi.

"I do not know what your emergency is, *señora* Sara. But I will tell you what I would say to my own daughter. That you should rush off like this alone and at night is not good. It is best to go back and face the situation with calmness. Whatever this emergency may be, you will see that it will be faster and better to let Don Luis and *el señor* Nicolás, your husband, deal with it. It is for just such difficulties that the good God above has given you a husband."

Sara could have screamed with frustration. *But they* are *my emergency!* How could she explain that to a loyal Cortéz employee? It was no use. But she wasn't going back!

The taxi had slowed to a crawl and Adolfo turned a tight circle in the mouth of the side road in preparation for heading back toward the refinery. Now, as the car started back up onto the highway, it was forced to a brief stop to allow one of the huge inter-city touring buses and a handful of cars trapped behind it to pass. Sara was already fumbling for the door handle. She threw herself forward just as Adolfo floored the accelerator.

She hit hard, sand and gravel biting through her nylons into her knees and scraping the palm of one hand and the fingers of the other where they curled protectively around the cell phone. The taxi, its open side door flapping wildly, had already jolted back up onto the asphalt and across both lanes of traffic before Adolfo realized what had happened. He squealed to a halt, eliciting another screech of brakes from an old Nissan jeep that almost plowed into him. A garbage truck, heading out to the city dump, skidded to a stop just inches from the back of the jeep. More angry honking followed. Leaning out his window, the truck driver bellowed his opinion of idiots who didn't know better than to drive when they were stone drunk.

Sara paid no attention to the chaos she'd caused. She was already scrambling to her feet. Without pausing to brush herself off, she sprinted across to the cover of the thick scrub jungle that pressed up against the highway everywhere that the clearing of fields hadn't cut it back.

She plunged between the thick bamboo-like stems of a tall cluster of reeds. Thorn bushes caught at the soft chiffon of her dress, and the ground underfoot was a mire of mud and water that oozed up over her sandals. Sara tugged impatiently to free her skirt, shutting from her mind all thoughts of snakes and frogs and other wild things that could be in here with her. The fabric came loose with a soft rip, but she wasted no time checking on it as she pushed forward to pull the reeds apart for a clear view of the highway.

Traffic was moving again. In the headlights of an oncoming truck, Sara could see that Adolfo had pulled his taxi off onto the opposite shoulder of the road. She tensed as he climbed out of the car, waited for the truck to pass, and then trotted across the highway. She didn't move a muscle when he slid down the shallow embankment and skidded to a stop only an arm's length away. This patch of reeds might not rank as the world's best hiding place, but she didn't dare risk the noise or the danger of heading further into the swamp.

To her relief, the taxi driver didn't even glance in her direction before hurrying past to peer down the side road where he'd turned his car around. Seeing nothing there, he walked along the shoulder of the highway until his moving shadow against the dark of the night disappeared from Sara's line of vision.

But not for long. Before she had time to consider her next move, Adolfo was back, pausing now at each step to peer into the tangle of reeds and bushes. Sara let the reeds she'd parted ease back together. She could no longer see Adolfo, but she could hear his heavy breathing and the crunch of his footsteps on the roadside gravel as he came abreast of her. She kept her breathing light and through her mouth, standing stock still for fear that he would hear the movement. Her nostrils quivered with a sudden need to sneeze.

She was rescued by a rustle in the bushes slightly behind her and several meters off to her left. Adolfo's footsteps crunched away. With utter relief, Sara raised a hand to give her nose a good rub before pushing apart the reeds just enough that she could see out again. The rustle came again, closer, before dwindling as the small creature causing it moved deeper into the scrub growth.

An exasperated *"Ay, caramba!"* exploded out of the night. Stalking back into Sara's line of sight, Adolfo threw one last glance around, then headed back across the highway. Climbing into his taxi, he maneuvered back onto the asphalt and roared off down the road toward the refinery.

Sara waited only until the taillights of the Toyota Corolla had been swallowed up by the night. She didn't blame Adolfo; he was only doing what he thought was his duty. She just hoped he didn't get into trouble for her escape.

But right now she didn't have time to worry about Adolfo's problems. She had only until the taxi reached the refinery—or even less with that CB radio—before Nicolás found out exactly where she'd bailed out. Then she could be certain there'd be men coming down the road to look for her, and they wouldn't be as squeamish as Adolfo about getting their shoes dirty. Speaking of which . . .

Pushing aside the reeds that masked her from the highway, Sara took a hasty step forward, her stomach churning with disgust at the sucking sound her sandals made as they came loose from the mud. She was feeling for a place to set down her foot when something live and cold moved against her ankle. Sara bit back a scream. She needed to get out of there—and fast. But fleeing through this scrub growth in the dark wasn't the answer. Even by daylight it was almost impenetrable without a machete. At night, with swamps and who knew what else out there, it just wasn't an option. The highway was the only way back to the city through all this tangle, but it was too far to walk, even if she didn't have to worry about Nicolás coming up behind her. The only way out of here was to hitch another ride. And the sooner the better.

One more step and a pause to loosen her dress from another briar brought Sara back onto the solid ground that edged the highway. The road was empty at the moment, but headlights on the horizon spelled her best chance for a quick rescue.

Hurrying a few meters back up the road, Sara melted into the shadow of a mango, whose unripe fruit the winds had scattered thickly underfoot. From the cover of the tree's branches, she should be able to see what lay behind the approaching headlights before they could see her. What she needed was some kind of transport that didn't belong to any guest returning home from the anniversary celebration. A touring bus or a garbage truck would be ideal.

A Nissan Patrol whizzed by. Then a taxi so much like Adolfo's that Sara caught her breath until she realized that it lacked the distinguishing Cortéz emblem on the side. Then, for so long a space that Sara began to panic, there was nothing.

She was debating whether she should settle for hiding herself in the sugar cane fields, rather than risk that the next vehicle turn out to be a Ferrari, when she saw a boxlike silhouette looming high above a pair of oncoming headlights. It looked like the sort of truck used to transport vegetables and fruit for the morning markets from places as far away as the Chapare or the Argentine border. The driver had most likely been traveling all day and night, and would have no possible knowledge of the evening's events.

Scrambling up the slope of the embankment, Sara ran out onto the highway, waving her arms wildly as the yellow beams of the approaching headlights touched her. For one awful moment, as the huge rig bore down on her, she thought that the driver hadn't seen her or had chosen not to stop. Throwing herself out of the way, she whirled around with shock to see the colossal wheels sweeping over the very spot where she'd just been standing.

But now the truck was slowing, its air brakes screaming as it pulled over onto the shoulder of the road. Sara sprinted after it as fast as she could in her heeled sandals. A damp, earthy odor greeted her as she trotted along the wooden sides. Potatoes.

By the time she arrived, breathless, at the front of the truck, the passenger door was swinging open. A dark shape thrust its head and shoulders out. "*Señorita?* What in the name of all the saints—?"

Sara didn't waste time on explanations. She was already clambering up, her scraped knees stinging as she kneeled onto the high step, then pulled herself upright with the aid of a metal bar beside the door. To make the next scramble into the cab itself wasn't easy one-handed—she still had the cell phone in the other—and her muddy sandals were slipping on the curve of the door frame when an arm emerged from inside to haul her the rest of the way up.

"*Señorita,* has there been an accident? Are you hurt?"

The light had come on in the cab when the door opened, and despite the urgency of the situation, Sara almost smiled at the blank astonishment on the face of the man who had pulled her in and on the weather-beaten features of the driver. But her smile faded before it reached her lips as she glanced down. Torn dress. Legs and shoes black with swamp mud. Skinned hands and knees. No wonder they thought she'd been in an accident!

"No, no, I'm not hurt, *gracias.*" Sara climbed further into the cab. "But I am without *transporte.* Please, *señores,* could you give me a ride into Santa Cruz?"

"*Claro, señorita!* Of course!" The man who had hauled Sara inside scooted over to make room for her on the seat, which had once been vinyl but was now one huge patch of duct tape. Gingerly shifting off a spring that had thrust its way up through the ripped upholstery,

Sara glanced with apprehension at the yellow glare of headlights in the outsized side mirror. She couldn't order these men to hurry up as she had Adolfo. But if that was Nicolás!

The driver shifted the engine into gear. Reaching across her, his partner pulled the door shut. Sara was only too happy to see the overhead light flicker off, even if it meant she was now alone in the dark with two strange men, both of whom had looked a bit rough in the glimpse she'd had of them. They were unshaven, and judging by their crumpled shirts and the odor of perspiration, they'd been in their clothes for considerably more than one day. The younger man, seated next to Sara, wore his hair in a ponytail halfway down his back, a style that Hollywood had popularized among Native Americans in the United States, but which she'd never seen before in Santa Cruz.

Both men were chewing something that Sara assumed to be tobacco until the driver leaned over and spat out his open window. A strange, acrid smell blew in and mingled with the other odors in the cab. Sara's nose wrinkled in the dark. But it wasn't until the driver reached into a paper sack on the dashboard and pulled out a wad of triangular leaves, adding them to the bulge in his cheek, that she realized the two men were chewing coca leaves. Nicolás had mentioned how long-haul truckers used the stimulant to keep themselves awake. At any other time, Sara would have been horrified to find herself alone on a night drive with such a pair. Tonight, she felt only gratitude.

Besides, the two men weren't giving her any cause for alarm. The younger one had his eye on her, but he slid over willingly enough to allow plenty of space between them. As for his partner, he was concentrating on his driving as though Sara wasn't even there. Sara glanced again, anxiously, into the side mirror. The headlights she'd been watching had drawn close enough to identify the vehicle as a local transport bus. But just as she relaxed, another pair of headlights appeared behind them, closing the distance as rapidly as though the two vehicles in front were standing still.

The streaking vehicle pulled out to pass the bus. Then, turning sharply and skidding across both lanes, the speedster bounced down off the asphalt and stopped very close, from what Sara could make out in the dark, to the spot where she'd flagged down the truck. The oncoming lights of the bus outlined the shape of a low-slung sports convertible as it swept on past. Nicky's Ferrari!

"Did your car break down, *señorita?*"

With a jolt, Sara realized that she was being addressed and that it wasn't the first time the question had been repeated. Despite his rough appearance, the driver's inquiry was formal and courteous. Unspoken was his real question: *What is a pretty* gringa *like you doing stranded on a dark road in the middle of the night?*

It would be simpler, Sara decided, to answer both questions. With complete truthfulness, she said, "There were some men chasing me. I had to jump out of the car to get away from them. I . . . I thank you for the ride. If you hadn't come along, I don't know what I would have done."

The trucker beside her made a sympathetic noise. "That is too bad. A young *señorita* like you. And a visitor to our country, are you not?" Without waiting for an answer, he shook his head. "What our country is coming to these days! You must know, *señorita,* that all of us here in Bolivia are not like those men."

The driver spat out the window again. "I have a daughter your age," he said, shaping the words around his wad of coca with a clarity that told of long practice. "I would kill the man who tried to touch her. You will be safe with us, *señorita.* Now, where did you wish to go in Santa Cruz?"

The truckers insisted on taking Sara well inside the city limits. She accepted gratefully. It would certainly be easier to give instructions to Laura to pick her up from some landmark that she knew. She kept an apprehensive eye on the side mirror for the fifteen minutes it took to reach the outskirts of Santa Cruz, but saw no further sign of the Ferrari. It would take some time for Nicolás to figure out that she was no longer hiding in that swamp.

The truckers dropped her off at the third ring, explaining regretfully that their heavy rig wasn't allowed any closer to the city center. The younger one shook his head doubtfully as he handed Sara down. "Are you sure you will be all right, *señorita?* It is very late to be alone on these streets."

Sara held up the cell phone. "I have friends I will call." She gestured toward a collection of lighted doorways and awnings along the street—bars and lower-class cafés that would be open until all hours of the morning. "And I can always wait for them in there."

Stepping up on the curb, Sara waited, her hand lifted in response to their waves, as the big truck made a slow turn that would take them around the third ring to the market that awaited their produce. *That'll teach me to judge by appearances!* The truckers' simple kindness had encouraged her, and now that she was back inside the city and off the highway, where any car coming up behind might be Nicolás, she was no longer inclined to panic at every sudden sound. She still couldn't quite believe her incredible last-minute escape. It really did seem miraculous, and for the first time since she'd run in terror from her father-in-law's office, she felt confident that she was going to get away. All that remained was to call the Histeds. By this time tomorrow, she might even be winging her way back to the United States.

As the taillights of the potato truck receded to two red dots in the distance, Sara turned away from the lighted doors and windows. Despite what she'd implied to her rescuers, she had no desire to give anyone in those cafés and bars a reason to remember an *extranjera* with long blonde hair. Besides, the kind of men who frequented such places at this time of night might not be as civil as the two truckers.

Instead, she headed toward a row of businesses, shuttered and dark at this hour, at the end of the block. She passed a hardware store and a mechanic's yard, the oblong shapes of half-repaired buses and trucks waiting for daylight behind a chain-link fence. The street that led off the third ring between the two businesses was unpaved, barely an alley by American standards.

Sara directed her steps onto the narrow lane, ignoring a low wolf whistle from a pair of youths emerging from one of the bars. The luminescent face of her Rolex read well past midnight, but there was still a fair scattering of traffic and plenty of people walking along the street or loitering on curbs and against buildings. It always astounded Sara to see how late people stayed up here as a matter of course. The social life of the city rarely came alive until ten o'clock at night, and even small children played outdoors until well past the time most American adults would be in bed.

She paused at the mouth of the alley and made a slow revolution, noting landmarks that could pinpoint the place for Laura. A water tower loomed above the cantinas like a UFO on stilts. A neon sign blinked its conviction that *Cerveza Ducal* was the best beer in the world. Those would do.

Sara flipped open the cell phone as she turned into the alley. The backstreet was dark once she got past the chain-link fence of the mechanic's yard, but it wasn't as empty as she'd hoped. A young couple was leaning against the wall where the fence met up with the repair shop at the back of the yard, arms and legs entwined so tightly around each other, it was a wonder they could breathe. But they showed no interest in Sara, and after a giggle and a quick glance, the girl whispered something to her partner, and the couple disappeared further back into the darkness.

Taking their place under the overhang of the repair shop's tin roof, Sara shivered as she reviewed Doña Inez's phone number.

Clouds had blown in while she was riding in the truck, and it had started to drizzle, turning the warm night cold. Her skinned hands and knees were stiffening up and sore, and she was just beginning to realize how exhausted she was. *Please, let her have Laura's number!*

The soft jingle startled her so much that she almost dropped the phone. She had the phone to her ear before it occurred to her that any call on this number wouldn't be for her, but for Reina. *"Sí?"*

"Reina?" The demand was sharp and peremptory. Then it changed to incredulity. "Sara?"

"Nicolás!" Whirling around, Sara searched the darkness of the alley wildly, as though he might be lurking somewhere close enough to see. "Where are you?"

"No, where are *you*? Oh, no, don't you hang up on me! What are you doing with Reina's phone? Where did that"—his description of his cousin was considerably less than flattering—"go, anyway? I told her not to let you out of sight! Trust her to screw everything up!" The angry crackle against her ear shifted to a harsh command. "Forget that! I'm coming to get you, Sara. Just tell me where you are."

Sara was now trembling so badly that her legs would no longer hold her up. She slid down the brick wall to a sitting position, her dress making a pale puddle of chiffon against the dirt of the alley. *He's not really here! He can't possibly know where I am!* she had to remind herself forcibly before she could speak. "Do you really think I'm going to tell you where I am? I saw you kill that boy! And you . . . you tried to shoot me!"

There was a pause.

"That was a mistake!" Nicolás said shortly. "I can explain everything. Look, Sara, you've got to understand . . . there were reasons! If you come back, you won't get hurt, I promise."

He waited for her answer. When it didn't come, his voice turned cold. "Enough, Sara! You tell me where you are, right now! If you don't, you're going to wish you had. I warned you once. There's no way you can get away from us. We're going to find you—the easy way or the hard! You come back now without any fuss, and we'll find some way to hush this whole thing up. If not—well, all I have to do is lift this phone, and you'll have every policeman in the country out there after you!"

"The police!" Something in the utter conviction with which he made that last statement sent a chill along Sara's veins. "Why would the police be after *me*? You're the one who shot that poor kid!"

She had a horrible premonition of what his answer would be even before he said coolly, "No, I didn't. You did!"

"No! You . . . you wouldn't!"

"I would!" The soft words were brutal in her ear. "If it's a choice between my neck and yours! I'm not going down for this, believe me. Papá has the story all ready. First, you cheated on me with this lover of yours. A young godson of my father's named Ricardo Orejuela. Then, when he broke off with you and threatened to tell your husband—me!—about your little romance, you shot him."

"I *what?*" Sara's outraged gasp drew a movement from the shadows where the young couple had retreated to cuddle. She lowered her voice to a furious whisper.

"You can't make that stick! All I have to do is tell them the truth—that you shot him to cover up your drug dealing. Once the police do any checking, they'll find out you're the one telling lies. I haven't been off anywhere on my own since I got to Bolivia, and I can prove it! All the police have to do is check up who I've been with, and they'll have to find out I couldn't possibly have been seeing this . . . this *kid!* As for shooting him, you wouldn't have one shred of proof. I never even touched that gun. All they have to do is check the fingerprints."

"What gun?" Nicolás asked blandly. "The only gun the police are going to find is the one you stole from Papá's collection—minus the silencer, of course—when you decided to get even with your blackmailing lover. The one you tossed away somewhere on the grounds of the sugar refinery after you wiped the fingerprints clean. And if you want to talk about proof, we have five upstanding citizens who witnessed the shooting. Including the wronged husband, who did his best to stop you before you went completely over the edge. And I can promise you this, *querida,* there is no authority in Santa Cruz that won't take the word of a Cortéz over any crazy story you might come up with!"

Sara's stomach was so cold she had to swallow to keep from vomiting her fear and dismay. "But . . . but that doesn't even make sense! There were people who saw me go in—*and* come out—and they can testify that I wasn't carrying any gun. Besides, who let that boy into the building in the first place? The guards had to have seen one of you with him! And . . . and what about the surveillance tapes? They're going to show I wasn't carrying any gun. And Jorge was with me, too! No decent police investigation is going to buy a half-baked story like that!"

"So we still have to work out some of the details." She had no difficulty imagining Nicolás's shrug. "We haven't made our statements yet. We have time. But don't think we can't make it stick! The chief of police is a personal friend of the family. He won't investigate any further than Papá tells him to. As for those surveillance tapes, thanks for reminding me! We'll have to do something about those before some nosy news reporter or police underling thinks of that too."

His mocking words were suddenly colder than the ice in the pit of her stomach. "Like I said, Sara, we own this country! You come back with me now, and we'll find another scapegoat for this. You don't, and I swear, my pretty wife, that by this time tomorrow you're going to find your picture on every TV screen and paper in the country. For murder! You won't be able to show your face anywhere without being turned in. Or didn't I mention that Papá's offering a reward for the whereabouts of his naughty daughter-in-law. If you're in the country, we'll find you. And don't even think of trying to leave! We'll have every road and every airport and every border crossing in this country watched. And if you're hoping to con some friend into helping you, forget it! Not even your DEA pals will lift a finger on this one. We have the law on our side this time!"

"The law!" Sara choked out. "You call that law?"

"In this country, the law is what we say it is! And it's about time you learned that, Sara," Nicolás said impatiently. Then, abruptly, horribly, his voice softened to a caress. "*Corazón,* it doesn't have to be this way. You tell me where you are right now, and we'll work something out. You know I wouldn't really hurt you, *mi bella mujer!*"

Sara clenched her fist against the intimate cajoling that even now could almost convince her of its sincerity. "I don't believe you! You tried to kill me once, and you'd do it again. And don't call me your *woman!* I'm not your 'woman' anymore, and I don't want to ever see you again! I wouldn't come back now if your pet policemen were going to throw me in jail for the rest of my life!"

There was a swift intake of breath on the other end. "Which is exactly what they will do if you don't do what you're told!" Nicolás said icily, abandoning any attempt at persuasion. "And, somehow, *querida,* I don't think you're going to appreciate the accommodations in the women's wing of Chonchocorro."

"You . . . you . . . you evil, perverted monster!" For once, Sara wished she could bring herself to swear. There just weren't adequate words in her vocabulary for what she was feeling. "I just hope someday you get what you deserve!"

She pushed the "End" key, unable to bear that hateful voice any longer. That Nicolás could even consider sending his own wife to prison—and for a crime he himself had committed! It was too diabolical to believe if she hadn't heard it with her own ears! And after she'd declined to help send him there, even though he deserved it! How could she have ever considered that he was worth saving? He was a monster and a murderer, and she didn't want to see him again as long as she lived!

Sara was sobbing with anger as much as fear as she tapped in Doña Inez's number. Well, he would see! Maybe the Cortezes did own the whole country. But she was an American, not a citizen of this horrible Third World hole. She'd follow her original plan. And once she told her story to the DEA, she'd have her own embassy behind her with all the protection that being a citizen of the most powerful nation on earth implied. They'd get her out, no matter what kind of lies Nicolás and his family dreamed up!

She keyed the numbers in too quickly and got only an angry beeping. The number she was calling was a cell phone. Sara had bought it herself for the administrator of the children's home when she'd found out that the only means of communication the orphanage had was an ancient phone in the front office. Sara tapped in the numbers again, more carefully this time: 0-1-3-4-6-2-0-4.

This time the call went through. But there was no answer. The drizzle was giving way to a soft rain now, a rising wind blowing it in under the overhang so that Sara had to bend over the phone to protect it from the water. Again and again it rang until at last a soothing female voice informed Sara that the user of the requested number was not responding to the cell phone service.

"Tell me something I don't know!" Sara muttered, stabbing the numbers in again. Doña Inez must be asleep. If only she'd kept the phone close enough to wake her up. She pressed "Send." *Please, PLEASE, pick it up!*

But this time the line rang busy. It took three more tries before at last a voice came on the other end. Not a sleepy voice, but crisp and wide awake. *"Sí? Hogar de Infantes."*

"Doña Inez!" Sara gasped out her relief. "This is Sara. Sara de Cortéz. Please forgive me for disturbing your rest."

"Sara!" The administrator's astonishment was evident. "No, you are not disturbing my rest. I was busy with one of the babies. I have just been calling the *pediatra*. Now I am filling out the report. But what are you doing awake yourself at this hour, Sara, *querida*? Is something wrong? We missed you this morning."

"Yes, I know. I am very sorry to have inconvenienced you. There . . . there was a family emergency, and it was not possible to call." It was a struggle to keep her distress from her voice as she dragged out the proper Spanish phrasing. "Please forgive me for bothering you at this late hour, but I have urgent need to contact the *señora* Laura Histed. Would it be possible that you have her number in your files?"

"Certainly, *querida*." Sara heard a rustle of paper. "It is right here. But did you not know? The *señor* and *señora* Histed have flown from Bolivia today. They are not sure when they will be back."

"What?" The words fell like a blow. "But—are you sure? I saw Laura just yesterday! She said nothing about traveling!"

"As with you, it was a family emergency. One of her grown children in *Inglaterra*—I do not know them by name. Her son—or was it her daughter?—has gone very ill into the hospital, and they are flying to their own country to be with their family. She called in a great hurry only to say that she could not help with the children and that she did not know when they would be back. . . ."

Doña Inez was still talking, but her words came from beyond a roaring in Sara's ears. Now what was she to do? Ask the children's home administrator herself for sanctuary? But no, Doña Inez had no car to come and get her, and the orphanage would be one of the first places Nicolás would look for her. It was, after all, the only place she'd ever spent much time away from the Cortezes themselves.

Sara forced several quick, deep breaths into her lungs. This was no time to panic. Maybe the administrator would have some other phone number in her file. One of the other volunteers from the English church who might know how to contact someone from the DEA, or even that tall, brunette pianist who worked with Doug Bradford. What was her name? Ellen Stevens, that was it.

"Wait! What is that?" Doña Inez broke off her cheerful explanation, and now Sara too could hear the hollow thuds that had caught her attention. Then she heard the shouts that were coming from somewhere in the distance. There was a screech as the administrator pushed back her chair. "Just one moment, Sara, *querida*."

Sara followed the sounds of her progress across the old reception salon where Doña Inez did her paperwork, the dull clang of wood against tile as she knocked over a stool. The thumps and shouting grew louder as the administrator entered the vaulted entryway, though Sara could not make out what was being said. Then Sara heard the metallic clink of the steel bar being lifted and the creak of massive doors swinging open. Her own heart stopped beating as she heard the frightened gasp. *"La policía!"*

"If you will permit us to enter. We would speak to you about one of your volunteers." The autocratic demand was so clear that Sara knew that Doña Inez must have dropped the phone away from her ear in her astonishment.

"Certainly." Doña Inez was bewildered but obedient. "Please come this way. Is there some difficulty?"

No, don't listen to them! Sara cried silently. But already she was punching the "End" key to break off transmission. So Nicolás had lied again! He hadn't given her any chance to come back before contacting the police. For them to have reached the doors of the orphanage so soon, Don Luis must have called them almost as soon as she'd fled his office.

Frantically now, Sara punched at the cell phone's small control panel, pulling up the directory of personal numbers Reina had programmed. There had to be something she could use! She flicked past Nicolás's personal cell phone number without even pausing for indignation. Good, there was Gabriela's home number. She'd always been friendly. On the other hand . . .

Sara hesitated even as her forefinger went to the "Send" button. Gabriela was after all a Cortéz too, and she liked Nicolás. Would she believe Sara's story over the convincing lies of her own relatives? Sara's hands were shaking again as she scrolled on down the list. It had seemed such a miracle when she'd escaped the refinery. Now she was back in the nightmare with safety once again receding from her.

"*Caray!* You get back here, or I'm going to kill you!"

"Try it! You're so slobbering drunk you can't even stand up straight!"

Sara's head jerked up at the angry voices. Scrambling to her feet, she searched the mouth of the alley. She was tensing to back further down the street when two men staggered past the alley. Arm in arm, they belted out a raucous drinking ditty, seemingly oblivious to the rain battering their faces. Behind them stumbled a third man, shouting obscenities at their backs. The tension left Sara's posture. Just some valued customers from the bars at the end of the street heading home for the night.

But as the revelers staggered out of her line of vision, the cell phone suddenly turned to a block of ice in Sara's hand. A car had just come into view, cruising slowly past the mouth of the alley. A small white station wagon. And though the alley itself was dark, there was more than enough light out on the main avenue for Sara to see the yellow-and-black checks of a taxi striping the side, and a three-pronged crown on the door. The front window was rolled down, the driver peering out as he crept along. Sara didn't dare move, not even to press further back into the alley. She had no doubt in the world as to what he was looking for. Though surely he couldn't see her here!

The taxi inched on. As the rear tires were rolling by, Sara started to breathe again.

Just then, the phone rang. The jangle was astonishingly loud above the soft patter of the rain on the tin roof overhead. Sara's stomach flew into her mouth as she stabbed for the button to turn it off.

"Sara! Who have you been on the phone with? Now, don't cut me off again!"

The angry static in her hand was Nicolás. She'd pushed "Send" by mistake. Fumbling for the power button, it took an eternity before she found it and cut off her husband's furious tirade. In a reaction born of revulsion and fear, she dropped the cell phone and ground it into the dirt with her sandal, stomping on it again and again until she felt it crunch and break underfoot. Only then did she sink back down to the ground. Her hands felt strangely naked without the small instrument, as though she'd lost her only weapon. But it had proved of no use to her, and now at least its shrill tone couldn't betray her again.

She was only dimly aware that she was being illogical—the phone wouldn't have rung anyway with the power off—but the close call with the prowling taxi and the knowledge that Nicolás's pursuit was already closing in behind her had been a greater shock than she realized, and terror had once again seized her mind, pushing her past rational thought.

She sat huddled into herself, the rain blowing into her face, for an immeasurable time. Something brushed along one bare arm, but she didn't even flinch. She knew she should move. She wasn't safe here anymore. But she had no idea where to go next. And how could she leave this dark lane if every taxi that cruised by, every night patrolman, every passerby on the street might be looking for her?

Resting her chin on her knees, she stared with blank and unseeing eyes at the black stretch of brick wall that wavered across from her through the soft curtain of rain. She was trapped. Daylight would find her still sitting here, quivering, like some small creature too petrified by fear to flee the approaching hunter.

Black. Where had she recently seen a big, ebony block just like that wall?

Gradually, as minute followed minute and nothing drastic

happened, Sara's sanity began to return and her mind stirred to sluggish movement. *Black.*

Of course! The security seminar at the Co-op's library. Nathan McKinley marking out a big black square on his poster board. What had he said? Black was the wrong way to respond to a threat. Freezing instead of reacting. Sitting paralyzed, without thought or plan, instead of moving. Exactly what she was doing right now! What was it she'd copied down in her notebook? *"An inappropriate response to stimuli. You are always better off doing something."*

Slowly, Sara pushed herself to her feet. Nathan McKinley was right. What was she doing groveling in the mud like a scared rabbit? Sure, her situation had taken another step backward. But she had more freedom now, more options, than she'd ever had on the refinery grounds, and she hadn't frozen then. *Get a grip on yourself, Sara! Where are your guts?*

Taking a step away from the overhang, she glanced cautiously up and down the alley. The young couple had long since disappeared in search of a drier spot for their snuggling, and the yellow glow of the one street lamp at the mouth of the alley showed no further movement out on the third ring. *Yellow.* That had been another one of McKinley's points. *Always be on the alert.*

Sara startled as again she felt the ghostly fingers that had brushed her arm earlier. But this time they were down at her feet and accompanied by a soft rustle. Forcing herself to bend down, Sara felt for the clammy thing that was now wrapping itself around her ankle. Her hands identified it even as she pulled it loose. A plastic bag. Blown down the alley by the wind. One of the big ones commonly used for garbage or carrying goods home from market. And black as the night itself.

Sara turned the bag over in her hands. What had been the next point of the security agent's lecture? *Orange.* You know you're in danger. Every nerve in your body is jangling with tension. So you make a plan—and fast! And then *Red.* Execute the plan. Don't just stand there. *Do something, Sara!*

She moved deeper into the alley, the overhang of the mechanic's repair shop sheltering her from the worst of the rain. She was still jumping at every noise, but her mind was working clearly again. Okay, so the Cortezes had their own taxi service alerted to look for her and perhaps others as well. Not to mention the police. But they were looking for an *extranjera* with long blonde hair. Fine! Let them look for that.

Sara stopped at the corner where another dirt street intersected the alley. Tucking the plastic bag securely under one sandal as the wind threatened to carry it away, she began plaiting her hair into a rough braid. There was no way to tie it off, but she twisted the braid around her small head and tucked the end into the coil as well as she could. Then she took the bag from under her foot and pulled it down tightly over her head, rolling up the edge where it was too big and bringing the excess around in front to tie it in a knot. The hairdresser had done something like this the one time she'd been crazy enough to get a perm, she remembered irrelevantly as she adjusted the makeshift turban around her ears.

Her hands were damp from handling the wet sack. Rubbing them into the dirt and mud at her feet, Sara smeared the result across her face and bare neck and arms, darkening them, she hoped, to a more respectable shade. Now if she could just find something to cover up the pale blue of her party dress. The disguise wouldn't hold water for an instant in daylight, but in the rain and dark it should at least make her less noticeable, and she would just have to be under cover before dawn.

Which was her next problem! Maybe she'd been crazy to smash that phone, but it was true that there was no one she could call for help now, certainly no one in Reina's directory. She didn't dare try Doña Inez again, not with the police there, and the only other numbers she knew by memory were family. The Cortéz family.

Still, she had two feet. She could walk. Only, where? Again, the places Sara knew around the city were the palatial houses of Cortéz family and acquaintances. Of the few expatriates she'd met, she'd never actually been in any of their homes—not even Laura's.

Except one!

The picture of a cool, ivy-grown stone house rose suddenly into Sara's mind. And with it, hope. Of course! The one person she knew who had the power and the authority to stand up against the Cortezes. And she knew more or less where his home lay. In Las Palmas, just a few blocks from the Co-op school. If she could reach Doug Bradford and the refuge of her own government, then she would be safe. And if there were taxis and policemen cruising the streets, well, there were thousands of unpaved side lanes and alleys like this where taxis wouldn't go, especially with the rain turning the ground underfoot into a quagmire.

Now that Sara had a plan, her despair dissipated. She thrust her turbaned head around the corner, following it with the rest of her body when she saw that the lane was abandoned, its narrow doorways shut up tight against the elements. The rain was coming down harder now, and a stiff south wind had blown up, making walking a cold and miserable pursuit. But Sara welcomed the stormburst. At least it would drive the night wanderers and drunks off the street and into bed. She spared a fleeting thought to the Cortéz anniversary celebration, which had not fully run its course by the time she'd left. The rain must be putting a damper on the festivities, even if her own dramatic exit hadn't!

And that led her to reevaluate her shock at seeing the taxi. It was really not surprising, Sara realized now, to find them searching for her here. Though she was well within the city limits, the route the truckers had taken was still the main thoroughfare leading into the city from the refinery. It was a logical place to start looking once Nicolás realized that she must have hitched a ride. Which meant that she needed to get as far from this neighborhood as she could.

Leaning forward into the wind and rain, Sara pushed on down the street. Las Palmas lay somewhere on the other side of town, though she had no idea how many miles from here. But Doug Bradford had turned onto the third ring that day he'd been driving her home, and she was walking parallel to the third ring now. So if she followed the curve of the circle long enough, she'd eventually have to come to Las Palmas. From there, she could easily find the DEA agent's house. Sara pushed her exhaustion and soreness to the back of her mind. She was in no condition for a long hike, but if she had to do it, she would!

Ummph! Sara grabbed for the nearest support as her feet skidded out from underneath her. She wound up wrapped around a lamppost, which was actually the lopped-off trunk of a palm with a sixty-watt bulb hanging from it. The dim light allowed Sara to inspect the slippery surface that had made her fall—a length of plastic trampled into the mud. Sara yanked at a corner. It was thick and heavy, the sort sold by the meter on huge spools in the marketplace and used for awnings by street vendors, or as a cheap tarp, or even, by the very poor, for a raincoat. Just what she needed.

Sara hesitated before pulling it loose. A broken brick weighed down one corner, and there was a mound of sand piled against a nearby adobe wall. Someone's humble building materials that the tarp had been sheltering before the wind jerked it free. But her need overcame her qualms. Kicking aside the brick, she dragged the plastic up onto the sand.

The piece was too long and wide for what she needed, but she managed to fold it and wrap it around her shoulders, grimacing at the grit it added to her already mud-streaked dress and limbs. At least it would cover her dress and keep off the worst of the rain. And it certainly added to her disguise. No one would recognize her now as a daughter of the city's wealthiest family. She looked more like one of the beggars who wandered these streets. If only she could leave something in return, it would feel less like stealing.

Sara stooped to tug off her sandals. She couldn't walk much further in these heels, anyway. Already they were giving her blisters. At the moment, the shoes were wet and muddy. But they were fine Italian leather, and when cleaned, they would be worth far more than the few *bolivianos* this plastic had cost. Maybe someone in the family could use them. Or sell them.

Setting the sandals carefully on top of the mound of sand, Sara weighted them with the brick that had held the tarp captive. Then she started walking again. She winced as her bare foot met a sharp stone thrusting up through the mud. It was going to be a long night!

Sara covered the first few blocks buoyed up with new hope and confidence. The storm was increasing in intensity, but with the heavy plastic holding in the heat of her exertion, she was actually warmer than she had been. And if the rain was also washing away the mud that had disguised her pale features, there was no one to notice. The street she was following was a hodgepodge of back sides to businesses that fronted onto the third ring and shabby doorways through which some of the poorer tradespeople had their rooms; an occasional neatly plastered wall indicated that a more prosperous merchant or shop owner had built himself a dwelling. Though there were still lights on here and there, and the occasional blare of a weekend party turned up full volume, the change in weather had, as she'd hoped, driven the merrymakers indoors.

She hadn't gone far, though, before she regretted the loss of her shoes. They might have made hiking difficult, but they'd at least protected her feet. Sara wasn't used to going barefoot, and the soles of her feet lacked the toughness of the Indian women who trudged shoeless along these streets every day. Where occasional stretches of sidewalk allowed her to scramble up out of the muck, the rough cement cut into her feet, adding new blisters to those rubbed raw by the sandal straps. The mud itself was softer, but these lanes had too long been a dumping ground for people's refuse.

When a stab of pain led her to unearth a broken beer bottle, Sara finally hobbled to cover behind a stack of oil barrels. Rinsing the nasty slice in her big toe in a mud puddle, she used the chunk of glass to hack off about six inches of the length of plastic. This she wrapped around her foot like the Ace bandage she'd learned to use in first-aid training. Then she tore a strip off the bottom of her dress to tie the makeshift footwear into place.

If you didn't look like a beggar before, you sure do now! she informed herself grimly as she repeated the process on the other foot. But though unsightly, her innovation definitely made walking easier, and she stretched her legs to make up for lost time, refusing to even think of the muck now swimming around inside that cut.

Orange. You're in danger. Keep your body on alert! Somehow, the idea that there were steps designed to deal with situations like this strengthened and steadied Sara—perhaps one of the things that seminar had been designed to do—and she found herself remembering other things Nathan McKinley had said. She checked repeatedly over her shoulder to make sure no one was following, her eyes constantly roving the perimeters of her vision. *Act natural. You're a street bum, remember?*

She must have been convincing, because when she stumbled across a stooped figure, wrapped in plastic against the rain and digging through a garbage bin outside a small open-air market, the vagrant turned on her with a snarl. "This one is mine! Find your own!"

Sara backed hastily away, making as wide a detour as she could. But that precaution, like the others, proved unnecessary. The vagrant was as close as she came to human contact all night. And one by one, the lights blinked out, and the music stopped, and Sara was left alone with the darkness and the empty streets. Every fifteen blocks or so, she had to cross one of the paved avenues that intersected the rings of the city like the spokes of a wheel. Twice she spied a white Toyota Corolla cruising along the well-lit width much too slowly to be trolling for a late-night fare. It took all her self-discipline not to freeze or increase her pace. But either they were too far away to see her or they were thrown off by her disguise.

She came closer to panicking when a policeman in an olive-green uniform crossed the street just meters away. But the officer didn't even glance at her, and a frantic scan of the direction from which he'd come showed a guard shack and a lighted doorway with a sign that announced *Precinto 6.* A policeman heading home from the night shift.

By the end of the first hour, Sara's concentration began to flag. She was too chilled through now for any amount of exercise to keep her warm, and the protests of her abused leg muscles grew more insistent with every added step. By the end of the second hour, she was no longer bothering to check back over her shoulder or even to raise her head. It was all she could do just to keep putting one foot in front of the other.

I'm clear back in White! she thought dully when she realized she had no recollection of the avenue she'd just crossed. *Head down, no idea what's happening! If someone came up behind me now, I wouldn't even notice!*

She tried to muster herself to care. But the last two sleepless nights and all the terror and exertion of this endless evening had drained Sara to the limit of her reserves. The demands of her tired body were drowning out every call to vigilance. What she wanted more than anything was to sink down into the mud of the alley and close her eyes. Just for a few moments. Then she could go on. But Sara had no idea how far she'd come, nor how much farther she had to go, and her dread of being caught in the open by the coming daylight was still stronger than her exhaustion. So she kept walking, like an automaton now, only occasionally coming to herself long enough to confirm that she was still moving.

Sara was never sure afterward whether she'd been awake that last hour or sleepwalking. And yet, such is the power of the human mind—or something else!—that she suddenly came to full consciousness to find that she was no longer moving. Directly in front of her, creaking gently in the wind, was a wooden sign that read Las Palmas Country Club. Sara stared at the sign with mingled elation and disbelief. She'd made it! This was the very street from which Doug Bradford had turned onto the third ring that day of the potluck.

She was wide awake now. Working her wrist out from under its covering, she peered at her Rolex. Three-thirty A.M. She'd been walking for three hours! Well, it wouldn't be much longer. She started up the cobbled street into Las Palmas, the nearness of her goal quickening her steps despite her weariness. The DEA agent's house was somewhere in these first few blocks, down one of these side streets. If she could only remember which! She did recall that Doug Bradford had turned onto this street from her left. She'd just have to check each one.

Some of her caution returned as Sara peered around the first corner. This kind of neighborhood had watchmen, and however unlikely it was that they would recognize her as Sara de Cortéz, a street beggar on these fastidious streets would be little more welcome than a fugitive. But she saw no one in the next few blocks, and the one guard shack she passed was dark. It would seem the night patrol of Las Palmas had little taste for doing rounds in the cold and rain.

She'd gone further than she'd expected to when she saw her first sign of life. A small yellow rectangle halfway down the second block to her left. The lighted window of a guard shack. She was studying it, her eyes just barely clearing the corner in her caution, when a larger rectangle of light appeared at the front of the shack. The dark outline of a man stepped through the open door. Sara let out a small sound of relief as she caught the silhouette of a rifle—or machine gun, or whatever it was; she knew absolutely nothing about guns—thrusting up plainly above one shoulder. The house behind the guard shack was just a dark mass against the night, but this had to be the place. No other guards she'd seen carried weapons like that.

The guard swiveled his head to scan the street, taking his time to study each angle. Here was one person, anyway, who wasn't allowing the weather to affect his vigilance. Sara waited until he finished and stepped back inside before she started forward eagerly.

She hadn't finished her first step before she stopped, then shrank back around the corner. What had she been thinking? It was three-thirty in the morning! Doug Bradford would be in bed and fast asleep! Was she just going to march up there and pound on the door?

And what about the guard?

Sara had been so intent on her goal, she hadn't even considered what might happen when she reached it. But now that dark figure with its deadly weapon slung so casually over one shoulder took on menacing proportions. What would his reaction be to some muddy, ragged vagabond walking up and demanding to see his superior? Would he even bother to call Doug Bradford? Or would he just throw her out into the street—or maybe even arrest her?

And if Sara did explain who she was and why she was looking for the DEA agent at this time of night—well, Nicolás had bragged about the contacts the Cortezes had within the anti-narcotics forces. Even if this guard wasn't among them, what was to keep him from repeating the story of the young *extranjera* who'd come looking for his *americano* boss in the middle of the night to someone who was?

Sara backed further away from the corner. Maybe . . . maybe it would be wiser just to wait. To try to catch the DEA agent when he left his house in the morning. She knew what kind of car he was driving, and if she intercepted him right here around the corner where the guards wouldn't see . . .

But no, that was stupid! By then it would be full daylight, and there would be any number of people and cars passing through here. And Nicolás had sworn that her picture and Ricardo Orejuela's murder would be plastered across the city by morning. Sara leaned against the wall, dizzy with indecision and exhaustion. She was so tired! If only she could think straight . . .

The throaty growl of an approaching automobile shocked Sara

back to reality. She spun around, her hand jumping to her throat. Blinding headlights were moving toward her, faster than would have been prudent during the day. They slowed for a speed bump less than a block away, slanting momentarily downward as they slid down over the cement obstruction. For just an instant, Sara could see the outline of the car behind the dazzling beams. A square-bodied vehicle with windows so black it might have been driven by remote-control, for all she could see of the driver.

Hope rose so suddenly, incredulously, that it brought a lump to Sara's throat. She recognized that car! A Land Rover with polarized window glass. It had to be! If she could just stop it before it reached the corner. As she'd done hours earlier out on the highway, Sara ran out into the path of the oncoming vehicle, wildly waving her arms. If she couldn't see past those darkened windows, he had to see her.

But the Land Rover wasn't stopping. It had picked up speed again as it left the speed bump behind, its driver in a hurry to get home and confident that nothing would be moving on the street at this hour. Sara dropped her arms, caught in the twin beams like a moth pinned in the dangerous radiance of a lantern. She had to move! She was going to be run over.

But this time her limbs didn't react to her command. She was just too weary, her brain too sluggish even for self-preservation. She took a half-step, her legs as heavy as though she were wading through glue. Then she swayed and fell.

Doug was thinking of his waterbed. This staying out half the nights of the week was for the birds! He eased over the speed bump, feeling the jolt in every bone of his body. Well, at least they'd gotten the Brazilians, though it had ended in a gun battle rather than peaceful surrender. Doug had called the FELCN in on this one, and Colonel Torres had cooperatively ordered in a chopper as well as the land troops who had ridden out with Doug in a FELCN army truck. By the time they'd reached the coordinates Ramon had given him, the rain had started, churning the road to mud and reducing visibility to practically nil—for the defenders of the downed Cessna as well as the FELCN troops.

But the Brazilians didn't have the sense to know when they were beaten. They'd started shooting as soon as they were ordered to come out of the plane. The FELCN troops, never at their most patient when sitting out in the middle of a rainstorm, had obligingly returned fire, resulting in two *narco* casualties. By that time, the downpour had developed into a torrential storm. Doug had at least been fortunate enough to fly back with the prisoners. Ramon and his NIFC team were no doubt still trying to four-wheel their way home.

Doug stepped on the accelerator as he left the concrete street impediment behind. How he hated those things! Why didn't they just put in a speed limit and save on the chiropractic fees? But that bump was the last one before home, which was just around that corner. And about time, too! He was wet through and starved and ready for some serious sack time! Doug's eyes flickered away from the steady swish-swish of the window wipers to the clock on the dashboard. Three-thirty! Maybe he'd even take tomorrow off. He returned his gaze to the road.

"For crying out—!" Doug was slamming on his brakes even as he registered the bizarre creature that had reared up against the glare of his headlights. A dark and winged entity, flapping in the wind and rain like some huge and monstrous insect. It wavered and fell. He wasn't going to stop in time!

Doug was out of the Land Rover before the engine stopped. Rain pounded down on his back as he bent to peer under the front bumper. He groaned inwardly as he took in the huddled shape just in front of the nearest tire. *Of all the—!*

Then he saw that the tire was stopped a full foot short of the limp heap, and he let out his breath. Climbing back into the Land Rover, he backed up, then climbed out again, leaving the engine off but the headlights on.

Now that he could get a good look at what he'd run down, Doug saw that his giant insect was in reality distinctly human in outline. A pedestrian, in fact, wrapped up in a cape of heavy dark-blue plastic— nothing unusual in this rain, though the black garbage bag over the head was a new twist. A street bum, drunk no doubt, or he'd never be out on a night like this. It had been his arms waving around that had given that impression of a winged creature. But why in tarnation did the guy have to be doing his flapping in the middle of the street?

Anger warred with concern as Doug felt under the plastic for a pulse. The shoulder under his hand was thin and small-boned—maybe a street kid rather than an adult, though some of these *campesinos* were scrawnier than a twelve-year-old back home. His fingers probed past sodden material to bare flesh, so cold that his heart sank. But the pulse he discovered at the base of the neck was strong, if uneven. With any luck, the poor guy had just fainted from the shock.

A stirring under his hands and a low moan reassured him. Doug eased the slight figure over. Then, as he caught sight of small, heart-shaped features, ghostly pale in the glare of his headlights, he stiffened. This was no street bum! It wasn't even a man!

Fumbling at the knot that kept the black trash bag in place, Doug pushed it away to expose the hair underneath. Sodden and twisted into some odd hairdo, but definitely blonde. Doug rocked back on his heels, astonished to an extent he couldn't remember since his first arrest had turned out to be a member of the vice squad working under cover.

What in the name of all creation was Sara Cortéz doing lying in the rain on his doorstep—*and* dressed in the rags of a street beggar?

CHAPTER TWENTY-TWO

The cold rain was pelting on her face. Sara swam up from the darkness. She lifted heavy eyelids. There was a face close above hers, its strong angles thrown into stark relief by a light that dazzled her eyes. She blinked away raindrops, and it came into sharper focus. A man's face—amazed and concerned and slightly impatient. Then she remembered the headlights bearing down on her and everything that had gone before. "D—Doug! Mr. Bradford!"

The exclamation echoed loud in the empty street, and she gasped in alarm, lowering her voice to a whisper. "It . . . it *was* you!" Sara struggled to a sitting position, clutching at the jacket front of the man hunkered down beside her just to reassure herself that he was real and wouldn't vanish into the dark and rain. "I was afraid—"

Doug's arm went around her shoulders, supporting her. "Are you all right?" The question was sharp, but with concern, not anger. "You're not hurt anywhere?"

Sara shook her head dumbly. Even through the plastic, the arm around her shoulders felt solid and comforting and warm, and she let herself relax for an instant against it as she might have against her own father's shoulder years ago. "I'm all right. I just . . . just fell."

Then she stiffened. Releasing her hold on his jacket, she pulled away from his firm hold and scrambled to her feet.

"No . . . no, I'm not all right!" she cried, hearing her voice rise but unable to stop it. "Nothing's all right! They . . . they killed him!" And then she did what she'd determined she wouldn't do. She burst into tears.

The warm tears blinded her, pouring down her cheeks to mingle with the cold rain. Taking a step away, Sara blundered into the bumper of the Land Rover. She had to grab at the hood to keep her balance, and in the process she lost her grip on her makeshift cloak. The plastic slid to the ground. Springing to his feet, Doug stepped to her side. His sharp eyes took in the details he hadn't been able to see before. The sodden braid tumbling down from where it had been tucked up under her hair. The torn and mud-streaked party dress clinging damply to her slender frame. The absurd foot coverings, tattered and unraveling now to show her bare feet.

The line of his mouth turned grim. "Okay, what happened?"

"I . . . I . . ." Sara's teeth were chattering so hard she couldn't get anything else out. Doug's arm came around her shoulder again, propelling her gently forward. "Never mind. Let's get you out of the wet and into the car."

Opening the front passenger door, Doug lifted her bodily up into the seat. Shutting the door behind her, he walked briskly around to the back of the Land Rover. Sara could hear him open the rear door and rummage around inside. She was struggling to control her sobs, but not successfully. She had been battling terror and exhaustion and the despair of fighting alone against a hostile world for hours now, forcing herself to exhibit a courage she didn't feel and doggedly pushing from her mind all but the next step she would take. But now that all the running and hiding was over and she could allow herself to believe that safety was hers at last, the shock and horror were setting in. Long tremors shook her, and her breath came in quick, shuddering gasps. She didn't realize that her body was reacting normally to the trauma of the last hours and the sudden relief of stress and fear, and she was bitterly ashamed at the spectacle she was making of herself. But she couldn't stop the tears that streamed down her face.

A fresh onslaught of wind and rain announced Doug's return. Without a word, he shook out a homespun wool blanket of Quechua weave that was part of a basic kit he kept in the back of the Land Rover for any emergency. Spreading it out over Sara, he tucked in the corners as gently as he'd once tucked in his own small daughter at bedtime. Then he walked around to the other side and climbed in behind the wheel. Switching on the overhead light, he rummaged for an old hand towel he kept to wipe condensation from the inside of the windshield. Unearthing it under an empty can of Pennzoil, he rubbed it over his face and hair, unobtrusively studying his passenger at the same time.

The girl was still shivering, even under the blanket. She'd evidently been out in the downpour for some time, because she was soaked through and blue with cold. Doug didn't like the look in her eyes as she stared unblinking at the windshield. He'd come across that bruised look before—in the eyes of children in a Nicaraguan refugee camp, human flotsam from that country's civil war, whose small lives had seen so much horror that they'd passed beyond terror to a dull listlessness that hadn't sparked back to life even when they were safe behind the barbed wire of the camp. It was obvious the girl had undergone some severe shock. And her showing up on his doorstep like this was a good clue that whatever had gotten her into this state would be of interest to Doug and the DEA.

But that could wait.

Digging into his pocket, Doug pulled out a neatly folded, if rather damp, handkerchief. "Here. It's a little soggy, but it's clean."

Sara's eyes didn't shift from the windshield, but she freed one hand to take the handkerchief with a tremble of her lips that might have been a "thank you."

"Good girl." Doug reached for the ignition as she applied the handkerchief to her nose and wet cheeks. "Now just lean back and don't try to talk. We'll have you to the house in just a few moments. Then we'll call a doctor."

It was just what Sara needed to shake her out of her daze.

"No!" Dropping the handkerchief, she reached with surprising force to strike Doug's hand away from the ignition. "No, please, I'm all right! I don't need a doctor! You can't let anyone see me—not even your guards! They'll . . . they'll kill me too if they find out where I am!"

From the expression on Bradford's face, Sara knew she was making absolutely no sense. But before she could add anything further, she was startled by the sound of a car engine. She twisted around in her seat, hampered by the heavy wool blanket. A pair of headlights was coming up the cobblestones behind them. They slowed to jolt over the speed bump. Sara's reaction was completely instinctive. Whirling back around, her hand shot to the overhead light, unerringly finding the right switch. The interior of the Land Rover plunged into darkness. She sat tense as the headlights came up alongside them, slowing still further to pass in the narrow street. The other car sat much lower than the Land Rover and had the contours of a sports car.

"Can they see in here?" she demanded, her voice made harsh by panic. The driver, a shadowed outline in a business suit, was turning his head as he inched past, and it didn't seem possible that he couldn't see her as she could see him.

"No, of course not," Doug reassured her out of the dark. "You've seen what these windows are like from the outside."

They sat in silence as the other vehicle eased past them. The driver showed no further interest in the Land Rover, and as the car

was illuminated by their own headlights, Sara could see that it was
indeed a sports car, but not Nicky's Ferrari or any automobile she
recognized. Gathering speed, it disappeared around a corner. Sara
let out her breath as the taillights winked out. Then Doug asked
quietly from beside her, "Now would you mind telling me what that
was all about?

"No, just wait a minute." He raised a hand as Sara's head turned
toward him in the dark. Groping for the ignition key, he switched
on the engine. At her small sound of protest, he explained, patiently,
as to a child, "It's okay. I won't take you to the house, if you've got a
problem with that. But we can't stay here in the street. There's a
little park just a couple blocks up the street. We'll pull in there.
Then I'd appreciate it if you'd let me know just what's going on here!"

Sara used the short drive to compose herself. To her relief, she
found that she'd stopped crying. At least that scare with the sports
car had been good for something! Drawing in deep breaths, she
managed to still the hiccups that were the aftermath of her violent
storm of tears, and under the heavy weight of the Indian blanket,
she gradually stopped shivering as well.

The park was actually a small plaza with walkways and ornamental
flower beds and trees. A line of vehicles was stationed for the night
along the curb. Since the concept of a two-car family was new to
Bolivia, even such well-appointed homes as those whose cool, plastered
walls fronted the *plazuela* often lacked garage space for more than
one vehicle. Pulling up behind a navy blue Mitsubishi Montero, Doug
switched off the engine and the headlights.

"Okay, we're just another car parked for the night." He reached
over and opened the glove compartment. The small light inside gave
off enough wattage to illumine the interior without being visible
from outside the tinted windows. "Now, would you like to tell me
what's going on? You said someone's trying to kill you. Who? And
why?"

"I . . ." Sara bit her lip. He sounded so cool, every bit the professional law officer, and now that she was sitting safe and reasonably
warm in this car, she was suddenly aware of how implausible her
story sounded, even to herself. "I'm not sure where to begin . . .
it's going to sound crazy. . . ."

Doug hadn't meant to sound abrupt. He was simply very tired
and wishing there was some way he could postpone the whole situation
until he'd had a few hours of sleep. When Sara didn't go on, he
prompted, "Look, Mrs. Cortéz—Sara—it's evident that something's
seriously wrong here and that you've been through a tremendous

shock. Whatever it is, I'm glad you came to me, and I'd really like to help. But I can't help you if you don't tell me what's going on. Does this have something to do with what we talked about the other night? That drug raid in Miami? Is that it?"

Sara nodded, swallowing a lump in her throat. The other night. A lifetime ago when she'd still had hopes that this would all turn out to be a misunderstanding. Then she shook her head miserably. "It . . . it didn't really start there. It's been going on for a long time, just . . . just like you told me. But that's when I found out about it."

"Fine. Then start there," Doug said as gently as he could, though fatigue tinged the edges of his voice. "How *did* you find out about that shipment of tapestries? What does this Julio Vargas and Cortéz Industries have to do with it? Just take it from the beginning, slow and easy, and go right on through everything that's happened until this moment. *Everything*—no matter how small or unimportant you might think it is. Can you do that?"

It was more a command than a question, but Sara, eyeing him uncertainly in the dim glow of the glove compartment, saw that he didn't look as stern as he sounded. She nodded a tremulous agreement and began to talk.

Doug was wide awake by the end of the first minute. This was unbelievable! Not the girl's story. The ring of truth there was unmistakable, and in any case, her testimony dovetailed too exactly with what he'd already learned about Julio Vargas to question its veracity. But this, in one fell swoop, was more intelligence than he'd managed to put together on the Cortéz case in—how many years? Almost since he'd come to this blasted country! It was all Doug could do to keep his exultation from showing through the impersonal expression of interest he'd learned to maintain during an interview.

Sara began obediently with the newscast of last Friday that had initiated this chain of events. This was matter-of-fact reporting and helped to steady her. She didn't bring in the party or that terrible disagreement that had taken her and Nicolás upstairs—that was no one else's business—but started in at her recognition of the tapestry on CNN. She went on to Nicolás's promise to deal with the situation, the conversation she'd overheard downstairs in her father-in-law's office, and the flurry of activity that had followed from the two men over the next days. Then her own growing doubts that had led up to her encounter with Doug himself after the security seminar. It wasn't until she began to talk about the aftermath of that interview that her voice faltered.

"He . . . he was so terribly angry when he found out I'd talked to you!" Sara whispered. Doug didn't have to ask who "he" was. "That's when I found out . . . and when I asked him how he could do it, he just laughed! He said it was just business."

Business, was it! Well, business for the Cortéz family was about to hit an economic downturn if he had anything to do with it! Doug's mind was working furiously even as he listened, only occasionally interrupting to prompt some added detail of what Sara had learned about the actual drug operation and how it worked. So Luis Cortéz, along with this Julio Vargas—really, he was becoming increasingly eager to meet this guy, preferably behind an interrogation table!— had been behind that mysterious gang of *volteadores* and those two hijacked cargoes of coke. It was gratifying, considering the scanty nature of his data—well, Kyle actually deserved most of the credit there—to see how close his speculations had come to the truth. But that was the way it worked in this business. You beat your head against a brick wall of unsolved mysteries until you were ready to give up. Then, all of a sudden, one more piece of the puzzle waltzed into place and the whole wall came tumbling down.

Already Doug was calculating manpower, examining—and discarding—possibilities. If he could turn this to his advantage, it could be the single biggest anti-narcotics operation the DEA had yet managed to put into the field during its tenure in Bolivia. And if they could really pull down one of the most powerful families in the country—and make it stick—the scandal might even put a measurable dent in these people's eagerness to indulge themselves in the drug trade. It would be a most satisfactory way to end his tour of service in Bolivia.

Turning his head to look across at Sara, he cut in abruptly, "You're saying they never once said where this hacienda is located? But surely . . . they must have given some indication! What direction were they flying? Didn't they even mention a general region?"

But he'd hardly got the words out when he caught himself. The girl had recovered well from her earlier hysterics and was making her testimony clearly, if tonelessly, stumbling only when she came to her husband's refusal to leave the country with her. But tears—silent ones—were again flowing down her cheeks, and her young face held such misery that Doug was stirred to pity and rage. It was so easy in situations like this to forget that the people involved—especially innocent bystanders like Sara Cortéz—were real human beings who suffered and hurt. The girl had outlined only the chain of events and what she could remember of the conversation, nothing of her own shock and terror, as she recounted her confrontation with the three men in Luis Cortéz's office and all she'd learned from Nicolás afterward. But Doug was an expert at reading between the lines, and he had no trouble imagining the emotions she must have felt when she'd found out the truth about her handsome young husband and his family. To him, this was the intelligence coup of his career. To her it was a tragedy of the highest order.

It would be a pleasure, he thought savagely, remembering that same young face glowing with happiness and pride in the man whose betrayal she'd just described, to find his fingers around a certain individual's neck!

"Look, I'm sorry," he said gently before she could respond to his interruption. "I really don't need to know all these details right now. Sometimes I let my enthusiasm for the job carry me away. Just go on to what's happened tonight. You were out at Cortéz Industries at their anniversary celebration. That much was on the radio. What happened then? From what I know of Luis Cortéz, he wouldn't make it too easy for you to walk off with enough information in your head to bring down his entire operation."

"Easy?" Sara straightened up hastily, mopping at her face with the now soggy handkerchief. "No—no, he didn't make it easy!"

Sara had managed in the last few minutes to push the evening's ending to the back of her mind as she chronicled all that had happened in recent days, leaving out not the smallest detail, as though by stretching her recital out, she could keep at bay its terrible conclusion. Now she found herself shivering again as she took up her narration of the anniversary celebration. It was as though she were living it all over again. The humiliation and helpless rage of the lie Don Luis had told to keep her captive. The sudden hope when Reina's cell phone had dropped into her hands. Jorge's appearance that had put an end to her plan of escape. The horror of that eavesdropped conversation in her father-in-law's office suite.

Doug's astonishment grew as he listened. He'd known too many women marrying into Sara's situation who'd chosen to shrug their shoulders and keep quiet when they'd found out what their new families were up to—in self-interest, if nothing else. In fact, after the other night's interview, he'd been more than half convinced that Sara was one of them. That she had instead seized the first opportunity to walk away was a welcome vindication of his own assessment of her character.

But he'd never expected anything like this! No wonder the girl had been in such a state of shock when he'd picked her up. And there was something in all of this that was striking a chord of memory.

He was still groping for the connection when Sara began describing the cross that had provoked such a sharp reaction from the Cortéz men and their young guest. Doug shot upright with a sharp exclamation. "Saint George! Why, sure! I remember that cross! Did they happen to mention the name of this boy?"

"Yes, they called him . . ." Sara had to think for a moment. "Richard . . . no, Roberto . . . no, it was Ricardo. That's what Don Luis was calling him."

"*What?* Not Ricardo Orejuela!"

"Yes, that was it. They called his father Pablo Orejuela. You know him?"

"I know *of* him! I was on my way to pick the guy up when he vanished into thin air. That cross was in the description the arresting officer gave us afterward. Not that it offered Orejuela a whole lot of protection."

So that's who Cortéz's supplier had been! And that was who had engineered Orejuela's escape and disappearance. One more mystery solved and one more crime to be laid at Luis Cortéz's doorstep.

"That's what Nicky said," Sara responded wearily. "That the cross would give him protection. That's why he started wearing it."

"Oh, he did, did he?" Doug let out a low whistle. "Well, well! If that isn't a dead giveaway! So your Nicky knew what *San Jorge* meant and believed it enough to wear it."

"What it means?" Something in the added grimness of his tone penetrated Sara's apathy enough to spark the question. "I . . . I thought it was just some superstition about Saint George being able to protect you from danger. Like he protected the villagers from the dragon."

"Not from danger; from the police!" Doug told her bluntly. "Or the authorities in general. *San Jorge* is the patrón saint of thieves and criminals—around here, anyway. Not to mention, drug dealers. We see it all the time when we catch these guys. A big picture of good old Saint George up on the wall. A candle to light in front when they pray to him. They even have their own ritual prayer that comes with it, if you can believe it. A pretty gruesome one, too. Asking *San Jorge* to blind their enemies—that's me!—and make our guns backfire on us and turn our knives to rubber and in general demolish anyone who tries to make them toe the law."

"Oh, no!" Sara whispered, aghast.

"Oh, yes! And young Ricardo's right. That *San Jorge* cross alone would have been enough to make our office sit up and listen. I don't imagine there's another one like it in the world. And if the boy had the coordinates of that hacienda—or even the general vicinity—he could have put a good-sized nail in Cortéz's coffin, all right! So what happened?"

But Doug could already guess the answer.

"He—he shot him! Just like that!" The horror of that last terrible, frozen moment when she'd seen Nicolás snatch the gun off her father-in-law's desk was back in Sara's eyes. "Like that poor boy was some . . . some piece of junk that had gotten in his way! I . . . I didn't think he'd killed him. It was all so quiet. He just looked . . . asleep, maybe. And then I saw the blood dripping down on the floor . . ."

Her teeth were chattering so hard that she could go no further. Doug waited patiently. He'd interviewed too many traumatized informants to push her. But his own thoughts were murderous. He'd sent that boy there to die. Oh, maybe not directly, and certainly no one could hold him responsible. But he'd planted the idea in the kid's head that Pablo Orejuela had met with foul play and sent him out to poke his nose around. Doug hadn't been surprised when Ricardo had never reported back. To expect him to trust the men who would have put his father behind bars had been a long shot. But he'd certainly never counted on the kid being foolhardy enough to challenge—and threaten—a man like Luis Cortéz. Why hadn't he come to Doug for help as this girl had had the sense to do? Well, this was one more score that he was going to settle with the Cortezes before this was all over!

When Sara could bring herself to go on, it was in little more than a whisper. The flight across the refinery grounds with Nicolás and his men on her heels. The last minute miracle of Adolfo's taxi. Escaping into the swamp and hitchhiking into the city. Her bald recital of events seemed totally inadequate to the terrible reality it had been, and though she twisted her hands together in the folds of the wool blanket, she couldn't stop shaking. Sometime in the middle of her recital, a warm, strong hand came down to cover her two icy ones. Its unspoken sympathy helped her through that heart-chilling moment when she'd thought herself safe at last only to find that the Cortezes were again one step ahead of her.

"He . . . he said they'd tell everyone that I killed that boy if I didn't come back. I couldn't believe he was serious! But when I called Doña Inez, the police were already there. And then I saw that taxi looking for me. . . ."

Sara felt as limp as a wet dishrag by the time she'd finished. She leaned her head against the back of the seat, closing her eyes. Then she opened them again and turned her head to look at Doug, trying for a wan smile that failed miserably. "I'm sorry. I really am behaving badly, aren't I?"

"You're—"

Doug broke off to study Sara with incredulity. This girl had been through more disillusionment and heartache in the last twenty-four hours than he'd wish on anyone in a lifetime. She'd witnessed a particularly distressing murder and had her own husband trying to kill her. Still, she'd managed to keep her head long enough to take advantage of the slimmest possibility of escape, make her own way to the city, put together a disguise and a plan, and trek more than three hours through a storm he wouldn't kick a stray dog out into. Shaken badly by the trauma of her ordeal, she'd nevertheless pulled herself together to make a credibly coherent report with a courage that made light of her own fear and exhaustion. And yet she felt she had to apologize!

"You're doing just fine," he told her gruffly. "If I'd gone through half of what you've been through tonight, I'd be a basket case by now."

Sara had her doubts about that! But her next attempt at a smile showed marked improvement. Sitting up straight, she pushed the damp strands that had escaped from her braid back from her face. "Then . . . you *do* believe me? About that boy? I was afraid . . . Nicolás said no one would! That they could make the police and . . . and everyone else think I was guilty."

Doug didn't answer immediately. Then he said slowly, "There's no denying that the Cortezes have an enormous influence in this country—with the justice system as well as the media. But if you're concerned about the American side, don't be! We're well acquainted with the Orejuela case, and your story fills in a lot of holes. As for Luis Cortéz, the DEA has had some serious questions about him for some time now—as you're aware. They'll believe you, all right."

"And you *can* get me out of the country?" The question was a rhetorical one. Sara's only anxiety had been whether the DEA would take her unsupported word against all the influence the Cortezes could bring to bear. Now that Doug had accepted her story, that worry was gone. Then a realization struck her. "My passport! I don't have it! It's locked in Don Luis's safe. That . . . that won't make any difference, will it?"

Doug's hesitation was brief enough that she didn't notice it. "We'll see what we can do. In the meantime, we're going to need to find you a place to stay. At least for the night. Which isn't going to be so easy at this hour. I'd take you home, but I'm afraid you're right about that. What you've told me here, not to mention the speed with which you say your in-laws had the facts of last night's raid, betrays some pretty high contacts in the FELCN. And it's the FELCN that supplies our guards. I'd like to think my own are trustworthy. They've worked with me for quite some time. But they have superiors and comrades who may not be, and until we've had a chance to nail Cortéz's operation—and get you out of the country—I'd rather not take any chances at tipping them off to the fact that you've come to us. Which rules out any other place connected to the DEA as well."

Doug's fingers drummed on the steering wheel as he thought aloud. "So what does that leave us? It's too bad Histeds aren't here. I'd trust them anywhere. One of the oil crowd from the church? No, I don't know any I'd care to wake up at this hour. And they've all got servants. . . ."

He fell silent. Then he nodded abruptly. "Sure, that'll do."

Doug started the engine, reaching across Sara to snap shut the glove compartment without any further explanation. Sara didn't ask for one either. The relief of having the whole story off her chest and onto someone else's broad and responsible shoulders was overwhelming, and as her body began to relax against the comfortable contours of the padded seat, the fatigue she'd been holding off so long settled down over Sara like a fluffy, down-filled blanket. No, more like one of her grandmother's heavy quilts. Or this cumbersome woolen thing that Doug had laid over her. Solid lead pressed down on Sara's eyelids. She'd rest them for just a moment . . .

Sara didn't wake up until she felt a hand gently shaking her shoulder. The soft purr of the engine had stopped. Reluctantly, Sara dragged her eyelids open. She sat up. The rain had moderated to a drizzle again, and in the glare of their headlights, Sara could see a long, high expanse of pink. The exact shade of pink of the candy hearts that had come with her valentines back in elementary school days. A wall.

In the wall was a gate, its metal doors standing wide open to the street. But that didn't make sense because it seemed that the candy-pink expanse was marching right on across the open gateway. Then, blinking, Sara saw that this was an optical illusion and that there was actually a second wall set back about ten feet from the gate and at a slant so that a vehicle could drive in through the gate and around it without giving anyone outside a glimpse of what lay beyond the entrance.

"Good, you're awake." Doug's hand dropped from her shoulder.

Sara dragged her eyes from the neon hue of the wall. She blinked
again. A stranger was sitting beside her. From somewhere, the DEA
agent had dug out a low-brimmed hat of the sort worn by the
Argentinean *gauchos,* that country's version of the American cowboy.
The sunglasses he wore below the tilted rim were so dark Sara
wondered that he could see out of them at all. Leaning over the
back of the seat, Doug hauled up a rag of some white material and
dropped it into Sara's lap.

"Tie your hair up in that. And when we get inside, just keep
quiet and let me do the talking. In fact, just stay down right there
and out of sight. If we have to get out, keep that blanket wrapped
around you and over your face. This isn't the kind of place people
ask questions, but there's no point in giving anyone a good look."

So that was the point of the Indiana Jones disguise.

"What kind of place is it?" Sara inspected the rag in her hands
with disfavor. It looked to be a piece of a ripped-up sheet and smelled
strongly of engine oil, but she obediently tucked up her braid and
tied the cloth bandanna-style around her head. As the Land Rover
rolled forward, she peered upward through the windshield to read
the sign outlined in alternating flashes of pink and purple above the
gate. *La Bon Cherry Motel.* Below the sign, scrawled in white paint on
the open portal beside her, was a price: *Diez Bolivianos.*

"Oh, a motel. *Le Bon Cherié,*" Sara interpreted the misspelled
French. "'The Good Sweetheart'?" She glanced around, trying to
reconcile the elegance of the French name with her surroundings.
They were past the inner wall now, and a paved courtyard opened
before them. Bordering the courtyard on their right was a parking
area, roofed over and divided by cement walls to form individual
stalls. Oddly, each stall had a curtain drawn across the entrance so
that the vehicle parked inside could not be seen. The curtains were
the same brilliant pink as the outside wall, and the row of cottages
across the courtyard to their left, which some designer had fondly
imagined to resemble miniature Swiss chalets, were pink as well,
except for the burnt-orange of the roof tiles and ornate carved doors,
painted to match. It was all utterly tasteless, and Sara couldn't imagine
anyone choosing to spend good money on the place.

"It's cheap enough!" she commented to hide her distaste. Maybe
the owner was a friend of Doug's. "Ten *bolivianos*—that isn't even
two dollars."

Doug glanced across at her. "That's per hour," he said shortly.

"Per hour? You mean—?" Sara was thankful for the scant illumination that masked her burning cheeks. "I . . . I see!"

"No, I don't think you do see!"

Sara looked at Doug in surprise. The DEA agent sounded angry, and the fluorescent tubing above the nearest cottage door outlined a jaw set in an uncompromising line. But before he could say anything else, a door slammed open somewhere beyond the line of cottages. Footsteps entered the empty courtyard, and a moment later, a knock came at Doug's window.

Sara drew the Indian blanket up over her mouth as Doug rolled down the window. A girl peered in, a length of plastic stretched above her head against the rain. She couldn't have been more than thirteen or fourteen, her hair still tied back in a schoolgirl ponytail, and Sara sincerely hoped that she was the manager's daughter and had no other reason for being out at this hour of night in a place like this.

"A room for two," Doug told her briefly. A flash of red identified the bill Doug passed out the window as a one hundred boliviano note. The plastic dropped as the girl grabbed for it. "For the rest of the night."

"*Está bien.* Number nine is empty."

The girl held a key up to the window, rising on tiptoe as she did so to give Sara a look that made her glad she'd covered her face. Sara could almost hear the girl wondering what a good-looking man like the one hiding behind those sunglasses and hat was doing with such a bundled-up wreck.

Then Doug took the key, and the girl stepped back to indicate a cottage with a large gilt 9 on the door. As she scuttled away, the plastic still shielding her from the rain, Doug made a tight turn to bring the Land Rover right to the doorstep of the cottage. Handing Sara the key, he ordered her with a jerk of his head toward the cottage door, "Go right on in. I'll park the car and be there in a minute."

Dragging the heavy Indian blanket around her shoulders and over her head while she clambered down from the Land Rover wasn't an easy task. But Sara managed it without showing more than a glimpse of the torn and wet clothing underneath. Doug waited until she had turned the key in the brass doorknob before driving away. Ignoring the girl, who was still lingering halfway across the courtyard, Sara pushed open the door and fumbled for the light switch. The girl scooted back indoors as soon as the light blinked on. Maybe she was just trying to be helpful.

Sara closed the door behind her. The room was no more than the outside had led her to expect. Pink. Frilled. Overcrowded. The bed, its gilt frame peeling in spots to reveal the original olive-green shade underneath, was squeezed tight against a full living-room set upholstered in fake velvet. There was no TV or phone, but Sara spotted an open door with relief. The bathroom was surprisingly ordinary.

Doug was there when she came back out. He still looked angry, and as he fastened a safety-chain into place, he said abruptly, sweeping the shabby room with a censorious glance, "Look, I'm sorry! I don't know what I was thinking, dragging you into a place like this! But the fact is, this is the only place in Santa Cruz where a man and a woman can drive in, openly trying to hide their faces, without anyone giving it a second thought. These motels are used to clients who don't want to be recognized. It's the only place, too, where an *extranjero* can find a room—especially at this hour—without being questioned or having to show some ID. Or maybe you're not aware that at any respectable hotel, you've got to register with your passport and that a listing of all foreign guests is turned over to the police along with passport numbers and other pertinent information."

Doug ran a hand through his hair, knocking off the Indiana Jones hat and leaving the damp crop underneath standing straight up in a disheveled thatch. "There's got to be a better idea out there, but I'm afraid this was all I could think of at this hour of the morning."

Sara, standing in the bathroom door with the Indian blanket dragging around her feet, listened to his explanation with a slightly opened mouth. *He's not angry with me!* she realized, blinking drowsily. *He's angry* for *me!*

He was also very tired, she could see now in the soft gleam of the frilled and tasseled floor lamp set beside the front door. The tight lines around his mouth were fatigue, not temper, and only now did it occur to Sara that if he'd been driving home at this hour, he probably hadn't been to bed tonight either. And hadn't Nicolás said that he'd been out on a case last night as well? And yet he'd stopped to help her without hesitation.

She came forward into the room. "Please, it's okay, really. I don't mind. How could I—especially when you're doing all this to help *me* in the first place? I . . . it's a great idea, really it is! Besides, they've already got people thinking I'm a murderer. So what difference does it make if that girl or . . . or anyone else gets the wrong idea about me? I'm going to be out of this country pretty soon anyway. Only . . ."

She hesitated, the soft color again rising into her cheeks. "What about you? If someone recognizes you, or your car coming out of a place like this . . . one of your friends from the church or something . . . I mean, you're an American government official. . . . I'd hate for anyone to think . . ."

The rigidity of his jaw was relaxing by the time Sara floundered to a stop, and there was something close to a twinkle in his gray eyes as Doug said dryly, "I appreciate your concern for my reputation, Sara. But it's not necessary. One advantage of a job like mine is that any of my acquaintances who catches me coming out of a place like this is going to assume—correctly!—that I'm here on the job. As a matter of fact, that's how I know this place. We busted a Paraguayan here over in number twelve just last year, though that young lady outside wouldn't recognize me from Adam. The place changed hands after the Paraguayan fingered the owner. Back then"—his voice grew dryer—"they had a nice pistachio motif."

The comment had the effect he'd intended. Sara smiled slightly. "I guess I'd better not complain, then, about peppermint pink!"

Doug yawned hugely, stretching so that his hands touched the low ceiling. "Well, now that we have that settled, we'd better salvage what we can of the rest of the night. Sara Cortéz, I've got a lot more questions for you, but they're going to have to wait until I can think straight."

He lowered his arms to give Sara a keen look. "I hope you don't mind if I curl up in one of those chairs over there. It would defeat the purpose of this charade if that girl out there saw me driving off home five minutes after we arrived."

"Oh, no!" Sara gave a quick shudder. "I . . . I couldn't bear it if you left me alone right now. But . . ." She looked from the uncomfortable chairs and short, plush sofa to Doug's large frame. "If you don't mind, I'll take the couch. You'll never fit."

Snatching up one of the pillows off the bed, Sara hurried over to the sofa. To her relief, the DEA agent didn't argue. While she was tucking the pillow up against an arm of the sofa and dragging the Indian blanket over her, he pulled off his jacket. Sara, curling her feet, still wrapped in the remnants of her makeshift coverings, up under the blanket, noted sleepily that he was wearing a shoulder holster. He unbuckled this as he walked over to the bed, placing it and the weapon it carried—a pistol, from what she could see—on a bedside table.

Then he walked back to the door. Pausing with his hand on the light switch, he asked abruptly, "Are you sure you're going to be all right there? Do you need another blanket? Maybe something to change into or a shower before you go to bed? Or any first aid? I should have asked earlier."

Sara shook her head against the pillow. "No, I'm fine, thank you." In actuality, her dress was still damp and a little chilly under the blanket and the scrapes on her hands and knees were beginning to make themselves felt now that she no longer had to concern herself with simple survival. But she'd taken up enough of the DEA agent's hours of rest as it was, and she was tired enough that she wouldn't notice anyway, once she was asleep. The room plunged into darkness, and a moment later Sara heard a thud and then another as a pair of boots hit the floor. There was a slow creak of the bedstead and a sigh of escaping breath. Then the room settled into a silence as profound as the blackness behind her eyelids. Sara settled herself to the sleep she'd been craving for so many hours.

But it didn't come. She lay rigid under the blanket, her heart beating fast with every rumble of traffic beyond the quiet walls. Was it really all over? What if, despite all her precautions, someone had seen her and recognized her? What if that sound of an engine slowing down outside on the street was Nicolás or Don Luis—or even the police? That safety chain wouldn't hold for an instant if someone tried to break down the door.

Sara sat up suddenly, feeling for a lamp she'd seen on a small table at the end of the sofa. The light, when it came on, was a ghastly pink, filtered through a fringed lampshade, but it was immensely comforting, for all that. She looked across the room. Doug Bradford was lying on his back on top of the satin bedspread, one arm folded under his head and the other flung out toward the bedside table so that his fingertips rested on the butt of his gun, his stockinged feet hanging over the foot of a mattress that was adequate enough for the smaller Bolivians, but a good six inches too short by American standards. He must have been very weary, because he was already sound asleep, his soft breathing coming in a slow, deep rhythm, the lines of fatigue relaxed so that he looked much younger than Sara had always thought him. But even sleep didn't diminish the resolute line of his mouth or the indefinable air of competence.

There was something solid and *safe* about that sleeping figure, and Sara knew with a sudden conviction beyond reasoned logic that no one would come through that door to hunt her down as long as Doug Bradford was there. Switching off the lamp, she lay down again and snuggled back into the blanket. Without stirring and without dreams, she slept.

CHAPTER TWENTY-THREE

The room was still dark when Doug awoke, but the slant of a sunbeam sneaking through the velveteen curtains over the cottage's one window told him that the morning was well advanced. He lay still until he was certain where he was and what he was doing there. Then he unfolded his left arm from under his head so that he could see his watch. Ten o'clock. Six hours of sleep. He could have used more after the last two nights, but it was all he could afford right now.

Swinging his feet over the side of the bed, he reached for his shoulder holster and buckled it on, grimacing at the rumpled condition of his shirt. He sure could use a shower! He ran a hand over his lower face. And a shave. Picking up his boots, Doug padded across the carpet—an outdated shag that smelled of mildew—and switched on the lamp at the end of the sofa.

The candy-pink glow of the lamp fell across a huddle of blanket and cushions. The Indian blanket was pulled up high over one slight shoulder, and the rag he'd made Sara tie over her hair had slipped down to cover her face, so that the only part of her that showed was one slim hand that had slipped out from under the blanket to hang over the edge of the sofa, palm up and curled into a loose fist. Doug could not detect any movement, not even in the rhythmic rise and fall of a person breathing. In fact, Sara was so motionless that Doug found himself reaching quickly for her limp arm.

He breathed a sigh of relief between his teeth and his own pulse returned to normal when he felt her wrist, which was warm and pulsing. Then, catching sight of the angry graze below the loose grip of his thumb and forefinger, he frowned. Squatting down on his heels, he peeled her curled fingers open, muttering to himself as he saw the full extent of the raw, blood-clotted scrape. He should have insisted on checking her over last night, no matter what she'd said. His own weariness was no excuse for falling down on the job.

Well, that oversight could be remedied. But not right away. Doug released Sara's hand. Her fingers curled back up immediately over her injured palm, but she made no other movement. Switching the lamp back off, Doug stood up. The scrape was ugly, but not serious. Sara might as well sleep as long as she could. But he really needed to get to the office, to find out what had been happening outside during the hours they'd been holed up. This was probably the best time to do it. If he left now, he might even be back before she awoke.

In the dim light offered by the stray sunbeam, Doug found and retrieved his hat and sunglasses from the coffee table where he'd dropped them the night before. Locating his jacket on the back of a chair, he pulled it on. He padded over to the door before tugging on his boots and clapping on the hat. He held the sunglasses in his hand until he was ready to crack the door open.

Sara was going to need a few things before he could leave her even for a short time. Something to eat, basic toiletries, a first-aid kit, clean clothes. And he'd better leave a note so she wouldn't panic when she found him gone. Everything but the clothing he could dig out of his emergency kit in the Land Rover. The clothes would just have to wait.

The courtyard was as empty as it had been in the early hours of the morning, and most of the parking slots were now empty as well. The rain had stopped, and the sun was bright and hot, steaming off the puddles that dotted the pavement. It was far too hot for a jacket, but unless Doug wanted to advertise to the world that he was carrying a weapon, he'd have to put up with a little discomfort until he could stash his shoulder holster and change his clothes.

Doug pulled the door shut softly behind him.

A door slammed across the courtyard and a girl emerged. She was now minus the ponytail and the plastic she'd held over her head against the rain, but Doug had no difficulty recognizing the same girl who had taken his money the night before. She was carrying a broom, with which she proceeded to attack the puddles in the courtyard, spreading out the water so that they would dry faster. Doug looked her over. She was far younger than Sara, of course, but only an inch or two shorter and chunky.

Looking up and noticing that she was being watched, the girl stopped sweeping, then drifted a few feet in Doug's direction. "*Sí, señor?* Is there something that you require?"

"*Sí*, perhaps there is." Taking a sheaf of Bolivian money from his wallet, Doug leafed through the bills until a two hundred *boliviano* note lay exposed to plain view. The girl's interest perked up noticeably. She edged closer. Pulling the bill free, Doug pasted on a smile that felt ingratiating even from the inside. "I'm in need of some assistance. The young lady with me was unfortunate enough to suffer an accident to her dress last night. The rains, you understand."

The girl's eyes flitted from the cash in Doug's hand to her own reflection in his sunglasses, and her glance was so cynical and speculative that Doug's smile hardened on his lips. A kid that age shouldn't be able to look like that! But that wasn't his concern right now. He had a job to do.

Holding the bill just out of her reach, he lowered his voice to a confiding note. "Maybe you can help me. The young lady is going to need something clean to wear once she wakes up. Unfortunately, I have to get to the office so I'm not going to have time to do any shopping." He nodded toward the skin-tight jeans and tank top the girl was wearing. "But the two of you are just about the same size. If you could see your way clear to lend her a change of clothing, I would be more than grateful to buy you some new ones for yourself."

The broom shifted from one hand to the other and back again. Then the girl shrugged, leaning forward to snatch the bill from his hand. "*Claro,* why not! But such nice clothing will need more than two hundred *bolivianos* to replace."

Doug knew better than that, but he didn't argue. Peeling off another two hundred note, he handed it to the girl, then ambled over toward the Land Rover. He glanced back when he reached the curtain that hid his vehicle. The girl hadn't moved and was staring after him.

"Quickly now!" he snapped as curtly as Luis Cortéz might have addressed one of his servants. He wasn't, after all, supposed to be a nice guy here! "I don't appreciate having to wait!"

The girl scurried off. Doug waited until the office door had slammed behind her before he pushed past the curtain and opened the rear hatch of the Land Rover. He always kept some basic supplies stashed there—extra MREs, a first-aid box, tools, the blanket Sara was using, a bedroll, even a change of clothing. But today he also had the military-issue backpack he carried for lab raids or any trip into the field.

Zipping open a pouch on the outside of the pack, he dug out a hotel-size bar of soap, a tiny travel bottle of shampoo, and a trial-size tube of Colgate. She'd have to settle for her finger as a toothbrush. Doug debated taking the time for a shower and change of clothing himself. No, that would have to wait until after he found out what was going on. It wouldn't be the first time his colleagues had seen him rumpled and disheveled after an all-night job.

Doug added a couple of MREs and the first-aid kit to his pile, then dug out a plastic bag and loaded everything into it. Scrounging in another pouch for a note pad and pen, he slid these items into a jacket pocket. He slung the plastic bag over his shoulder and was about to lock the rear hatch when he paused. There was something else that Sara might need right now. Striding around to the front of the Land Rover, Doug rummaged in the glove box.

The manager's daughter—or whoever she was—had returned by the time he got back to the cottage. Taking the pile of clothing she handed him, Doug shook it out for inspection. There was a pair of jeans, somewhat worn but still in reasonable condition, a T-shirt with the insignia of a gangsta rap group across the front, and clean underwear and socks. Shoes would have to wait.

Nodding his approval, Doug passed the girl another two hundred note. "We may be staying for another day or so. You will not disturb the young lady while I am absent—not under any circumstances. She is tired and wishes to sleep. Do you understand?"

The girl shrugged her indifferent agreement. Tucking the money down the front of her tank top, she slid the DEA agent a glance that conveyed a different kind of speculation this time. "If there is anything else you should need, *señor?*"

Doug waved her off, quelling the impulse to give her a fatherly talk about looking like that at men old enough to be—well, her uncle, anyway! A moral lecture wouldn't exactly be in keeping with the character he was supposed to be playing. Still, there was something vastly wrong with a world where a girl barely into her teens had to survive in this kind of environment. Where was her father, anyway?

This world sure is one big mess! He addressed his thoughts skyward as he balanced the pile of clothes and the plastic bag in one hand while sliding the motel key into the lock with the other. *There's not a whole lot I can do to change it, either, except to do my job and clean up the bits you push into my path. Still, maybe you could send someone into that kid's life, Father. Someone who can reach her the way you know I can't right now!*

Using a booted foot to shut the cottage door behind him, Doug shifted the contents of his arms again to remove his sunglasses, then threaded his way through the dim room to the coffee table. Dumping his load, he flicked the lamp on, then stopped, his hand still on the switch.

Sara had rolled over during his absence, and the ghastly pink light now lay full across her face. Nothing could ever make Sara Cortéz ugly, but there was no denying that she was almost unrecognizable as the spotlessly groomed and well-dressed young woman he had met in their few prior encounters. Her movement had thrown off the Indian blanket, revealing the muddied and torn chiffon party dress she had worn to the Cortéz anniversary celebration. The rag around her head had come loose, and her hair had worked itself out of its braid, leaving a matted tangle around her small face. She was still sleeping the deep, tranquil slumber of an exhausted child, not even stirring under the lamplight, but her eyelids were still red and swollen, a silent reminder of the tears that had traced pale channels down her dirt-streaked cheeks the night before.

Doug's mouth tightened into a straight line. What would it be like to find out that the man you had loved and trusted with your life was actually a crook and a murderer?

His eyes fixed on Sara's unhappy young face, he prayed silently, *Father God, I know how to do my job. But I'm not so great at helping people who are hurting—and this young woman must be hurting pretty bad right now! I don't know what her relationship is with you, but I know that you love her and care about her a lot more than I could. So I just ask that you watch over her and let her feel your presence and find some of the comfort you've given me when I've needed it so badly.*

Doug blinked and pulled his eyes away from Sara. It was time to get moving before he lost the whole day. He emptied the black plastic bag onto the coffee table, making a neat stack of its contents next to the pile of clothing. Scribbling a quick note, he slipped it inside the Bible he'd taken from the glove compartment. He placed the Bible on top of the clothing. Sara was still dead to the world. Reaching over her, Doug extinguished the lamp.

As he pulled out onto the street in front of the motel, Doug made a routine scan for surveillance even as he shifted his thoughts away from Sara. As expected, he saw nothing suspicious. No cars pulling in behind him. No loiterers showing too much interest from behind their newspapers. But he made a few expert turns all the same, confirming that no one was tailing him, before taking the most direct route to the office. Setting aside just enough attention to navigate his way through the Santa Cruz traffic, he played over, step by step, the story he'd be telling Grant Major in a few minutes.

The prospect of approaching his boss wasn't entirely pleasurable. Whereas last night Doug had been buoyed by the exhilaration of having his suspicions vindicated and the pieces of a major puzzle come together, today, with a few hours sleep to stimulate his soggy brain, he could see the warning flags and the implications he'd been too tired to consider until now. Sara's story was no less compelling in the light of day, but it boiled down to the same problem as always. Evidence! Clear, prosecutable evidence! Whatever Sara had confirmed about the Cortezes' past activities, she'd admitted that Cortéz Industries—and the warehouse where she'd seen the tapestries—was clean at the moment. As for the mysterious hacienda, there were tens of thousands of country places to be found within a Cessna's flight of Santa Cruz. Without some clue as to its location, the hacienda—and the eight tons of cocaine—might as well be mythical. That is, if the Cortezes hadn't destroyed the drugs altogether by now.

No! It wasn't that easy to destroy eight tons of cocaine—certainly not overnight. And Doug was banking that the Cortezes would be reluctant to walk away from that kind of money before they were absolutely forced to. First they would try to get Sara back before she had a chance to tell her story to someone who might listen. As long as they didn't know she'd contacted the DEA—Sara's instinct had been right there—they'd sit tight and wait for developments.

Which gave Doug a little time, but brought him face to face with his other big problem: Sara herself. She wasn't safe as long as she remained within range of Luis Cortéz's long-reaching arm. But getting her out of the country and back onto American soil wasn't as simple as Doug had allowed her to believe. Especially if Nicolás Cortéz's threat last night was genuine and not just an attempt to force his wife to come home.

Doug eased the Land Rover into the faster traffic flow of the second ring. Some people—particularly those whose political education came from the gleanings of fiction—got the craziest ideas about the DEA's ability to do just about anything. In actuality, the agency was bound by as many rules and regulations as any other—especially when overseas. And while Grant Major was a good man, the best Resident-Agent-in-Charge Doug had ever served under, he was a stickler for going by the book—in this case, the DEA *Handbook,* a volume even larger than the Holy Scriptures. If it wasn't in there, you didn't do it. It was that plain and simple!

Offering DEA cooperation to an American citizen looking for witness protection from a band of cocaine traffickers might be covered under one regulation or another, but getting a girl out of the country who was accused of murder—falsely or not—and who was actively being hunted by the local authorities, was something else entirely.

He could already imagine Grant Major's pithy comments when he heard that Doug had committed their office to doing just that!

Well, Doug had endured the rough edge of Grant's tongue before without any permanent scars. And surely the RAC would understand the urgency of the matter. Besides, notwithstanding the police, who had showed up so quickly at the children's home last night, there was always hope that Nicolás was bluffing. The Cortezes were obsessed when it came to protecting their good name. If they could deal with their recalcitrant daughter-in-law quietly and without a scandal, they would. Even if it meant dumping young Ricardo's body into the Pirai River for the piranhas to dispose of.

As for evidence, at least Sara's story opened up some new lines of investigation. The first thing would be to put Kyle onto a title search for that hacienda, although, unless Luis Cortéz was very stupid —and he wasn't—it was unlikely to be listed under his family name.

Then there was the Orejuela connection to check out. Birth records might confirm Pablo Orejuela's blood relationship with the Cortéz family. More urgent would be an around-the-clock surveillance team on Luis Cortéz and his son. Airplane flights, every movement of goods in and out of their warehouse, any departure from their daily routine. Maybe a tracking device on their planes? That might be risky with a trained military pilot like Julio Vargas around, but it was worth considering.

Whatever they did would have to be discreet if they were to avoid tipping off Luis Cortéz or any of his flunkies. The last thing the DEA needed was to spook them into dumping those eight tons. The trouble was that being discreet took time, and Doug had a hunch that time was something they didn't have.

✠

Grant Major had every reason to be home on a Saturday morning, and Doug had expected to call him from the office. But when he entered the front hall, he spotted his boss at the foot of the stairs, a steaming cup in one hand. Doug's nostrils flared tentatively. "Licorice? Well, at least it beats that haystack mixture!"

"Anise tea," Grant answered complacently. "Best stuff for heartburn I've come across yet. Doesn't taste half bad either."

He turned a shrewd gaze on Doug. "You look like a candidate for a cup yourself. What's up? After last night, I figured you'd be taking the weekend off."

"Last night," Doug repeated wryly. "That's what I need to talk to you about, boss. You got a few minutes? I've had some major intel come in on the Cortéz case that you need to hear."

"The Cortéz case?" Grant paused at the foot of the stairs, his eyebrows shooting into his hairline. "I wasn't aware that there *was* a Cortéz case."

Doug refused to rise to the bait. "Just hear me out, boss. It's real this time—and big!"

Grant's foot was already on the first step. "How big?"

"Drug dealing, murder, you name it! I knew they were dirty, and it turns out I was right. For starters, you remember those two big cargoes that were hijacked a while back? Turns out it was Cortéz who took them out. It's all still in the country, too. And I know how they're planning to move it. We weren't so far off with that raid, after all. They've been playing us for suckers all this time!"

Grant turned slowly and surveyed Doug's face. The man was serious all right! But then, he would be. Luis Cortéz had never been a joking matter to Special Agent Doug Bradford.

"And you came up with all this since last night?" He couldn't keep his skepticism out of the even question. "Is this hard intel, Bradford, or some more of your speculation?"

"It's hard intel, sir! Cortéz's daughter-in-law—Nicolás's wife. She found out what her husband and his family were up to, and she wants out."

Grant grunted. "Oh, she does, does she? Well, that's gotta be a first! Never known one of these coke wives yet who didn't just shut her eyes and lap up all the luxury. Nor have I met one who would split on the family business even if they did care what was going on! Does this woman actually have a conscience, or did someone cross her the wrong way? And what is it she wants from us?"

Doug ignored the sarcastic first question and cut right to the chase. "She wants us to help her get out of the country. She's an American, and she wants to go home. She's also scared to death of Cortéz—says he'll take her out to keep her from talking. And I think she's right. If we'll help her get home, she'll give us everything she knows about their operation. And that's a lot, sir, believe me!"

"Enough to make it stick this time?" Doug had his boss's attention now.

"Well, no, not yet. But it's enough to open some interesting new lines of investigation. I'm not saying it'll be a walk-through, but I think we can get them this time, sir. If you'll just back me up on this."

Grant jerked his head, indicating that Doug should accompany him upstairs. "Okay, come on up and tell me about it, and we'll see what we can do. It's not like La Paz really needs those reports I gave up my golf game for anyway."

"Thanks, Grant. Mind if I grab a cup of coffee and something to eat? This may take awhile, and I haven't had breakfast yet." Doug didn't wait for permission. Things weren't that formal here. But he cocked an eyebrow at Grant as he turned away.

"Something for you? To go with that . . . uh, drink?"

"Smirk all you want," his boss said, unruffled. "Your time will come. But sure, bring me one of those cinnamon rolls that Ellen brought in yesterday."

Just then, the foyer door slammed open, hitting the plastered wall with a crash that made both men wince. The RAC leaned over the railing. "That you, Ellen? I thought I sent you home last night. What ever happened to a little thing called the weekend around here?"

"Just making a few Brownie points for my performance report, boss."

The administration officer kicked the door shut with a high-heeled foot, her arms loaded with an oversized handbag, a pair of bulging black plastic sacks, and a rolled-up newspaper. "Actually, I'll just be here for an hour or two. I've got to get that shortfall in the work receipts figured out before the auditors come down from La Paz on Monday."

Ellen Stevens dropped the plastic bags beside Doug. "I'm glad you showed. Saves me looking for you. Here's the rest of those clothes the church got together for the children's homes. You took the rest Sunday, didn't you? I'm afraid you're also going to have to get them on out to the kids, since Laura's out of town. You don't mind, do you?"

Without giving him a chance to answer, she brushed past him and started up the stairs after Grant Major. She paused on the first step to give Doug a motherly once-over. "Been sleeping in your clothes again, honey? What did you do, stay out all night? I thought you and Ramon were back by three!"

Doug couldn't help grinning as he picked up the bags of clothes and headed down the hall toward the kitchen. How that woman kept track of every movement "her agents" made was a mystery to all of them!

Behind him, he heard Grant ask Ellen, "That isn't *El Deber* you've got there, is it? Maybe you'd let me take a look through it when you're done."

"Go ahead and take it now," Ellen replied. "I won't have a chance to read it before lunch anyway."

Doug heard a rustle as the newspaper changed hands. He'd like a look at that paper too! There was bound to be something on the Cortezes' anniversary extravaganza last night. And maybe on Sara's disappearance, too. The wild flight through the crowd she'd described was bound to have aroused some interest in the reporters there to cover the event.

And if Nicky-boy was serious about siccing the police on Sara, he added grimly as he reached for a clean mug. *Though it's a little early for that to be hitting the streets.*

It wasn't.

"Bradford! Get your rear up here–*now!*"

Doug had just set down the coffee pot and was rooting in the fridge for the cinnamon rolls, when Grant Major's roar reached the kitchen. It was never the most positive sign when his boss called him "Bradford," especially in that tone of voice. Abandoning his coffee and the rolls, he jogged quickly down the hall and up the stairs to the RAC's office.

Grant Major wasn't a profane man, but he was cutting loose a few choice phrases when Doug entered his office. He slapped the newspaper down on the desk and spun it around to face Doug.

"What is this, Bradford?" he demanded, stabbing a thick forefinger at the banner headline.

Doug picked up the paper and shook out the front page. Sara gazed up at him from beneath a bold, black headline. *Homicide Mars Cortéz Anniversary. American Daughter-in-Law Shoots Lover and Disappears.* The photo was a good one, taken in the dress she'd been wearing last night, no doubt by one of the society photographers who flocked to such events. The fixed smile was there, the lifted chin, and the sadness around the eyes that a casual observer would never notice. The *El Deber* staff must have been up all night resetting the newspaper for this.

"Just reassure me of one thing, Bradford!" Grant demanded with deceptive calmness. "This isn't the girl you're wanting us to get out of the country, right? Your great new intel source on the Cortezes?"

"Yes, that's her," Doug admitted, skimming through the headlines with growing anger. "But there isn't a word of truth in this, believe me, boss! That's what I was going to tell you about. It's all a frame. Nicolás Cortéz killed the kid, not the girl. Then they set the girl up to take the rap because she knows about their drug operation and was planning on coming to us with it!"

"A frame, is it? And who did you get that from? The girl? The same young woman that half the country is hunting down for murder?

Read the article, Bradford! They've got her cold on this, with a whole handful of eyewitnesses who actually saw her shoot the guy! And they aren't all Cortezes, either."

Grant's blood pressure was visibly rising again. "For your information, Bradford, Luis Cortéz was in to FELCN headquarters just a couple weeks back. I know you've never liked the guy, but he expressed a very sincere concern over what drugs are doing to the youth of this country. And he backed that concern with a donation large enough to put new uniforms on half the underpaid police force of this city. The man's a personal friend of the president, for Pete's sake! Businessman of the year, you name it! And for all your digging, you have yet to come up with a single concrete piece of evidence that links him to drug trafficking. Not in the past. Not now. So you tell me, Bradford! Why should we take the word of this girl"—he gestured toward the newspaper—"a girl who's got every reason to lie her teeth out if that'll con us into helping her slip past the legitimate authorities of this country—over the eyewitness account of not one, but five . . . count 'em, Bradford, *five*, of Santa Cruz's most solid citizens?"

"Because they're all as guilty as sin!" Doug snapped, tossing the newspaper down on the desk. "And you know it, Grant! Let me guess who the five upstanding citizens were. Let's see . . . besides Luis and Nicolás Cortéz, I'd be willing to bet that the other three are Luis Cortéz's two sons-in-law and his personal guard. Am I right?"

Grant Major settled back in his seat. "And just how did you know that?"

"Grant, here are those work fund reports you were asking for. They're ready except for your initials." Ellen Stevens drifted in the open office door. She didn't seem to notice the tension between the two men, which was no reflection on her powers of observation. Personalities got a little hot around here at times, and the administration officer had learned not to take seriously a shouting match that could end in a new plan of operation five minutes later.

"What's all the hollering about, guys? I can hear you clear down the hall!" Dropping the forms on the desk, she glanced over the RAC's shoulder. "Why—didn't I see that girl at church a few weeks back?"

Snatching up the paper, she studied the photo on the front page with avid interest. "Sure, that's Sara Cortéz! You remember her, Doug. She came to that barbecue at your house. In fact, didn't you give her a ride home?"

Grant shot Doug a sharp glance. "So! You're acquainted with the girl, Bradford. You didn't tell me that part!"

"Barely," Doug answered shortly. "Just enough so she thought of me when she found herself running for her life and with the intel for a major drug op in her head."

Ellen was shaking her head over the headlines. "Oh, I can't believe this is true! She seemed like such a nice girl. She's even been helping at the orphanage. Did you know that, Doug? Laura Histed told me. Laura says she's great with the kids. I'm sure Doug's got to be right, Grant. There's got to be some mistake. Sara wouldn't kill anyone!"

"Thanks for the vote of confidence, Ellen!" Doug said dryly. Turning back to the RAC, he added with a quietness he didn't feel, "We do have more than the girl's word, if you'd give me two minutes. And as far as lying, why don't you just talk to her yourself and see what you think! Come on, Grant. When have I ever steered you wrong?"

"Plenty! And I seem to remember the same name being involved!"

Grant caught himself short. He wasn't being fair, and he knew it. The Cortéz raid debacle had caught everyone in the office as flatfooted as it had Bradford. He himself had seen the same evidence, after all, and he'd been the one to authorize the operation, even if it had been Doug who'd put it all together. It wasn't as though it had been the first time an op had gone bad—nor would it be the last. It was just that the Cortéz raid had been more high-profile than most.

He sighed, rubbing a hand over his woolly scalp. "Okay, Doug, give me what you have!"

Doug accepted the unspoken apology as it was intended. "Yes, sir. For starters, just take a look at the victim's name in that article. You remember Operation Motacusal?"

Doug gave a quick rundown of Sara's story, adding in what he knew of the Orejuela case and his and Ramon's own involvement with Ricardo. Then he covered the data that had surfaced on Julio Vargas. He left out only two things—Sara's arrival on his doorstep last night and where she was now. That information could wait until it was needed. Grant's only reaction to his report was an occasional grunt, but Doug could tell he was making an impression.

"Sure, I remember Orejuela," he admitted when Doug had finished. "Okay, I'll concede the possibility that the girl might be telling the truth."

He raised a quick hand before Doug's response made it out between his teeth. "Fine, so maybe she *is* telling the truth. I've never denied that Luis Cortéz might be dirty." Grant chose to disregard the sudden throat clearing from the other side of the desk. "All I've ever asked is that you get me some proof that will stand up in court. Which we still don't have. Oh, sure, we can follow up on these leads. Maybe we'll even get lucky. But as for this Sara Cortéz, I'm not sure what you're asking here."

Tilting his chair back so that the front legs were off the ground, Grant formed a steeple with his fingertips. Doug recognized the habitual gesture, which usually occurred when the RAC was about to make an unpleasant point.

"The girl's facing criminal charges, remember? She's got the local authorities after her and even Interpol, according to the paper. Not to mention that Cortéz is offering a hefty reward for information leading to the girl's arrest. And however much we might personally sympathize or feel she's been wrongly accused, we don't have one shred of evidence that she's innocent and that these men are lying. So what are you expecting me to do? Our business here is to stop drug traffickers, not to get involved in the personal problems of American civilians, however worthy they might be. That's what they've got their consulate representative for."

Grant shook his head regretfully but firmly. "No, it looks to me like this is a case for the State Department, not the DEA."

That his summation was just what Doug had predicted didn't make it any more palatable. "And what's the embassy going to do?" he demanded. "They're not going to get her out of the country! They've got more rules and regulations than *we* do, and the way they move would make a snail look like Speedy Gonzales."

Ellen Stevens had been listening with patent fascination. The two agents' conversation might have been strictly classified as private, but the open office door was a standard invitation that anyone was welcome, and the two men hadn't asked her to leave. Nor was she going to offer. This was too enthralling. Besides, her security clearance was as high as their own, wasn't it?

"So why can't they just stick her on a diplomatic flight—or even one of our own helicopters or something—and fly her out?" she interjected. "Isn't that what they did when that State Department johnny—what was his name?—was accused of using diplomatic connections for trafficking Inca artifacts a while back? I seem to remember they had him on the first flight home. And he was facing criminal charges too! It was all over the news here."

The two men exchanged a wry look.

"Rogers worked for the embassy—" Grant began.

"Yeah, remind me, Ellen, to give you a lesson sometime on the legal rights of the average American civilian overseas," Doug added, with unnecessary irony, the administration officer believed. "Oh, maybe there was a time twenty years back or so when your run-of-the-mill ex-pat could wave his American passport around a Third World country and expect special privileges. But not anymore!

"Take right here in Santa Cruz. We've got an American citizen now who's been in the local jail for months! He isn't even accused of a crime—except maybe lending money to the wrong crowd. The man came down here to strike it rich, invested all his capital with some local agro company, then lost it when they absconded with the dough. So he squawked to the police, like any good citizen would, and the next thing he knew, the locals had filed a lawsuit against him for slander—and he was the one who ended up in jail!

"The locals never did present any charges against him. The proofs were too overwhelmingly on his side. But that didn't matter. You see, the way the legal system works around here, you aren't innocent until proven guilty. You're guilty until proven innocent. And without that stolen money, the poor guy can't even afford a lawyer or the paperwork to have the case dismissed. Our consulate has been trying for weeks to get the guy out on bail while the thing is settled. But the judges won't budge. Personally, I think they're enjoying the opportunity to show an American who's boss!"

Doug turned back to face the RAC. "No, what I was thinking of was more—well, of course, Cortéz is going to have the police watching every border crossing and airport. But there's a lot of jungle between here and Paraguay, or even Brazil, and if the drug dealers can get across, so can we. Maybe even on one of those trafficking routes we've hit. It's a problem that she doesn't have a passport, but if we can get her to the embassy in Asunción or Brasilia—"

"What?" Grant's chair crashed back onto the floor, his steepled fingertips flying apart. "Are you crazy, Bradford? You're seriously suggesting that this office mount a covert operation to sneak a wanted criminal over the border? And away from the police force of a friendly democracy that is also one of our strongest allies in the drug war we're supposed to be conducting around here! I can just see the headlines! 'Americans Interfere with Bolivian Justice! DEA Caught Red-handed!' And don't think it wouldn't come out! Because it always does! Oh, no, Bradford! We've worked long and hard to get an extradition treaty with Bolivia. The ink's hardly dry on it, and we're just now working on getting our first major trafficker out of here and onto U.S. soil for prosecution. If they catch us trying to short-cut their legal process by smuggling out an accused felon, they'll pull the rug out from under that treaty so fast, it'll take us years to get another!"

Grant shook his head adamantly. "And what if we did get her out? They'd have every right to demand that she return to stand trial. The Cortezes wouldn't even have to buy them off this time! Murder is one of the crimes listed under our treaty with them. No, I'm sorry about the girl, Doug, but I can't allow you to drag this office into anything that will jeopardize our position here in Bolivia. If you want to help this . . . this young woman, then tell her to turn herself in to the proper authorities."

Doug rolled his eyes and rocked back in his chair. "Okay, so maybe the legal system here isn't the best," Grant continued, "but we can ask the State Department to keep an eye on the situation, get her a good lawyer, maybe lean on things a bit. They'll make sure she gets a fair shake."

"A fair shake?" Doug leaned over the desk, his palms hitting down with a crack against the polished wood. "You know better than that, Grant! When the Cortezes are controlling the entire police investigation? Or didn't your newspaper tell you that Colonel Encinas from the PTJ is a close family friend? As for our esteemed State Department, if they can't get one old man released on bail, what are they going to do for Sara Cortéz with a pile of phony evidence stacked a mile high against her? She'd be rotting in jail for the rest of her life! Which wouldn't be long, since they're trying to kill her! Or maybe you'd forgotten that!"

Grant's flinty gaze didn't give an inch. "We'll pass your concern on to the State Department, whose competence I'm sure you're grossly underestimating, by the way! If the girl calls you again—I assume she *was* going to contact you again?"

"She didn't say, sir," Doug said woodenly. Which was true, because *he* would be contacting *her*. If Grant wanted to assume that Sara had contacted him by phone, this wasn't the time to tell him otherwise.

Grant eyed him sharply, but let it pass. "Well, if she contacts you again, tell her to give the American consul a call and place herself under that lady's protection."

With a shrug, Doug lifted his hands from the desk. "Sure. If she contacts me again, I'll pass on your advice. But she'd be foolish to take you up on it, and I'll tell her that, too."

"That was an order, not a suggestion," Grant said sternly. "As for you, Bradford, it's clear to me that you are too personally involved in this case. I want you out! Any further investigation, I'm handing over to Ramon. You turn over what you've got to him. Including a full contact report on this girl. And don't let me find out you're playing a lone hand behind my back. This one's going strictly by the book from now on! Do you understand?"

Doug's only answer was the tightening of his mouth. Grant considered his best agent critically—the inflexible set of his jaw, an expression that could only be described as mulish, the steely determination in the gray eyes. But he met Doug's unyielding gaze with an equal determination in his own.

"Douglas, you're a good man. But you're walking a mighty thin line here. May I remind you that you've sworn an oath of duty to this office. And that means following the rules, whether you agree with them or not! Don't think personal friendship puts you above discipline. Penalties are pretty stiff in our business for a man who won't obey orders! I'd hate to think one of my agents would be foolish enough to risk his entire career over a girl he's met—what, twice? Three times?"

"My career!" Doug bit off the word. Then, after a moment, he said slowly, "Tell me, Grant. If you were"—he started to say "me," then modified it—"in this hypothetical situation you're suggesting here, and it was *your* career you were worrying about. And you knew . . . oh, not just conjecture or speculation—you *knew* that following these precious rules of yours would mean a miscarriage of justice, maybe even a death sentence for an innocent person. . . . What would you do with that handbook of yours?"

This time it was Grant who was silent. Doug let out a short, hard laugh. "I thought so! Maybe I know you better than you do yourself, *sir!* Now, if you don't mind, I've had a hard couple of nights carrying out my duty to this office, and if you don't object, I'm going to take the rest of my weekend off!"

Spinning around on his heels, he strode across the room. His hand was on the door when he swung back around. "Just give me this much, boss. If anyone asks, Sara's never contacted this office, okay? *Anyone*—her in-laws, the police, even the State Department itself. If you can't give the girl a hand, at least don't help put a noose around her neck."

"I know my job, Bradford!" Grant said stiffly. "I've been keeping the affairs of informants confidential since long before you were in diapers, and I'm quite capable of grasping the need to keep from tipping Cortéz off to the fact that we've learned about his dirty little game. You just go make your report, and let me worry about this case."

Doug left with an abrupt nod. As the door slammed behind

him, Ellen Stevens turned on her boss, mouth open. Grant raised his hand. There was something about his expression that wasn't as severe as she'd expected. "No, don't say anything! In fact, I don't want to hear another word about this anywhere. This conversation has just been ruled classified. And that's an order!"

✠

Doug left the RAC's office satisfied that the Cortezes wouldn't be learning Sara's whereabouts from the DEA. If only his boss weren't so hard-nosed about everything else! He grabbed a cinnamon roll as he passed through the kitchen, but decided to forego the coffee. There was no point in hanging around here any longer. He'd make his report like the good little agent his boss had ordered him to be. But not now. Right now he was heading home for a well-deserved hot shower—and some hard thinking!

Retrieving Ellen's clothing bags from where he'd dropped them in the kitchen, Doug headed for the back door. His footsteps echoed along the empty corridor. Then his sharp ears caught a low murmur ahead. The place wasn't so empty after all.

Turning the corner, he stopped in an open doorway. Ramon Gutierrez was standing beside his desk, the pieces of the M-16 he was cleaning lined up neatly in front of him. The voice belonged to Kyle Martin, who was sprawled out in Ramon's swivel chair, his long legs propped up on a footlocker. It *would* be these two! The other agents, all married with small children, were where they should be on a Saturday morning with no urgent cases looming—home with their families. Doug didn't need the sight of the *El Deber* that Kyle was reading aloud to know that the news had preceded him.

The intelligence officer lowered the paper as Doug stepped into the office. "So, what were all the fireworks? We could hear Chief Honcho bellowing clear down here!" Without giving Doug a chance to answer, he rustled the newspaper. "Have you seen this? This *is* the young lady you asked me to run through the files a while back, isn't it? Who'd have ever thought from that spotless profile that she'd be capable of shooting a guy!"

Doug kicked the door shut behind him, dropping the bags he was hauling. "She didn't shoot him!"

"Oh, really! And who told you that? The girl?" Kyle's and Ramon's voices overlapped in chorus, but their eyes held more curiosity than disbelief. Doug sat down on the corner of the footlocker, shoving

Kyle's feet to the floor, and told them the same story he'd just told his boss. The two agents, who were both aware of Doug's encounter with Sara after the security seminar, listened with rapt attention and satisfying noises of incredulity.

"Well, what a stuffed shirt!" Kyle exploded when Doug had finished. "So Major really thinks you're supposed to hang the girl out to dry?"

"Hey, don't blame Grant," Doug said quickly. "He's got the good of the whole office to be thinking about here—not just one case or one girl. And he's right, I guess, technically. I mean, I was a cop once myself, and I've got to admit that if some bunch of foreigners had tried to interfere in the course of a police investigation, and on *our* soil, or harbor a criminal suspect—well, we'd have had every right to throw the book at them. And we'd have done it, too, diplomatic immunity or not."

Kyle made a rude noise. Doug ignored it. "Anyway, he's ordered me off the case. It's yours now, Ramon. I'll get the contact report to you as soon as I get a minute to type it up. Kyle can get you the rest. You might want to check on that hacienda. Maybe put a watch on the Cortezes and their planes. You know what to do, only be discreet about it, okay? If they get even the slightest suspicion that Sara's been talking to us, we'll never get near them again. I don't need to tell you guys that it's now or never if we're ever going to catch these suckers. And"—he paused to slide a sideways glance at Ramon—"I know Grant's pretty adamant that I stay out of this, but you *will* keep me updated on what you find out! I'll give you a call if any more data comes in."

The two agents' eyes met in perfect understanding. Ramon's thin lips curved in a grin that would have looked hungry on a wolf. "You bet, man! You can count on me, *mano!*"

"And all this while I was sleeping!" Kyle added with disbelief, missing the interplay between the two men in the process. "It's like a plot for a book or something! The dastardly villains. A murder. A beautiful damsel in distress."

"Who happens to be married!" Doug broke into his fantasies dryly.

"Oh! Yeah!" Kyle's hopes were dashed. "So where *is* the fair damsel, anyway? You can't tell *me* that you left her without making arrangements to keep in touch! Or did you stash her somewhere you haven't told Chief Honcho upstairs?"

A dead silence settled over the room. Ramon busied himself cleaning his already impeccably clean fingernails with a letter opener that had once been a switchblade from the backstreets of L.A. After a moment, he counseled Kyle softly, "Hey, *mano!* Don't ask the man so many questions! And maybe you won't get told no lies!"

✠

Doug was encouraged as he tossed the bags of clothing into the back of the Land Rover and drove away from the DEA office. It felt good to know he had friends he could count on. But now he had to decide where to go next. And he didn't just mean home!

He tightened his hands on the wheel. He wasn't angry at Grant, though he had been when he'd slammed out of his office. As he'd told Kyle, he understood the RAC's position only too well. Unfortunately. Despite the acrimonious exchanges they'd had on the subject, Doug knew good and well that Resident Agent-in-Charge Grant Major held no brief for whatever position and influence the Cortezes wielded in this country. Nor for what the media—local or otherwise —had to say about his department. As evidence, Doug had the fact that he himself was still around despite the Cortezes' efforts to have him thrown out of Bolivia.

On the other hand—and this is the point Grant was always trying to pound into his head—you couldn't get too far working in this country if you were going to antagonize the very people who ran the place. If there was one lesson the RAC had taught Doug, it was that you had to pick your battles. The Drug Enforcement Administration was an equal-opportunity law enforcement agency, and they cared little how wealthy or powerful their targets might be by local standards. But if you were going to hit someone who had the clout to hit back, you'd better make sure you could win. It was like back home when he'd been a young beat cop with the Miami PD. No one asked a lot of questions if you considered it necessary to kick in the door of a downtown Miami flophouse. Kicking down the mayor's door, though, would be something else. It wasn't that you couldn't do it. But you'd better have plenty of "just cause," as the legal establishment termed it, and be willing to stake your career on it.

And that was the rub here. They didn't have just cause. Not yet. And maybe they never would—unless something broke open in the next week or two. And as long as that was the case, he'd been unrealistic to expect Grant to risk his own position and that of the entire DEA office by collaborating on something that was beyond doubt illegal by any standard of international law.

So where did that leave Sara?

Rather, where did it leave him? Doug didn't regret for a moment having helped her, but there was no denying that he'd opened up a far larger can of worms than he'd counted on when he'd scooped Sara Cortéz off the pavement last night. And the question Grant had posed was a real one, made by someone who had his best interests at heart. A government agent was supposed to uphold the law, not break it, and Grant was right that there was little future for an agent who defied a direct order from his boss. Was he prepared to risk a career he enjoyed and hoped to spend the rest of his life at for a woman who had no real claim on him at all?

Did he have any choice?

The newspaper photo of Sara, with her brave smile and terror-haunted eyes, swam between Doug and the steering wheel. Maybe he *was* underestimating the State Department's competence. But Grant was underestimating the ruthlessness of Luis Cortéz. Had he forgotten that this man had already engineered the helicopter rescue of Pablo Orejuela and then had him killed to keep him from revealing his link to the Cortéz family? The very speed with which the senior Cortéz had seized onto his son's impulsive stupidity—how could you call it anything less?—in shooting young Ricardo, and the sheer brilliance of his tactical use of that disastrous mishap to neutralize Sara's escape, showed an adversary more formidable than even Doug had considered.

Sure, the easiest course of action would be to follow Grant's advice. Tell Sara, "Thanks for the intel, but there's nothing I can do," and then drop her off on the steps of the new American consular office over in Equipetrol and hope for the best. It was a decision for which no one would fault him. After all, he'd done what he could to help, and his boss had the facts straight. Dealing with American citizens in legal difficulties was the bailiwick of the State Department, not the DEA.

Except he wouldn't give a plugged nickel for Sara's life once Luis Cortéz found out where she was. Which would be just as long as it took for the American consul to hear Sara's story and call up the chief of police. That dear lady was an even greater stickler for following the book than Grant Major.

But every oath Doug had ever taken, whether as a policeman or in government service, dealt first of all with justice. The U.S. Department of Justice. That's what the government institution he worked for was called. And if the day ever came when he would even consider putting his own best interests and career security ahead of the life of an innocent person who had turned to him for help, that would be the day he turned in his badge. Grant could argue all he wanted that Sara wasn't his responsibility. But sometimes you didn't choose your responsibilities. They chose you! And somehow, in the weeks since he'd first met her hostile gaze across the Co-op school pavilion, Sara Cortéz had become his responsibility. No harm would come to her as long as he could do anything about it, and that was all there was to it!

"Okay, so what's our tactical situation?" he asked himself aloud as he jolted over the first speed bump into Las Palmas. He didn't like the answer. Sara was safe only as long as no one could find her. And she couldn't stay where she was for long. The motel had been his best option for last night, but sooner or later—and he'd better figure on *sooner* with Luis Cortéz involved—it would occur to someone to check the motels and fringe *residencias* that were known to wink at a guest's ID. And though most motel owners were notoriously reluctant to discuss the comings and goings of their clients, they were even more reluctant to give the police an excuse to sniff around their operation. They would cooperate. Which meant that Sara had to be moved—and fast.

And then what? Doug had never reckoned on having a fugitive on his hands indefinitely. His initial thinking had been simple:

1. Get Sara's testimony.
2. Use her testimony to hit Luis Cortéz.
3. Turn her over to the proper American authorities.
4. Let the State Department worry about getting her home.
5. Offer to pay for her ticket out of his own pocket if State chose to be tightwads.

A day or two at the most, and Sara Cortéz would be safely gone.

Well, that plan was scuttled now—thanks to Luis Cortéz's rapid action and Grant Major's decree. Somehow, he had to come up with a sanctuary where Sara could lie safe and undiscovered until he could find a way out of this dilemma. Which wasn't going to be easy. Where was he supposed to find a safe haven in this city full of eyes and ears?

Doug pulled up in front of the guardhouse that protected his home. He offered the guards no explanation as to where he'd been all night. That was none of their business, and they wouldn't ask. Slinging Ellen's bags over his shoulder, he headed indoors. Maybe he should just bring Sara here. If he parked the Land Rover inside, Sara could get indoors without being seen by the guards. And he had no servants except for a twice-a-week cleaning girl, who'd be glad for a vacation as long as it was paid.

Doug rejected the idea almost as quickly as he'd considered it.

The guards didn't usually enter his home, but they did carry keys to run a security check, if necessary, and they had use of the bathroom in the maid's quarters at the back of the property. They'd have to know someone was in his house. It wasn't that he didn't trust them. The same contingent had been alternating shifts for more than two years now, and he knew each man well. But money did strange things to people, and the $10,000 reward Luis Cortéz was offering for information on Sara's whereabouts was an awfully big temptation for someone who made less than $200 a month. It was better to not test their loyalty too far.

Besides, continued contact between himself and Sara was not such a good idea. In fact, it was downright dangerous. Doug was not forgetting that it had been Sara's contact with him at the security seminar—brief though it had been—that had precipitated this entire situation. And both Cortezes had heard her threat to go to the DEA. Doug would likely be one of the first people to undergo scrutiny as Luis Cortéz searched for his missing daughter-in-law. If he wasn't being watched already!

Laying a change of clothing out on his bed, Doug walked into the bathroom to turn on the shower. No, he'd have to be very careful. He was probably safe enough so far. There was no way the Cortezes could have tailed him last night on the job—nor would they have any idea of his chance encounter with Sara. And any inquiry about his whereabouts would simply confirm that he'd been out all night on a case.

But from this moment forward, he'd have to assume that Luis Cortéz had him under surveillance—whether at home, the office, or both. Consequently, Doug needed to get Sara as far away from himself as possible. In fact, for Sara's safety, it was imperative that anyone digging into Doug's affairs would find him going about his life and job as publicly and normally as possible. Luis Cortéz couldn't be sure that Sara had contacted him, and it would be up to Doug to convince him that she hadn't.

Doug grimaced as another crucial matter came to mind: The contact report Grant had ordered him to write. Falsifying a report had to be one of the quickest crash-landings there was for ending a law enforcement career. Not that he planned on lying, but there were details about last night that he had no intention of adding to the DEA's official file on this case. The same things he'd left out of his oral report. Namely, how he'd picked up Sara Cortéz and where she was now—not to mention, of course, what he planned to do with her. Those files could find their way far beyond the local office, and despite the half-promise he'd gotten from Grant, until he found some way out of this mess, he had no intention of allowing knowledge of Sara's whereabouts to go any further than between his own two ears.

Well, that might be one more nail for Grant Major to hammer into Doug's professional coffin, but he'd just have to deal with the issue when the time came. Which reduced his problems to only three. First—find Sara a place to stay where she would be safe, and away from him, for as long as it took to resolve this situation. Second— figure out some way to get Sara out of the country and back to the United States without involving the American government or leaving her stuck with an unresolved homicide charge on her record. Third— find enough evidence to arrest Luis Cortéz before he managed to move those eight tons of cocaine across the border. Complicating these problems was his need to accomplish everything without drawing attention to himself—and without stepping over the line that Grant Major had drawn in the sand.

And with that, Doug came to a dead end. He hadn't the slightest idea where to begin. As he padded across the room to pull on his clothes, he did what had become his habit when he was perplexed or troubled. He turned to the only one he knew who was more than capable of handling the situation.

"Well, Lord, you can see I'm kind of in a mess here! I'm not quite sure if this is something I've gotten myself into or whether it's something you've brought into my life for your own purpose. But I really don't see where I could have done anything different, and— sure as shootin'—no one but you could have dropped Sara into my path like that last night. So I've got to believe this is your doing and that you have a plan for all of this. Either way, I need your guidance, because the truth is, I haven't the slightest idea where to go next."

Doug continued to pray as he moved around the house, his hands busy with the supplies he was packing up. It had been almost eight years now since a pretty and very determined young social worker named Julie Gates had dragged the undercover cop who kept sticking his nose into her caseload of troubled teens to a Sunday evening service at her small neighborhood church. Doug had gone with initial cynicism, but he'd returned repeatedly in the weeks and months that followed, oddly drawn to these people who took the Bible so seriously and yet welcomed a rather profane young law officer into their midst with a warmth he'd never expected.

Three months later, Doug and Julie had married in that same church. By then he had found what he'd been looking for ever since his rocky teenage years, when his parents had split up and he'd been forced to watch the Arizona ranch that had supported three generations of Bradfords get sold in the bitter divorce settlement that followed. He'd discovered and embraced a personal relationship with the God of the universe, who cared enough for Doug Bradford and this whole messed-up world to come into it himself in the person of Jesus Christ.

Still, Doug had always been more prone to action than prayer. Family devotions had been Julie's department. It wasn't until those months after all he'd held dear had been ripped away, that Doug had learned to fall on his knees and cry out to God—until now prayer had become so much a part of his life that at times it seemed he had only to open his eyes a little wider to see the Friend whose presence he could feel so plainly.

"I guess what I'm really afraid of here is that I'll screw the whole thing up—and maybe get someone hurt, too—by following my own crazy ideas and not yours, Lord. So I pray that you'll shed a little light down my path and show me where to go from here. What I'd really like to ask is that you drop some real big piece of intel—maybe that helicopter or the location of that hacienda—into my lap so I can nail that sleazeball Cortéz and get Sara's life—not to mention my own—back on track before things blow sky high around here. But I guess you know better than I do what you're wanting to do here, so I'll just ask that you work this whole thing out somehow according to your will and your glory. And since I can be a little deaf at hearing what you're telling me, I'd ask that you make it clear enough that even a hardheaded guy like me can be sure it's *your* will and not my own."

No brilliant ideas immediately sprang to mind, but a gradual calm began to settle over the churning of his brain. The God who could keep the universe in balance was in control, even if Doug wasn't. As to his prayer, he realized that he knew *exactly* where to go from here. Back to the motel and Sara. After that, he'd just have to trust that God would make clear the next step before he had to take it.

Doug zipped shut his overnight bag. If he had no idea what was up ahead, at least he'd be prepared! Grabbing a spare travel bag from the storeroom, he tossed in a new toothbrush and a fresh bar of soap. To that he added an unopened bottle of shampoo, some disposable razors he'd received in a care package from the States and wouldn't be caught dead using, a towel and washcloth, and a brush that one of the church ladies must have left at his house after the last barbecue.

What else would a woman need? For sure, more clothes than the kid at the motel had supplied, but acquiring another few outfits would be difficult. It was likely that by now Luis Cortéz had established some kind of monitor on his movements. Doug was an expert at shaking a tail—and would follow his usual set of cautions on the way back to the motel—but to wander around town looking for women's clothing would be just plain foolishness.

Wait a minute! What was he thinking? He had clothes enough to spare right here! Doug loped into the guest room, where he'd just added the two plastic bags from Ellen Stevens to a waist-high mound. The clothing in those sacks wasn't just for small children. Pastor Sam had announced at church last week that women's and men's clothing were also needed for the older teens (and, no doubt, some of the workers) at the children's homes. And Sara was a slim little thing. There ought to be something in those bags that would fit her.

So on top of everything else, now I'm stealing from the poor! Doug told himself ironically as he tore open a plastic bag and then another.

Well, he'd add his own economic contribution to make up for it. He was grateful to find what he needed at the bottom of the third bag. Another pair of jeans, a simple corduroy skirt that looked as though it would fit, a couple of tops, a faded but warm and serviceable sweatshirt, and another T-shirt—which was decorated with cutesy flowers, but was still a marked improvement over the gangsta rap shirt the girl at the motel had provided. Nothing fancy, but then Sara wasn't going to be hitting the town anywhere.

Shaking out the worst of the wrinkles, Doug folded the clothing into the travel bag, adding on top two pairs of flat sandals and a pair of *chinelas*—those plastic flip-flops common to bathers and *campesinos*.

"I may be taking off for the weekend with a friend," Doug answered the mildly inquisitive glance of the guards as he lifted the two travel bags into the back of the Land Rover. "It isn't for sure yet, so if it turns out I'm coming back, I'll call and let you know."

Doug's surveillance of his surroundings was a lot more thorough this time as he drove away from the house. And, as usual, when you started looking for possibilities, the quiet street suddenly seemed crowded with suspicious characters. A beggar stopping his shuffling way down the street to watch the Land Rover go by. A street sweeper whisking busily at the cobblestones halfway down the block. A pair of older youths loitering on the corner. Neighborhood teens hanging out—or something else? A policeman in olive green, standing under the Las Palmas Country Club sign, swiveling his gaze to follow Doug's slow jounce over a speed bump. Any, or all—or none—of these characters could be following his departure with overly curious eyes, or digging out a cell phone as soon as the Land Rover was around the corner.

Doug didn't bother to speculate. The procedures for dealing with these circumstances were so familiar that they were almost automatic. Turning out of Las Palmas, he drove in a straight line long enough to give a tail time to pick him up. Then he began to turn at random, one eye on his rearview mirror. There were a couple of possibilities that seemed to be sticking with him. When two more leisurely turns failed to lose a white Toyota Corolla with an easily identifiable dent in the front bumper, Doug decided it was time to shake the tail. The sheer chaos of the traffic helped. Accelerating as he came up on the second ring, Doug sped through an intersection so close to an oncoming gravel truck that he found he'd been holding his breath when he came out on the other side.

Doug glanced in his rearview mirror. The station wagon had skidded to a stop almost under the wheels of the gravel truck. Now it was trapped as the heavy load rolled ponderously through the intersection, followed by a solid line of vehicles that had been held up behind it. Doug turned the Land Rover in the direction of the motel, keeping to the unpaved side streets where few other cars cared to jolt through the ruts. Despite his precautions, the thought of driving the Land Rover into the motel in plain light of day didn't thrill him, and he didn't relax his vigilance, keeping his gaze flickering constantly from the road to his mirrors.

When he saw no signs of another tail in the remaining distance to the motel, he drove swiftly through the gate and pulled into his parking stall. Then, just to be sure, he sat for a full five minutes—timed precisely on his wristwatch. When no other vehicle or person followed him through the gate, he reached for his hat and sunglasses and climbed out. Leaving the two travel bags in the back of the Land Rover, he drew the curtain across the back bumper and walked briskly across the courtyard. A door slammed open at the tap of his footsteps, but the girl, recognizing a paid-up customer, didn't bother to come out.

Cottage number nine looked even more tawdry under the unforgiving brilliance of the midday sun than it had by moonlight, its candy-pink exterior chipped and peeling. Doug's steps slowed as he approached. He'd been gone for more than two hours. Would Sara be awake yet? And how was she going to respond to this latest setback? The news he was bringing was hardly what she would be expecting, and though she'd shown exceptional courage and presence of mind until now, it was going to be a real blow to find that she was trapped indefinitely in Bolivia, with even her own government ranged against her.

Well, there wasn't going to be any easy way to do this, so he'd just have to do the best he could. And from what he knew of Sara, she'd rather have the unvarnished facts than any attempt to play down the gravity of her situation.

Doug dug from his pocket the heavy gilt key with its ornate #9 embossed on the grip. His hand was still on the doorknob when he heard from inside the low, despairing sounds of her grief.

CHAPTER TWENTY-FOUR

Sara stirred. Without opening her eyes, she groped sleepily for the pillow that had slid out from under her head. It was oddly hard and slippery as she tucked it back under her cheek. The blanket around her shoulders felt heavy and hot. Pushing it away with her free hand, she rolled over.

And fell off the sofa.

The crash jolted her awake. Untangling her legs from the blanket, Sara pulled herself back onto the sofa, unsure for a moment what she was doing sleeping in the sitting room or why she felt so stuffy-headed and sore. She turned her head stiffly to take in the dim, unfamiliar shapes of the furniture around her and the one slim finger of pink light that a crack in the curtains had laid across the shag, and then she remembered. All of it!

Reaching for the light switch, she almost panicked when she saw the empty bed, the satin bedspread still rumpled where the DEA agent had lain. The bathroom door stood wide open, and the only sound in the room was her own heartbeat. Across the room, the safety chain dangled on the doorjamb. He was gone. He'd left her.

Then her eyes fell on the neat mound of supplies on the coffee table, and the tension left her muscles. Sara touched the first-aid kit on top of the heap. She might be alone, but she hadn't been abandoned. She pushed aside the first-aid kit, wincing at the stiffened scrapes across the palms of her hands. She'd have to take care of those before they got infected. She glanced through the rest of the pile. Toiletries. Clothing. Doug Bradford had thought of everything. Just to be clean again would be heaven!

Sara lifted a flat, oblong package; she had no idea what it was. She read the stenciled lettering: Meals Ready to Eat. The words prompted an empty churning in her stomach. She peered at her Rolex and saw that it was already lunchtime. This brown, plasticized envelope sure didn't look as though it could contain a whole meal.

She laid the MRE hastily back down as she caught sight of a

piece of note paper jutting out from the pages of a small, reddish-pink book. A note. Snatching the book from the stack of clothing, she discovered that the leather cover wasn't really the garish color suggested by the reflection from the gaudy lamplight, but a deep rose, almost a burgundy. She eagerly flipped it open to where the pocket-size sheet of notebook paper marked the center like a bookmark. The note was scrawled in a masculine bold, angular cursive.

> *Sara,*
>
> *It's 10 a.m. now, and I have to leave for a while. I may be gone for some time, so don't be alarmed if I'm not here when you wake up. You're safer here than anywhere else right now. But please don't leave the room or allow anyone in. Here are a few things to tide you over until I get back. Not much, I'm afraid, but the clothes are clean at least, and the MREs are edible, though that's about all you can say for them.*

(There was a small break on the page and a scratched-out section that looked as though the writer had been trying to decide how to phrase the next line. Then the note continued.)

> *I noticed you had your own Bible at church and are used to handling one, so I thought maybe you would find this one useful. There hasn't been anything that has helped me more in times of trouble and hurting. The Psalms have been a special comfort to me. If anyone knew what it was to be alone with enemies on his heels and friends stabbing him in the back, it was David.*

(There was another scribbled-out section. Then the note finished.)

> *I'll be back as soon as possible. DON'T LEAVE THE ROOM UNDER ANY CIRCUMSTANCES!*

The last sentence was underscored heavily and followed by Doug Bradford's signature.

Sara returned to the top of the page and read the note through again. *Times of trouble and hurting,* Doug had written. Was it possible that this utterly competent and self-sufficient DEA agent knew what it meant to be alone and pursued and afraid? Though why she should be so surprised, given the job he had, she didn't know.

Her eyes dropped from the note to the open Bible in her hands. Doug had tucked his note into the first pages of Psalms, and her eye was immediately caught by a line in Psalm 10: *"In his arrogance, the wicked man hunts down the weak, who are caught in the schemes he devises."*

Sara had heard bits of the Psalms before in Bible readings at church and had even memorized *"The Lord is my Shepherd"* in Sunday school. But she didn't recognize this one. Her heart chilled as she read on. It could have been written about the men who were after her! *"He boasts of the cravings of his heart; he blesses the greedy and reviles the Lord. In his pride the wicked does not seek him; in all his thoughts there is no room for God. His ways are always prosperous; he is haughty and your laws are far from him; he sneers at all his enemies. He says to himself, 'Nothing will shake me; I'll always be happy and never have trouble.'"*

That last line could have come straight from Nicolás's lips! No one could touch the Cortezes, he'd told her smugly. They were too powerful and rich. They didn't need to fear the law. They owned it! And it was just too bad for any of the small and ordinary people who were caught in their schemes.

Sara skimmed through the next lines. *"He murders the innocent . . . he lies in wait to catch the helpless. . . . He says to himself, 'God has forgotten; He covers His face and never sees.'"* What was it Nicolás had said when she'd asked if he was afraid of God's judgment? *Religion is one thing. Business is another.*

And the worst thing was, he seemed to be right! The Cortezes *had* prospered, and even now it was Sara who was in hiding, and an innocent boy lay dead, and who knew how many other helpless people had been hurt while the Cortezes laughed through their teeth at the thought that God might intervene.

Oh, Nicky, how could you?

As quickly as the thought arose, the truth became obvious. Like countless others before him, Nicolás had chosen power and wealth and personal ambition over righteousness and justice and even the people he claimed to love.

Sara sank back onto the sofa, the Bible still open in her hands, her hunger and the pain that wracked her body overcome by the greater pain in her heart. The horror and terror of the past twenty-four hours, and her own desperate need for survival, had crowded out every other thought. But now, safe, at least for the moment, she was free to think about the future—and the past. Tears blurred an image of impossibly blue eyes laughing down into hers, of passionate arms holding her close.

They were such beautiful memories—that's what hurt! Memories of love, and a warm sense of belonging, and a breathless joy beyond anything she'd ever dreamed. It had only been three short months, but she had been happier than she'd ever been in her life. That it had all been a lie, a mirage even while it had been happening, was an agony that twisted in her like a knife.

Sara drew her knees up, tucking her feet under the torn edge of her skirt, and huddled into herself as though for protection against a cold that was no longer there. How had it all come to this? *How could you let it come to this?*

It was only then that Sara realized who it was she was addressing. She tugged loose the Bible, which had slid down into her mud-splattered lap, and as she smoothed out the crumpled pages, a quick hand across her eyes brought back into focus the first verse of the psalm she'd been reading. *"Why, O Lord, do you stand far off? Why do you hide yourself in times of trouble?"*

She averted her eyes, but a cry from across the page jumped out at her as though she herself had screamed it aloud. *"How long, O Lord? Will you forget me forever? How long will you hide your face from me? How long must I wrestle with my thoughts and every day have sorrow in my heart? How long—"*

With a sudden violent motion, Sara flung the Bible across the room. It landed with a flutter of pages on the carpet. Throwing herself face down on the sofa, she burst into a storm of tears.

Yes, God, why? she raged. The eternal question became a racking sob. *Why are you doing this to me? Why are you letting this happen? Where have you been while the Cortezes were building their dirty little cocaine empire? Where were you hiding when that boy was killed and my own husband tried to kill me? For that matter, where were you when my mother was crying for help with an eighteen-wheeler coming through her windshield? Where have you been every time I've needed you all these years? How long does a person have to scream before you hear?*

Sara burrowed her face into the cushion as a decade of unanswered questions broke loose within her, and the bitterness and anger she'd bottled up for all these years poured out like acid rain.

"Oh, God, can't you see that's why I quit talking to you?" she wailed. "I don't even want to think about you! It hurts too much! It's easier to stay frozen up inside—to ignore you as you've ignored me all these years—than to keep battering myself bloody on the brick wall of your indifference! Maybe if I could really doubt that you're up there, it wouldn't be so bad! But I *know* you're there, somewhere, keeping the atoms of the universe from flying apart and the history of this miserable planet on the track you've got planned for it. And I know that every word I'm crying is registering somewhere in that awesome mind of yours, between the DNA code for a caterpillar and the molecular structure of a star. You just don't care enough to answer!"

Something in her last accusation arrested the flood of her pain. Could she really say that God had never answered? In her mind's eye she relived the last terrible moments of her mad flight across the refinery grounds when, exhausted and at the end of every resource, and utterly certain that the end was only a heartbeat away, she cried out to God. Had she forgotten?

And beyond any hope, help had come! Had that taxi been a miracle? Maybe. And what about the truck ride into Santa Cruz? In fact, every time she'd been certain she was at a dead end, another timely door had opened, right down to the incredible coincidence of Doug Bradford's arrival on the streets of Las Palmas last night.

But for what?

"Why did you even bother, God? I'm so miserable now, I might as well be dead anyway! I just don't get it! If you could stoop down to save me last night, why didn't you just stop all this from happening in the first place? It would have been so easy for you to just put your hand down that night in Seattle and keep Nicky and me from ever meeting! Or why couldn't you have kept him from turning into such a monster? Why didn't you? Why did you have to let it end up this way? Oh, God, we were so happy! I loved him so much! Was it so much to expect—that happily-ever-after ending? Was it too much to ask for—a family, children, someone to love—that you had to take it away from me—again? Couldn't you leave me with anything?"

Her anguish threatened to overwhelm her, and she wept again. She wept for the losses that had mounted in her life—the loss of her mother, the detachment of her father, and the betrayal by Nicolás. She wept for her dead dreams of happiness and love—and for a future that now stretched gray and empty and barren in front of her as far as her mind's eye could see. *Oh, God, it hurts so much, I can't stand it!*

In her agony, she didn't hear the door open and shut. It wasn't until she felt a light touch on her shoulder that she realized she wasn't alone. She recoiled, her last sob catching in her throat as she struggled to take a controlled breath.

She heard Doug Bradford's quiet voice. "It's okay, Sara. Go ahead and cry. I know you've got to be feeling pretty scared and alone right now. But it's all going to work out. You'll see."

His hand fell away as Sara scrambled to a sitting position, tugging her skirt hastily down across her knees. Pushing aside the pile of clothes and other supplies, Doug sat down on the edge of the coffee table and offered Sara his handkerchief. She took it gratefully and blew her nose unself-consciously—which, in itself, was a sign of her misery.

"I . . . I know it's going to work out," she shuddered. "I'm not really afraid. Not anymore. I was just . . ."—she swallowed the sob that was still in her throat—"thinking."

"Thinking?"

Sara caught Doug's swift glance at the Bible, which lay face down between an armchair and the bed. "I . . . I'm sorry about that. It was just . . . I was thinking about Nicky. . . . I still can't believe he could—"

Doug's mouth tightened. Could she still be making excuses for that jerk even after the guy had tried to kill her?

"I . . . I guess I never really knew him," Sara continued, as she twisted the handkerchief into a tight ball in her hands. "I didn't know any of them. I was just . . . I was just so stupid! And even when you tried to warn me—all those things I said to you . . . I was wrong, and you were right about everything. I can't blame you if you say 'I told you so.' I . . . I deserve it!"

Doug put out a hand to interrupt her. "No, don't say that," he told her quickly. "There was no way you could have known. I just wish I *had* been wrong and that you didn't have to go through all this."

Sara raised her head, and Doug—despite years of dealing with angry and hurting people—was appalled by the misery he saw in her face.

"That's what I don't understand! Why *am* I going through all of this? Why is all of this happening? You're supposed to be a Christian— right? You go to church. You know the Bible, at least a lot better than I do. So maybe you can tell me! Where is God in all of this? Like those verses in there said. Why isn't he stopping the Cortezes? And if he knew what Nicky was like, if he knew all this was going to happen, why did he ever let me marry Nicky in the first place?"

Doug was silent for a moment before he said, "Did you ask him?"

"Did I ask him!" Sara cried bitterly. "Now you sound like my pastor! No, maybe I didn't ask him! I just fell in love, that was all! Was that so wrong? Are you trying to tell me that's why this is all happening? That it's some kind of punishment because I didn't ask God's permission to get married?"

"That wasn't what I meant," Doug said gently. He met her angry eyes with a steady gaze of his own. "Look, Sara, I'm the last one to judge another person's relationship with God. And I can't say why he's allowed all this to happen. I've been kind of wondering that myself, to be honest. But I do know that when I'm hurting and mixed up and wondering what in creation God is doing with my life, the best thing I can do is to ask him. Maybe I don't always go away understanding why he's doing what he's doing, but at least I know he's listening and that he cares. And that he *does* have a purpose behind what he's doing, even if I can't see it right now. I guess that's what I was hoping you'd get out of the psalms. David did a lot of crying out to God. But he also found a lot of answers, if you read far enough."

He checked himself suddenly, a rueful half-smile replacing the seriousness of his tone. "I'm sorry, I didn't mean to get preachy."

"No!" Sara said quickly. There was a touch of wonder in her eyes as she considered the man sitting across from her. He was a surprising person, this DEA agent. *He really cares!* she thought with a shock. *He cares about mixed-up girls who drop themselves on his doorstep just like he cares about those druggies on the street.* The realization warmed her voice as she apologized. "No, *I'm* sorry. I had no right to be dumping all my personal problems on you. Or"—she tried for a ghost of a smile—"to be picking another fight! You've been more than patient, and I really do appreciate everything you've done to help." She glanced over again at the book on the carpet. "Even that."

Sara blew her nose again, more discreetly this time. Then drawing a deep breath and visibly bracing her slim shoulders, she said, "Please, I've wasted enough of your time. I'm sure you didn't come back here just to hear me complain. What . . ."—her voice dropped involuntarily in volume—"what did you find out?"

Doug watched with admiration as Sara pulled herself together. The girl had grit. He reached for the newspaper he'd laid down beside him. "I'm afraid there are some complications," he said carefully, flipping the paper open and passing it over to Sara.

Sara blanched white as she took in the picture and headlines splashed across the front page. "Oh, no! Then he did do it!"

She scanned quickly through the article. *The police . . . Interpol . . . wanted for murder.* The ugly phrases were like fingers at her throat, and it didn't take a genius to grasp the implications. She raised her eyes from the paper. "Can . . . can you still get me out?"

Doug's expression—or lack of one—was all the answer she needed. Sara dropped the paper as though it was burning her. "But your people—the DEA—they can't really think I did it! Not . . . not after all the information I gave you!"

"It isn't a question of what we believe. It's the evidence that the State Department has to work with. And right now, unfortunately, all the evidence—and international law—is on the side of the Cortezes."

Sara was speechless, and Doug went on to explain. "Our hands are pretty well tied—unless we can come up with some overwhelming evidence that the Cortezes aren't the solid citizens they purport to be."

"Then Nicolás was right," Sara said dully. "Not even the DEA can stand against them! They win clear across the board."

Somehow, this turn of events was no real surprise. It was too much to hope that she might actually find herself free of this nightmare. Jumping to her feet, Sara moved blindly across the room, stopping only to pick up the Bible from the carpet. Smoothing the bent pages, she closed the cover carefully and dropped the book onto the bed.

"So—that's the end of it, then." Her voice was steadier than she felt and gave away none of her despair. "Well, at least you tried. Thank you for that, anyway. And . . . and don't worry about me. I'll work something out." She stared without seeing at the crumpled pink bedspread, then began aimlessly to straighten it out. "If . . . if you'd just shut the door on your way out."

Doug was on his feet and at her side in one long stride. "Now, just one moment! Haven't we already been through this once? You don't really think I'm just going to walk away and leave you here. . . ."

Abandoning her efforts to make the bed, Sara whirled around to face the DEA agent. "And what can you do if your own office says no? What . . . what can *I* do? If I can't get out of the country, they're going to find me sooner or later. I know they will!" She fought to keep the fear out of her voice as she glanced around the room. "Even here!"

"Look, Sara, would you please sit down?"

Doug pushed her gently into a sitting position on the edge of the bed. Hauling over an armchair for himself, he perched on one arm, his strong hands clasped over his knee. "Sara, I'm not going to kid you. The situation is"—he groped for a word—"difficult. The way I see it, we've got just two options. First, I can drive you from here over to the American consulate. You can march in there, give yourself up to the consul, and trust yourself to the workings of the Bolivian justice system. You'd probably have to go to jail until the trial, but the consul's a good lady. She'd do everything she could to help, and she'd keep a close eye on the proceedings—make sure it's all legal."

"No! You can't be serious!" Sara was shaking her head frantically before he even finished, renewed terror in her eyes. "Luis . . . Nicky . . . Do you really think it would matter if I was in jail? They'd kill me for sure. They grabbed Orejuela right from under the noses of all those policemen, remember?"

"I remember!" Doug said with grim emphasis. "I said it was an option, not that it was the best option. But the only other option that I can see"—he unclasped his hands from around his knee—"is for you to trust me."

"Trust you?" Sara echoed his words blankly. "To do what?"

"I haven't the slightest idea," Doug admitted. "Yet. But I'll think of something, don't you worry. The Cortezes haven't won this match—not by a long shot."

Doug shifted his position on his precarious perch. "Look, I know it's a lot to ask for you to trust me when even I have no idea where I'm going. And I'm not saying it'll be easy. It won't. For starters, it will mean hiding out until I can figure a way to get you out of the country. I can't even say how long! But if you're willing to take the chance—put yourself in my hands and do exactly what I tell you—I can promise you this much. One way or another, I won't rest until I get you out of this! And if there's any possible way on this earth to do it, I'll bring the Cortezes down too!"

Sara, blinking at the flat conviction of his tone, found herself believing him. She could almost make herself think that everything was going to work out after all. "I do trust you," she said soberly. "And of course I'll do anything you tell me. But . . ."

She hesitated even as her heart was stirring to accept this new hope. "I'd like to say yes, of course, because to be honest, I don't know what else to do. But isn't this going to get you into trouble with your superiors? And what about my in-laws? They're . . . they're dangerous! If they find out you're trying to help me, they might go after you too. It . . . it was one thing to be asking for your help when . . . when I thought the DEA would want to get involved. But if it's going to cause problems for you in your job or . . . or maybe even put you in danger too—well, I just don't know if I should be letting you get mixed up in all of this!"

"Letting me?" Doug said wryly. "Don't kid yourself, Sara! This isn't just your fight here! I've been in this a lot longer than you have, and I can tell you this. With or without you, I'm going after the Cortezes. They're not going to walk away from this if I have anything to do with it!"

Leaning forward, he added firmly, "Look, Sara, this is what I'm trained for, okay? So why don't you just let me worry about my job and any hypothetical danger to either of us. All I want to know is, are you with me or not?"

Doug held her gaze until she nodded slowly. Then he went on briskly, "Good. Now, we're running short on time here, so we've got to make some plans. The first order of business is to get out of this place. You hit that nail right on the head. Nobody saw you last night, and I think we're safe enough for the moment. But sooner or later, Cortéz—or someone wanting that reward of his—is going to come knocking on every door in this city. In fact, that's our biggest problem, right there. Finding any kind of a place where you can lie low without someone spotting you and running to Cortéz. You don't exactly blend into the local crowds around here, and that picture of you is going to be plastered all over town."

Doug's remarks were accompanied by an absent half-smile, but it was obvious to Sara that he was thinking out loud rather than holding a conversation.

"What we've got to do," he continued, "is get you out of Santa Cruz. That's where Cortéz is going to be concentrating his search—at least to start with. Unfortunately, any place in this country where there are people, we're going to run into the same problem. In fact, I don't know any place that's going to be safe from either Cortéz or the police, except maybe out in the middle of the jungle." He paused for a moment and rubbed his chin. "Which actually wouldn't be such a bad idea, if I could go with you. There's thousands of square kilometers out there where you won't find another living soul, and if I didn't have to stay here and keep an eye on Cortéz—and let him keep an eye on me—I'd just take a stash of MREs out there and we could hole up somewhere until this all blew over."

"You . . . you're not coming with me?" The news came as something of a shock. It was the first time Sara had considered that Doug might not be accompanying her to wherever she would be going. She immediately recognized how foolish that assumption had been. Of course the DEA agent had more important things to do than sit around and baby-sit her. "No, of course you're not," she corrected herself quickly. "I . . . I wasn't thinking."

Doug understood what she wasn't saying.

"We don't have much choice here, Sara," he explained gently. "Cortéz is going to assume you'll try to contact me. If we're going to pull this off, we've got to convince him that you haven't. And that means I've got to be seen going about my regular business. I also need to be where I can investigate this case. While you—"

"I know," Sara broke in hastily. "I just . . . it's okay, really. And I wouldn't mind staying out in the jungle somewhere," she added without conviction, "if you think that's the safest place. I can manage just fine on my own, if . . . if you just leave me some supplies."

"That's what you think!" Doug snorted. "There's a lot more dangers out in the jungle than just people. No, the jungle idea was just a thought. Now, if there was some little *finca* out there where I could leave you . . . someone I could really trust, and where Cortéz would never think to take a look . . ."

Doug's voice trailed off as his words set a wheel turning in his mind. "You know," he said slowly, "maybe that isn't such a crazy idea." He traced one thought to another and then to another. *Yes, that could work! No, we'd need . . . wait, that would do it!*

Doug snapped his fingers. "That's it! I think I've got it."

He turned to Sara, who had been watching with bewilderment the rapid procession of thoughts across his face. "I have a friend who just might be able to help us. If you wouldn't mind roughing it for a while. It would be rather primitive."

"No, of course not—!"

"Great!" Doug was already slipping his cell phone from his belt. "I'm going to have to make some phone calls. In the meantime, why don't you go ahead and shower and change. I'd like to be out of here in half an hour, if we can."

Flipping his phone open, Doug punched in the number of the DEA office. He relaxed when he recognized the laconic "Yep!" on the other end. It had been a toss-up who would answer the phone.

"Kyle, is Ramon still there?"

"Sure! Coming right up!"

Ramon's decisive voice came on the line. "Doug, what is it?"

"Ramon." Doug slid from the arm of the chair and settled into its seat as Sara, her arms piled high with clothes and toiletries, closed the bathroom door behind her. "I need a favor, and quick. You remember those SatTracks we got in a month or so back?"

There was a brief silence before Ramon responded. "I seem to recall a memo from Grant talking about those things, but I can't say I've ever had call to use one."

"It's a tracking device," Doug reminded him impatiently. "Kind of like the one you slapped on that pickup you were tailing last night, only sized-down by about three-quarters. The military just released them to us. One of their newest toys."

"Okay. I'm with you," Ramon conceded. "And—?"

"I need you to call the tech agent right away. Tell him you need a SatTrack fixed up in . . . oh, I don't know—maybe one of those big shoulder bags that women like to carry shopping, or a leather purse, or even a backpack, if he can't get anything else. . . . You know, something you could keep with you all the time, but that's bulky enough so the tracker can be sewn into the lining without anyone picking up on it. I'll meet you at McDonald's in one hour to pick it up."

"An hour! You've got to be kidding! It's Saturday, *mano*, in case you've forgotten. The tech agent isn't even here. In fact, he's hosting a barbecue at his house—I know that because he invited me to drop by, which was kind of where I was heading right now."

"Yeah, well, we all have our share of interrupted dinners," Doug said, cutting into Ramon's protest with scant sympathy. "And since he lives only four blocks from the office, it shouldn't take him too long to get over there, do his thing, and get back to the grill. Oh, and Ramon, if anyone asks you, keep me out of it. This is for a case of yours, got it?"

"Oh, really! And which case is that?" Ramon demanded.

"Don't ask—!" Doug began.

"Yeah, I know, and you won't tell me any lies," Ramon retorted. "Okay, I'm not stupid! I'll see what I can do. But you watch your back, *mano*. I'm not always going to be around to cover for you."

Grinning, Doug ended the call and keyed in another number. He heard the hollow signal of another cell phone. Regular phone lines had yet to reach the far regions of the Chapare. In fact, only in the last two months had an additional tower made cell phone service available over the two hundred-plus kilometers of distance. There was a burst of static, then the cautious tones of someone not used to electronic devices.

"*Sí?*"

"Benedicto," Doug greeted his friend pleasantly. *"Hermano, como está?"*

✠

When his conversation was completed, Doug returned the cell phone to his belt and began tidying up the few belongings he'd brought into the room. He was dumping MREs and the Bible into the middle of the Indian blanket when Sara came out of the bathroom. She yawned and stretched, shaking loose the damp, shining fall of hair down her back.

"Need anything out of here before I pack up?" Doug waved the first aid box as Sara crossed the room. "Those gashes on your hands looked pretty nasty."

Sara held out her hands, palms up. They were still red and sore, but clean and scabbed-over. The scrapes on her legs had washed clean too, though she couldn't help wincing as her borrowed jeans rubbed at her skinned-up knees. Even the shallow cut on the bottom of her foot had somehow not become infected. "I think I'll be okay, thanks. Actually, I'm feeling pretty good."

And she really was, she discovered, somewhat to her surprise. It was almost as though the steaming cascade of water had washed away, along with the dirt and the tear stains, much of her despair and panic and self-pity. The situation Doug had outlined was worse than Sara had anticipated, but wallowing in her fear wasn't going to improve matters. She'd just have to take it one step at a time and not look too far ahead. At the very least, she could offer a cheerful face to this man who—for motivations of his own, he'd said, but out of kindness and compassion, too—was going so far out of his way to help her.

So it was with a genuine smile and a flash of her former humor that Sara added almost gaily, "I have to admit, though, that I'd kill for something to eat! I can't even remember how long it's been."

Doug turned her hands over, inspecting them thoroughly with a practiced eye before, satisfied, he tossed the first-aid box onto the blanket and used his pocket knife to spear an MRE. Slitting the pouch open, he fished out a granola bar and handed it to Sara. "Here, this'll tide you over. We'll be getting some real food in just a bit. Now, if you want to toss your stuff in here . . ."

Sara retreated to the bathroom, returning a moment later with an armful of toiletries and the wadded up remnants of the clothing she'd slept in. Doug added them to the heap on the blanket, then bundled the whole thing together and slung it over his shoulder. After a last quick check around, he dropped the room key onto the coffee table and nodded to Sara, whose mouth was crammed full of granola bar. "Okay, if you're ready, let's get out of here."

The tile courtyard was still sleepy and empty under the blaze of the afternoon sun, but Doug made Sara wait inside the motel room while he backed the Land Rover up to the door of the cottage. He was opening the door to climb out when he had a sudden thought.

Reaching over to open the glove box, he found what he wanted underneath his flashlight, the car's papers, and a bunch of other odds and ends—a small leaflet that Pastor Histed had passed out at church a few Sundays back. On the front was a picture of a deep chasm. On one side of the chasm was the Spanish word for GOD and on the other side MAN. Spanning the gap was a bridge shaped like a cross. Shaking the pamphlet loose, he took it with him, dropping it beside the key on the coffee table. Then he stepped back outside and opened the passenger door so that Sara could scramble in unseen.

It was really breaking cover to leave the leaflet and might even arouse some unwanted questions, but it made him feel a little better about the night's adventure to think that the girl, who seemed to be the only one running this joint, would pick up the brightly colored tract and read through it.

There was already an increase in the number of olive-green uniforms on the streets, Doug noted grimly as he pulled out of the motel and went through his usual evasion routine. Not just an added number of traffic cops peering into bus doors and the windows of taxis, but military police sauntering along the sidewalks and stopping to show what could be a flyer to bystanders. Yes, it was time to get Sara out of town, before the MPs shifted their interest from public transport to private cars.

As he drove, Doug explained his still-developing plan to Sara.

"I met Benedicto when I was training some anti-narcotics units down in the Chapare a few years back. That's Bolivia's main coca-growing region. Mostly jungle. But you'd be surprised how many little villages and towns the *campesinos* have tucked away back there. Not to mention, of course, all the clearings they've cut for planting coca and other crops.

"Anyway, we'd been out on night patrol and were heading back to base when I heard some singing. Nowhere near on key, but I recognized the song. It was a hymn my wi—uh, my church back home used to sing. And there on the side of this jungle track was a *pahuichi*. Just this open A-frame of thatch over some bamboo scaffolding. Inside were all these *campesinos* clapping their hands to the beat of a drum and a couple tambourines. That's when I realized it was Sunday morning and this was a church. I don't know who was more dumbfounded when I stopped the jeep—my unit or the congregation.

"Benedicto was the pastor. He's a little guy—barely up to my shoulder—and I know he must have thought there'd be trouble when all those soldiers marched in. But he didn't bat an eye—just stopped the service to make us welcome. Even invited my men and me to eat lunch with them afterward. After that, I'd stop in every time I was through the area. Over the years we've become good friends."

"So that's where you want me to stay?" Sara asked doubtfully. "At this church?"

"Oh, no! That area isn't even jungle anymore. As you'll see. But Benedicto has some church members he says can be trusted. A Quechua family well off the beaten track up in the hills."

Doug slowed as the golden arches of McDonald's came into view.

"In fact, that very inaccessibility is going to be our one real problem. It'll keep you safe from visitors, but once we get you up there, you're going to be pretty well cut off from the outside. The hills there don't allow for cell phone reception, even if these people had electricity to keep a battery charged. Of course, they'll always be able to get a message out to me through Benedicto. Still, we've got to allow for the possibility of some emergency." Turning off the avenue, Doug eased over a speed bump into the McDonald's parking lot. "Which is why we're stopping here."

Sara nodded understanding and assent, though she couldn't imagine how McDonald's could possibly fit into the plan. Despite her earlier bravado, the thought of being left on her own in a thatched hut in the middle of the jungle, with who knew what kind of *campesino* Indians and not even a way to call for help, was an appalling prospect.

You're going to show some courage here, if it kills you! she told herself sternly, then grimaced at her poor choice of words.

"This Benedicto . . . what did you tell him about me?" she asked Doug. "I mean, does he know? About Ricardo and . . . and the police?"

"He knows I have a friend who has run afoul of the *narcos* and needs to drop out of sight for a while," Doug said briefly. "Benedicto knows what my job is, and he may have his own ideas of what I'm doing here. But he won't ask any questions. Or talk. You can count on that."

Turning into the parking slot, he switched off the engine and swung around to face Sara. "Look, if you're having second thoughts about this, now is the time to say so," he said gently. "I know this is a lot to ask."

Sara glanced at him in surprise. He was devising a plan to get her out of the mess she'd dug herself into, and yet *he* was apologizing to *her*? "No second thoughts," she said firmly. She turned her head to look out the tinted window of the Land Rover. "Why are we stopping here?"

"A friend is dropping off a package for me. To solve that communications problem I mentioned. Then we're going to head out of town. Benedicto won't be ready for us until tomorrow afternoon, I'm afraid. He won't be able to contact his people until they come in to church in the morning. But I don't like the looks of all those cops out there. We have to assume they'll be watching the main roads, too. So I'm figuring we'll head right on into the jungle. There's plenty of small tracks out there that'll eventually get us where we want to go. It may take a lot longer, but once we clear the city limits, we're not in any big hurry. And if we run too long on time, we can hole up somewhere for a few hours."

Doug reached for the door handle. "Okay, I'm heading in. I'll pick up lunch while I'm at it. What'll it be? Big Mac? Shake? Hey, don't be shy!" he urged when he saw Sara hesitate. "It might be the last decent meal you get for a while."

Sara did feel shy. It was just beginning to sink in that she didn't have so much as a penny, and everything from here on out—not only the cost of her lunch but even the clothes on her back—was coming out of Doug Bradford's pocket.

"Whatever you have is fine with me," she told him in a constrained voice. "I'm . . . I'm not very hungry."

Her little white lie was immediately betrayed by the audible rumbling of her stomach. Doug gave her a sharp glance, but his words were mild. "Okay, two Big Mac combos it is. Oh, and would you mind climbing into the back there before I open the door? We've got a lot of people out here, and I'd just as soon no one noticed that I've got someone else in the car. I know that must seem a little extreme, but—"

"No, not at all," Sara said hastily as she scrambled over the back of the seat. She was no more anxious to be noticed, especially at McDonald's, a popular hangout for much of the expatriate community and upscale members of Bolivian society who could afford the prices. Though comparable to McDonald's back in the States, prices were three times what an ordinary noonday meal would cost at the average family restaurant here. She and Nicolás had dined here on occasion, and never without seeing people they knew.

Doug waited while Sara crawled in between his military backpack and a small metal drum of extra gas. "That's good. While you're waiting, you might want to check that flight bag back there. You should find a pair of shoes that fit—and maybe some other clothes you'd prefer."

There were still five minutes left of the hour he'd given Ramon, but when Doug entered the fast-food restaurant, the younger agent was already at the counter, his black eyes flitting impatiently from the attendant who was counting out his change to the door. Doug caught his glance, then swung on his heel and strode into the bathroom. He'd just checked the two stalls for occupants and turned on the water to wash his hands when Ramon joined him.

Doug nodded toward the black plastic bundle under his arm. "That it?"

"That's it." Ramon dropped the bundle on the counter. "You're lucky. Tech had already been experimenting with this and had it more than half ready to go. Otherwise, you'd have been waiting all afternoon." As Doug picked up the parcel, Ramon peered gloomily into the paper sack that held his carry-out order. "I'll tell you what, man. You owe me! A steak, for one. You know how hard it is to show up at someone's house for lunch after you've just dragged him out for what's supposed to be some last-minute op? Not to mention the chewing out I got for requisitioning the thing on such short notice!"

Doug was already peeling back the plastic to disclose a small canvas knapsack of the type used for school books. "Yeah? Well, that does happen to be his job! Next time, don't let him give you any flak."

"Easy for you to say! You're not the new guy in town," Ramon replied. But he dropped his grumbling to briskly explain the tracking device, with one eye on the bathroom door as he talked. "The SatTrack's sewn into the bottom of the satchel. Not bad, eh? Can't tell it's there even if you look! The antenna's in that trim running up the side."

He passed Doug a scrap of paper with a series of numbers scrawled on it. "The computer program and sat link are set up and ready to go. Here's your password number. Just type it in, and you've got your coordinates. Go easy, though, on how often you call it up if you want that battery to last more than a couple of days."

Tucking the piece of paper into his shirt pocket, Doug ran a hand over the bottom of the knapsack and around the edges. It was a good job, all right, undetectable even to his experienced fingers. The SatTrack was a distant cousin of the tracker the DEA used for surveillance. But this newest toy of the tech department was hardly larger than a credit card and less than a half-inch thick. And unlike its predecessors, it didn't depend on proximity to a scanner or any other kind of computerized surveillance grid. Instead, it contained in its slim insides a GPS—or Global Positioning System—that permitted a satellite uplink to locate its signal anywhere on the face of the planet. It was only this capability that had allowed Doug to consider removing Sara to such a distant locale.

The system wasn't completely satisfactory, of course—he'd have much preferred to have a more direct means of communication—but then there was little about this case that was satisfactory, and if he wasn't able to talk to Sara, he'd at least be able to confirm that she was safe and sound where he'd left her. As long as she kept the SatTrack with her. . . .

Shoving the knapsack back into the black bag, Doug tucked it under his arm and clapped Ramon on the back. "Thanks, pal. I really do owe you one—a steak, I mean. How about we settle on Monday? Lunch at *Don Miguel's,* my treat."

Ramon looked unimpressed, but before he could respond, the bathroom door banged open, and a small boy dashed in, his shorts already half down, a harried-looking man at his heels. Taking leave with a grin and a raised eyebrow, Doug caught the door before it swung shut and went out.

Ramon walked out the front door as Doug stepped up to the counter to place his order—two Super Size Big Mac combos with a couple of vanilla shakes for dessert. Paying the tab, he took the sack of food, collected straws and a handful of ketchup packets from the roving waitress whose job it was to dole out such precious commodities, and quickly exited to the parking lot. Already he was mentally mapping out the route they would take into the jungle. There was a spot where he'd once camped with his Leopard team, and if they could get that far by dusk—

"Bradford!"

Doug checked his stride in midstep. Slowly, casually, he turned, schooling his expression into an impassive mask even as adrenaline tensed every muscle. No, he hadn't mistaken the supercilious tone with its slight accent. He gave a curt nod.

"Cortéz."

CHAPTER TWENTY-FIVE

The bright yellow Ferrari was in the drive-through line a few paces away. With a yank of the steering wheel, Nicolás pulled aside, bumping over the curb of a meridian divider, and squealed into an empty parking slot only two spaces from the Land Rover. Climbing out quickly and slamming the door behind him, Nicolás rounded the back of the Ferrari with brisk, angry strides and planted himself in Doug's path. "I want to talk to you, Bradford."

His glance darted around the crowded parking lot even as he nodded toward the large McDonald's sack in the crook of Doug's arm. "Hungry today, aren't we?" he sneered, as though he could see the double order inside.

Doug made no attempt to push past Nicolás. Instead, his eyes narrowed in what Sara had termed his "suspect look" as he took in each small cue of the other man's body language. He hadn't seen the Cortéz heir since the Fourth of July gala when Nicolás, urbane and insufferably pleased with himself, had made such a point of introducing Doug to his new bride.

The arrogance was still there, but it was clear from the petulant smirk on his face and the angry aggression with which he thrust his hands into the pockets of his baggy white pants that something—Daddy perhaps?—had seriously punctured the carefree aplomb with which he normally sailed through life.

There was a feverishness, too, in Nicolás's darting glance that Doug didn't like at all. They'd had a bull once, back in Arizona, with that look in his eye—a sleek, powerful-looking animal that had been real popular with the females, too, until it had taken to savaging them when it was in the same pen. Doug's father finally had to shoot the creature. It had ended up as fairly tasty salami.

But Doug allowed neither this assessment, nor the warning signals that Cortéz's gibe had raised, to show in the casualness of his shrug. "You might call it breakfast and lunch in one. I was out on a case all night."

The impatience of Nicolás's hand gesture made it clear this was no news to him. Doug made a mental note to check out those FELCN connections Kyle had dug up. It took someone in Colonel Torres's own office to get the news out this fast. Doug glanced pointedly past Nicolás to the narrow aisle on the driver's side of the Land Rover. "I don't have time for a chat about eating habits here, Cortéz. What do you want?"

"What do I want?" Nicolás abandoned any interest in Doug's lunch. Though the DEA agent hadn't moved, Nicolás put an arm out to bar his way, and his feverish blue eyes were fixed on Doug's face. "I want my wife! Have you seen her?"

"Your wife?" Though Doug felt as if he were tiptoeing through a minefield, the arch of his eyebrow was a masterpiece of mild surprise. "Sure, I've seen your wife. Why?"

Nicolás ignored the question. "You saw her? Where is she? When was this?"

"Why, just the other night." The knapsack was still tucked under Doug's left arm. Shifting his McDonald's order to the same side, Doug made a show of digging out his keys as he elaborated indifferently, "It was at a security seminar the embassy hosted for the expatriate community. Over at the Co-op, as a matter of fact. It's too bad you couldn't make it too. It was really quite interesting. Your wife seemed to find it so, anyway. In fact, we talked a little about it afterward—I'm sure she told you. She seems pretty concerned about the drug situation here. Had all kinds of questions about some raid she'd seen on the news. Not that I had any answers. It wasn't even local. Why is it that everyone thinks we've got time to keep up on every drug-related bust that happens around this planet? Or that we'd give out that intel to anyone who walks up and asks! But we sure do get a lot of those kinds of questions—especially from the women."

Had his sarcasm been a little too forthcoming? Doug didn't relax beneath his casual posture until he caught the flicker of satisfaction that crossed Nicolás's face. *Gotcha!*

"Don't get cute with me, Bradford!" Nicolás sneered. "You think I care what my wife babbled about at some *gringo* seminar? Or are you going to tell me you haven't read the paper today!"

"The paper?" A dawning comprehension crept into Doug's expression. He let his keys slide slowly back into his pocket. "Oh-h-h! Is that what this is all about? Yeah, sure, I saw the paper. Haven't had a chance to give it more than a glance, but it would have been hard to miss the headline about your party last night, if that's what you mean. Are you trying to tell me that was all for real? I've got to admit I just assumed there had to be some sort of mistake. That pretty little bride of yours up and shoots someone in the middle of a party? And then she disappears in plain view of a few thousand spectators? Seems a little far-fetched!"

"Oh, it's true, all right. I was there," Nicolás said shortly, but his eyes slid away from Doug's as he told the lie. "Are you trying to tell me you haven't heard from her?"

Doug allowed his eyebrow to register even more surprise. "Is there any reason I should?" He glanced pointedly at his watch, his voice frosting over with the impatience of a busy man who has been courteous long enough in the face of inexcusable rudeness. "It seems to me you've got the wrong department here, Cortéz. The DEA deals with drugs, not homicide—or missing persons. Even Americans. You did say your wife is a U.S. citizen, am I right? If you think she is out there, trying to turn herself in to her own government—I assume that's the point of all these questions—then it's the State Department she's going to want to contact, not us. Maybe you should try talking to the American consul. Unless"—his tone sharpened to a sudden professional interest—"you have some particular reason why you feel she'd want to contact our office?"

That did it.

"No, of course not!" Now it was Nicolás's turn to look at his watch, as though he'd just remembered an urgent appointment. "You're right. My wife can have no possible interest in your office. It's just that we've been checking with any—ah . . . foreign acquaintances she might have tried to contact. When I saw you here, I remembered that my wife had mentioned speaking to you, and so I thought I'd ask. On a long shot, as you Americans say."

He spread his hands in a very Latin gesture. "You will, of course, let us know immediately if she does contact you or anyone else from your office. I'm sure you can understand our concern to find her as soon as possible. As has become obvious, my wife has some serious emotional problems. Even delusions and hallucinations, from what the doctors can tell us. For her own safety, as well as for that of others, she needs to be under professional treatment as soon as possible. We'd hate for someone else to get hurt!"

His tone carried a very proper regret, but Doug detected a chilling malice lurking in Nicolás's blue eyes. This guy was a killer all right!

Well, Nicky-boy was going to find out that Doug could be dangerous too. And now it was time to finish this little tête-à-tête. He had made his point, and Nicolás seemed to be buying it, but if Doug had to stand here one more minute, exchanging platitudes with this creep, he wasn't going to be able to keep his fingers off the guy's neck!

Doug slid an expression of utter boredom over his anger. After all, considering their past relationship, the guy would be suspicious if he was too polite. "Look, Cortéz, I'm sorry about your domestic problems. Really, I am! But I've been out all night, okay? I'm tired, I'm hungry, and this food isn't getting any warmer. Right now I'm heading out of town to salvage what little remains of my weekend. If you want to start giving orders to the DEA, I suggest you go talk to my boss. Now, if you'll excuse me . . ."

Drawing his keys from his pocket, Doug took a purposeful step forward. If Cortéz wanted to get physical, fine! But Nicolás was already stepping aside, allowing him to brush past. Doug checked his side mirror as he reached the Land Rover. Nicolás was staring after him, but even as Doug inserted the key into the lock, the Cortéz heir turned on his heel and stalked back to the Ferrari. A glance inside the Land Rover showed no sign of Sara. Praying the girl had enough sense to keep her head down, wherever she was, Doug let the car door swing wide open, allowing a clear view of the interior as he leaned over to set the sack of food carefully on the next seat.

But Nicolás seemed to have lost interest in the DEA agent, and he was already backing out the Ferrari with great dispatch. As Doug tucked the black sack Ramon had given him behind his seat and climbed into the Land Rover, Nicolás accelerated out of the parking lot, apparently having forgotten the snack that had brought him to McDonald's in the first place.

Following at a more leisurely pace, Doug took note of the direction in which the Ferrari had roared off and turned the opposite way. He'd covered the first block before Sara emerged from hiding. Doug grabbed at the sack of food as she climbed over the back of the seat. She'd found some sandals that fit, he saw, and had changed into a rumpled but less objectionable T-shirt. She was also pale as a sheet.

"I saw Nicolás," she said unnecessarily. She slid down into the seat beside Doug, lifting the food order onto her lap and cradling her arms around it as though she had no idea what she was holding. "When he came over to the car like that . . ."—a shudder ran up her body—"he was looking right in the window. I could have sworn he'd seen me and that he was going to open the door any minute!"

She controlled another shudder with a visible effort. "What . . . what did he want?"

"You!" Doug told her bluntly. "He wanted to know whether you'd been in contact with us. And he did his level best to give the impression that last night's shooting was some mental aberration of yours and—just in case you *had* been in contact—that anything you might have to say should be discounted as psychotic babbling."

Sara drew in a sharp breath and closed her eyes. "And what did you tell him?"

Doug threw her a wry glance. "What do you think? That I had you tucked behind my back seat, of course!" He regretted the ill-timed joke when he noticed the white lines of fear pinched around her mouth. *Me and my cop humor!*

"Hey, it's okay!" Doug reached over to turn her chin toward him. Holding her gaze as she opened her eyes, he said gently, "Sara, you know I wouldn't have let him touch you back there! I *won't* let him touch you! Will you believe that?"

Doug waited until she made a small nod of assent before releasing her and turning his attention back to his driving. And just in time! He spun the steering wheel hard left as the right tires skidded in the gravel of the shoulder.

"Actually, other than the fright it's given you, I'm not sorry we ran into Nicolás back there. I think—no, I *know*—I managed to convince him that we've had no contact with you. And just as important, I made him believe that I never attached any real significance to our little conversation the other night. And since he's also under the strong impression that I'm leaving town for the weekend and that I have absolutely no interest at all in his personal affairs . . ."—Doug offered what he hoped was an encouraging grin—"with any luck, he'll leave us alone from now on."

From McDonald's, Doug had turned onto the wide boulevard that led out toward Viru Viru airport, where it became a broad, paved highway running out through the Chapare to the highland cities of Cochabamba and La Paz. The Land Rover was now approaching the city limits, with the airport control tower clearly visible across the palm-dotted fields to their right.

Letting his tone grow plaintive, Doug nodded toward the food sack still clutched tightly in Sara's arms. "Is there any chance of getting something to eat out of there before it's all stone cold? I don't know about you, but yesterday's dinner seems a long while back!"

His wry lament provided the desired distraction. With a quick apology, Sara busied herself digging out straws and napkins and adding ketchup to the hamburgers. But the tension in her posture didn't subside, and her tendency to glance back over her shoulder didn't abate, until they were well out of the city, and Doug had to prod her several times before she picked up her Big Mac. Then her hunger overcame her apprehension, and she dug in with relish.

Sara was piling the empty food containers back into the sack as the Land Rover crossed a long suspension bridge. On the far side, Doug turned the car off the highway, jolting down the embankment onto a narrow dirt track. At first the track was open, with clearings cut away on both sides of the road. The torrential rains responsible for the dense vegetation had driven the rural Chapare *campesinos* to build on stilts, and their thatched homes rose high above the clearings on great hardwood pilings like a series of children's tree forts. At the base of the pilings grew banana plantings and citrus, avocado, mango and papaya trees. Beyond the houses were small fields of rice, manioc, corn, and other crops that Sara didn't recognize.

Then the Land Rover turned onto another trail, this one narrower and showing little signs of use. The thatched houses grew farther apart until they disappeared altogether, and the jungle canopy closed in above the trail. Doug eased back on the throttle. Reaching over to turn off the air-conditioning, he rolled down the front windows. A rush of air, sultry but clean and sweet-smelling, blew through one window and out the other. With it came a chattering of birds and the raucous scream of a macaw, and then the furious chattering of an angry monkey somewhere off to Sara's right. The only manmade sound was the gentle purring of the Land Rover's finely tuned engine.

The tautness slowly ebbed from Sara's muscles. For an uncounted passage of time, she watched the jungle flow by, letting the peace and silence seep into every pore of her troubled mind. Doug Bradford seemed to feel the contentment of the jungle afternoon as well. Sitting easily back against his seat, he was humming something softly under his breath, his fingers tapping leisurely against the steering wheel. The glimmer of a smile lit his gray eyes as he caught Sara's glance.

She smiled back shyly. "It's so beautiful! And green. All those crops. I never realized they grew so much around here."

As the Land Rover jolted left onto yet another narrow track, she waved a hand toward a clearing of luxuriant green bushes opening up beside the trail. "That one there. I've seen it growing everywhere. What is it?"

Doug followed her gesture, and the smile left his eyes. "Coca," he said briefly. He nodded toward the long-legged house on the edge of the field. Instead of the traditional wooden railing, this one had a cement-tile roof and bricked-in sides. Under the pilings, Sara could see a brand-new Toyota pickup and a Mitsubishi Montero. "And maybe more than just the leaf, judging by the price of those vehicles."

A cold chill descended over Sara, and some of her new found

peace left her. So that innocent-looking green bush was the deadly leaf she'd heard so much about.

"Why don't they do something about it?" she said with sudden violence. "I mean, what is the point of running around catching drug dealers if they're just going to let people keep growing the stuff? Why don't they just . . . just go cut it all down or something?"

"You're starting to sound like an agent," Doug said dryly. "Hey, you won't get any argument from me. The easiest solution to this whole problem would be to waltz in here and dig up every one of those coca beds. Except for one thing. It isn't illegal to grow coca in Bolivia. Just to process it into cocaine.

"You ask any one of these *campesinos*, and they'll be quick to tell you"—his tone grew even drier—"that *their* coca is just for tea or for traditional chewing. The ninety-five percent or more that ends up as cocaine always belongs to the next guy."

"So can't they encourage them to grow something else?" Sara asked incredulously as they rolled past another vast planting of coca bushes. "If they know most of it is going to end up as cocaine. I saw plenty of other crops growing back there."

"They do," Doug answered patiently, easing the Land Rover down the bank of a creek. "The U.S. government has poured half a billion dollars into the Chapare in the last couple of decades to encourage alternative development. Roads. Schools. Clinics. You name it! They'll actually pay the *campesinos* to tear up their coca plantings—give them machinery and seed and farm equipment. Help them put in new crops. Benedicto and his people are some of those who have taken advantage of the program, as you'll see tomorrow.

"But the Bolivian government has absolutely refused to make the eradication of coca anything but voluntary. There's just too many people with too much to lose putting pressure on them. Not just the *narcos* working behind the scenes but the *campesinos* themselves. In fact, there are plenty of *campesinos* who'll take our handouts and then move back into the jungle and plant themselves another field."

Doug glanced over at Sara as the Land Rover lumbered through a creek bed and up the other side. "It's simple economics, really. As long as the *narcos* keep the price up, the *campesinos* can make several times the income off a field of coca as they can off rice or tea or any other legitimate crop. Not to mention that with the coca, there is virtually no labor involved. Just strip the bushes of their leaves a couple times a year and pack them up for the *narcos*. Why bother with all that planting and hoeing and weeding?"

The track dead-ended suddenly at a deserted clearing. The pilings of the house were toppled to the ground and its cultivated area was already reverting to brush. Guided by some landmark that was invisible to Sara, Doug swung in under the branches of a huge, spreading hardwood. Another track opened up ahead of them, this one smooth and hard-packed.

"So what do they do for the rest of the year?" Sara asked curiously. "If they're not farming?"

Doug shrugged without lessening the concentration with which he was negotiating a deadfall in the path. "A lot of them work for the *narcos*. We figure there's probably ten thousand maceration pits out in that jungle. That's where they tread out the leaves to get the raw cocaine paste," he explained. "Or in the actual labs." He gestured back the way they'd come. "That place we just passed turned out to be a coke lab. Back when I was running training exercises on these trails. Gave us the excuse to go in there and rip up the guy's coca patch. He should be out of prison by now, but from the way those fields are grown over, I guess he never came back."

Sara listened to his matter-of-fact reply with amazement. She'd been too preoccupied with her own problems to wonder exactly what it was that the man beside her did with his days. Running around on jungle trails? Training the soldiers of a foreign government? And he talked about finding cocaine labs and hunting down dangerous criminals as casually as though he were strolling downtown.

"But isn't that dangerous? I mean, what if one of those people tried to shoot you?"

"It wouldn't be the first time." There was amusement in the glance Doug shot her that Sara didn't understand. "Anything can be dangerous, even crossing a street. That's what keeps life exciting."

"Exciting!" Sara stared at him in disbelief. "Is that why you do all this? Because you *like* danger and . . . and shooting and all that?"

She broke off, reminded suddenly of her manners and of why Doug Bradford was sitting in this car in the middle of the jungle. "It just seems so—different!" she went on lamely. "Your life, I mean. My own life has always been so ordinary and . . . and *safe*—until now, that is!" She managed a ghost of a smile, which told more than anything the effect the jungle serenity was having on her nerves. "And to be honest . . . well, I guess it just goes to show what a coward I am, but after these last few days, I'm beginning to think that's all I'm cut out for. Ordinary, I mean. And safe. So I've always kind of wondered, when I see policemen and firemen and people like you on the news and all, what would make someone choose a job"—her gesture encompassed a thousand cocaine labs and a land filled with men like Julio Vargas and Luis Cortéz—"that's going to put them in danger on a regular basis. Is that why? Because of the excitement? Like the way you hear of people spending their lives bungee jumping or diving over waterfalls?"

Doug slammed on the brakes with a violence that slid Sara forward off the seat. But before she could be dismayed at his reaction, she saw the animal that had burst into the road. It was the size and shape of a small pig, with inch-long brown bristles, but with the stringy tail and elongated pointy face of a rat.

"*Jochi*," Doug commented as the animal disappeared with a rustle into the underbrush on the other side of the path. "If I'd brought my rifle, I'd go after it. It'd make a nice change from MREs for supper."

He drove on in silence for a minute or two, but just as Sara was beginning to think he'd forgotten her question, he picked up as though there'd been no interruption. When he spoke, his voice was reflective. "That's it for some people, I suppose. Excitement. Adventure. The need for a challenge bigger than you're going to find in a desk job. Some men are just born to it, I guess. I know I'd never settle down to a nine-to-five career. Most of the guys I work with feel the same way."

His hands were firm on the wheel as he jolted through a series of chuckholes that had Sara's teeth vibrating. "But there's got to be more than that. If all you want is excitement, then bungee jumping and waterfall hopping is a whole lot easier than what we do. The DEA doesn't want people who are in this just for kicks. There's got to be a sense of responsibility—of duty, if that isn't too old-fashioned a word. Not just to your country, but to other people. You see people getting hurt, and you realize that someone's got to stand up and do something about it or the bad guys are going to win. And then no one's going to be living that safe, ordinary life you were talking about. So you decide to be that someone."

Something in his tone told Sara that he wasn't just making a hypothetical statement, and she asked gently, "Is that what happened to you? You saw someone getting hurt, and you decided to do something about it?"

Noticing his sudden change of expression, she added quickly, "I'm sorry, it's none of my business. You don't have to tell me."

Doug glanced across at her. "No, that's okay," he said as though he were faintly surprised. "I don't mind—if you really want to hear it."

"Yeah, I'd really like to hear it," Sara responded.

Doug was silent for a moment as though gathering his memories.

Then he started slowly, "It was when I was still a kid. Thirteen—maybe fourteen. I don't remember exactly. We were living in Arizona then. My dad had a ranch—cattle mainly—passed down to him from my grandpa and from his grandpa before him. It was right on the Mexican border, and I can't remember a time when we didn't see folks crossing over from Mexico. But it was a big spread, and they never came near the house, so we didn't really pay them any attention, except the border patrol would come by the house from time to time to ask permission to camp out down on the southern edge of the ranch."

Doug eased down into another creek bed, this one with rushing water deep enough to splash up onto the bumper. As the Land Rover emerged onto the bank, shaking off the water like a wet dog, he went on, "Then one day—I guess I was in eighth grade—a patrol officer stopped by the school. Said he'd been sent to pick me up. There'd been a big shoot-out on the ranch. Not illegal immigrants this time, but drugs. No one from the ranch was hurt—they were all out on the range, except my mom, who was in town shopping—but two federal officers were down, shot dead right in our front yard. There was still blood all over the ground when I got home and bullet holes in the siding of the house. One of the officers had a boy on my basketball team.

"I guess it was the first time I really saw that drugs weren't just something you said 'no' to, but something that could wreck people's lives. Regular people, not just those inner-city street gangs I'd seen on the news that were so far removed from our rural community they might as well have been fiction. And so, as kids will, I made this vow to myself that I was going to do something about it! You know, the Batman-Flash Gordon 'Save the World from Evil' syndrome. A year later, my parents split up, and I ended up in Miami with my mom. But it stuck. I never did consider anything seriously after that but a career in law enforcement. I was actually thinking of criminal law, but I got tired of nothing but theory, so as soon as I got my political science degree, I signed up at the police academy. Three months later, I was out on the streets with the MPD. That's the Miami Police Department."

He gave Sara a wry grin as though mocking his own seriousness. "A little corny, eh? Kid comes in contact with the seamy side of life. Vows a lifetime revenge on the bad guys!"

"I don't think it's corny," Sara said softly, feeling as though she were understanding something of this man for the first time. "You could have just walked away. Instead, you turned a bad experience into a career of helping people. I think that's . . . special." She felt her cheeks grow warm at the quizzical glance he gave her and added quickly with an impishness that had Doug turning his head to give her a longer look, "Of course, if you'd been really smart, you'd have sued the government for psychological trauma and spent the rest of your life on a government subsidy."

Doug laughed out loud at that, and Sara was encouraged to ask, "So if you were a policeman in Miami, how did you end up in Bolivia with the DEA? Isn't it a completely different kind of work?"

"Oh, that came a couple years later. By that time, I was working undercover in anti-narcotics. And I'd gone on with night classes to finish my masters in criminal justice. My captain told me I was over-qualified for what I was doing and encouraged me to buck for DEA. It sounded interesting, especially the chance to go overseas some-day, so I did. As soon as I had in my minimum time stateside, I put in for an overseas post. Bolivia was the first to open up."

Doug broke off his narrative as a sudden motion caught his pe-ripheral vision. The Land Rover was passing under the branches of an avocado tree, and a spider monkey, bored with branch-hopping, had chosen that moment to launch itself at the car. Sara gasped as the Land Rover swerved sideways across the track. The quick action brought the monkey's swing up short, less than a meter from the windshield. The vine to which it clung carried it back to the tree, its black, hairy limbs splayed so that it looked like the spider it had been named after. Chattering furiously, it grabbed a cantaloupe-sized fruit and tossed it at the Land Rover. The avocado hit the roof and splatted, leaving yellow-green splotches as it rolled down over the windshield and off the hood. Doug winced. "There goes the wash job!"

He scowled at the victory dance being gleefully enacted in his rearview mirror. "You sure you're wanting my life history here? It's not exactly pleasure reading."

Sara eyed his frown covertly. Was he joking again, or did he consider her interest too personal? She didn't know him well enough to tell.

"I really would like to learn more about what you do," she said diffidently. "If you wouldn't mind. It just . . . it all sounds so fascinating—your job and all. Besides,"—she turned her head to study a particularly unexciting clearing—"I thought it would help pass the time. I . . . I'd rather talk than just sit and think. And you already know everything about me!"

Sara managed to keep her tone light, but Doug, casting a sharp glance at her averted profile, saw there a desolation that had been missing for some minutes, and he gave himself a savage mental kick before saying aloud, "Sure, we can talk."

Not that he was any great shakes for talking—just ask the new agents who had the misfortune to sit through some of his lectures. But if it would help keep her mind off her troubles, he'd talk from here to kingdom come.

Doug cleared his throat. "Shall we start with basic training? That's always a good cure for insomnia."

He was rewarded with a glimmer of a smile, and as the track unrolled beneath the treads of the Land Rover, he went on to tell Sara about the U.S. Marine Corps base in Quantico, Virginia, where the DEA agents-in-training shared instructors and classroom lectures with the FBI. He described the Ranger training at Fort Benning that made Quantico look like a sissy's stroll on the beach. He told her about sitting up all night outside a drug dealer's mansion and learning to pass himself off as any one of a dozen different personas for undercover work.

After a while, Sara shifted her eyes back to the jungle, asking Doug a question every time he slowed down just to show that she was paying attention, but otherwise just listening. There was a lavishness of creation here that she'd never seen before, even in the cooler rain forests of her native Washington State. Trees with huge, spreading branches like oak or maple; and other tall, thin trees with virtually no branches at all, just leaves like green paper streamers. *Paraísos* blooming peach and lilac and pink and orange and white. Palms shooting up straight and tall as telephone poles, and ending in one small tuft of fronds. Smaller palms with fronds fringed like the trim of a buckskin shirt. And tying it all together into an almost impenetrable mass were the flowering vines that made a machete the first and most necessary tool for every Chapare inhabitant.

Doug, keeping an eye on Sara, along with the road and the surrounding jungle, saw her hands slowly unclench to lie loosely in her lap and was satisfied. "Then there's the times you run into Murphy's Law," he said lightly, backing the Land Rover away from a drop-off where the rains had washed out the track. Murphy's Law had been in play the afternoon Doug climbed six flights of stairs to arrest a cozy trio of Jamaican brothers who were holed up in a Fort Lauderdale housing project.

"Theoretically, you're supposed to shout 'Police!' and then give them a reasonable amount of time to get the door open. But if you think the guy inside is dangerous, you'd be pretty stupid to give him time to go for his gun. So, in real life, the time lapse between shouting

'Police' and kicking down the door is maybe a tenth of a second. And I'm not saying which comes first!

"Only this time the door was a little on the flimsy side. The kick—along with half my leg—went clear through the paneling." Sara's giggle drew a quick glance and a smile from Doug. "So here I am with my leg buried up past the knee, hopping in on one foot, with three big black guys, mean as they come, starting to come after me across the room. And while I'm trying to keep my gun on all three of them at once, the door just keeps swinging open, taking me with it."

"So what happened?" Sara demanded. The last vestiges of trouble had left her amber eyes, and they were alight with laughter at the image he'd invoked. "I notice you're still alive."

"That's why you bring back-up," Doug told her dryly. He was surprised to find that he was enjoying himself. Sara Cortéz was a good listener, and her patent interest and the shy intelligence of her questions encouraged him to continue every time he could have sworn he was boring her to death. As the slow kilometers rolled away under the tires of the Land Rover, Doug found himself wracking his brain for other past incidents that could be milked for a humorous twist.

He downplayed the danger that had often accompanied his work, and as for the degradation and sheer human filth that were a lot bigger part of the job than the occasional ludicrous moment, he left that out altogether. He was trying to cheer Sara up, not depress her!

Only occasionally did they encounter another human being—an Indian woman trudging along the track, or a stooped figure in a clearing. But Doug had rolled the windows back up some time ago, so all that could be seen from the outside was the reflection of the surrounding greenery off the tinted blackness of the glass.

"As for my boss, I don't know what aggravated him more—that we almost got nailed by our own side, or the ammo we laid out without landing a single shot. He ordered us back to the firing range every afternoon for a month."

Doug slowed to turn the Land Rover onto the narrowest and least-traveled track they'd been on yet. If the internal compass that had served him well so far wasn't mistaken, the spot he'd chosen to wait out the night was somewhere just up ahead. And about time, too. The sky above the jungle canopy had deepened from rose to the palest of greens, and the tangle of vegetation on either side of the track had grown dark and mysterious. A bat swooped down over the hood of the Land Rover, the first one out for the night's hunting, and from somewhere, a rooster crowed. Not a tame one from some nearby *chaco,* but some wild jungle bird. The shadows lay thick across the track, and inside the vehicle, Sara could no longer make out more than an indistinct outline when she turned her head to look across at Doug.

"All your stories are about the States," she said. "Hasn't anything interesting ever happened to you here in Bolivia?"

She could have bit her tongue immediately. The long pause was enough to tell Sara that the same "interesting" episode that had jumped to her mind was going through Doug's mind as well. Two years had passed since the raid on Cortéz Industries. And it still wasn't funny.

But before the silence became awkward, Doug said lightly, "Not a whole lot. I guess I'm just too good these days to make those kinds of mistakes."

He reached over and switched on the headlights. "I think I've made a fool of myself enough for tonight. Are you hungry?"

The abrupt question caught Sara by surprise. She glanced around as though a restaurant might materialize somewhere up ahead. But the road was empty, and Sara suddenly realized that they hadn't seen a single living soul—not even as much as an abandoned coca field or deserted hut—since the last turn. Doug slowed to a crawl, leaning out his window to study the dark mass of uncut brush that edged the track. Sara was opening her mouth to ask him what he was looking for when he slammed on the brakes, backed up a few meters, and cranked the steering wheel hard to the left. Sara could have sworn he was turning into a solid wall of undergrowth, but before she could comment, the Land Rover had pushed its way into a hidden clearing—a perfect circle ten meters in diameter. Bumping into the center, Doug switched off the headlights. "This is where we'll park for the night," he told Sara. Climbing quickly out of the driver's seat and reaching behind the seat for a flashlight, he walked around to the back of the Land Rover.

Sara stepped down from the vehicle and tilted her head back to look at the sky. The last tinges of twilight were fading, blurring the distinction between the tossing sea that was the treetops and the somber expanse above, until she could see a star blink on and then another. The brush through which the Land Rover had crashed was already springing up to hide their passage, and for a whimsical moment, it seemed to Sara that they'd stepped out of the real world onto some small and remote island beyond the reach of men. Some-where mystical and starlit, where evil and violence could not intrude.

Then Doug lit a fluorescent lantern, and suddenly this was just another clearing in the jungle, though perhaps a little more symmetrical than most.

Sara wandered over as Doug dimmed the lantern to its lowest setting and set it beside the rear tire where the bulk of the Land Rover would shield its pallid beam from the direction of the road. Reaching again into the rear of the car, he brought out a heavy canvas tarp and spread it out beside the car.

"So, what'll it be?" Digging inside his backpack, Doug brought out a couple of the food packets he'd left for Sara at the motel. "Baked beans or beef stew?"

Sara eyed the packets doubtfully. The heavy, sealed plastic gave no hint as to what was inside. "I'm not sure. Am I eating it cold or hot?"

"Oh, we'll cook it, don't you worry!" Diving back into his pack, Doug brought out a block shaped like a cube of margarine but several sizes larger. With his pocket knife, he cut into the block, peeling back the wrapping. The contents looked like a white putty or Play-Doh. Doug cut off a large chunk and molded it into a flattened ball.

"What's that stuff?" Sara asked.

"It's what's going to cook our dinner. Here, take it just a minute." Dropping the ball into her hands, Doug sliced into the MREs. Sara pinched at one edge gingerly. It was just the slightest bit crumbly, like homemade Play-Doh rather than the store-bought stuff. Doug was emptying the food packets onto the tarp, when he added nonchalantly, "It's a plastic explosive."

"Explosive!" Sara dropped the putty as though it had burned her. "You mean—like a bomb?"

Doug laughed heartily as he recovered the ball of explosive from the ground. "Hey, it's safe enough. Here, look!"

Pinching off a fingernail-size dab, Doug tore a match from one of the matchbooks included in the MRE packets and struck it. Sara sucked in her breath as he held the flame to the tiny ball in his palm. But there was no explosion, just a sudden whoosh of flame. Doug dropped the burning stuff to the ground where it blazed up with an astounding amount of white heat for such a small amount of material. Grinding it out with his boot heel, he grinned at Sara. "See? Perfectly harmless!"

Doug showed Sara how to remove the metal base from one of his army canteens, folding open the collapsible handles to form a makeshift saucepan. "It's called C-4," he explained. "It's a military explosive. We use it for blowing up cocaine labs—or cooking. I carry two or three of those bars in my backpack all the time. It's really great stuff. You can carry it around, drop it, burn it, whatever, but it takes an actual explosion to set it off. We carry fuses for that. Then— well, you don't want to be too close. It packs a real punch."

The food was surprisingly good, or maybe Sara was just hungry. She opted for the beef stew, which she dumped into a saucepan and held over the unorthodox campfire. The chunk of C-4, no bigger than the palm of Doug's hand, burned with a steady white flame that had the stew bubbling in less than a minute.

While they ate, Doug told her how his Leopards had shaped out this clearing as an FOB—a forward operating-base—when they'd been running training exercises in this part of the Chapare. Sara listened, fascinated, as he described night marches to sneak up on jungle cocaine labs, and confrontations with angry *cocaleros*, who fought pitched battles to keep the anti-narcotics troops from destroying their maceration pits. Not once during the meal did Doug mention the present circumstances. The two of them could as easily have been on a camping trip.

"Your life is so different from mine," Sara said again, almost wistfully, as she mopped up the last of her stew with a piece of bread. She looked across the weak beam of the fluorescent lantern to where Doug was hunkered down over a fresh chunk of C-4, heating water for coffee.

"Thank you," she said softly. "For this afternoon."

Doug didn't pretend not to know what she meant. Pouring half the hot water into the cap of his canteen, he stirred in some Néscafe and leaned around the flame to pass it to Sara. "You feeling any better now?"

Sara stared down into the inky interior of the canteen cap. "A little, I guess. As long as I can keep from thinking about it." She lifted her head to give him a direct look. "I've been wanting to tell you how grateful I am for everything you've done. I know you say the Cortezes are part of your job, but all of this . . ." Her glance went around the campsite. "You didn't have to do all this just for your job. And the way you've been so kind and patient with me when . . . when I've been so upset."

A restless movement and grunt of protest from the other side of the fire made clear Doug's discomfort at her praise, and she finished quickly, "Anyway, thank you."

She added with a faint smile, remembering when she'd thought the government agent thoroughly deserved his single status, "You know, for a bachelor you really *are* pretty good at this! Most men I know wouldn't know what to do with a girl in hysterics. It's hard to believe you've gotten this far without some lucky girl snatching you up."

The comment was rhetorical, meant only to change the subject to a less serious vein, and there was nothing unusual in Doug's brief pause before he resumed pouring some water into his canteen cup. But Sara had the distinct feeling that a door had slammed suddenly in her face, and she found herself stammering, "Did . . . did I say something? . . . I didn't mean any—"

"No." Setting his canteen on the ground, Doug stood up to grind the last flaring remnants of the C-4 into the scorched earth with his boot heel. Then he picked up his coffee and walked over to the Land Rover to sit down an arm's length from Sara, his back against the front tire. "I was married once," he said reflectively, more to the night than to Sara. "Her name was Julie. You'd have liked her, I think, and she would've liked you."

Sara looked at Doug in the dark, but didn't say anything. After a brief pause, he began telling her about Julie, and about little Esther Rose. It had been so long since he'd spoken of his loss that he was astonished to find he was recalling more of the good times than the tragic end. The sweetness and laughter were no longer memories he wanted to push away but a release to share. It took a swiftly drawn breath from beside him before Doug realized that tears were running down Sara's cheeks.

"Hey," he said remorsefully. "I didn't mean to make you cry!"

"I know." Sara brushed a hand across her lashes. "It's just so sad! I'm really sorry for you!"

"Don't be! It was a long time ago. I've learned to live with it." Doug stopped to look at Sara with some of the same surprise he'd felt earlier when he'd been carrying on about his youthful law enforcement ambitions. "You know, I don't think I've told anyone about Julie and the kids in years. Most of my acquaintances here in Bolivia don't even know I was ever married. I don't know exactly what it is, Sara, but it's hard to believe that we've only really spoken to each other two or three times."

"I know what you mean. Even when we were arguing, it seemed like I'd known you for a long time. And now we're sitting here talking like old . . ."

Sara broke off, suddenly shy at what she'd been about to say, and Doug finished quietly, "Friends? I hope you'll consider me a friend, Sara."

Sara felt a fresh stinging behind her eyelids at the gentleness in his tone. It hadn't been so long ago that she'd counted this man an adversary, and now he was maybe the closest thing to a friend she had left in the world. Certainly in this country.

"I . . . thank you. I'd like that." Setting her coffee down on the ground beside her, she attempted a smile. "And I'm glad you told me about Julie. She sounds very nice."

Her smile faded as she looked at her empty hands. "At least your memories are good ones. I . . . with Nicolás, I can't even think of the good ones now. They've all been spoiled by what he did. I think it might be easier to accept him dying than . . . than all this!"

With the stars glittering cold above the black circle of the jungle and the fluorescent lantern casting only the palest finger of light across the grass, Sara couldn't see the expression on Doug's face, but his shadowy bulk was a comforting nearby presence, and she found herself talking about how she'd met Nicolás, trying to explain a little of how it had been.

"I know now how naive and . . . and *stupid* I was! But I was so tired of being alone . . . of watching my friends go home to their families for the holidays while I went back to an empty apartment. It's the most terrible, *rootless* feeling, knowing that there isn't one person on the face of the earth to whom you really belong. Even when people are kind, you're always the guest, the outsider. And then . . . then Nicky came along, and he said he loved me. My friends told me I didn't know him well enough . . . that I should wait . . . find out more about him. And they were right, I guess. But I was so crazy in love, and I had to decide—Nicky was leaving— and he was so . . . so—"

"I know what he's like!" There was more than a hint of dryness in Doug's tone. "And don't be so hard on yourself! You'd lost your mother and brother and grandparents at an early age. Then your father."

Sara didn't question how he knew the details about her family. If he'd been investigating the Cortezes, he'd probably had her checked out as well.

"You were lonely and looking for someone to love—that's only natural," Doug was saying. "And there's no denying that Nicolás Cortéz is as charming as they come. You couldn't have known what he was!"

Doug hesitated, not quite sure how to phrase what he wanted to say. "But—look, Sara, I know this is a bad time for you, but I hope you won't consider it trite if I tell you that you're really not alone in all this. Maybe you don't have a family you can fall back on, but you do belong to someone who cares about you very much."

"God, you mean!" Sara hunched her shoulders disparagingly. "Oh, sure, I know I belong to God. I went to Sunday school. I was practically raised on John 3:16: 'For God so loved the world that He gave His only begotten Son' and all that. But that's the whole point! God loves the *world*. All of it, right down to the murderers and rapists and . . . and narcos! That doesn't exactly make me anything special! Just . . . just one more dot among billions. And if you've got billions, who's going to notice or care if one dot gets lost in the shuffle. You know, like people talking about how much they love all the heathen over in Africa or somewhere. Which is fine, except that isn't going to help one lost kid who is in some crowded corner of a refugee camp!"

Sara dropped her head onto her knees, her words becoming muffled. "I . . . I guess I just wanted someone who would love me as *me*. Because . . . because he saw something about *me* that was worth loving! That's what I thought I had with Nicky. He made me feel beautiful and glamorous and . . . and special, even though I knew I really wasn't. But it was never real! He wasn't really loving me, just someone he thought I was. Someone exciting and sexy who could kick up her heels and dance and swing and party. Not just a . . . a dull, ordinary girl who takes life too seriously and doesn't have a bone of excitement in her body."

Doug shook his head in amazement. How could anyone with so much to offer have such a poor opinion of herself? He shifted his position to get a better view of Sara. She was sitting with her knees drawn up to her chin, her head buried in her arms, her long hair spilling down to brush the tarp. The lantern was turning her hair into a shimmering curtain, and Doug found himself reaching out to touch one of those silky golden strands before, shocked at the impulse, he snatched his hand back.

A sudden, burning fury shook him. What had Nicolás Cortéz done to this girl? He'd destroyed her self-confidence, chipped away at her self-esteem—and all because she had too much strength and human dignity to fit into his selfish playboy existence! The brief glimpse he'd had of Sara comforting a blood-stained and sobbing little boy rose into Doug's mind. Such a wealth of love and human kindness—and all wasted on a rotten scoundrel who hadn't hesitated to sacrifice his wife to maintain his millionaire lifestyle and illicit pursuits!

Doug cleared his throat roughly. "Is that what Cortéz has been telling you? Well, take it from me, he doesn't know what he's talking about! You're worth ten of any one of his crowd, and don't you ever forget it!"

Forcing his eyes away from her huddled shadow, he fixed his gaze on the black silhouette of a coconut palm that loomed above the other trees at the edge of the clearing. When he spoke again, his voice was quiet. "As for God loving you—well, I don't see it that way at all. That we're just one out of billions for him, I mean. The Bible says he *knows* us. Not just as part of some big, impersonal world, but as very special individuals who he personally designed and breathed into life. Every personality trait, every talent, every dimple. I can't remember where it says it exactly—somewhere in Psalms, I think— but there's a verse that talks about how God knitted us together while we were still in our mother's womb. Just think of it—every cell and gene and DNA code in our body! You put that kind of work into someone, and you've got to care about them.

"It's just like being a parent. You can have more than one kid, and every one of them completely different in personality and appearance. But you don't have to split up your love in order for each child to get a share. And you don't use up all your love on one kid so that there's none left for the others. Every one of your children is just as special and wonderful and unique as the others, and you love each one so completely that you'd give your life for them."

Doug broke off as he heard the pain and longing that had crept into his voice. Sara raised her head from her knees to look at him. Then, wordlessly, wanting to return some of the comfort he'd offered her, she reached over to squeeze the big hand that had clenched on one bent knee. His other hand came up to cover hers, and their eyes met in silence and complete understanding.

Then Sara drew her hand away, and Doug continued reflectively, "I guess that's the way I see God. He really *is* our Father, just like the Bible says. Not like a human father, who messes up and maybe forgets his kids in his own problems. But the way a father really should be: loving and kind and compassionate. And when we need a little discipline, he supplies that too.

"And even though I might not be able to tell my kids apart after the first dozen or so, God knows every one of us—all the billions he's created—and he can think about us and listen to us all at the same time. Kind of like one of those big Cray computers that can do millions of transactions in the time our human brain can add two and two. Only so much more vast and powerful that we can't even picture it. Except that God isn't just some big, impersonal machine. He loves us far more than we can even imagine."

Sara didn't answer. She'd turned her head to look at the lantern, as though it held some momentous secret that could only be ferreted out by intense concentration. But after a moment, Doug caught a small sound—a choking sound like a sniffle that has been quickly stifled. Pulling out a clean handkerchief, he tucked it into her hand. Sara closed her fingers over it without a word, then unfolded it to wipe her cheeks dry and blow her nose. Glancing down at the sodden linen, she managed a watery chuckle that broke off into a sob. "I'm sorry. It seems like all I ever do around you is bawl! At this rate, you're not going to have any handkerchiefs left."

She drew in a deep, shuddering breath. "It's just . . . I used to think like you. That God was my Father. That he loved me and that I . . . I loved him. And then, after I lost my family, it was like he just—went! And all these years, it's like I've been frozen up inside. Like God was out there somewhere, but I couldn't reach him because he'd gone so far away."

She swung around suddenly on Doug. "That's what I don't get! You talk about God being this loving heavenly Father. Well, a real father takes care of his children! He doesn't let their world fall apart! How can you see God like that when he lets so many bad things happen—like my family and Nicky and . . . and your wife and kids? How can you be so . . . calm about it all? Doesn't it make you angry that God would let a couple of juvenile delinquents destroy the people you love and then walk away without a scratch? Don't you ever want to just scream at him and ask why?"

"Sure, I've wanted to scream at God," Doug said wryly. "And I've done plenty of it, too. Especially those first few months after Julie and the kids. Julie was always the strong one as far as faith went in our home, and without her I wasn't even sure I wanted to go on. I quit going to church for a while. But . . ."—he stopped to give Sara a keen glance—"you sure you want to hear all this? Seems like I've been doing a lot of talking around here."

When Sara nodded, Doug shrugged. "Well, okay. But if I get to rambling, just tell me to shut up." He fell silent for a moment before he went on, "I guess maybe it was the thought of Julie looking over my shoulder that made me pick up a Bible instead of a bottle of booze like I might have a few years earlier. And I guess you could call it a coincidence that my Bible opened up at the Psalms, since they do come smack in the middle of the book. Either way, they grabbed me. This guy David was asking the same questions I was! Where is God? Why is he turning his back on me? Why should decent people have to suffer and hurt while bad guys walk the streets with everything they ever wanted?"

"Yeah, well, it's fine to have questions!" Sara put in bitterly. "But it'd be nice to have a few answers!"

"But that was the whole point," Doug countered swiftly. "The more I read those psalms, the more I saw that there weren't just questions there. I mean, here was David telling God about how bad things were, and then all of a sudden he'd be praising him! And as I started looking for some explanations instead of just screaming, I began to see some things that . . . well, they didn't make an empty house any less painful, but they did help me come to terms with it.

"For one thing, I was acting as though I was the only person in the world who'd ever lost a loved one. But I wasn't! The world was full of people suffering just as much as I was—and maybe a whole lot more! Parents who have to watch their children slowly starve to death. Children cowering under the unspeakable abuse of evil men—if you'd seen some of the things I have, it would make you sick! The fact is, we live in a sick, messed-up world. All you've got to do is switch on the news to see that. And being a Christian doesn't make you any more exempt than anyone else. Just look at how many Christians are being martyred for their faith around the world right now. The question isn't 'Why should anything bad happen to me?' It's 'Why *shouldn't* it?' It happens to everyone else!"

"But that's just it!" Sara cried out. "Why should it happen to *anyone*? Why *do* we live in such a sick world? Why do people get away with being so . . . so evil? If God is so powerful and loving, how could he ever let things get this bad? And why doesn't he just stop it all instead of sitting up there on his hands while people get hurt and the world falls to pieces around us?"

"Hey, wait a minute." Doug shifted to a more comfortable position against the hard rubber of the tire, stretching his long legs out in front of him. "We can't go blaming the state of our world on God! *We're* the ones who've messed things up, not him! Humankind, that is. I mean, just look at what God started us out with. A world so perfect and incredible that we're *still* uncovering its treasures. And the freedom to do what we wanted with it. Which we promptly used to go our own way and do our own thing!

"Oh, sure, I suppose God could have kept us from making such stupid choices—if all he wanted was a bunch of wind-up dolls. But he created us as independent, thinking beings, not robots. He wants us to love and follow him because we *choose* to, not because he's forced us into it. And that means giving us the freedom to choose our own destiny. Even if he knew he wasn't going to like a lot of the choices we were going to make. So if we've got to live with the consequences of a few thousand years of bad choices, it's kind of hard to blame anyone but ourselves!"

Sara looked at him sharply. Was he preaching at her? But Doug was gazing thoughtfully into the night as though he were reflecting on something from his own past, not hers.

"Anyway, that's a little off the subject. You asked why God lets bad things happen at all. Why he doesn't just put an end to the whole thing right now—or at least protect his own children from having to live with the consequences of our messed-up world like everyone else. That's what you were getting at, wasn't it? Well, like I said this morning, I don't have any great answer. The Bible says a lot about how trials can help our faith to grow, and how even the bad things in our lives can work out for good in the long run if we love God and are following His will. I'm sure that's a big part of it. But maybe it just comes down in the end to the fact that God doesn't look at time the way we do—or trouble and death either!"

Doug paused for a long swallow of coffee. It was stone cold. He set the cup down on the ground beside him. "You see, God started all this with a happy ending in mind, and he's still working on that happy ending, in spite of all the mess man's made of things. He's got no intention of letting evil and injustice and murder—or the people doing them—go on forever, believe me!

"But he's got his own timetable for taking care of it, and if it seems to us that he's taking his time about fixing the state of the universe, you've got to remember that to God, all of human history isn't much more than a moment. He's looking at the whole thing from beginning to end, not just our little part. And if it doesn't always make much sense from where we're standing down here, it's all clear from where God is sitting."

"Isn't that what I've been saying?" Sara cried, but her tone now was less bitter and more questioning. "God's up there in heaven working out his master plan for the universe, and I'm sure it's all going to turn out great. But in the meantime, what about us—here and now? Is that all we are—just one more pawn among the billions he's moving around, and if we get hurt in the process, tough luck?"

Doug smothered a sigh. This was turning into a regular preaching session—or another argument! But he couldn't just leave it like this. "That's not what I meant. Look, I told you I wasn't much good at this. But just because God allows suffering and loss to come into our lives doesn't mean he doesn't care. Or that he isn't there with us. It's . . . well, let's go back to my 'parent' example. Sometimes you've got to take your kid to the doctor, right? And sometimes there's a big, ugly needle involved. Now, you as a parent know that shot's necessary and that your kid has to go through with it if she's going to get better. But I can tell you this! When that long needle pokes into your kid's arm and she's screaming at the top of her lungs, your head may say one thing, but your heart is feeling her fear and pain every bit as much she does. And you'd give just about anything to take her place!"

Doug's throat was getting dry, and he considered another swallow of his coffee. But army instant was bad enough without drinking it cold.

"Here, maybe this'll make more sense! There's a story my pastor read at the funeral. I'm sure you probably know it—the death and resurrection of Lazarus. I've never heard a funeral without it. Anyway, Lazarus and his sisters Martha and Mary were special friends of Jesus, right? So you can imagine, when Lazarus gets sick, they're expecting Jesus to be there right away to heal him. Only he never came! By the time Jesus finally showed, Lazarus had been dead for four days.

"Well, of course, Jesus had his reasons. He knew that Lazarus' death was necessary to pave the way for a miracle that would give hope of the resurrection to every generation since! But Mary and Martha didn't know that. All they knew was that their friend hadn't come and their brother was dead. So when they went out to see Jesus, they were really hurting! Now, Jesus knew they had nothing to cry about, because in just a few minutes they were going to be seeing their brother again. But what did he do? It's the shortest verse in the Bible, John 11:35: 'Jesus wept!' Even though Jesus knew there was going to be a happy ending, if they'd just trust him and hold on a bit, his friends were hurting *now!* So he wept with them. Because he loved them and felt their pain."

Doug's legs were starting to fall asleep. He was also beginning to think maybe he'd overdone the lecture. But Sara seemed to be listening attentively enough. Rising gingerly to his feet, he picked up his canteen cap and walked over to the edge of the tarp to pour the cold coffee into the grass. Then he swung around to look down at Sara with a rueful smile.

"I'm afraid you got a sixty-four-dollar answer to a pretty simple question there. But if you ask what I got out of all my own screaming out at God, I guess that pretty well sums it up. God never made us any promise of a pain-free life. In fact, as long as we're still on this earth, you can just about count on problems and heartache. But he doesn't leave us alone with it, and he cares enough to cry with us when we're hurting. It's like Pastor Histed said a few Sundays back. God doesn't go anywhere. He's right where he's always been, loving us, holding his hand out to us, waiting for us. We're the ones who do the running. Only question is, which direction are you going to run? Do you run from God, or do you run toward him?"

CHAPTER TWENTY-SIX

Do you run from God, or do you run toward him?

The words stayed in Sara's mind, despite her best efforts to thrust them away. With nothing to occupy the evening and already yawning with weariness, she had retired for the night as soon she'd helped clear away their simple meal. The back seat of the Land Rover was comfortable enough, with the Indian blanket tucked around her against the coolness of the night and a sweatshirt rolled up under her head as a pillow. But her sleep was restless, full of troubled dreams that escaped her as soon as she awoke. Doug slept outside—if he slept at all. More than once during the night, Sara was awakened, and when she peered out the window of the car, there was Doug sitting upright on the tarp, his head turning to watch the night. One time, the tarp was empty, but she could see the DEA agent's dark shadow prowling around the edge of the clearing.

The next morning, when Sara crawled, stiff and bleary-eyed, out of the Land Rover, Doug was busy folding up the tarp. He was also, Sara noted with some disfavor, freshly shaved, wearing a clean shirt that had hardly a crease, and looking indecently wide awake. When he heard the door of the Land Rover open, he raised a hand in cheerful greeting.

Mumbling an inaudible "Good morning," Sara took the canteen and towel he offered her, mercifully without comment, and disappeared with her flight bag behind a thicket. When she emerged a few minutes later, she was feeling almost human again.

They breakfasted on more MREs—black beans and ham this time, which were tasty enough, though an unusual choice for breakfast; but Sara, abandoning the last of the gooey mess in the bottom of her canteen holder, could see how one could quickly grow tired of the traveling rations.

She was relieved to hear that it wouldn't take more than two hours to reach the rendezvous point where they would meet Benedicto and his people. They wouldn't have to leave the clearing until noon. In the meantime, Doug brought out the SatTrack-equipped knapsack and explained its purpose to Sara, showing her the invisible line of stitching that concealed the antenna and the slightly padded bottom that disguised the GPS unit hidden inside.

"Keep it with you at all times, even if you're just going for a stroll—or to the bathroom, which is going to be pretty much the same thing, I'm afraid! I need to know that wherever the SatTrack is, that's where you are too. I'll try to check in twice a day. At that rate, the battery should last a couple of weeks, at least. If things don't come together by then, I'll see about getting another unit out to you."

For the rest of the morning, Doug reviewed Sara's statement, this time in greater detail, grilling her on every scrap of conversation, every minute aspect of the scene in the warehouse, and every interaction she'd had with her father-in-law—right down to the expression on his face—until Sara's head swam with the effort to recall it all. She was beginning to comprehend what a squeezed lemon must feel like by the time Doug released her and began tossing his gear back into the Land Rover. Even then, as they jolted their way through the brush that masked the clearing and back onto the trail, he kept retracing points of her story until he knew as much as she did about the Cortezes' operations—drugs and otherwise.

When Doug finally ran out of questions, Sara, still exhausted after her restless night, took the opportunity to doze a little, her body braced against the jolts and bumps of the trail. When the track beneath the Land Rover's tires abruptly became smooth, she reluctantly pulled herself upright. Rubbing sleep from her eyes, she gaped at the wide gravel road and neat orchards of young orange and grapefruit trees that had replaced the jungle. "What . . . where are we?"

Doug glanced over at her. "Good—you're awake." He nodded out the window. "Benedicto's experimental plantation. We're going to be picking up your hosts fairly soon now."

Sara sat up further, pushing the hair back from her face for a better view out the windshield. The scene bore no resemblance to the haphazard clearings she had seen in the jungle. The citrus orchards soon gave way to the vine-covered frames of a grape arbor. Beyond the vines on one side of the road she could see a huge corn field. A tractor stood abandoned at its edge. The road itself was empty on this sleepy Sunday afternoon, but beyond the corn field she spotted a cluster of small adobe houses and, to one side, a larger white-washed building with a tin roof.

"The new church," Doug said, following her gaze. His swift grin held a measure of pride at what she was seeing. "Really something, isn't it? Would you believe this was all jungle just five years ago?"

"It's incredible," Sara said slowly.

"They have fish ponds on the other side of the village. And cows and chickens. The politicians here and the *cocaleros*—the coca growers—themselves do a lot of spouting off about how the poor *campesino* has no choice but to plant coca if he is to feed his family. Benedicto and his people show just what kind of a lie that is. Maybe it takes a little longer, and it certainly takes a whole lot more hard work. But there is a good living to be made in this soil."

Doug braked as the jagged stump of a hardwood reared up on the side of the road just ahead. It marked a dirt track that wound through the vineyards. "This'll steer us clear of the village," he explained to Sara as he made the turn. "Everyone and their dog should be bedded down for *siesta* right now, but these people know my Land Rover, and I'd just as soon not do any unnecessary advertising that we came through here this afternoon. Benedicto says this track will take us right up into the hills where we're going. He and his people are going to meet us somewhere along the trail."

The hills to which Doug referred were the beginning of the Andes mountain chain that formed the boundary between the Chapare and the rugged and barren heights of the Bolivian highlands. The experimental plantation was right at the base of the first range, and no sooner had they left the vineyards behind than the trail began to climb steeply. Intended for an oxcart, not a motorized vehicle, the track was deeply rutted and narrow enough that the brush scraped against both sides of the Land Rover. Even with four-wheel-drive, they were soon reduced to little more than a walking pace.

Several kilometers and almost an hour later, they finally bounced around a bend and came upon a small line of people walking single-file along the side of the trail. It was the first group of more than one person that Sara had seen since they'd left Santa Cruz the day before. At the sound of the Land Rover, the *campesinos* turned and stopped.

"Benedicto." Sara could hear the relief in Doug Bradford's voice. "And that must be your hosts. I never expected them to get this far without us."

There were four people in all. A man in city clothing. A second man in the loose cotton pants and open-necked shirt of the *campesino* laborer. Trailing behind the second man was a woman with the long braids and multilayered skirts of the Quechua. Both the man and the woman were bowed under packs so large, Sara wondered how they could stand up. A small girl no more than seven or eight years old brought up the rear.

Sara studied the group incredulously as Doug pulled up in the middle of the track. "They walked all the way from the plantation like that? Look at the size of those packs!"

"Three or four hours down for church on Sunday mornings. Then back with the week's groceries in the afternoon," Doug said, opening his door. "Better them than me, I must say."

Sara was silent as he climbed out. Would she bother attending church if it meant several hours hard walking in each direction? She didn't think so! Reaching for her own door, she scrambled out of the car.

The man in city clothing hurried forward as Doug strode around the front of the Land Rover. *"Don Doo-glaas, mi amigo!"*

Even without the greeting, the pleasure on both men's faces told Sara that this must be Doug's pastor friend. Benedicto was a little man, no more than five feet tall, with the stocky, barrel-chested build common to the Quechua *campesino*, and he had to reach up high to pound Doug's shoulder in the traditional *abrazo* greeting.

Sara watched the genuine warmth of Doug's response with some wistfulness. Here was another side of this DEA agent's complex character. Doug turned and motioned her forward. "Sara, I want you to meet a very special friend, Benedicto Choque."

Sara stepped forward hesitantly, offering the little pastor her hand without venturing close enough to risk an *abrazo*. "It is a pleasure to meet you," she said in formal Spanish. "Doug showed me your plantation. It is very beautiful."

Benedicto looked at Sara's hand as though he wasn't sure what to do with it, then briefly touched her fingers with his own. "God has blessed us, yes," he said simply. "But we would have nothing were it not for the kindness of our great friend *Don Doo-glaas*. It was he who made the arrangements with the *americanos* so that my people and I could build a new life. Did he tell you of this?"

Sara glanced up at Doug's suddenly blank face. "No, he didn't."

The pastor was already edging away from Sara, his body language making it clear that he had other things on his mind than small talk. With a brief smile down at Sara, Doug turned his back to follow Benedicto's shift in position. Feeling dismissed, Sara backed up against the Land Rover.

Benedicto waited until Sara was out of earshot before he spoke. "My cousins—Rafael and Josefina. They have agreed to do what you ask. They will take the girl and keep her safe. And not just because of the money you have offered them. It is true that they have needs because they will not grow the coca and live too far from the road for the programs of the *americanos.* But beyond that, they hate the *narcotraficantes* very much. Their oldest son was caught last year when he walked by error into a *fábrica de cocaína,* and it was not until days later that they found his body."

Benedicto glanced past Doug to where Sara was leaning against the Land Rover, and lowered his voice. "I must tell you, though, my friend, that we too have the radio. There has been much news—about a crime—and a girl. The name—"

Doug cut him off with a swift hand. "No, no names." With a quick glance at Sara, he lowered his own voice. "Look, I know what you've heard, but it isn't true, believe me! The woman is innocent. As for the men who have sown these lies abroad—you know that I cannot tell you the things that I learn in my work, but I assure you that they are more evil than you can imagine. If they are allowed to harm her, then they will go on to do greater damage, not only to my country, but your own. And to prevent that, I have given my word to do all in my power to protect her."

The Quechua pastor was silent, his eyes turned down to his dusty shoes so that Doug could see only the top of his dark head. The enormity of what he'd requested of his friend hadn't really hit him until now, and it no longer seemed such a brilliant brainstorm. Justified or not, he was asking these people to risk a clash with their own legally constituted authorities, not to mention some very nasty and powerful criminals. And all for a young woman they didn't even know!

As another endless second passed, and then another, he cleared his throat.

"Look, I'm sorry, Benedicto. I had no right to expect—"

The Quechua pastor raised his head and said as matter-of-factly as though there had been no hesitation, "Your friend will be safe enough at the *rancho.* There are no other *chozas* so far up the mountain. And my cousin's two remaining sons have gone to the city to work and study. They will not be home for many months."

Doug's breath whistled out between his teeth. "Thank you, Benedicto. This means more to me than I can express."

"You are my friend," Benedicto said simply. "And I trust you. The news tells lies and so do the *políticos,* and even those men whose names are greatly honored in our country. But you do not lie. And you give of your life to fight the evil that is choking my country. So if I can help you, then it is my responsibility before our God to do so."

Sara's misgivings returned as she watched the two men talk—

about her, she was sure. Her eyes went to the little pastor's three companions standing silently to one side. Was Doug really going to abandon her with these people? They seemed so—so *alien!* Not at all like the city people with whom she'd had contact in Santa Cruz, even the poorer ones. Except maybe the beggars who were always pestering people for coins at the intersections.

She looked at their bare feet—thick and splayed, as though tramping these trails without shoes had grown an extra hide on them.

And the smell! It settled over the car in an overpowering wave as Doug ushered the new passengers into the back seat. Sara had never been at close quarters with the peculiar odor of the Bolivian *campesino*—a combination of infrequent washing, hand-woven wool, no deodorant, and hours spent walking under a tropical sun—and she had to bite her lip to keep her nose from wrinkling with distaste.

Summoning all her self-discipline, she managed a friendly greeting as Doug slammed the door shut and stepped around to the driver's door. But while the pastor returned her hesitant smile, the others only stared back at her impassively, the solemnity of their eyes seeming to echo her own misgivings. Had they even understood her? Or was it possible that her own fair coloring, and maybe even her smell, was just as alien to them, like some blanched creature that had crawled out from under a dark rock?

I can't do this! she told herself with sudden panic. *He can't expect me to! He'll just have to take me back with him—anywhere!*

Just then, Doug slid into the driver's seat beside her. He showed no indication of even noticing the smell that permeated his vehicle, and as he started the engine, he glanced back over his shoulder to inquire cheerfully in Spanish fluent enough to startle Sara, "Any of you ever hear the story of the little old Quechua *mamita* and her *bulto*?"

The Land Rover lumbered into gear, and Doug went on with his story without waiting for a response. "Well, our little *mamita* is walking down the road with this heavy pack on her back. She's getting pretty tired when a truck driver comes along and offers her a ride. She accepts and climbs on board. Now, the truck is already full of other people doing the same thing, but they make room for our *mamita*, and there she stands, watching the road go by, only too happy not to have to walk any farther. But she hasn't been standing there long when one of the other passengers taps her on the shoulder. 'Señora, why don't you lay down your pack? You must be tired from carrying that heavy thing!'

"The little *mamita* turns to him, shocked, and says, 'Oh, no, I couldn't do that! This kind señor has already been so good to give me a ride in his truck. How can I possibly ask him to carry my *bulto* too?'"

The ensuing laughter startled Sara, but answered her question about whether her hosts spoke a language she knew. Their dark faces were no longer impassive but creased with mirth, and when the man in the *campesino* clothing spoke rapidly to his wife in what Sara assumed to be Quechua, she too laughed, her hand flying up to cover her mouth, her black eyes squeezed together with an enjoyment so infectious that it drew a smile from Sara.

This time the Indian woman returned her smile, her hand dropping away from her mouth to reveal the missing teeth she'd been trying to hide. The little girl at her side added a gap-toothed grin of her own before both mother and daughter were overcome by bashfulness and ducked their heads away. And with that instant of human contact and shared mirth, her proposed hosts no longer seemed so alien, but people who, despite being vastly different from her in terms of culture and living standard, were not really so very unlike herself.

Which might have been just what Doug had in mind.

The Land Rover inched upward for another hour, halting occasionally for the men to drag deadfalls out of the way. Sara was again surprised by the absence of human traffic, though she did spot an occasional path branching off into the brush. The Chapare jungle might have its inhabitants, but they sure seemed well hidden!

Finally, when the track narrowed to a trail barely wide enough to allow a donkey to pass, they were forced to abandon the Land Rover. Sara came around to the back as Doug lifted down the flight bag of clothes and toiletries he'd put together for her. Rafael and Josefina had already retrieved their packs and were waiting patiently with Benedicto a few meters down the trail, their shoulders stooped under their burdens.

It all had to be as awkward for them as for her, Sara thought, taking the flight bag from the Doug's hand. Would she be so willing to put herself out for a bizarre-looking foreigner—and a potentially troublesome one, too!—if the situation had been reversed? Probably not!

She eyed the group unobtrusively as she slung the flight bag over her shoulder and adjusted the strap. The little girl seemed to be trying to make up her mind as to whether these two pale *gringos* were going to bite her, sidling forward a few steps, then scurrying backward half the distance before darting forward again.

Sara could put a name to her small face now, Consuelo. She

waited until the child was just a few steps away before raising her hand in the smallest of waves. Consuelo scuttled backward.

Doug was digging into his backpack now, pulling out anything that might be of use to Sara in the days ahead—mosquito repellent, a bottle of Tylenol, a travel-size first-aid kit, a roll of toilet paper, a pocket flashlight. Catching the exchange between the two girls, he straightened up to give Sara a searching look. "You sure you're going to be able to handle this? I know these aren't the kind of folks you're used to, and I'm afraid their house isn't going to be much better. I guess I've been down here so long I'd forgotten how these people strike Americans for the first time."

Sara blushed. So Doug hadn't missed her earlier expression of disgust. "Sure I can handle it! It was just—a surprise. I'll be fine once I get used to . . . well, everything."

Out of the corner of her eye, she watched Consuelo sidle forward again. "I really do like your friends. They seem—nice."

"That they are." Gathering his collection together, Doug dumped it into the knapsack that held the SatTrack. "These people may not have much by our standards, but they're the salt of the earth, let me tell you! And I can promise you they'll do whatever they can to keep you safe, even if it might not be so comfortable. I'm sorry I can't do more about that. But it shouldn't be for long—I hope!"

He handed the knapsack to Sara. "I just wish I could have come up with a better means of communication. You've got some things in here for basic emergencies—what we carry in the field, pretty much. But I'd feel a lot better if there was some way for you to make contact if you get sick or need me in a hurry."

Consuelo chose that moment to make the final dash to Sara's side. Slipping her hand into Sara's, she leaned confidingly against her. Sara, blinking back a sudden rush of tears at the feel of those hard, dirty little fingers in her own, looked down to give the child her warmest smile before turning back to Doug. "I'll be fine, really. Besides, we already decided this was the only way, remember?"

She slung the knapsack over her other shoulder. "And you've certainly given me anything I could possibly need. Except . . ."— she hesitated—"would you mind . . . I was just wondering—is it okay if I borrow that Bible I had this morning? I . . . well, I don't have anything else to read, and I thought . . ." Her voice trailed off.

"Absolutely." Doug made no other comment as he dug the Bible from the pile that had been in the Indian blanket. Passing it over to Sara, he followed it up with the strip of sheet material she'd used to tie up her hair the night before. "That hair of yours is your most distinctive feature," he responded to Sara's grimace. "There aren't any other *ranchos* between here and Rafael's. But I'd prefer you keep it tied up anytime you're outside. Just as a precaution."

Sara agreed reluctantly, but she categorically refused to touch the grease-stained rag that Doug was holding out to her. "I'll tear up that T-shirt from the motel. At least it's reasonably clean!" She fished the garment from her bag and fashioned it into a bandanna. As she knotted the fabric in place, Doug slung his own backpack onto his back—he wasn't about to leave his military gear unattended in the middle of the jungle, however small the likelihood of someone coming along—and used a remote control to lock the Land Rover.

The other three adults were still patiently waiting down the trail. They started off single-file as Doug and Sara joined them, except for little Consuelo, who insisted on clinging to Sara's side. Sara lost her load almost immediately when Benedicto insisted on taking her bags. Even so, she was envying the others' easy stride within the first five minutes. How did they manage it with those heavy loads? And all uphill! Even little Consuelo was doing better than she was. But before Sara had to embarrass herself by asking for a rest, the trail leveled off, opening up into bright sunshine and a clearing.

This was hardly large enough to be termed a *rancho*—just a small natural plateau, of perhaps five acres, tucked between one fold of the foothills and the next. But it had a stream running through it and was dotted with banana and citrus and mango trees, as well as newly planted patches of corn and potato.

As they entered the clearing, Consuelo ran on ahead to open the gate of a roughly built corral. A herd of goats and sheep stampeded out, bleating and maaing as they scrambled for the hillsides above the clearing, where either the elevation or a machete had thinned the vegetation enough to allow for some open meadow.

Behind the corral, in the center of a baked-earth yard, stood an adobe house. Beside it was a *pahuichi*, its steep thatched roof held up by an open scaffolding of logs. A blackened cooking area lay at the back, and there were hammocks slung between the rafters.

Rafael and Josefina were already carrying their packs into the shade of the *pahuichi*. Doug drew Benedicto aside, and Sara saw him press something into the pastor's hand before the two men walked off together to take a swift turn around the house and yard. When they returned, Sara was collecting her flight bag and knapsack from where Benedicto had dropped them. Doug came over to Sara as Benedicto ambled over to speak to his cousin. Tilting his low-brimmed hat forward to shield his eyes, Doug made a slow revolution, scanning the perimeter of the clearing, before looking down at Sara.

"Everything seems to check out okay. Benedicto says he'll keep in touch if there's any kind of problem."

There was a moment's hesitation before he went on. "Sara, I've got to get back to town tonight. And I don't like to leave the car alone out there any longer than I have to."

Sara had known it was coming, but she was unprepared for the stab of desolation that hit her in the pit of her stomach. Despite her earlier resolution, she had to fight a sudden, ridiculous impulse to grab onto Doug and beg him not to go—to take her back to the Land Rover and just keep on driving through the jungle forever, or at least until she found herself somewhere familiar and safe.

Instead, she straightened her shoulders, lifted her chin high, and dug out her brightest expression. "Of course you need to go now. Thank you for bringing me, and . . . and for everything."

She waited for Doug to turn away so that she could relax her resolute brightness, but he made no immediate move to leave. He glanced again around the hard-baked earth of the yard, the fine lines at the corners of his eyes crinkling into a frown under the shade of his low brim.

"I'm beginning to have some second thoughts about this, Sara. Leaving you here alone—I don't know what I was thinking. It's just too . . . too isolated! And I never expected conditions to be quite this bad. If anything should happen to you . . ."

Doug pulled his hat off, running his other hand through his hair in a gesture that Sara had come to associate with exasperation or concern. "I've just got a bad feeling about this! For two cents, I'd march you back to town and forget this whole crazy idea."

Perversely, his own misgivings stiffened Sara's wobbling courage. She pivoted around to make her own survey of the ramshackle adobe hut and the noisy livestock and her hosts, already stolidly digging through their packs as though they'd forgotten they had visitors. Consuelo was hovering close by again, not understanding a word, but staring with dark, wondering eyes from one *gringo* to the other.

"It doesn't look so bad!" Sara said bravely. "I've always wanted to try sleeping in a hammock. It'll be like camping out. Besides,"—her eyes met his directly—"what choice do I have? Isn't that why we're here? Because there's no other alternative? I mean, what would happen if you did take me back with you?"

Doug took his time replacing his hat before he admitted, "Cortéz would find you. Maybe not right away, but sooner or later he would."

"Then I'll take my chances here." Sara was suddenly anxious to have the DEA agent leave before she changed her mind again. She held out her right hand. "Well, I . . . I guess this is good-bye. You need to get going if you're going to be down off that awful road before dark, so please don't feel you have to wait around any longer for me. I can get settled in on my own. You just—"

A sudden lump in her throat choked her words. She swallowed as unobtrusively as she could. "Just go and stop the Cortezes before it's too late!"

Doug took her hand, his keen gaze intent on her face as though he could read every qualm that lay behind her brave words. "You're not afraid?"

Sara considered the question. "You know, I'm really not!" she discovered with surprise. "I *was*—terribly afraid. And I guess maybe I should be. But . . ."

Consuelo, who had inserted herself between the two *gringos,* chose that moment to wrap her thin arms around Sara's waist in a fierce hug. Stooping to hug her back, Sara said over her head, defiantly, to convince herself more than Doug, "You see? I'm going to be just fine here. In fact . . . I think I'm going to enjoy myself!"

✠

And she did, in an odd way that buried at the bottom of her mind the circumstances that had brought her here. The life was poorer than she ever could have imagined—one room, two cooking pots, and only enough cutlery and enameled dishes to set the table for three, which meant that Josefina and Consuelo ate after Rafael and Sara had eaten and the dishes had been washed. Sara knew Nicolás would have sneered to see her scrubbing her clothes down at the creek, without any soap, or ducking down in the six inches of water to rinse her hair. Interestingly, after a day or two, Sara no longer even noticed the body odors.

It was quiet up here in the hills, infinitely peaceful and oh, so beautiful, with the Andes rearing up to form a stark wall against one horizon and the jungle tumbling down the hillside in a restless tangle to the other. And above it all, the boundless arch of the sky. In another month the rains would start, and the clouds would come down to touch the hilltops in an endless gray. But for now the overhead expanse was a flawless blue.

Never-ending breezes wafted the scents of a hundred flowering plants out of the jungle and into the clearing, and added sound effects to the illusion of a great, sighing ocean. Nothing but the chatter of parrots and monkeys ever disturbed the lazy contentment of grazing sheep and goats, and there were times—lasting perhaps ten minutes to an hour—when Sara could forget that there was a world outside this small landholding that held evil and hate and betrayal.

Sara's hosts didn't seem to notice how barren their lives were. Nor did they seem to mind the long days without any contact with other human beings, apart from their weekly trek to church. There was plenty of work to fill the hours. Rafael spent his days out in his *chacos,* chopping the encroaching jungle growth back from his young crops with a machete and hoe. Josefina worked right alongside him when she wasn't stirring her pots over the clay trough where burning firewood made a primitive stove, or grinding corn and peanuts to a tedious fineness between two flat rocks, or spinning a cotton-candy mass of raw sheep's wool into rough thread on a handheld spindle. But there was always time to swing lazily in the hammocks during the heat of the day.

And in the evenings, when their supper of potatoes and rice and fried plantains had been scraped up to the last crumb and the cooking fire had died down to embers, the little family sat out on the mud-brick steps of the snug adobe house and sang—choruses whose tunes Sara recognized from long-ago years in Sunday school, though she didn't understand the Quechua words, and haunting melodies that had no counterpart in Western music. Their untrained voices were appallingly off-key, but they held a joyous exuberance and contentment that Sara, who spent most evenings swatting the mosquitoes that lined up for a taste of Doug's army-issue repellent, couldn't remember having known even when life had held everything she wanted.

Her biggest frustration was that she couldn't talk to her host family. Josefina spoke only Quechua, and though Rafael was fluent enough in Spanish, the necessity of conversing with a pallid *gringa* from the big city was so obviously painful to him that Sara only approached him for essential exchanges of information. The rest of the time she listened wistfully to the normal family exchanges between husband and wife and daughter in a language she couldn't comprehend.

At first, she tried to help with the household chores, but even when Josefina would allow her to peel a few potatoes, it was evident to Sara that it made her hosts uncomfortable to see their guest working. They had, in fact, shown as much horrified dismay as she had ever seen from her mother-in-law when, the first day after her arrival, she'd shown up in the corn patch to work beside Josefina. Rafael had for once managed to look her straight in the eye and ordered her to rest in the shade, where the sun wouldn't burn her pale skin.

So Sara ended up spending much of her time with little Consuelo. It was the little girl's chore to shepherd the flock of sheep and goats up to the hillside pastures, and after that first awkward day, Sara went with her. This proved to be an acceptable activity to her hosts, and each morning thereafter, Sara and Consuelo would eat their breakfast of bread and sweet black coffee, then set off to spend their day up on the hillsides behind the *rancho,* wandering slowly with the sheep and goats from one grassy patch to another, making their way back down in the late afternoon to count off the flock into the corral for the night. Consuelo spoke only broken bits of Spanish, but hand gestures and smiles and hugs filled in the rest of their undemanding communication, and the two were soon fast friends.

The first week slipped by with no word from Doug. Not that Sara expected any. He'd told her there'd be no possibility of communication. But somewhere in the back of her mind, she'd cherished an illogical hope that a solution might have presented itself back in Santa Cruz and that he would return quickly to take her away.

And she hadn't anticipated how much she'd miss him. It wasn't that she didn't feel safe without the protection of his presence. Mindful of Doug's orders, Sara kept the knapsack with her at all times, using it to carry lunch for herself and Consuelo out to the grazing land each day. And though she'd soon gotten rid of the ripped T-shirt headdress, she kept her blonde hair braided and carefully tucked-up inside a wide-brimmed straw hat that Josefina had woven. But as the slow days passed without incident or so much as a sign of another human being, she ceased to worry that Nicolás and his father might find her here.

Still, the DEA agent been someone to talk to, and she found him intruding into her thoughts at odd intervals. The keen gray eyes that could soften so quickly to gentleness. The quiet firmness of his voice. The things he'd said . . .

Sara had thought once before that Doug Bradford would be a friend worth having, and so he'd proven to be. But that was a friendship without a future, because, even if she ever got out of here, the paths of their lives were not likely to cross again. So each time he invaded her thoughts, she pushed him back out.

Only that left room for other, more worrisome thoughts. What was going on back in Santa Cruz? What other evil had Don Luis and Julio Vargas hatched since her disappearance? What was happening with the eight tons of cocaine that Nicolás had boasted no one could find? What had Doug found out? What was he doing about it? And how long would she be in exile here in the Andean foothills?

And what was Nicky—the man she had given her heart to—doing right now? What was he thinking? About murder? Or the wife he'd driven away into a cold, rainy night? Or both? A helpless rage began to rise again in Sara.

I hate him! I hate him! I hate him!

Deliberately, before the flood could overwhelm her, she pushed those thoughts away as well.

Consuelo had a capacity for silence born of her solitary, though not unhappy, life. She could go for hours without speaking as she wandered along behind the sheep and goats, swishing at their nimble heels with a stick, or sitting motionless on a rock, watching her flock graze until it was time to urge them on to the next meadow.

And so, with nothing else to distract her thoughts, Sara found herself reaching more and more often for the Bible she kept tucked into her knapsack. She started in the middle of the book with the Psalms that Doug had made such a big deal about, then branched out to other Old Testament books, not with any plan but flipping through the pages and stopping occasionally to read, her eyes drawn to the pleas and complaints of the prophets that echoed her own quarrel with God.

Psalm 22: "My God, my God, why have you forsaken me? Why are you so far from saving me, so far from the words of my groaning? O my God, I cry out by day, but you do not answer, by night, and am not silent."

Psalm 69: "Save me, O God, for the waters have come up to my neck. I sink in the miry depths, where there is no foothold. . . . I am worn out calling for help; my throat is parched. My eyes fail, looking for my God."

Sara flipped to the next page, and her eyes fell on Psalm 74: "Why have you rejected us forever, O God? Why does your anger smolder against the sheep of your pasture?"

Sara raised her eyes and gazed at the flock of sheep and goats resting peacefully under the shade of a lilac *paraíso*, where they'd taken refuge from the noonday heat. At the moment, they appeared to be the embodiment of serenity, but she had already learned that they could be both stupid and recalcitrant. There had been times when it took Rafael's strong arm to start them from their comfortable huddle in the corral up the steep mountainside to pasture. She'd seen rebellious sheep that would only kick up their heels at Consuelo cower down on the ground under Rafael's angry, uplifted rod. Was that the picture of God that had leapt to the psalmist's mind?

Sometimes David's entreaties uncannily mirrored Sara's own experience. One morning, when the pages of her Bible fell open to Psalm 55, she felt tears spring to her eyes as she read her heart's own cry, recorded thousands of years ago:

"My thoughts trouble me and I am distraught at the voice of the enemy, at the stares of the wicked. . . . My heart is in anguish within me; the terrors of death assail me. Fear and trembling have beset me; horror has overwhelmed me. I said, 'Oh, that I had the wings of a dove! I would fly away and be at rest—I would flee far away. . . .'"

At once Sara was back in the trembling horror of her night flight from Cortéz Industries, when she too had felt death at her heels. She quickly scrabbled through the thin pages of the Bible until her eyes came to rest in the book of Jeremiah. The prophet's sardonic criticism of God's justice system struck an immediate chord:

"You are always righteous, O LORD, when I bring a case before you. Yet I would speak with you about your justice: Why does the way of the wicked prosper? Why do all the faithless live at ease?"

"Yeah, God, where is your justice?" Sara demanded aloud, earning a puzzled stare from Consuelo, sprawled on her belly in the grass at her feet. "Why *do* you let the wicked kick back in their cocaine-financed mansions and prosper while the decent people suffer and go hungry . . . and hide on some backwoods *rancho* in the middle of the jungle?"

But Sara found no real satisfaction in searching for other people's complaints. As she'd told Doug, she was looking for answers, not more questions. Yet her curiosity began to stir. All these pleas for help. All these anguished cries of the soul. Why were they recorded in these pages? Hadn't David been a king, a great warrior, a giant slayer? Hadn't Jeremiah been a famed man of God, preaching in kings' courts? Wasn't Job supposed to be the richest man in the world or something like that? So why were they crying out to God in bitterness and anger and pain as though they were . . . *her*?

Sara had been to Sunday school as a child, and once she and her father had settled in Seattle, she'd attended church almost every week. But the Bible stories she remembered had touched the *high* points in people's lives, the great victories that made for exciting sermons. Moses crossing the Red Sea. Joshua watching Jericho's walls tumble down. David chopping off Goliath's head. Daniel emerging triumphant from the lions' den.

That these same servants of God had experienced trials and

bereavements and long years of loneliness of their own amazed Sara as she went back to pore over those stories for herself. David had slain Goliath, then he spent long years on the run from King Saul, hiding in caves, separated from his wife and family, with a price set on his head by his own father-in-law. Often he escaped only a step ahead of the soldiers who were hunting him. Sara noticed in a study note at the bottom of one page that many of the psalms she'd been reading had been written during these years of exile. Huddled in a damp cave over a small campfire, with a harp in his hands and anguish burning his tongue, had the young warrior David envisioned the crown that lay ahead and the golden age of Israel?

Then there was Moses, wandering around with the sheep and goats—just like Sara. Only, not just for a couple of weeks, but for forty sand-choked *years!* Or Daniel, marooned in a strange land in what amounted to little more than slavery. And Job. Not the wealthy and influential patriarch of his early and later years, but the broken father who wept at the loss of his children; he'd been stripped of his health, along with everything else, and raged against the groundless accusations of his friends.

It wasn't easy reading. Biographical details were often sandwiched between the most bizarre death-and-doom orations against countries she'd never heard of, like Moab and Tyre and Assyria and Cush. But Sara persevered, shaking her head in disbelief over Isaiah, who had gone around stripped and barefoot for three whole years just to illustrate a point God was trying to make to his people. And Jeremiah. Beaten, forced into hiding, thrown into prison, half-drowned in a mud pit. All because he persisted in warning Israel of God's impending judgment if they didn't repent of their evil ways.

Yes, these men had as much reason to cry out against God as she did. And yet . . .

Turning back to those cries of anger and pain, Sara read them again, no longer skipping over pages, but puzzling through entire chapters and sections. There was something different here! Something that caught Sara's attention and filled her with an indefinable longing. Sure, these men had challenged God, railing out at him in bitterness and rebellion. But they hadn't stopped there. They'd gone on to find the kind of answers she was searching for and that same calm resignation—no, not resignation, *peace*—that Sara had noticed and been baffled by in Doug Bradford.

David, the same fugitive who had accused God in Psalm 10 of hiding himself—"Why, O Lord, do you stand far off? Why do you hide yourself in times of trouble?"—had gone on to write Psalm 40, where he said, "I waited patiently for the LORD; he turned to me and heard my cry. He lifted me out of the slimy pit, out of the mud and mire; he set my feet on a rock and gave me a firm place to stand."

And Job, who had wished for death and defended his own righteousness so vehemently, had from the very ash heap where he sat scratching his boils with a shard of pottery, interrupted his self-defense with an incredible statement of faith: "I know that my Redeemer lives, and that in the end he will stand upon the earth. And after my skin has been destroyed, yet in my flesh I will see God."

It didn't make sense. How could these men argue with God one minute, then turn right around and speak with such assurance of his love and goodness?

"I remember my affliction and my wandering, the bitterness and the gall," Jeremiah cried out in the book of Lamentations. "I well remember them, and my soul is downcast within me. Yet this I call to mind and therefore I have hope: Because of the LORD's great love we are not consumed, for his compassions never fail. They are new every morning; great is your faithfulness."

There it was again! That paradoxical conviction in the midst of chaos and pain that God is somehow loving and good. Not that Jeremiah had ever seen that hope realized, from what Sara could see, at least in his lifetime. He'd lived alone and died alone, after watching one after another of his dire prophecies come true. Jerusalem destroyed by the Babylonians. Tiny children starving in the streets. Parents practicing cannibalism. Disappointed and angry, Sara slammed the Bible shut on that last depressing chapter.

"Come on, God! He did everything you wanted. Couldn't you have allowed him at least one bright spot?"

Sara smiled wryly to herself when she realized she was talking aloud. How silly could you get, working yourself up over some man who'd been dead and buried for twenty-five hundred years?

Twenty-five hundred years. Sara repeated the number thoughtfully. It was a long time! In fact, by comparison, Jeremiah's entire life was hardly a dot on the time line of history. What had Doug said about God looking at time differently than men did? Was that the answer to that incomprehensible affirmation of hope? Would all this nightmare in her own life one day seem just such a breath of time?

One thing was abundantly clear, she had to admit, however unwillingly. Nowhere in the Bible had God guaranteed a carefree existence, not for his people, not for anyone. The whole world was full of tragedy and violence and grief—and always had been. And if God could let his own servants in for such a bad time, then who was Sara to think that she should be exempt?

It was as though the foundations of her world had shaken under her feet. For too long Sara had looked at God through the assumption—an arrogant one, she could see now—that she had been badly mistreated. That God had no right to allow tragedy to touch her life as it had so many others. That God had turned his back on her, and therefore she was justified in turning her back on God.

But now what?

Oh, God, was I wrong? Were you really there all the time?

CHAPTER TWENTY-SEVEN

Halfway through the second week, the little *rancho* had an unexpected visitor. Sara and Consuelo had just finished chasing the last of the flock into the corral, and Sara was down at the creek, bathing. She was just wringing out the skirt of her chiffon party dress, which she wore in the water for modesty, when she glanced up to see a stranger—a young man, dressed in city clothing but with the strong features of a full-blooded Quechua—watching her with total concentration from the bank of the stream.

Her startled scream brought Josefina and Rafael running from the corn patch. By the time they arrived, Sara had determined that the man, though stockily built and a good six inches taller than Rafael, was very young—possibly still in his teens. And he was even more astonished to see her than she was to see him. He was certainly not a Cortéz spy.

Ramon and Josefina seemed no less astonished at their unexpected visitor. After the usual abrazo, they launched into a rapid dialogue in Quechua, and it was some time before Sara managed to piece together that the young man was their oldest son, Epifanio, who had been off studying in the highland city of Cochabamba, and that his unexpected return was not entirely welcome.

There was no singing that evening, and when Sara retired to her hammock under the *pahuichi*, she could hear Epifanio arguing with his parents through the open door of the adobe house.

"Speak Spanish, Papá! We are not ignorant *campesinos* anymore. What good is an education if you are to continue speaking in the tongue of an illiterate?"

"You will be respectful to your mother, young man!" Rafael bellowed, but Sara noticed that he had switched to Spanish. Consuelo crept outside and crawled into the hammock with Sara as the volume and pitch of the voices inside the house continued to rise and fall. Rafael sounded more annoyed than Sara had ever heard him, and

Josefina offered an occasional cry of protest, but the argument was dominated by Epifanio's strident, demanding voice.

"Papá, I have finished my *bachillerato,* is that not enough? Have you done so much? And José will finish his high school next year. Let *him* go on to university. I am tired of studying. . . . Yes, you have slaved that we may study, Papá! But so have we, working long hours in the city for people who despise us, only so that we can spend more hours at night with our books. And for what? There are opportunities right here in our own Chapare that are faster than a university degree. . . . Papá, you are old-fashioned, can you not see that? And so is Tío Benedicto."

Rafael responded with words that Sara couldn't hear, before Epifanio erupted again, his voice loud and angry. "What do you know, you who have never left this poor piece of land you call a farm? You are an old man, and your day is past! The teachers at the university say that it is we—the new and educated youth of Bolivia—who must decide what our future will hold! Not a generation that cannot even read and write!"

Rafael exploded in a stream of Quechua and the bamboo door suddenly slammed shut, reducing the argument to a low grumble of voices behind the thick mud walls.

When morning came, Sara was glad to escape into the surrounding hills with Consuelo and the sheep and goats. She had no idea how Epifanio's parents had explained her presence here, but she didn't like the way his eyes followed her wherever she moved. Nor did she like the troubled look in Josefina's eyes and the angry silence between father and son.

Before the door had slammed on the previous night's argument, Sara had gathered that Epifanio had quit school against his father's wishes, and she couldn't help but hope that he wasn't going to be hanging around the *rancho* the whole time she was there. Though, of course, it was his home, and he had a lot more right to be here than she did.

But when Sara and Consuelo returned that evening with the flock, Epifanio was gone. He had returned to school, Rafael explained without elaboration. With his departure, life returned to the usual routine, and Sara went on with her reading, with increased urgency, no longer concentrating on the writers' laments, but searching out with curiosity and wonder what God had to say in response. Maybe somewhere she'd find the answer to the bedrock of faith and peace that these wandering prophets—and Doug Bradford—seemed to have found.

On the second morning after Epifanio's visit, she opened her Bible to Job, chapter 40. "'Will the one who contends with the Almighty correct him? Let him who accuses God answer him. . . . Brace yourself like a man; I will question you, and you shall answer me. Would you discredit my justice? Would you condemn me to justify yourself?'"

She continued reading through to the end of the book of Job, then turned over to where she had left off the day before in Isaiah, and in chapter 43 she found God speaking more gently to his people.

"But now, this is what the Lord says—he who created you. . . . 'Fear not, for I have redeemed you; I have summoned you by name; you are mine. When you pass through the waters, I will be with you; and when you pass through the rivers, they will not sweep over you. When you walk through the fire, you will not be burned; the flames will not set you ablaze. For I am the LORD, your God, the Holy One of Israel, your Savior.'"

I will be with you! That's what Doug had said about God! He hadn't promised to keep the floodwaters away, but he'd promised to be there, a shelter and a rock in the midst of the storm. Was that the secret the prophets had discovered? Could it really be that God was closer than Sara had ever dreamed possible? So close that she could— well, argue with him? Because, come to think of it, you wouldn't pour out your rage and frustration to an adversary. You'd cry out to a friend, a parent, a lover.

Isaiah 49 brought back bittersweet memories of loving arms holding her close. "'Can a mother forget the baby at her breast and have no compassion on the child she has borne? Though she may forget, I will not forget you!'"

The black shapes of the letters blurred suddenly on the page, and Sara flipped quickly forward, only to be caught again by Isaiah 54: "'In a surge of anger I hid my face from you for a moment, but with everlasting kindness I will have compassion on you, says the LORD your Redeemer. . . . Though the mountains be shaken and the hills be removed, yet my unfailing love for you will not be shaken.'"

Slowly, as another week passed and the pages between Sara's hands grew dog-eared, a picture began to emerge from the stories and prophecies—the tangle of disasters and wars that Israel's own sin repeatedly brought sweeping over them. This was not the image of a distant and uncaring God that had dominated Sara's thinking for so many years, but that of a husband wooing back a beloved bride who had inexplicably chosen another. Or a father yearning over his recalcitrant children, even as he was forced to discipline them. Watching their needless stumblings with infinite love and compassion. Waiting patiently for his children to turn back and take one step toward his outstretched hands.

"See, I have engraved you on the palms of My hands," she read in Isaiah 49, and its image of God's tender possessiveness brought with it a longing so intense, it caught at Sara's breath. If only she could go back! Not to the blissful early days with Nicolás, but further. Much further. Back to when she'd known God's tenderness and had felt his very arms close around her! Back before she'd ruined it all with her own stubbornness and rebellion.

The next morning, Sara stumbled across a passage that seemed to sum up all the deep pain and longing that had been growing within her. She and Consuelo had made a good start to the day—the sheep being more cooperative than usual—and pink still edged the horizon when Sara settled herself on a favorite rock to watch Consuelo chase the last of the ewes into the pasture. She sat unmoving, listening to the cacophony of whistles, warbles, squawks, and caws as the jungle's feathered life greeted the day. When the last of the sunrise had lightened to blue, she reached somewhat reluctantly into her knapsack for the Bible.

But her ambivalence vanished as soon as she removed the blade of grass she was using as a marker and flipped the page open to Habakkuk 3. When she reached the seventeenth verse, she recognized the same passage that Sam Histed had read the one morning she had visited the English church.

"Though the fig tree does not bud and there are no grapes on the vines, though the olive crop fails and the fields produce no food, though there are no sheep in the pen and no cattle in the stalls, yet I will rejoice in the LORD, I will be joyful in God my Savior."

Sara read the words again, this time more slowly. "I will rejoice. . . . I will be joyful." That was it! That was what these people had that she didn't—the cool, steady undercurrent that flowed beneath the arguments and storms and turmoil, and every so often broke to the surface in inexplicable expressions of hope and praise. She'd seen it in Rafael and Josefina, despite their meager lifestyle. And in Doug Bradford, when he'd talked about the wife and children he'd see again some day. Joy. Plain, simple, sheer joy. Not because things were going well, but because . . .

Because they had you, God! That's why they could rejoice, all of them! Even when they were yelling at you and confused like Jeremiah and Habakkuk. They didn't have anything else, but they had you! And that was enough, wasn't it?

The tears burned at Sara's eyes until she could no longer hold them back. Jumping restlessly to her feet, she reached for the knapsack and slung it over her shoulder. She had to get away! Mumbling an explanation to Consuelo, who excused her with a sleepy shrug, Sara started off across the pasture. At the edge of the meadow, she broke into a stumbling run, scrambling up the hillside as though her life depended on reaching the top of the bald-headed rise that overlooked the wild citrus and flowering shrubs.

"Though the fig tree does not bud and there are no grapes on the vines, though the olive crop fails and the fields produce no food . . ."

It was quiet on the hilltop, except for the wind gusting across the knoll. The sky above her was brilliant and the day already growing hot. A single little marshmallow cloud floated straight overhead. Beyond the clearing, the hillsides tumbled down to merge into the endless expanse of the Chapare jungle. What if that abundant growth suddenly dried up and withered, no longer producing the fruit it now brought forth in such abundance?

"Though there are no sheep in the pen and no cattle in the stalls, yet I will rejoice in the LORD, I will be joyful in God my Savior."

Sara dropped her knapsack to the ground. "Oh, God, I mocked when Sam Histed read those verses! I didn't think I needed to hear because I had it all! A family, a home, everything I wanted. And now it's all gone. But even if I had it all back, it wouldn't matter, because that wasn't really what I wanted. It was you! And it wasn't you who turned away. It was me! I ran away from you as soon as things got hard, and then I got lost and I couldn't find my way back. And all these years that I've been missing you, and searching for you, and thinking you'd abandoned me, you've been right here, waiting for me! Oh, God!"

Throwing herself down on the prickly grass, Sara wept one final torrent of tears. But this time, not for the broken dreams of family and home. And not for the laughing, utterly charming young husband she'd adored and lost. She wept for the cold, empty years she'd squandered without God—her best friend—for the loneliness and bitterness that had been so unnecessary because God had been there all the time.

"Oh, God, I want to come back!" she gasped. The dirt against her lips tasted as bitter as her anguish. "I don't care about anything else now! I just want you! I want to love you again and know that you love me, like I used to when I was a kid. If you can still love me when I've run away and turned my back for so long! Can you, God? I've been so stupid! Can you still want me? Oh, God, please, I can't take it anymore. I can't go on alone. If you really care, if there's still any chance for me, *please,* just say something!"

She couldn't even pray anymore. She just clenched her hands and felt the agony and grief and lostness sweeping over her in a wave so intense she didn't even realize that she was digging her fingernails into her palms.

And then it came. Not in a trumpeting proclamation from heaven. There was no blinding revelation. No vision of a man in white robes reaching down to comfort her. There was only a still, small voice deep within her. A voice so still that she hadn't heard it until she'd quieted herself enough to listen. The voice offered no promises, no deliverance from the straits in which she found herself. It just whispered, *I'm here, my child. I will always be here, and I love you.*

A slow peace seeped into Sara as she lay there; it did not remove the pain, but made it somehow easier to bear. At last she rolled to a sitting position, wiping away the worst of the tears and dirt with her sleeve. The shift in the sun's position told her she'd been lying face down in the dirt for longer than she'd realized. The morning was well advanced, and, halfway down the hillside, the herd was already drifting toward the next pasture. She could see Consuelo's small figure dashing down the path after a wayward goat. The birds had finished their morning performance, and the only sound was the distant hum of a helicopter.

UMOPAR, Sara guessed, a reminder that the beauty and tranquillity that lay around her wasn't as innocent as it looked. But even that thought didn't disturb the peace that had calmed her tears. She reached for the Bible, flopped open on the grass where she'd let it fall, its pages fluttering in the breeze. Clutching it to her as though it were a lifeline in a sea that was making one last attempt to pull her under, she raised her face toward the single white cloud overhead.

"*Though the fig tree does not bud . . .*"—she whispered the words as a vow—". . . and there are no grapes on the vines, though the olive crops fail and the fields produce no food . . ."

The verses suddenly changed and became her own prayer. "Though I never see Nicky again. Though I never again in this life know human love. Though everything I have and love and dream is stripped away. Yet I will rejoice in the Lord, I will be joyful in God my Savior."

Her fingers relaxed and she felt the sting of the cuts in the palms of her hands. She looked at them in surprise. Wiping the spots of blood on a tuft of grass, she opened the Bible again, and for the first time, she read the next verse in Habakkuk.

"The Sovereign Lord is my strength, he makes my feet like the feet of a deer, he enables me to go on the heights."

She looked down the long slope that she had scaled in her anguish. How easily and quickly a deer could bound up this hillside. Right now she felt like a crippled rabbit creeping along in the shadowed valleys. But perhaps someday God would bring her through to the heights. She had only to endure. Someday this too would pass, even if, like Jeremiah, it wasn't until she found herself in God's own presence.

You are my strength, O God, she vowed silently. *My only strength. And you are enough.*

The thought lifted her chin and dried her tears. It stayed with her as she slipped and slid down the mountainside, and as she stopped at the stream to wash the dirt and tears from her face. It was still there when she heard Consuelo scream. It stiffened her spine when she saw a helicopter that was unmistakably military settle down so close to the *pahuichi* that the wash of its rotors was blowing Josefina's freshly ground corn flour out of the *tacú*. And it gave her the strength to walk forward with dignity to meet the men who were holding machine guns on her frightened hosts.

CHAPTER TWENTY-EIGHT

The scene outside the *pahuichi* was in such sharp contrast to the peace on top of the hilltop knoll that it took a stunned moment for Sara to assimilate what was happening.

The wide open yard between the corral and the *pahuichi* seemed suddenly small and crowded with the ugly mass of the helicopter, settled dead-center and looking like a leftover prop from a Vietnam War movie—long and sleek and a dull gray-green, its propellers churning up vast billows of dust. It was the coloring and shape that marked the helicopter as military to Sara, because there were no actual numbers or lettering on the body.

That and its occupants.

Sara counted four of them as she walked into the clearing, two crouched down in the open side-door of the helicopter, and the other two on the ground, fanned out on either side of the helicopter. All wore the standard khaki military field dress. One of the men was stalking toward the *pahuichi*, where Josefina cowered down beside the huge, hand-carved *tacú*, while his partner kept his weapon leveled at Rafael.

Sara made no attempt to escape. Even if she thought she could make it to the cover of the surrounding brush, there was no way she could leave Rafael, Josefina, and little Consuelo to face those deadly looking guns.

So she walked forward, one hand holding her hat down against the blast from the rotors. And if there had been any doubt in Sara's mind that these men were here for her, it was dispelled in an instant. The pilot's door was opening now, and she could see through the plumes of dust a man she would recognize anywhere. Solid black clothing. Slicked-back ponytail. Gold earrings. Erect military bearing that made no allowances for the force of the wind striking between his shoulder blades. With a thin smile of satisfaction, Julio Vargas strode toward Sara.

When he reached her, he ripped the straw hat from her head,

tossing it to the wind. The thin line of his mouth twitched ever so slightly as the flaxen coils of Sara's braids were revealed. With a snap of his fingers, Vargas summoned the nearest soldier.

"*Sí*, this is the one. We will inform Don Luis that we have found her."

He turned to Sara. "You have given us a good deal of trouble, *señorita*. Now you will come with me. Your father-in-law wishes to speak to you."

Sara didn't move. These past peaceful weeks had lulled her into believing that her worst remaining threat was boredom, and she was still struggling with the reality that after all this time, the Bolivian authorities had somehow caught up with her. And Julio Vargas, of all people! What was her father-in-law's crooked head of security doing here with these soldiers? And flying their helicopter?"

"Ju . . . Julio, what are you doing here? How did you find me?"

"Did you think we would not in the end?" Vargas swept the small farm with a contemptuous glance. "Though I did not believe until I saw you with my own eyes that a Cortéz—even an *extranjera*—would be willing to hide herself in the pigsty of a *campesino's choza!*"

He snapped his fingers again, his sharp order rising above the noise of the helicopter. "We must go quickly. Find the woman's things."

In response, the soldier nearest the *pahuichi* aimed a deliberate kick at Josefina's *tacú*. Weeping as the stone mortar tipped and her corn flour spilled into the dirt, the little Quechua woman scurried over to Sara's hammock. The soldier followed.

"Señorita Sara."

Sara turned her head to see Rafael lowering his hands and his hoe as he hurried toward her across the yard. One of the soldiers shifted the aim of his machine gun threateningly. Rafael darted a fearful glance toward the gun, but he kept coming, his short, thick-set body thrust pugnaciously forward, until he was close enough to ask with quiet dignity, "Do you know these men, señorita Sara? What is it that they want of you?"

The Quechua farmer came to a stop halfway between the soldier and Julio Vargas. No, Sara realized suddenly, between that machine gun and her! Her heart went out to her taciturn little host in a rush of gratitude and affection. She had been nothing to this man but a burden and a troublesome guest. And yet, though she knew he must be terrified of these armed strangers, he was trying to protect her!

But there was nothing Rafael could do, and the last thing Sara wanted was to provoke an incident that might bring harm to her host family. "It's okay, Rafael. I know these men. They are . . ."

Sara paused. What message could she leave without arousing

suspicion in the men who had come to get her? "I . . . I have to go with them. But you must not be concerned. This man works for my husband and my father-in-law. They have come to take me—home."

Julio Vargas gave a grunt of approval. The prisoner was being cooperative. Rafael relaxed ever so slightly, his face settling from truculent determination to the stolid impassivity characteristic of Quechua peasants. But Sara knew he understood. She swung back to face Julio Vargas. "You didn't say how you found me. Who told you I was here?"

The security chief let his gaze rove over Sara from her tousled braids down the dirt-stained T-shirt and jeans to the plastic *chinelas* on her feet. In his cold scrutiny there was none of the deference to which she'd been accustomed as the wife of Nicolás Cortéz.

"You can hide your hair, *señorita,* but you cannot hide that pale skin or the *gringo* stiffness of your stride. A boy who treads the pits for the *cocaleros* saw a foreign woman dwelling in his father's *pahuichi,* so far into the jungle that they didn't know enough to turn you in for the reward. It didn't take many days for the story to travel to our ears. I myself dismissed the tale as unlikely. Apparently, I was wrong."

The insolence of his remarks hardly registered against the shock of what he said.

"Epifanio!" Sara whirled around toward the helicopter in horrified realization. "Oh, no!"

Josefina, hurrying out of the *pahuichi* with Sara's flight bag clutched to her chest, caught sight of her son at the same instant. Dropping the bag into the dirt as the stocky teenager clambered down from the doorway of the helicopter, she broke into a loud wail.

"*Mi hijo,* what have you done?" Rafael shouted. "Epifanio! How could you do this?" The stocky Quechua father started toward his son with an angry roar. But as he charged past the soldier who stood between him and the helicopter, the man raised his machine gun, slamming it against the back of the farmer's head. Rafael pitched forward onto his face. Sara gasped in horror. She would have run forward, but Julio Vargas caught her by the arm. Josefina was screaming. Consuelo raced wailing across the yard to her mother's side. The soldiers in the helicopter jumped down and raised their machine guns to firing position. In the middle of it all stood Epifanio, his young face showing utter bewilderment at the chaos his appearance had wrought.

Sara spun fiercely and snapped at Julio Vargas, "Tell your men to leave them alone, you hear me! You wanted me, and now you've got me. But they have nothing to do with this. Just leave them alone!"

"You are no longer in any position to give orders here, *señorita,*"

Julio said coldly. But he made a gesture to the soldiers. They lowered their guns. Releasing Sara, the security chief snapped his fingers at the soldier who had clubbed Rafael. "Leave the man alone and search those bags. We do not have time to waste."

He jerked his head toward Sara's knapsack. Giving Rafael a last jab with the machine gun, the soldier strode over to wrench the knapsack from Sara's shoulder. It was with effort that Sara restrained herself from yanking it back. Helpless anger choked her as the soldier trotted over to snatch up her flight bag as well.

The pandemonium was subsiding now. Sara saw with relief that Rafael was struggling to his feet. There didn't seem to be any blood. Josefina had broken off her hysterics to hurry over to her husband, Consuelo clinging to her skirts. The soldier with her belongings ripped open the flight bag without any regard to the zipper, dumping its contents onto the ground. He and his companion crouched down to poke through the pile.

"And now, *señorita,* you will answer *my* questions. You have cost us many days of searching, and it is evident now how you have done it. So you will tell me. Who is it that brought you to this . . . this *choza?*"

"I . . ." Sara wracked her brain for an answer to Julio's demand. Any answer. But she was distracted as the soldiers began to rummage through her knapsack.

"Come! I am no fool!" Julio Vargas took a step forward, blocking Sara's view of her meager personal effects. He was so close that she could smell his cologne, a heavy musk that reeked of arrogance and power. A month earlier, she'd have told him to back off in no uncertain terms. But this man was no longer the Cortéz underling she'd met. This was the army colonel Nicolás had told her about, and Sara, reluctantly bringing her gaze back to meet his flat, black eyes, found that she didn't dare give him another order or even step away.

"You will tell me now. It was your low-class associates from the *Hogar de Infantes* who arranged this, is that not so?"

"What! Why, . . . whatever gave you that idea?"

Julio misinterpreted Sara's start of surprise. His thin mouth curved in a sneer. "It is a simple deduction of logic. Who else do you know who would have contacts within such a class of people? I personally have investigated every acquaintance you have, and there are no others you know who would stoop to such a place as this. Certainly not the *americanos.* Now that I see where you have been hidden all these days, it is easy to deduce who is responsible, however much they have sworn they have not seen you. Now, you will tell me who it was!"

The security chief shifted his position as he made the demand, losing Sara's attention again as she caught sight of a soldier giving her knapsack an upside-down shake. It was a struggle to keep her face from betraying her sudden tension. Was the SatTrack as well hidden as Doug had said, or was that sophisticated piece of equipment about to betray her connections with the American DEA?

But the soldier gave the knapsack no more than a cursory glance before dropping it to kick through the pile of well-worn clothes and toiletries that had tumbled to the hard-packed dirt of the yard.

"Come!" Julio snapped his fingers in her face. "I have no patience for this!"

Sara allowed only the slightest slump to betray her relief before she turned her full attention back to her father-in-law's second-in-command. "Do you really think I'd tell you?" she demanded, torn between elation at Julio's wrong assumption and a new worry for Doña Inez and the others at the orphanage. "Why? So you can go and kill them too?"

"Don't be absurd! Do you think we have an interest in avenging ourselves on peasants?" Julio spat with such contempt that Sara actually believed him. Swinging around on his heel, he shouted at the two soldiers who were picking through Sara's belongings. Sara caught only the interrogatory inflection, not the words, but the meaning she could easily guess as one of the soldiers raised his hand in a side-to-side shake that means "*nada*, nothing!"

Julio jerked a thumb toward the helicopter, and the two men scrambled to shovel Sara's possessions back into the bags. Then the security chief swung back around to face Sara. "Enough of this! It does not matter so much now if you will not answer. What matters is that you have been here and not with the *americanos*. The rest you can answer for yourself to Don Luis. Let us go. But first, we will check you as we have your bags."

He was running his hands over Sara before she had even taken in his meaning. To his credit, he did it as impersonally as a doctor, but it was utterly humiliating, and Sara was biting back tears by the time he finished. Satisfied that she was hiding nothing, Julio pushed her toward the helicopter. Grabbing up her two bags, the soldiers fell into step behind.

Julio gave Sara no chance to say good-bye. As she started to turn, hands grabbed her and pulled her into the helicopter. Consuelo started forward with a wail as she saw Sara leaving, but Josefina snatched her back, her own wails rising above her daughter's. The last sight Sara had of her host family was Consuelo burying her face in an outburst of tears in her mother's apron, Rafael shaking an angry fist at the helicopter, and Epifanio's loud defense, "But, Papá, she is a criminal!"

The soldiers shoved her into a seat against the far wall. The knapsack and flight bag landed at her feet. Julio Vargas was already climbing into the pilot's seat. He tossed out a wad of paper before slamming the door shut. The wad scattered into bills as it hit the ground. Sara caught a glimpse of Epifanio scrambling for the money as the wash from the rotors blew the bills in all directions. Then she could no longer see the ground because the helicopter was rising. Even as hard hands fumbled to fasten a strap around her waist, the helicopter banked into a sharp turn. The open door framed only blue sky. The little *rancho* that had become such a part of her heart was gone.

As soon as the helicopter leveled off, Sara snatched up her knapsack off the floor. In a world that had once again turned topsy-turvy, it suddenly seemed as vital to her comfort as a child's security blanket. How had this all happened so fast? Ten minutes ago she had finally found some measure of tranquillity. And now here she was, a captive again.

Sara hugged the knapsack close as she turned her head to take in her newest prison. The machine had certainly not been built for comfort. The only real seats belonged to the pilot and copilot. Her own perch was no more than a bench, narrow and hard. The rest of the interior was stripped bare, leaving the soldiers to hunker down on the floor. The side door of the helicopter stood wide open, but the wind wasn't as bad as she would have expected, just enough to cool down the heat of the engine. The noise, though, was excruciating. Gritting her teeth against the thunder of the blades, Sara wondered that these men didn't even seem to notice.

She glanced ahead at the pilot's seat. Julio Vargas hadn't so much as looked back at her since the helicopter had lifted off. He had the advantage of headphones over his ears, and he appeared to be talking into a handheld mike.

The four soldiers squatting on the floor in the back hardly took their eyes off her, their machine guns still unslung and cradled across their arms. She might have been some dangerous criminal they were guarding!

Sara sighed unhappily. That was probably exactly what they thought! If these men were from the *policía militar,* as they appeared to be, they'd undoubtedly been given the same story Don Luis had fed to everyone else. "Consider armed and dangerous."

Her captors fit that category a lot better than she did. They all looked tough and seasoned, and their eyes on her were cold and watchful, even a little cruel. Though that could be her imagination. They probably trained police to look mean when they were making an arrest!

Sara hugged the knapsack tighter. There was far too much noise to ask where they were taking her. But she didn't need to. Where else but back to Santa Cruz? She shuddered. She'd heard such horror stories about Bolivian jails. Tiny unsanitary cells with no food or water—or anything else—except what you could provide for yourself. And other, even worse, things!

A black tide of fear and hopelessness rose in Sara's chest, threatening to sweep her back out to the sea of despair from which she had so recently struggled ashore. She held tightly to the moment of peace she'd felt up on that sunny knoll.

And then it was there again! The knowledge of God's presence was so close, she felt she could almost reach out and touch him. What had that verse said? "When you pass through the waters, I will be with you. . . . Fear not, for I have redeemed you. . . . You are mine . . . you are mine . . . you are mine. . . ."

Slowly Sara relaxed her hold on the knapsack, lowering it to her lap. In any case, there was no reason for despair. Once she was back in Santa Cruz, she'd be able to contact the American consulate. At least there'd be people who knew where she was. And Doug Bradford would be there. He might have come up with something during these past weeks. Maybe now he even had a solution. At least she would know soon.

Reaching for the coil of braid around her head, Sara loosened the plaits and shook them out. It was the one silver lining in this particularly gloomy cloud—getting rid of that hat and these awful braids! The thought brought to mind the man who'd made her wear them. How long would it take Doug Bradford to find out that she was no longer safe at the *rancho*? Even if Rafael was in any condition for hiking, it would take hours for him to get the news out to his cousin, Benedicto. More likely, Doug wouldn't find out that Sara was back in Santa Cruz until he next checked the SatTrack. Or would the humiliation of her capture be all over the news the instant the helicopter touched down?

Running her fingers through her hair to untangle it, Sara shook the length back from her face. Her glance bumped into the watchful gaze of one of her guards. He grinned as he caught her eye. Then, in a totally unexpected gesture, he brought a hand up in a slicing motion across his throat.

Sara hurriedly turned her head away. What a horrible man! She fastened her eyes instead on the panorama of jungle racing past outside the door. It was a dizzying feeling, but it was better than facing stares that were as relentless as a hawk eyeing the field mouse it has chosen for lunch. The drop-off didn't seem to bother the soldiers. They weren't even belted in!

They were flying low, almost skimming the treetops, though the ground was probably further down than it looked. Then, suddenly, a ridge rose up in front of the windshield, and the helicopter rose so abruptly that the soldier nearest the door grabbed for a strap on the wall. The wind whistling past the open door grew chilly as they soared upward. Range after range of foothills spread out below like a wrinkled green bedspread.

The helicopter banked to run between two ridges. Here again was evidence of the isolation of the Bolivian countryside—lone adobe houses tucked away in little valleys or perched on stark hillsides, without so much as a trail to show how they had gotten there. Only along the banks of a brown, snaking river did clusters of thatched roofs mark small villages or an occasional town. Sara longed to ask where they were. Surely a straight flight across the Chapare jungle would have been the most direct route to Santa Cruz.

The helicopter dropped again and they were back in the lowlands. They flew across a scattering of cultivated areas, clearings of bananas and rice and potatoes interspersed with uncut scrub jungle. Then, as they flew on, Sara saw clearing after clearing of low, thick bushes that were like no food crop she had ever seen, the coca plants a green stain on the face of this beautiful land.

And yet, was her own country any better? Could those who chose to buy claim any less guilt than those who chose to sell?

Soon even these clearings were left behind. The trees grew taller until they were giants that looked as though they could have sheltered the helicopter in their branches. There was no sign of the unpaved tracks that had crisscrossed the Chapare. Sara's unease grew as kilometer after unbroken kilometer flowed away beneath the belly of the chopper. They had been flying for more than an hour. So where were the towns and roads that should have marked any approach to civilization?

She'd almost worked up her nerve to question the nearest soldier when she realized that the helicopter was setting down. Enormous branches rose up to draw them in, so close it seemed she could reach out the open door and grab one. Those trees must be a hundred feet tall, maybe even twice that, she realized with awe and then dismay as the helicopter continued to sink down through their branches. This wasn't Santa Cruz, or anywhere close. It looked like—like virgin rain forest!

The skids of the helicopter touched the ground. The beat of the rotors dropped to an idle throbbing. Yanking off his head gear, Julio Vargas swung down from the cockpit. The soldiers piled out of the helicopter after him. From her belted-in position, Sara looked around for some reasonable explanation for their descent. But there were no *chozas* or cultivations or people that she could see out there. Just an opening in the jungle canopy.

Why had Julio and these soldiers brought her here? There weren't many possibilities that jumped to mind, and Sara's unease grew to panic. She buried her face against the coarse weave of the knapsack, tensing for the grab of rude hands, blanking all from her mind but a promise. "I will be with you . . . when you go through the waters, I will be with you . . ." *Oh, God, are you here?*

The scuffle of heavy boots died away and Sara raised her head. She was alone in the helicopter. No, not quite alone. There was a soldier standing guard outside the open door. Sara recognized him as the same one who had made the threatening gesture. He grinned again as he caught Sara's eyes on him. Stepping forward, he thrust his head and shoulders through the open door. "Want some company, pretty *señorita?*"

Sara would have shrunk away, but there was nothing but the wall behind her. Instead, she straightened her back and gave him a withering look. It had no effect except to widen his grin enough to show blackened front teeth, but the shout behind him did. "*Hola,* Papo, give me a hand here!"

The guard drew back at the shout. His companions were returning. Not Julio, but the others. They were no longer carrying their weapons, but burlap sacks slung over their shoulders. These had to be heavy, judging from the way the men were staggering under the load. As one sack slid loose, Papo hurried forward to catch it. The soldiers tossed the sacks onto the floor of the helicopter and left again at a trot. Slinging his own weapon across his back, Papo climbed into the helicopter and began pushing the sacks to the back wall.

By the time he'd finished arranging the heavy bags, the other soldiers were back with another load. Sara watched with astonishment as the burlap sacks piled up around her. They could have been flour or sugar except for the acrid chemical odor they gave off. Like a hospital, or a lab, or one of those test-tube experiments she'd done in high school. It wasn't an unpleasant odor—at first. But as the sacks were piled higher around her, the smell intensified until Sara was breathing out her mouth. What in the world was this stuff?

Then a last bag slammed down in front of her with a force that ripped at the drawstring that held it shut. The top of the sack stretched open. Not enough to spill its contents, but enough to give Sara a good look at what was inside. The sack was jammed full of flat packets that looked like cellophane bags of powdered sugar.

Sara's first reaction was actually elation. So it was still here—the eight tons of cocaine that were supposed to be her father-in-law's farewell to criminal activity. By the timetable Nicolás had once mentioned, the stuff should have been long gone by now, dispersed to a dozen ports and millions of victims. Sara had wondered and worried about that during the weeks of silence from Doug. The downside of convincing Don Luis that she hadn't gone to the DEA had been the likelihood that he would press on with his shipment plans. But from the looks of what was piled up around her, it appeared that Don Luis had chosen the more cautious course of laying low until he could track down his fugitive daughter-in-law. Which meant there was still time to stop this poison from leaving the country.

When they had finished loading the bags, the soldiers retrieved their weapons and crawled in on top of the burlap sacks. Julio settled into the pilot's seat and lowered his headphones over his ears. Sara watched him reach for the radio mike as the whine of the rotors rose from idle to full throttle. This stop—and those radio calls—made sense now. Of course the security chief would be communicating with his boss, and once he'd informed Don Luis that Sara had been harmlessly parked in a *campesino* hut instead of with the DEA or some American friend, her father-in-law must have given the order to pick up the cocaine and finish the job that Sara's escape had interrupted. Nicolás had told her they were keeping those eight tons stashed somewhere that could never be traced to the family. What better spot than this lonely opening in the middle of the untamed jungle?

Except . . .

Sara's elation abruptly evaporated. She'd been too engrossed in watching the loading procedure to think through the obvious implications. If these "soldiers" were out here in the middle of the jungle loading cocaine, then they couldn't possibly be soldiers.

Sara slumped against the vibrating metal wall behind her. How could she have been so stupid? Despite the obvious incongruity that Julio Vargas was flying this thing—and throwing out orders left and right—she'd assumed that these men constituted some proper Bolivian authority, because . . . well, for one thing, because this was a military aircraft, and where would Don Luis get a military helicopter without somebody knowing about it?

Nicolás had told her once that Julio Vargas flew his own helicopter, but she never would have envisioned that he was talking about something like this. It certainly explained how Julio had been able to force down those drug flights to hijack all this cocaine that was piled high around her. How he had managed to secure a combat helicopter, Sara couldn't begin to imagine. But that mattered little now.

What mattered was that she could no longer assume that the Bolivian authorities even knew she'd been found. What was it Julio had said? "A boy who treads the pits"? Epifanio had not returned to school as his father had assumed. Instead, he had apparently found work trampling coca leaves in one of those maceration pits Doug had told her about. Epifanio had gone to work for the *narcos!* And through those underworld connections, not the police, word of Sara's whereabouts had trickled back to Don Luis.

Sara stared up at the tiny patch of blue sky she could see above the sacks of cocaine. Poor Rafael and Josefina! They'd had such hopes for their son. They'd taught him right from wrong and done their best to give him a start in the outside world that was the future of their country. And yet it was clear that Epifanio had opted for the easy way out. With one son already dead by the hand of *narcos,* this had to be a devastating blow for them.

And for Sara? An hour ago, she'd panicked at the thought of a Bolivian jail cell. Now she could only wish that she were being hauled back to Santa Cruz, where at least she might be able to contact Doug and where the presence of the U.S. consulate might invoke some semblance of fair play. But this latest development put an end to even that small anticipation. With a few hundred kilos of cocaine on board, the last place Julio would be heading was the city. And Sara didn't have to stretch her mind too far to guess his real destination. There was only one place where Julio Vargas would be delivering a load of Cortéz cocaine. And Sara along with it!

It took another twenty minutes to confirm Sara's suspicions. By then, her head was spinning from the acrid fumes of the cocaine. At last she felt the helicopter begin its descent, but with the cargo piled high around her, she could see nothing until she caught a glimpse of a red tile roof, and then a whitewashed stucco wall.

As the helicopter settled to the ground, Julio killed the engine. The whine of the propeller blades throp-thropped to a stop, and Sara was able to hear shouting from outside the aircraft. Within seconds, a procession of *peones*—judging by their cheap cotton clothing—began scaling down the piles of burlap sacks, hefting them onto their backs, and staggering away. As the stacks diminished, Sara could see a wide veranda running the length of the whitewashed wall.

Sara fumbled for the strap that held her in her seat. The soldiers no longer seemed interested in her as they slung their weapons over their shoulders and strode off in a body around the side of the helicopter. Slinging her knapsack over her shoulder, she stepped over the remaining sacks to the door. She saw her flight bag appear, rather flattened, from under a burlap sack. Then it too disappeared onto someone's shoulder. Stepping down, Sara walked forward toward the nose of the helicopter. Not one eye turned in her direction. It was as though her presence had been forgotten. Then, as she caught her first glimpse of what lay beyond the helicopter, she gasped.

This was the rustic country hacienda that had played such a role in recent events?

She turned a slow circle, forgetting for a moment the circumstances that had brought her here. The house was enormous, rising three full stories. Flower beds edged the veranda, and from where Sara was standing, a lawn as neatly trimmed and extensive as the one at *Industrias Cortéz* stretched away to the edge of the jungle, which had been trimmed back to make an even border around the property. Far off to the left, she saw what appeared to be a gravel airstrip.

Much closer, an enormous satellite dish lifted its face from the middle of the lawn. Above the dish, a needle-shaped tower stretched toward the sky. What had Nicolás said about no cable TV or room service at the hacienda? But then, why should she be surprised by one more lie?

Sara's initial awe cooled as she picked out two soldiers patrolling the perimeter, with Dobermans—the Cortéz trademark in watchdogs—pacing beside them. No, not soldiers, despite the army fatigues that had fooled her earlier. Security guards might be a better term. Though why they were needed in the middle of virgin rain forest . . .

"Ouch!" A sudden jab in her side startled Sara. She whirled around as she was jabbed again. "What—!"

The sight of an ugly, knobby-looking gun choked off her furious protest. It was too big to be a pistol and too short for a machine gun or rifle. But Sara didn't need a short course in firearms to recognize its deadliness. She raised her eyes from the barrel that was jammed into the base of her rib cage.

"You were going somewhere, *señorita?*" Julio Vargas asked coldly.

The pressure on her ribs eased as he used the gun to motion her toward the house. "You will be pleased to precede me."

Sara shot the security chief a look that would have shriveled him to ashes if mental heat could manifest itself in physical power. But she obeyed, quickly and gingerly. She'd never had a gun aimed point-blank at her before, and she wasn't entirely convinced that it wouldn't accidentally go off. She was almost as rankled by Julio's continued use of the term *señorita* as by the weapon. That this Cortéz underling would feel so free to toss aside her married title drove home more than anything the change in her position.

"Why did you bring me here?" she demanded over her shoulder as she stepped onto the veranda. "I thought the whole idea was to drag me back to Santa Cruz and throw me into jail for the death of that poor boy that Nicolás shot."

The gun in her back prodded her toward the main entrance, a set of those huge double doors that Sara had seen on every old-style mansion in Bolivia. "That will no longer be necessary, *señorita*. You solved that difficulty for us when you chose to run away. The police are well satisfied with your guilt, and now that we have been able to recover you without their involvement, it is my consideration—and that of Don Luis—that it would be sheer foolishness to allow you the opportunity to confuse them with other stories."

Sara felt a chill despite the blazing sun, and she bit back any further questions. So she'd been right! The Bolivian authorities had no idea she'd been captured. Nor did Don Luis have any intention of letting them know.

The impression of a rich man's residence ended at the front door. The entry hall was spacious, with high ceilings, but it was empty except for sacks of cocaine stacked against one wall. The plaster was crumbling in spots from both walls and ceiling, and the treads of the wide staircase were unpolished and scuffed by countless boot marks.

As Julio pushed Sara forward, a man in a white lab coat stepped quickly out of her way, his glance carefully blank as it went from Sara to the gun at her back. He disappeared under the balustrade of the staircase. Shifting his weapon to grip Sara by the arm, Julio steered her in the same direction. A narrow door showed itself beneath the stairs. With his gun hand, Julio pushed it open, and Sara gasped again.

The place looked like the cockpit of a jumbo jet—or a computer lab. The man in the white coat was bent over a console. Static and the murmur of voices came from some sort of speaker above his head. It looked like no radio setup Sara had ever seen, but she had no doubt this was the explanation of that communication tower and satellite dish out on the lawn. If only she could gain access to this room and somehow figure out how to send a message to Doug Bradford . . .

Raising her glance from the console, Sara caught the communication technician's eye. The malice she saw there told her that she might as well have shouted her thoughts aloud. "Marcelo," Julio ordered coldly, "you will inform Don Luis that we have arrived with the girl. And continue to monitor the military channels. If there is any new activity, I wish it reported immediately."

The door clicked shut on Sara's fleeting hope, and the security chief was prodding her back across the entryway through another set of double doors opposite the stairs. Sara stopped short as the doors swung shut behind her. One quick glance told her she had now reached the hub of the Cortéz drug operation.

The room was even bigger than the ballroom at the Cortéz mansion, and it was clear that it had once served the same purpose. But the bank of arched windows that had once let starlight in on the dancers was now bricked over, the chandeliers replaced with fluorescent tubes. On the platform where once a band had filled the jungle night with the alien sounds of music, two men in lab coats were breaking bags of cocaine into a row of bathtubs. Stacks of Indian weavings and llama-skin rugs were piled high beside the tubs.

On the dance floor itself, more workers bustled around rows of long tables. Already, several of the burlap sacks lay slit open, and at the nearest table, Sara could see a technician using a funnel to channel scoops of cocaine into wine bottles. An elderly *peón* was pouring wine in on top of the crystals. Despite enormous and noisy air-circulation units set in the wall above the bricked-over windows, the acrid smell of chemicals was far stronger than it had been in the helicopter.

"Move!" At Julio's jab, Sara started down an aisleway between the rows of tables, her outrage growing as she took in each new aspect of the processing lab. Rough shelving along the walls held other products waiting to be processed. Jugs of molasses. Crates of rubbing alcohol. Five-kilo bags of sugar. Racks of clothing. Sara spotted an embroidered blouse exactly like one she herself had bought recently in a Cortéz boutique. And there were other items that Sara hadn't even known Industrias Cortéz produced. Shampoos. Conditioners. Fine liquors.

Piled in one corner were stacks and stacks of cardboard shipping boxes. All with an off-centered Cortéz emblem up in the right-hand corner!

At the far end of the room, Sara paused to watch a wrinkled old Quechua man knead a one-kilo bag of cocaine into a mound of raw clay on a potter's wheel. Already fired pieces of his craft lay on a table beside him, stylized representations of the Inca earth goddess, Pachamama. They were lying on their sides, and Sara could see they were hollow. But as she watched, another worker picked one up and emptied a bag of white powder into the base.

"It sure didn't take them long to get started!" she commented caustically, her eyes sweeping the room with disgust. "Though I imagine they've had plenty of practice by now."

"They have been working since I radioed the news of your capture," Julio said coldly. "You have cost us a good many days, *señorita*. Now that you are found, Don Luis has given orders to finish our work as soon as possible. A week from now—poof!—this will all be empty to return to the jungle." Vargas turned his head to survey the room with some distaste. "I for one will be pleased to see the end of it. *Pfaah!* The place stinks!"

It was the first personal comment Sara had ever heard Julio Vargas make, but any chance that it indicated an actual spark of humanity in the man was dispelled when he stabbed her hard in the kidneys with the barrel of his gun, pushing her forward toward a door beside the platform. She gasped with a mixture of pain and fury. That one had really hurt!

Grabbing at the doorjamb to catch her balance, Sara rounded on her captor furiously. Gun or no gun, she'd just about had it! Maybe she wasn't "Señora Cortéz" anymore, with all the privileges that implied, but he didn't have to treat her like—like that poor girl at the factory. "Would you stop doing that? I am quite capable of walking on my own if you'll just tell me where you want me to go. And I don't think poking me every two seconds with that . . . that *thing* was part of any orders you got from Don Luis!"

Without waiting for his reaction or giving him a chance to prod her again, she whirled back around and grabbed for the door in front of her, a gesture of defiance that proved meaningless because the door was locked. Sara hated the thin smile on Vargas's face as he reached past her to unlock the door, but he did step back, using the gun to wave her through the door in a gesture of exaggerated courtesy. Ignoring the mockery, Sara gathered up the remnants of her dignity and stalked into the room.

Immediately she was greeted by a cool breeze. Air-conditioning!

Sara looked around. This was the first part of the residence she'd seen that had been maintained in its original splendor, and it was immediately apparent that she had stepped into Don Luis's office. Her father-in-law's sense of style was written all over it. The huge mahogany desk. The red leather chairs, which she knew from experience were more impressive than comfortable. Over the desk, a painting in an ornate gilt frame. Like most of the paintings Sara had seen gracing the Cortezes' walls, it had the marks of an old Spanish master. A knight in *conquistador* armor rearing high on a white horse.

And to the right of the painting, a door.

"The door will do you no good, *señorita*," Julio said coldly from the doorway, following Sara's eyes. "It is locked, and there is a guard outside."

Julio stepped back out of the room and reached for the doorknob. In another moment, Sara would be locked in.

"Wait! Don't leave me here." Her voice wavered between panicked and authoritative. "I want to speak to Don Luis or . . . or Nicolás."

Julio paused with his hand on the doorknob. "Your husband has no interest in speaking to you, *señorita*. Or so I have been informed. But you will have the opportunity to speak with Don Luis soon enough. He will be flying in shortly from Santa Cruz. He has already given orders that, when he arrives, he wishes to interrogate you. Personally."

His glance was indifferent, his tone flat. But there was something in the way he said the last word—almost with regret—that sent a fresh chill down Sara's spine. She looked at the security chief—it was perhaps the first time she'd ever truly looked at him—and was suddenly afraid.

Sara had disliked Julio Vargas since that first day at the refinery warehouse when she'd seen his temper exercised at the expense of an innocent young woman. But though she'd known he was capable of criminal behavior, her perceptions had perhaps been colored by her husband's arrogance toward him. Even as he was taking her captive this morning, she had still thought of him as Don Luis's lapdog—as Nicolás had once snidely called him. A follower. A taker of orders.

Now Sara saw the casualness with which he held the huge and unwieldy pistol, and she noticed, as she had once before, that his eyes were as unblinkingly hard and cold and dead as a black stone. This man was no lapdog. More like an attack dog, if there was any canine analogy. A killer. Like Nicolás. Only far more dangerous, because this man wouldn't kill in a drunken rage; he'd kill for business.

"And then?" Vargas was pulling the door shut before Sara realized that the words hadn't made it past her throat. Even when she repeated them, they came out in a whisper. "And then? What are you going to do? What is he going to do with me?"

Julio Vargas paused. He'd heard her. He turned around and regarded her with his flat, lifeless eyes. Then, horribly, his tongue flickered out, just the pink tip, wetting his lips as though an offered treat had set his mouth to watering. Sara realized in that moment that Julio Vargas had never forgiven her for the scene in the warehouse when she'd dressed him down in front of his subordinates—and now he was relishing his answer.

"Then?" The corners of his mouth turned up ever so slightly. "The jungle out there is many thousands of kilometers, *señorita*. You will not be the first fugitive who has disappeared into its boundaries never to be seen again. Now—if you will excuse me, I must supervise the work. I trust these accommodations will be satisfactory until Don Luis arrives."

Again, his tongue flicked across his lips. Sara ran forward to catch at the edge of the door as it started to close. "You can't do this, you know. If Epifanio's been talking, there are probably others who've heard by now where I was staying. There's going to be a lot of questions if I don't show up in Santa Cruz. And my friends are going to be able to tell them exactly what happened . . . how I was picked up by a military helicopter and everything. You'll have my embassy crawling all over you. I *am* an American citizen, after all. They're not going to let me just disappear into thin air."

Her plea was as weak as it was desperate, Sara knew even as she finished. Unfortunately, Julio Vargas knew it too. He paused long enough to sneer. "Do not fool yourself! You are a criminal fugitive. Do you truly think your *campesino* friends are going to tell the world that they have been hiding you? They know only too well that they will be in jail if they say a word. If I thought otherwise, they would not be alive now. Don Luis does not wish to spill unnecessary blood, but I—I have no such difficulties!

"And if your friends were so foolish, what proof can they give that you were ever there? There are many who have made such a claim of seeing you since your disappearance, hoping for some reward for their tales. But if they check, they will find that no military aircraft have flown in that area. You see, my machine does not exist.

"As for the *americanos,* as far as they are concerned, you have already disappeared—and of your own free will. If you are not found, they will be only too happy to be spared the embarrassment of a public trial for one of their citizens. Do you think we have not considered that? Now, please, I must go."

Sara groped for a seat as the lock clicked into place and she was left alone. The worst of it was that Julio Vargas was probably right. Except for Doug Bradford, the American authorities would probably be content to write her off as lost in the jungle and thereby avoid an international incident—her story was bound to hit CNN and every other news service. That would certainly not enhance her country's overseas image.

The knight on the white horse watched Sara smugly from the wall behind the desk. His eyes were blue, his face impossibly handsome under the plumed helmet. They did have a thing for heroic portraits, those Cortéz ancestors. Sara shifted her eyes to the woman standing behind the horse. She was Spanish and plump. Another Cortéz bride? Behind her, up on a hill, was a church that was a twin to the San Lorenzo cathedral on the main plaza of Santa Cruz. It was a familiar scenario.

Sara sat up suddenly in astonishment. Yes, it *was* a familiar scenario! But not because of those hated Cortéz features. The maiden. The church. Yes, there was the dragon, too, shadowed under the belly of the horse, its blood streaming away from the spear in its chest to the edge of the painting. That was—St. George! The patron saint of drug dealers!

No, wait a minute. This painting had to predate the saint's present connection to the drug trade by at least a century or two. Nor was the St. George legend an unusual portrait setting for Spanish colonial art. Still, Sara could see why Don Luis had chosen to move the painting down here to the hacienda. Like the St. George cross, the painting could give rise to comparisons that an uneasy conscience would find unwelcome. Sara studied the painter's interpretation of the legend. The dragon was a very small and shriveled dragon, the knight and his spear very large, and to the girl huddled in a chair beneath them, they seemed to symbolize all the might of the Cortezes and the impotence of the authorities against them. Julio Vargas had every reason for his confidence. After all, this wouldn't be the first time they'd made an enemy disappear into thin air. It wouldn't be a difficult task to do it again.

Or so they thought!

Slipping the knapsack from her shoulder, Sara hugged its comforting bulk tight. Julio and Don Luis and Nicolás might think they had won. But they'd badly miscalculated when they had chosen to bring her—and her wired knapsack—to the hacienda. Maybe even now a silent signal was making its way skyward to tell Doug Bradford where she was. As soon as he found she was no longer safe where he'd left her, he'd come after her. And when he did, he wouldn't just find her but those eight tons of cocaine and the lab Don Luis had hidden so successfully for so many years in full production.

The smallest bubble of excitement rose in Sara to combat her fear of Julio Vargas and Don Luis. Could it be that the whole chain of events that had started with Epifanio's unexpected visit and led to this moment was no accident?

Is that why you let them find me, God? So Doug would find the hacienda and catch them in the act with all that cocaine? Could this . . . could this even be why you brought me to Bolivia? Why you never stopped me from marrying Nicky? Is it like Doug says, and this is all part of a plan of yours? Even my mistakes?

But even as her excitement welled, the doubts and fears attacked. Was she taking this too far? How could she be so sure that thing in her knapsack was even working anymore? Doug had said the battery would last a couple of weeks. It had been far longer than that already. And why—*why*—had he never come back? Not even to bring her the replacement tracker he'd promised. Had something gone terribly wrong out there while she'd been cut off to the world? Maybe even to Doug himself? After all, he was in a dangerous profession where people actually used guns like those the guards and Julio Vargas were carrying! Was it possible that—

No! Sara shook the terrible thought from her mind. Doug was alive and well. She had to believe that. And he would come. If Rafael got her message and the description of her captor to Doug, he would know who had taken her and why.

But would it be in time?

She couldn't allow false hope to mislead her. Even if Doug had found out by now that she'd been moved, he would still have to reach Benedicto and then Rafael and Josefina. That would take time. And once he found out what had happened, it would take even more time for Doug to reach the new position marked by the SatTrack signal. Was he a pilot? Sara realized she didn't know. But even if he could reach this isolated spot in the middle of the jungle, what could one man do against this fortress? The thought of Doug walking into those guards and weapons she'd seen out there chilled Sara more than the danger she herself was facing. He wouldn't—couldn't—be so foolhardy!

But if she had to wait while he returned to Santa Cruz to talk his boss into authorizing a raid, what chance was there that she would still be here when they arrived? Even now, Don Luis was on his way to see her, and he would be here far sooner than any force Doug might be able to put together.

Huddled down into the red leather chair, her knapsack clutched so tightly that the tendons of her fingers were turning pale yellow under their tan, Sara fought the terror that was turning the room dark around her. She couldn't lose her newfound faith. She had to believe that God had a plan in all of this. But Don Luis had a plan for her too, and the problem was, those two plans didn't have to be mutually exclusive. Once Doug had traced the SatTrack signal and had located the hacienda, it wouldn't require that Sara be found alive and well in order for him to finish the job of bringing down the Cortezes.

With infinite weariness, Sara bowed her head and rested it on the knapsack. And would her death really be such a loss? It wasn't as though she had any place to go when this was all over. Nor any purpose that she could see for the long years ahead.

"Though the fig tree does not bud and there are no grapes on the vines . . ."

Sara let the words steal into her mind, calming her. The fig tree had never budded for Jeremiah. Not in his lifetime. Why should she expect any more for herself? But even if they killed her now, they couldn't really hurt her. Not anymore. And if all that came of her brief lifetime was an end to Luis Cortéz and his evil empire, then she could no longer feel it had been a total waste.

And yet, though such a short time ago she had been dreading the future, she found suddenly that she wanted to live—if only to see this finished.

Sara lifted her chin and looked straight on at the triumphant glitter in the painted blue eyes of St. George.

"God, I know you're with me right now," she prayed aloud. "And I know you care about me and that anything you decide to do with my life has got to be right. So I guess I shouldn't be afraid anymore. But I am! I'm scared to death—and so confused! I don't understand how all those prophets could rejoice even when people were putting them to death. But I really need some of their courage now! Please, God, help me to hold on to what you've taught me these past weeks, no matter what happens here today! And, God—no, Father! I haven't called you Father in years, but I want to now. Father in heaven, if I can't be brave when they walk through that door, at least help me not let them see my fear!"

CHAPTER TWENTY-NINE

Ramon slapped the rusty metal cylinder. "Okay, let's blow this baby and get out of here."

Doug pulled a stick of C-4 explosives from his backpack and prepared to attach it to the massive ether synthesizer they had seized in the raid. Along with a squad of NIFC soldiers, the two agents had been staked out in this forsaken stretch of jungle since before dawn, and it was finally time to head for home. For once, though, the outcome had been worth every minute of lost sleep. In fact, it just might make sense to leave the cocaine processing lab intact for a while. It would make a nice tour stop for those junketing congressmen who would be descending on the DEA office next week.

With that thought in mind, Doug glanced around the small clearing as he peeled back the foil from the plastic explosives. There was no clear apron where a helicopter could set down, just a rough camp hacked out of the brush under a grove of wild rubber and cacao trees. But the bright-red Toyota T-100 the troops had discovered hidden under a tarp was proof that a vehicle could make it in all the way.

As if to further confirm Doug's assessment, the small army truck in which they'd covered all but the last two kilometers from Santa Cruz came bumping into view along a narrow jungle track, horn blaring. The driver backed the truck around beside the red pickup, and Lieutenant Olivera, the officer in charge of the NIFC squad, waved for his men to begin loading the confiscated equipment that was small enough to move. In addition to a refrigerator—which seemed to have been reserved for liquid refreshment for the workers—there were dozens of *garrafas*, the small natural gas cylinders which most Bolivians used for cooking, five-gallon cans of alcohol, plastic containers of other chemicals, a power generator, and a freezer.

And, of course, there was the recycler—a fifty-five-gallon drum scorched black by all the fires that had been lit underneath it—and all the usual paraphernalia for processing cocaine. Too much to be carried in by mule or on the backs of *peones*, like many of the smaller operations did. This camp was an elaborate set-up and far better planned than most. The thickness of the jungle canopy camouflaged both site and track from any snooping aircraft, and it was far enough off any beaten path that they'd never have known the place existed were it not for a disgruntled *peón* turned informer who had tired of working long, dangerous hours for peanuts while his boss walked away with all the profits.

Splitting the chunk of C-4 lengthwise, Doug laid the two pieces side by side on top of the ether synthesizer, which had been crafted from a cast-iron gas cylinder left over from the days of the American oil companies. Now it lay on its side in a cradle of welded metal pipes, with an iron tube about two feet high thrusting upward at one end. The tube was topped by a manometer, and from the side of this device a length of copper tubing ran out at right angles to coil down into the well and up the other side, where it ended in the mouth of a five-gallon plastic jerry can.

The contraption was a jury-rigged affair that any decent engineer would have sneered at. But it worked, which was all that mattered. Even in its rusted condition, the cylinder alone was worth about $2,000 to a chemical trafficker, and since it was too heavy to cart in as evidence, Doug was going to make sure that no one came along later to put it back into use. Hence, the C-4 explosives. The recycler had been easier to decommission. They'd simply split the barrel in two with a fire ax.

That the site existed at all was due to one simple reason. It wasn't the coca leaves, which existed in ever-increasing abundance, that limited the amount of pure cocaine hydrochloride a country like Bolivia could produce. It was the availability of essential chemicals. So many were needed. Quicklime and kerosene to leach the cocaine out of the coca leaves in the maceration pits. Sulfuric acid to precipitate the resulting mash into cocaine paste. Potassium permanganate and common baking soda to filter out impurities, leaving behind the pure cocaine base. Hydrochloric acid, ether, and more sulfuric acid to transform the base into the cocaine hydrochloride crystals that would dissolve in the user's bloodstream to bring the craved high.

Tens of liters of sulfuric acid were required for every kilo of cocaine that hit the streets. Consequently, it was now possible to make as much money smuggling chemicals *into* Bolivia as smuggling cocaine *out*—which fueled an entirely new criminal racket. A ton of sulfuric acid purchased in Paraguay for $400 could be sold on the

Santa Cruz black market for $30 *per liter.* The same for ether. So it was no surprise when some resourceful locals came up with the idea of bypassing government controls by synthesizing their own ingredients. After all, the process for producing ether, needed in mass quantities for cocaine production, wasn't much different than the procedure used by Appalachian bootleggers to make moonshine whiskey. All you needed was a mixture of alcohol, caustic soda, and sulfuric acid, and a gas cylinder under the tank to heat the concoction until it turned into a gas. From there, the gas boiled through the copper tubing down into the water source, which cooled it enough to turn it back into liquid ether, which was then collected in plastic containers at the other end.

The recycler was then used to reheat the liquid ether, run it through another water source, and condense it again into pure diethyl ether. The final product could be sold at a profit of several hundred percent on the black market.

The *narco* who had set up this camp had apparently decided to work both ends of the market. Instead of selling the ether, he was using it to process his own cocaine, thereby increasing his profits several times more. And with the recycler, he could reprocess the liquids left over from making the cocaine, redistilling the ether again and again.

Well, not anymore! Doug had already radioed back enough information to arrest the *pez gordo,* a certain Las Palmas resident who at the moment was probably enjoying the last good night's sleep he would have for a while.

Ramon cut a length of blasting fuse long enough to allow himself ninety seconds to clear the area, and inserted one end into the igniter cap. Meanwhile, Doug grabbed a black plastic bag and collapsible shovel from his backpack and began filling the bag with dirt and rocks. The dirt reeked of chemical waste that had been dumped on the ground for untold months. It made Doug's skin crawl to think of how many tons of the stuff had been poured out onto the soil of Bolivia during the twenty years of the cocaine boom. If these people didn't start shaping up, their entire country was going to be one big ecological catastrophe.

By the time the bag was full, Ramon had inserted the other end of the time fuse into the C-4 and glued it down with a piece of the plastic explosive. Knotting the mouth of the bag shut, Doug placed it on top of the charge. Its weight would help direct the force of the explosion downward into the metal of the old gas tank. Doug had learned by experience just how hard these things were to destroy.

Two full sticks of C-4 in a tank full of ether would hardly even dent it. Trial and error had proven the bag technique to be the easiest and most effective use of the explosives.

Ramon glanced up at Doug as he twisted the igniter cap to make sure it was tight. "You ready?"

Doug scanned the camp to make sure all their men—and the prisoners who had been captured during the raid—were well distant from the blast site, then nodded. Ramon pulled the thin loop of wire that was the cotter pin from its hole in the side of the igniter cap, then gave the igniter pin on top of the cap a one-quarter turn before yanking it loose. A thin thread of smoke emerged. The two agents walked away. With the hundreds of times he'd done this, the thought of that burning fuse no longer bothered Doug, though he was careful to obey the foremost safety rule—don't run.

In any case, Ramon must have cut the fuse a little long, because the two agents had ample time to join the rest of the men at the edge of the lab site, turn—and wait. No matter what the scientists said, anyone who worked with explosives could testify that the second hand of a watch invariably slowed in proximity to a burning fuse and continued to slow in direct proportion to the inches remaining on the length of fuse.

Boom! The explosion rocked the rusty old cylinder. Doug waited until the rock and dirt had settled back to the ground before he walked over to inspect the damage. The synthesizer tank was still in one piece, but now there was a jagged, basketball-size hole in the top. No one would be putting this can into use again. He gave the thumbs-up signal. "Okay, let's load up and head out!"

Lieutenant Olivera repeated the order to his men, and they began herding the prisoners into the back of the red pickup.

Ramon walked over to Doug. "You got all the shots we need?"

Doug called out to one of the NIFC operatives who was walking slowly around the disabled recycler with a Hi-8 video camera to his eye. "Hey, Carlos, did you get this yet?"

Carlos didn't raise his glance—or the camera—from the shattered oil drum. "*Sí, señor.* Every centimeter."

"And what about still shots?"

This time, Carlos stopped and lowered the camera. "I have taken pictures of everything that is needed for evidence, Señor Douglas," he said pointedly. "Do you wish to take my job over for yourself?"

Doug smiled to himself at the soldier's air of offended dignity. His habit of checking up on his subordinates was maybe a bit strong, especially with the new generation of NIFC operative, whose professional expertise was often more than a match for the DEA agents. Carlos, for example, had earned a degree in telecommunications before being recruited for his present job. "Sorry, I shouldn't have asked."

Carlos put his camera away and climbed into the driver's seat of the Toyota. Doug was following Ramon over to the army truck when he suddenly remembered that he had one more thing to do.

Striding purposefully past the disabled synthesizer, Doug stooped under the branches of a rubber tree. Part way up the trunk, a block of wood had been nailed to form a rough shelf, which held a half-dozen melted blobs that had once been votive candles. Just above the shelf, also nailed to the tree, was a gilded picture frame. Mounted under the glass was a garishly cheap representation of St. George, the armor glaringly gold, the dragon a brilliant scarlet, the sky an impossible blue. Even the damsel in distress looked more like an over-endowed barmaid than a saintly maiden.

Ripping the picture from its nail, Doug dropped it deliberately, face first, into the dirt and placed his boot smack in the middle. When he felt the crackle of splintering glass, he lifted the shattered frame and shook off the loose shards. Sliding the print from the frame, he took out his lighter and flicked it open. A sheet of paper loosely pasted onto the back curled and writhed as the flame licked at the thin cardboard. The inscription quickly turned black and crumbled away. Doug didn't need to read the words to know what they said. He knew them well enough by now, and they made him see red every time.

> *Glorious San Jorge, the valiant,*
> I petition you with three Pater Nosters and an Ave Maria
> that my body be not imprisoned nor wounded nor my blood
> spilled; that I will walk as free as Jesus Christ walked in the
> womb of the Virgin Mary.
> I petition you with one Lord's Creed
> That my enemies will have eyes and will not see me, hands and will
> not lay hold of me, feet and will not overtake me;
> If they come against me with arms, that they will backfire;
> if with stones, that they will turn to earth;
> if with knives, that the points will double back on them;
> That the enemies of my body and my soul be deceived
> and the authorities be brought to nothing as they seek
> to pursue me and trample me under foot

until they are forced to submit themselves at my feet
as Jesus Christ submitted Himself to the Holy Cross.

It wasn't exactly the most peaceful prayer. Theoretically, this St.
George was supposed to represent protection in the face of evil. But
to the underworld here in Bolivia, *San Jorge* wasn't about protection,
nor was there anything milquetoast or kindly about him. *San Jorge*
was the warrior saint, the dragon slayer. And that was how these
guys saw themselves. Warriors fighting against the big, mean establishment that had the temerity to expect them to obey the laws by
which the rest of society had to abide. It was a whole lot easier on
their egos than admitting they were nothing but common criminals.

"Hey!" The shout was from one of the prisoners. "You can't do
that! That is private property. It is *santo,* holy."

The expletives that followed as the print continued to burn were
far from holy. Doug ambled over to the Toyota, St. George's faithful
steed turning to ash in his hand. Leaning his free elbow on the side
of the truck, he looked coolly down at his heckler.

"For your information, Justiniano, you don't have private property
anymore." Doug's glance moved deliberately from the shiny-red paint
of the new pickup to the refrigerator and freezer in the rear of the
army truck and back again. "I'm sure there are a lot of good government programs that will appreciate your generosity. As for
this . . ."—his cool gaze lingered on the prisoner's handcuffs as the
blackened cardboard fluttered from his fingers to the ground—"I
don't know why you'd want to keep him anyway. I'd say he's kind of
fallen down on the job, wouldn't you? Or maybe *San Jorge* here just
doesn't like drug dealers."

Snuffing out the last bit of flame under his boot, he turned on
his heel. "See you in prison!"

A stream of curses followed Doug as he climbed into the cab of
the army truck. Ramon slid in behind the wheel. He looked over at
Doug as he turned the key in the ignition. "That *San Jorge* stuff
really gets under your skin, doesn't it, *mano?*"

Doug had the grace to look a little shamefaced. "It just makes
me so mad that anyone would use the name of God to be dealing in
this—this . . . Well, anyway, the guys are used to it, but it always
makes the druggies madder than where they think good ol' St. George
is going to save them from!"

"Hey, man, I understand." The truck groaned as Ramon shifted
into first gear. "My mamá back in the barrios—she prayed to the

saints until the day she died. Burned candles and everything. Don't know what good it did, but I know what she'd have said about lowlifes like these guys figuring one of the holy *santos* was on their side. And I can tell you this, *mano*. If my mother were here, they wouldn't have got off so easy. Mamá had a tongue that could raise blisters."

The incident with the San Jorge painting brought Sara to Doug's mind. He'd been too busy with the raid to spare a thought for how she was faring—until now. Ramon cast his companion a thoughtful glance as Doug lapsed into silence, then turned his eyes to the track through the jungle. Doug stared out the window, but he wasn't seeing the scrub brush and low-hanging trees that crowded the narrow trail. *Two-and-a-half weeks and still no solution!*

The search for Sara had been full-blown by the time Doug had returned from dropping her off with Benedicto. The story was in every newspaper and on every radio and TV channel in the country—except CNN. Doug still wondered whether Grant Major had been involved in that little oversight, but the RAC would never admit it. Within a day, thousands had come forward insisting they'd seen Sara getting off a bus, ducking into a shop, or lurking in their neighborhood. Doug was certain there wasn't so much as a pebble unturned within the boundaries of Santa Cruz by now. Add to that the airport checks, police searches, and transport inspections—he'd been caught in one of those on his way home from the Chapare—and it hadn't taken long to affirm the wisdom of Doug's decision to get Sara out of the city.

But that was about all that had gone right. Ramon followed up on the new information Sara had introduced into the Cortéz case as competently—and discreetly—as Doug himself could have done. The grand total of results had been absolutely zip! The Miami investigators had traced their cocaine-laden hangings to the Quechua weavers of the Lake Titicaca *altiplano,* but whether the Bolivian or Peruvian side couldn't be determined without finding the individual artist. Which had proved fruitless. Certainly no connection had developed that could point a finger at Industrias Cortéz. They bought and exported native handicrafts, but so did dozens of other companies.

And so it had continued. The search for the hacienda had turned up a Beni cattle ranch that was registered to Industrias Cortéz, from which regular flights brought back beef for the Cortéz restaurants. But discreet inquiries revealed that the owners had not personally visited the ranch in the working memory of the present cowhands. The ranch was in a well-settled area with plenty of neighbors, and the overseer's house was a small, four-room affair. Further, there were no noticeable security precautions for keeping out visitors. Doug, looking over the report, had to agree with Ramon that the place didn't fit the profile for the level of illegal activity Sara had described.

The Orejuela lineage had proven equally elusive. Though Kyle had managed to trace Pablo Orejuela's registry of birth, and that of his father, Salvador, Salvador's father was listed as "unknown," and the place of birth was registered simply as "Santa Cruz province." With both Pablo and Ricardo out of the picture, the only real tie Doug had to connect them with the Cortezes was the *San Jorge* cross the arresting officer had seen around Pablo Orejuela's neck. And all Luis Cortéz would need to say was that the piece of jewelry had been stolen sometime in the past and that he hadn't seen it since. There were people who might be able to testify otherwise, but having to keep this investigation under such tight wraps was putting a real crimp on the gathering of evidence.

As for Luis Cortéz and his son, they were going about their business as usual, apart from the necessary fanfare surrounding Sara's disappearance and the police investigation. There had been one press conference—Nicolás had been notably absent—at which Luis Cortéz had gravely requested the public's cooperation and expressed in sonorous and measured tones his regrets and deepest sympathy to the bereaved family of the murdered boy.

Surveillance on Cortéz Industries had produced no better results. Ramon had gotten an operative into the warehouse as a packing girl, but she'd been expected to work, not wander around, and had reported little except that none of the crates and boxes she'd seen had carried the misplaced emblem that Sara had described.

A more distant watch had tracked the comings and goings of Cortéz aircraft. But it had proven impossible to inspect their cargo without demanding an open police search. Unauthorized personnel didn't just wander around the airstrip, and the only cargo the surveillance team had been able to identify through their high-powered binoculars was a load of beef that had been shipped in whole, unwrapped sides rather than boxes or crates. In any case, there'd been few plane flights, and the two Cortéz men themselves hadn't left the city once.

Doug himself had been back at his job within hours of returning from the Chapare. Not just because it had taken him less than two minutes to spot the tail loitering across the street from the office, but because there was nothing else he could do as far as Sara was concerned. Besides, several cases in which he'd invested a couple of months of hard work had begun to pull together. Grant had said little, beyond commenting that Doug's weekend off didn't seem to have been very restful. He hadn't asked Doug about Sara again, although he did comment that she had never turned herself in to the State Department.

Doug had raised an innocent eyebrow. "Oh? I guess maybe she figured out exactly how much help they were planning to give her. I can't say I'm sorry."

Grant hadn't responded to that and had seemed more than satisfied to see Doug hard at work again, though it was impossible to say with any precision what was going through his wily mind.

Then there'd been an unexpected break in an investigation of a small Paraguayan airline whose personnel had been augmenting their salaries by running cocaine from Santa Cruz to Asunción in their carry-on luggage. The company's assets had been confiscated by the Bolivian government, and with all the excitement, Sara and the Cortezes had dropped from the front-page news.

Grant hadn't mentioned Sara again until just two days ago, when he'd called Doug in and slapped a fat file binder down in front of him.

"There it is—Ramon's report. And not one word in it to indicate that Luis Cortéz is anything less than pure as driven snow. Not one disputable air flight. Not one questionable shipment. No criminal antecedents among any of Cortéz's overseas business associates. Not one misstep. What do you have to say to that, Bradford?"

Doug hadn't backed down under the RAC's choleric gaze. "You could say that about plenty of people we investigate—right up until we catch them with their hands in the powder. Cortéz isn't stupid! He's just waiting for all this to blow over. As soon as he thinks he can get away with it, he's going to be shipping that coke, you wait and see."

"Fine." Grant had dropped the file into a drawer. "Let me know when he does. In the meantime, I've got more urgent matters that need Ramon's attention."

So it had settled down to a stalemate. Luis Cortéz wasn't going to move any more cocaine until he knew where his daughter-in-law was and exactly who she'd been talking to. If the recent disappearance of the tail who had dogged Doug over the past couple of weeks was any indication, the Cortezes had concluded that she hadn't run to the DEA. But with the extent of the search they had mounted, they would also have every reason to be confident it was only a matter of time.

Doug was determined to make sure that their confidence was misplaced. But he couldn't do anything more until Luis Cortéz made a move. The problem was, Cortéz could afford to wait longer than Doug. Those eight tons of cocaine would keep indefinitely. Sara wouldn't!

Doug roused abruptly as the massive bronze statue of the *Cristo*, its arms outstretched above the second circle, loomed up at the intersection just ahead. Meeting Ramon's thoughtful glance, he suddenly realized he hadn't spoken once in the entire fifty kilometer drive. "Drop me off here, will you? I'm going to hump it over to the office while you're taking care of this load."

Ramon was on his way to Bienes Incautados, the warehouse where goods confiscated from drug raids were stored until they were no longer needed for evidence. Despite the inevitable corruption and mysterious attrition of inventory, the department had benefited a lot of good causes over the years. There were children's homes and shelters for abused women and teen addicts now enjoying the lavish accommodations of a drug lord's *finca*, or mansion, as well as lesser expropriations, such as the refrigerator and freezer in the back of the truck.

Ramon would have all the help there that he needed to unload. As the truck pulled up to the light, Doug clambered down from the cab, taking with him the Glock pistol in his hip holster but leaving behind the M-16 he'd carried on the raid. Lifting a hand to his companion, he set off on foot through the snarl of traffic. While Ramon was delivering the truck and its contents, Doug would get the DEA-6 form written up on this morning's bust, then head home for lunch and maybe even a bit of a siesta.

Doug's nod to the guard as he entered the office was perfunctory. Sooner or later, Luis Cortéz was going to decide that Sara was no longer a danger to him, that if she had not been found by all the forces looking for her, then she was no longer to be found. There had to be some way to push him into making that decision sooner rather than later.

Doug stopped dead in his tracks in the middle of the hall.

And if he was wrong? What if Cortéz had already made his decision, and that decision had been to cut his losses? Luis Cortéz had already shown himself to be a very cautious man, and if he decided to stop right where he was, he could turn the present stalemate into checkmate. He'd be out a lot of money, but he'd still have plenty of funds to do anything he needed to, if not all he wanted. And Nicolás would be clear of the murder rap he'd earned.

And Sara? She'd be hung out to dry in the Chapare.

Doug had maintained a determined optimism even as Sara's leads had trailed off into dead ends, one after another. Now the reality of the situation hit him head on, and a feeling of helplessness, such as he'd known only one other time in his life, swept over him. If Luis Cortéz chose to stand pat, it would be the end for Sara. It wouldn't even help to get her over the border. In Sara's absence, the State Department had been more than willing to accept the Cortezes' story, especially in light of the convenient "corroboration" of Sara's mental state from the Cortéz family doctor. A few pithy comments by the ambassador when she'd visited the DEA office last week had made it clear where she stood on the subject, and it had taken all of Doug's self-control not to set the record straight. As it now stood, unless Doug somehow managed to convict Luis and Nicolás Cortéz of drug dealing and murder, Sara would never be able to go home again.

Father, I'm stumped! I promised I wouldn't let her down, but I just don't know how I'm supposed to keep that promise. I've done everything I can do, and I haven't the foggiest idea where to go from here. I need that next step! Just a little break to show me I'm still on the right track!

"Daydreaming, Bradford? Or just a little heavy meditation?"

Grant Major's sardonic question brought Doug's prayer to a quick close. It was only then that he realized that he was blocking his boss's progress down the hall. He moved to one side, though the RAC easily could have walked around him had he chosen to.

"Sorry, boss."

Grant's glance as he strolled past was thoughtful. "Is it too much to hope that's a case you're chewing over that hard? Speaking of which . . ."—he continued to move his massive bulk down the hall as he spoke—"I didn't see the Paraguayan report on my desk. I need that for a debrief with La Paz this afternoon."

"Aye, aye, sir. Coming right up." The tone was respectful; the parody of a Quantico marine salute was not.

"I saw that," Grant said without glancing back. "Just get it done!" He paused, then looked back over his shoulder. "By the way, Doug, this morning? That was a good job!"

"Thank you." Doug acknowledged the compliment with a brief smile, and this time there was nothing sarcastic in the hand he raised in salute. "I'll have that report done by noon."

As far as bosses went, Grant could be worse, Doug admitted as he picked a half-finished DEA-6 form out of his "in" basket. Even if he was a stickler for the desk side of the job! The truth was, Doug had totally forgotten that the RAC from the La Paz office was flying in this afternoon to confer on the Paraguayan case. Well, he'd better get this thing finished.

But instead of reaching immediately for a pen, Doug switched on the computer. When the menu came onto the screen, he called up the program he wanted. In the first days after he had left Sara at that lonely mountain *finca*, Doug had been unable to resist checking on her whereabouts every few hours. But as one routine day followed another, and the coordinates flashing on his screen remained unvaried, Doug had gradually accepted that he'd managed her getaway undetected and that she was safe.

After the first Sunday, when Benedicto had called with the cryptic message that his cousin's family was doing well, other than some loneliness due to lack of visitors, Doug had reduced his monitoring of the SatTrack to once a day. There was the battery life to consider, and with the workload attendant to his latest cases, it hadn't been so easy to stop in to the office at unscheduled hours. (For obvious security reasons, the DEA's highly classified computer network was not designed to be accessed by modem from his home PC.) The last time he'd called up the SatTrack was just before he'd left the office for dinner the evening before.

The process wasn't complicated. Like the device itself, the program was designed to be user-friendly for even the most ham-fingered and technically handicapped agent. After a few seconds, a message flashed onto Doug's monitor: *Password Requested.*

Doug keyed in the five-digit number Ramon had given him, then added *SatTrack #199.8013. Identify yourself.*

The display shifted to show a satellite slowly turning on its axis. It would take a little time for the request to bounce to the satellite orbiting somewhere overhead, travel from there to the knapsack in Sara's possession to activate the GPS locator, and then for that signal to return to the satellite, bounce down to the satellite dish in the DEA's back yard, and back to the computer on Doug's desk.

Doug lounged back in his desk chair to wait. One way or another, he was going to have to make some decisions. At the very least he needed to get a new battery pack for the SatTrack out to the *rancho*— and soon. The battery had already lasted longer than Ramon had led him to expect, but yesterday's signal had been delayed in returning and had been accompanied by a warning that battery power was low. A day or two more and it would be dead.

Less urgent, but still imperative if this stalemate continued indefinitely, was the need to find someplace more permanent for Sara. Maybe it had been wishful thinking to expect a speedy solution to the Cortéz situation, but he'd never expected to leave Sara in such squalid conditions for so long. How had she, a city-bred girl who'd never been out of an upper-middle-class environment, been coping?

Even if she had adjusted to her mean surroundings, he couldn't let the situation just continue to drift.

His legs shifted restlessly under his desk. What he really needed was to talk to Sara, to see how she was doing with his own eyes. Now that the Paraguayan bust had gone down, Doug could afford a day or so out of the office, and with Cortéz's clumsy tail off his back, the risk of delivering a replacement battery pack in person, instead of through Benedicto, would be minimal.

Admit it, Doug told himself ruefully. *You just want to see her again.*

Instantly, he took himself sternly to task. *There's no future in that sort of thinking, Bradford! She's a married woman, and just because her husband is a jerk and a criminal—that doesn't change anything. Your job is to bust the bad guys so she can get on with the rest of her life.*

Doug deliberately set aside every thought of Sara beyond the business at hand. But all the self-discipline he mustered up couldn't suppress a pang—as though something very precious had just gone out of his life. It was an ironic twist of fate that the one person, in all the long years since Julie and the kids had died, who'd ever managed to touch that empty place in his heart should turn out to be as far out of his reach as the satellite rotating on the screen in front of him.

No, not fate. Something bigger than fate was in control here, even of such vagaries as Doug's wayward emotions. *Father, just help me get her life back for her before she gets out of mine, okay? That's all I'm asking here.*

The 3-D image of the satellite was still making its slow revolutions. Doug leaned forward to joggle the mouse. Had the battery gone dead more suddenly than he had anticipated? No, now the screen was fading into a line of numbers and letters.

LATITUDE: 18*03.724S.

Doug's mind was elsewhere as he glanced through it. He'd made his decision. As soon as these reports were out of the way, he was heading out, whatever kind of excuse it took. He'd get Ramon to pick up the replacement battery. Just so Tech didn't demand to check the SatTrack unit for himself. His eyes went impatiently to the second line.

LONGITUDE: 042*11.28W.

Doug was already reaching to close down the program when it sunk in that the coordinates he'd just scanned so hurriedly were not the same as the ones engraved by repetition into his memory. His hand fell away from the mouse as he read the coordinates again—slowly this time and with full attention, as though concentration alone would change the sum of the two lines blinking ominously on the screen.

Then, as though a hand had reached out from the screen and slapped him hard on the face, he reacted, scrabbling through the mess on his desk for the piece of paper where he'd scribbled that unvarying set of numbers and letters. No, his memory wasn't at fault. The sets of coordinates on the screen were not only different, they were nowhere close!

Doug pushed his chair back violently and vaulted across the office. A pile of rolled-up cylinders lay on the table beside the radio. Finding the one he wanted, Doug unrolled it with one quick flick of his wrist, sweeping the others to the floor as he spread it out flat in their place. The map he was now looking at was the most detailed that satellite photography could produce. Doug ran a finger across the grid markings at the top, then down the side. It took all of five seconds to find what he was looking for. Snatching the cell phone from his belt, he punched in a number.

"Buenas—"

Doug didn't give the Quechua pastor time to finish his greeting. "Benedicto, where's Sara?"

The answer came back slow and puzzled, and Doug's heart was sinking before the first words were out. "*Sara?* What do you mean, *mi hermano?* Has there been a difficulty?"

Benedicto, it turned out, hadn't heard from his cousin in more than a week. Rafael hadn't been to church the last Sunday, but Benedicto hadn't been surprised, because he knew that Rafael didn't like leaving the women alone on the rancho. And since Doug had not called with any concerns, Benedicto hadn't worried.

"If something has happened, then someone will be coming to tell me. I will let you know as soon as I hear. No, that will not serve. If you are right about this device of yours, then perhaps there is no one there to come. I myself will go to see. But I am afraid that this will take some time, my brother."

Yes, it would take time, Doug thought bleakly as he rang off. That had always been the weakness of this plan. He didn't even know how many hours it had been since the SatTrack had begun its change in location. Staring down at the unfurled satellite map, Doug tried to conjure up one innocent reason why the SatTrack unit would show movement almost two hundred kilometers—as the crow flies— to a location that, according to the map, was smack in the middle of some of the densest and most unpopulated jungle in Bolivia. A glitch in the satellite tracking system? A condor had carried off the knapsack and dropped it into the jungle? No, what he had here was the worst-case scenario he'd feared when he'd left Sara on that Chapare hillside with such inadequate communication.

Somehow—it didn't matter now how—the Cortezes had discovered Sara's hiding place, and they'd come to take her away. He would bet his life on it!

Rolling up the satellite map he'd been using, Doug left the others on the floor as he strode out of the weapons room and down the hall. "Kyle!"

The intel analyst winced as his door crashed against the wall. "Hey, careful of the hinges!"

"Sorry." Doug caught the door and closed it. "Kyle, I really need—"

It was then that he saw Ramon, bent over a keyboard on the other side of the room. "Back already? What did you do? Fly?"

Ramon shrugged without slackening the speed of his fingers over the keyboard. "You walked. I took a cab. It's not so far from Bienes Incautados. I've been in for five minutes or more."

"Then you can tell me. Who's got the latest on the Cortezes? Just the two men, Luis and Nicolás. I need to know what they're up to—*now!*"

"I really couldn't say." Ramon pushed the "enter" key, then waited as a series of beeps and whirring noises indicated that the file he was loading was coming on line. "We don't have anyone on them anymore."

"What!" Doug almost choked with anger. "And who was the crazy idiot who ordered that? There was supposed to be someone on those two night and day!"

Ramon straightened up to give Doug a steady look. "*I* ordered it. There was nothing there, *mano,* okay? And we had other jobs to do. We needed the men."

"Well, get them back on now!" Doug stopped and took a deep breath, running his fingers through his hair. "I'm sorry, Ramon. You're right, it was your call, not mine. But could you at least find out where they are right now? Even if you have to call their office and ask right out. There's no time for pussy-footing around anymore."

"Sure, man." Ramon was already reaching for the phone. Doug took an agitated turn around the office as the other agent gave a few crisp orders. He hated to make a move on so little intel, but there was no way he could wait the hours it would take for Benedicto to make it out to the *finca* and back. He had the SatTrack's last position. It would have to do. The problem was reaching the location. There were no roads showing on that map, and what wasn't on that map just plain wasn't there. Without the resources of the DEA to draw on, that meant he was reduced to begging, borrowing, or stealing an aircraft—and a pilot. There were a couple of private airfields around town, but, again, it would take time. *Oh, God, just keep her safe until I get there.*

The phone rang just as Ramon was setting the receiver into its cradle. It took two rings for Doug to realize that it was his cell phone and not the desk unit across the office. He grabbed at his belt. *"Sí?"*

It was Benedicto. "Rafael is here," he said briefly. "I will let him speak."

"Señor, it is *la señorita* Sara!" The words came laden with grief, carried on the raspy breath of a man who'd just finished a hard race. It hit Doug like a load of bricks in the belly.

"What happened?" he managed to say.

"It was my own son, *señor.* He was working for the *narcotraficantes.* Oh, *señor,* I am so sorry! And now they have taken her away!"

Rafael was babbling so fast that Doug could barely understand his strongly accented Spanish.

"Okay, let's calm down here. Just take it slow and tell me what happened."

Rafael took another ragged breath and brought himself under control before continuing with the details of the morning's ordeal. A military helicopter; men dressed as soldiers, led by a man dressed in black; they had taken Sara away.

Julio Vargas! Doug concluded grimly. It couldn't be anyone else. Luis Cortéz's hatchet man. And he'd had Sara in his filthy hands for—Doug checked his watch—right on two hours. No wonder Rafael was breathing so hard. The man must have run the whole way to have reached the plantation so fast! Obviously Vargas couldn't bring Sara into Santa Cruz in a military chopper that had supposedly been destroyed years ago, but why had he chosen that particular compass point in the middle of virgin jungle?

Why, indeed?

Even as fear for Sara's safety mounted within Doug, a certain exultation was beginning to grow. He didn't even notice the map crumpling under the pressure of his fingers. This was it! Beyond all odds, it had come—the break he'd been waiting for! Based on the information Sara had provided, Rafael's news could lead to only one possible conclusion. Those SatTrack coordinates pointed to the location of a certain mysterious hacienda, whose jungle surroundings ensured that a military aircraft could easily lie hidden when it wasn't being used for illicit activities. And where eight tons of cocaine were waiting only for Luis Cortéz to get his hands on his daughter-in-law!

And that changed Doug's entire position!

The office phone rang while Rafael was still speaking. Doug's eyes followed Ramon's response. At the other agent's thumbs-up signal, he cut into the Quechua farmer's stricken apologies. "No, Rafael, you must not blame yourself! These things happen. We will get her back. Now I must go after her."

"Both Cortezes are still in the city," Ramon reported as Doug clipped the cell phone back on his belt. "In their offices at Cortéz Industries. But there's a plane warming up on the field."

"Good! Then we may be in time yet. Tell them to let us know when the plane takes off." Doug was already heading for the door.

"Hey, man, we've been pretty patient here!" Kyle called after him. "You going to tell us what this is all about?"

But Doug had already disappeared as abruptly as he'd come. Ramon and Kyle exchanged a speculative look. Then Kyle drawled, "You know, *amigo,* if that boy doesn't start communicating, I'm going to be seriously tempted to do bodily violence!"

Doug caught the RAC in his office, but not alone. Grant took one look at the determined set of Doug's jaw and said quietly, "Just leave the expense reports, Ellen. I'll get back to you later."

Doug waited for the administration officer to close the door behind her before striding over to the desk. This time he didn't want an audience. He wasted no time on preliminaries. "You said not to come back until Cortéz made a move. Well, he's done it. He's got the girl. And we've got the location."

Shoving aside a pen holder, the RAC's brass nameplate, and an assortment of reports that had been in neat piles before Doug got his hands on them, he unrolled the satellite map in front of Grant Major. Grabbing a highlighter that had spilled out of the pen holder, Doug drew a bold yellow circle around a point at the bottom of the map. This time Grant was going to listen to him. And Doug wasn't going to take "no" for an answer!

"There! That's where they took Sara Cortéz. And that's the place we've been looking for. Luis Cortéz's hacienda. How much do you want to bet they're not already starting to move that cocaine, now that they've got her! We take in a few choppers and hit the place, and you're going to find all the proof you've been wanting. But it's got to be fast, before Sara gets hurt."

"Sara," Grant echoed. Doug couldn't quite read the tone of his boss's voice as he lifted his eyes from the yellow circle on the map. "That's this Cortéz girl you've only met once or twice, right? And how exactly did you come by this incredible piece of information? Did Cortéz call you up and give you the news? Or maybe the girl did herself?"

"Well . . ."

Doug paused. He'd known it would have to come out sometime. In a way, it would be a relief to get this over with. Deceiving Grant, necessary though it might have been, had been the most distasteful part of this business. And there was no longer any tactical advantage in keeping it to himself. "The truth is, sir, I have a bit of a confession to make."

"Now you hold it one moment." Grant held up his hand to stop Doug. "If you're going to tell me you've been keeping tabs on that girl, don't! You think that's news? I know you a little too well, Bradford, to think you'd ever give up so tamely. But as long as it's private—well, this office doesn't know anything about it. You bring it to my attention now, and it's official DEA business. So you'd better be sure you know where you're going here!"

Doug was struck dumb for an instant. After all the years they'd worked together, the RAC was still capable of astonishing him. Grant read his thoughts with a fleeting smile. "I'm really not on the other side, Doug. If these guys are dirty, I want to catch them as much as you do."

Doug began to explain, but as he spoke, Grant's expression darkened. By the time Doug brought up the SatTrack unit, the RAC was no longer bothering to control his ire. "You did *what?* he bellowed. "You're telling me you expropriated a piece of equipment that couldn't possibly be traced anywhere but to this office and placed it on a fugitive? And what were you planning to do if the authorities picked her up? Which is still a distinct possibility here!"

Doug started to protest, but Grant would have none of it.

"No, don't give me any rubbish about how well hidden it is! They're not all fools in the police department, no matter what you think! Wouldn't that be a nice thing to explain to the Bolivian government *and* the media? How a highly sensitive and very recent development of the U.S. military turns up on a criminal suspect with whom we've already sworn up and down we've had no contact! What were you thinking, Bradford?"

Doug stood rigid under the hail of furious words. "I didn't see any alternative, sir," he said woodenly when his boss had run out of choice phrases. "I admit I wasn't considering the good of the office at the time, and I'll take full responsibility and any discipline you want to hand out, including my job. Tomorrow! Today we've got an American citizen who is in trouble. And eight tons of cocaine to pick up."

"Eight tons. You sound pretty sure about that." Grant's tone didn't relent, but some of the choler left his complexion. "From where I'm sitting, it looks like a pretty flimsy house of cards you've got here, Bradford." He leaned way back in his chair as he recounted Doug's story. "Let me see if I've got this straight! So Vargas picked up the girl from where you had no business hiding her in the first place. I'll buy that. Your man's got no reason to lie. But you've got nothing illegal so far, unless you can prove he has no intention of bringing her in to the proper authorities. The helicopter is another matter—again, if it checks out not to be an authorized military flight. Which I assume you haven't done yet. As for *this*"— he launched himself forward and stabbed at the yellow circle on the map with a large forefinger—"all you've got here is a dot on the map. What makes you so sure this hacienda is even out there? Or those eight tons of cocaine? Because if you're seriously asking the DEA to storm in there to seize the place and rescue a girl who still happens to be a wanted fugitive, you'd better have more than wishful thinking to back you up! For that matter . . ."

Grant's inflexible gaze softened just a fraction, and he paused a full heartbeat before going on. "You do realize that if you're right about Vargas, there's a more logical explanation to those SatTrack coordinates than some hypothetical hacienda out in the middle of the jungle."

The statement hit Doug with the chill of a deluge of ice water. It wasn't that the same thought had never occurred to him. He'd been forcing back the image of Sara's lithe young body lying like a broken doll at the foot of a massive jungle hardwood ever since he'd registered the hostile territory the SatTrack was marking. There was hardly an easier way to get rid of an unwanted prisoner than to slide open the door of a chopper and—

"No!" Doug shook the picture from his mind. "I won't buy that for a minute, sir. Just look at the map here. Okay, so the proportions aren't much. But you can see the size of that clearing. There's plenty of room to put a good-sized place in there. And Rafael overheard Vargas specifically telling Sara that her father-in-law wanted to interrogate her. Since Vargas hasn't brought her into town, that's a pretty good indication that Cortéz is planning on flying out there. And we've got his plane warming up right now to back that up. No, that hacienda is out there, and so is the coke. Call it a gut feeling if you like, but I'd stake my life on it!"

Grant might have scoffed at that, but he didn't. This business wasn't based on feelings, but hard facts and solid data. But he'd developed every respect for a hunch when it came from the man pacing impatiently in front of his desk. Not that there was really anything so nebulous as "feelings" involved. Doug Bradford just happened to possess a rare and remarkable knack for extrapolating right conclusions at a subconscious level from scraps of data too scanty for conscious logic. It was a trait that made for the best cops—and government agents. Call it a hunch or a gut feeling or whatever you wanted, but it was worthy of attention.

Tilting back in his chair again, Grant brought his fingers together to form a steeple and looked at Doug with every indication of interest and no sign of what he was thinking. Doug felt desperation well up inside him. The minutes were ticking away. Luis Cortéz could be lifting off right now!

"Come on, Grant! Are you still worrying about the political implications here? So Cortéz had lunch with the ambassador and plays weekend golf with the president. If we find that cocaine, it's not going to matter how many political connections he has."

"And if we don't?"

"Sometimes you have to take some risks. You taught me that, sir, remember? If nothing else," Doug added bitterly, "you can get your SatTrack back."

The RAC's inflexible gaze didn't shift so much as to blink, and Doug tasted the sourness of disappointment in his mouth. He couldn't believe it. After all this, the old fox was going to say no! He leaned far over the desk with the feeling that he was burning a bridge behind him. But it was too late to care. "I'm going in there whether I've got your backing or not, Grant! I don't care if it's as an agent of this office or unemployed. And if I get there too late, it's going to be on your head."

He slapped his hands down suddenly and hard on the map. "Can't you see it, Grant? This is our last chance—our *only* chance to take these guys down. It's exactly what we've been waiting for, and it just dropped into our laps like—like it was meant to happen! And you're just kissing it off. Where are your guts? Twenty years ago, you'd have been the first in line!"

"My guts are right where they've always been," Grant said imperturbably. "And I haven't said no, if you'd stop arguing long enough to listen. I'm just considering all the angles."

He fell silent, his eyes dropping at last to the yellow circle on the map. Then he said in measured tones, "You realize, Bradford, that if anything goes wrong, you're finished in this country. I can't let the agency take a fall on this. You don't find anything, and you're a rogue agent who's already broken the rules and is on his way out."

Doug stiffened. For a moment he was sure he'd misinterpreted Grant's words. Then his breath went out of him, and his hands unclenched. Picking up the satellite map, he rerolled it as he said quietly, "Thank you, Grant. You won't regret it."

The RAC made a shooing motion. "Just go, before I change my mind. You've got the op. Oh, and by the way . . ."

His raised voice stopped Doug's long, rapid strides to the door. "Good luck, Doug. However it turns out, I respect a man who's willing to stake his life—and his career—on what he believes."

CHAPTER THIRTY

Sara explored every inch of her prison, not with any real expectation of finding the assortment of articles that a genius—or a script writer—could piece together into a means of escape, but because it was the natural thing to do when one was locked in a strange room.

The office turned out to be only a facade. There wasn't so much as a document, an old letter, or a computer printout to show that it was ever used for business. The desk was empty except for a handful of pens, some Cortéz letterhead, and one old newspaper that had been shoved into the top drawer. Wherever Don Luis kept the files for his cocaine operation, it wasn't here.

The newspaper supplied a few moments of distraction. It was several months old, and a double photo on the front page showed a red-and-white Cessna and a blue pickup. The headline announced the escape of a minor *narcotraficante* named Pablo Orejuela. The only other item of interest was the melted-down remnant of a votive candle set inside a carved bracket that had once held an ornamental lamp up on the wall next to the St. George painting. Sara couldn't imagine her father-in-law placing that token of superstition there. More likely, it had been one of the workers from the other room.

Sara examined the door locks that held her prisoner. They were very large and as solid as the doors. She was still fiddling with the handle on the outside door when it suddenly turned under her hand. She jumped back guiltily as a guard thrust his head inside and gave her a surly look, but recovered quickly enough to demand to use the bathroom, a need that had become conveniently urgent.

The guard showed no change of expression, but stalked across the office and slid open a wooden panel that had looked like part of the wall. Then, to Sara's relief, he retired back outside. But not before Sara was able to see that the door led onto the veranda, with the airstrip no more than a hundred meters straight ahead, and the jungle beyond it.

Like the office, the bathroom would not have been out of place at the Cortéz family mansion in Santa Cruz. Turning on the brass taps, Sara used a hand towel to sponge down her face and arms. She was surprised to realize that she was hungry. It made sense, given that she'd had only a piece of bread for breakfast and it was now past noon, but she wouldn't have expected to feel hunger at a time like this. Returning to the office, she dug into her knapsack for the lunch she'd put together for herself and Consuelo. Whatever was going to happen might as well be on a full stomach. The boiled *yuca* and potatoes were gritty with dirt from where the soldiers had dumped the food onto the ground, but she was able to eat almost half before she could no longer stomach the grainy texture.

She glanced at the hand-carved cuckoo clock up on the wall. Only about a half-hour had elapsed. With nothing left to occupy her, she huddled onto a chair and pulled out the Bible. She would read and pray until they came for her. But anticipation and fear are exhausting emotions. She'd hardly rested her head back against the red leather of the chair before she fell asleep.

The steady drone grew closer and louder until at last it penetrated even the sound-proofing that the original owner of the hacienda had installed to keep his business transactions private from any party guests who might have been inclined to eavesdrop.

Sara raised her head reluctantly. She'd been far away from this office, but the dream was already fading, and she knew only that it had been a nice dream and that she didn't want to leave it. Rubbing at a crick in the back of her neck, she blinked sleepily at the Swiss cuckoo clock. Two hours!

Uncurling herself from the leather chair as the last tatters of her dream dissolved into nothingness, she wasn't even aware at first of the sound that had disturbed her slumber. Then it grew loud enough to distinguish itself from the throb of the air-conditioning. Sara's stomach gave a sickening twist. It was the sound of an aircraft engine. And it was coming this way.

She was instantly on her feet, her ears straining to follow the steady vibration. If only this office had a window! But she didn't really need one. That wasn't the rhythmic beat of the helicopter coming in with another load, but the dull drone of a plane. It roared in directly overhead, shaking the walls with a thunder no amount of soundproofing could keep out.

The roar dwindled in the direction of the airstrip. Mentally, Sara followed the sharp bank of the plane and the wheels touching down. Then the sound of the engine faded back into the drone of the air-conditioning. Her reprieve was over. Don Luis had arrived.

Sara paced restlessly as she waited for someone to come for her. Much as she'd been dreading the appearance of her father-in-law, the wait now seemed interminable. At last she heard the tap of quick footsteps on the veranda and a murmur of voices just outside the door. She wiped her palms on her jeans. She'd been steeling herself all day for this moment, but now that it was here, she wasn't sure she could face it. The lock clicked. The door handle turned. Her breath was coming now in quick, short gasps.

Oh, God, I'm not ready! I'm so afraid!

Then her breath caught in her chest and stayed there. The door opened, and the dark outline silhouetted against the brightness of the afternoon sun had the self-assured bearing, the arrogant lift of the head, and the angry tenseness she'd dreaded. But it wasn't her father-in-law who stepped over the threshold. It was Nicolás.

"Sara." He kicked the door shut behind him. Sara stood in stunned immobility as he crossed the office with quick strides. If she hadn't been ready for Don Luis, she was even less prepared for Nicky. It wasn't until he reached out to draw her into his arms that she reacted. Knocking his hands away, she twisted out of his embrace. "Don't you touch me!"

Her back slammed into the wall. Nicolás didn't move. Raising his hands in capitulation, he said caustically, "Fine. I'm not going to touch you, see?"

Throwing himself into the nearest chair, he lounged back against the red leather, his long legs stretched out to cross at the ankles. It was a familiar pose and graceful, one that a month ago would have brought Sara flying into his arms. But the sight of it now sent such a wave of bitterness and betrayal through her that she almost cried out. How could he sit there so unmoved by the actions that had smashed her world to bits?

Closing her eyes against the pain, she demanded harshly, "What are you doing here, anyway? I was told you didn't want to see me! Or did you decide to do your own dirty work again, instead of leaving it to Julio or Don Luis?"

"Sara, don't talk like that!" The pain in Nicolás's voice was so genuine that Sara's eyes flew open again. More quietly, he went on, "Look, I just want to talk to you, okay? Papá doesn't even know I'm here. He didn't want me to come. I had to sneak out while he was calling around to get his cocaine shipments set up again. He isn't going to be too pleased when he finds out I took the Cessna. But I don't care! I had to see you again."

Sara listened with astonishment. Apparently her husband wasn't as unmarked by these last weeks as she'd thought. It always surprised her, whenever she saw Nicolás after a lapse of days—or hours— just how spectacular his good looks were, as though her memory had to be exaggerating. Today was no exception. His white polo shirt and Bermuda shorts set off perfectly the tanned and well-muscled length of his limbs. The chiseled features of the Spanish aristocrat commanded attention, as always, above the bronzed column of his throat.

But a closer look showed that he'd lost a good deal of weight. His clothes were hanging loose on his lean frame. His face was thinner than Sara had ever known it, and his blue eyes were overly bright and sunken into dark hollows. He looked haggard and ill—and very unhappy.

Involuntarily, Sara took a step forward. "What is it, Nicky? Why do you want to see me? Have you been ill?"

"Ill!" Nicolás rubbed a hand over his lower face, which was carrying at least a day-old stubble. "I guess you could call it that. These last weeks have been pure hell, what do you think? Not knowing where you were, or who you were talking to, or even if you were still alive! Police all over the place, and Papá going crazy about postponing his deliveries again."

"Yeah, well, it hasn't exactly been easy on me either!" Sara interjected. But Nicolás continued as though he hadn't heard.

"As to why I want to see you—you're still my wife, aren't you? I couldn't believe it when they told me they'd found you. And in a *campesino* hut, of all places! No wonder we never found you. Though I should have thought of it—all those revolutionary ideas of yours. We looked for you everywhere else! Every contact you've ever made here. The hotels. Motels. Even the hospitals, after a while. The DEA too. I talked to Bradford myself. And Papá's had them staked out since you left. But nothing! They've just been going about their usual business, stirring up trouble for a lot of good Bolivian citizens. Especially Bradford. He's made some big hits these last couple weeks. That's what convinced Papá more than anything that he wasn't poking around in our affairs. In fact, he pulled in an old contact of Papá's just this morning."

Doug was alive! Sara knew her expression had given away the sudden surge of joy. But Nicolás wasn't even looking at her. He was moodily studying the tips of his Nike loafers.

"Anyway, it didn't take long to figure out you couldn't have turned up there, or they'd have been snooping all over the place. The embassy, either. We couldn't figure out where you could have gone. You didn't have any money or travel documents. And then, of course, Papá had to blame me for warning you about the police. But who was supposed to guess you'd slip through every net we threw out there? We must have followed up thousands of people calling in for that reward. I was beginning to think you were dead! And to have Papá on top of all that, acting like the whole thing was my fault and insisting we dump the entire operation if we couldn't find you before the police did. Three hundred million dollars! And then there's Mamá and the girls. They've been all over me."

Nicolás slid Sara a sideways glance. "They're wanting me to marry Reina, you know. Of course, they don't know that you didn't really . . . well, you know! But Papá's been making hints too. He says she'll understand our ways better. But then, he'd push any girl at me right now if he thought it would make me forget I ever met you."

Reina! Sara's earlier instinct to sympathize had been waning under Nicolás's tone of self-commiseration. Now it popped like a bubble. Yes, she could imagine Reina had been making the most of these past weeks. And Mimi had always favored the girl as a daughter-in-law. It was really no great surprise, and it certainly could make no difference to Sara now. And yet the news still came like a kick in the stomach.

"And you, Nicky? What do you want?" she asked bitterly. "Is that why you're here? To ask for a divorce?" Her damp hands pressed hard into the fine wood paneling behind her. "But then, who needs a divorce? It'll be so much simpler for the whole family if you're a widower, won't it?"

The expression on Nicolás's face said it all. He lifted his eyes to hers for an instant, and she read the shame and torment there. Then he dropped his face into his hands with a groan. "Oh, Sara, I never meant it to turn out this way! You've got to believe that! It's just—one thing led to another until it all got out of control. You. The boy. Oh, if only I'd never picked up that cursed piece of jewelry! But I never wanted anyone to get hurt, I swear. You've got to understand. I was drunk. And angry. And he was threatening us. You heard him! I . . . I just lost it!"

"And me?" Sara said evenly. "Are you trying to tell me you didn't really want to hurt me? You shot at me, remember? You'd have killed me, too, if I hadn't gotten away."

Nicolás shook his head miserably. "I don't know. Maybe. *Then.*

All I could think about was what you'd tell the police if you got to them first. And Papá had it all worked out. But afterward—no, I would not have hurt you. I . . . I haven't been able to sleep or eat, thinking about it. Thinking about you running away from me with that terrified look on your face. Wondering if you were dead. Or if Papá—"

He shook his head again, his words muffled against his hands. "It's just not fair! I didn't want any of this. I just wanted . . ."

His misery was so evident that Sara again felt the unwilling tug of compassion. Leaving the reassuring stability of the wall, she walked across the office to look down at her husband's bent head. It was ironic, that here at this late date, she was at last seeing her husband clearly. He wasn't—and never had been—a hero or a savior. She'd merely perched him on a pedestal, and he had inevitably crashed. But neither was he the heinous monster she'd built him up to be these last weeks. He was just a spoiled and rather weak young man who, because of his looks and wealth and family name, had never had to deny himself anything he wanted. And because he'd never had to learn self-denial, he'd become convinced that the world owed him anything he desired. And now, to his bewilderment, he was finding out that there were things that money couldn't fix.

No, Nicolás hadn't wanted any of this to happen. But neither would it have occurred to him that he could lift a finger to avoid it. He was really very young—young enough to lash out and smash without thinking when his world was threatened.

And young enough to regret the smashed pieces afterward.

Sara herself had been very young and unwise when she'd married Nicolás. But through these weeks of testing, she'd grown up. Nicolás had not. Sara could now see that the passionate adoration she'd felt for him had been nothing more than the infatuated idol worship that too many adolescent girls wasted on pop singers and movie stars, without any consideration of the real man behind the public image. Under different circumstances, and if Nicolás himself had chosen another course, that infatuation might have matured into real love and a real marriage. But that would never happen now. Still, she could no longer hate him for what he'd done to her life. If she felt anything, it was pity, because he was far more miserable than she.

With that realization, the festering bitterness—the hurt and anger—left her, and she felt curiously free. Kneeling down beside Nicolás, she said quietly, "Just tell me one thing, Nicky. Did you ever really love me?"

"Love you!" His face was drawn, his eyes pained. "Of course I loved you! You were the best thing that ever happened to me. You have something Reina could never have in a million years. I haven't been able to forget you, no matter how hard I tried. That's why I had to come. Just to see you one last time. Oh, if only I'd never brought you into this."

This time when he pulled her toward him, Sara didn't resist. She cradled his head against her shoulder, stroking the hair—which she'd once caressed as a lover—as a mother does with a child that needs comforting. She felt immeasurably old, which was a sign of just how young she was! "Then help me now, Nicky. You said you had the Cessna. You can help me get away from here. Or come away with me yourself. You can still walk away from this. I don't know what we need to do, but if we tell the truth—"

Nicolás was already shaking his head. "It's too late for that, Sara. Don't you understand? I'm a murderer! They'd send me to jail. No, it's too late! For you. For me. Not even God could change things now."

He dropped his head against her shoulder again. "A murderer! Do you know what that feels like, Sara? The cocaine was one thing. Papá pays plenty to the priests to make that right. But murder—that's a mortal sin! Papá, all that bothers him is the fuss it's caused. But he didn't pull that trigger! And he's not the one with the nightmares. I keep seeing that boy's chest erupting in blood, and I know it's God's judgment! I'd give anything to undo it. But it's just too late!"

"Oh, no, Nicky, you're so wrong! It's never too late. If there's anything I've learned these last few weeks, it's that!" Pulling back in his arms so that she could see his eyes, Sara took Nicolás's face between her hands. "I know you think I'm pretty religious, Nicky. But I really haven't been. Oh, sure, I went to church, and I've tried to live a decent life. But, well, I'd pretty well shut God right out of my life. Then all this happened! And it's taught me a lot of things. I found out that God really cares about me. Me, Sara, as a person! And it's never too late to turn back to him."

Nicolás stared at her with haunted eyes. Sara searched her mind for something that would get through to him. "Do you remember the story they tell at Easter? About when Jesus was crucified on the cross with those two thieves up on either side of him?"

Nicolás looked baffled, as though she'd inexplicably changed the subject. "Sure," he said irritably. "Everyone goes to mass for Holy Week. What does that have to do with anything?"

"Those thieves were murderers too," Sara explained patiently.

"But one of them turned to Christ and repented, even as he was dying. And Jesus forgave him! That's what the Bible says. Jesus told the thief that he'd be with him in Paradise that very day. Nicky, don't you see? He can forgive you too! It's never too late. Maybe . . . maybe you'd have to go to jail or something. But it wouldn't be forever. Not like an eternity. And God would be with you. And I would too, Nicky. I'd stay by you, no matter what. I promise you that!"

For a long moment, Sara saw longing and indecision warring with the pride and fear on Nicolás's face. She saw, too, the exact instant when pride won out. Pushing her arms away, Nicolás got to his feet, and that familiar arrogance settled down like a shutter over the guilt and shame.

"No, I can't! It's too much to ask, Sara. You want me to let the whole world know what I did? To have them calling the Cortezes criminals and taking away our homes and businesses? And for what? Spending the rest of my life in jail isn't going to bring back that kid!"

Kicking his chair backward, Nicolás moved away from Sara. "No, Papá is right. All we have to do is hold on a little longer, and everything will be fine. We just have to get through this without panicking. Besides, who knows if any of that religious stuff is really even true. Anyone would get nightmares after an experience like I had. It's a shrink I need, not confession!"

He was in a hurry to get away from her now. "Look, I've got to go. Julio needs me to help get that cocaine ferried over here. Papá wants it all out of here before something else goes wrong. I'll . . . I'll see you later."

Sara stood straight as an arrow, watching him stride over to the veranda door. "Will you?" she asked quietly. "Don Luis is going to be here any minute. And you know what he's got planned. I can see it in your face, Nicky. Are you really going to just walk away and let him *murder* me?"

Nicolás winced at the brutality of the word, but he kept his eyes averted from hers as he rapped on the door. "Of course not. I'll talk to Papá. There's got to be something we can work out. Now that you've been found, maybe we can get the charges about Orejuela dropped. It shouldn't be so hard. Papá's got the chief of police in his pocket. You could go back to the States and pick up your life again. If we could just be sure you'd keep your mouth shut."

Sara looked sadly at the back of his shirt. "I can't do that, Nicky. And your father knows it. That's why he isn't going to let me walk away from here. You know it, too, if you'd just pull your head out of the sand. Please, Nicky! If you won't come with me, at least give me a chance to get away."

The door opened and the guard thrust his head in for a curious look around before stepping aside for Nicolás. Nicolás's gaze barely touched Sara as he stepped out of the room. "I'll think about it," he said as he closed the door.

CHAPTER THIRTY-ONE

F ive minutes to destination."

Doug stuffed the last of his granola bar into his mouth and drained his canteen lid of juice before detaching himself from the vibrating wall of the Huey. It could be awhile before he had a chance for another meal. Rising to a semi-crouch under the low ceiling of the aircraft, he swung his pack to his back, fastening the straps across his chest, then slung his M-16 over his shoulder. The other DEA agents around him were doing the same—adjusting their packs, checking their weapons, pulling on gloves, shaking out coils of rope. Doug slid the nylon harness of his rappelling gear up over his legs.

"Three minutes."

A row of metal loops ran along the top of the door on both sides of the helicopter. Threading his rope through the nearest loop, Doug tied it off tight. He tugged at the knot, letting the rope take his full weight—including his pack—before he was satisfied. It was his own neck if the thing didn't hold!

The sides of the chopper were sliding open now. Pulling a pair of heavy leather gloves over the green wool ones he was already wearing, Doug made sure his rope was threaded through the safety loop on the front of his harness before he stepped to the edge. Off to his right, a second Huey was keeping pace. It was close enough that Doug could identify the broad back of Major Ernesto Ramirez, commander of the NIFC forces, as he supervised the placement of his own team's rappelling gear. Doug didn't need to look to know that two more Hueys completed the diamond-shaped formation.

"Two minutes."

The jungle canopy beneath the shadow of the chopper hadn't changed in the last forty minutes, but the pilot, his eyes glued to the instrument panel, reached for the throttle. The tempo of the engines eased a fraction. Doug felt the thrill of adrenaline shoot through him. Show time!

And none too soon. Doug had broken his own record for getting this mission off the ground, but it still hadn't been fast enough. They'd covered the better part of two hundred kilometers since they'd lifted off from Santa Cruz, but it had now been three hours since Rafael's despairing call, more than five since Sara had been taken from the mountain *finca* by Julio Vargas and his men.

Gathering the slack on his rope into his right hand, Doug glanced around to assure himself that every man in the insertion party was ready: packs balanced, rappelling harnesses in place, ropes hooked to the safety loop. It wasn't necessary—these guys were pros and knew how to handle themselves—but it was a habit that leadership of men had drilled into him. Ramon, making a swift check of his own, caught Doug's eye and gave him thumbs up.

Doug returned the gesture with the briefest of grins. Finding willing candidates for this mission hadn't been a problem. In fact, there wasn't a single agent in the office who wouldn't have jumped at the opportunity. And if not for Sara, Doug would have felt the same quiet enthusiasm he saw in the face of every man on board. This was the kind of op that had drawn these men to join the DEA, and which only too seldom came their way amid the usual routine of interviews, surveillance, and paperwork. To rappel down into alien territory, hump fifty-plus pounds of pack for hours on end through heat, mud, and insects, then face an opposing force of unknown size and training—it was dangerous, exhilarating, . . . even fun!

Availability at such short notice had been the limitation. Besides Ramon and Doug himself, there'd been only three other agents in the office and free to go when Doug convened a frenzied planning session after leaving Grant's office. A call to the NIFC commander had scrambled a dozen more troops who hadn't yet headed home for lunch, and the commander had chosen to accompany the mission personally. For Major Ramirez, too, this was an adventure as well as a job. Doug wouldn't have taken any more men, even if they'd been available. This was to be a covert insertion, not an aerial attack, and a smaller group would be a whole lot easier to move quickly and quietly.

"One minute," the technical sergeant intoned.

Doug positioned himself at one side of the open doorway while Mike Simmons, a rangy African-American, took up his place beside him. Four would make the initial drop: Mike and Doug from this side of the chopper, Rocky and Carlos from the other.

That left only Ramon for a second drop. Not a large group, but the Hueys didn't carry nearly the size of force that their outside appearance might suggest. Once the pilot, copilot, and technical sergeant had climbed aboard, you couldn't squeeze more than five PACs (passengers-and-equipment, that was; exactly how the acronym fit into that, Doug had no idea and cared even less) into each chopper.

Hunkering down on the balls of his feet, Doug nodded his readiness to Mike. The newest member of the Santa Cruz DEA team, Mike was also the tech agent who had unwittingly supplied the SatTrack in Sara's knapsack. He'd shown surprise but no anger when he'd discovered where the unit had ended up. Grant had been more than generous in sparing the other agents the unofficial nature of Doug's involvement in the case. Which would last only as long as things worked out today!

There'd been a lot more of a stir when Doug announced the target of the afternoon's mission. Ramon had known more of what Doug was up to than anyone else, and had guessed the rest by the time Doug had gotten off the phone with Rafael. But Kyle, who had been following Sara's whole story as though it were a soap opera staged for his entertainment, had been astounded enough to shut up altogether. As for the rest, Grant's veto of any further expenditures of time and resources on the Cortéz case had made the rounds of the office.

But satisfaction had far outweighed surprise. The industrialist's well-publicized opinion of their agency hadn't exactly made Luis Cortéz popular in DEA circles, and the agents represented around the briefing table had known too much corruption in high places to find any difficulty in accepting that the month's biggest news story was a carefully orchestrated lie and that the country's most prominent family was dabbling in murder as well as drug trafficking. The general consensus was that it would be a pleasure to put an end to both.

"Thirty seconds . . . twenty . . . ten . . ."

And there it was, opening up right on schedule. It always puzzled Doug how these clearings would suddenly appear in the middle of otherwise unbroken jungle. A fire, whose devastation had since grown over? Or some Indian tribe that had cleared and planted there in such a distant past that they were a memory even to the soil? Whatever the case, enough time had gone by that the opening in the jungle canopy was not a true clearing, just a spot that had shown as less dense vegetation on the satellite map. There were trees, though they were small enough and dotted far enough apart to show the ground in between. The thick growth that carpeted the clearing promised to be thorny, even from above.

"Okay, let's get this show on the road!" Doug was kicking his rope over the edge even before the Huey slowed to a hover. His back to the door, he slid out after the rope until his boots encountered the helicopter skids. At his side, Mike Simmons was doing the same thing. The Huey had dropped so that some of the hardwoods at the edge of the clearing were now above eye level, but the ground was still a hundred feet below. Doug leaned back against his rope so that the weight of his pack pulled him down into an almost sitting position. His right hand held the rope out to the side so that it would feed easily through the safety loop on the front of his harness. His left hand was at the small of his back, keeping the rope wrapped across his front and side to control the speed of his descent.

"Go! Go! Go!"

At the technical sergeant's call, Doug kicked himself away from the helicopter. His hands burned through both pairs of gloves as the rope whipped through them. A branch slapped at his pack. Then the ground was coming up at him. Doug leaned left into the rope around his side to slow his descent. Even so, the jar of his landing was enough to send a shock up both legs. His knees came up and hit him in the face with a force that brought water to his eyes.

Releasing the rope, he fell with a sideways roll so that he took the force of the landing instead of his pack. The undergrowth was as thorny as it had looked. Doug rolled back to his feet. All around the clearing, the rest of the task force was hitting the ground in a rain of bodies. Beside him, he heard Mike let out a mild oath in his soft drawl as the tech agent extricated himself from a bramble. Then Ramon hit down, and the Hueys were curving off back toward Santa Cruz, the technical sergeants scrambling to haul up the ropes the insertion team had left dangling. The whole exercise had taken fewer seconds than the time to describe it.

Doug helped Ramon to his feet before stripping off his rappelling harness. The combined roar of the departing helicopters seemed loud enough to his noise-conscious ears to be heard back at Trompillo airport, where they'd lifted off, but experience reassured him that their arrival would be inaudible to anyone more than five kilometers distant. And their target was more than five kilometers away. Which meant they'd better get cracking!

The first order of business was to get under cover. If the sun could see them, people could, too. He waved to the stocky figure of Major Ramirez, who was dog-trotting across the clearing toward the five Americans. Two minutes later, the whole team was assembled under the shelter of a towering mahogany tree. There'd been only one injury in the descent, a deep gouge from a branch that one of the NIFC troops had caught across the face. Doug, who was humping the first-aid kit, already had out the bandages and hydrogen peroxide.

"Your man going to make it okay?" Doug called.

Rocky waved a length of gauze. "No problem. Just a scratch."

Reassured, Doug crossed over to where Mike was setting up the sat-phone he'd unloaded from his backpack. No bigger than an executive briefcase, the black box was a miracle of modern communication, packed with technology of incredible complexity. But all the agent in the field had to know was a phone number to reach any place on the face of the earth serviced by AT&T. Lifting the receiver, Mike glanced up at Doug.

"You want to talk to Kyle?"

Kyle would be monitoring the phone and the high-frequency radio that Doug was carrying until the insertion team was back home and safe, even if it meant staying at the office all night. Doug shook his head. "Just let him know we're down safe and see if he's got anything new for me. Oh, and have him get on the horn to Shannon over at Trompillo and make sure he gets those choppers refueled and ready to head back this way if we need them. We scrambled this so fast, I think I missed a couple of bases."

Trompillo, the military airport in the center of Santa Cruz, was home to the *Diablos Rojos,* the Bolivian Air Force division assigned to support the anti-narcotics effort, including the Hueys that had just flown them in. Brian Shannon was the American coordinator who served as liaison between the Red Devils and the DEA. His ability to set up this afternoon's transportation with less than an hour's notice was a mark of why he'd been selected for the job.

Leaving Mike to make the call, Doug spread out the satellite map on top of his backpack. Major Ramirez and the other American agents bent over it with him. Ramon tapped a curving line on the map that corresponded to a stream only a few hundred meters due east of their position. The stream led within a half kilometer of their target before making a sharp curve further east to meet up with a bigger river.

"That stream's going to be our quickest way in, by a long shot. The water'll be low this time of year, and we can make pretty good time along the banks. The only risk would be if they've got surveillance aircraft. And that doesn't seem too likely."

"That—and the alligators," Doug added dryly. The nasty reptiles that infested the streams around here were small brutes compared to the monsters Doug had seen in the Florida Everglades. But they were vicious and agile and loved nothing better than to slide up to some unwary hiker and jerk him down under the water. Doug had lost a man that way once and had no intention of doing so again. "You wait until you've had a run-in with a gator or two and you won't be in such a rush to take the quick way. Besides, if there are any people at all out in this neck of the woods, they'll be living along that stream. No, we'd better stick to the woods."

"He is right," Major Ramirez agreed. "The *caimanes* are very dangerous here. It would be foolish to risk them if it is not necessary."

If this had been the impenetrable scrub of the Chapare, Doug might have risked the riverbanks anyway, rather than waste hours fighting their way through several kilometers of brush or searching for a game trail that would lead where they wanted to go. But they were in triple-canopy rain forest here, meaning that there were at least three full layers of trees spreading their branches above them at differing elevations, ending with the massive rosewoods and mahoganies, some of which grew to a height of 150 feet or more above the jungle floor. This overhang made for a perennial gloom at ground level that kept plant growth down enough to require only an occasional slash of their machetes. The hard part would be finding their way through an area where every clump of trees looked the same as each one they'd encountered before. The jungle canopy blocked any glimpse of the sun or stars, and more than one person had wandered around in circles out here until they'd died of thirst or starvation or worse.

But here modern technology came to their aid.

Doug removed a global positioning unit from his backpack and set it on top of the satellite map. No bigger than a cell phone and much like a handheld video game in appearance, the Magellan GPS-4000 was yet another example of what was once highly classified military technology that had made its way, in a streamlined and much improved version, to the civilian market. Doug had found this model at a sporting-goods store, and had willingly paid the steep price out of his own pocket when he'd seen how much smaller and lighter it was than the army-issue units that the Justice Department had supplied the DEA.

Working on the same principle as the SatTrack and sat-phone, the Magellan was even now searching out one of the satellites speeding unseen through the stratosphere above. After locating three separate satellites, it would use their signals to triangulate its own position, then flash it onto the crystal display panel. With the GPS, it was impossible to get lost, even in the deepest jungle, unless the battery ran out. And to guard against that possibility, Doug carried a handful of extras.

Major Ramirez shook his head admiringly over Doug's shoulder as their new coordinates flashed onto the display panel. The NIFC commander had been sitting down to his noon meal when Doug had called, but he had responded immediately to the American's sense of urgency. It was one of the things he'd learned to respect about the DEA. The *gringos* would piece together their bits of information with a meticulousness that had driven him wild in the impatience of his earlier years. But when they chose to react, it was always with lightning speed. His own military could take lessons. "You *americanos* think of everything!"

Not everything, but the GPS had certainly changed the way the DEA was doing business in places like Bolivia. Calling up the menu, Doug selected Route Map. He'd already programmed in the coordinates he'd gotten from the SatTrack. Now he added the drop site coordinates. The screen cleared, and a compass grid appeared. Their destination was a dot marked POS 1. Below it appeared another dot marked POS 2. Their present position. An arrow pointed from one to the other. The distance—5,900 meters—appeared next to the arrow. All Doug had to do now was keep the arrow lined up ahead of him. That, and six kilometers of walking, would run him straight into his target.

Mike was packing up the sat-phone by the time Doug finished. "Kyle said to let you know he's been checking on the SatTrack like you asked. The coordinates haven't budged since we left. Looks like you called this one right."

He glanced up at Doug as he slid the black case back into his pack. "That's not all. Kyle's got some new intel from the Cortéz place. One of their planes took off just after we did. A Cessna. It wasn't Cortéz senior, though. It's the son, Nicolás."

Doug nodded. "Well, it's what we've been expecting. If he's headed the same way we are, he's going to beat us by a few hours. But there isn't much we can do about that."

Despite the urgency of the news, Doug felt almost as cool and collected as his tone conveyed. It wasn't that he was not still terribly afraid for Sara. He was! There were no guarantees that she was unharmed—or that she would still be okay by the time they could reach her. But now that he had a course of action, that unfamiliar and unwelcome feeling of helplessness had dissipated. Worrying wouldn't change Sara's situation anyway. It just reduced the alertness he needed to do the job. So he kept those fears pushed into a corner compartment of his mind and concentrated on the one thing he could do to help her. This operation was what he was trained to do, and he was good at it. Which didn't mean he was taking matters entirely into his own hands.

Father, I'll keep this mission moving. You just watch over her until I get there, okay?

Doug glanced around the circle of men. Rocky had finished taping up his patient and was repacking the first-aid kit. The rest of the team were shaking down their gear, packing away rappelling harnesses, and giving their weapons a last check, all the while keeping a wary watch. Doug nodded to Major Ramirez. As the NIFC commander called his men around, Doug used a twig to scratch out a representation of the GPS screen.

"Okay, this is where we are. Our target's over here. We're talking a little under six klicks as the crow flies. We can't be sure of what's waiting for us on the ground, but we can count at least five on Vargas's security team, an unknown number of civilians—*and* a hostage. Now, the point here is to get the hostage out alive, so the last thing we want is to spook them. And that means, time considerations or not, we do it by the book—slow and *quiet*."

Doug's briefing was simply to remind everyone of the situation. He wasn't telling them anything they hadn't already heard. His fellow DEA agents had been briefed before they'd ever left the office. The others hadn't learned the actual details of the mission until right before they boarded the helicopters at Trompillo airport. That included Major Ramirez, the pilots who'd flown them in, and even the American coordinator, Brian Shannon. This wasn't because Doug didn't trust every one of these men implicitly. Like many other things, it was simply standard procedure, part of the tight security that had developed as a result of the long history of leaks that had plagued the anti-narcotics effort here in Bolivia. If no one apart from the agents involved—from the coordinator to the Red Devil pilots to the NIFC troops who were gathered around him—knew ahead of time the place and purpose of the mission, the chances of any one of them opting for a pay raise by picking up the phone before liftoff were vastly minimized.

Shannon and his pilots had been told only how many PACs and how far, while Major Ramirez had known only that his men would be making an airdrop into the jungle and to make their preparations accordingly. Even now, outside of the DEA agents, only Major Ramirez knew the probable identity of their target. This *wasn't* standard procedure, but the political implications on this one were big enough that Ramirez himself had dictated the level of secrecy. It was better not to give the men any unnecessary distractions.

"We've got some serious hiking ahead of us," Doug continued. "Even with minimal ground cover, we're going to have to figure two hours to close in. And, say, two more for reconnaissance. That means first dark is the earliest we can hit the place. The good news is, it's going to make it a lot harder for them to see us coming. Any questions or suggestions?"

There were none. The task force reshouldered their packs and weapons. Doug frowned as he saw the injured soldier take a swig from his canteen before returning it to his belt. It was Ibañez, a skinny little man with pockmarked, weasel-sharp features, with whom Doug had worked several other missions. From the tilt of his head as he guzzled, the canteen was already half empty. And he wasn't carrying a spare. Ibañez had done the same thing on their last mission and had ended up begging Doug for water when a transportation breakdown had turned the mission into an overnighter. Would the man never learn?

Doug's frown deepened as he noticed that none of the Bolivian task force was carrying more than one canteen, except for Major Ramirez, who carried two. Doug himself was carrying four, two on his pack and two more on an additional LBE—load-bearing-equipment —harness fastened around his hips and under his backpack. His pack alone probably weighed twice what any of theirs did, even without the extra twenty pounds added by the HF radio. By the time you threw in the Kevlar vest that he, like the other DEA agents, was wearing under his camouflage fatigues, and the dozen extra banana clips for his M-16 in the front pouches of his LBE harness, Doug was carrying a full third of his body weight. And though, having ordered the raid, Doug had felt obliged to pack the heaviest load, none of the other Americans was carrying much less.

It was this propensity for preparedness—not training or competence—that was probably the biggest difference between the American agents and their local counterparts. Major Ramirez and his men believed that the *americanos* went overboard when it came to packing extra gear, and they tended to sacrifice weight for speed by carrying only what they figured to actually use on a mission. Which was fine as long as everything went according to plan.

"An ounce of prevention is worth a pound of cure" was an axiom the DEA took seriously. Whether it was carrying a plastic bag to put dirt in for blowing up a recycler instead of scrambling in the middle of the jungle for a container, or packing extra food and water, or bringing an HF radio in case the sat-phone went out, the Americans preferred to hump the extra weight rather than be caught short by an emergency.

Well, it couldn't be helped now, and in all fairness, the FELCN had a whole lot less inventory than the Americans did. But Ibañez had better not come begging for water two hours into the mission this time.

Waving his arm in a forward motion, Doug moved out. Behind him, without further instruction, the rest of the insertion team spread out into the double-arrow formation that Doug and Major Ramirez had worked out. Doug, with the GPS-4000 in hand, took the point of the first formation, with four men fanning out at two-meter intervals on either side in the shape of a flight of geese. Ramon and Rocky took up positions at the two ends of the V. Major Ramirez followed a few meters directly behind Doug, with eight of his men fanned out behind him and the two remaining Americans, Mike and Carlos, taking up the last two positions.

The formation allowed each man to see two or three of his companions at all times, preventing the task force from being separated or spread out too far. Lining himself up with the arrow on the GPS route map, Doug checked on the two men nearest him. The operative to his right stepped on a branch just as Doug glanced back, his face registering an apology under his floppy hat when he saw Doug wince. To his left—where *was* the man?

The olive and brown splotches on the camouflage fatigues had been designed with just this kind of environment in mind, and it was only the movement and the fact that Doug knew the guy had to be there that allowed him to see that what looked like another bit of vegetation was actually a hat whose owner had taken time to crown it with a tuft of greenery to break up its unnatural outline. The hat flitted forward in utter silence and stealth through the tangle of ferns and elephant ears. It was Ibañez. One canteen or not, the guy was good!

The last of the sunlight filtering in from the clearing was gone after the first ten meters, leaving a green dimness like that at the bottom of a deep pool. But the gloomy shadows brought no relief from the heat. It had rained during the night, and the lush vegetation and overhead canopy had trapped the moisture, turning the jungle into a vast sauna. Doug's fatigues, already none too fresh after the morning's dawn hike, were soon patched with sweat, and a dozen itches developed under his pack and the Kevlar vest.

But he scarcely noticed. All of his senses were concentrated ahead of him and behind and around, filtering the sights and sounds of the jungle for anything out of place or man-made. He heard nothing unusual. After the initial stretch of jungle, his team was moving well, avoiding even the use of their machetes. But that did not diminish his alertness. There were more dangers in the jungle than *Homo sapiens:* snakes and insects that were far more lethal than any man, and a tiny tree frog no longer than his thumb that could spit a poison more deadly than a rattlesnake's. And the bigger hunters, jaguar and puma, were always on the prowl.

But if anything was watching their passage, it chose to avoid the aliens invading its territory. The only game they flushed was a pack of *jochi,* the pig-sized rodent native to Bolivia. Doug paused every fifty meters to realign the group on his compass markings. After an hour, he called a five-minute halt. They had made good time, the sparseness of the ground cover allowing them to cover three full kilometers. Breaking formation, the men gathered and hunkered down in a loose, outward-facing circle, not losing their vigilance even as they unstoppered canteens to replenish the fluids they'd lost through perspiration.

Doug was draining the first of his canteens—Ibañez, he noted, was already running on empty—when he heard a distant hum that was not a part of the jungle symphony. His hand constricted around his canteen as the hum grew to a drone. An aircraft! And coming up fast behind them on the same trajectory they'd been following for the past hour. Every head was up, every face straining upward to where nothing could be seen but gently waving leaves. If just for once the canopy would open up to show a bit of sky!

Not that Doug needed a visual sighting. He knew the distinctive beat of the engine and the throp-throp of the propellers. A Huey! And there were no military flights scheduled out here beyond their own. And then he was glad for the leaf cover as the helicopter roared in directly above their heads. It swept on by, heading straight down the path of the arrow on Doug's GPS route map.

Ramon got the word out first. "Vargas."

And headed into the hacienda—Doug would bet his life on it! But from where? And why? And if that was Vargas, where was Sara? This fresh confirmation that he was on the right track brought no self-congratulation. If that chopper had flown in an hour earlier, it would have caught them flat-footed at the clearing. Or seen the helicopters that had brought them.

Doug got grimly to his feet. The five-minute rest period wasn't up yet, but no one objected as he moved out after the dwindling drone of the Huey. The encounter had slammed home as nothing else that this mission was for real and that there would be men with guns and military training waiting for them when they reached their destination. With sobered faces, the men fell into formation.

The helicopter swept overhead twice more in the next hour, and once, at a greater distance, they heard a drone that was not a helicopter but a small plane. Doug's tension grew. Could Cortéz possibly know they were coming? It didn't seem possible, with all their precautions and the speed with which this raid had been put together. But then, the DEA had thought that on other occasions!

They were moving more slowly and cautiously now as they drew closer to their destination, and they had covered something less than two kilometers when Doug call the next halt. But they were now only a thousand meters from the target. Doug made a small detour to where the slightest of openings in the jungle canopy had allowed a rampant growth of elephant ears. The broad fronds waved gently well above a man's height as the insertion team eased their way into them. Here they would establish their forward operating base.

While Doug called up this new position on the GPS, the rest of the task force stripped off every bit of gear they would not be needing for the evening's raid. From here on out they would carry as little weight as possible. Backpacks, the sat-phone and radio, canteens— all of it was heaped together and cached well back into the thicket. Major Ramirez told four of the men to stand guard. The others settled themselves silently around the cache of supplies. Here they would wait and rest while Doug and Major Ramirez went forward to do an initial reconnaissance of the target.

The new coordinates were coming onto the display panel now. Doug keyed them into his route map. That gave him a third dot, marked POS 3, on his screen. His tracking skills were good enough to get himself and Major Ramirez back to the group—he hoped! But he'd rather not have to waste the time using them. Other than the GPS unit and his walkie-talkie, Doug had stripped himself of everything but his LBE harness and his M-16. Major Ramirez was carrying even less, just the Colt service revolver he favored over the DEA's Glock. Doug walked over to where Mike was dismantling the sat-phone again.

"Everything's still 'all systems go,'" the tech agent informed him. "I told Kyle not to expect to hear from us again until it's over. Oh, and Luis Cortéz hasn't left the city."

Well, that was one piece of good news! Doug looked down at Ramon and the other two agents, sprawled out against their packs. "Okay, we're heading out now. Ramon, you're in charge until I get back," he reminded the younger agent.

That had been decided before they ever lifted off from Santa Cruz. Rocky and Carlos both actually had more seniority in the Santa Cruz DEA office than Ramon, but Ramon's army service had included a lot more deep jungle training than either of those two agents had received. Even if he hadn't run into gators before.

"We're a thousand meters out here. Give me forty minutes to get there. Say, fifteen minutes to reconnoiter. Another forty minutes to get back. That's what? An hour and a half? If we're not back in two hours, you'll know something's gone seriously wrong. Then—"

Ramon came to his feet in a lithe motion, his sudden grin wolfish on his narrow features. "Then we storm the place and take it apart, one brick at a time!"

Doug knew Ramon well enough to know that he was entirely serious. "No! I don't come back, you call Santa Cruz," he said firmly. "Get Grant and Shannon and tell them to get a team in here on the double."

He paused and offered a brief and very grim smile that mirrored Ramon's. "*Then* you storm the place!"

Doug and Major Ramirez did the final kilometer on their bellies, inching forward from one clump of vegetation to the next so silently that Doug once found himself eyeball to eyeball with a jungle tortoise that hadn't heard his approach. The creature's beak could easily have taken off Doug's nose, but after an eternity of contemplation, the reptile blinked and trotted off with a speed that belied its reputation.

The caution of their advance proved unnecessary. Not once did Doug detect any more sign of human presence than he had all afternoon. Sometimes it felt a little foolish, all this crawling and sneaking around, like a kid playing ninja. Especially when your belly hurt from crawling over rocks, your gun was digging into the small of your back, and retrospect showed you could have saved considerable time and trouble by strolling right up to your target.

But just when you started thinking that way, that's when you found yourself face-down under a bush no bigger than a house plant, with a *narco* armed to the teeth walking by so close you could have untied his shoelaces. It was better, Doug had decided a long time ago, to feel foolish nine times than wind up dead the tenth!

At four hundred feet, there was a sudden shift in vegetation. Major Ramirez was up to his knees in swamp before Doug recognized the reason. Detouring around the swamp, with its thick growth of ferns and water plants choking the edge, added an extra fifteen minutes that Doug hadn't counted on. But if the area continued to have as little security as they'd seen so far, they'd make up the time by simply hiking back to the FOB.

Doug heard the dogs before he saw a shaft of sunlight strike a branch up ahead. Adrenaline tightened his belly so that he didn't feel the rocks. He felt Major Ramirez's hand on his heel as he wormed deeper into a patch of grass that marked the jungle's edge. Doug lay motionless for a full minute, listening, muting his own breathing so that he could be sure it belonged to him and not someone else. The only sounds were the soft soughing of the wind through the trees and his own heartbeat. Cautiously, Doug parted the grasses.

The late afternoon sun slanted across the lawn that swept away from them up to the big house. Doug's first reaction was exultation. He'd called it right! This place was just too crazy for anyone but a *narco* to have dreamed up. In fact, it was a little too crazy for Luis Cortéz. The industrialist didn't have the flamboyance or conceit to bother wasting money on something like this. Then years-old bits of rumor and speculation clicked together, and Doug knew what he was looking at. So those old stories about Gonzalez, now rotting in the California state pen, had been true. Though how in tarnation had Cortéz come by this place? It spoke volumes about his past relationships.

Doug's professionalism took over. He wiggled his boot under the NIFC commander's hand. As the major crawled up beside him, Doug began a second, slower scan of the clearing, starting with the perimeter closest to their hiding place. A good fifty meters away, he saw a security guard in military khaki patrolling with the dog he had heard. A Doberman pinscher. He hated those brutes! Doug noted his pattern of patrol, a measured and unvarying pace set twenty meters in from the border of mowed grass that marked the perimeter. Both the man's head and the dog's turned toward the house far more often than they did the jungle, as though they expected any trouble to come from inside, not out.

Doug and Major Ramirez had approached the clearing from the left side of the main hacienda building, but more than halfway up the width of the clearing so that they could see the front of the residence. Doug paused briefly to study the satellite dish and radio uplink. Interesting! If that was what it looked like, then maybe Pablo Orejuela's lightning "rescue" and a few other aspects of this case weren't such a mystery.

Doug's careful gaze moved over to the airstrip. It was empty as far as he could see, except for another strolling guard and Doberman patrolling the edge. Doug picked out one more guard-and-dog pair far to his right, at the extremity of the property, still marching a measured twenty meters in from the perimeter.

The level of security was a lot less than he'd expected, but there was plenty of activity at the hacienda house itself. The helicopter had returned and was dropping into the clearing. Even at a distance, Doug could see that it was a Huey. But it was coming in on a different flight path than the one that had taken it over the insertion team, angling instead across the airstrip. People came boiling out onto the veranda as the chopper settled down onto the lawn in front of the house. Worming a pair of pocket binoculars from his LBE harness, which he'd shifted around so that the pouches rested above his rear instead of under his stomach, Doug raised them to his eyes.

It was Vargas, all right! The distinctive black clothing that was the security chief's egotistical fashion statement was impossible to miss. Also disembarking were the rest of the guards Doug had expected to see. In all probability, they were the ones who had hijacked Sara. Doug made a careful pan with his binoculars. No sign of a blonde head. So what were they doing that was vital enough to pull that many men off guard duty?

Doug focused the binoculars on a burlap sack that a worker was hefting to his shoulder, estimating with the ease of practice the weight and molding of its contents. Cocaine. It could be nothing else. Which explained those helicopter passes that had troubled Doug. Eight tons took a lot of moving. He should have guessed that Luis Cortéz would be too wily to keep the stuff at his own place, whether registered to him or not. They must have stashed it somewhere out in the jungle, though not too far away, judging by the intervals at which the Huey had come and gone.

Of course, that didn't explain this new flight path—unless Cortéz had cached the two hijacked plane loads at two separate locations. That made as much sense as anything, and was certainly in keeping with the extreme caution he had shown so far. And now that he had Sara, he was bringing it all in with the supreme arrogance that there was no one left to stand in his way.

Well, he was about to learn otherwise! Doug's jaw set hard as he studied the train of burlap sacks moving up onto the veranda and through the front door. *We've got you now, man! You're going down!* Doug tapped Major Ramirez on the shoulder. "I'd like to check the other side," he mouthed.

Major Ramirez nodded his agreement, and the two men wormed their way back until the sunlight faded from view. This time they didn't bother with the belly crawl. There were no guards out here, and they were running out of time. When they had skirted the clearing far enough to offer a full view of the opposite side of the house, they dropped back to the ground and slithered forward.

From here, Doug could see that the hacienda house was set far too close to the back line of jungle for proper security. Studying the vegetation through his binoculars, Doug saw why. There was a swamp back there. The same morass they'd edged around to get here. That would be a plus in getting close to the house without crossing the open lawn.

He could also see the entire stretch of the airstrip. It was empty right back to where it ended at the tangle of brambles that marked the beginning of the swamp. If Nicolás Cortéz had indeed arrived, he'd already departed. Maybe that small plane they'd heard? Doug's stomach tightened again, but not with adrenaline this time. Had he taken Sara with him? Was all of this for nothing?

"Look, *Douglas,* there! The girl?"

The surge of relief that welled up inside Doug as he followed the jerk of the major's chin was a reflection of just how rigidly he'd been keeping his heart on hold these last hours. He raised his binoculars. The veranda they'd seen on the other two sides of the big mansion ran down this side as well. Halfway down was a very solid-looking door. Through Doug's binoculars, the door appeared to be of considerably more recent construction than the rest of the house, and it had a lock better suited for a bank vault than a country house. Outside the door, a security guard was shifting his feet. But if he looked bored, there was nothing but business about the AK-47 slung over his shoulder, and Doug had no illusions that he was standing outside for a breath of fresh air.

"The girl," he affirmed quietly. "Let's go. We've seen what we came for."

✠

Sara couldn't settle down. She moved restlessly around the office, pacing back and forth between the desk and the far wall. She stopped to listen to an aircraft taking off, staring up at the painting of St. George and willing Nicolás to come back.

But he didn't.

As the sound of the engine dwindled into the distance, she went into the bathroom and took a drink. She washed her hands, then dug into her knapsack for a brush. Anything to fill another minute. A dozen times she sat down on a chair, then sprang back up. She checked her watch. The hands had reduced themselves to slow motion.

The one bright spot in all her restless fidgeting was the information Nicolás had tossed to her—Doug Bradford was alive and well and going about his business as usual. The joy and relief that bubbled up every time her mind went back to that fact were a mark of just how worried she'd been. That he was up to his neck in other cases didn't sound too promising, but at least he was still out there, and who knows? It had been hours since her capture. By now he had to know she was gone. If Rafael had managed to get word to Benedicto, Doug would know exactly what had happened. And every minute that ticked by gave him more of a chance to do something about it.

Sara made another turn around the office. No, she couldn't let her hopes get up too high. Though he might be competent, Doug Bradford was still just one man, and even if he did come for her, he'd need an army to get through all the security out there. If only she could let him know about the sacks of cocaine piled up in the old ballroom. Maybe then he could convince his boss to come after the Cortezes.

But that possibility wasn't even worth dreaming about. Don Luis was still due any minute. She couldn't count on Doug getting here first. No, her best hope right now was Nicolás. Guilt and shame and some remnant of the feelings he'd once had for her had driven him here this afternoon. If those emotions weren't strong enough to impel him to turn his back on crime, she just had to hope that he cared enough to help her get away. If only Don Luis didn't show up before he made up his mind. It would be just like Nicolás to put off any decision until it was taken out of his hands.

Sara stopped pacing, shamefaced. *Father, I said I was going to trust you on this. But I was doing better when I didn't think there was any hope at all! You know where Don Luis is now, and Nicky—and Doug. Help me to wait for what you choose to do. Whatever that might be!*

She forced herself to sit down. Retrieving the Bible that had tumbled to the floor when she'd fallen asleep, she opened it and began reading. But she couldn't concentrate. Her eyes ran aimlessly over the pages of print. Finally, she gave up and just sat there, sometimes praying, sometimes not thinking at all.

An hour passed, and then another, and still Nicolás didn't come back. Unwillingly, she began to face the fact that he wouldn't. At intervals she heard the sound of an aircraft. But the flight path was not over the house now, and the sound-proofing of the walls was sufficient that she couldn't tell if it was a helicopter or a plane, or whether it was arriving or departing. Each occasion brought her to her feet, her ears straining for the sound of approaching footsteps or voices, until enough time had passed to convince her that it must be Julio Vargas, bringing in another load of cocaine. Then she would sink back into her chair, and her racing heart would gradually subside, though it never quite reached its normal rate. Maybe Don Luis had found other matters more important than his runaway daughter-in-law. Or, more likely, confident that Sara wasn't going anywhere before he had a chance to deal with her, he'd chosen to get those interrupted cocaine shipments underway first.

She was beginning to think that even her father-in-law's appearance would be preferable to the prolonged agony of waiting when she heard the distant rumble of another aircraft, and this time, after long, tense minutes, a sound at the door. Not the veranda door, but the solid, reconstructed door that led into the old ballroom.

The Bible tumbled from her lap. This was it. She knew it! It had to be getting close to dusk outside, and if her father-in-law was coming at all tonight, it had to be now. And now that the wait was over, she knew that the agony of anticipation had been far preferable.

But it was Nicolás, not Don Luis, who careened through the doorway, propping himself up against the frame as though completely out of breath. "I'll do it, Sara," he gasped. "I . . . I can't go with you, but I can't just stand by and—"

His face was pale, his eyes feverish and even more hollow than they had been two hours earlier. His words tumbled out almost too fast for Sara to follow. "It would be Julio that would do it, I know it. He does all Papá's dirty work. To have him putting his hands on you—no, I'm not letting that slimy toad touch you!"

Nicolás pulled himself upright at Sara's apprehensive glance toward the open door. "What are you looking at? None of that bunch out there speak English."

But he did move away from the entry, removing the ring of keys before kicking the door closed behind him. Sara was at his side before the latch clicked shut. She stopped short of hugging him, but she put her hand on his forearm, her face alight with gratitude and relief.

"Then you're going to help me get away? Oh, Nicky, thank you! I . . . I was beginning to think you weren't coming back."

Nicolás glanced down at her softened expression, and his own tortured look eased for an instant in response. Then he looked away, his eyelids blinking rapidly, and she felt the muscles bunch under her fingers before he shook off her hand. Brushing past her, he headed across the office toward the outside door. "Yes, I'll help you. But it has to be now! The radio operator just told me. Papá has already left Santa Cruz."

Sara stared thoughtfully after him. Something was wrong here.

Something more than simple worry that his father would be here before they could get away. Turning to the desk to snatch up her knapsack, an action that had become automatic by now, she asked quietly, "Okay, Nicky, what is it you want me to do? That guard out there isn't going to just let us just walk out of here, is he?"

"The guard?" Nicolás didn't even seem to understand the question. "Why shouldn't he? I'll just tell him I'm tired of sitting. If I'm going to interrogate you, I'm going to make you walk while I do it. You don't think any of these guys are going to argue with an order from me! Besides," he added, not so irrelevantly, "Julio's gone to get another load of coke."

Nicolás inserted a key into the lock, tried to turn it, and pulled it out. "But we don't have much time. I've been helping bring in that second planeload we hijacked. Julio's making the last run now. And that means Papá isn't going to be stopping by there on his way in like he'd planned, either. So he could be here any minute. No, leave the bag." Nicolás had just noticed what she was slinging over her shoulder. He yanked out a second key from the lock. "People don't take bags on walks."

Sara reluctantly abandoned the knapsack. "So we're just going to wander over to the plane and fly off? I guess I didn't realize it would be so easy."

"The plane?" Nicolás gave up trying to unlock the door and gave it a sharp rap. "Forget the plane! The Cessna is out. This has got to look like you got away on your own. Besides, the fuel gauge is just about on empty, and we don't have time to refuel."

"Then—" Sara was bewildered. What other avenue for escape was there from this place? "Then what are we going to do?"

Nicolás's eyes didn't quite meet hers. "Easy. We'll walk around out there for a bit, get over near the perimeter. Then, when no one's looking, you make a dash for it. I'll try to give you a good head start. You know, thrash around in the bushes a bit before I let security know you got away. They'll come after you. I can't stop that. But Julio took most of the guards to load the coke. Besides, it's going to be night soon. You should be able to get away. Anyway, that's as far as I can go!"

Sara was listening with incredulity. Was this the help Nicolás was offering her? An escape into trackless jungle without so much as food or water? Not to mention the wild animals that lived out there! And armed men on her trail! "That's your plan? But—what am I supposed to do then? There's nothing out there for a hundred kilometers! I'd never make . . ."

She lapsed into silence as the truth sank in. Nicolás knew good and well the odds of her ever making it out of the jungle alive. His averted gaze was testimony enough of that. But her husband had made a compromise with himself. He couldn't stand to see her die. Not stone sober. Especially at the hands of a man he despised. But if Sara just disappeared into the jungle and was never seen again, then he could argue with his not-very-touchy conscience that he'd given her a chance. And block out of his mind just how nonexistent that chance had been. He'd probably end up convincing himself that he had done his best to save her life.

Still, Sara wasn't going to argue with the chance he was offering her, no matter how slim. Nor did she consider her chances to be quite as slim as he did. Doug Bradford was out there somewhere, and if she could just get away from here—hang on for a few hours more—sooner or later he would surely be coming after her.

She took a furtive glance at the knapsack on the desk. If he *could* come after her without that tracking device. But there was no way to bring it along now without raising suspicion, so she pushed the thought from her mind, along with the catalog of other dangers that might be awaiting her in the jungle. At least her position was better than it had been five minutes ago when she'd had every expectation of Don Luis walking through that door.

"Would you get a move on?" Nicolás snapped irritably. Sara suddenly realized that the veranda door was standing open. "I told you, Papá is already on his way! You want to do this, or not?"

Impatiently, he grabbed Sara's arm and herded her ahead of him. The guard snapped to attention as they emerged onto the veranda. "Your gun!" Nicolás barked.

The guard started to unsling his machine gun, but at Nicolás's impatient gesture, he shifted it back and drew a revolver from his hip holster. Slapping the weapon into Nicolás's hand, he snapped back to attention.

"The *señora* is going to walk with me," Nicolás told him brusquely. "I will not be long. You will remain here on guard."

The guard's eyes shifted from the revolver to Sara, but he showed no other reaction to the order. Nicolás had been right. These men were trained to obey orders, not question them, and Sara began to suspect that they weren't just regular security guards, but probably old army buddies of Julio's. Or more likely, subordinates.

Nicolás accounted for the revolver as he herded Sara across the veranda. "So he thinks I'm really guarding you. I'd take the M-16, but it'd be a lot harder to explain how I missed when you get away."

The sun was no longer visible except as a band of orange on the horizon, and though back in Seattle this would have given way to a leisurely twilight, here in the tropics, with its quick passage from day into night, it would be dark within fifteen minutes. Sara was encouraged to see only one patrol besides her own guard, who was still standing rigidly at attention when she glanced back over her shoulder. She could thank Julio's hurry to move the cocaine for that! All in all, Nicolás's timing had been perfect, though how much of this had been planning and how much was due to her husband's last-minute attack of conscience, Sara didn't even try to guess. Stepping down off the veranda, she surveyed her new surroundings.

The helicopter had delivered her to the front of the big residence with its rainbow of flower beds and unbroken sweep of lawn, but her father-in-law's office opened onto the side of the house. Perhaps a hundred meters away, directly ahead of her now, was the landing strip she'd glimpsed earlier, running in a straight line from one end of the clearing to the other. The guard she'd seen was strolling along the edge of the runway, a Doberman pacing along at his side. Beyond him, a twenty-meter-wide strip of grass separated the runway from the jungle that formed the perimeter of the estate.

Sara looked to her left and sighed with relief. This looked a lot more promising. The builders of this place had been far less assiduous in pushing back the jungle from the rear of the house, and no more than ten meters separated the veranda from the tangled vegetation there. Sara took a step in that direction.

Nicolás yanked her to a stop. "Where are you going, *idiota?* Can't you see that's swamp back there? Why do you think they haven't cut it down?" His fingers biting deep into her arm, Nicolás gestured with the gun toward the landing strip. "That way."

"But—the guard!" Sara protested. "We're going to run right into him."

"And if we do? I'll tell him to move along. He won't be there for long, anyway. He's got to patrol clear down to the end of the runway. All we have to do is wait until he walks on by. Unless you want to try around the front of the house," Nicolás added sarcastically. "That would give you a full audience."

He didn't loosen his grip on Sara's arm as he steered her toward the landing strip, and she had to break into a trot to keep up with his rapid strides. She opened her mouth to inform him that no one was going to mistake this for an outdoor interrogation *or* a walk if he didn't slow down a bit. But she held her tongue when she saw the determined look on his face. His concentration was set on a towering line of hardwoods beyond the landing strip.

He's in a hurry to get rid of me now, Sara thought sadly, and from his perspective she couldn't blame him. Nicolás didn't look down at her or speak, even when she stumbled on a stone and he had to yank her to her feet. She made no attempt to break the silence. What was there to say now, anyway? One way or another, this was good-bye. What would happen to Nicolás once she was out of his life? Would he ever marry Reina? Or was he going to end up in jail when Doug arrived to find him in the middle of a full-fledged drug operation? Sara refused to even think about that. Nicolás was out of her hands now and into God's. And she couldn't even begin to guess anymore what God had in mind.

The twilight had faded even in the time it took Nicolás and Sara to reach the landing strip. The runway itself was still a bright slash against the mown grass, but the edge of the jungle was now a dark shadow against the sunset. The guard back on the veranda was no more than an indistinct outline. Sara's heart began to race as she felt gravel under her sandals. Only seconds to go. At least . . .

As Nicolás had promised, the guard and dog patrolling the edge of the runway had moved on by the time they reached the edge of the strip. But thanks to the rapid pace at which Nicolás had dragged her along, the sentry was still too close. It would have been hard for anyone exercising even the slightest degree of vigilance to miss their approach, and Sara had seen the guard turning his head to watch them more than once as he made his way along.

Now, as the gravel crunched under her and Nicolás's feet, both dog and handler halted. Making an about-face, the guard cupped his hands to his mouth and called down the runway, "Is there a difficulty, *jefe?*"

Nicolás swore under his breath. Sara echoed his sentiments, if not the words, as she recognized the human half of the patrol. It was the soldier from the helicopter who had drawn his forefinger across his throat in the age-old threatening gesture. Papo. Even at fifty meters and in the growing dusk, there was no mistaking the gleam of curiosity in his eyes.

"There is no problem, Papo," Nicolás called back irritably. "Continue on your rounds. The *señora* and I will be walking for a time."

The guard did not move immediately. "You do not wish an escort?"

"If I wished for an escort, I would have requested one. Now, you will move on before I am forced to discuss your performance of duty with the coronel!"

Generations of Cortéz arrogance were conveyed in the ice of his voice, and when Nicolás emphasized his order with the revolver in his hand, the guard sprang immediately to attention. *"Sí, señor!"*

Spinning smartly on one heel, he clicked his tongue at the Doberman and the patrol continued its slow pace down the runway. But after two strides, Sara saw the guard look back over his shoulder. After two more strides, he looked again. Then, after two more steps, he stopped and turned around, the Doberman curving around his legs. Nicolás's fingers dug angrily into Sara's upper arm. "That nosy little . . ."

He shouted at the guard, using a few choice Spanish epithets that had the man snapping to attention before moving off again.

Nicolás had barely swung back around to Sara when he stiffened at a new source of annoyance. "Well, if this isn't all we need! Vargas!"

Sara had heard it, too, still distant but increasingly louder, the rhythmic beat of a helicopter. She spun around to search the skyline. Then she spotted it, still just a black shape high above the jungle but coming in fast at a course that looked to carry it right over the landing strip. Sara pulled frantically at Nicolás's hold. "Let me go! I can make it now! Nicky, please, let me go! He'll be sure to see me if he flies over here."

The guard was glancing over his shoulder again, and Nicolás hauled Sara back hard against him. "Oh, no you don't, *querida*. I'm not going to have that jerk telling Papá I didn't try to stop you. Besides, how far do you think you'd get with that dog coming after you?"

His arm was tight around her shoulder now. "But maybe you're right. Julio's bound to see us. Maybe we should just head back to the hacienda. This isn't going to work anyway, if we're going to have an audience."

"No! You can't be serious." Glancing up at him, Sara saw with a lurch in her stomach that he meant it. His offer of help had been an impulse, lasting only so long as it was easy and sure and with no risk to himself. But now that things were getting complicated, he was having second thoughts.

Sara forced herself to stand still in his grip. "Please, Nicky, we can still do this. The helicopter won't be landing for a few minutes. Look, the guard is further away already. Just . . . just give me this chance!"

"Fine. Then just keep walking. Nice and easy. No, not straight across! Are you trying to give the guy ideas?"

Sara let Nicolás steer their steps to the left in a gradual trajectory that would eventually take them across the landing strip while continuing to widen the gap between them and the security guard. All the while, Sara's stomach was knotted in an agony of apprehension as the powerful beat of the propellers drew nearer. The tautness of Nicky's arm across her shoulders and the rigid set of his face added the fear that he might back out altogether at any moment. And still, even as he drew further away, the guard was showing no signs of losing interest. Had he guessed what they were up to?

The helicopter was coming in now, and to Sara's immense relief, it swept in over the landing strip—still high enough to clear the enormous crown of the jungle canopy—and angled toward the front of the hacienda. In doing so, it accomplished what Nicolás's sharp commands had not: it drew the attention of the sentry away from Sara. As the Huey continued on its approach, the guard stopped in his tracks to stare up at it; then, casting a final glance over his shoulder, he started off at a brisk trot toward the house, the dog loping along beside him on its leash.

Sara waited only until his boots touched the grass. "Now! Let me go!"

Without a word, Nicolás dropped his arm. They were halfway across the runway now. Another ten meters would bring Sara to the other side. From there it was just a short sprint to the dubious shelter of the jungle. Sara tensed herself for the dash, then found herself checking involuntarily. Night was almost upon them now. Her husband's face above her was no more than a pale oval whose features could not be read.

"Good-bye, Nicky!" she said softly.

She couldn't tell which emotion prompted the violent twist of his body. "Just go!" he said hoarsely. "Go!"

Sara turned away again, her heart lightening as her muscles tensed. It really couldn't be better. The guard was now running rapidly toward the house. Everyone there would be occupied unloading this last load of cocaine. She would have the head start that Nicolás had promised. And by the time they came after her, it would be pitch dark.

The plane almost landed on them. Or so it seemed. The sound of its engines had been hidden in the powerful roar of the helicopter. Dropping in over the house from the opposite direction, the pilot banked sharply to line up the plane's nose with the landing strip. Sara's legs were stretched for their first step toward freedom when the thunder of the approaching craft, now rising above the settling beat of the helicopter, drew her startled glance.

She gasped in horror. The plane was coming straight at them, as though it had materialized out of nothing, or the solid wall of jungle swamp behind it. And this was no Cessna, but a far larger, two-prop machine.

Nicolás was staring upward with the same frozen horror that gripped Sara. She caught a glimpse of the pilot, glaring down at their upturned faces with a malevolent rage that must have been communicated by some other sense than sight, because she could not possibly have seen that blur of features so clearly.

Don Luis had arrived at last.

Then the plane was on them, the undercarriage flashing only meters overhead, the wind of its passage knocking Sara off her feet. Sand stung her eyes, causing her to cry out in pain. She felt Nicolás's hands helping her to her feet, and she clung blindly to them as she pulled herself upright. It took precious seconds to rub her eyes clear, and when she could see, the wheels of the airplane had already touched down. The air reverberated with the protest of its brakes. But though the plane was slowing, it wasn't stopping.

As Sara watched with gape-mouthed astonishment, the pilot threw the plane into an impossible curve. Its wings were wobbling so precariously that, for an instant of hope, Sara was sure it was going to overturn as the reckless speed of the ground-loop carried the aircraft out to the edge of the grass. But the sturdy craft, a DC-3—which, with its third wheel had earned the appellation "tail-dragger" from pilots—had a stability the lighter Cessnas didn't have. Although one wing hit the ground, hard, the very force of the impact bounced the plane back onto the wheel that had left the ground. The fuselage rocked wildly, then stabilized.

And then the DC-3 was rocketing back toward Nicolás and Sara, the glass of the windshield glinting with the last of the twilight like the eyes of some huge avenging insect. The horror of its approach released the two people in its path from their frozen trances. Sara saw Nicolás making a dash out of the path of the oncoming plane, and she at last began to run.

She was going to make it! It takes distance and some seconds to land even a small plane, and by the time the DC-3 had slowed enough to make its crazy U-turn, it had been carried well down the runway. The edge of the landing strip was just strides ahead. She would be well into the shadows of the first line of overhanging branches before the plane reached her.

But Sara had forgotten who she was dealing with and that the pilot of the DC-3 could see how close to escape she was. She heard the plane screeching to a halt, its engines abruptly dropping from their squeal of acceleration. Above the noise of the turbines, she heard her father-in-law shout, "Shoot, Nico, you fool! You've got the gun! Shoot the girl!"

She knew she shouldn't look back. But the spot between her shoulder blades was ice cold, and she had to see. The impetus of her stride carried her toward the perimeter of the strip as she turned her head, the long strands of her hair flying across her face so that she had to waste a hand to brush them away. Her peripheral vision caught Nicolás standing immobile across the runway, the revolver he'd taken from the guard hanging loosely in his hands. But her eyes settled on the DC-3, still far down the runway, and Don Luis, running forward from under the wing with a deadly looking shape in his hands.

As her foot touched down on grass, Sara heard a rapid-fire *tat-tat-tat* that she'd often heard on the screen but never in real life. Gravel sprayed up around her so that she stumbled, and as she recovered her balance, she saw—incredulously—two holes in the sleeve of her T-shirt where a bullet had passed through the fabric just an inch below her armpit.

And then she heard her husband's voice, filled with fury and anguish. "No, Papá, don't shoot her!"

Her whole body turned, slowly, like a leaf tumbling in the wind. And as she scrambled to maintain her balance, she saw a sight that would never leave her as long as she lived. Dropped to one knee in front of the DC-3, Don Luis was raising his weapon to take better aim.

In Sara's heightened awareness, the gun barrel came up no faster than molasses being poured on a cold winter day—but she was moving even slower. Even as her body braced for the impact of the bullets, she saw Nicolás running. Not toward her or toward his father, but straight into the line of fire, each footstep touching down leisurely and silently as Sara's heart slowed to a century between beats.

Her mouth opened to scream a warning, but it was too late, too slow. Don Luis was already squeezing the trigger.

A spurt of flame split the twilight. Sara saw Nicolás fly off his feet and hurl backward as the bullets stitched their way across his chest. The staccato gunfire died abruptly, leaving his still form sprawled awkwardly in the gravel like a broken doll.

With that, time resumed its normal tempo, and Sara could move again. Her scream finally sounded, mingling in the heavy air with a wail of anguish from beneath the plane. Then she was running again, not toward safety and escape, but back across the landing strip. Don Luis was running too, his gun still in his hand. Some unconscious corner of Sara's mind noted that Don Luis must have been alone in the plane, because no one else was coming, but she wasn't thinking about her father-in-law, only of Nicolás.

It was bad, she knew at once, dropping on her knees beside the spread-eagled body of her husband. He was on his back, one hand limply at his side, the other flung out above his head, the revolver still tangled in his fingers. His eyes were closed, his face untouched, and he might have been asleep, were it not for the stain that was spreading across the tattered remains of his polo shirt—not red in this light, but a dark gray. A larger stain spread out beneath him, soaking into the gravel. Sara could feel the warm stickiness through the knees of her jeans. There was too much blood to even think of trying to stem it, and she could not see how his shattered chest could still hold breath, until a bubble made its way through the bloody mess and popped. She felt a feeble movement against her legs.

"Sara." His eyes were open now, although dulled by pain. His arm moved again against her knees, and Sara helped him lift it to her face. "Shh! I'm here now. Don't try to talk."

"No." His voice was just a thread of sound, the words coming out laboriously between the bubbles of his escaping breath. "The story . . . about the thief . . . with Jesus . . . on the cross. Is it true?"

Sara nodded violently, tears pouring down her face as she cradled his bloodied hand against her cheek. "Yes, of course, Nicky. Don't worry about it now. We're going to get you to a hospital."

"No . . . too late. . . . Go."

The last word was a movement of his lips rather than a sound. His fingers moved briefly against her cheek. It might have been a caress. Then they went slack, and his head rolled back against the gravel so that his eyes were no longer looking into hers but were staring upward to where the last fading green of twilight was giving way to the first stars. But there was no sight in them anymore, and Sara knew he was gone.

Her head fell forward, her body shaking with sobs. "Oh, Nicky!"

The resounding *crack* of a gunshot reminded her that she was not alone. She raised her head. Don Luis had covered about half the distance from the plane, and he was still running, a lone, dark outline against the night. Another shot sounded, not automatic fire but a single volley, and the spark of flame from her father-in-law's upraised arm showed that it was directed toward the sky rather than at her. If it was a signal, it was working, because already there were shouts of men's voices. From the direction of the house, two shadowy figures were racing back toward the landing strip. The guard and the Doberman.

It was only then that Sara realized how little time had elapsed since her father-in-law had tried to gun her down and hit his son instead. Still, although he had a lot more distance to cover than she had, it seemed odd that he hadn't reached her yet. And why was his approach so cautious and dodging? Why wasn't he shooting at her?

Her eyes fell on the black shape of the revolver against Nicolás's outstretched hand, and it occurred to her that Don Luis didn't know if she was armed. Nor could he shoot at her without the risk of hitting Nicolás again. She had one last chance to escape.

But still Sara didn't move, kneeling in the cooling puddle of blood as one long second passed into another while Don Luis narrowed the distance between them and the patrol team drew nearer. It seemed a betrayal of her own to abandon Nicolás now.

Go! Her husband's last word registered in her brain. *Go!*

Sara looked one last time at Nicolás's lifeless face. Yes, she had to go. There was nothing more she could do here. Carefully laying down the hand she'd held to her cheek, Sara got to her feet. She looked dazedly down at the blood that coated her hands and spattered the front of her shirt. Then, still carefully, as though she were sleepwalking, she wiped her hands on her jeans and reached for the revolver. It was heavier than she'd expected, and she almost dropped it. She wasn't even sure how it worked, but she took a firmer hold on the butt and straightened up. Unsteadily at first, but then finding her stride on the loose stones, she ran.

But her hesitation had cost her, and all too soon, a cry of anguish told her that Don Luis had reached Nicolás. This time she didn't look back. It was too dark to see, anyway. She stretched her legs to the limit, her whole body tensed for the bullets that would surely be coming. But nothing happened, and soon she was at the edge of the landing strip and back on the grass. Black and gnarled branches reached down to pull her under their cover.

She was almost in their grasp when she heard boots pounding across the gravel behind her and the sharp report of a single shot. This time it was no signal, because she heard the bullet whistle past her ear and a smack as it buried itself in a tree trunk.

"Don't shoot, you fool!" she heard Don Luis shout. His voice was ice cold and far deadlier than any fury. "I want her alive."

Sara felt soggy bark under her outstretched fingers. With another step, the jungle swallowed her up.

✠

Don Luis had never known such rage, not even when he'd found out that his father's egotistical incompetence had cost him his inheritance. For the first time in a life that had included many questionable acts, he experienced the lust to kill, to feel a life choked out by the strength of his own bare hands. He lowered Nicolás's limp body to the ground. In a moment he would grieve, but first there were things to do. His son, his heir, was dead, and someone was going to pay.

Sara was already gone by the time the guard and his dog reached Don Luis's side. He started to continue in the direction that Sara had fled, but Don Luis stopped him with a chopping motion of his hand. "No, it is too dark to find her this way. We need men and equipment. Your radio!"

The guard was pulling the walkie-talkie from his belt even before Don Luis impatiently snapped his fingers. As soon as the radio was in the sentry's hand, Don Luis snatched it away. The orders he gave were short and succinct, and the immediate sound of a whistle and running feet from across the lawn told him he was being obeyed. Not that he would have expected otherwise. Settling back on his heels to wait, he gazed coldly at the guard. The man was staring with horror at Nicolás's sprawled body. The Doberman crouched at his handler's feet, emitting a continuous low whine .

"Now you will tell me how it was possible that this should have happened! Were not orders given that this woman was dangerous and was to be kept strictly under guard? And who was the incompetent fool who was to be patrolling this section?"

"I—it is I who have been patrolling this section, *señor*. But it was Señor Nicolás himself who released the woman. I . . . I spoke to him myself, because *el coronel* had given strict orders that the woman should be secured until your arrival, and I thought it possible that she—but your son was carrying a weapon, *señor*, and he did not seem to be under compulsion. He ordered me to leave, said that he wished to walk with the *señora*."

The guard was stammering in his hurry to excuse himself. "There was something strange in their comportment, and I thought it odd that Don Nicolás should choose to walk with the prisoner this close to the perimeter. It was for that reason that I left my duties, *señor*. It was the orders of *el coronel* that anything out of order—however small— be reported to him. When I saw the helicopter arriving, I felt there was sufficient reason to do this in person. Forgive me if I have misjudged, *señor*."

"Never mind!" Don Luis cut him off curtly. He didn't need the guard's nervous explanation to know what had happened here. Nicolás, that young fool, still had not mastered his weakness for his *americana* woman. And now he had allowed her to talk him into this madness. It was for fear of just such an occurrence that he had ordered his son to stay away. Why . . . *why* . . . when all was finally falling into place, did the boy have to choose rebellion?

Other men were arriving now. The swamp was all the security the back side of the house had ever needed. But there had been guards patrolling the front and opposite borders of the hacienda, and they had left their posts in response to the gunfire and the signal that followed. Don Luis ignored them, sitting back on his heels with his head bowed, until Julio Vargas arrived with the remainder of his security force. Illuminated by the beam of his powerful flashlight, the security chief's narrow features were set in the same icy anger as his boss's.

"Do not be concerned, *jefe*. We will have her back, in one piece or many!" he told Don Luis tightly, and the coldness in his black eyes made it clear he had no preference. He tossed something to the ground. It was Sara's flight bag. The clothing inside spilled out onto the ground. "The woman's. Let the dogs get the scent."

The Dobermans were already tugging at their leashes, whining with eagerness, as Vargas snapped out his orders. There were four dogs and eight men, including himself. "Does every man have a lantern and a radio?" He didn't need to ask about weapons. "Then you will spread out and follow the dogs, two to a patrol. We will not return without the woman."

He snapped his fingers at Papo, the guard who had been patrolling the landing strip. "You! You know which direction the girl has taken. You will come with me. Lead out."

The security chief raised a hand as the men and dogs began to spread out. "And do not forget! The woman is armed. You will consider this as you search. You know what to do."

"No!" Don Luis's contradiction was harsh. "I do not want the girl harmed. Whatever it takes, you will bring her back alive."

Julio didn't argue, but set off at a trot, waving for his men to follow. The Dobermans had already picked up the trail. As the dogs bounded across the landing strip, the searchlights of the hunting party bobbing up and down behind them, Don Luis knelt down again to lift the lifeless form of his son. Now he could allow his grief to fill him. There was a savagery in his expression, as he cradled Nicolás's lolling head against his breast, that his conquistador ancestors would have recognized.

No, he did not want his pretty little daughter-in-law harmed. Not yet! He had things to discuss with her. And this time when he was through, there would be no calling Julio Vargas to finish the job.

CHAPTER THIRTY-TWO

The insertion team heard the spatter of gunfire while they were still some distance from the target. Drifting forward now from behind the gnarled trunk of a *toborochi*, Doug caught the flicker of moving lights in the jungle beyond the airstrip. The lights wavered and went out.

"Do we check it out?" Major Ramirez murmured into his ear.

The landscape glowed a faint green in the infrared light of his night-vision goggles as Doug turned his head in a slow sweep from left to right. It was quiet now. Too quiet! There were lights on in the main building—unnaturally bright through the lenses of the NVG—though only on the first floor. The Huey sat at the same spot he'd seen it last. He'd heard the throp-throp of its propellers only minutes before the shots. But it was abandoned now and silent.

Far beyond the building, on the airstrip, Doug made out the dark outline of two aircraft stationed perhaps twenty meters apart. A small single-engine plane, a Cessna. And a larger two-engine craft with the fat body of a DC-3. So they'd come at last! But the aircraft, too, sat dark and abandoned. Nowhere was there any sign of human life. Or canine. Where were the guards he'd picked out less than an hour earlier? If he were lucky, it was a sign of the lack of discipline on which this place ran!

"No. It could be anything. We stick to the plan."

The plan for the raid had been made before they'd ever left the FOB, and each man knew exactly what his part was. But there would have to be one small change now. Doug pushed the visor of his NVG up onto his forehead. Beside him, Major Ramirez did the same. They had been able to scramble only three of the bulky headsets for the entire task force, which had made the last ten minutes of their approach challenging. But now that they were out of the jungle, the twinkle of the house lights and the glimmer of stars and moon above the clearing would be ample for their night-adjusted vision to do the job.

Without the illumination of the NVG, the men clustered silently around Doug were black shadows whose presence could be felt more than seen, and only the height and proximity of one allowed him to direct his whisper in the right direction. "Rocky, your party's ready, right? I'd like you to check out the airstrip. See what's going on down there. Mike, you'll have to put one of your own men on the chopper."

The plan for the raid divided the task force into three parties, each with its own job to do. Rocky, along with five of the NIFC troops, was to form the outer perimeter party. His men would split up into pairs, covering each of the three main approaches to the house, to keep patrolling guards or other outside forces from coming to reinforce the enemy inside once the action started. Those with the farthest to go to reach their positions would move out first.

Mike and three others had been assigned the inner perimeter. They would stake out the four sides of the main residence. As the outer perimeter party focused its attention toward the jungle, the inner perimeter party would focus on the house itself, trusting the outer party to watch their backs while they concentrated on stopping anyone who tried to escape from indoors.

That left the rest of the task force, led by Doug and Major Ramirez, as the "snake," or raiding party, that would hit the house itself. The whole thing was as choreographed as an exercise of ballet, and no one would move from his assigned position without specific orders, regardless of what he heard or saw happening at another location. Only now, they would need a fourth party.

"Carlos. Ibañez." Two shadows glided forward. "It looks like the Cortezes decided to show for the party. You two stake out those planes. Don't disable them. We might need them later. But if someone tries to take off—well, you know what to do."

That was going to cut the main raiding party a little short, but Doug wasn't going to offer anyone a chance to escape in that direction. If it hadn't been for Sara, the sight of those two aircraft would have afforded him considerable satisfaction. This trap wouldn't have been complete without the Cortezes. But now his stomach tightened at the thought of Sara inside somewhere with those two men. Time had run out. He only hoped they weren't too late!

Father, we're going in! The rest is up to you.

Hardly louder than his silent plea, he gave the order. "Okay, perimeter, aircraft, you've got four minutes to get in position from—"

Every team member looked at the faint phosphorescent glow of their wrist watches. They'd been synchronized back at base. *"Now!"*

Rocky dropped the visor of his NVG, and the perimeter team, along with Carlos and Ibañez, was gone at a run. Not out across the lawn that lay dark and open under the rising moon, or back into the black tangle of the jungle, but around the edge of the clearing where the thick foliage overhanging the mowed border offered invisibility as well as speed. Only when each pair reached the closest point to their assigned positions would they drop down to belly crawl the rest of the way.

Doug led the rest of the team at a trot in the opposite direction. Here the jungle curved close to the main residence as dry land gave way to swamp. At the edge of the swamp, Doug stopped and waited, his eyes roving in a continuous pattern from his watch to the deserted veranda, now only a dozen meters away, then back to his watch. Sweat was trickling again under his Kevlar vest and through the oily camouflage makeup on his face. He could smell around him in the dark the same tension that was building up within himself. Not fear, just the keyed-up anticipation that tightens the muscles of a jockey at the starting gate or an athlete awaiting the kickoff of a championship game. Doug counted down the seconds: *5 . . . 4 . . . 3 . . . 2 . . . 1.*

"Go! Go! Go!"

And then they were sprinting, noiselessly at first across the grass, then up onto the veranda, their boots thudding as they abandoned stealth. Mike's party split in two, running hard in either direction. Doug had already chosen his raiding party's own entry point—a door halfway down the side of the house that was neither newly installed nor boasting a new lock. It crashed down off its hinges as he kicked it in.

It was the kitchen. Not a *Better Homes & Gardens* kitchen, but a big, bare room with a sink built like a horse trough and a configuration of metal tubing and open gas burners that served as a rough camp stove. There were open baskets of rice, potatoes, and onions, and a single unit of metal shelving against one wall.

Two Quechua women in flared skirts and braids raised startled faces and screamed at the guns and military garb of their unexpected visitors. They screamed again with sheer terror as the fluorescent lighting illuminated the stripes of green and black that made Doug's face an inhuman mask below the raised visor of his NVG. Wailing with fear, they scuttled back into the farthest corner, raising trembling fists with forefinger and pinkie thrust out in the two-horned sign that Inca tradition promised would ward off this evil spirit.

Doug didn't pause for pleasantries. He was already across the kitchen, kicking open the opposite door. He didn't need to check over his shoulder to know that Ramon and the others were right at his heels.

The next room was a storeroom, complete with freezer and refrigerator. Doug crossed it in two strides. He could have taken the more sedate route of trying the door handle, but there was something eminently satisfying about the crash of splintering wood under his boot. The next *narco* who chose to take over this place was going to have a major repair bill first!

The hall that he burst into was long and lined with doors. To his left, it ran clear to the back of the building. To his right, it opened out into a wide foyer whose high mahogany portals appeared to be the main entrance to the mansion. The hall had only one occupant, a white-coated male emerging from beneath an unlit staircase, his head bent over an open file in his hand. At the clatter of the insertion team's running boots, the man glanced up. The file fell with a flutter of pages to the tiles. His mouth dropped open—to scream, to warn, it didn't matter.

Sprinting down the hall, Doug slammed the butt of his machine gun against the side of the technician's head. At the same instant, he used a foot to sweep the man's legs out from under him. The technician crashed down on top of his scattered pages. The blow hadn't knocked him out, but he made no further attempt to speak. Major Ramirez had his M-16 at the man's throat now, and the NIFC commander's right boot was planted in the center of his chest.

Doug left him moaning and clutching at the side of his face to stride to the open door from which the man had emerged. The room was empty of other occupants, but even with the advance clue of the powerful satellite dish outside, its contents were enough to give Doug pause. There had to be enough communications gear here to monitor half the airwaves of Bolivia! Or make a sat-link call directly to Moscow or Hong Kong. And how in the world had Luis Cortéz gotten his hands on an Israeli army encryption unit, whose flip-side capacity just happened to be the decoding of secure military communications? Not to mention unscrambling ordinary cell phone traffic. Since when were those available on the civilian market?

But this wasn't the time for a closer examination. Behind him, Doug could hear the pounding of feet and splintering of wood as the rest of the raiding party fanned down the hallway. Cries of "Clear! Clear!" indicated that they too were finding only empty rooms. Doug was swinging back around from the open door when Ramon came dashing into the foyer.

The younger agent jerked his thumb toward the staircase to signal his intentions. Then he was running lightly up the worn treads, slinging his M-16 back over his shoulder as he pulled a flashlight from his LBE harness with one hand and his Glock pistol with the other. As the rest of the raiding party pounded into the foyer, two men peeled off to follow the bobbing of Ramon's light upstairs.

The third soldier, along with Major Ramirez, fell into step behind Doug as the DEA agent headed purposefully across the foyer for the last set of closed doors, which matched exactly the doors of the abandoned salon on the other side of the entryway. Three boots crashed against the wood simultaneously.

This time they hit pay dirt.

The room was huge, easily a full quarter of the ground floor, the floor-to-ceiling arch of its boarded-up windows and remnants of polish on the plank floor evidence of what the place had once been. It was also easily the largest cocaine processing set-up Doug had ever come across in all his years with the DEA. At least two dozen heads shot up to stare at the intruders with varying degrees of astonishment and shock and dismay. The loud hum of the air-circulation units explained how the raiding party had managed the element of surprise after all the racket they'd been making outside.

Major Ramirez carried the actual authority of Bolivian law here, not Doug, and he used it without delay. Raising his voice above the noise of the fans and the sudden buzz of dismayed voices, he shouted, "This is the *Fuerzas Especiales Contra El Narcotráfico*. You are all under arrest. You will drop your weapons. If you resist, you will be shot."

There was no resistance. Nor any weapons in evidence. Every hand shot into the air. Every eye followed the movements of three M-16s cradled in three rock-steady pairs of hands. As his own weapon came up and around, Doug took in the white packets spilling out of open burlap sacks, the long tables laden with merchandise and scales heaped up with the sparkle of snow—and everywhere, the stylized *C* with its three-pronged crown—and tasted victory. His quest was over. There was enough evidence in this room to put away the whole Cortéz clan ten times running. But he wasted no time on self-congratulation. This had been way too easy!

Major Ramirez said it. "Where are the guards, Douglas? And where are Don Luis and Don Nicolás, whom you said would be here?"

"I don't know!" Doug said grimly.

His gaze swept down the long room, pausing to hold the eyes of one of the workers, whose white lab coat seemed to denote a higher rank and who had started to lower his arms. His M-16 shifted an inch, and the man hurriedly raised them again. Doug's gaze moved on past the stage. The door set into the back wall of the ballroom was precisely where he had calculated it must be. He stepped forward between the rows of tables, then broke into a run, leaving Major Ramirez to shout for the lab workers to begin moving back against the wall.

He wouldn't be able to kick in this door, Doug realized while he was still meters away. It was too new and too solid, the striker plate in which the lock was set a massive thing of tempered steel. Nor was his usual Plan B a much better option. Even disregarding the danger to anyone on the other side, a bullet against that lock was as likely to ricochet back at him as it was to have any effect on the steel.

But in any event, he didn't have to make the choice. The door was unlocked. And the room on the other side of the door was unoccupied.

Running a hand beside the doorjamb, Doug found a light switch and flicked it upward. As the fluorescent tubing steadied into a blue-white glow, he glanced around, taking in with no real surprise the incongruent luxury of the office furnishings and the painting of Saint George on the wall across the room. *One more nail in your coffin, Cortéz!*

Then his eye fell on the huge mahogany desk, and his heart gave an undisciplined jolt. No, he hadn't been so far off. She'd been here all right!

Striding across the office, Doug snatched up the knapsack and unzipped it, dumping its contents out onto the desk. He smoothed out a corn husk. There were crumbs clinging to its inner surface, but they had been eaten hours ago. Had he been wrong in his assumptions, his hopes? Had the Cortezes already come and gone? And Sara—?

Picking up the Bible, he flipped through it. The pages were dog-eared and marked with smudges of dirt and grass and what looked suspiciously like tear stains. Doug's throat tightened as he laid the Bible down.

Where are you, Sara? What have they done?

✠

She was running. Running desperately through a night blacker than she had dreamed possible. As she ran, unseen hands reached out thorny fingers, tearing at her clothes, tangling in her long, fine hair. A nightmare creature snaked out of the blackness to wrap a slimy tentacle around her neck. Sara screamed before the horrible thing resolved itself into a fungi-eaten length of jungle vine.

A guttural shout answered. There was a sound of thrashing in the underbrush. Then, off to her right and dangerously close, a dot of light stabbed at the darkness. Sobbing now with terror, Sara threw herself to the left, tripping over tangles of vines, thrashing at the plant life that impeded every step as she plunged blindly through the night. If only she could see!

But there was no pale glimmer of starlight, not even one gentle moonbeam filtering through the invisible canopy of the hardwood giants far overhead. The blackness was so complete that she couldn't even see the outline of her hands, which she was holding up to shield her face.

It hadn't been so bad at first. The gunfire had ceased as soon as the underbrush had swallowed her up. Perhaps the discovery of his son's death had distracted Don Luis. Or maybe he'd realized the impossibility of pursuit in this blackness and concluded it would be simpler to abandon Sara to the merciless hand of the jungle.

Whatever the reasoning, she had accepted the respite gratefully, slowing her initial mad dash to feel her way carefully into the foliage. The last of the fading twilight had dissipated within the first meters, but the passage ahead of her groping hands and feet was less congested than she'd anticipated. She had pressed forward, refusing even to contemplate what the ooze squishing up between her sandaled toes might contain. By dawn she would be far away.

But then had come the shouts and the lights crashing into the jungle behind her. How could she have been so stupid as to think a man like Luis Cortéz would give up the hunt so easily? They had simply gone for searchlights. And they would not relent until they had hunted her down.

She had been running full tilt ever since. For an eternity, it seemed. She'd lost the revolver in the first minutes of the stumbling chase. And the plastic *chinelas* on her feet soon after that. And now the surge of adrenaline that had brought her this far was wearing off.

Sara slowed as the dot of light winked out again. The broad leaves of what felt to be elephant ears or dwarf palms were slapping her in the face, but her arms dropped to her sides, unable to batter through another meter of jungle growth. She was perilously close to exhaustion, her fine hair plastered in strands to her skull with sweat and mud, her gasping breaths drawing no refreshment from the hot, humid air that hadn't dropped one degree with the falling of night.

Still, she forced herself on, driven by the sounds of the hunt behind her. This simply made no sense! With all her frantic twistings and turnings, she had yet to lose her pursuers for more than a few moments. How had they clung so inexorably to her trail as though . . . as though they could see her in this darkness?

A startled yelp and a curse from somewhere too close behind gave the answer. The dogs! Lean and swift and tenacious, the Dobermans were trained for attack and for just such a task as this. And at least one of them was back there, sniffing out her scent, guiding the hunters.

Despair made Sara stumble. She could evade the men, but not the dogs. Not by night. Not by day. Already she could see pinpoints of light blinking into view again over her shoulder. And she was so tired! Why bother waiting until those silent, vicious creatures came up on her unawares in the dark? Why not just turn around right now? Drop down right here in the bushes and give her body the rest it craved? It would only hasten the inevitable!

Her feet made the decision for her. Stumbling down a slight incline, Sara found the ground suddenly smooth and hard. As she flailed to recover her balance, she felt only empty air in front of her. She had blundered into some sort of shallow ditch, with just enough width and depth to hold her feet in its channel. She had no idea that she had stumbled onto a game trail worn deep into the forest floor by generations of the jungle's larger beasts, but the sudden ease of passage underfoot gave her the impetus to stretch her legs back into a run. Maybe resistance was futile and senseless, but to give up so tamely now was to demean the sacrifice Nicolás had made to get her this far. If they were going to capture her, she would be kicking and fighting with every last ounce of strength she possessed.

Nicolás! The wonder and sorrow of his death were still fresh wounds. Weak and spoiled and utterly self-centered. Willing to do almost anything, including murder, to protect his own selfish interests. And yet in the end he had thrown away his own life to save hers! Why . . . why had he done it? One last impulse that hadn't measured the consequences to himself? Or some remnant of the feelings he had once held for her? She would never know. New tears streamed down her face and she stumbled again, though her tears could not possibly blind her more than she was already. *Oh, Nicky!*

She ran straight into a thorn bush. When she had yanked herself free, her groping hands determined that she had reached a T-junction in the trail. Which way to turn? To the right or to the left? Her last sprint down the game trail seemed to have thrown off her pursuers, at least momentarily. But now she was completely disoriented. She had no idea where she was in relation to the pack following her. Either direction might take her right back into their arms.

Her hesitation dragged out, her ears reaching for any sound that might give a clue to her pursuers' position. But the jungle was so noisy! The incessant, shrill whine of the cicadas. The rustle of a small nocturnal mammal looking for dinner somewhere above her head. A high-pitched scream—like a mortally wounded woman! It died away, becoming a gurgle of agony, reminding Sara that the pursuers she was straining her senses to locate were not the only hunters at large out here.

How was it that she had once thought the jungle night lovely and exotic? Now it seemed full of cruelty and death and unseen enemies. Any of those sounds could mask one of them—human, canine, . . . or something else!—stealing up behind her. Every hiss and rustle hammered at nerves already stretched past breaking, and she had to bite her lip to keep from screaming again. A sense of unreality dizzied her. What was she, Sara Connor, a city-bred and university-educated woman, doing in this primitive and alien place, so far from her own cool northern climate?

A loud, rapid hammering directly underfoot startled Sara into renewed action. Her blundering flight barely missed the tiny tree frog whose delicate throat had produced the awful clamor. She had no idea which direction she'd finally chosen, but instinct kept her to the smooth footing of the game trail despite the terror that was driving her on. She splashed through a stream, still running faster than she thought her body was capable. On the other side she lost the game trail, but she sped on, her arms flying up to protect her face as she crashed through some sort of undergrowth.

A protruding root sent her sprawling. Sara fell hard, barely suppressing the cry of pain that rose to her throat. She lay still for a few seconds, or a minute, or an eternity, every muscle in her ill-treated body pleading to stay where she'd fallen. It had rained here earlier in the day, and the ground under her hands and face was unpleasantly spongy. A scent rose from it that was vaguely familiar, like a dinosaur exhibit she had once visited at Epcot Center in Orlando, though there the scent had been artificially reproduced. Musty and damp, it was unpleasantly reminiscent of thousands of years of decaying organic matter. Then, as sheer stubbornness pushed Sara to her hands and knees, another scent caught at her night-sharpened senses. Slowly, with infinite caution, Sara lifted her head.

Her last desperate scramble had brought her into a small clearing. For the first time since her initial mad rush into the jungle, she could actually make out the hands that were pushing her away from the ground. She could also see the moss-blurred length of the colossal hardwood, bigger around than a man was tall, whose toppling had created this opening in the jungle canopy. Padding silently forward from the shelter of the fallen giant was a long, shadowy form. Two small green lamps floated with it across the starlit grasses, and as Sara rose too quickly to her feet, a low rumble shook the hot night air.

✠

"Doug!"

Doug strode back to the office door. Ramon was trotting his way down the center aisle. Beyond him, Major Ramirez was herding their prisoners into one small group against the boarded-up windows. Doug made a quick count of the green-and-brown fatigues that stood out amid the chaos of screams and protests and milling people. The raiding party was all safe and accounted for.

"We're all clear here. There was no one else in the house except those guys." Ramon jerked a thumb back toward their captives. "No sign of the two Cortezes at all, or Vargas and his men."

Ramon's sharp eyes held a question as they shifted to a point past Doug's shoulder. Doug moved aside so that Ramon could see the knapsack sitting on the desk. "She was here all right."

He lifted his Motorola from his belt. "Mike, we're all clear in here. You got anything out there? Everyone okay?"

The hand radio crackled. "We're all clear out here. I'm outside that door you mentioned. There wasn't any guard. In fact, we haven't seen a living soul. But I did see lights a couple times out in the woods."

Ramon was at Doug's heels as he walked briskly back through the office. The door leading onto the veranda was unlocked. Doug moved immediately to one side as he stepped out onto the veranda. Highlighting yourself against a lighted doorway wasn't a smart thing to do in these situations. Mike was standing at the edge of the veranda, studying the night. Doug stepped up beside him. He could make out the faint glimmer of the airstrip, but any twinkle of lights was well lost in the jungle by now, and dropping the visor of his NVG made little improvement. He lifted his Motorola back to his mouth.

"Rocky, you out there? We're all clear here, but no sign of uniforms or the girl. What do you have for us?"

Doug caught the excitement even through the static. "This is

Rocky here. We're all accounted for. No sign of the guards or the dogs. Repeat, no sign of the guards or the dogs. But we've got a body here. Repeat, we've got a body here."

"A—body?" Doug would have sworn that his voice didn't change its even tone, but Ramon was suddenly at his side, wresting the radio from his rigid fingers.

"Hey, Rocks, you taking lessons in insensitivity or what? What do you got there, man?"

"That's right, a man," the Motorola crackled back. "He's been shot. More than that—practically cut in half, I'd say. I think you'd better get down here and take a look, Doug. I—well, I've only seen the guy on the news, but I think it's one of the Cortezes. The younger one."

Nicolás Cortéz! Doug snatched the walkie-talkie back from Ramon. "Are you sure? It's not a girl? Blonde?" The demand received as much response as it deserved, and he added, "Okay, Rocky, I'm sending a team right away. You've got Romero with you, don't you? Have the rest of your men fall back to the perimeter of the house."

He swung around on Mike. "Take a couple of your guys and get down there to back Rocky up. Get some lights up, will you? See if you can get us some answers. And watch your back. We still don't know what's out there. Ramon—"

The sudden deadly chill in Doug's voice brought Ramon's head around sharply.

"Do you think we might be able to persuade someone inside there to tell us just what's been going on here?"

✠

Don Luis watched with mounting fury from the jungle's edge as the *americano* flicked on a flashlight and played its beam over Nicolás's body. It was past time to call others down from the house, but the unaccustomed tears he'd shed were not for others to witness, and so he'd remained on his knees, the still form of his son cradled against his shirt, his mind emptied of all but his pain and grief and rage.

Only when his iron will had reasserted its control had he lifted his head—just in time to see a dark shape running along the veranda. The running figure had been distinguishable only as human, but there had been no mistaking the long-barreled shape of an automatic rifle. Don Luis's first thought had been that it was one of his own security detail arriving late for the hunt. But something furtive in the silent sprint had stifled the angry call that rose to his lips. Laying down the burden in his arms, Don Luis had retrieved his own weapon and retreated soundlessly from the airstrip.

Don Luis had been safely under cover when two more dark shapes detached themselves from the black shadow of the Cessna and became suddenly visible against the paler gray of the gravel. The outline of weapons had been there too, and one of the figures was far too tall to be anyone in his employ.

Then they'd stumbled over his son's body. He hadn't understood the radio communication that followed. But he hadn't needed to. He'd recognized the language. Somehow—it did not seem possible given the precautions he'd taken, but there was no denying the evidence of his own eyes and ears—the *americanos* had traced him here. By now, they were uncovering his entire operation. And with his marks all over it. All his carefully laid plans—no, the whole structure of his life—was crumbling to pieces around him.

Don Luis tightened a forefinger on the trigger of his Uzi machine pistol. The backs bent over Nicolás's sprawled form made a perfect target for his rage. Then he reconsidered. There were new lights now on the veranda. Whatever momentary satisfaction there might be in giving way to that vengeful impulse wasn't worth drawing attention to his own position. Besides, he knew where to put the blame for this. It was the girl! However it had happened, she was responsible. Just as she was responsible for everything else that had gone wrong since his son had made the mistake of bringing the *gringa* home, with her seductive fairness and whining middle-class morality.

But the *americanos* had not won yet. Was he not Luis Cortéz Velásquez de Salazar? The ignominy of public disgrace and prison was not for someone such as he! There had to be a way out. Even as Don Luis lowered the Uzi, his fertile brain was reviewing his options.

The planes. Silent and abandoned beyond the two intruders, they were the only escape route he could see. If he could get into the cockpit and take off before the Americans discovered his presence . . .

Don Luis drifted from the concealment of one tree trunk to the next. The Cessna would lift off faster, but the DC-3 was in the best position for a takeoff. It galled him to leave his son to the *americanos*, but beyond his grief was the instinct for survival—and a burning hatred for the young *gringa* who had dared to assume the honored name of Cortéz. Already, the story was coming together in his mind.

He had never been here. He knew nothing of this place. It had been the girl who was responsible. Was not her relationship with young Ricardo Orejuela widely known? And had not his father been arrested for this very crime of drug trafficking?

And Julio Vargas, too. It was unfortunate, but his assistant would have to be sacrificed for credibility. The *coronel* had betrayed his employer, as his daughter-in-law had once naively suggested, using the resources of *Industrias Cortéz* for his own debased activities. Did he not have witnesses who could place Vargas this very day with the girl? There was the *campesino* boy whose babbling to his *cocalero* boss had trickled upward to Don Luis's ears. And the parents themselves, who would not dare to testify to anything else.

As for Nicolás, it was a terrible tragedy that his son, having discovered the perfidy of his fugitive wife and her accomplice, had with his usual impulsiveness chosen to fly down here and confront them himself instead of waiting for wiser heads. Which of the two had murdered his son had yet to be worked out.

Don Luis was almost smiling by now. That there were holes in the fabric of his narration large enough to engulf *Industrias Cortéz* didn't trouble him. He had once told his illegitimate cousin Orejuela that the police were no fools. If the evidence was clear enough and public enough, it could not be ignored. But then, Orejuela had not been a Cortéz. He would see who his countrymen preferred to believe—the accusations of the *americanos* or the word of a Cortéz.

That he was abandoning the man who had been his most faithful and trusted associate troubled Luis Cortéz even less. Loyalty to one's staff made good business sense, but not at the cost of one's own skin. And a scapegoat was necessary. Let Vargas try to explain himself to the *americanos*. His past record and the convenient presence of the stolen *Fuerzas Armadas* helicopter would do little for his credibility.

But there was one last task for Vargas to finish. Easing back toward the jungle to put another tree trunk between himself and the landing strip, Don Luis raised the handheld radio to his mouth.

Sara didn't move a muscle. The starlight filtering down through the broken canopy was not enough to make out more than the long, black outline and the phosphorescent gleam of the creature's eyes. It was cat-shaped, though an oddly squat cat with a pendulous belly that dragged at the short grasses. But that was its only resemblance to a domestic animal. The lifted head was as large as a mastiff's, and the twin lights drifting toward her were at waist height. At any other time, Sara would have collapsed from sheer terror or run screaming for the nearest human presence. But tonight, earth's most vicious hunter was loose in the jungle, and this creature was of secondary concern. So she remained where she was, rigid, her eyes held by the almost hypnotic lure of the cat's unwavering stare.

It was the best thing she could have done. The jaguar had fed well that night and was simply curious about this invader of his hunting ground. The strange upright creature smelled like no flesh it had hunted before, but it was quiet and unalarming, and the jaguar was too lazy and belly-full to exert itself unnecessarily. Its rumbling growl softened to an inquisitive purr, and the big cat lowered its green gaze. Sara held her breath as the jaguar strolled majestically by, so close that the rank musk of its fur caught at her throat and she could feel the heat of its sleek, powerful muscles.

Then it was gone, a dark shape moving silently away until it was swallowed up by the rotting carcass of the fallen hardwood. Sara didn't move until the faint rustle of leaves had died away. She unclenched her hands, which were wet with perspiration. One hunter was gone. But where were the others? It was too much to hope she had lost them too.

"Por aquí!"

A beam of light caught Sara right in the face, dazzling her. She heard Julio Vargas's triumphant call, the crackle of twigs breaking under heavy boots, the low, eager whine of a dog. But all she could see was the brilliant kaleidoscope that danced before her eyes. She whirled from the light, heading blindly to where she knew the nearest edge of the clearing must be. But her muscles had tightened when she'd stopped running, and her flight was more of a stagger than a run. A thrashing of bodies followed the light through the under-growth, and panting that could only come from the slavering jaws of a Doberman. At any second, sharp teeth would tear at her clothing or an angry hand would grasp her shoulder.

She had no idea that the rules had changed until a sharp *crack* split the night. Though it could easily have been the sudden snap of a dry branch under a boot heel, Sara's reaction was instant, born of these last terrible hours. She dove for the ground as the bullet thwacked into the moss of a massive log beside her. Crisscrossing beams of light stabbed the darkness above her head, followed by a single long burst from an automatic weapon. By then, a frantic belly crawl had carried Sara the last few feet to cover, and she was scrambling around the base of a huge rosewood tree before the first bullets stitched their deadly pattern across its bark.

"Idiotas!" The furious exclamation belonged to Julio Vargas. "Can you not shoot one woman? It is your necks if she escapes."

A veritable explosion of gunfire followed. Spots of light bobbed wildly as the bombardment raked back and forth across the clearing with an abandon that seemed more likely to get one of their own men shot than her. To Sara, cowering with her face buried in her arms, it was like the inside of a thunderstorm. Apparently they were no longer concerned about taking her alive.

The adrenaline rush that accompanied that realization freed her stiffened muscles. As the barrage slackened, she scrambled to her knees. Thanks to the powerful searchlights that were probing the clearing, she could see just far enough ahead to guide her next move. When the searing beams bobbed away for a split second, she dove for a tangle of ferns, glancing incredulously over her shoulder as she came out on the other side into darkness. Why weren't they on her?

Then she heard an angry roar rising above a spatter of gunfire and the fearful shouts of men. They had stumbled across the jaguar! And the dogs were fully engaged, judging by the hisses and yelps and howls that were now erupting behind her. Another spat of gunfire drowned out the fight, but Sara's feet had already made their own grateful discovery: the hard earth of another game trail through the jungle.

Without regard for the battle behind her, Sara broke into a run.

And doubled over in agony.

She knew it had to be a stray bullet. The pain was too severe for anything else. Her hand clutched at her waist, her heart constricting in panic as it came away moist and sticky. Stumbling, she collapsed to her knees.

But already, as she remained doubled over, the pain was easing a little. When a closer probe revealed no injury, she felt as foolish as her panic would allow. The stickiness staining her fingers and mingling with the mud from her latest tumble had to be Nicky's blood, not her own!

Still, she didn't move on. An attempt to rise brought a fresh stab of pain to her side, and she could only watch helplessly as the first spot of light brushed across a tree trunk nearby and another caught the glitter of startled eyes on a branch far above her head.

But, incredibly, the searchlights drew no nearer. A sloth blinked sleepily at the beam that illumined it. Then the lights veered sharply away, and the accompanying noises receded. How could Vargas and his men possibly have missed her trail? She couldn't have been more than a dozen meters away from them. Unless . . .

Unless they no longer had the dogs! Had the big cat killed them or driven them off? It didn't matter which, though it wouldn't hurt her feelings to think that those vicious animals had been put permanently out of commission.

Sara remained where she was, kneeling in the middle of the jungle trail, until the cramp in her side had completely dissipated. Then she got slowly to her feet and began wandering down the game trail, her feet feeling out the slightly sunken edges. She couldn't have run, even if she'd tried. At intervals she stopped, making a slow turn to search out the blackness around her. But not once did she catch a glimpse of light or hear the sounds of men. The night had gone silent. The frogs had finished their chorus. Even the strident song of the cicadas had died away.

Sara had enough presence of mind to realize that this sense of lessened danger was only an illusion. Vargas and his men were not about to give up their search. And there were other perils out here in the dark. But as she further slowed her pace, a certain serenity that she would never have thought possible in such a situation eased through her mind and heart and tired muscles, so that the jungle night, with its muted sounds, seemed almost beautiful again. She'd prayed for a miracle once before, in just such desperate circumstances as these, not really believing it would come. Now she asked for nothing.

Lifting her face toward the heavens that lay somewhere above the dank blackness overhead, she whispered, "God—Father—I have no idea what you did back there. I have no idea what you're doing right now. But I'm really beginning to believe that you do!"

There was no warning. The path simply fell away.

Sara slid helplessly downward, the soft earth crumbling away under her feet as they scrabbled for purchase. She was gaining speed when a painfully solid object, a rock or a stump, jammed against her bare toes. Thrown off balance, Sara pitched forward, landing with a splash that drove the breath from her lungs. Coughing and spluttering, she sank downward. Fluid, warm and vile—too thick to be water, too thin to be mud—closed over her head.

✠

"*Por aquí!* Over here! I know I heard something!"

A dot of light sprang from the night as Sara broke the surface, gagging and choking. Distant cries answered the first shout before the light winked out far to her right. Treading to keep afloat, Sara groaned silently. She couldn't believe that Vargas and his men had managed to track her this far without her hearing or seeing them. No, it was just her misfortune that their search had veered into this area just in time to hear that noisy splash.

At least the one brief flash of light had shown Sara where she was. She'd fallen into a jungle swamp, like the one Nicolás had warned her about behind the hacienda. Just ahead, before the darkness closed in again, she'd glimpsed the gaunt silhouette of a wind-felled branch, whose length slanted upward, out of the water.

Sara kicked frantically in the direction of the branch, visions of venomous snakes and alligators lending strength to her efforts. The weight of her wet clothing made it a fight to keep her head above the surface, and twice more the muck closed over her head—awful, slimy stuff filled her mouth and nostrils as she fought her way upward.

She was sinking again, helplessly, when her flailing hand made contact with something solid. Digging her fingers into rotting bark, Sara struggled to pull herself up onto the slippery surface of the branch. Pausing only to wipe the muck from her eyes, she began crawling, hauling herself upward with the help of smaller boughs that had not yet rotted away, her teeth gritting as things she could only guess at crunched beneath her knees.

One foot had just touched solid ground when her fingers closed on a length that was smooth and as thick around as her wrist. At last, a dry vine! Taking a firmer grip, Sara began to pull herself up the muddy bank. But she had only managed the first step when her makeshift rope began to move under her hands. Sara recoiled with horror as it wriggled away from her grasp. Releasing the "vine" in a violent reflex, she clawed her way up the steep bank in one long, frantic scramble. Behind her, a disgruntled python recoiled its mistreated tail around the limb where it had curled up for the night and returned to its interrupted slumber.

Falling to her knees on the bank, Sara retched again and again, shock and the foul poison of the water she'd swallowed shaking her with long, uncontrollable spasms.

At last, when nothing remained in her stomach but the burning of acid, she raised her head. The night around her was again black and silent. Wiping a filthy hand across her mouth, she pushed back the sodden mass of her hair and staggered to her feet. She groped underfoot for the trail she had lost, then stopped. How many other swamps were waiting for her unsuspecting feet? Her latest blunder had underscored just how dangerous her blind wandering could be. Besides, any direction she took might head her straight into the arms of Julio Vargas and his men. Better to find a dry spot under some thicket to wait out the night. Morning would be soon enough to decide what to do next.

"I swear I heard something. It was over here! This way!"

Sheer desperation threw Sara to the ground as a beam of light swept across the place where she'd been standing. Before the beacon could return, she rose reluctantly to a crouch, tensing her exhausted muscles for another desperate dash into the night.

Will this never end?

As she lifted her head, she saw that running was no longer an option. Small points of light were now springing up on all sides. Spreading out to form a glittering semicircle among the trees, they began to converge in her direction.

Her only avenue of retreat was the swamp—an impossible option. She would have to hide. The jungle undergrowth that had given her so much trouble was now her only ally. The plant life she could make out dimly in the bobbing dots of light was broad-leafed and thick. Closing her mind to thoughts of snakes and oversized insects, she worked her way backward inch by inch, careful not to break so much as a leaf or twig as the tangle behind her swallowed her up. She shuddered as a whiplike length brushed dry and smooth across her face. Fighting back a scream that would have spelled sure doom, she forced her trembling fingers to investigate. This time it was a real vine. She inched back another foot. Then two. If they still had the dogs, this wasn't going to work. But without them, she had a chance.

An army boot crashed only inches away. Sara's breath remained in her lungs as a powerful beam played over the broad, palmlike fronds that screened her hiding place. The floodlight hovered for a moment, then moved slowly on and did not return. The heavy footsteps crunched noisily away. Her breath emerged soundlessly between her teeth. It had worked! She had only to stay here until the searchers passed on, then slip again into the night. She eased noiselessly into a more comfortable position and prepared to wait.

Sara wasn't sure when she first realized she was not alone. There was no sound but the pounding of her own heartbeat in her ears, and even if she'd dared to turn her head, it was too pitchblack to see anything. But, somehow, she could sense another presence close by. She could smell a faint musk that was not her own fear or sweat; she could feel the animal warmth of another body crouched motionless under the fronds that concealed her from her enemies. Something— *someone?*—was in that dark hiding place with her!

Sara's muscles quivered with the effort to hold them still, her eyes wide, like a frightened fawn, against the dark. The seconds ticked on, and still there was no sound or movement from the unseen presence beside her. A terror stronger than anything she had felt in all that terrible night seized her. If it was one of the hunters, why wasn't he shouting in triumph? Was he toying with her? Like a cat with its prey?

Her breath came through her mouth, shallow and quick. The crashing of boots continued in the surrounding jungle, punctuated by the guttural shouts and curses of impatient and angry men.

Don't move, Sara! Maybe it hasn't seen you! But even as she gave herself the order, she knew she was going to crack. She couldn't stay alone in the dark with this nightmare. A twig snapped as her leg shifted in an involuntary spasm. A beam of light swept back in her direction.

"*Por aquí!* Over here!"

It was too much! No longer caring if she was seen, Sara pushed herself to her hands and knees. She would make a run for it, lose herself again in the jungle. She could make it past that searching beam. She knew she could!

At that very instant, she sensed movement behind her. Hard, forceful fingers bit into her cheeks, cutting the scream in her throat. She couldn't breathe! Tearing a hand loose from the steel arms that held her, she struck her assailant in the face. But horror made her drop her fist, for there was no face there, only a hard, knobby mass! Then a brutal strength pinioned her arms and legs to the ground, and a heavy body pressed her down into the mud.

The searchlights were very close now. Her assailant rolled suddenly away, offering Sara one last chance to attempt a desperate escape. But there was no fight left in her. Beyond caring now, beyond even terror, Sara lay inert, facedown in the mud, as the hunt swept over her.

Chapter Thirty-Three

Sara."

The name was only a breath of sound, too low to tell if it was male or female or even human. But hard hands were turning her over now, and the breath of sound came again. "Sara, it's me! Doug."

Doug. It couldn't be! Doug Bradford was far away and wasn't coming. Not in time for her, anyway. She'd known and accepted that for an eternity now. Groping in the dark, Sara felt the texture of cloth and something underneath that was too hard and unyielding to be flesh. But as her hand traveled tentatively upward, she traced out the firm line of an unshaven jaw and a mouth that was very human. The hard, knobby mass above resolved itself into some kind of helmet.

"Doug! Oh, Doug, I thought you weren't coming! I . . . I thought I was dead!"

A warm hand clamped lightly again over her mouth, and she realized that her cry had risen well above a whisper. Then Doug's hand left her mouth, and his strong arms pulled her close. Sara collapsed against the solid security of his body. She had *known* that death was with her in that thicket, and the release from terror was so sudden that she felt more dizziness and nausea than relief. She couldn't cry—mustn't make a single sound—and she shook with her efforts to remain silent. Doug held her tightly, stroking the dank mass of her hair in wordless comfort. His clothing smelled of sweat and exertion, but it was the most wonderful scent in the world, and she burrowed her head against the hard shield he was wearing underneath his shirt until her tremors gradually eased enough for her to pull away in embarrassment.

Doug released her immediately. His mouth was close to her ear, and his whisper rose to a timbre she could recognize as his voice. "They should be well gone by now. Let's go."

She wouldn't have known that he'd left her side if she hadn't felt the loss of his body warmth. A moment later, his low voice came back. "It's all clear out here."

An invisible hand reached down out of the dark to help her to her feet. Behind her she heard the release of air through someone's nostrils and the movement of a boot in the undergrowth.

"Don't be afraid," Doug's quiet voice reassured her. "It's just one of my men, Ibañez. He'll follow right behind you." Without releasing her hand, Doug added even more quietly, "Look up, Sara."

Sara tilted her head back to see two small strips of light floating in the darkness just above her head. They glowed with the unearthly green of phosphorescence, and the angle at which they were set brought to mind the long ears of a donkey or mule or some such creature.

"You see those two rabbit ears? They're right on the back of my hat here. You just keep your eyes on those, and you won't be able to lose me, okay? Now let's move out before someone decides to check back in this direction."

Sara was grateful for his hand holding hers as he moved off into the blackness, not hesitantly or groping or tripping as she had done, but as confidently as though he could see exactly where he was stepping. The rustle of her passage was loud in her ears compared to Doug's silent stealth. The "rabbit ears" floated this way and that in front of her, disappearing altogether at times as Doug turned his head from one side to the other. She could no longer hear the faintest whisper of sound from Ibañez, who was, presumably, somewhere behind her. Her muscles protested as she stretched them to keep up with Doug's impossibly long strides. The damp clinging of her clothes didn't help.

But the hike didn't last long.

No more than five minutes had passed before Sara emerged from an overhanging tangle of branches and felt mowed grass under her feet. She gaped in astonishment. Just a few meters ahead of her was the pale gleam of gravel and, off to her left, the black shapes of two small planes. The moon had risen high overhead during her desperate flight, giving gentle illumination to a long stretch of lawn, beyond which flickered the bluish-white cast of fluorescent lights. After all her running and dodging and hiding, she'd ended up right back where she'd started! The swamp she had fallen into had to be the very one that stretched away from the back of the hacienda.

Sara could now make out the broad-shouldered figure at her side. Some sort of futuristic goggles covered his eyes, and the hand that wasn't firmly gripping hers held the long shape of a weapon.

Now that she could walk without stumbling, she tugged her hand self-consciously from his grip. He let her go, using his free hand to flip the goggles up onto his forehead.

Other shapes began emerging from the woods. Two—three—no, four others! She hadn't heard even a rustle of their approach!

Doug's lack of concern at their appearance reassured her, but she found herself instinctively stepping behind the solidity of his rangy frame as they drifted closer.

Each man carried a weapon, and two of them appeared to be wearing the same type of goggles as Doug.

"Rocky, I'm going to take Sara right on up to the house," Doug said quietly to one of the newcomers, who was a good head taller than his companions. "If you'd give the perimeter another good check. . . . Then go ahead and fall back to the veranda."

Doug's hand was at Sara's back, urging her forward toward the airstrip when he turned back. "Oh, and Ibañez, good work! And thanks!"

Sara couldn't see what Doug was removing from his belt, but she heard the slosh of water as he tossed it to a shadowy form behind her. There was a low laugh as the man caught the toss. Then, as Doug signaled for Sara to accompany him, the others scattered in a quick lope along the perimeter of the hacienda. Sara hung back. "Doug, I need to tell you! There's other people up there at the house. A lot more than you have here. And I think they might have guns too!"

"Don't worry about it, Sara." If Doug felt any amusement at Sara telling him how to do his job, it didn't show in his voice. "It's all taken care of. We've got the place secured."

Sara had no idea what he meant by that, or who, exactly, this "we" entailed. But she didn't need to. Doug did, and she'd learned by now that she could trust his handling of any situation. She stopped worrying and trudged on beside him, her muscles relaxing to lassitude now that there was no need for adrenaline to drive them. Her feet gradually slowed from the pace she'd maintained at his heels in the woods.

Doug matched her pace, but didn't push her. As they crossed the airstrip, Sara's eyes went instinctively to the gravel, searching for a dark stain. But they had come out of the jungle well down the runway from where she'd gone in, and as her feet touched the grass on the other side, a sigh of release suddenly went out of her. Looking up at Doug's broad shoulders and the blurred shadow of his face, she said simply, "I still can't believe you came! I was sure they had me! I . . . I thought I was dead! How did you ever find me in time?" A shiver went through her, and Doug paused in midstride to look at her.

"I'm not so sure myself," he said quietly, "except there had to be a whole lot more than me controlling this mission! I'm only sorry we didn't make it sooner, and that you had to go through this kind of trauma first. I'm going to have a hard time forgiving myself for that." At Sara's sound of protest, he cleared his throat. "Anyway, you've probably guessed that it was the SatTrack that led us to the hacienda. We must have hit the place just as you were getting away. Our reception was a bit of a surprise—we were expecting considerably more resistance than we got. Then we found your knapsack."

His voice was calm and matter-of-fact, betraying nothing of his own emotions at the time. "Once we found out you were no longer on the property, we rounded up the workers and asked what happened. It didn't take long to learn that you'd escaped and that Julio Vargas and his men were out after you.

"Finding you wasn't so difficult. We've got three pairs of these night-vision goggles here, and we'd been told Vargas was tracking you with the dogs. So we just went after him and let him lead us to you. We knew where you'd gone into the woods. From there, it was just a matter of heading out until someone spotted a light, then coming back together to trail the bunch. That was easy enough, since we could see in the dark and they couldn't—especially with the kind of racket they were making.

"We were just coming up on Vargas when we heard all the fireworks." Doug's voice tightened. "We were afraid . . . well, anyway, we finally gathered from all the shouting that you'd gotten away. Then we found out they'd lost the dogs. Without them, we knew there wasn't a chance in a North Pole blizzard that anyone was going to track you down tonight. But I—we—figured that if we couldn't find you, we could at least stick around in case Vargas and his men happened to stumble over you in the dark. Ibañez and I were between them and the swamp when we heard you. Actually, it was Ibañez who heard you first. I've got to admit I'd have gone right on by, and I even had the NVG. That guy's got ears like a bat! I guess you know the rest."

He'd had the delicacy, Sara noted, not to mention just *what* they'd heard. She peered up at Doug's face in the moonlit shadows. "So, are you just going to leave them out there? Don't you have to . . . arrest them or something?"

"Are you kidding?" The shake of Doug's head was emphatic.

"With the kind of ammo that bunch is carrying? Oh, sure, we could take them, but they're not worth putting my guys in the line of fire. Besides, there's no need. Sooner or later, they're going to get tired of wandering around in circles and head back this way. It's pretty clear that Vargas hasn't figured out yet that his security's been breached, and we aim to keep it that way. When they walk in, we'll pick them up, plain and simple. And if they don't come back—"

Sara interpreted his shrug with an involuntary shudder. Thousands of square kilometers of jungle out there, and she'd already encountered some of its pitfalls. They'd take jail if they were smart!

Doug and Sara had reached the veranda now, and as he gave her a hand up, the dark shadow of his silhouette shifted suddenly to full color under the fluorescent lights outside the house. Sara had never seen him in anything but civilian clothing, and she stopped in her tracks to stare up at him uncertainly. With a sense of shock she took in the camouflage fatigues, the green and black stripes that had blurred his face, and the casual fit of the ugly weapon over his shoulder. He looked bigger than she remembered and more formidable than the man who had told her humorous anecdotes in the Land Rover, and who had listened patiently to her hurts and complaints around a campfire.

And then she noticed that he was looking down at her with the same measure of shock. He took a step backward, his eyes hardening as they raked over her, his mouth thinning to a straight line. "Sara, are you all right? Were you hurt?"

Following his eyes downward, Sara saw herself for the first time since her ordeal. The unmistakable reddish-brown of blood that still splotched her T-shirt under the stains of mud and swamp water. The algae and filth that coated the mat of hair falling over her shoulder. The long scratches on her arms, made by thorns, that burned where the swamp muck had penetrated. And the crackle of drying mud and slime that was tightening the skin of her face.

For an instant it seemed a replay of another scene outside the doors of a ballroom a month ago, and she recoiled under his hard gaze. But it wasn't the same. Concern, not anger, was sharpening his tone and thinning his mouth, and with that realization, she lost her uncertainty, and the man in front of her was no longer a stranger.

"I'm okay, Doug; really," she said softly. "The blood—it isn't mine. It's—" Sara looked away, swallowing a sudden lump in her throat, before she went on with difficulty. "Do . . . do you know about Nicky?"

"Yes, I know." Doug added nothing to the grim statement, and though Sara wanted to ask more, she didn't. Striding across the veranda, Doug pushed open a door. "Come on, Sara, let's get you inside. At the least, we can get you a shower, maybe even scrape up some clean clothes." His mouth twisted wryly as he motioned for her to precede him. "Picking you up in this condition seems to be turning into a habit!"

"I know. I was just thinking that some things seem to happen over and over. . . ." Sara trailed off as she saw that they were back in her father-in-law's office. Her eyes went against her will to the handsome face staring down from the wall, and she flinched under the icy glare. Seeing her recoil, Doug called himself something rude under his breath and herded her quickly across the room.

It really was silly, but Sara could feel the tension leave her as the door shut between her and the painting. She glanced around. There had been major changes in the old ballroom since she'd last passed through. The long tables were abandoned, the pottery wheel stilled. The laborers and white-coated chemists were huddled in a group against the boarded-up windows, sullenly eyeing the pair of automatic rifles trained on them.

And everywhere were men in olive-and-brown-splotched army clothing. Sara's eyes widened as she counted the soldiers. There must have been a dozen just in this room! And that didn't include the men who had emerged from the jungle with her and Doug. Who were these men, and where could they have all come from?

With growing rage, Don Luis watched as Sara and the search party emerged from the woods and made their way across the hacienda grounds to the house. So Vargas had botched even that simple task! And that changed everything again! Don Luis had figured to be long gone from here by now, but it hadn't proved as simple to get to the plane as he'd anticipated. On the heels of the *americanos'* discovery of his son's body had come lights and a squad of soldiers who had combed the area all the way to the planes and back, even taking pictures with their bright lights held high. As he was absorbing that setback, another force had arrived, heading into the woods so silently that Don Luis had barely managed to scuttle under the cover of a thicket before they flitted past.

He'd been forced to cower in that humiliating position until the lights finally moved away from the airstrip. Emerging at last, he'd felt the snags of thorns in the expensive Armani shirt and slacks he'd imported from Miami and found his son's body gone from its place. But he could not leave yet. He had to be sure that the *americanos* had really left the area unguarded.

Then, just as he'd begun to make his move, the soldiers from the jungle had reappeared as silently as they'd come, and with them was the smaller, slimmer, unmistakable shape of a woman, with hair too pale in the moonlight to be black. Again he'd been forced to wait and watch, fuming, while his hated daughter-in-law receded forever from his grasp and the *americanos*—and their toadying allies among his own countrymen—prowled around his property with that absurd caution of theirs, even intruding a few meters into the woods so that he was forced to cower again in his thicket.

Now at last they were gone, retreating back to their base—*his* house. And this time he would go, too, without further hesitation, lest they choose to snoop around again. But go where? With the girl dead, there would have been no one to gainsay his version of the story, whatever their suspicions might have been. Now, with all that had been found here today and the girl still alive to spill her testimony into their eager ears, he had no hope that the *americanos* would ever again listen to him. And if their State Department spoke, the Bolivian government would have to listen. Was his influence strong enough to stand against all the evidence they could throw against him? Many of his countrymen would indeed believe it was all a lie, a fabrication of the *gringos*, if he, Luis Cortéz Velásquez de Salazar, stood up and declared it to be so. Or at least they would have the courtesy to pretend that they did.

But would there be enough of those who counted? Or would his compatriots give in to the demands of politics and abandon him as he himself had abandoned others? The thought was one he did not want to consider, but perhaps the time had come for him to do what others of his countrymen had been forced to do. Disappear. To leave the country of his birth forever. After all, the money would still be there. Enough, anyway, in Swiss bank accounts and Panama and Libya.

The prospect of exile filled Don Luis with a murderous fury. It would not be just a home and a business that he would be giving up. Those could be bought anywhere. It was the respect and honor and position that his name and his family connections gave him here and nowhere else. Still, if there was one reason that the Cortezes had survived when other families had fallen, it was because they had always known when to give up and move on—all the way back to the first Bolivian Cortéz, who had left his homeland of Spain under his own set of clouded circumstances. Luis Cortéz had wrested triumph from defeat before; he could do it again. In time, it might even be possible to bring his family, too. The *gringos* would not touch them. Their judicial system was soft that way. Maybe they would even return to the homeland none of them had ever known.

But first, the plane.

The DC-3 was only a few meters ahead of him now. Don Luis stepped out onto the gravel of the airstrip. It left him in full view of the moon floating overhead, but there was no one close enough to see him. He circled the nose of the plane. His hand was on the door. It swung open. He set his foot to the step.

Too late, he saw a pale shadow reflected against the white fuselage of the plane. He heard a voice from behind him, in foreign-accented Spanish. "You going somewhere?"

As Doug urged Sara forward past the pottery workshop, she saw one of the men in camouflage fatigues training a camera on a statuette of Viracocha, the Inca sun god. Another was videotaping a market scale heaped high with cocaine. He lowered the camera as they approached. Sara recognized him even through the makeup. It was the young DEA agent she'd seen with Doug at the embassy security seminar. His black eyes narrowed just a fraction as he took in her bedraggled appearance.

"Mrs. Cortéz. I'm glad to see that Doug found you. He's been a little worried." Ramon met Doug's sardonic expression with an impish grin. He was clearly enjoying himself. "Hey, Doug, Mike wants to see you when you have a minute. He's in checking out that com gear. Would you believe Cortéz was tapping into FELCN headquarters? And he had a cell phone tap on half our list, not to mention a good number we don't have a thing on. Their tech says that's how they found out about those two loads they hijacked. Oh, and another thing. Mike says half the stuff they got in there is classified gear donated by the Israelis and our own government to Bolivian army intelligence. There's going to be some heads rolling!"

Sara listened with dawning understanding as the two men exchanged information. When Ramon had turned his camera lens back on the silvery mound in the scale, she asked incredulously, "Doug, all these men—they're DEA, aren't they? I . . . I didn't think your boss would let them come! Does that mean he believes me now? That they know it was the Cortezes and not me?"

"Well, let's just say he was prepared to give me—you—the benefit of the doubt," Doug said dryly, steering Sara around a rack of boutique clothing that had spilled over on its side between them and the smashed-in doors leading out into the foyer. Kicking aside a pile of garments, he glanced around at the bustle of activity with grim satisfaction. "I don't think we're going to have any problem convincing anyone after today!"

His swift scan reached a point near the main entrance into the ballroom, and his satisfaction suddenly fled, leaving only grimness. He shifted quickly to block Sara's view. "Uh, . . . Sara . . ."

But Sara had already seen it. One of the long tables had been cleared off and placed against the wall near the double doors. Laid out on the table was a sheet-covered form. Moving like a sleepwalker, Sara left Doug's side. He caught at her arm. "No, Sara. Don't look."

Doug saw her amber eyes darken with both anguish and resolution as she shook her head. "I have to, Doug. Let me go."

Folding back the sheet, Sara looked down at her husband's placid face. Someone had closed his eyes and sponged away the blood, and there was no sign of the damage that she knew was concealed by the rest of the sheet. It was a beautiful face, chiseled and remote and very young in its repose, and it held a peace that had never been there in life, the restlessness and petulance and self-indulgence somehow smoothed away. Sara stood looking down until a droplet of water splashed hot against the cold, pale flesh. Then, as she felt Doug's arm go around her shoulder, she turned away to release her tears against his chest.

Doug's arm tightened around her. "Sara, he was a criminal," he said gently. "You didn't have any choice. It wasn't your fault."

Sara's head turned from one side to the other against the hardness of the Kevlar vest. "It *was* my fault! He died to save me! I know he was a criminal, but he gave his life to save mine! He didn't have to, but he did!"

"Sara, what are you saying?" Doug released her abruptly, his hands sliding down to grip her arms and ease her away from him. "Sara, you'd better tell me what happened out there," he said urgently. "According to the workers, *you* shot Nicolás while you were trying to escape."

"And you're telling me you believed them? They weren't even there! How was I supposed to shoot anyone without a gun?" Sara pulled herself as far away from him as she could, her body stiffening with anger under his grip. "Can't you recognize another one of my father-in-law's stories when you hear it? *He* shot Nicolás, trying to hit me!"

Doug gave Sara a gentle shake. "Hey, Sara, I believe you, okay? We're not trying to accuse you of anything."

Under his steady gaze, the stiffness left Sara's body along with her anger. "I . . . I'm sorry. It's just—"

"I know. You've suffered from too many of Luis Cortéz's fabrications. But you don't need to be afraid anymore, Sara. After today, Cortéz will never be able to touch you again. I can promise you that! Speaking of him, do you have any idea where he is? We've searched the place twice and still haven't turned up as much as a hair."

The Motorola at Doug's belt crackled before Sara could respond. Doug let go of her to grab the radio. "Yes?"

"Doug, this is Carlos. I think you might want to hop down here. We've got a situation brewing."

"What kind of a situation? Carlos? Carlos!" There was no answer to Doug's question, just the crackle of static. "Carlos, are you still there? Come in, Carlos!"

Doug glanced across the ballroom, where Ramon was still bent over the viewfinder of the camcorder. "Ramon, lose the camera! I'm going to need you. Sounds like we got a problem down by the planes."

As Ramon shoved the camcorder into the hands of the nearest soldier, Doug raised the Motorola again to his mouth. "Carlos, what is going on down there? Come in?"

The hand-radio crackled to life. "Carlos here, Doug. Everything's under control. Repeat. Everything's under control. I think I've just resolved that little situation."

Doug's breath left him slowly. "Report. What's going on?"

"Well, some guy came in from the woods, and he was sneaking around the planes. Though if he'd been any noisier about it, you could have heard him from up there! Anyway, it was clear the guy was trying to make a break for it, and I'm betting he's a pilot, too, because he headed straight for the cockpit of the DC-3 and tried to climb in. Who he is, I haven't a clue. But he ain't no soldier and he sure ain't no *campesino*. Not unless they've started wearing ties and sports jackets out in the coca patch."

Startled, Sara looked up at Doug. "Don Luis," she said with conviction.

Doug broke in impatiently. "Carlos, would you just spit it out? What is the situation now? Where is the suspect?"

"I collared him," Carlos summed up simply. "He's standing in front of me right now, simmering like a Texas longhorn in mating season. He ain't said a word yet, but I took an Uzi off of him. Been fired recently, too."

"That must be the gun that took out Cortéz junior," Doug answered. "Okay, Carlos, start the suspect up to the house. We'll sort it out here. I'll send Rocky and Ibañez down to take over your watch. Ramon, can you give me a hand?"

Finishing his instructions, Doug turned to Sara and said gently, "Sara, your father-in-law is on his way up, and I don't think you're going to want to be here. Why don't I have one of the men take you to where you can clean up and change. I'm told your bag turned up in one of the storerooms."

"No!" Her vehement response drew a look of surprise from Doug. Sara shook her head emphatically. "No, I'm not running away." Walking over to the table, Sara looked down again at the lifeless form of her husband. "My father-in-law did this."

She wasn't just speaking of Nicolás's violent death that the sheet hid mercifully from her view, but the whole of that careless, merry young life that her father-in-law had warped with his arrogance and greed so that perhaps the only truly unselfish thing Nicholás ever did was that impulsive act that saved Sara's life.

He looked so peaceful now! What had he been thinking when he'd spent his dying words asking about the thief on the cross? She would never know, but she could hope that he'd somehow made his own peace with God before it was too late.

Gently, she pulled the sheet back into place. When she turned around to face the two agents, the tears and anguish were gone, and her face was set like flint. "Don Luis did this," she repeated flatly. "I want to see him."

Doug looked down at her for a long moment, then glanced over at Ramon. At the other agent's shrug, he nodded abruptly. "Fine! Just stay behind me, and do what you're told."

✠

The door to his office was standing wide open, the light inside laying a bright rectangle across the tiles, as Don Luis was herded onto the veranda. But the man waiting just outside was not one of his own guards, despite the similarity of uniforms. Don Luis wouldn't have recognized the face under the stripes of makeup were it not for the gray eyes, cool and watchful.

"Bradford!" he hissed the word as though it were an obscenity. He might have known! So the girl *had* gotten to him despite all those reassuring reports to the contrary. Heads would roll for this! Or maybe they wouldn't.

The taste in Don Luis's mouth was unfamiliar and bitter as his gaze swept past Bradford and settled on another of the DEA stooges—though this one might even be one of his own countrymen, from his appearance. And standing a safe distance behind the two men, as filthy and bedraggled as if she had met the death she deserved out there in the jungle, was the author of his defeat. His daughter-in-law. Don Luis glanced longingly at the Uzi automatic pistol thrust carelessly into his captor's belt, then at the M-16s cradled easily across three pairs of arms. But the failure he could taste in his mouth was not evident in his arrogant stride as he stepped onto the veranda.

"So—you have found my fugitive daughter-in-law. Good! I do not know what she has been telling you, but I fear that you are laboring under a misunderstanding. To my regret, I had no conception before today of what this woman and my associate *Coronel* Vargas have been doing here. When I discovered their betrayal, I was fortunate enough to escape. I was attempting to leave, to bring the law, when your agent found me. Of course, had I known that it was you and your men from whom I have been hiding myself, and not more of Vargas's hired assassins . . ."

His shrug under the alpaca broadcloth was elegant and persuasive. "But now that you are here, I will with relief leave the arrest of this woman and her accomplices in your hands. You will have discovered that they killed my son, who was foolish enough to confront his wife alone. He never could believe that she would be willing to hurt him, even after young Orejuela. And he has paid for that trust!"

The bitterness in his voice was genuine, and the light of the veranda captured the ice-blue glitter of his eyes, narrowed with pain as well as fury and contempt, as they raked across Sara's unkempt appearance. Sara didn't even try to defend herself against his accusations. She'd had no clear idea of what she planned to do upon confronting her father-in-law. Scream at him, maybe. Force him to take back the lies he'd told about her. Somehow pierce through that imperturbable shell of his until he saw himself as she did—cruel and wicked and utterly contemptible.

Now she saw that she didn't need to do anything. Don Luis was finding his own punishment without her help. He'd lost his only son—perhaps the person he cared most for in all the world. And now everything else was falling away too. The business empire and wealth he had sacrificed all honor to obtain. The prestige and position that was his by birth and accomplishment. His very freedom. And to Luis Cortéz Velásquez de Salazar, prison was going to be far more galling than to any ordinary criminal. Nothing she could do or say would punish him more.

So she said nothing, only lifting her chin to meet his contemptuous gaze without flinching. It was Doug who interrupted the smooth recital. "It's not going to wash, Cortéz," he said dryly. "We know just how Nicolás died."

"Yeah, and we've seen what you've been up to inside the house." Ramon's narrow features were wearing their wolfish look. "We've got you cold, Cortéz. Not even you are going to walk away from this one!"

Don Luis looked from one unyielding profile to the other and chose to change his tactics. "Come, *caballeros,* this is not necessary. Let us be reasonable. Every man has his price. You have only to name yours. I know the paltry sums with which your government rewards you for this thankless job. What is it that will satisfy you? One million? Two? For each of you, of course."

The flick of his fingers included Carlos, but ignored Sara. "You may have the glory of your arrests. You may keep this place for your 'evidence.' There is more than enough here to satisfy your superiors. I ask only that you turn your back for a few moments. You arrived a moment too late. I had already escaped. In return for so little, you will never have to soil your hands with this . . ."—for just an instant, he let contempt slip into the smoothness of his tone—"this *profession* again. Come, gentlemen, let me go!"

His cold eyes swept over the three agents—arrogant, confident, his command carrying all the authority of a man who'd never had to repeat an order. Doug didn't even dignify the offer with an answer. Ramon said it for the rest of them.

"All men aren't for sale, Cortéz! As for your filthy dough, you know just where you can stuff it!" Ramon's indignation took on a mock-injured tone. "And whose income are you calling paltry here? There isn't a *mano* in my barrio who's done better! Other than a few lowlifes like you. And I can tell you where they're spending their money now. Right where you're going to be spending yours for the next few years!"

Doug slung his M-16 back over his shoulder and stepped away from the door. "Let's get this over with, Cortéz. I'm sure you know the routine. Carlos, take him on in."

Don Luis knew dismissal when he heard it. He'd delivered it often enough himself. This could not be! He was a Cortéz. It was his place to be pronouncing the fate of others with such calmness and finality. For him, there had always been a way out. It was the way the world ran, the way it was meant to be! His mind was seething even as he raised his hands wide in surrender.

"Very well, gentlemen. If you will not profit from our association—"

His fury and desperation gave Don Luis a swiftness and strength that caught the DEA agents off guard. Lunging sideways and back, he hit Carlos with the force of an American football tackle. The impetus of the attack carried both men over the edge of the veranda.

Carlos took the impact of the landing, his breath going out of him with an audible groan, the M-16 flying out of his hands to land out of reach across the grass. Don Luis grabbed at the Uzi in the agent's belt. He had it out. Rising to a crouch, he began to turn, his finger tightening on the trigger.

"Drop that gun and get your hands on your head, or I swear I'll blow it off!"

Don Luis froze, the Uzi still no higher than his hip. His face a mask of hate and fury, he turned his head in the direction of the sharp order. Only a meter away, the cold metal barrel of an M-16 shifted to center more exactly on the lapel of his alpaca sports jacket. Ramon's steely black eyes above the barrel were no less cold.

Doug Bradford had pushed Sara to the floor, but he was already rolling back to his feet, his M-16 no longer over his shoulder but in his hands. "You heard him! Drop that gun!"

Don Luis glanced to his right, where Carlos was sitting up now. The agent was still winded, but his hand held a Glock-17, rock steady.

Don Luis raised his hands slowly, but he did not release the Uzi. He had played his last card, and he knew there would be no more. There was only one thing left for a man of honor to do. He drew upon all the hauteur of his Cortéz ancestry as he glared coldly across at Doug Bradford. "I am Luis Cortéz Velásquez de Salazar. Can you envision me in Chonchocorro?"

Tightening his grip on the Uzi, he brought it down, leveling on Sara, who was just getting to her feet behind Doug. Maybe he'd even make it before—

Carlos shot him through the heart.

On the veranda, Doug turned Sara's face into his shoulder as the single cry of agony died away. Down on the grass, Carlos knelt over the body. Looking up, he shook his head. "He's gone!" The agent's eyes were stricken with shock and his face was ashen beneath the colorful camouflage. "I didn't want to kill him, Doug! Why didn't he just drop the gun?"

Doug walked over and gripped Carlos hard by the shoulder. "It wasn't your fault, Carlos. Cortéz knew just what he was doing. He wanted to die."

EPILOGUE

They're releasing the girl to travel. She's out of here tonight," Grant Major informed Doug with a certain relish. "That's got to be some kind of record, although it's easy to see why they're in such a hurry. This whole thing's been a real embarrassment. That the *gringa* turns out to be innocent and one of the president's own buddies is guilty as sin doesn't exactly make great headlines. I figure they're hoping that with her gone, the story will peter out."

Grant paused, drumming his fingers against the blotter on his desk before he went on, "That goes for you too, Douglas, I'm afraid. You did a fantastic job out there. I know it, and so do they. But Cortéz had a lot of friends in high places. And for all the public hoopla about the dent this has put in the *narcotráfico,* there are those who are downright unhappy about the way this whole thing has turned out. Unhappy enough that someone just might decide to take a potshot at the man who brought Cortéz down. At least that's the excuse. They want you out of the country. For your own protection, they say."

The RAC raised a warning hand before Doug could argue. "I've got to tell you, Doug, upstairs agrees with them. I'm going to miss you—you're the best man I've got—but the fact is, you're just too high profile to be effective in this country any longer. I'd sure like to know who splashed your involvement all over the press. Vargas, probably. He practically foams at the mouth every time he mentions your name. Yours and the girl's. But that doesn't matter now. You're out of here. Tonight. We'll have your stuff packed up and shipped after you."

Doug's furious protest was to no avail.

"I'm sorry, Doug, but it's already settled! It won't be so bad. Your term was almost up here anyway. This is just anticipating things by a few months. And with the commendations you're getting out of all this, you can just about have your pick of open slots. Stateside, that is. You won't be going back overseas for a couple of years. You know the rules! In the meantime, how long has it been since you've had a vacation? Take a month off. Take two!"

Doug shook his head and started for the door. Grant stopped him on his way out. "By the way, the Bolivian president is awarding you a medal for your 'distinguished years of service here,' as he puts it. The *Emblema de Oro*—the Gold Emblem—no less. Of course you won't be able to pick it up in person, but it'll look great on your record."

"Sure, give him my thanks!" Doug replied sardonically as he walked out the door.

✠

"Emma's last checkup was absolutely clear. Of course, the doctor says she can't do any heavy lifting. And the tennis will have to wait a little longer. But she's back to just about everything else she was doing before the surgery. It does help that the boys are in school all day. They're such adorable little scamps. It was hard to leave, thinking how big they'll be next time we see them. But Sam said it was time we got back to Bolivia."

The shrill ringing of the phone broke into Laura Histed's recital. "If you'll excuse me, Sara, I'll be just a minute."

Hurrying across the wide landing at the top of the stairs, Laura reached for the phone on the wall. "Histed residence. . . . Why, yes, she's right here!"

Sara bolted straight up on the sofa. "Is it Doug?"

Laura shook her head even as she was saying into the phone, "Yes, . . . great. . . . Yes, that's wonderful. . . . Yes, of course I'll tell her!"

Hanging up, she turned excitedly to Sara. "That was the American consul. The charges against you have been dropped. You're free to leave the country. And if that isn't some kind of record, I don't know what is!" Her narrow-bridged nose was almost quivering with delight as she bustled back to Sara's side. "And that isn't all! The consul has your tickets—you're leaving tonight! She's sending someone to drop them by. You'll be on LAB as far as Miami. Then you'll have a voucher from the State Department to book a flight anywhere you want to go within the United States. Sara, you're going home!"

Going home!

Sara stared without really seeing across the landing to where an unframed painting hung on the wall above the staircase. It was a scene from northern Bolivia—a river with a canoe drawn up onto the bank, and a *pahuichi* surrounded by the bright green foliage of the jungle. The days since she'd left behind those same vine-choked trees had been a blur of debriefings and out-and-out interrogations—conducted by the DEA, the State Department, the FELCN, and, it had seemed, every branch of Bolivian law enforcement.

Getting the charges against her reversed might have been more complicated had it not been for Julio Vargas. When the Cortéz security chief discovered—after leading his men back to the hacienda, where they were immediately placed under arrest by the FELCN commander—that Don Luis had tried to set him up to take a fall, and with the indisputable evidence against him represented by the stolen Huey, he decided to talk.

And he'd had a lot to say. He revealed the existence and whereabouts of a financial ledger that the accounting department of Industrias Cortéz had never seen, and some computer files that Don Luis would certainly have destroyed if he'd made it back to Santa Cruz. The result had been dozens of additional arrests, both inside the borders of Bolivia and in several of the overseas shipping ports that handled Cortéz products.

Yes, things had moved quickly. Still, in this country, where justice held that you were guilty until proven innocent, the dismissal of charges was a bureaucratic process that could have taken months. Sara couldn't imagine what kind of strings the State Department must have pulled to have accomplished her release in less than a week!

"What is it, Sara?" Laura's pleasant features reflected her concern as Sara brought her attention back to her hostess. "I thought you'd be excited about the news. Aren't you happy to be going home?"

Sara shifted her legs restlessly. "Yes, of course, I'm happy. It's just—"

"Oh, Sara, I'm sorry! How could I be forgetting?" Dropping down on the sofa beside Sara, Laura reached over to pat Sara's knee. "I know how difficult this all must be for you! No—that isn't true! I have *no* idea how difficult it's been or what you've gone through these last weeks. I can't even imagine it! But I know it has to have been terrible! Losing your husband in such a way, and when you were so happy! Sam and I felt so bad when we got back from England to find out that you were missing and being accused of that boy's murder. Not that we ever believed it, even before Doug called and told us the truth. Still, we've been in this country long enough to know how impossible it is to make a stand against a family like the Cortezes."

Laura gave Sara's knee another comforting pat. "But it's all over now, dearie, and it really has turned out so wonderfully well that it does seem like a miracle! For all our praying, we never guessed the Lord would work it out like this. 'Oh ye of little faith,' I guess you could call us, like the Bible says. And though it might seem hard to believe now, Sara dear, someday you'll see that this won't hurt quite so bad as it does today. Oh, excuse me! There goes the doorbell again. I tell you, I'm ready to unplug that thing—and the telephone too! I just hope it's not another reporter."

As Laura trotted down the stairs, Sara got up from the sofa and wandered over to the landing's lone window. It overlooked the brick wall that ran around the Histed's simple home, giving a clear view of the broken glass imbedded on top and the unpaved alley beyond. A scissor grinder was peddling a rusted bike along the alley, his grinder trundling along behind. This was a far cry from the Cortéz mansion.

Yet Laura was right, Sara had to admit. It had worked out wonderfully well. Unbelievably, she'd done exactly what she'd set out to do. Those eight tons of cocaine were safely off the streets. Don Luis's organization had been put permanently out of commission. Julio Vargas was facing the long prison term she'd envisioned for him—as were Nicolás's two brothers-in-law, and a certain high-ranking army officer whose longtime acquaintance with Julio Vargas had provided Don Luis with the classified military equipment he had used to pry into the highest levels of the drug underworld and spy on the anti-narcotics efforts of the government. And beyond all expectations, Sara herself had come out of this whole nightmare with both her life and her freedom.

So why wasn't she happier about it? Everyone else seemed to be! The FELCN commanders were basking openly in the glory of the largest drug bust in their history. The DEA was doing much the same in its own quiet fashion. The State Department was relieved to have settled an unpleasant international incident to their own political profit.

As for the media, once the spate of arrests had made the city's leading family fair game, they'd shown as much ecstasy in ripping apart the Cortezes as they had earlier in trumpeting Sara's alleged guilt. Julio Vargas had told the truth about both Ricardo Orejuela's and Pablo Orejuela's deaths, and the poetic justice of Don Luis's demise was a news story they still hadn't let drop.

Sara knew she had every reason to be happy. She was free at last to leave this alien country that she had once thought so beautiful, but which had brought her only pain and sorrow. Tomorrow she would be back in the familiar surroundings and security of her own country. So why the emptiness inside when she thought about boarding that plane this evening? It wasn't as though she had anything to hold her here! The only acquaintances she had made in the past few months had been friends of the Cortezes. Only Gabriela, of all of them, had made any effort to contact her; she had called briefly to say how sorry she was about everything and to wish Sara good fortune in her future. But her grief at her cousin's and uncle's deaths had been evident, and she hadn't even broached the subject of the Cortezes' cocaine dealings.

Sara had called the *Hogar de Infantes* to apologize for the difficulties she had caused there. Doña Inez had been pleasant and understanding, but Sara had detected a reserve that hadn't been there before, and the administrator had not suggested that Sara return to her volunteer work.

Sara had also spoken briefly with Rafael and Josefina and little Consuelo. Doug had arranged the call for her through Benedicto. But though the Quechua family was glad to hear she was safe, Sara would never be able to return to the relationship she'd had with them. Their worlds were just too different. Epifanio was back at home, though his return probably had more to do with the arrest of his employers and the destruction of the maceration pit where he had worked than with any genuine remorse.

As for her former in-laws, Sara hadn't seen or heard from them at all. Nor had she attended the funeral, a huge, televised event carried out with as much pomp as would have been expressed if the deceased were national heroes instead of indicted criminals. Mimi had called the Histeds to make it abundantly clear that Sara wasn't welcome. Not that she had wanted to go. She'd said her good-byes to Nicolás and could not have sat through a service pretending to mourn her father-in-law. But she had genuinely liked Delores and Janéth, despite their feather-brained lifestyles, and had come to respect her mother-in-law, and she would have preferred to have left on different terms.

Well, she couldn't blame them for hating her. To their way of thinking, she was to blame for the deaths of Nicolás and Don Luis and for everything else that had befallen their family. And to a certain extent, they were right.

Sara let out an unhappy sigh. No, the only farewells she would have to say, before boarding the plane tonight and closing the door forever on this nightmare chapter of her life, would be to Laura and Sam. And to—

The footsteps on the stairs were too definite to be Laura's and too quick to be Sam's. Sara spun around. "Doug!"

She glanced down over the balustrade, looking for Laura. But Doug was alone. This wasn't the first time she had seen him since he'd brought her here and left her that first night. Despite a busy schedule of his own, he'd insisted on staying by her side during all of the interrogations and depositions. She had been too grateful to refuse, though she hated to take up so much of his time. The DEA and State Department officials had at least been courteous. But some of the other interviews had been less pleasant. Especially the one with the police chief crony of Don Luis, who had grilled her unmercifully until Doug put a firm stop to it.

Still, Sara hadn't been alone with the DEA agent since he'd dropped her off at the Chapare mountain farm, and she felt suddenly shy as he strode toward her across the landing.

Doug showed no signs of sharing her feeling of awkwardness. "Hey, I've got something for you!" he greeted her with a smile.

Withdrawing his right hand from his slacks pocket, he dropped a glittering object onto the coffee table. Sara picked it up with wonder and amazement. It was the Cortéz cross, its emeralds gleaming richly against the gold as though they held within themselves another source of illumination than the sunbeams slanting over Sara's shoulder.

"We found this at the hacienda—tucked in behind that painting in the office. The police ordered all your husband's and father-in-law's personal effects released to the family when the bodies were returned for the funeral. I figured if anyone should have this, it should be you."

Sara turned the precious trinket over in her hand. The tiny painted mouth of St. George curved triumphantly up at her as he plunged his spear into his scaly victim. With a shudder, Sara dropped the cross back onto the table. "I don't want it!"

"Are you sure?" Doug's eyes on her face were sharp. "I didn't expect you'd want to keep it for a souvenir, but that gold and those emeralds have to be worth quite a bit, and I got the impression from Laura that the Cortezes haven't left you much in the way of cash—or anything else."

Sometimes Laura talked too much! Her warmhearted friend meant well, Sara knew. But she really hadn't wanted Doug to know her financial embarrassments.

"I have enough," she said carefully. Which was an accurate statement, depending on one's definition of enough. The truth was, the only possessions she had were the supplies Doug had scrounged for her and some additional clothing, rather ill-fitting, that Laura had put together out of her own modest wardrobe. Of course, she had a whole closet full of clothes and other belongings at the Cortéz mansion—if Mimi hadn't taken them out and burned them by now. But Sara had no intention of returning there to claim them.

As for money, she had exactly one ten centavo piece she'd picked up off the sidewalk outside police headquarters. The State Department had returned her passport and American driver's license, which had been locked in Don Luis's safe. But the credit cards she'd had before her marriage had long been canceled, and Nicolás's personal bank account, to which she didn't have access anyway, had been confiscated by the anti-narcotics authorities.

The assets of Industrias Cortéz, with all its branches and business accounts, had also been seized, as the law allowed when properties or businesses were involved in the trafficking of drugs. But like many *narcos* before him, Don Luis had been astute enough to deed large portions of his estate over to his wife and daughters and other family members. The big mansion might have to go, but Mimi and her daughters wouldn't be hurting financially. Despite the origin of their inheritance, Sara couldn't help being glad that Delores and Janéth and her mother-in-law wouldn't be left destitute.

As Nicolás's widow, she could undoubtedly have sued for her own share, but she'd rather starve in the streets than touch so much as a cent of Cortéz money!

Picking up the gold ornament, she handed it back to Doug. "I've got everything I need," she repeated definitely. "But if you really think I can do what I want with this, could you see that it's sold and the money given to the *Hogar de Infantes*? Maybe they can melt it down or something, and get rid of that St. George! I'd give it to Doña Inez as is, but if she tried to sell it, someone would be sure to think it was stolen."

"I'd be glad to." Doug dropped the cross back into his pocket with a look of approval that brought color to Sara's cheeks. "Somehow I thought you'd say something like that. Okay, then, I have one more thing here that belongs to you."

Sara made no move to take the envelope that appeared in his hand. She was already certain of what it contained.

"It's your tickets home," Doug explained patiently. "The consul asked me to drop them by." Reaching for one of Sara's hands, he folded her fingers around the envelope. "There's a little something extra in there, too. The guys in the office felt bad about the deal you got from the Cortezes, and they wanted to express their appreciation for helping us crack the case."

Sara could see the dull green of American money peeking from the unsealed envelope. The guys—or Doug? But she knew better than to press the point. There was a time when she would have indignantly refused the offer of help. Now she accepted the gift in the spirit of kindness with which it had been offered. "Thank you," she said simply.

"It's nothing much. Just to help you get started again stateside." Doug leaned back against one of the wooden pillars that supported the balustrade, his eyes keen on her face. "What's going through that little head of yours, Sara?" he asked softly. "I expected those tickets would be received with a little more enthusiasm. Isn't this what you wanted?"

When Sara didn't answer, his gaze sharpened further. "It's all been a little sudden, hasn't it? I certainly never expected you'd be flying out this quick. Do you have any idea of what you'll be doing? Where you'll be heading after Miami? I understand you were living in Seattle. Do you have family there?"

No, she didn't have family in Seattle—or anywhere else that she knew of. Her father had never been much on maintaining family ties after her mother died, and though surely she must have relatives somewhere, Sara had never met them.

But there were college friends and a few couples she knew at her old church. Surely one of them would allow her to borrow a sofa for a few days while she figured out what to do next.

Sara managed to meet Doug's keen gaze with a smile. "I . . . I don't really have much family. But Seattle's as good a place as any, I guess. It's too late to get a teaching position for this school year, but I can put my name in for subbing. Or tutoring. They always need tutors who can speak Spanish."

Sara dropped her eyes to the envelope. Rubbing a thumb along the V-shaped flap, she said in a low voice, "So . . . I guess this is good-bye then."

The pang that hit somewhere in the region of her heart told Sara the truth. How had she deceived herself so? It wasn't leaving this country that she was having a hard time with, or Laura and Sam, dear as they had become to her. It was Doug!

It took all her strength of will to keep a smile on her lips as she met the questioning look in Doug's eyes. It *would* be now, as she was about to leave, that she would finally recognize just what this man had come to mean to her! He had been her savior, her comforter, and a solid bulwark against the confusion of these last days of police and reporters and government officials. More than that, he'd been a friend. And now, with a flight ready to snatch her away in just a few short hours, she did not want to say good-bye!

And Doug? Sara's smile faded despite her efforts. What was he thinking behind those keen gray eyes? Never once had he complained or shown any reluctance for the task he'd taken upon himself on her behalf. But there was no denying that she'd been a terrible drain on him and his time. He was probably relieved to see her go, though he'd never be discourteous enough to show it. So she would make this easy for him.

Dropping the envelope onto the armchair beside her, she tempered her voice to maintain self-control. "Thank you for bringing this by and . . . well, for everything! I can't tell you how much I've appreciated everything you've done for me and . . ."

Sara closed her eyes to block out his penetrating gaze. This wasn't working! But she wasn't going to be able to take much more. "Anyway, good-bye! Maybe . . . maybe we'll run into each other again sometime. And—please, when you leave, if you could let Laura know that I—I'd like to be alone for a while."

She turned swiftly to the window, her eyes fastening blindly on the scissor grinder, who had stopped halfway down the alley to sharpen a set of knives. Her shoulders were set rigidly as she waited for the sound of Doug's departing footsteps. She'd botched that thoroughly, but later on she'd send him a nice thank-you note. And then, at Christmas, maybe a card. Wasn't that what you did with friends when you both went separate ways? He might even write back out of sheer kindness. And that would be the end of it. She'd never see him again!

The view out the window blurred as Sara battled the desolation that welled up within her. Doug Bradford had been a friend when she'd needed one. But he belonged here. As for Sara, she belonged—nowhere!

Again she fought the rising tide of despair. During these past few days she'd been allowing herself the illusion that she was not alone. But that was all it had been—an illusion. Now it was time to start facing reality.

No! she reminded herself fiercely. *I'm not alone! I can't forget that again!*

Blinking the scissor grinder back into focus, she whispered again the words that had burned into her memory on the slopes of a small mountain farm in the Chapare. "'Though the fig tree does not bud and there are no grapes on the vines, though the olive crop fails and the fields produce no food, though there are no sheep in the pen and no cattle in the stalls, yet I will rejoice in the Lord, I will be joyful in God my Savior.'"

Oh, God, you've brought me this far. You'll take me the rest of the way—wherever that might be!

Behind her came a soft cough, a barely audible clearing of the throat, and Sara suddenly realized that she had never heard Doug leave. She didn't dare turn around, but she didn't have to. Strong hands did it for her. Through the shimmering tears in her eyes, she met Doug's steady gaze. She saw compassion—and something else!

"Sara, this doesn't have to be good-bye!"

Slowly, reluctantly, Doug released her, stepping back so that half the length of the coffee table was between them. "I've been doing some thinking ever since I heard about your flight tonight. I don't want to say good-bye like this. I—if you're really not sure what you want to do next, I've got a mother in Miami who's rattling around in an empty house and happens to love company. She'd be happy to have you stay there awhile. At least until you have other plans."

Sara stared at him, uncomprehending, even as everything in her soul wanted to cry out her acceptance. "Oh, no, I couldn't do that! Your mother doesn't even know me. She can't possibly want a total stranger descending on her out of nowhere!"

"You wouldn't be descending on her," Doug said patiently. "I'd be taking you. I'm flying out tonight myself."

Sara stood stock still. It was suddenly hard to catch her breath. "*You're* flying out? But—why?"

The slant of Doug's mouth was ironic. "I guess we're both *personas non grata* around here. The higher-ups have decreed that I'm out of Bolivia. They say it's for my own protection, in light of everything that's happened."

"Oh, Doug, that's terrible!" Sara started. "I mean—you—"

She dropped her sentence when she saw the intensity in his eyes. Doug stepped forward and rapped his shin on the corner of the coffee table. Pushing the offending piece of furniture out of his way, he ran his fingers through his hair with an uncertainty that Sara had never before seen.

"Sara, you must know how I feel about you! I . . . since Julie died, I never thought another woman would come into my life, my heart. But you're there, and I can't just let you go like this! I know it's too soon, and I certainly never meant to rush you like this. I thought there'd be more time. But—I can be patient. All I ask is your friendship, a chance. And that you don't just walk out of my life!"

Sara couldn't get a word past the tightness in her throat. Whatever she had allowed her heart to dream, it wasn't this! She raised her eyes to meet Doug's. There was in him none of the flamboyant charisma or the easy charm or the sheer physical beauty that had drawn her to Nicolás. But Sara had grown up enough to know how little those qualities really mattered.

And enough to value the differences that made Special Agent Doug Bradford of the DEA the man he was. The steadiness and self-discipline—yes, and stubbornness, too—that showed themselves in the firm line of his mouth, and the stern set of his jaw that made him seem older than his thirty years. The sharp mind behind that keen gaze that saw deep beneath the surface of people's lives. And the kindness and caring that could soften those cool gray eyes to gentleness, like they were softening now. Something inside of Sara that she had never thought to feel again unfolded its wings inside of her.

"What is it?" Doug asked quietly. "You look like you've just been offered the sun."

The warm smile rising into Sara's amber eyes was like the first morning light after an endless and tempestuous night that had despaired of the coming of the dawn. "I think I just have!" she said softly.

Sometimes the fig tree does bud.